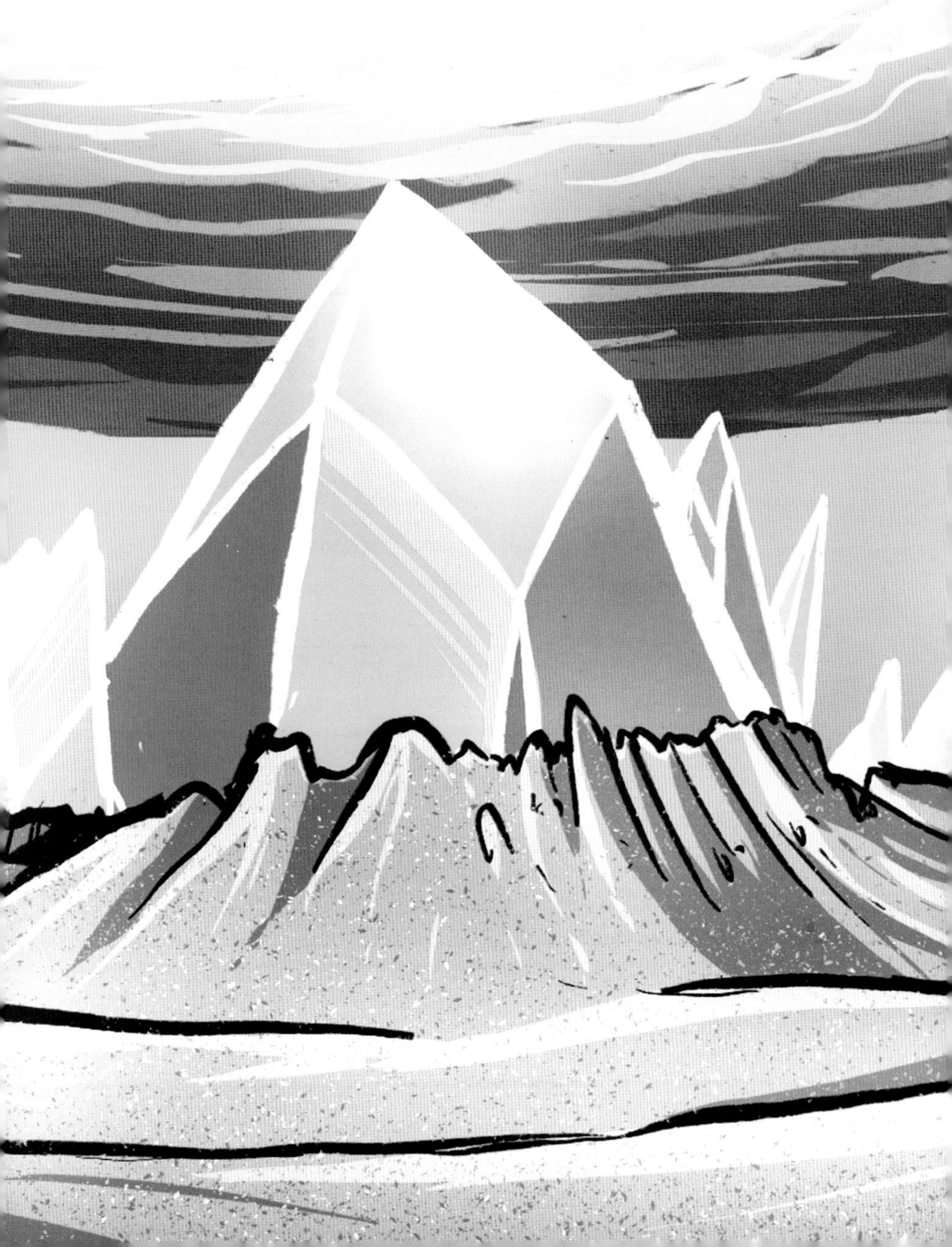

Also by
Lucas Turnbloom

STEVE L. McEVIL

STEVE L. McEVIL
and the Second Wind

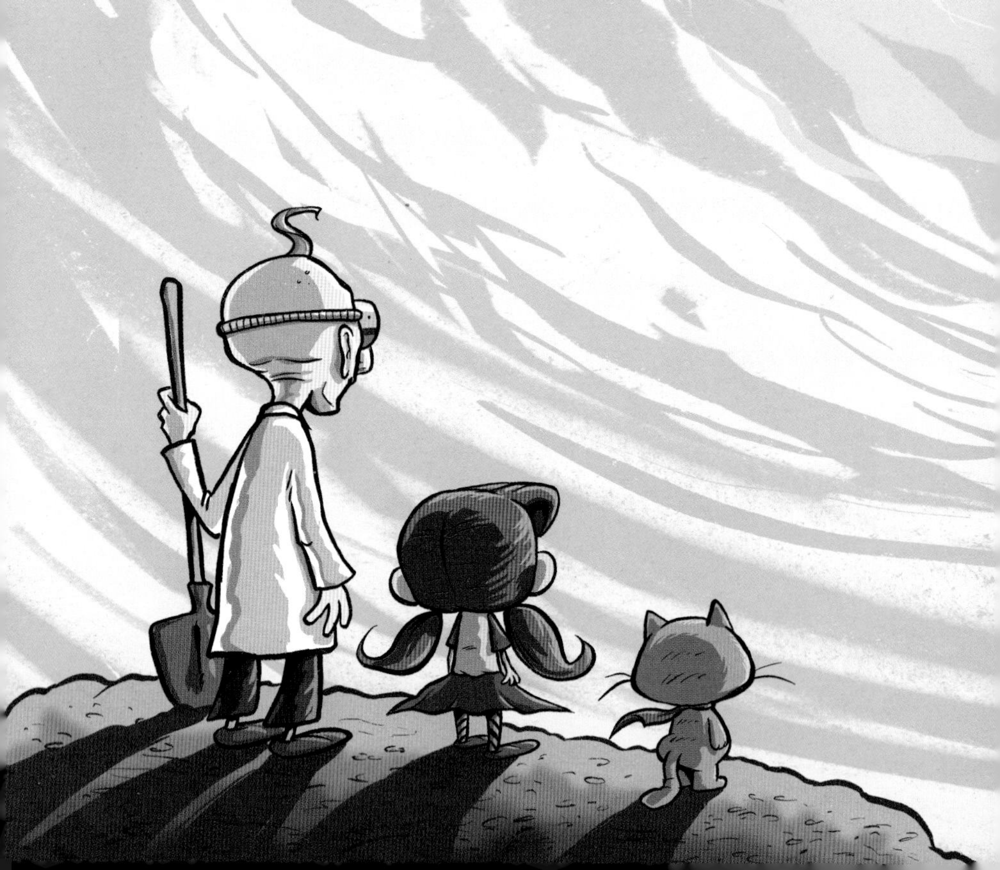

STEVE L.

McEVIL

and the
TWISTED SISTER

Lucas Turnbloom

Colors by Marc LaPierre
and Lucas Turnbloom

CROWN
BOOKS FOR YOUNG READERS
NEW YORK

All rights reserved. Published in the United States by Crown Books for Young Readers, an imprint of Random House Children's Books, a division of Penguin Random House LLC, New York.

Crown and the colophon are registered trademarks of Penguin Random House LLC.

RH Graphic with the book design is a trademark of Penguin Random House LLC.

Visit us on the Web! rhcbooks.com

Educators and librarians, for a variety of teaching tools, visit us at RHTeachersLibrarians.com

Library of Congress Cataloging-in-Publication Data is available upon request.

ISBN 978-0-593-64958-9 (trade) | ISBN 978-0-593-64959-6 (lib. bdg.) | ISBN 978-0-593-64960-2 (ebook)

Interior design by Bob Bianchini and Jules Buckley

MANUFACTURED IN CHINA

10 9 8 7 6 5 4 3 2 1

First Edition

FOR
ZOE, PENNY,
JUNIPER, PAISLEY,
ISABEL, EVAN, MADELYN,
NATHAN, NAIA,
CAMERON, AURORA,
LIAM, WYATT & LILLI

CHAPTER 1

The Twisted Sister

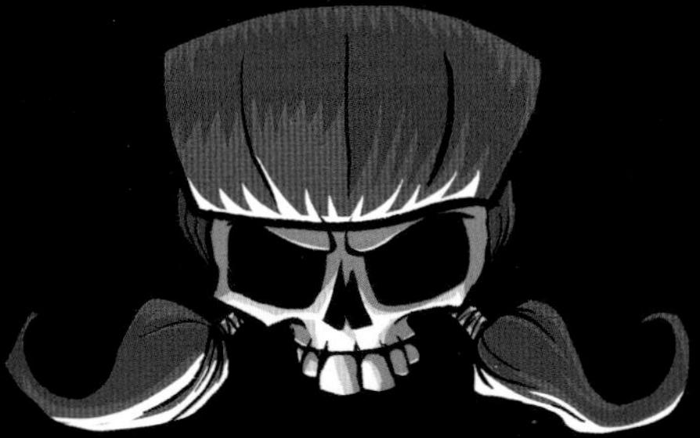

McEVIL HOUSEHOLD: 7:54 P.M.

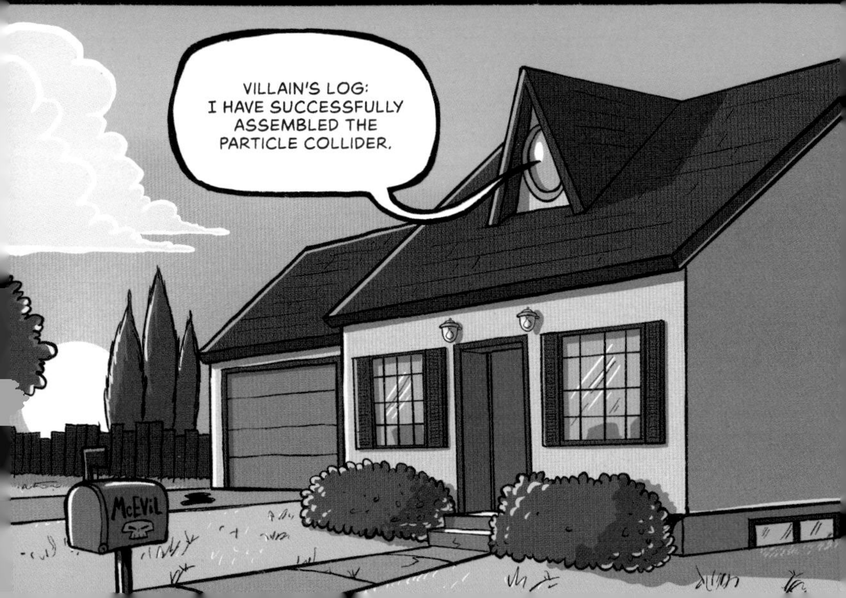
VILLAIN'S LOG: I HAVE SUCCESSFULLY ASSEMBLED THE PARTICLE COLLIDER.
McEVIL

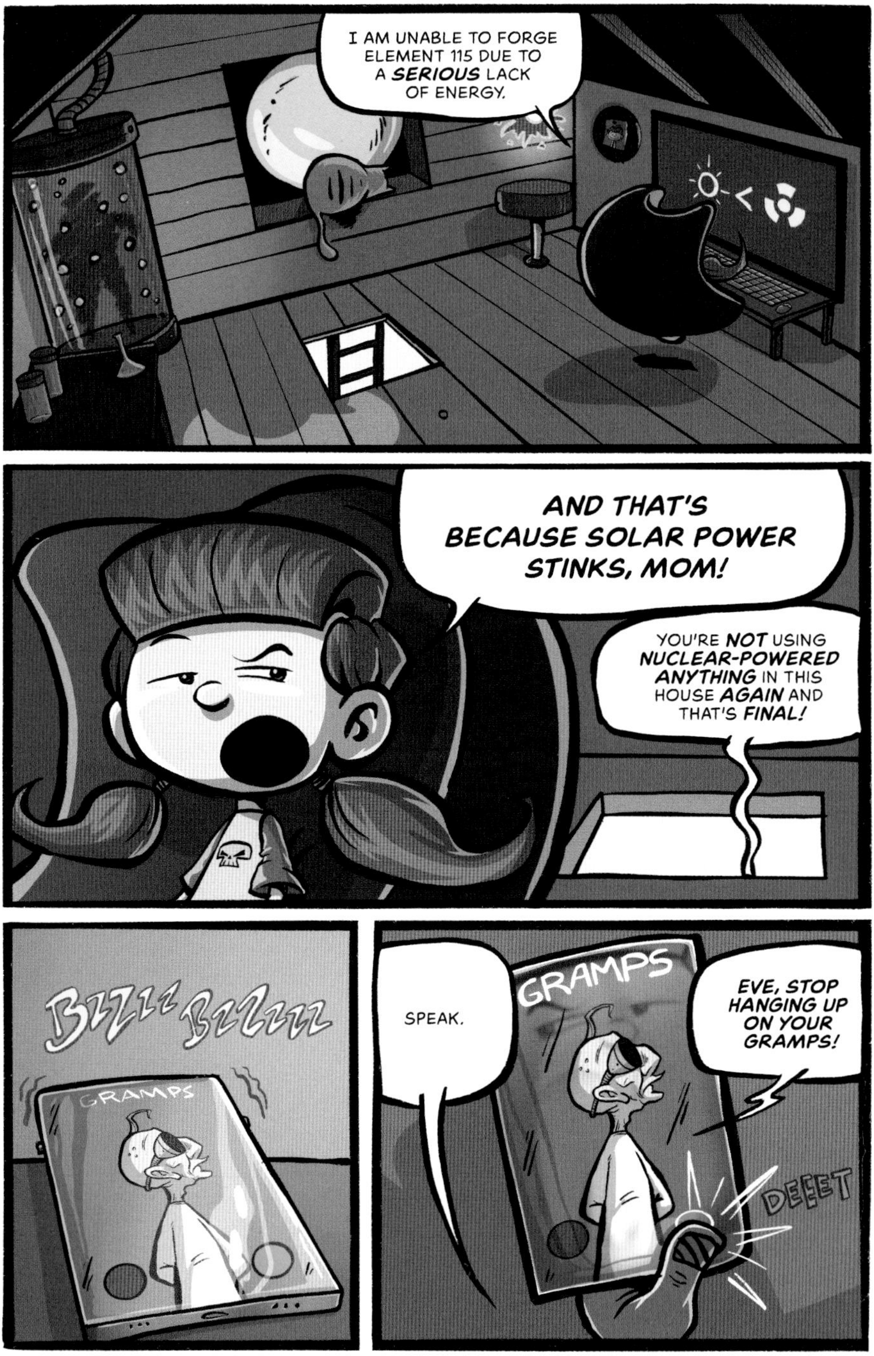

I AM UNABLE TO FORGE ELEMENT 115 DUE TO A SERIOUS LACK OF ENERGY.
AND THAT'S BECAUSE SOLAR POWER STINKS, MOM!
YOU'RE NOT USING NUCLEAR-POWERED ANYTHING IN THIS HOUSE AGAIN AND THAT'S FINAL!
BZZZZ BZZZZZ
GRAMPS
SPEAK.
GRAMPS
EVE, STOP HANGING UP ON YOUR GRAMPS!
DEEET

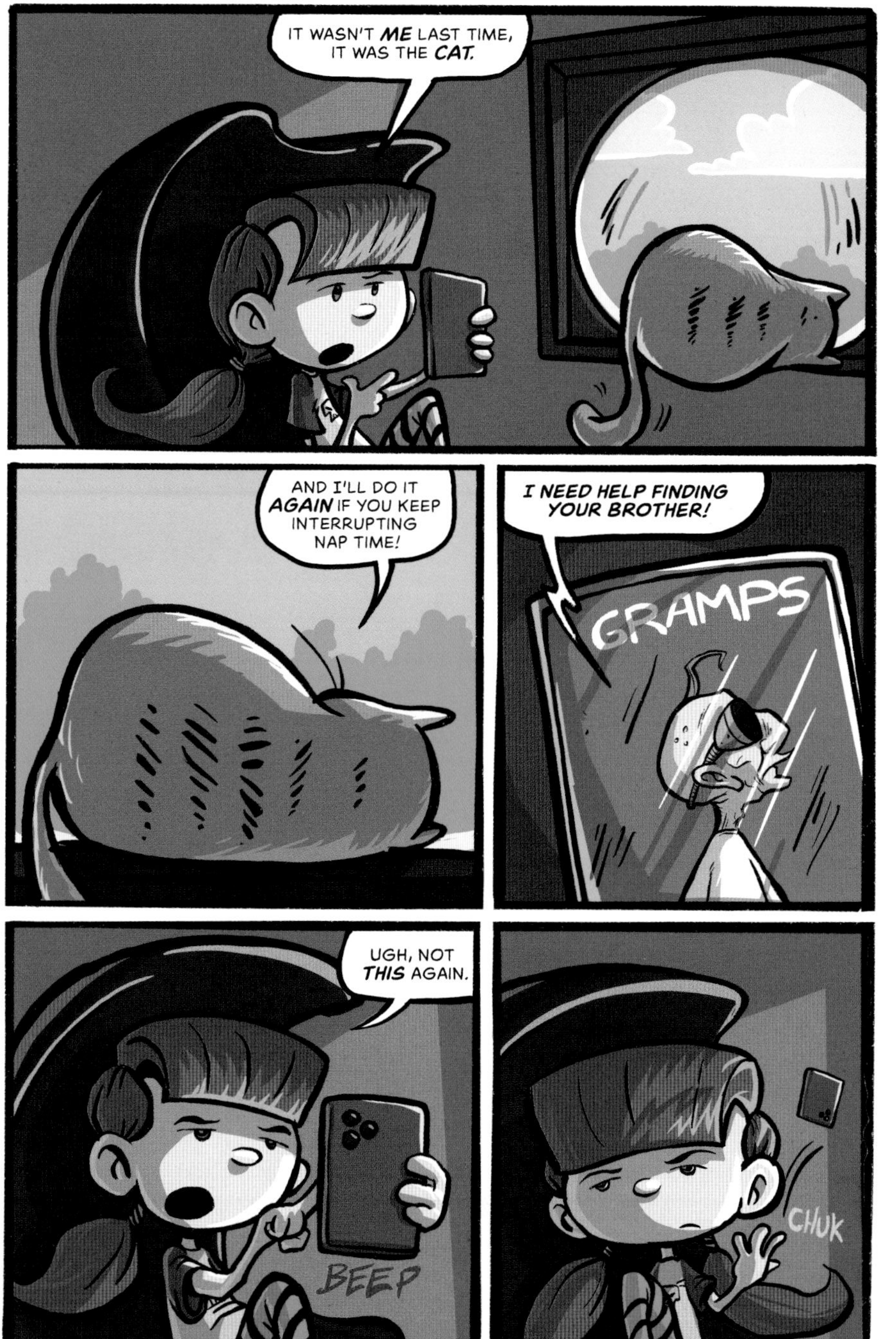
IT WASN'T ME LAST TIME, IT WAS THE CAT.
AND I'LL DO IT AGAIN IF YOU KEEP INTERRUPTING NAP TIME!
I NEED HELP FINDING YOUR BROTHER!
GRAMPS
UGH, NOT THIS AGAIN.
BEEP
CHUK

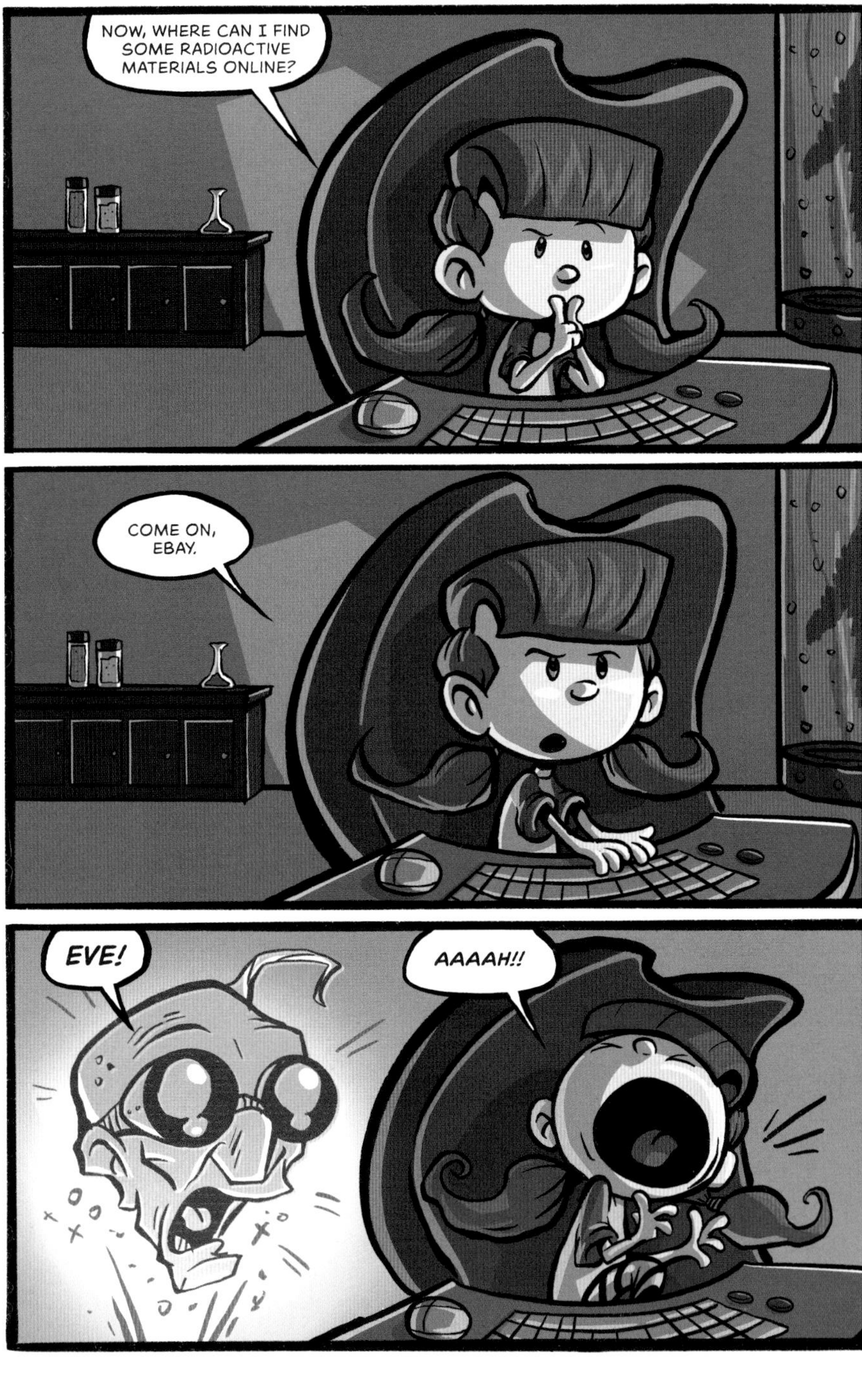
NOW, WHERE CAN I FIND SOME RADIOACTIVE MATERIALS ONLINE?
COME ON, EBAY.
EVE!
AAAAH!!

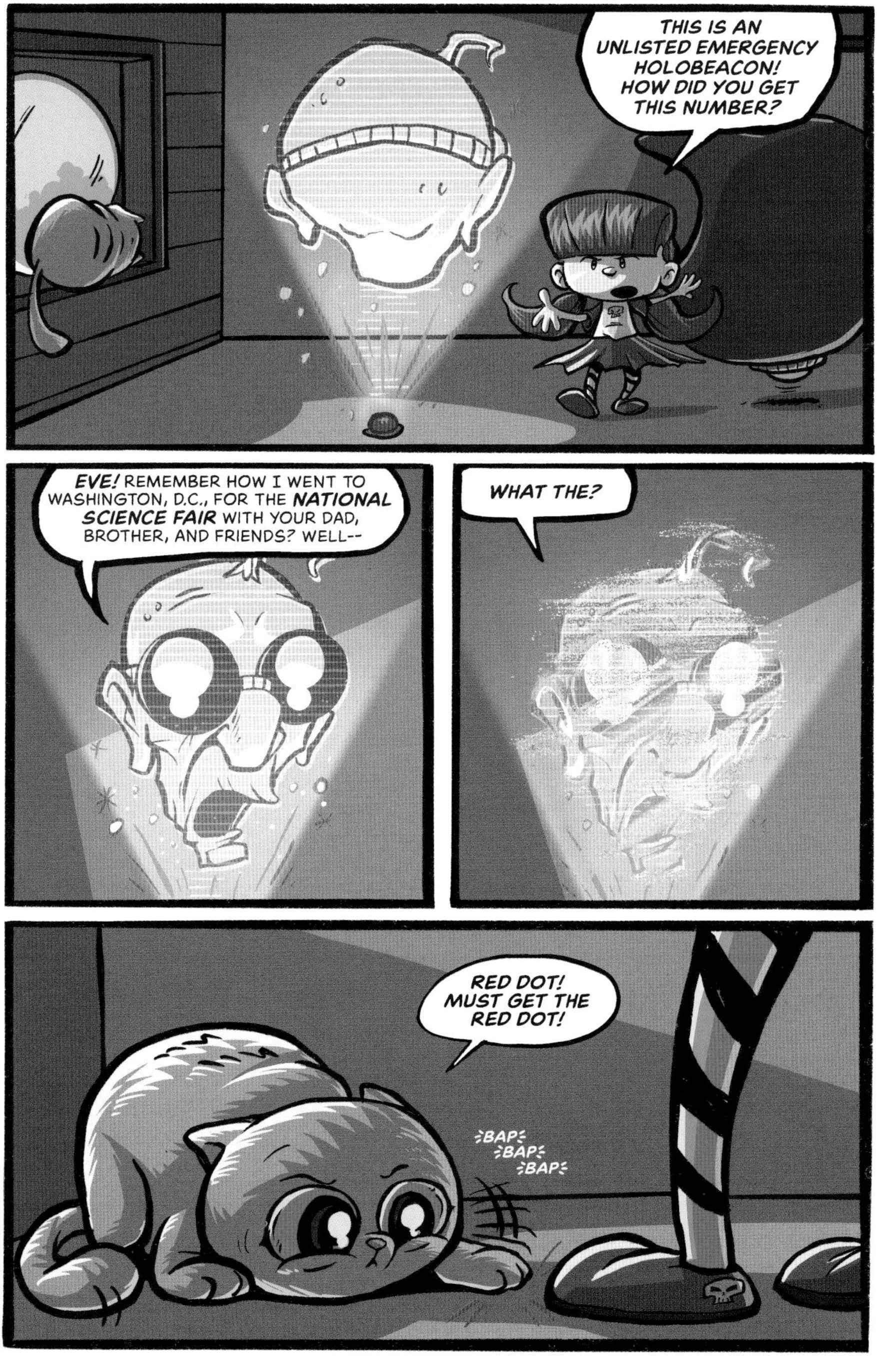
THIS IS AN UNLISTED EMERGENCY HOLOBEACON! HOW DID YOU GET THIS NUMBER?
EVE! REMEMBER HOW I WENT TO WASHINGTON, D.C., FOR THE NATIONAL SCIENCE FAIR WITH YOUR DAD, BROTHER, AND FRIENDS? WELL--
WHAT THE?
RED DOT! MUST GET THE RED DOT!
BAP
BAP
BAP

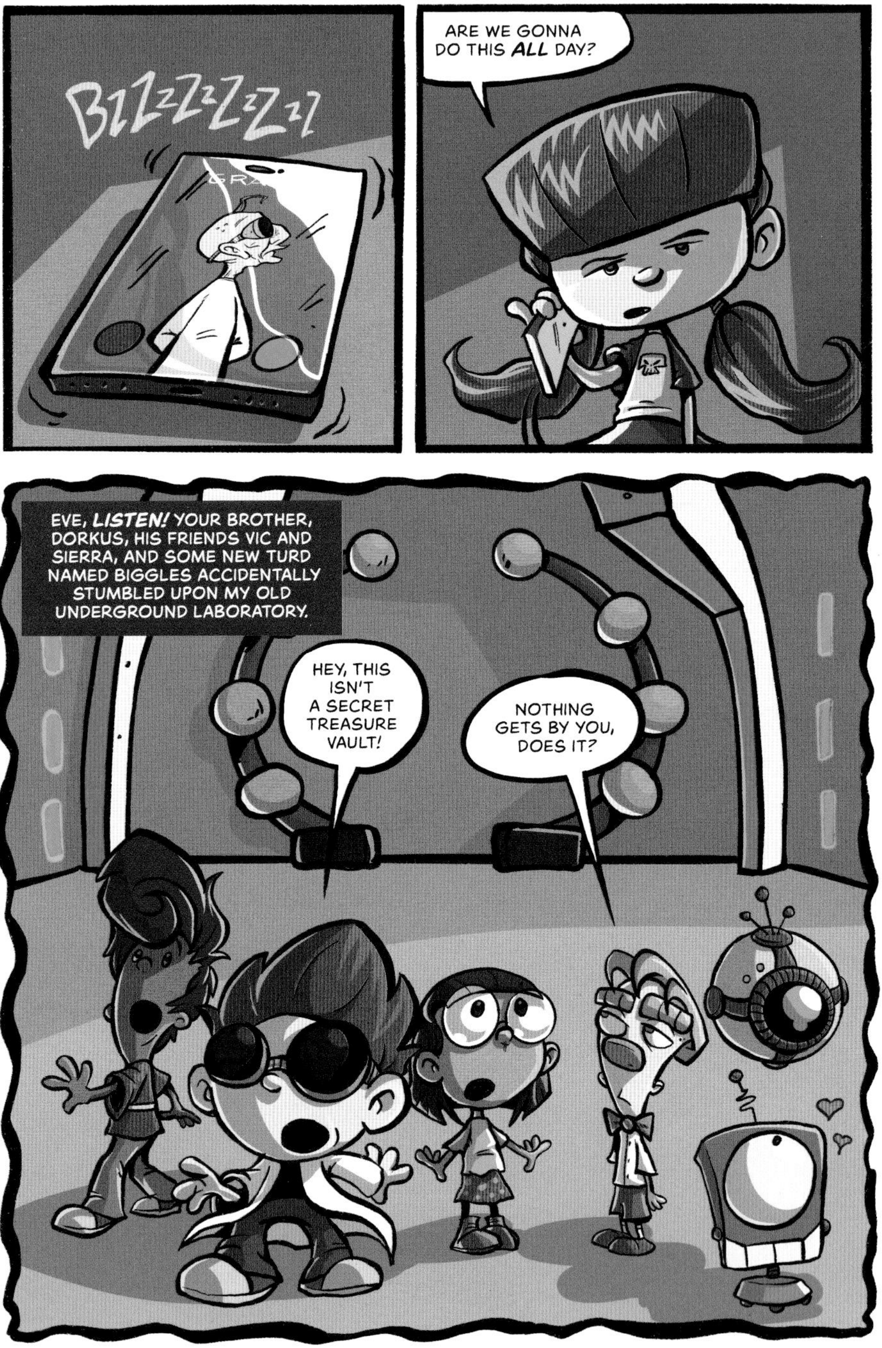
BZZZZZZZZZ
ARE WE GONNA DO THIS ALL DAY?
EVE, LISTEN! YOUR BROTHER, DORKUS, HIS FRIENDS VIC AND SIERRA, AND SOME NEW TURD NAMED BIGGLES ACCIDENTALLY STUMBLED UPON MY OLD UNDERGROUND LABORATORY.
HEY, THIS ISN'T A SECRET TREASURE VAULT!
NOTHING GETS BY YOU, DOES IT?

ALONG WITH A SNEAKY VILLAIN NAMED CODEX!

I TOLD EVERYONE I WAS A *GOOD* GUY SO THEY WOULD HELP ME WITH MY EVIL PLOT! *HA!* KIDS ARE SO GULLIBLE.

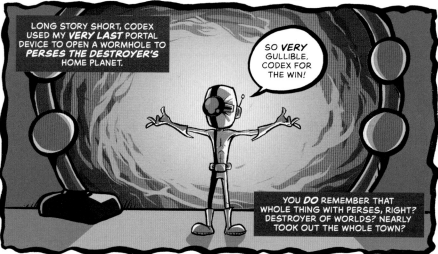

LONG STORY SHORT, CODEX USED MY *VERY LAST* PORTAL DEVICE TO OPEN A WORMHOLE TO *PERSES THE DESTROYER'S* HOME PLANET.

SO *VERY* GULLIBLE. CODEX FOR THE WIN!

YOU *DO* REMEMBER THAT WHOLE THING WITH PERSES, RIGHT? DESTROYER OF WORLDS? NEARLY TOOK OUT THE WHOLE TOWN?

NO, NOT REALLY.

OH, *RIGHT.* I FORGOT YOU WEREN'T INVOLVED IN ALL THAT.

STORY OF MY LIFE.

TOSS

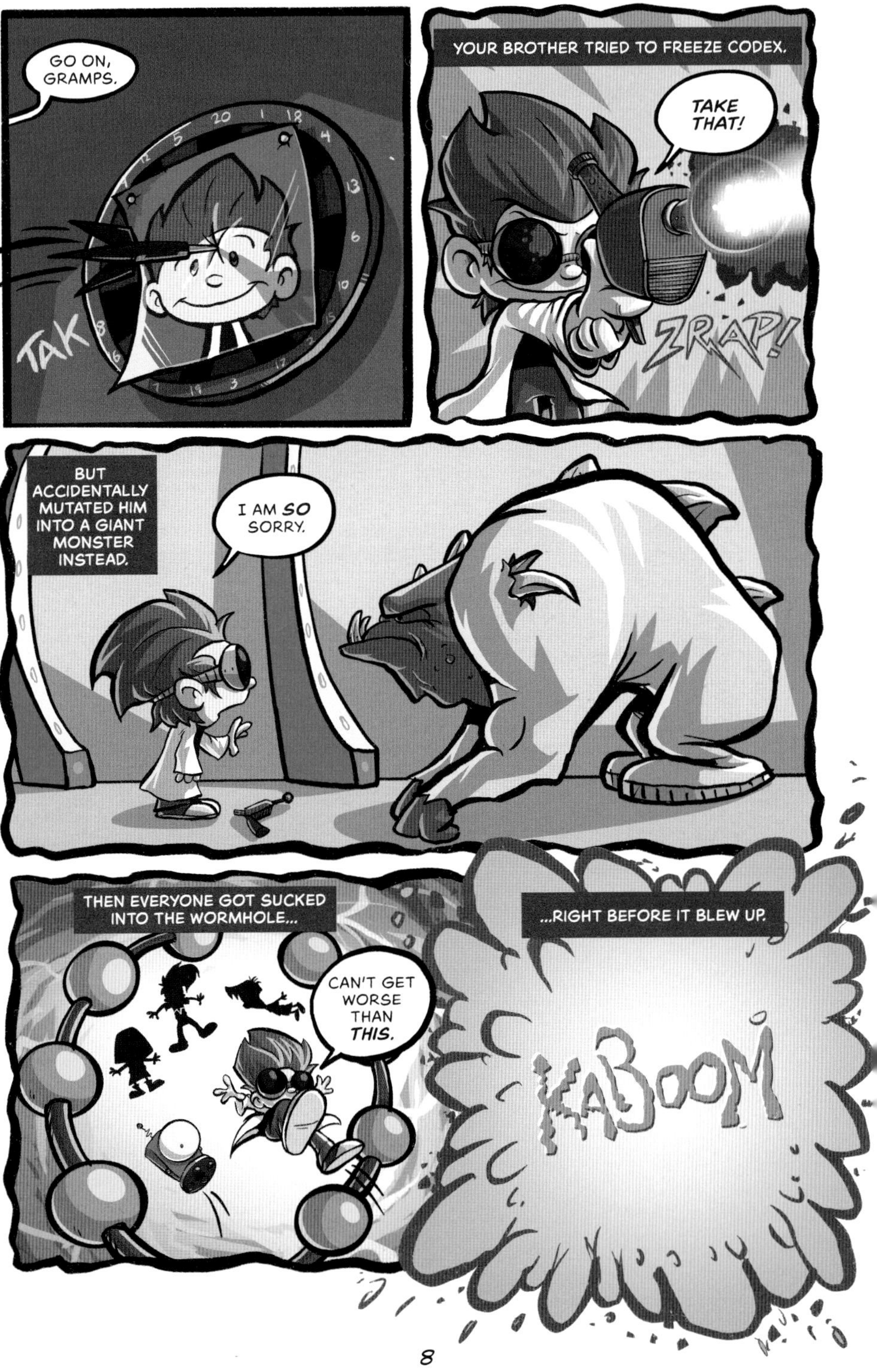
GO ON, GRAMPS.
TAK
YOUR BROTHER TRIED TO FREEZE CODEX.
TAKE THAT!
ZRAP!
BUT ACCIDENTALLY MUTATED HIM INTO A GIANT MONSTER INSTEAD.
I AM *SO* SORRY.
THEN EVERYONE GOT SUCKED INTO THE WORMHOLE...
CAN'T GET WORSE THAN *THIS*.
...RIGHT BEFORE IT BLEW UP.
KABOOM

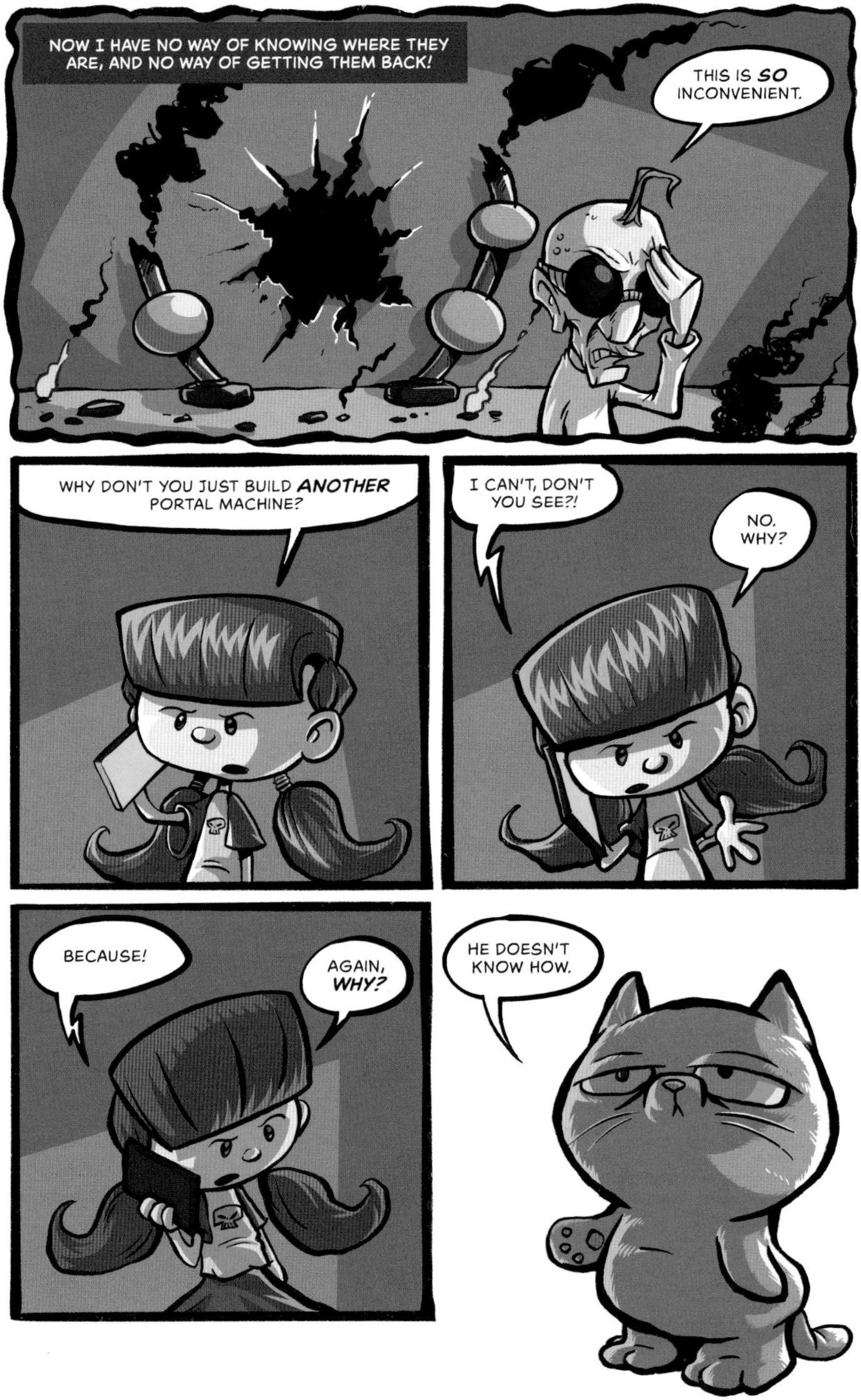
NOW I HAVE NO WAY OF KNOWING WHERE THEY ARE, AND NO WAY OF GETTING THEM BACK!
THIS IS *SO* INCONVENIENT.
WHY DON'T YOU JUST BUILD *ANOTHER* PORTAL MACHINE?
I CAN'T, DON'T YOU SEE?!
NO. WHY?
BECAUSE!
AGAIN, *WHY?*
HE DOESN'T KNOW HOW.

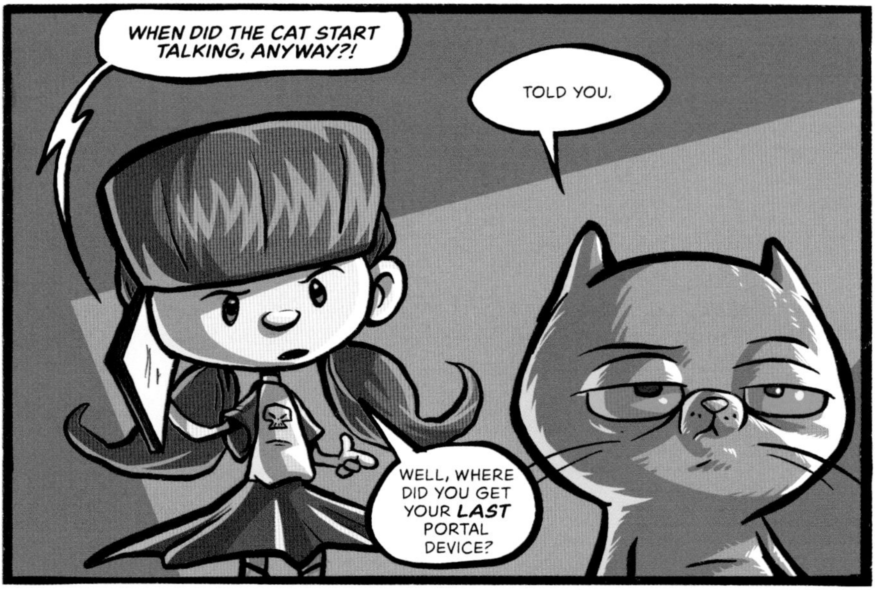
WHEN DID THE CAT START TALKING, ANYWAY?!
TOLD YOU.
WELL, WHERE DID YOU GET YOUR **LAST** PORTAL DEVICE?

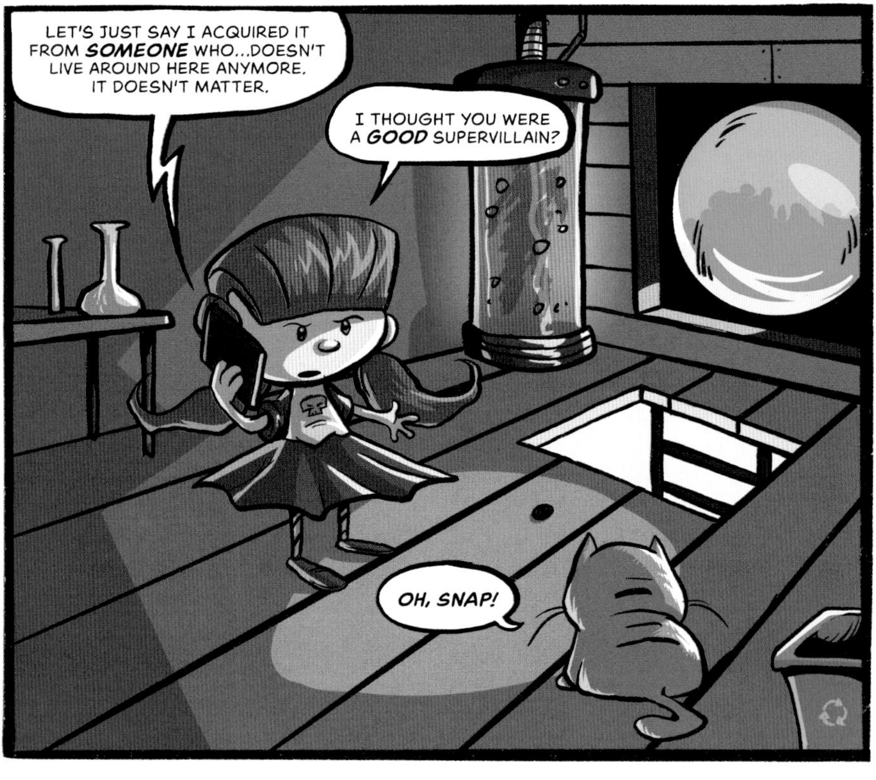
LET'S JUST SAY I ACQUIRED IT FROM **SOMEONE** WHO...DOESN'T LIVE AROUND HERE ANYMORE. IT DOESN'T MATTER.
I THOUGHT YOU WERE A **GOOD** SUPERVILLAIN?
OH, SNAP!

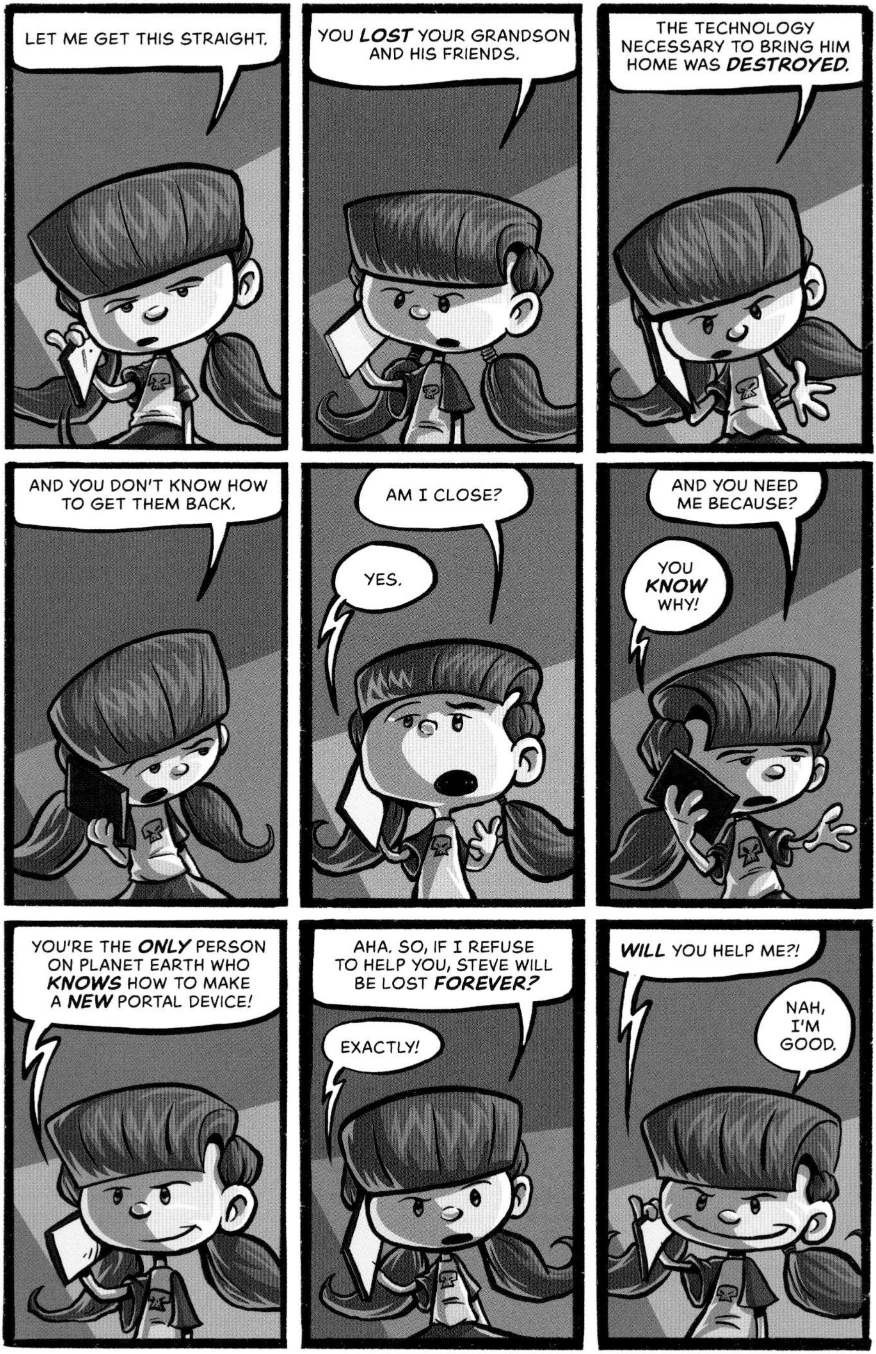
LET ME GET THIS STRAIGHT.
YOU **LOST** YOUR GRANDSON AND HIS FRIENDS.
THE TECHNOLOGY NECESSARY TO BRING HIM HOME WAS **DESTROYED.**
AND YOU DON'T KNOW HOW TO GET THEM BACK.
AM I CLOSE?
YES.
AND YOU NEED ME BECAUSE?
YOU **KNOW** WHY!
YOU'RE THE **ONLY** PERSON ON PLANET EARTH WHO **KNOWS** HOW TO MAKE A **NEW** PORTAL DEVICE!
AHA. SO, IF I REFUSE TO HELP YOU, STEVE WILL BE LOST **FOREVER?**
EXACTLY!
WILL YOU HELP ME?!
NAH, I'M GOOD.

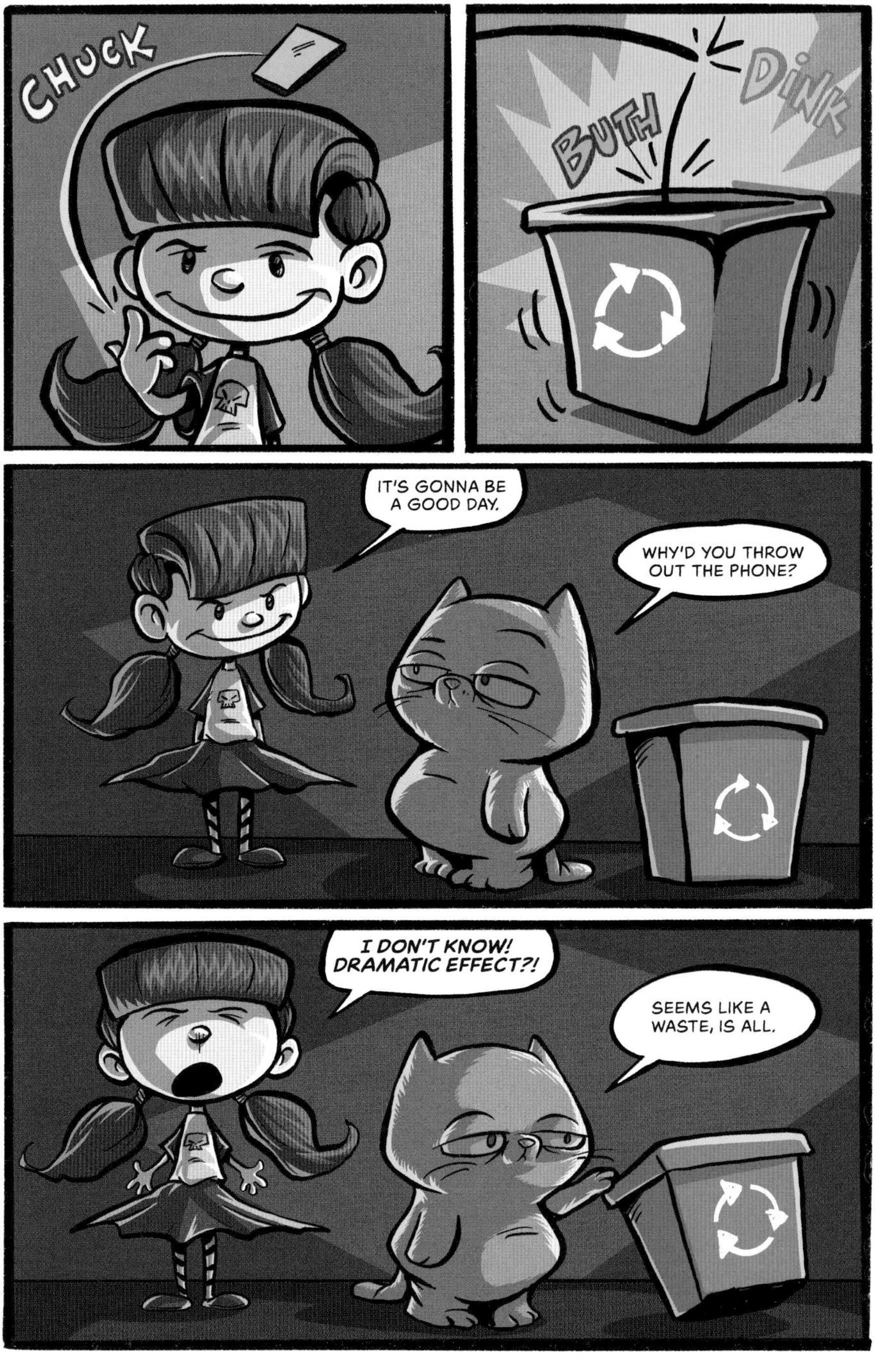
CHUCK
BUTH
DINK
IT'S GONNA BE A GOOD DAY.
WHY'D YOU THROW OUT THE PHONE?
I DON'T KNOW! DRAMATIC EFFECT?!
SEEMS LIKE A WASTE, IS ALL.

CHAPTER 2

Lost and Found

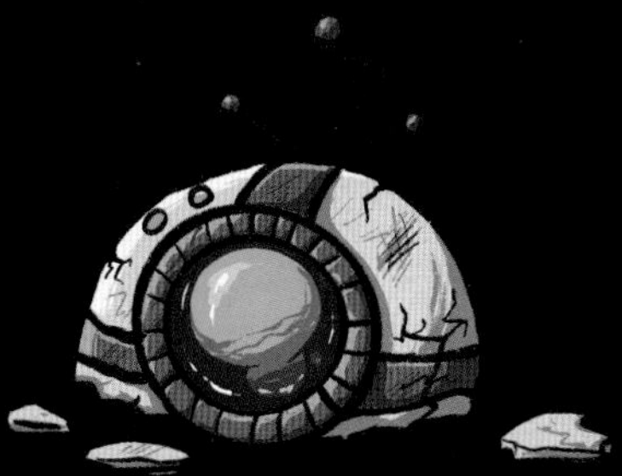

THE OTHER SIDE OF THE GALAXY...

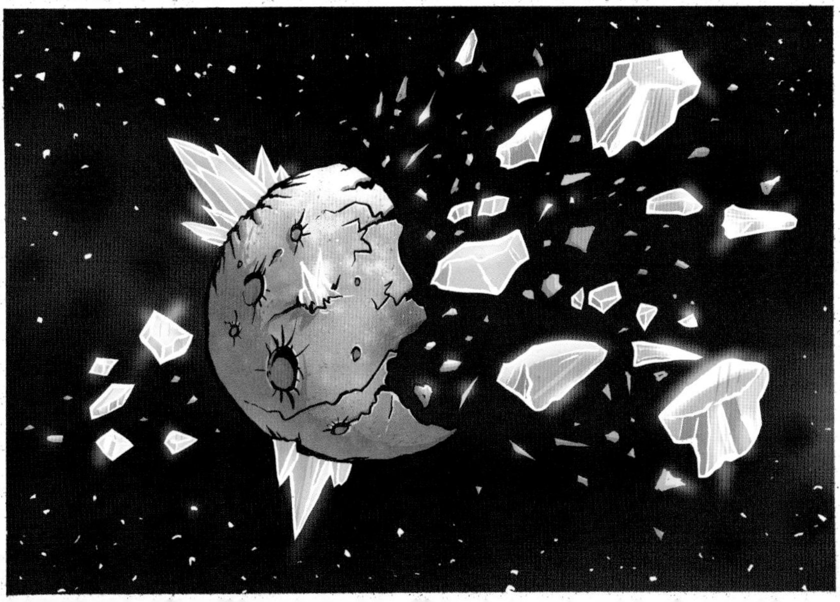

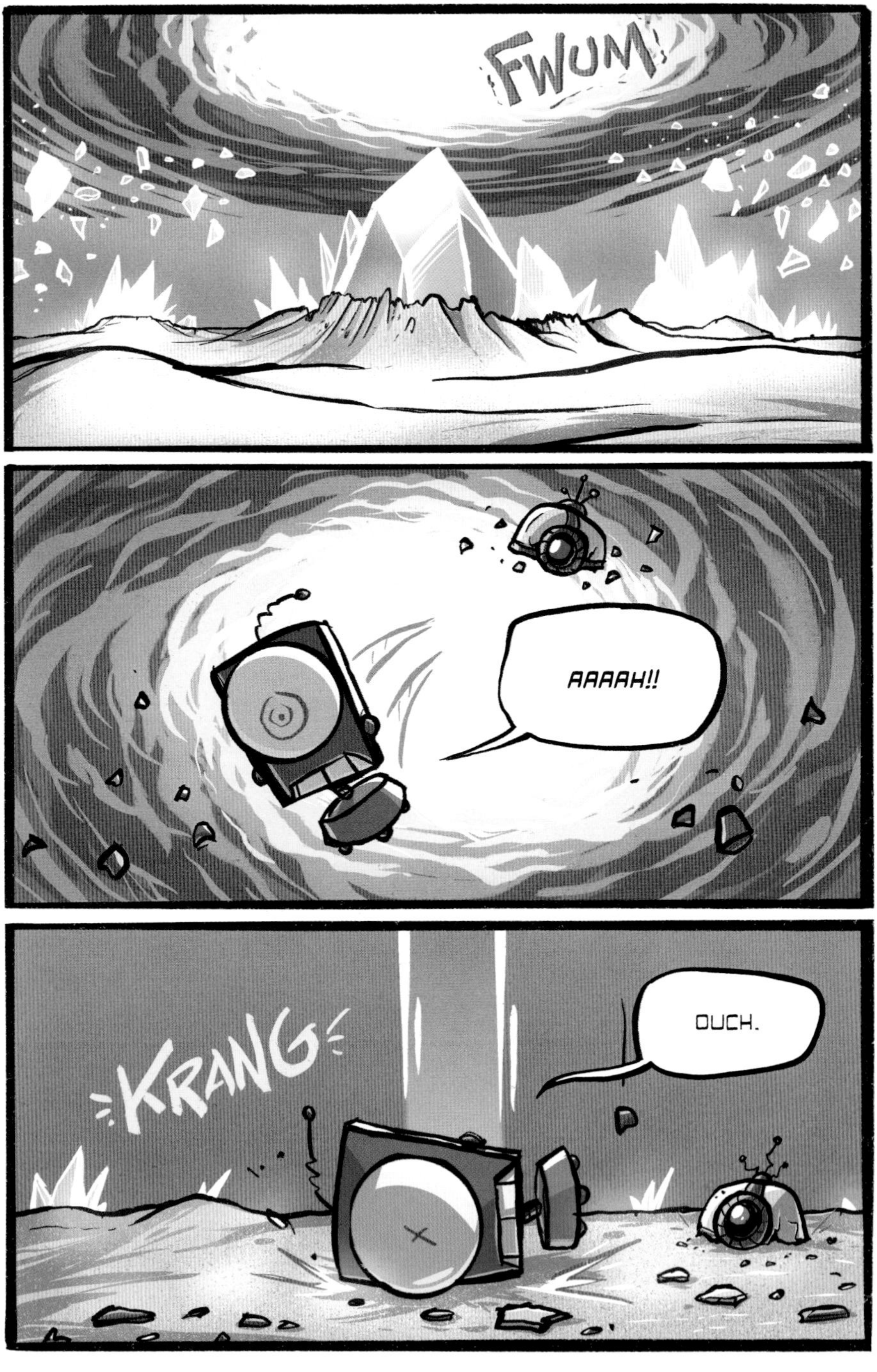
FWUM
AAAAH!!
KRANG
OUCH.

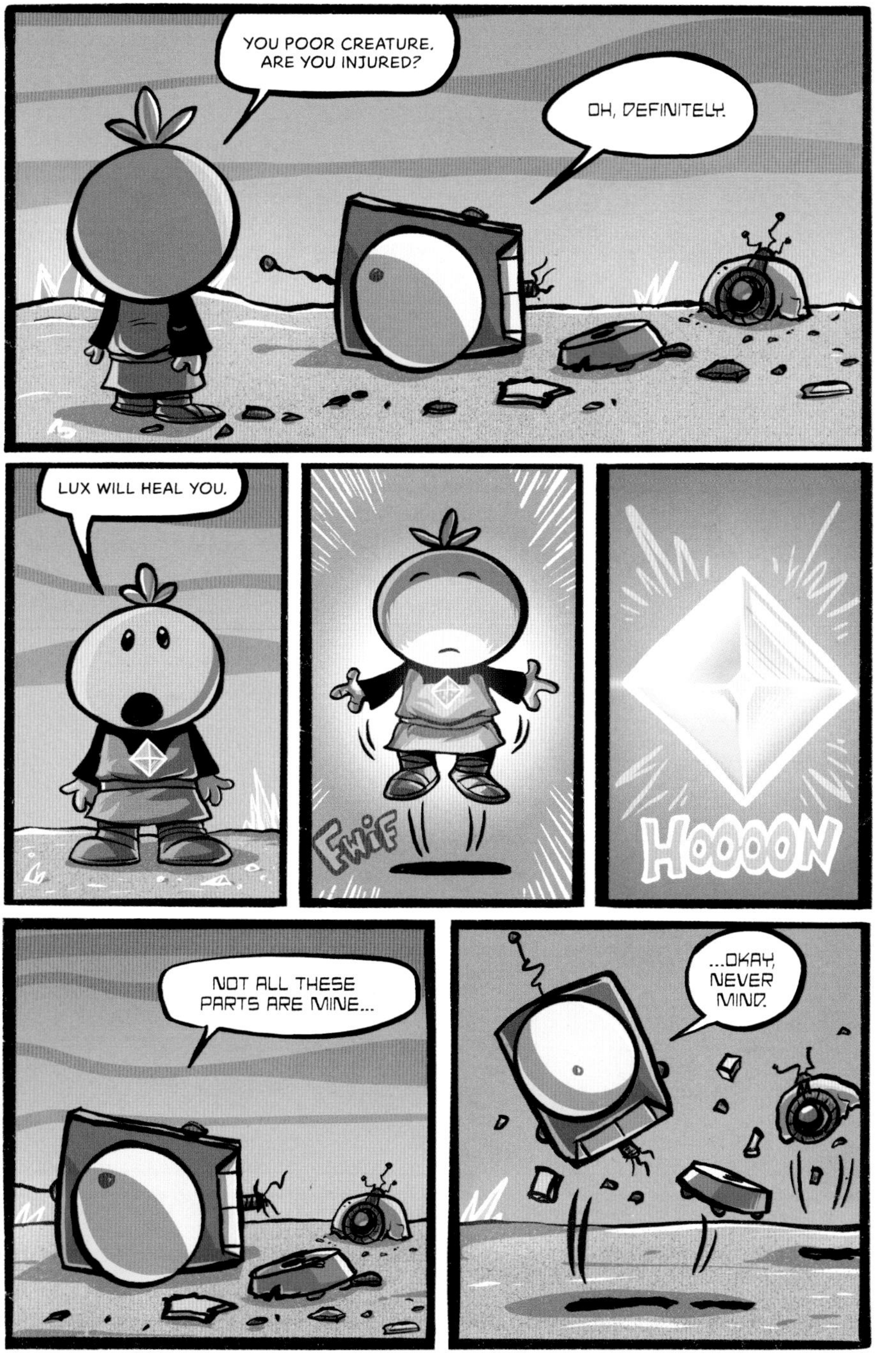
YOU POOR CREATURE. ARE YOU INJURED?
OH, DEFINITELY.
LUX WILL HEAL YOU.
FWIF
HOOOON
NOT ALL THESE PARTS ARE MINE...
...OKAY, NEVER MIND.

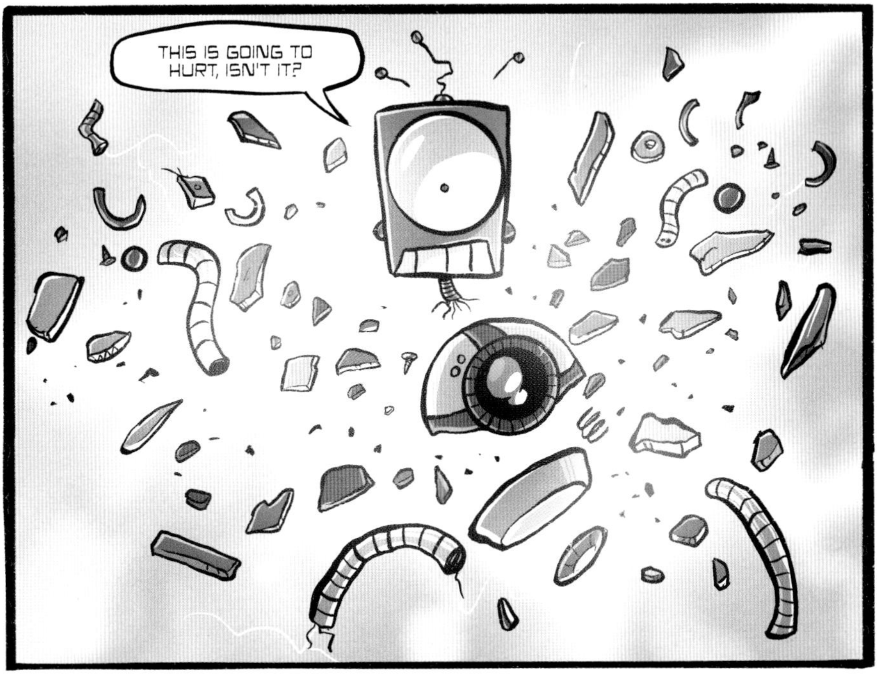
THIS IS GOING TO HURT, ISN'T IT?

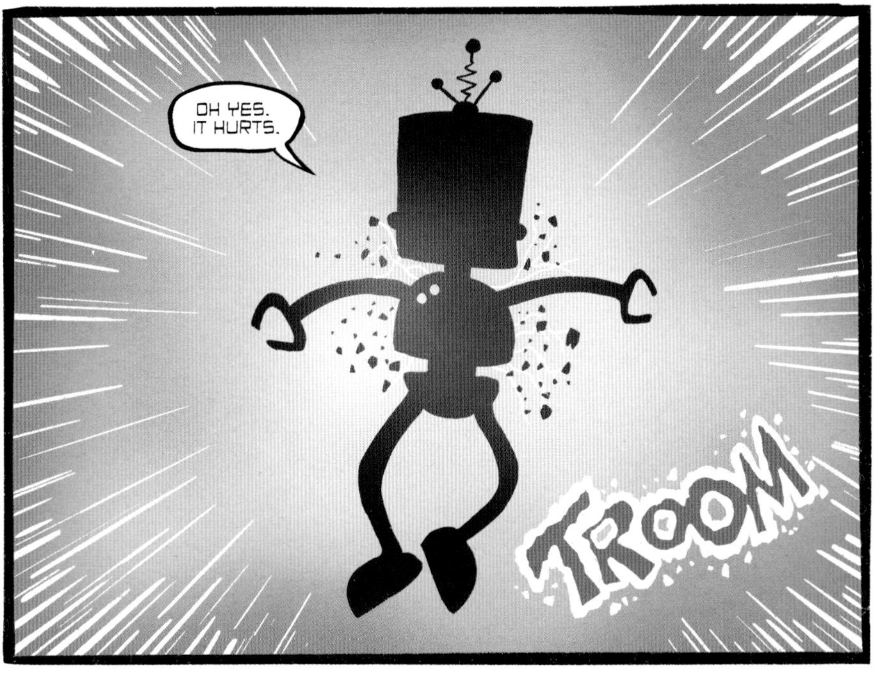
OH YES. IT HURTS.
TROOM

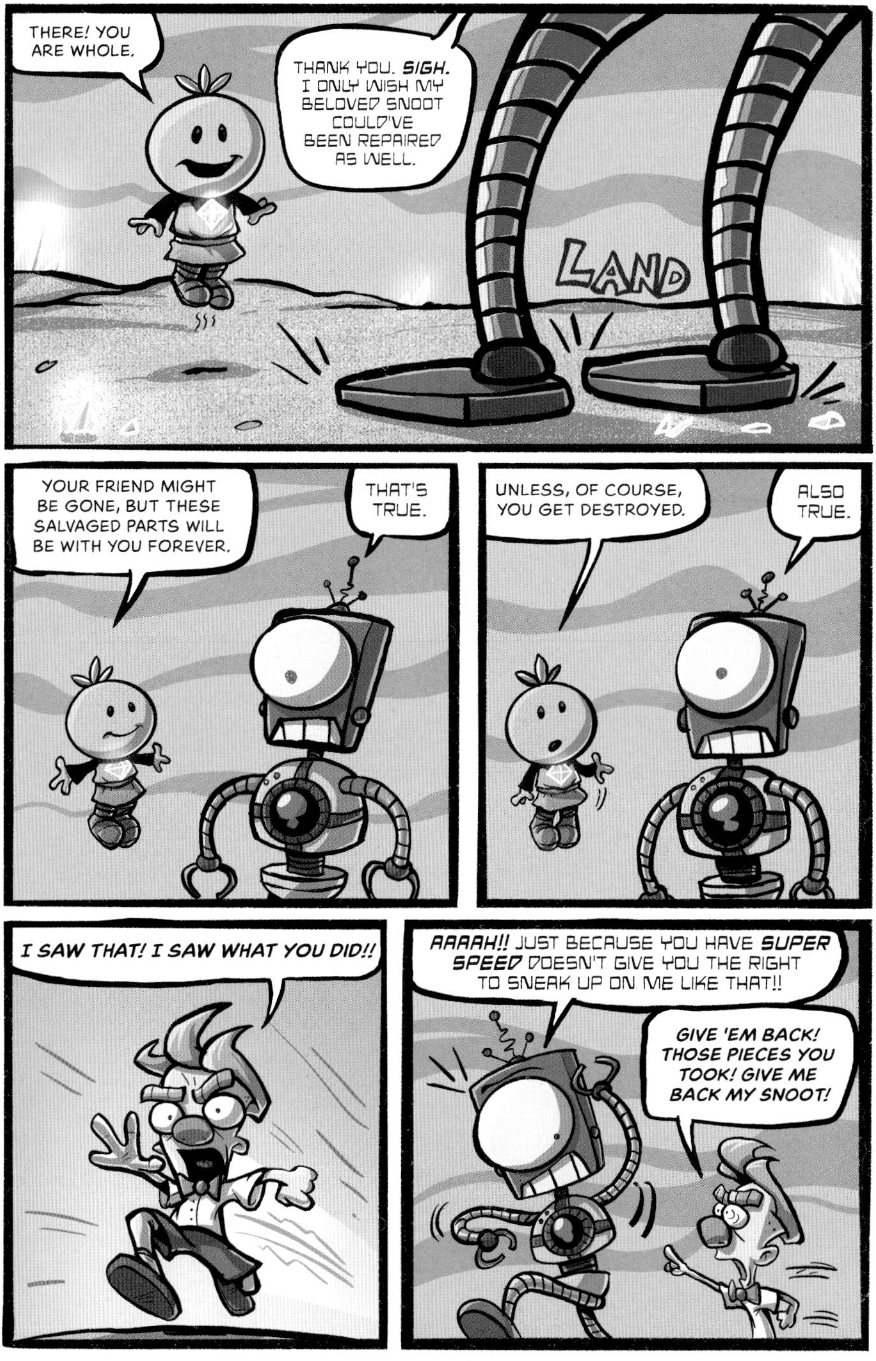
THERE! YOU ARE WHOLE.
THANK YOU. SIGH. I ONLY WISH MY BELOVED SNOOT COULD'VE BEEN REPAIRED AS WELL.
LAND
YOUR FRIEND MIGHT BE GONE, BUT THESE SALVAGED PARTS WILL BE WITH YOU FOREVER.
THAT'S TRUE.
UNLESS, OF COURSE, YOU GET DESTROYED.
ALSO TRUE.
I SAW THAT! I SAW WHAT YOU DID!!
AAAAH!! JUST BECAUSE YOU HAVE SUPER SPEED DOESN'T GIVE YOU THE RIGHT TO SNEAK UP ON ME LIKE THAT!!
GIVE 'EM BACK! THOSE PIECES YOU TOOK! GIVE ME BACK MY SNOOT!

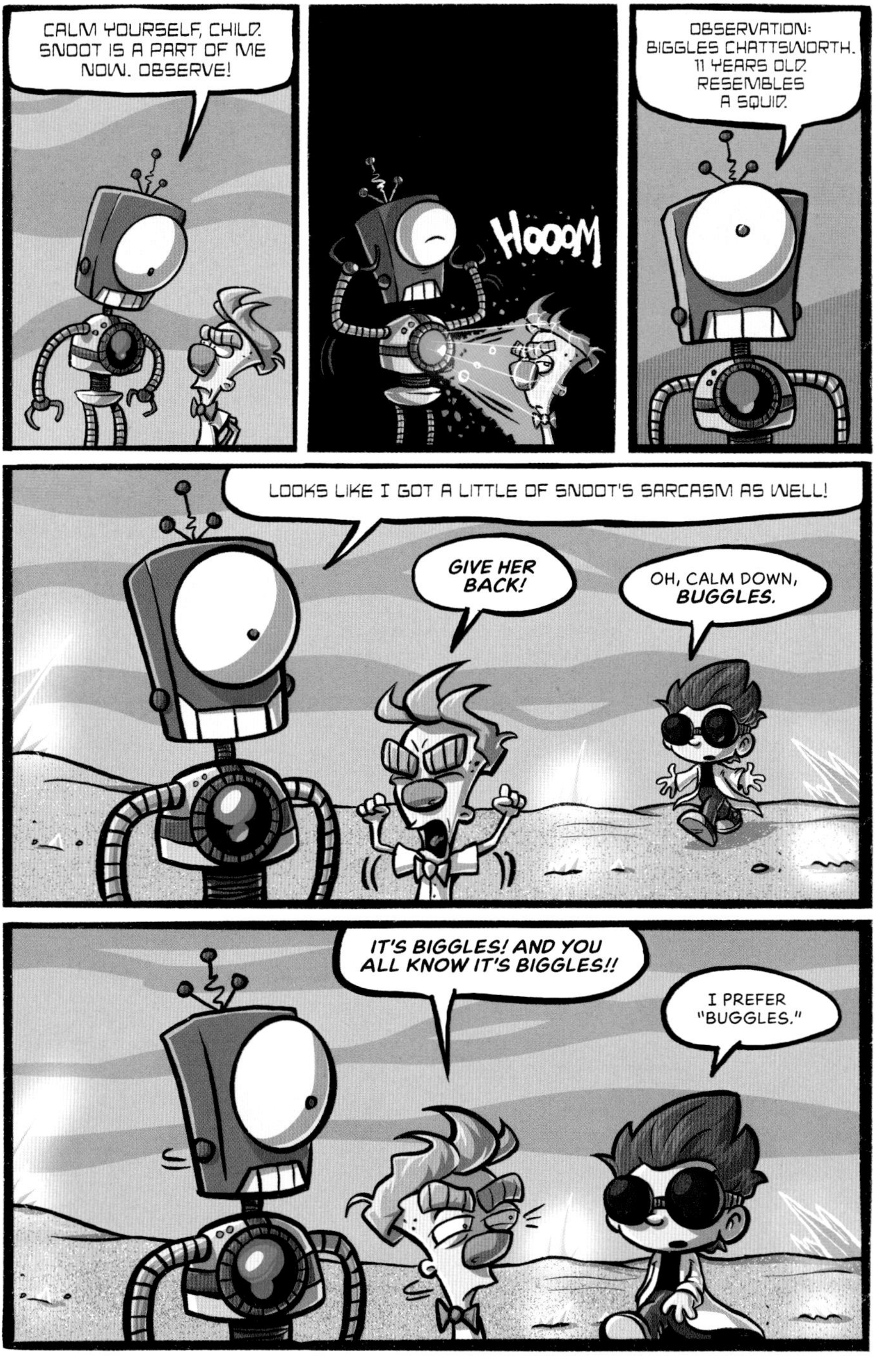
CALM YOURSELF, CHILD. SNOOT IS A PART OF ME NOW. OBSERVE!
HOOOM
OBSERVATION: BIGGLES CHATTSWORTH. 11 YEARS OLD. RESEMBLES A SQUID.
LOOKS LIKE I GOT A LITTLE OF SNOOT'S SARCASM AS WELL!
GIVE HER BACK!
OH, CALM DOWN, BUGGLES.
IT'S BIGGLES! AND YOU ALL KNOW IT'S BIGGLES!!
I PREFER "BUGGLES."

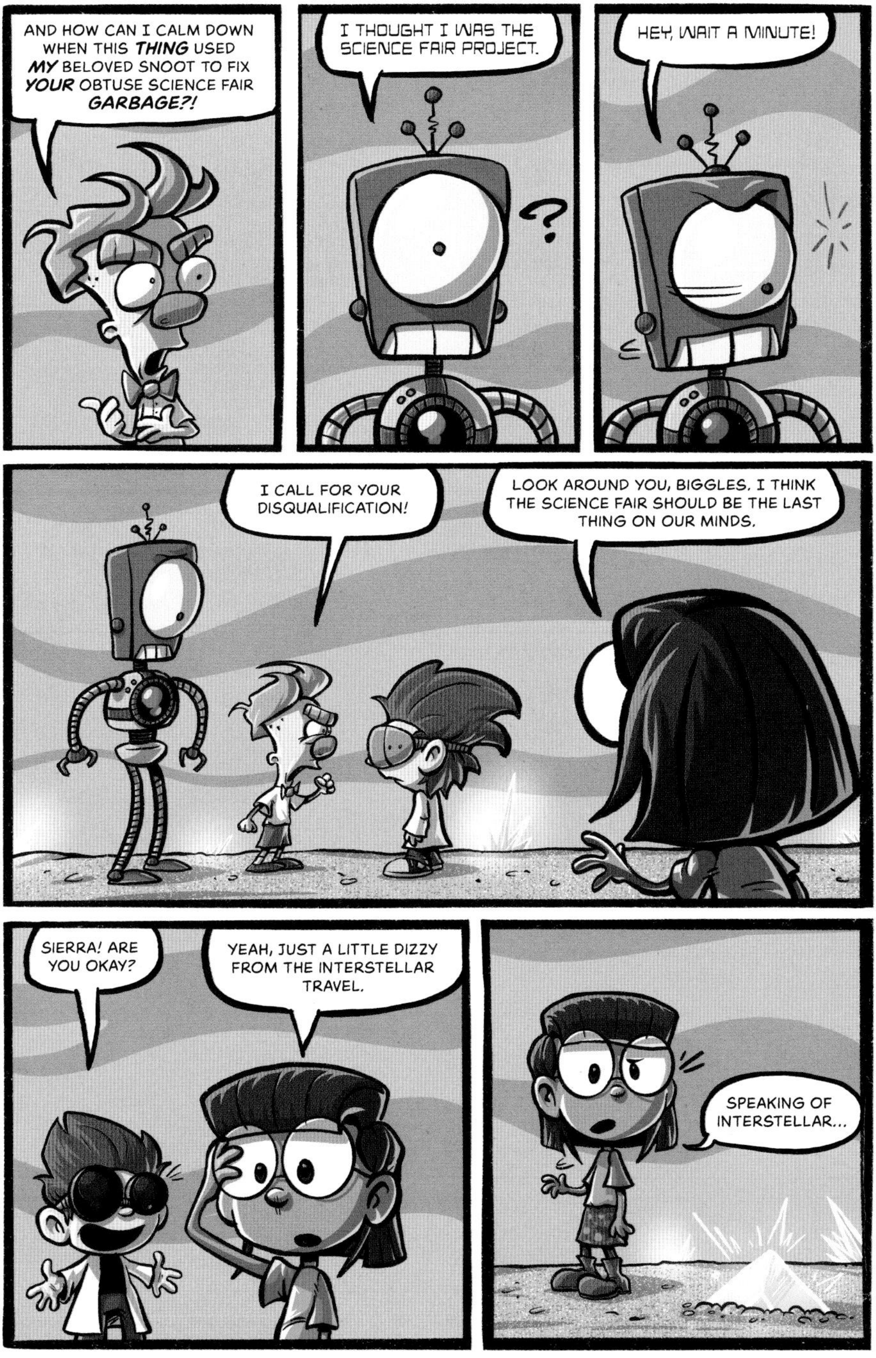
AND HOW CAN I CALM DOWN WHEN THIS **THING** USED **MY** BELOVED SNOOT TO FIX **YOUR** OBTUSE SCIENCE FAIR **GARBAGE?!**
I THOUGHT I WAS THE SCIENCE FAIR PROJECT.
?
HEY, WAIT A MINUTE!
I CALL FOR YOUR DISQUALIFICATION!
LOOK AROUND YOU, BIGGLES. I THINK THE SCIENCE FAIR SHOULD BE THE LAST THING ON OUR MINDS.
SIERRA! ARE YOU OKAY?
YEAH, JUST A LITTLE DIZZY FROM THE INTERSTELLAR TRAVEL.
SPEAKING OF INTERSTELLAR...

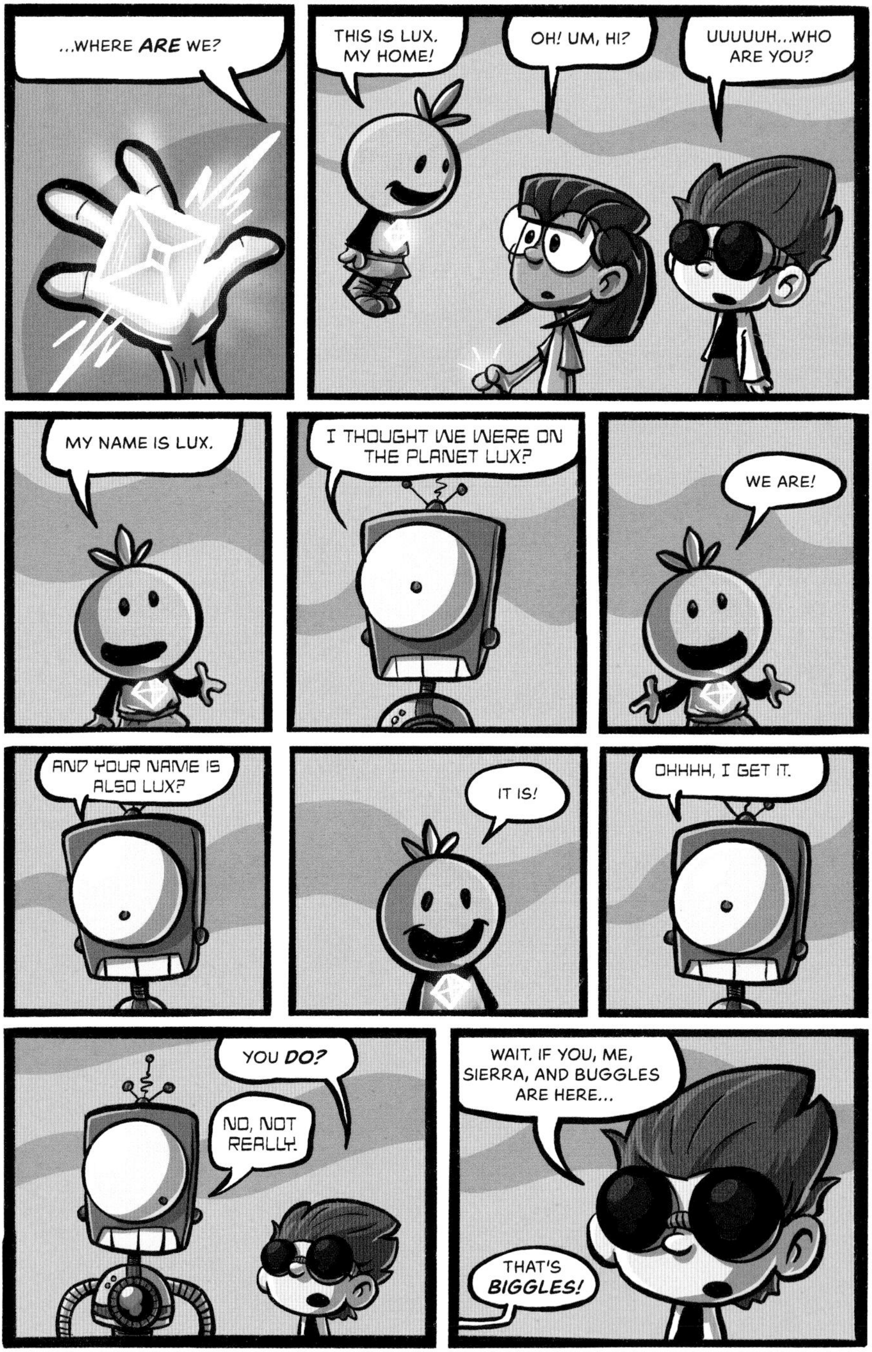
...WHERE ARE WE?
THIS IS LUX. MY HOME!
OH! UM, HI?
UUUUUH...WHO ARE YOU?
MY NAME IS LUX.
I THOUGHT WE WERE ON THE PLANET LUX?
WE ARE!
AND YOUR NAME IS ALSO LUX?
IT IS!
OHHHH, I GET IT.
YOU DO?
NO, NOT REALLY.
WAIT. IF YOU, ME, SIERRA, AND BUGGLES ARE HERE...
THAT'S BIGGLES!

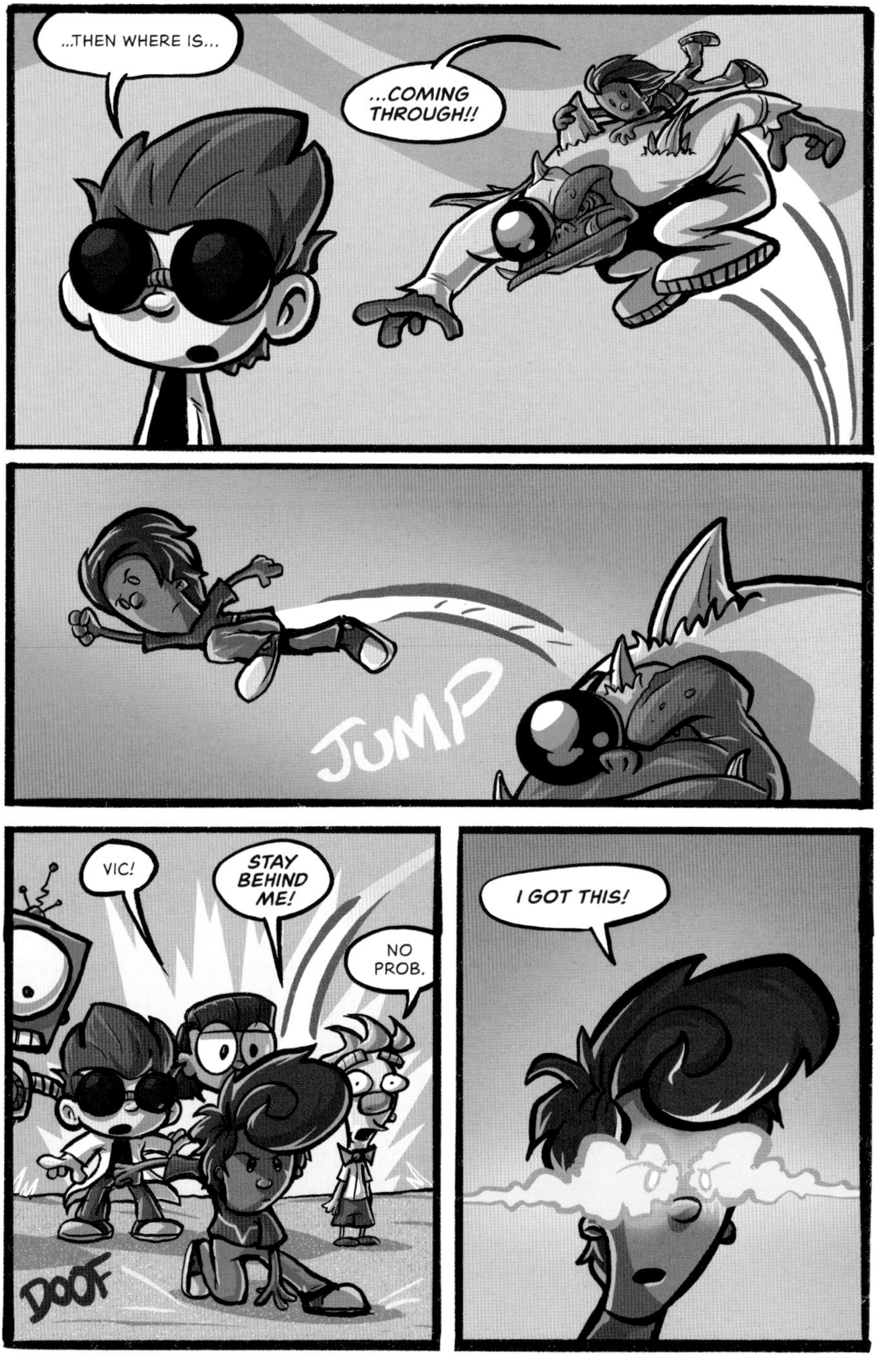
...THEN WHERE IS...
...COMING THROUGH!!
JUMP
VIC!
STAY BEHIND ME!
NO PROB.
DOOF
I GOT THIS!

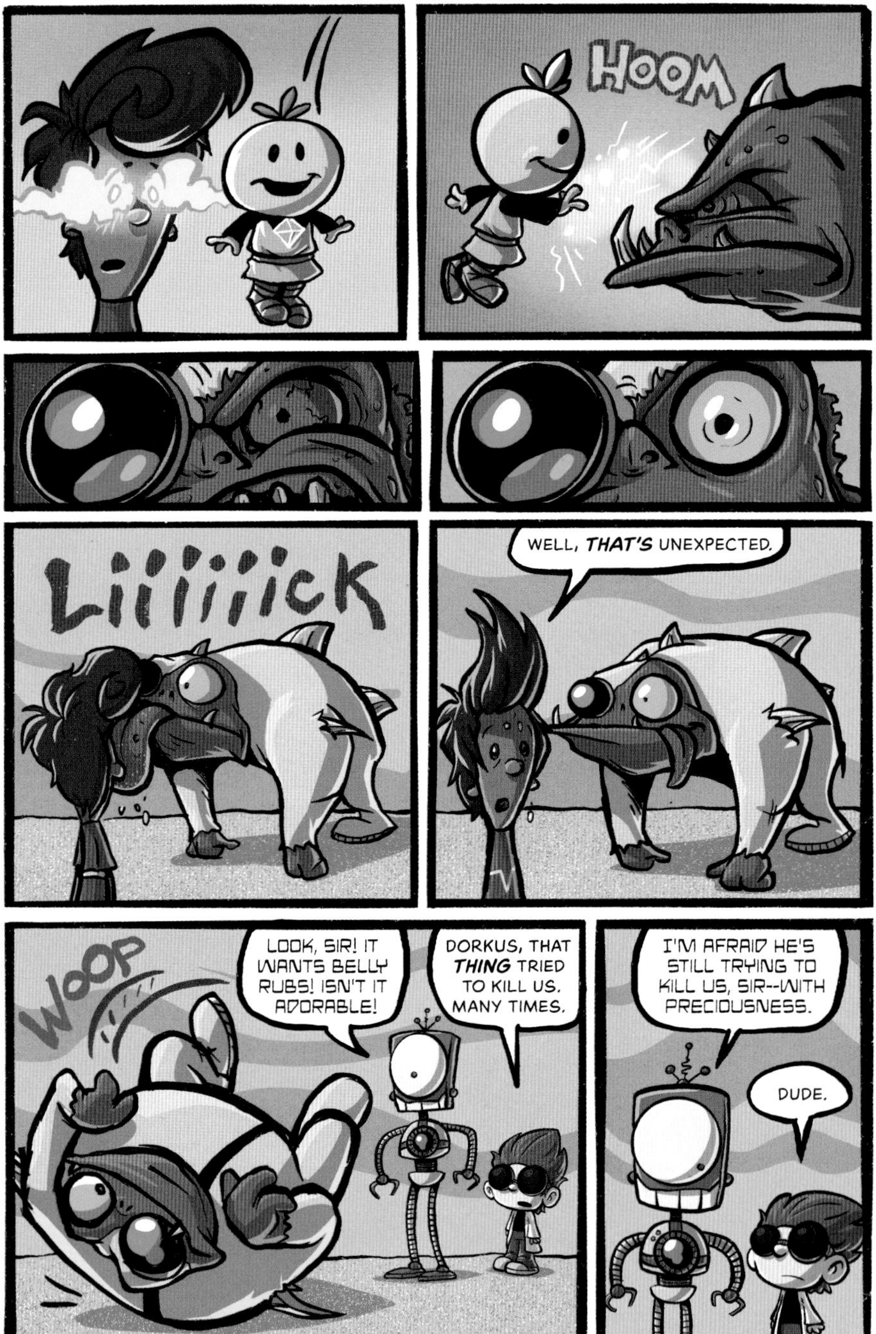
HOOM
Liiiiick
WELL, THAT'S UNEXPECTED.
WOOP
LOOK, SIR! IT WANTS BELLY RUBS! ISN'T IT ADORABLE!
DORKUS, THAT THING TRIED TO KILL US. MANY TIMES.
I'M AFRAID HE'S STILL TRYING TO KILL US, SIR--WITH PRECIOUSNESS.
DUDE.

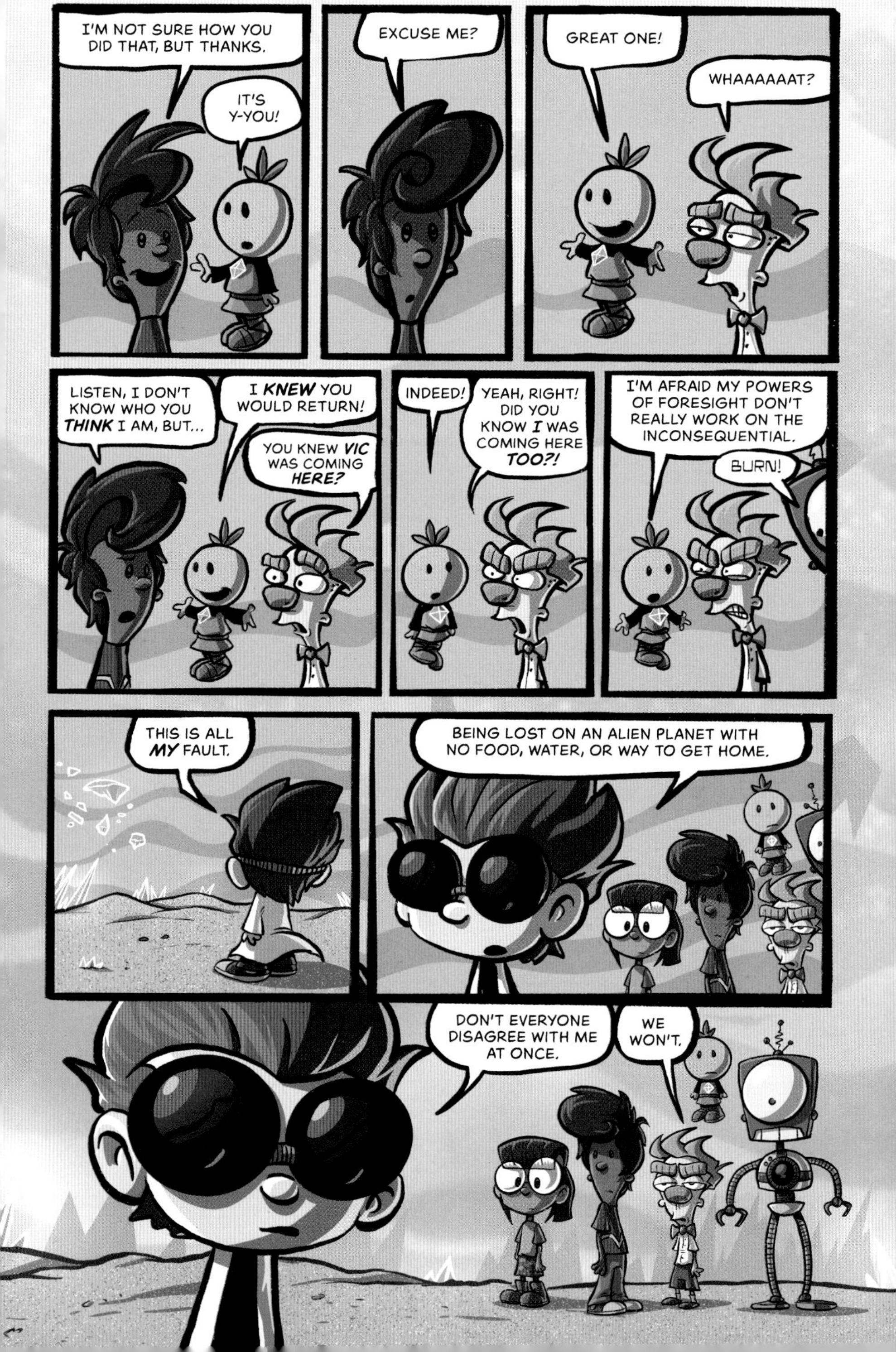

I'M NOT SURE HOW YOU DID THAT, BUT THANKS.
IT'S Y-YOU!
EXCUSE ME?
GREAT ONE!
WHAAAAAAT?
LISTEN, I DON'T KNOW WHO YOU *THINK* I AM, BUT...
I *KNEW* YOU WOULD RETURN!
YOU KNEW *VIC* WAS COMING *HERE?*
INDEED!
YEAH, RIGHT! DID YOU KNOW *I* WAS COMING HERE *TOO?!*
I'M AFRAID MY POWERS OF FORESIGHT DON'T REALLY WORK ON THE INCONSEQUENTIAL.
BURN!
THIS IS ALL *MY* FAULT.
BEING LOST ON AN ALIEN PLANET WITH NO FOOD, WATER, OR WAY TO GET HOME.
DON'T EVERYONE DISAGREE WITH ME AT ONCE.
WE WON'T.

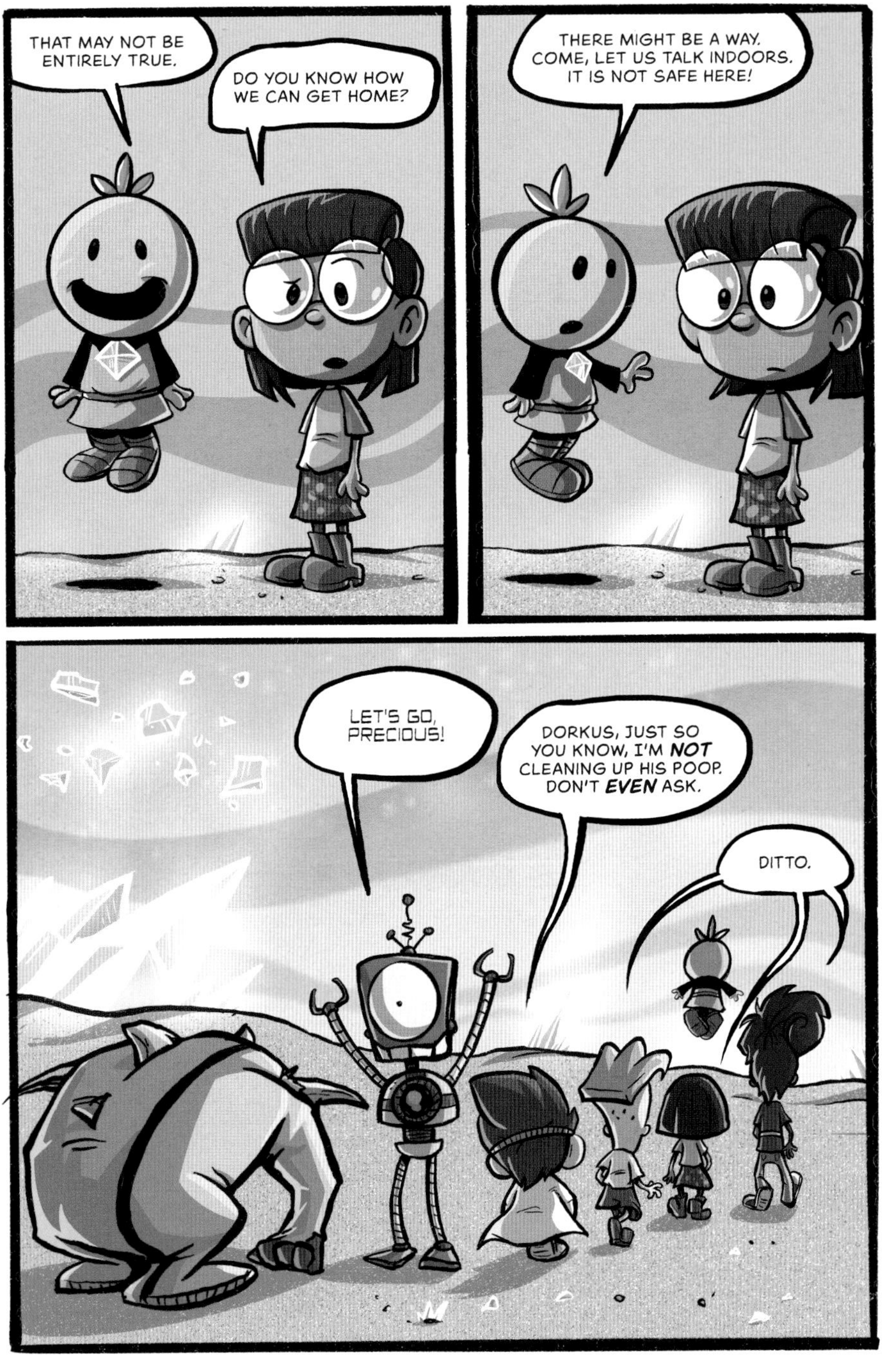
THAT MAY NOT BE ENTIRELY TRUE.
DO YOU KNOW HOW WE CAN GET HOME?
THERE MIGHT BE A WAY. COME, LET US TALK INDOORS. IT IS NOT SAFE HERE!
LET'S GO, PRECIOUS!
DORKUS, JUST SO YOU KNOW, I'M **NOT** CLEANING UP HIS POOP. DON'T **EVEN** ASK.
DITTO.

CHAPTER 3

A Walk to Forget

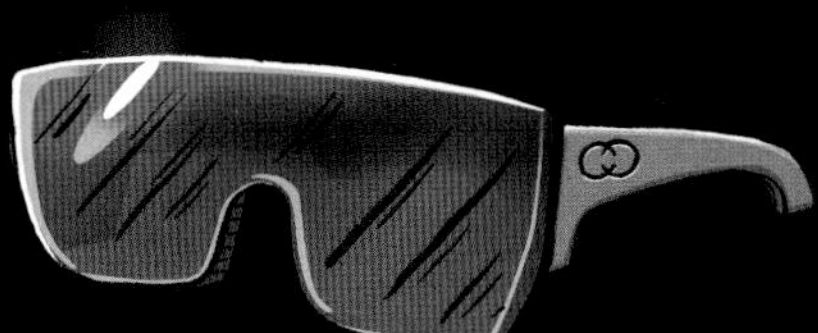

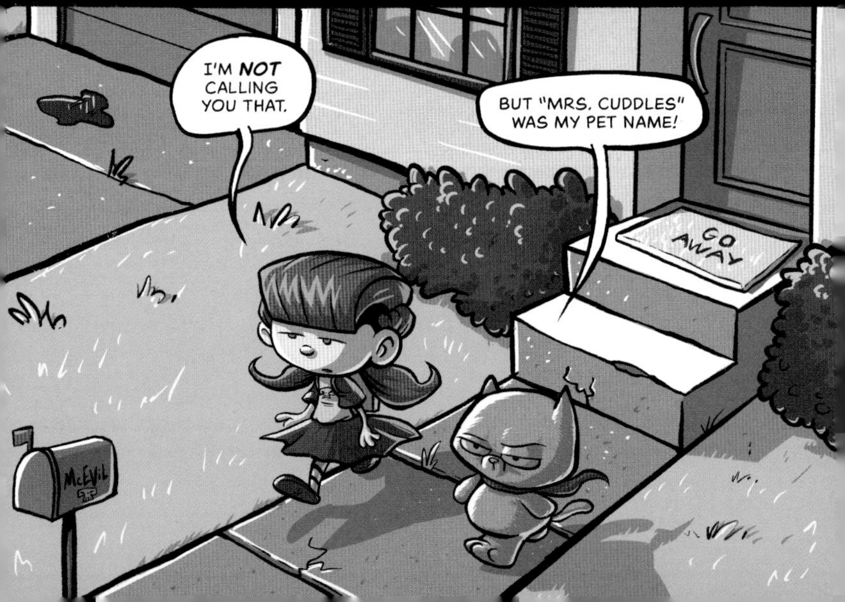

I'M **NOT** CALLING YOU THAT.
BUT "MRS. CUDDLES" WAS MY PET NAME!
GO AWAY
McEVIL

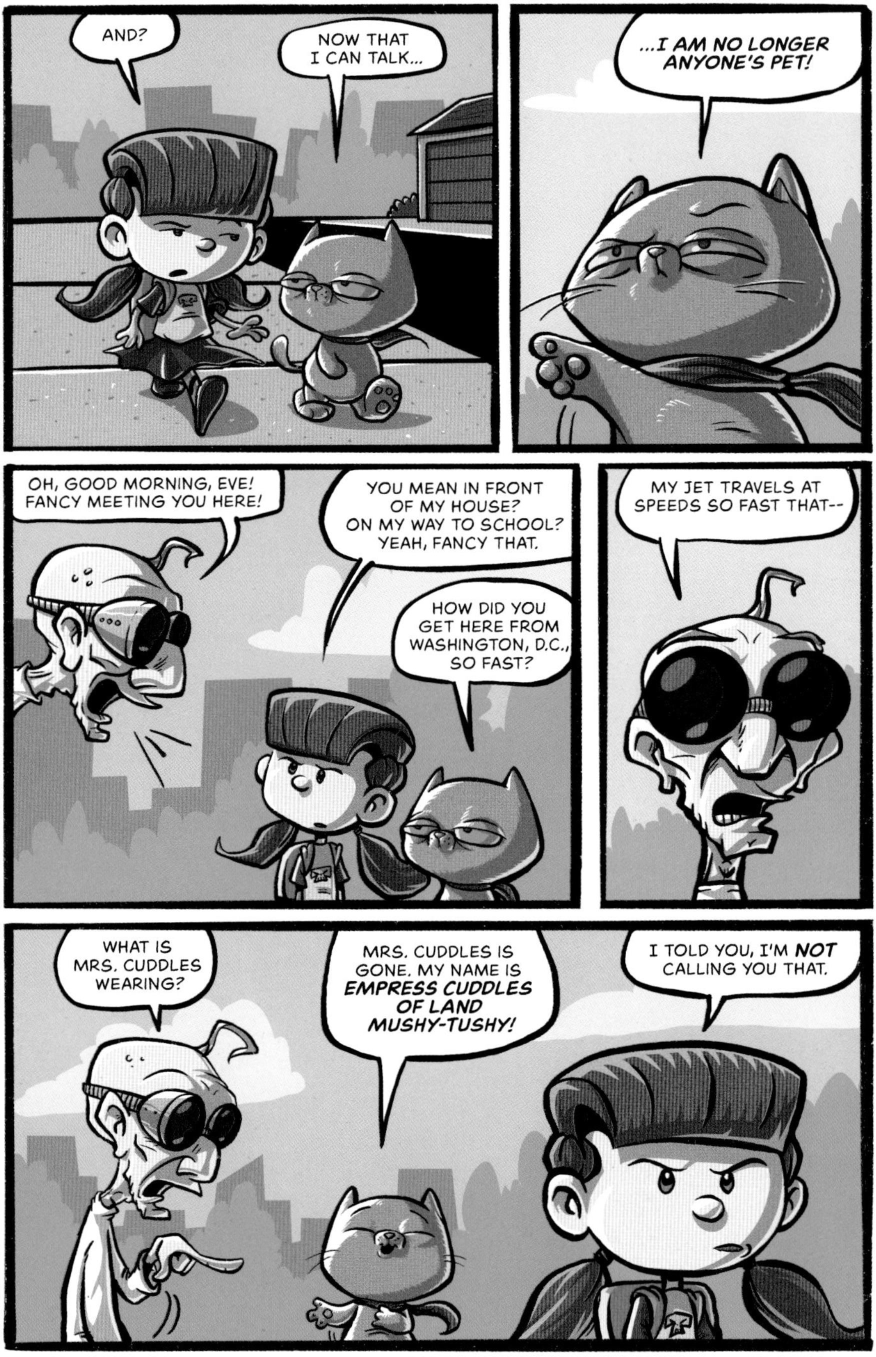
AND?
NOW THAT I CAN TALK...
...I AM NO LONGER ANYONE'S PET!
OH, GOOD MORNING, EVE! FANCY MEETING YOU HERE!
YOU MEAN IN FRONT OF MY HOUSE? ON MY WAY TO SCHOOL? YEAH, FANCY THAT.
HOW DID YOU GET HERE FROM WASHINGTON, D.C., SO FAST?
MY JET TRAVELS AT SPEEDS SO FAST THAT--
WHAT IS MRS. CUDDLES WEARING?
MRS. CUDDLES IS GONE. MY NAME IS EMPRESS CUDDLES OF LAND MUSHY-TUSHY!
I TOLD YOU, I'M NOT CALLING YOU THAT.

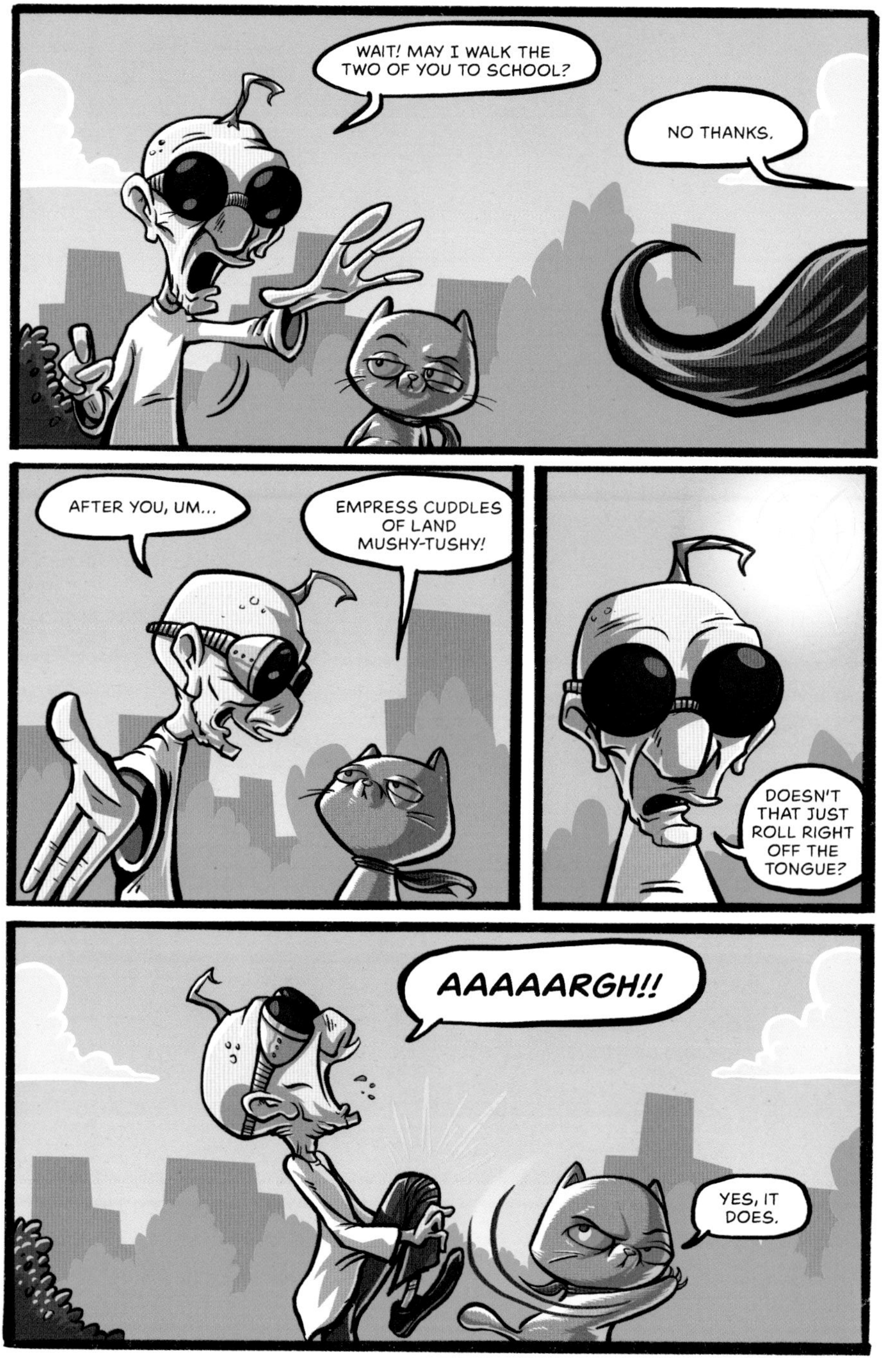
WAIT! MAY I WALK THE TWO OF YOU TO SCHOOL?
NO THANKS.
AFTER YOU, UM...
EMPRESS CUDDLES OF LAND MUSHY-TUSHY!
DOESN'T THAT JUST ROLL RIGHT OFF THE TONGUE?
AAAAARGH!!
YES, IT DOES.

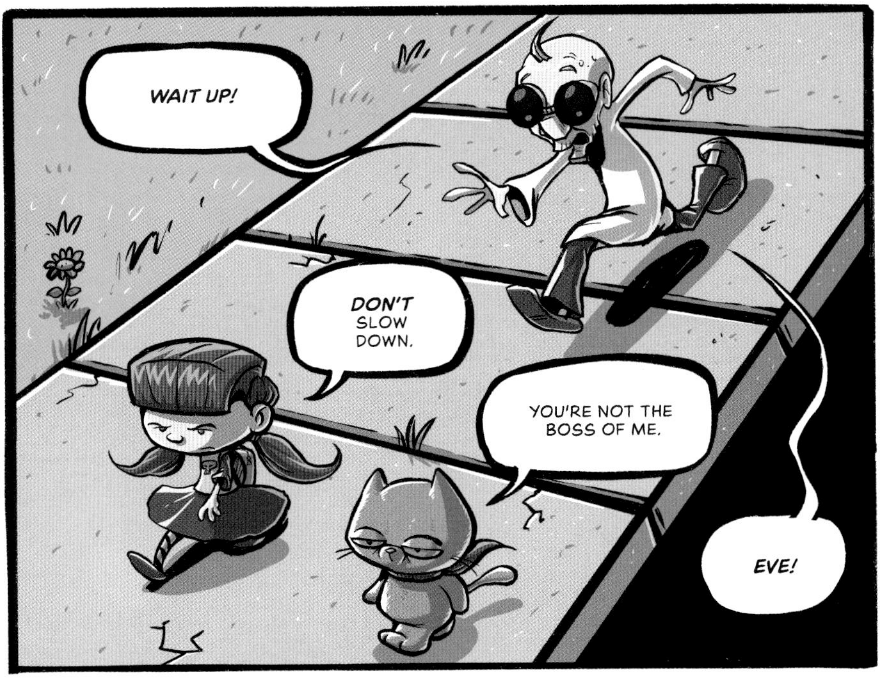
WAIT UP!
DON'T SLOW DOWN.
YOU'RE NOT THE BOSS OF ME.
EVE!

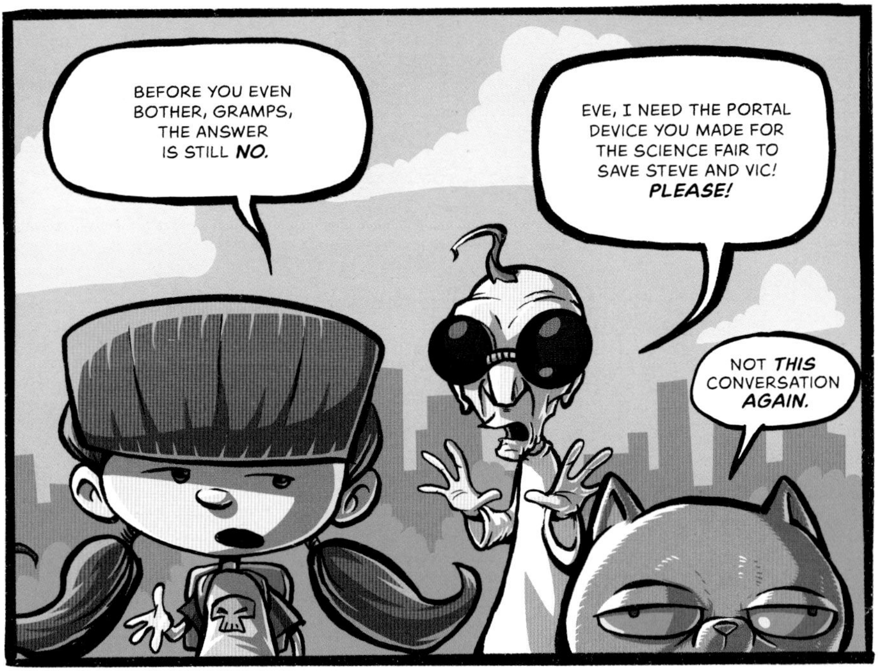
BEFORE YOU EVEN BOTHER, GRAMPS, THE ANSWER IS STILL NO.
EVE, I NEED THE PORTAL DEVICE YOU MADE FOR THE SCIENCE FAIR TO SAVE STEVE AND VIC! PLEASE!
NOT THIS CONVERSATION AGAIN.

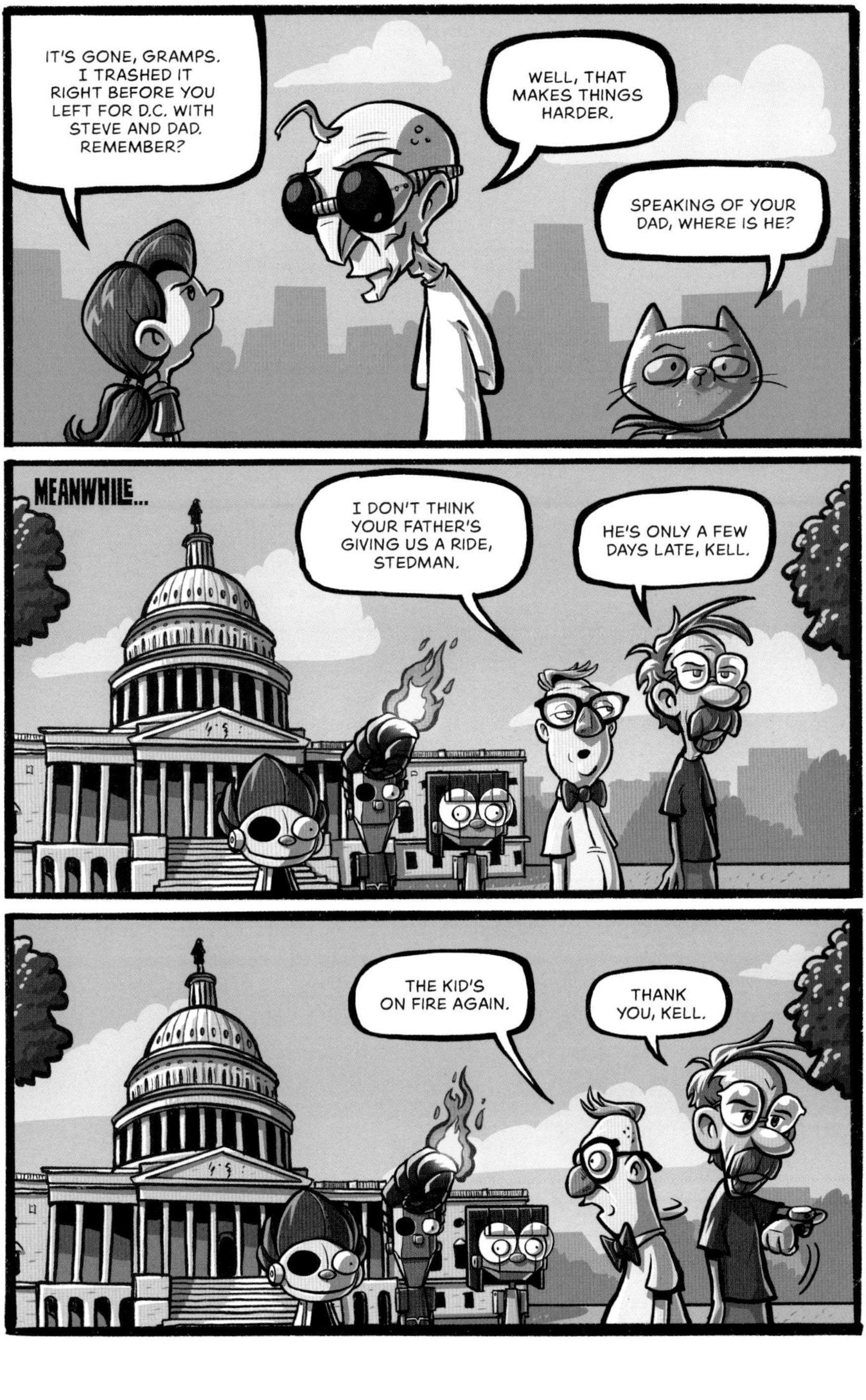
IT'S GONE, GRAMPS. I TRASHED IT RIGHT BEFORE YOU LEFT FOR D.C. WITH STEVE AND DAD. REMEMBER?
WELL, THAT MAKES THINGS HARDER.
SPEAKING OF YOUR DAD, WHERE IS HE?
MEANWHILE...
I DON'T THINK YOUR FATHER'S GIVING US A RIDE, STEDMAN.
HE'S ONLY A FEW DAYS LATE, KELL.
THE KID'S ON FIRE AGAIN.
THANK YOU, KELL.

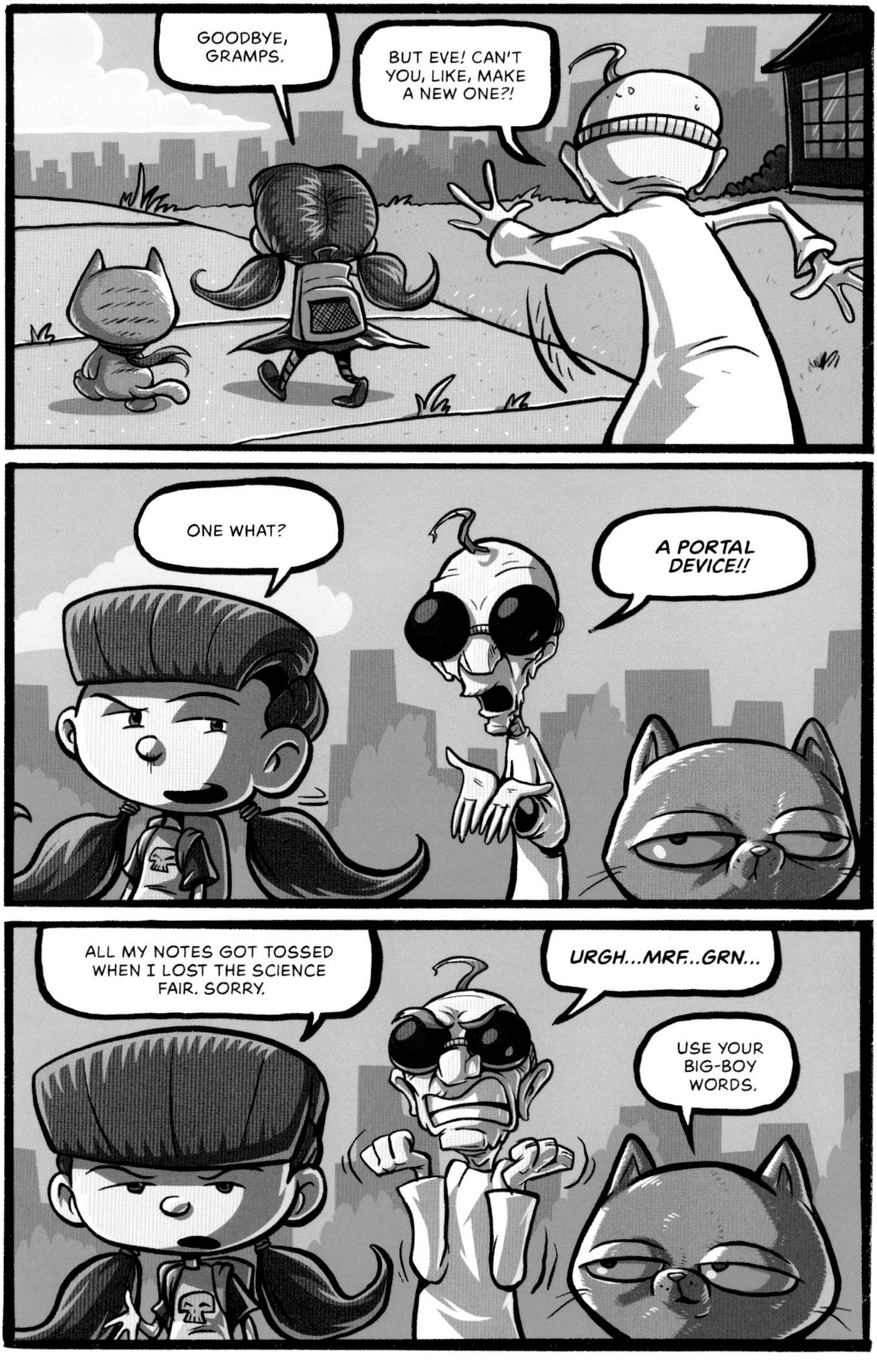
GOODBYE, GRAMPS.
BUT EVE! CAN'T YOU, LIKE, MAKE A NEW ONE?!
ONE WHAT?
A PORTAL DEVICE!!
ALL MY NOTES GOT TOSSED WHEN I LOST THE SCIENCE FAIR. SORRY.
URGH...MRF...GRN...
USE YOUR BIG-BOY WORDS.

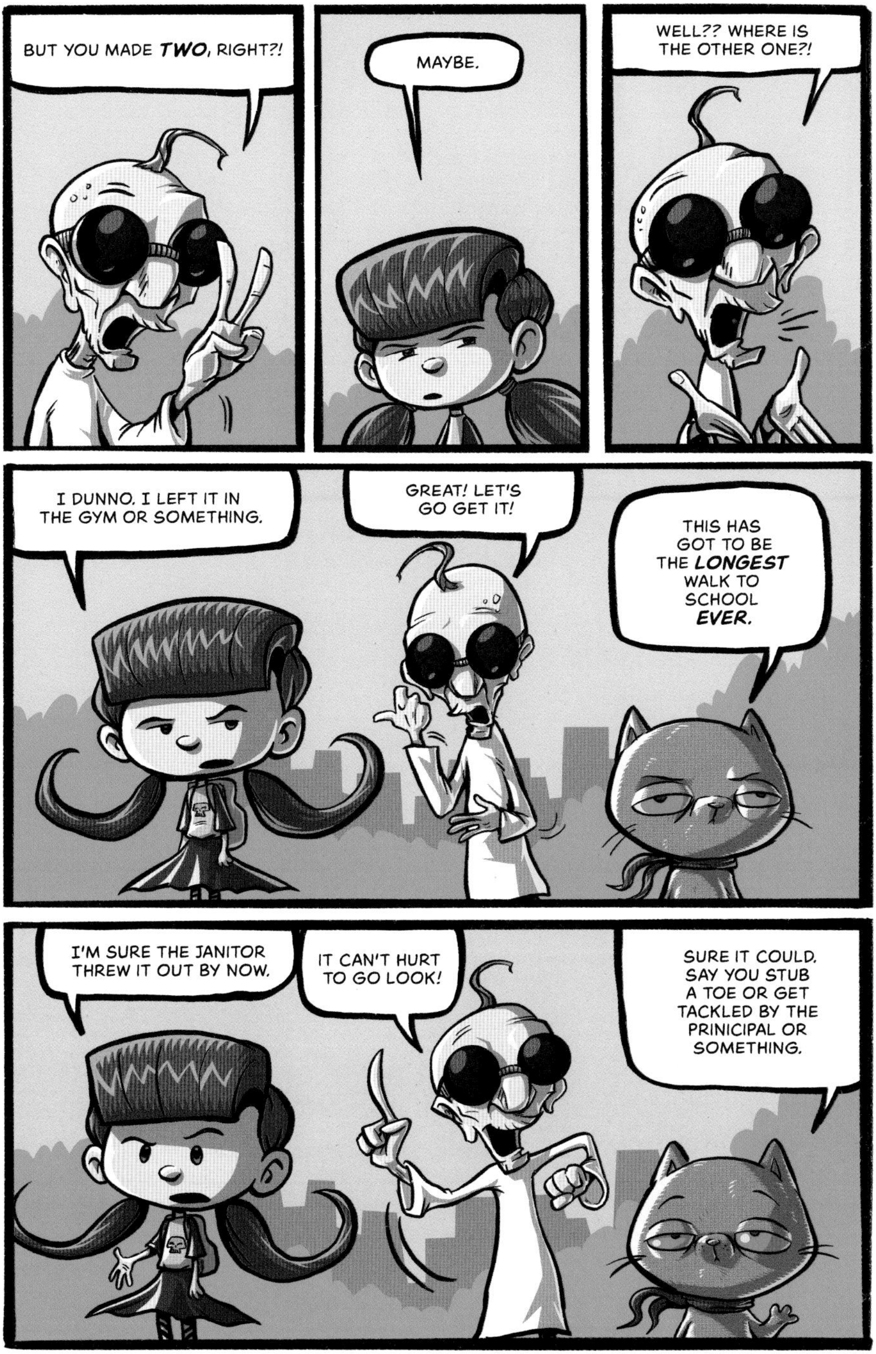
BUT YOU MADE **TWO**, RIGHT?!
MAYBE.
WELL?? WHERE IS THE OTHER ONE?!
I DUNNO. I LEFT IT IN THE GYM OR SOMETHING.
GREAT! LET'S GO GET IT!
THIS HAS GOT TO BE THE **LONGEST** WALK TO SCHOOL **EVER.**
I'M SURE THE JANITOR THREW IT OUT BY NOW.
IT CAN'T HURT TO GO LOOK!
SURE IT COULD. SAY YOU STUB A TOE OR GET TACKLED BY THE PRINICIPAL OR SOMETHING.

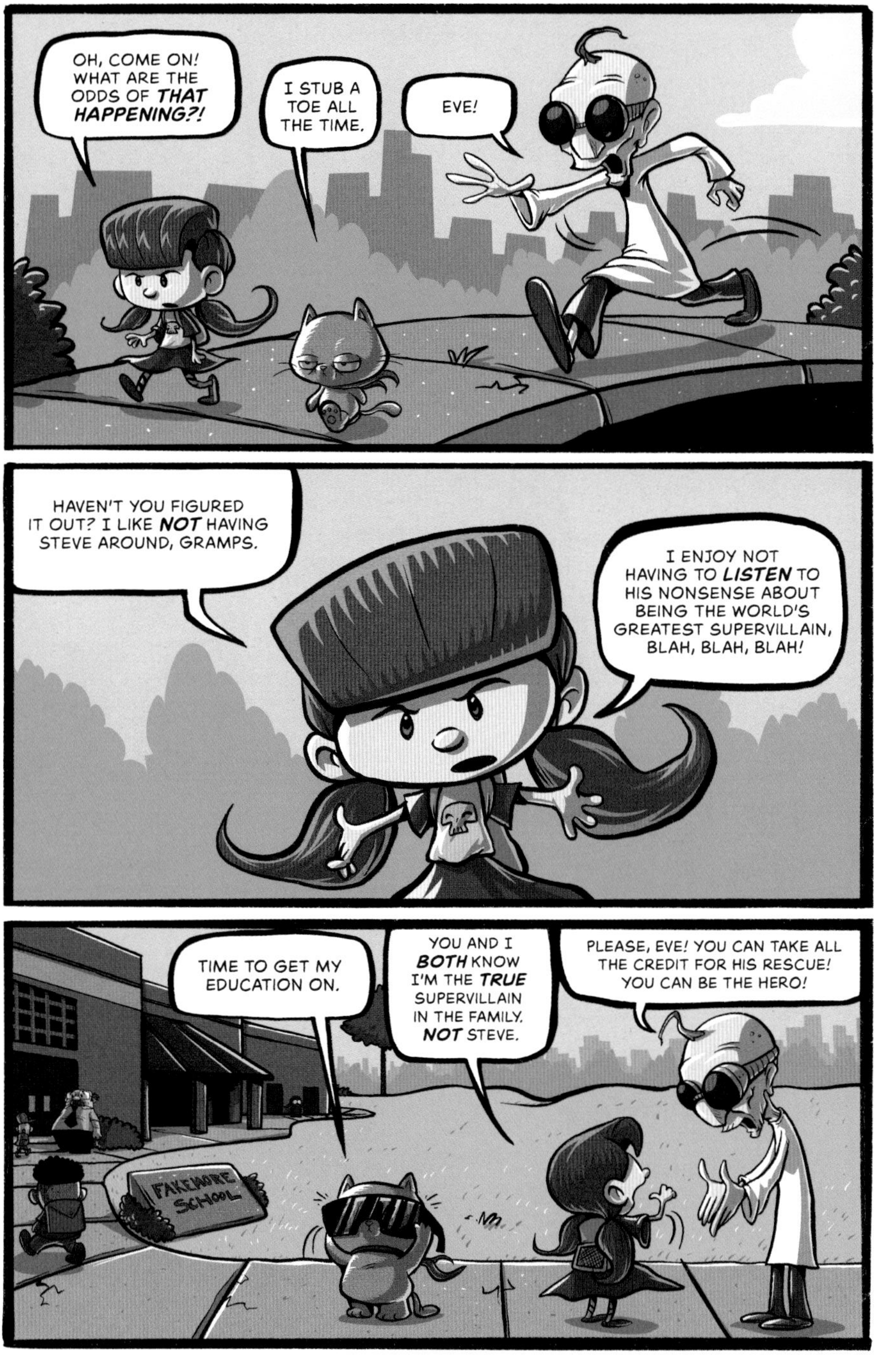

OH, COME ON! WHAT ARE THE ODDS OF **THAT HAPPENING?!**
I STUB A TOE ALL THE TIME.
EVE!
HAVEN'T YOU FIGURED IT OUT? I LIKE **NOT** HAVING STEVE AROUND, GRAMPS.
I ENJOY NOT HAVING TO **LISTEN** TO HIS NONSENSE ABOUT BEING THE WORLD'S GREATEST SUPERVILLAIN, BLAH, BLAH, BLAH!
FAKEMORE SCHOOL
TIME TO GET MY EDUCATION ON.
YOU AND I **BOTH** KNOW I'M THE **TRUE** SUPERVILLAIN IN THE FAMILY. **NOT** STEVE.
PLEASE, EVE! YOU CAN TAKE ALL THE CREDIT FOR HIS RESCUE! YOU CAN BE THE HERO!

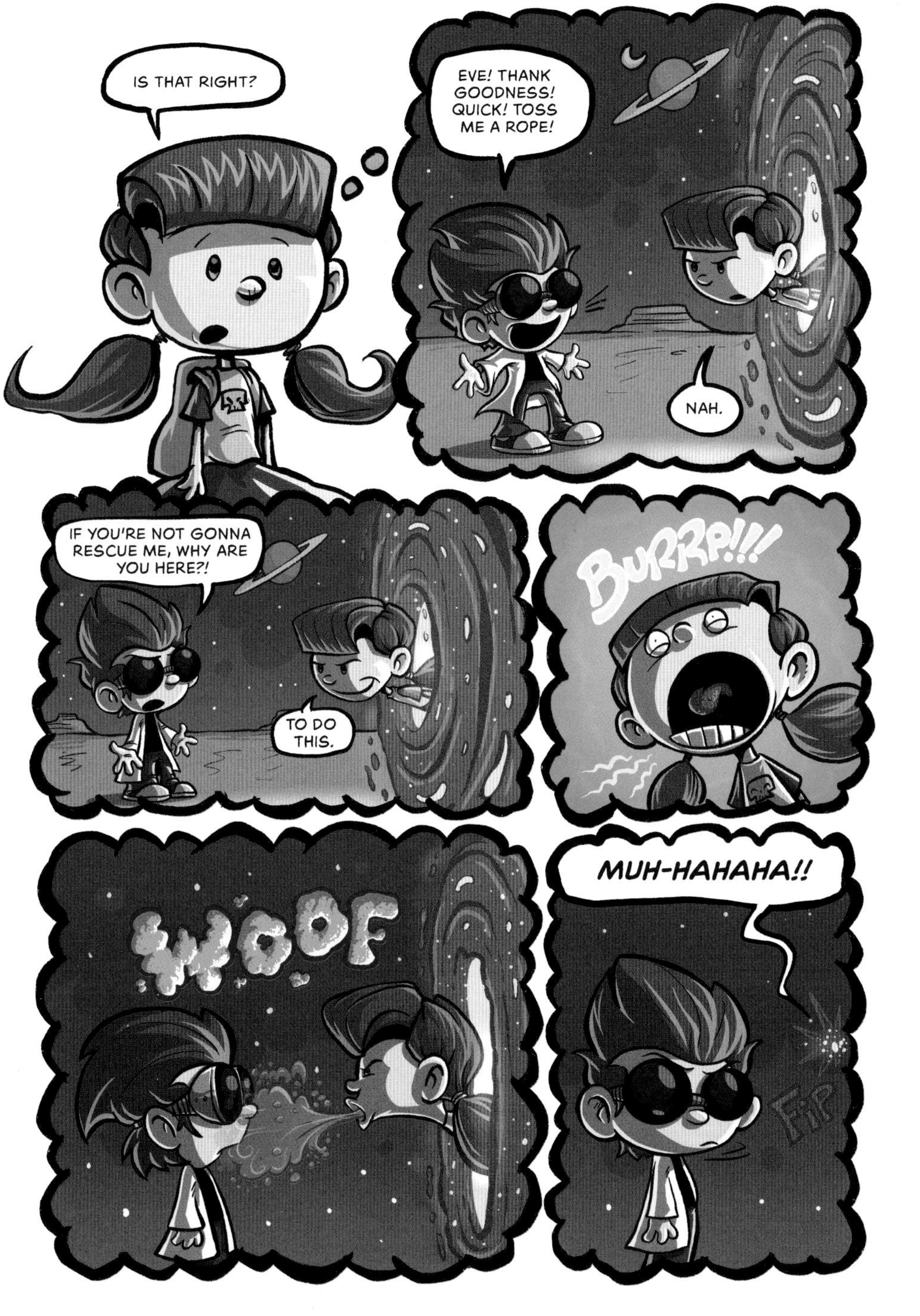
IS THAT RIGHT?
EVE! THANK GOODNESS! QUICK! TOSS ME A ROPE!
NAH.
IF YOU'RE NOT GONNA RESCUE ME, WHY ARE YOU HERE?!
TO DO THIS.
BURRP!!!
WOOF
MUH-HAHAHA!!
FIP

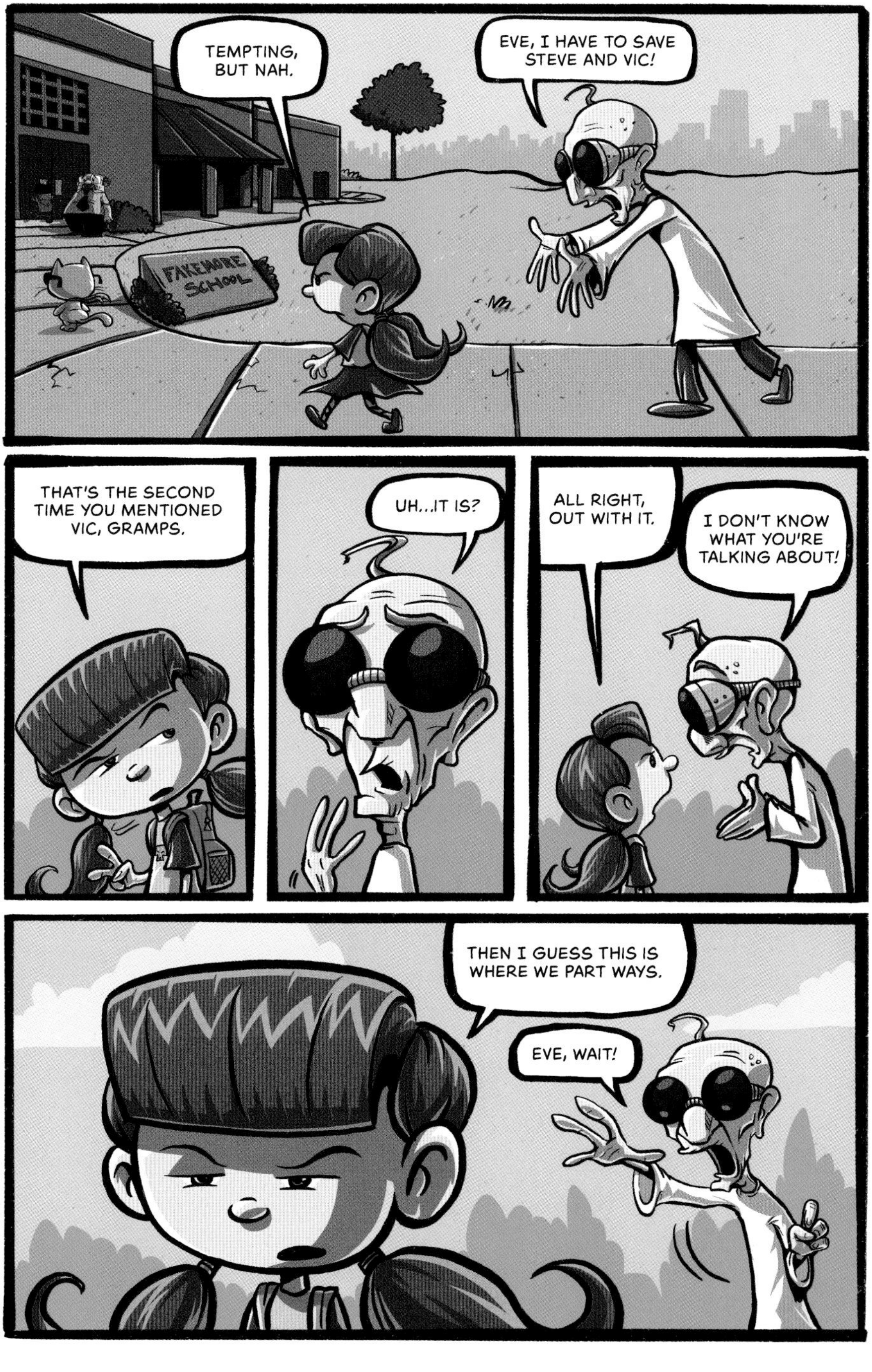
TEMPTING, BUT NAH.
EVE, I HAVE TO SAVE STEVE AND VIC!
FAKEMORE SCHOOL
THAT'S THE SECOND TIME YOU MENTIONED VIC, GRAMPS.
UH...IT IS?
ALL RIGHT, OUT WITH IT.
I DON'T KNOW WHAT YOU'RE TALKING ABOUT!
THEN I GUESS THIS IS WHERE WE PART WAYS.
EVE, WAIT!

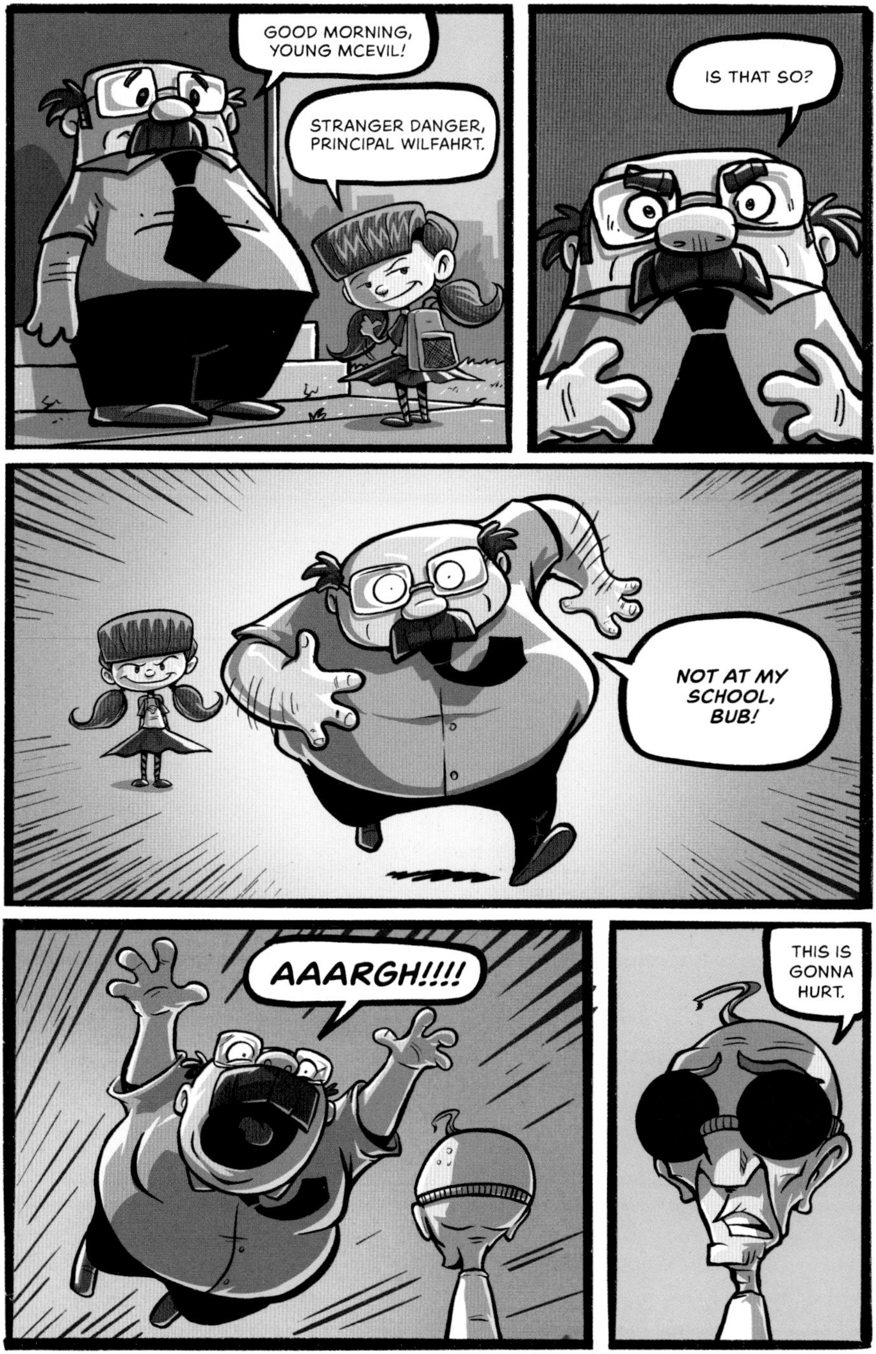
GOOD MORNING, YOUNG MCEVIL!
STRANGER DANGER, PRINCIPAL WILFAHRT.
IS THAT SO?
NOT AT MY SCHOOL, BUB!
AAARGH!!!!
THIS IS GONNA HURT.

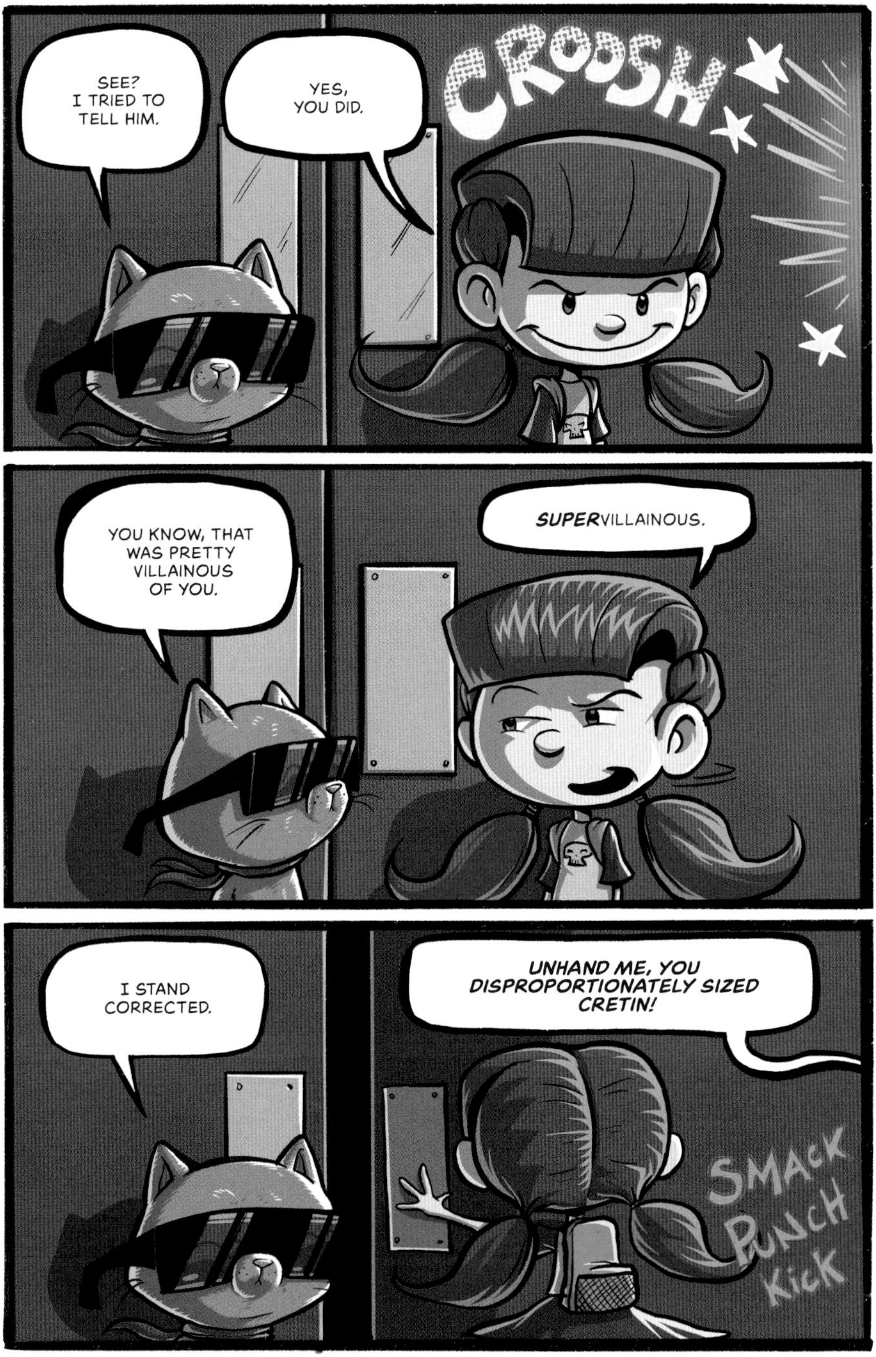
SEE? I TRIED TO TELL HIM.
YES, YOU DID.
CROOSH
YOU KNOW, THAT WAS PRETTY VILLAINOUS OF YOU.
SUPERVILLAINOUS.
I STAND CORRECTED.
UNHAND ME, YOU DISPROPORTIONATELY SIZED CRETIN!
SMACK
PUNCH
KICK

CHAPTER 4
Family's History

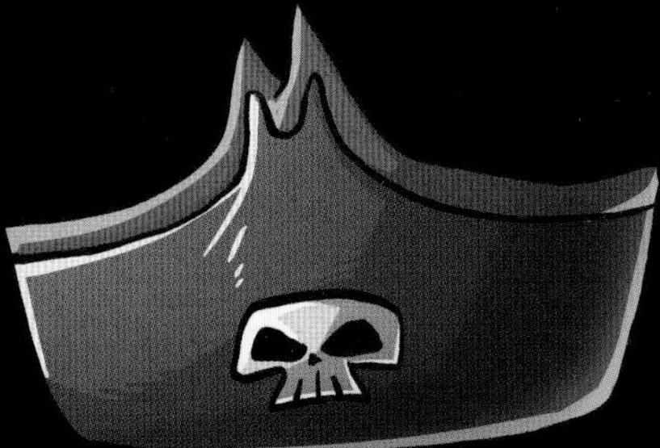

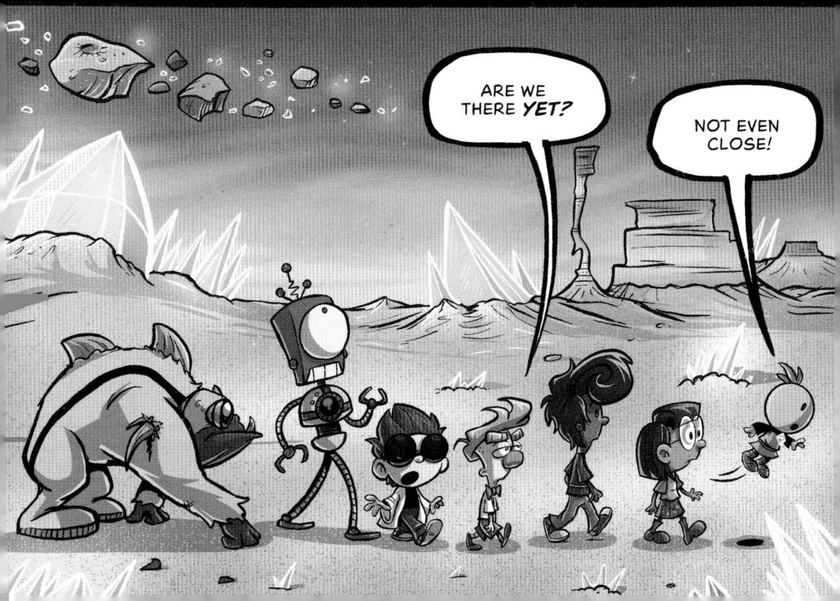
ARE WE THERE *YET?*
NOT EVEN CLOSE!

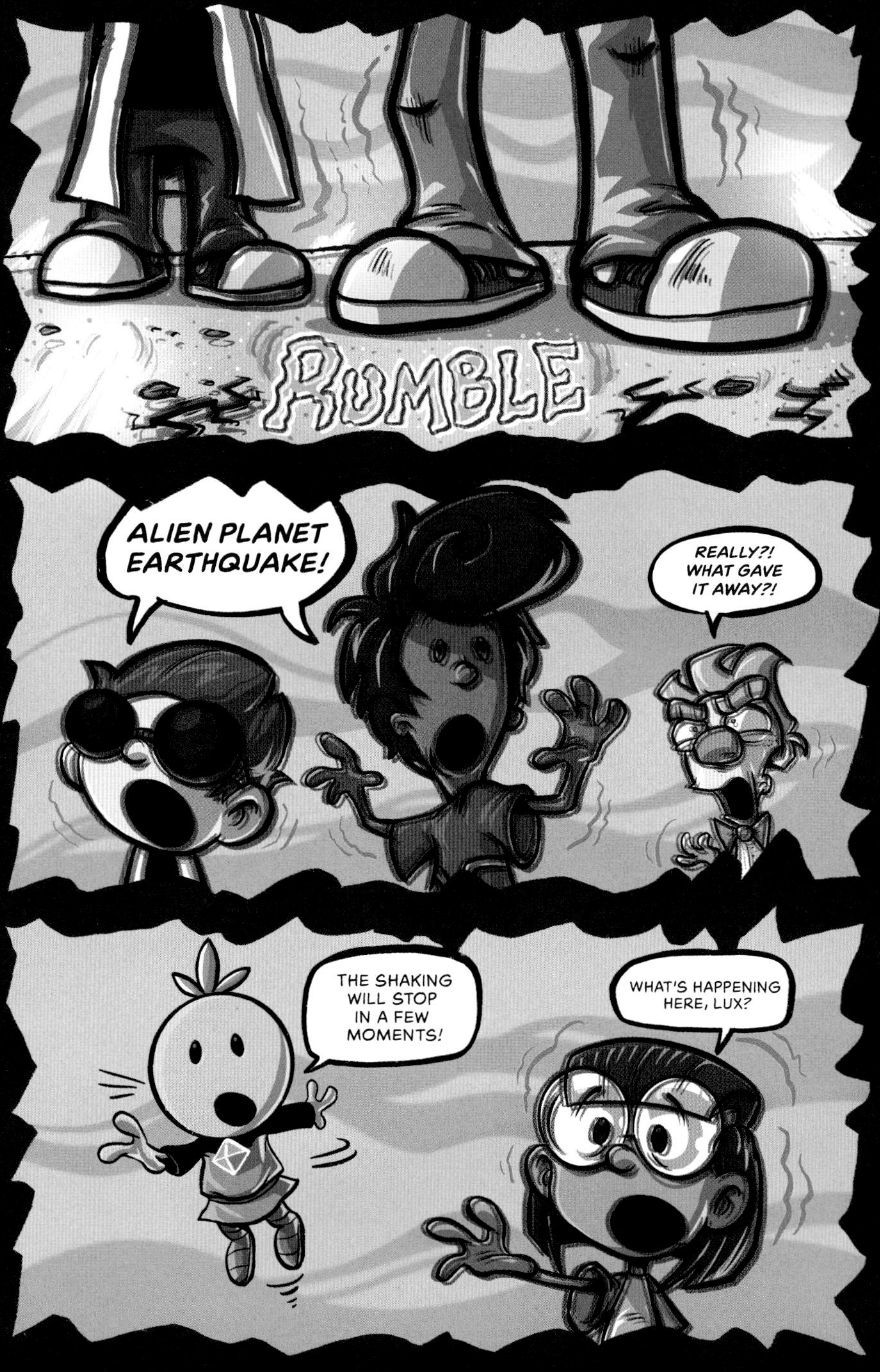
RUMBLE
ALIEN PLANET EARTHQUAKE!
REALLY?! WHAT GAVE IT AWAY?!
THE SHAKING WILL STOP IN A FEW MOMENTS!
WHAT'S HAPPENING HERE, LUX?

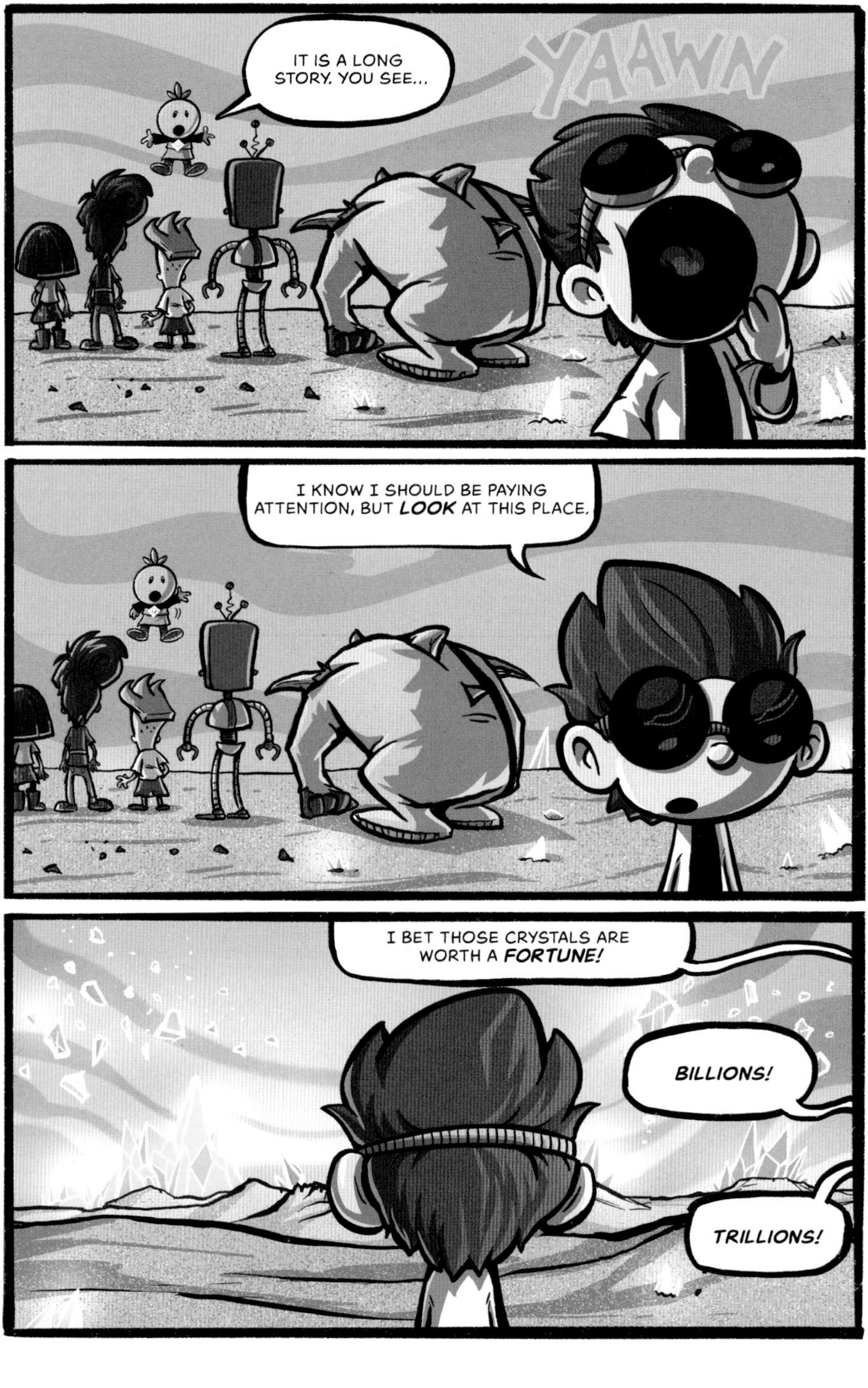
IT IS A LONG STORY. YOU SEE...
YAAWN
I KNOW I SHOULD BE PAYING ATTENTION, BUT LOOK AT THIS PLACE.
I BET THOSE CRYSTALS ARE WORTH A FORTUNE!
BILLIONS!
TRILLIONS!

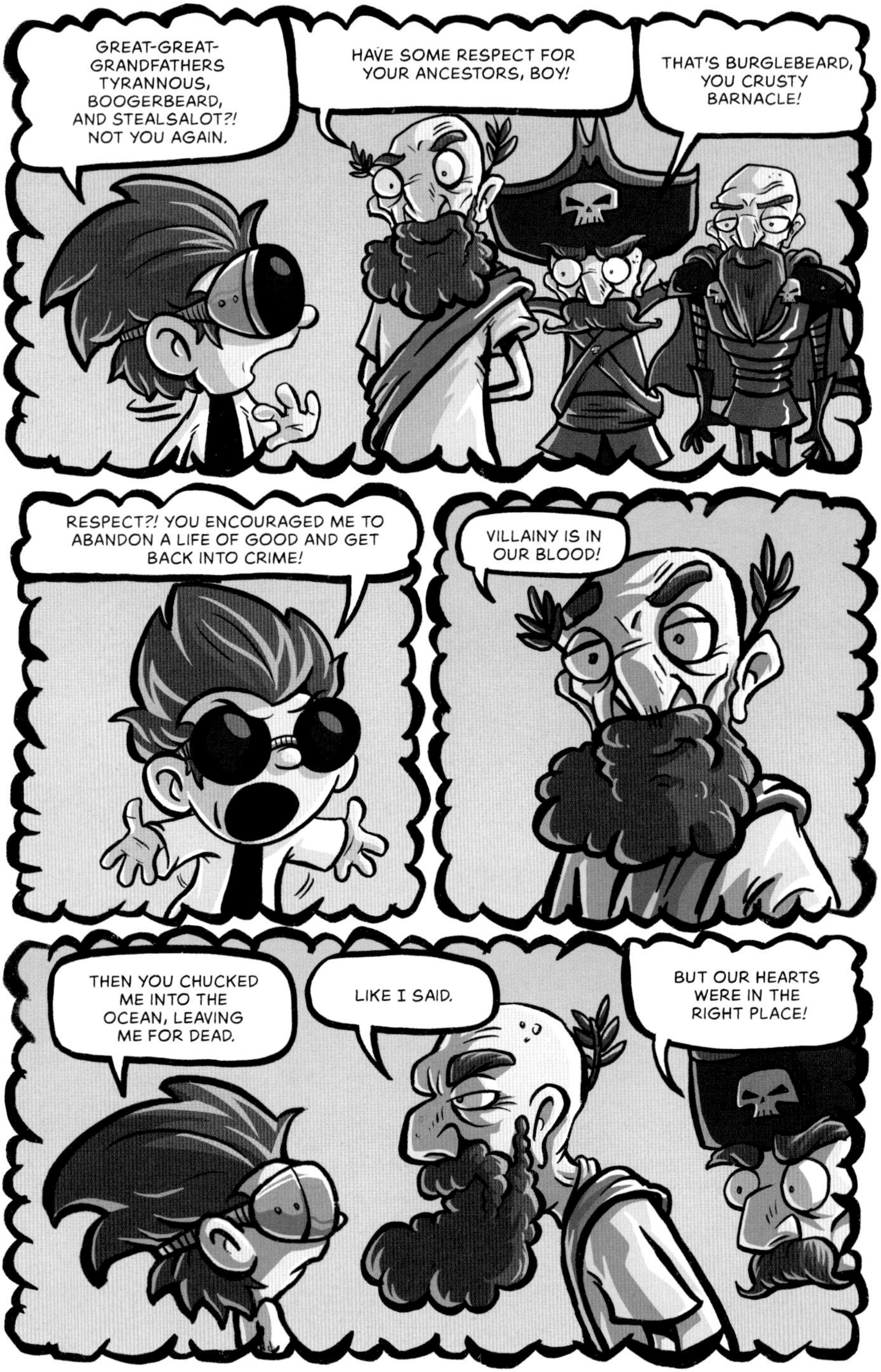
GREAT-GREAT-GRANDFATHERS TYRANNOUS, BOOGERBEARD, AND STEALSALOT?! NOT YOU AGAIN.
HAVE SOME RESPECT FOR YOUR ANCESTORS, BOY!
THAT'S BURGLEBEARD, YOU CRUSTY BARNACLE!
RESPECT?! YOU ENCOURAGED ME TO ABANDON A LIFE OF GOOD AND GET BACK INTO CRIME!
VILLAINY IS IN OUR BLOOD!
THEN YOU CHUCKED ME INTO THE OCEAN, LEAVING ME FOR DEAD.
LIKE I SAID.
BUT OUR HEARTS WERE IN THE RIGHT PLACE!

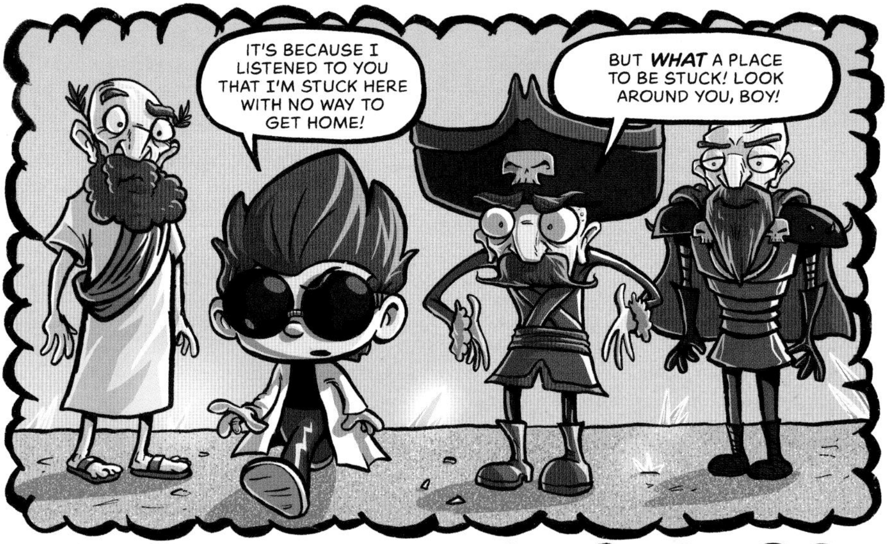
IT'S BECAUSE I LISTENED TO YOU THAT I'M STUCK HERE WITH NO WAY TO GET HOME!
BUT **WHAT** A PLACE TO BE STUCK! LOOK AROUND YOU, BOY!

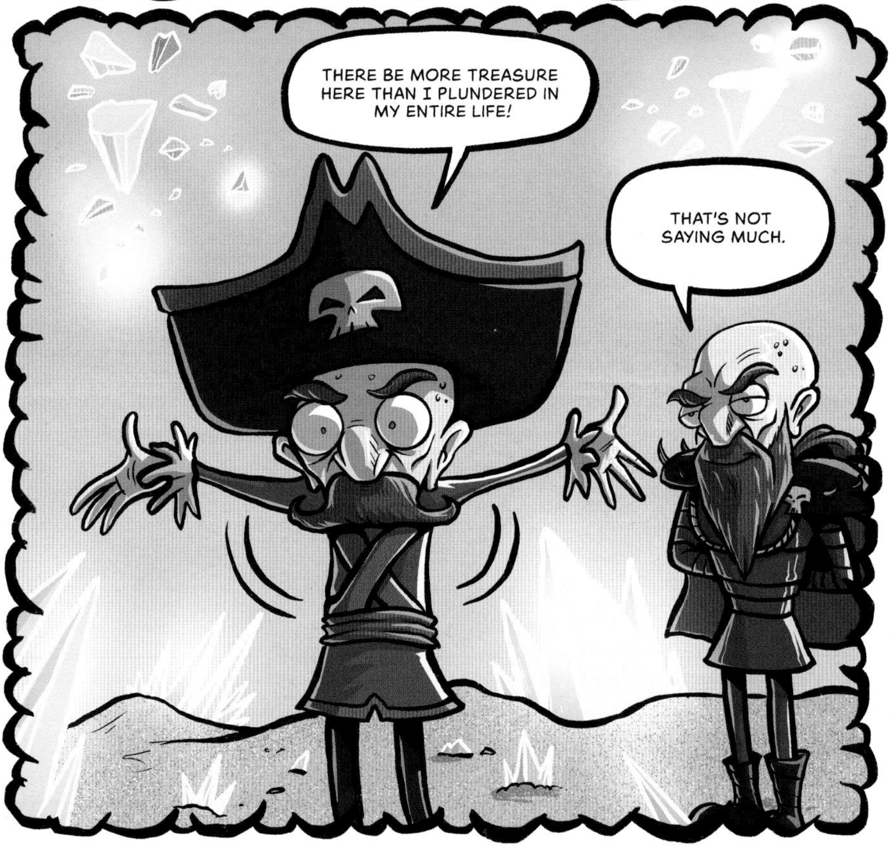
THERE BE MORE TREASURE HERE THAN I PLUNDERED IN MY ENTIRE LIFE!
THAT'S NOT SAYING MUCH.

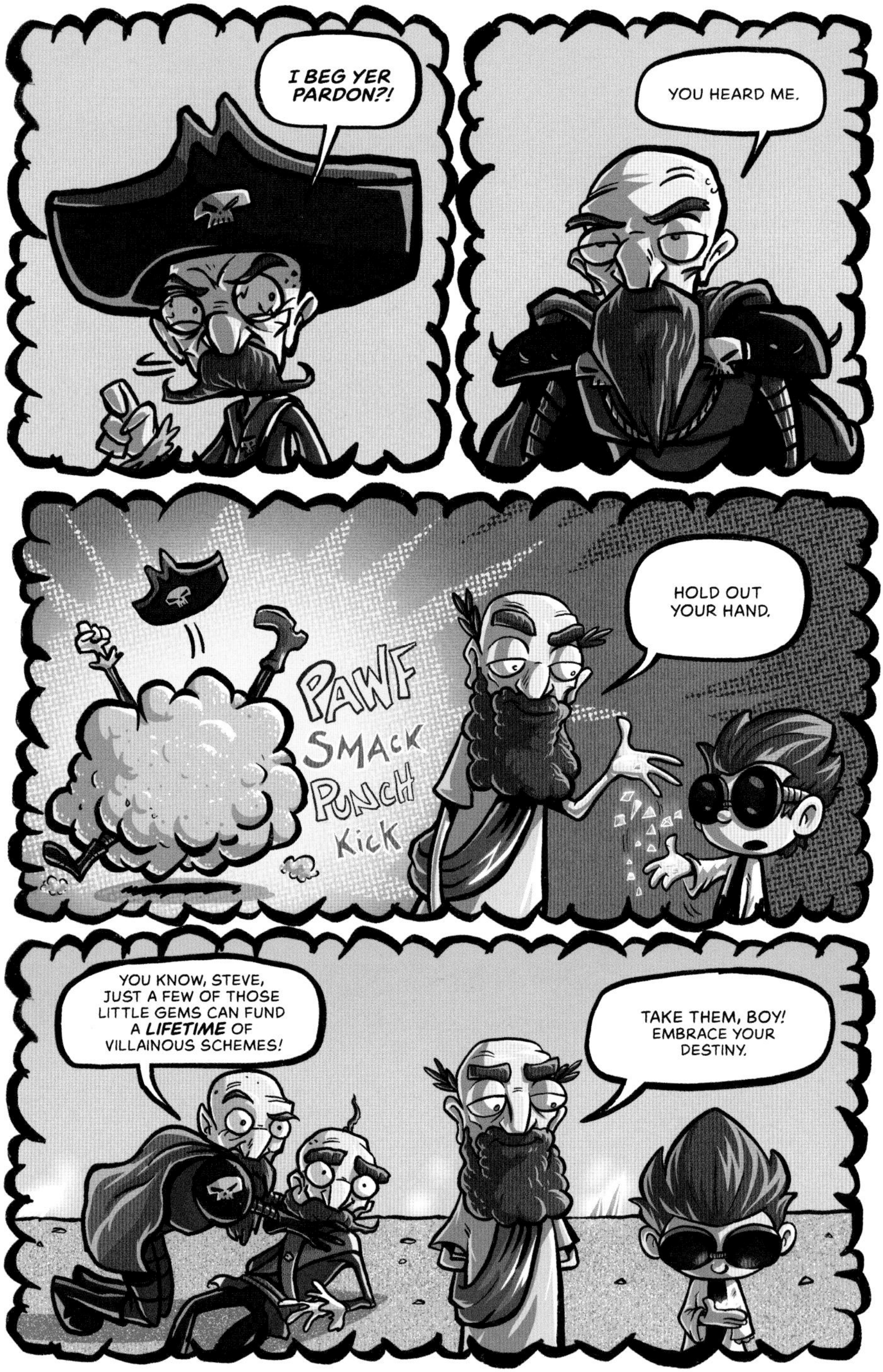
I BEG YER PARDON?!
YOU HEARD ME.
PAWF
SMACK
PUNCH
KICK
HOLD OUT YOUR HAND.
YOU KNOW, STEVE, JUST A FEW OF THOSE LITTLE GEMS CAN FUND A **LIFETIME** OF VILLAINOUS SCHEMES!
TAKE THEM, BOY! EMBRACE YOUR DESTINY.

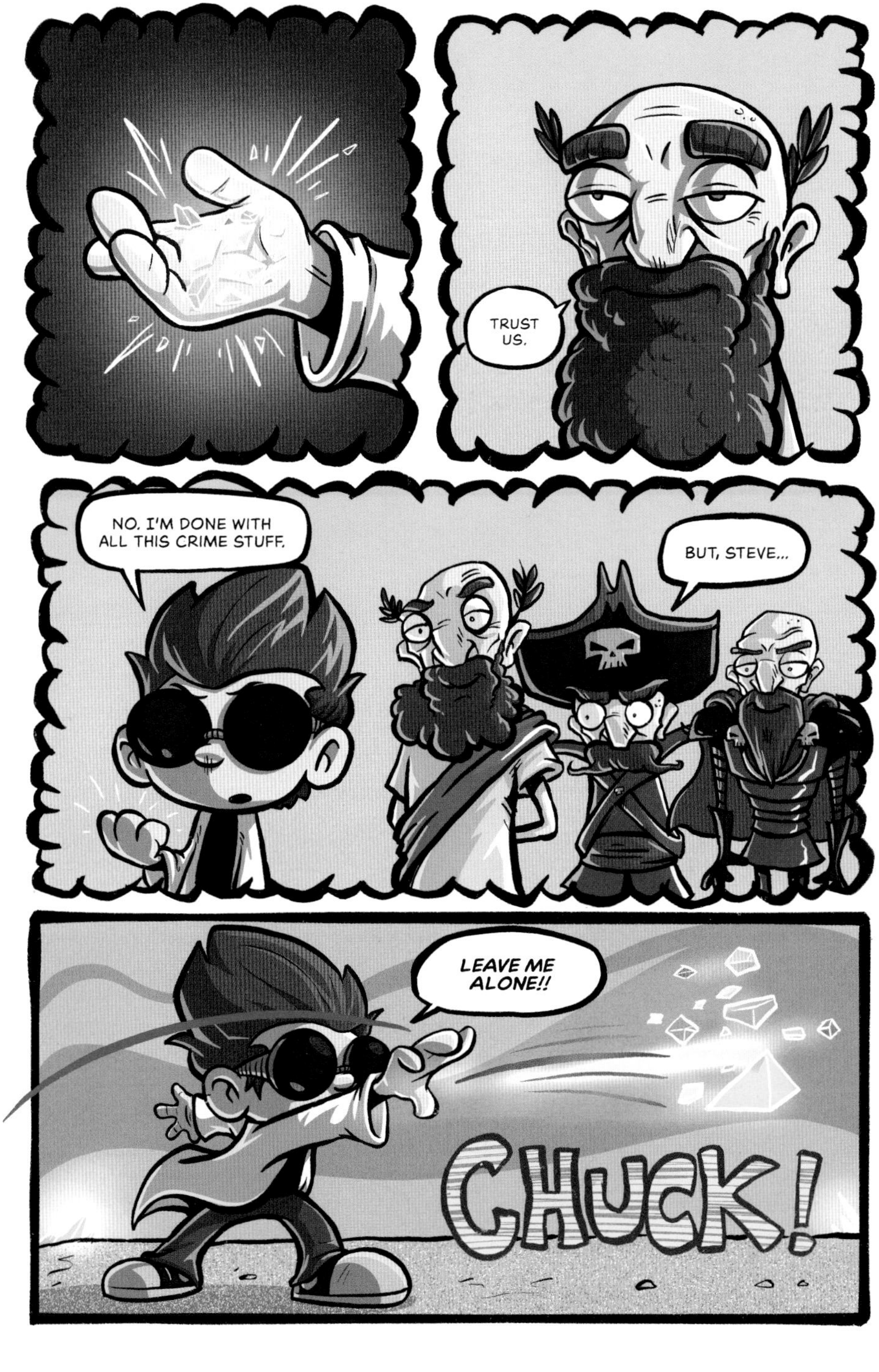
TRUST US.
NO. I'M DONE WITH ALL THIS CRIME STUFF.
BUT, STEVE...
LEAVE ME ALONE!!
CHUCK!

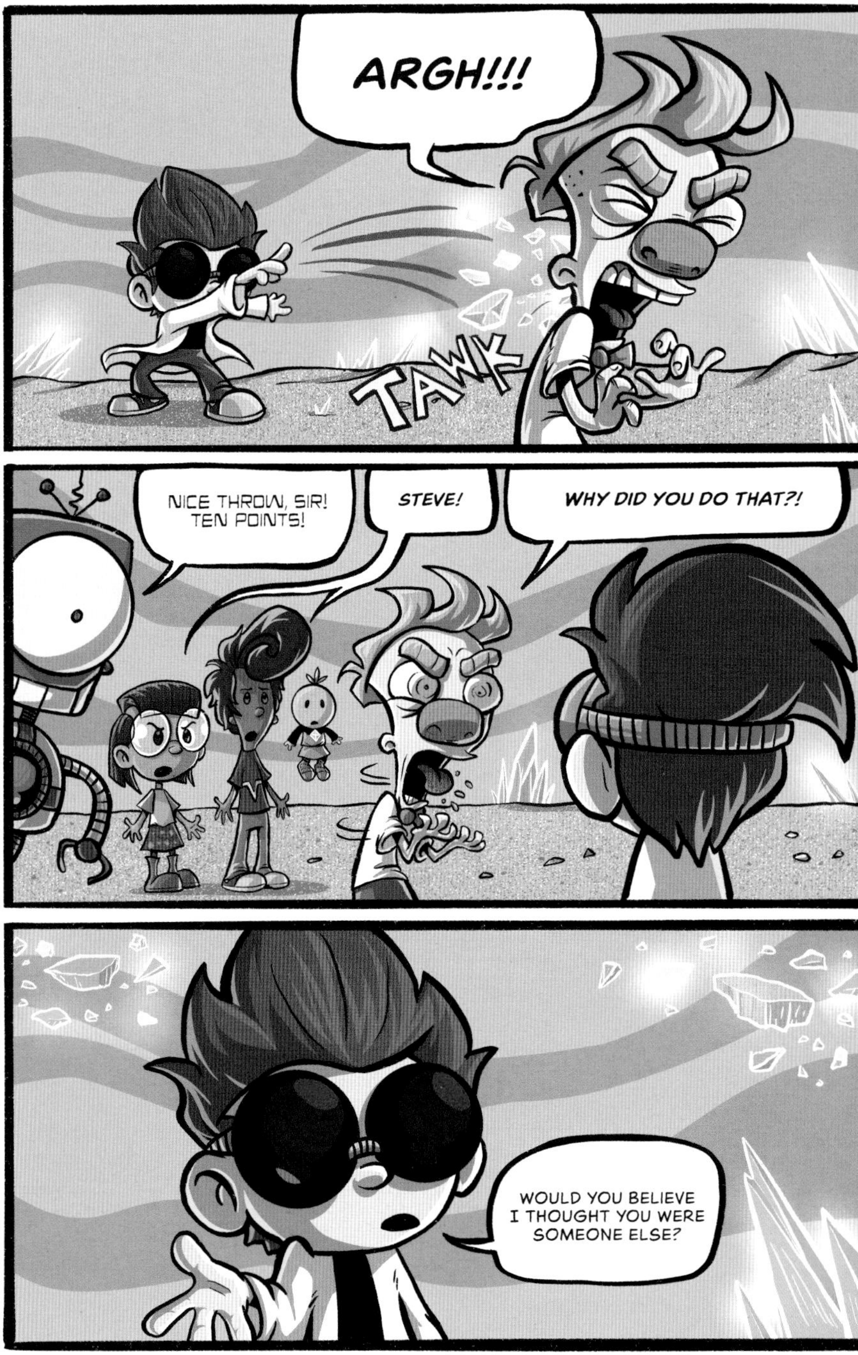
ARGH!!!
TAWK
NICE THROW, SIR! TEN POINTS!
STEVE!
WHY DID YOU DO THAT?!
WOULD YOU BELIEVE I THOUGHT YOU WERE SOMEONE ELSE?

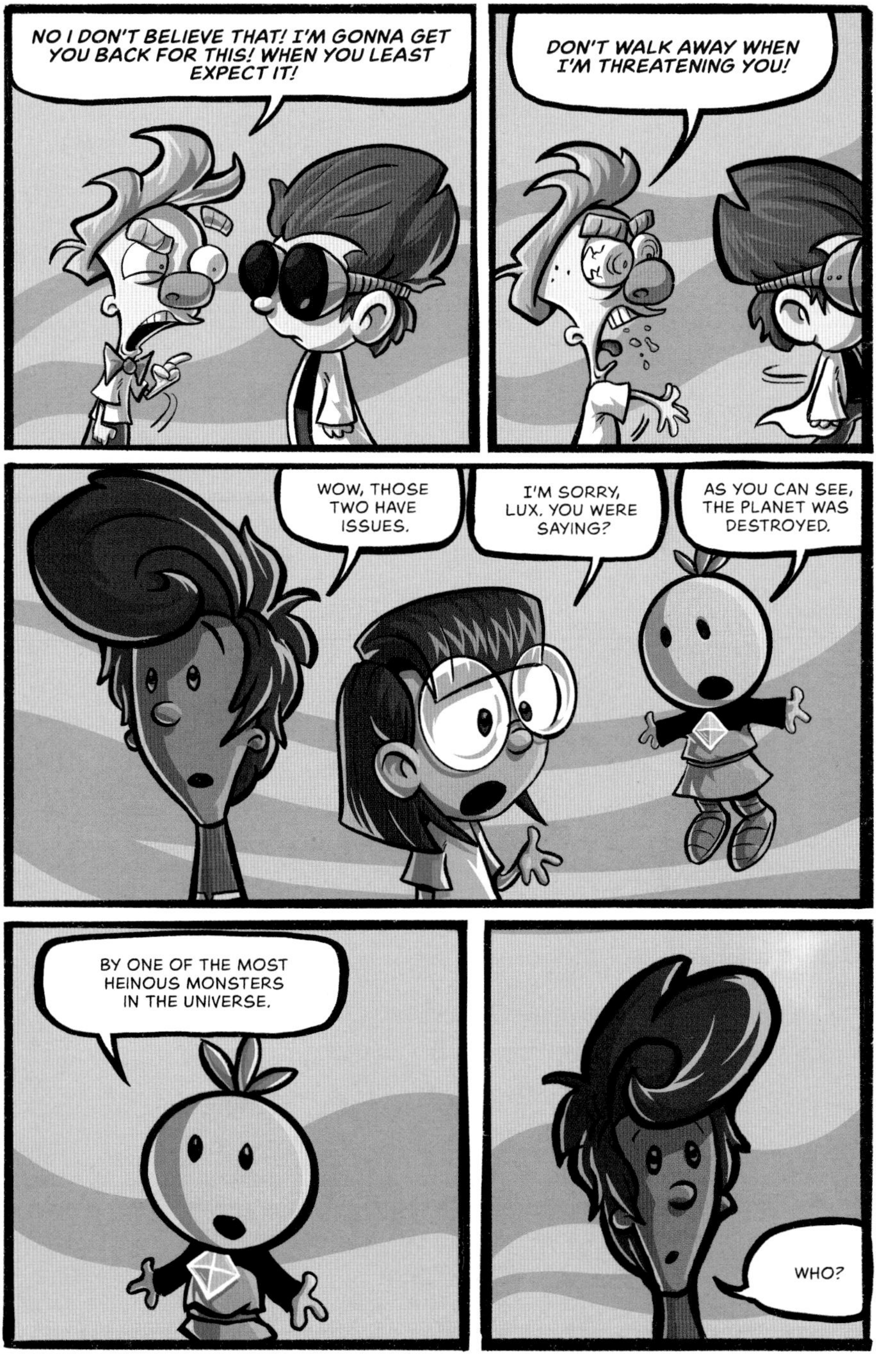
NO I DON'T BELIEVE THAT! I'M GONNA GET YOU BACK FOR THIS! WHEN YOU LEAST EXPECT IT!
DON'T WALK AWAY WHEN I'M THREATENING YOU!
WOW, THOSE TWO HAVE ISSUES.
I'M SORRY, LUX. YOU WERE SAYING?
AS YOU CAN SEE, THE PLANET WAS DESTROYED.
BY ONE OF THE MOST HEINOUS MONSTERS IN THE UNIVERSE.
WHO?

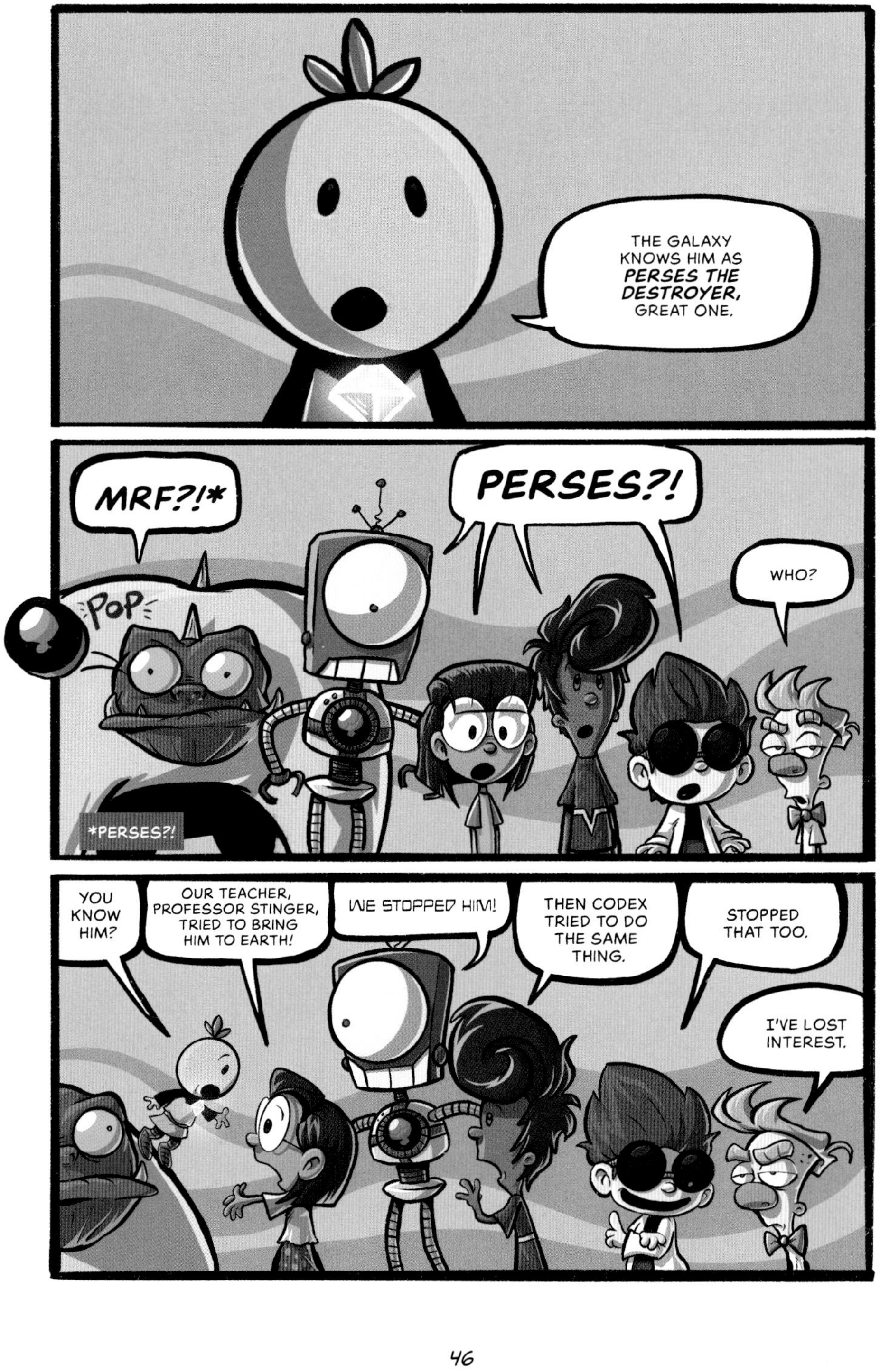
THE GALAXY KNOWS HIM AS **PERSES THE DESTROYER,** GREAT ONE.
MRF?!*
PERSES?!
WHO?
POP
*PERSES?!
YOU KNOW HIM?
OUR TEACHER, PROFESSOR STINGER, TRIED TO BRING HIM TO EARTH!
WE STOPPED HIM!
THEN CODEX TRIED TO DO THE SAME THING.
STOPPED THAT TOO.
I'VE LOST INTEREST.

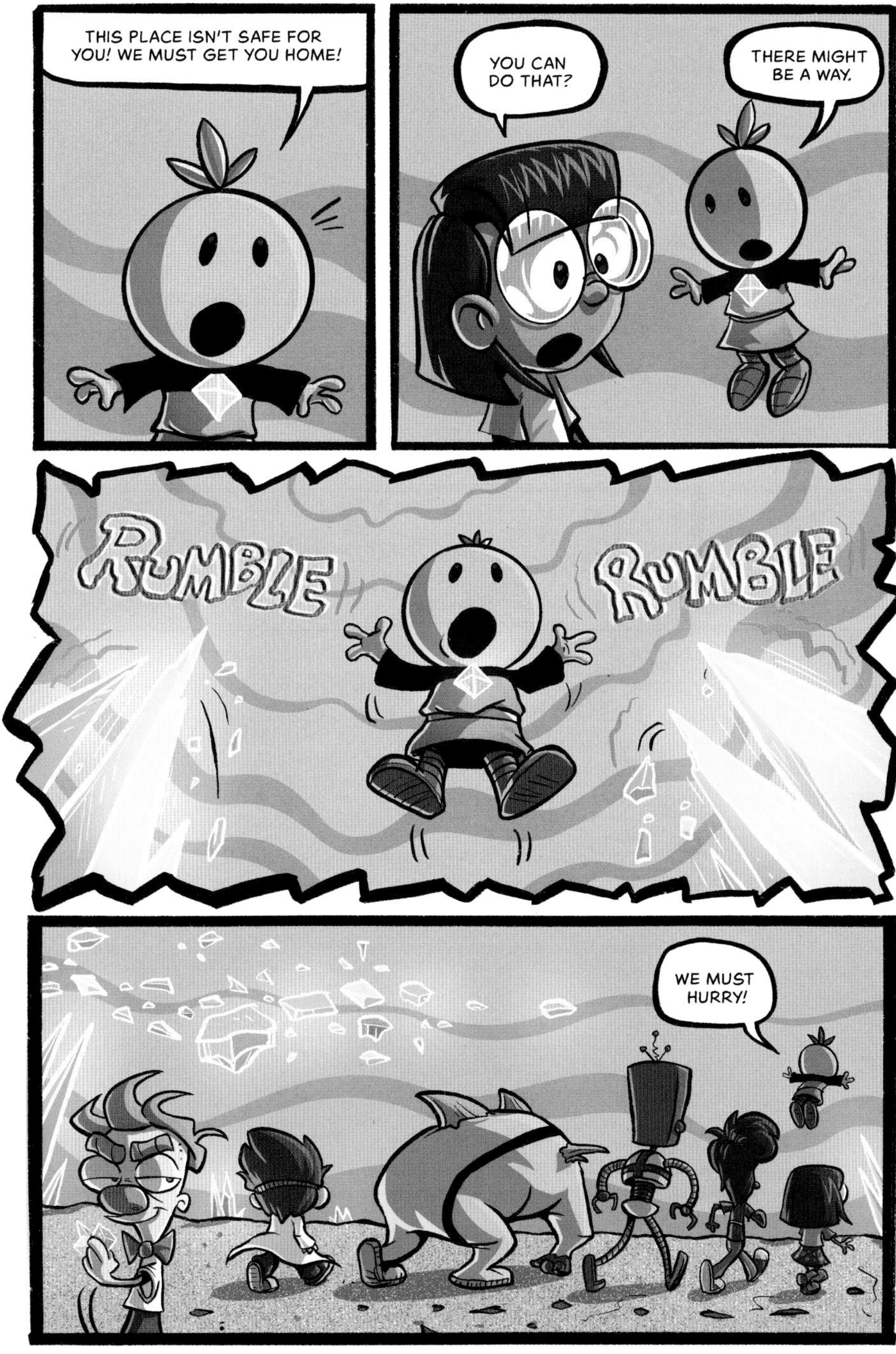
THIS PLACE ISN'T SAFE FOR YOU! WE MUST GET YOU HOME!
YOU CAN DO THAT?
THERE MIGHT BE A WAY.
RUMBLE
RUMBLE
WE MUST HURRY!

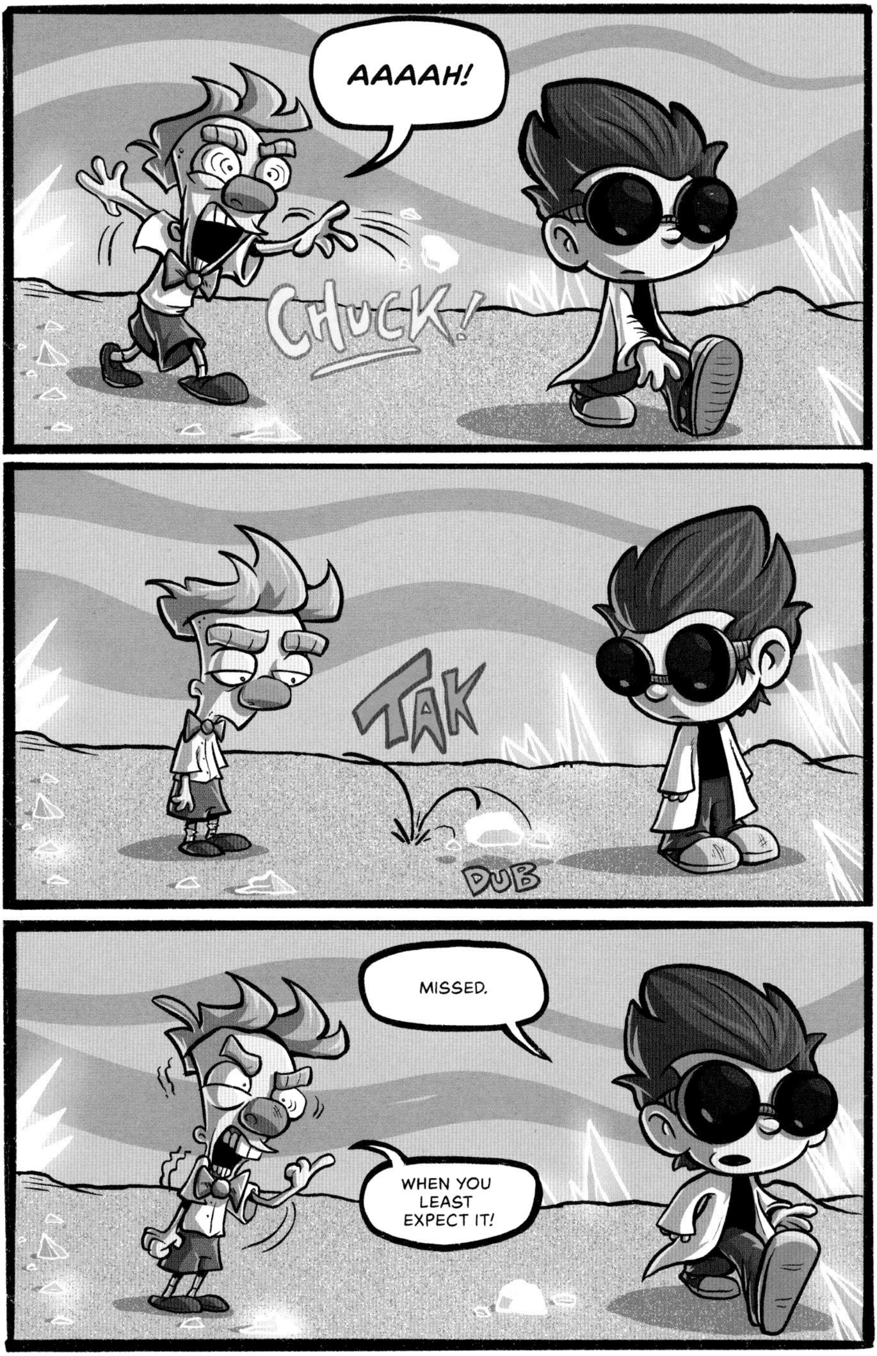
AAAAH!
CHUCK!
TAK
DUB
MISSED.
WHEN YOU LEAST EXPECT IT!

CHAPTER 5

Old School

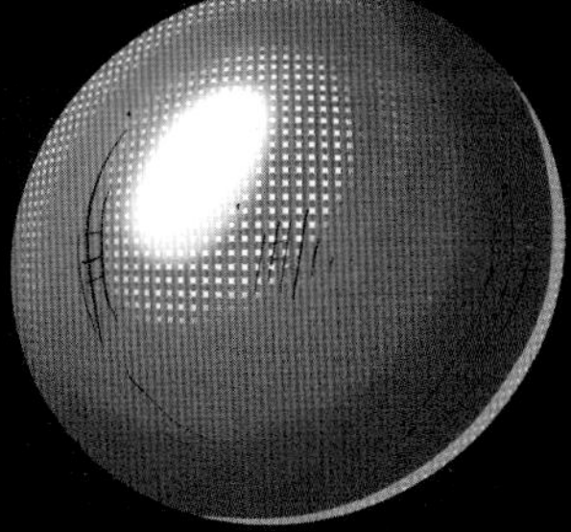

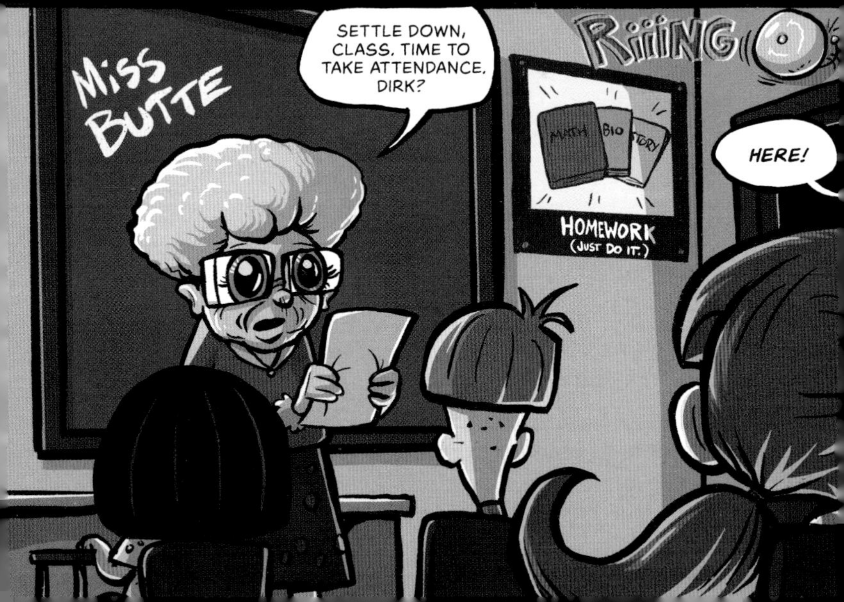
MISS BUTTE
SETTLE DOWN, CLASS. TIME TO TAKE ATTENDANCE. DIRK?
RIIING
MATH
BIO
STORY
HOMEWORK (JUST DO IT.)
HERE!

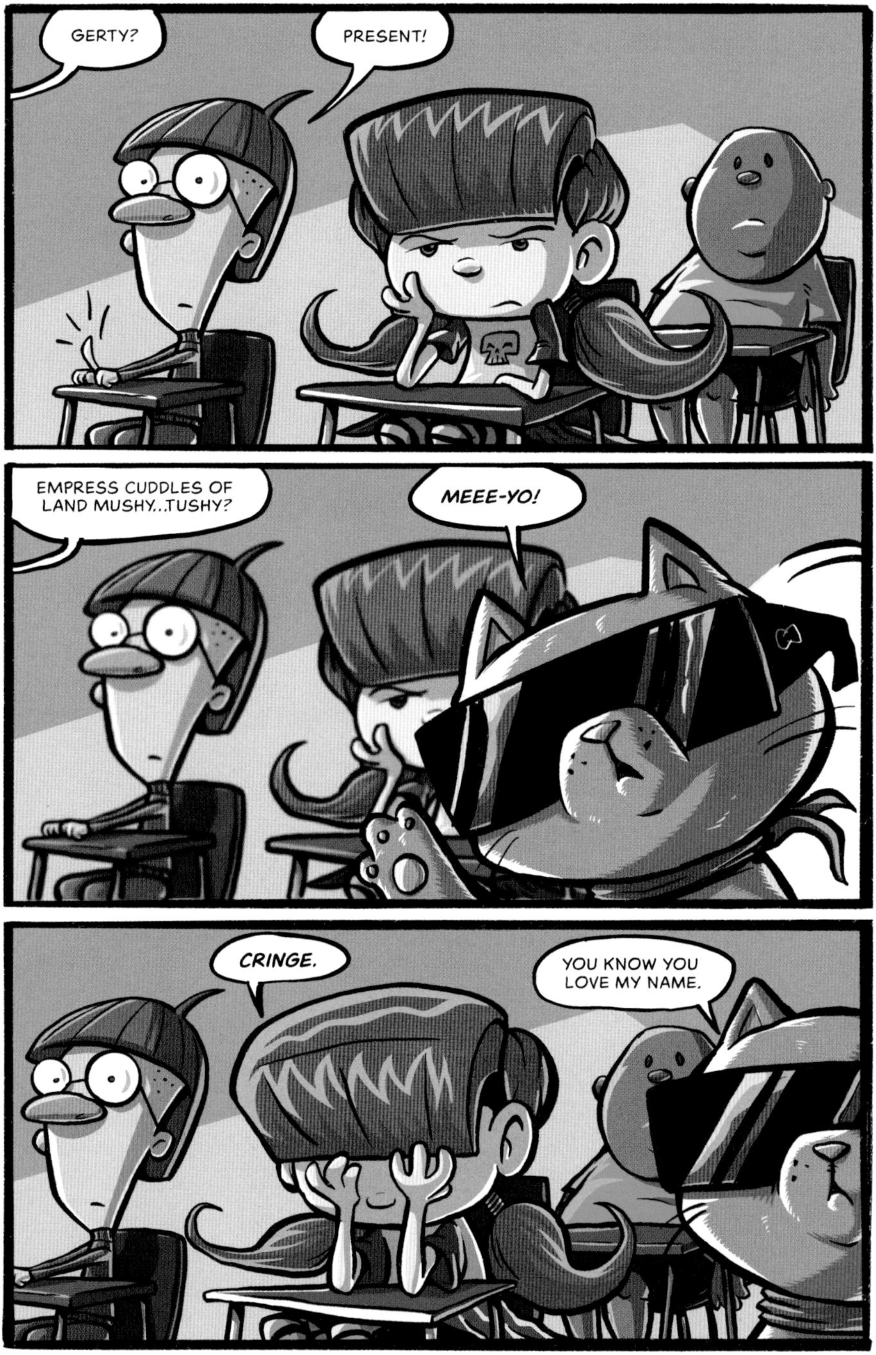
GERTY?
PRESENT!
EMPRESS CUDDLES OF LAND MUSHY...TUSHY?
MEEE-YO!
CRINGE.
YOU KNOW YOU LOVE MY NAME.

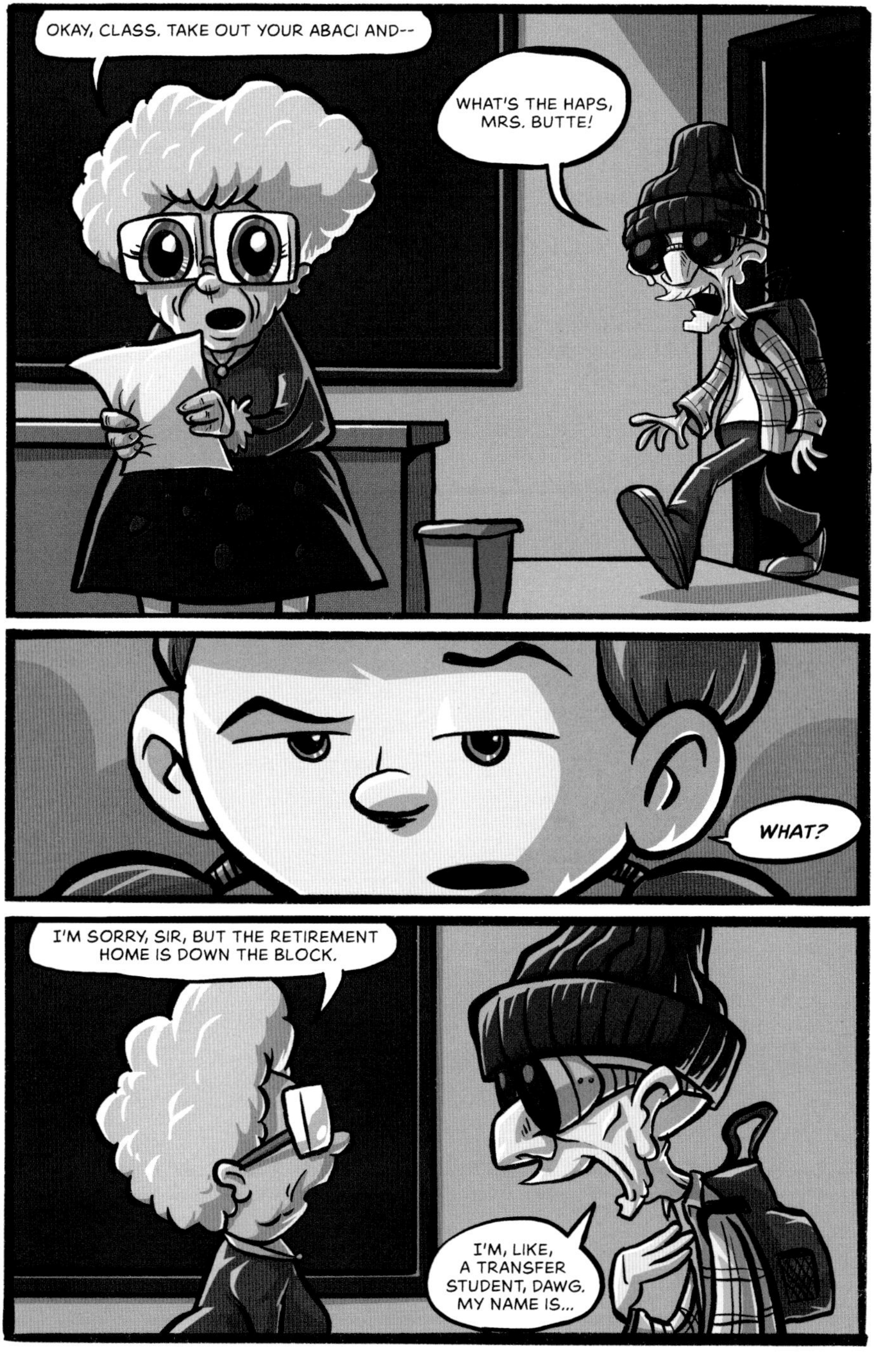
OKAY, CLASS. TAKE OUT YOUR ABACI AND--
WHAT'S THE HAPS, MRS. BUTTE!
WHAT?
I'M SORRY, SIR, BUT THE RETIREMENT HOME IS DOWN THE BLOCK.
I'M, LIKE, A TRANSFER STUDENT, DAWG. MY NAME IS...

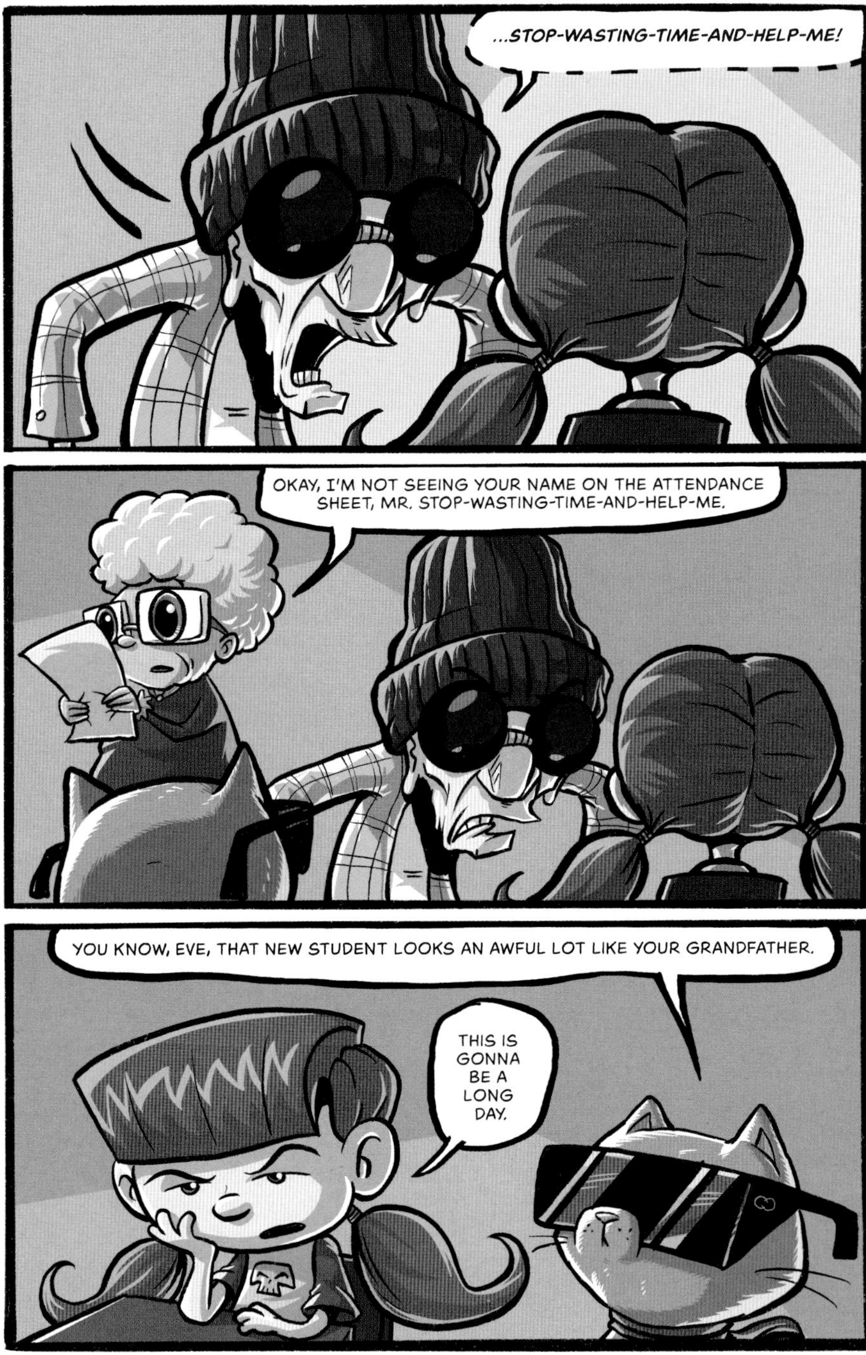
...STOP-WASTING-TIME-AND-HELP-ME!
OKAY, I'M NOT SEEING YOUR NAME ON THE ATTENDANCE SHEET, MR. STOP-WASTING-TIME-AND-HELP-ME.
YOU KNOW, EVE, THAT NEW STUDENT LOOKS AN AWFUL LOT LIKE YOUR GRANDFATHER.
THIS IS GONNA BE A LONG DAY.

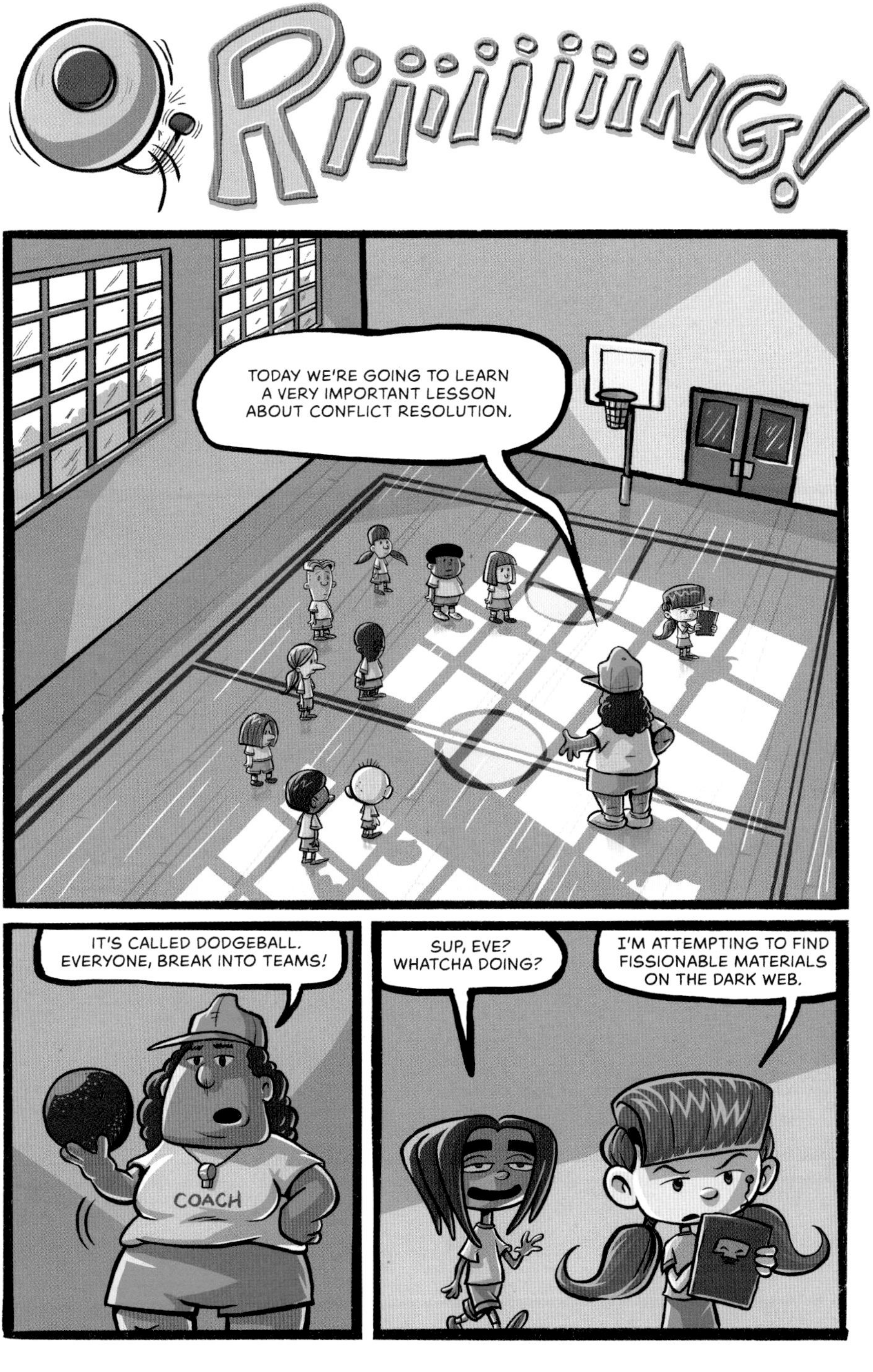
RIIIIIIIING!
TODAY WE'RE GOING TO LEARN A VERY IMPORTANT LESSON ABOUT CONFLICT RESOLUTION.
IT'S CALLED DODGEBALL. EVERYONE, BREAK INTO TEAMS!
COACH
SUP, EVE? WHATCHA DOING?
I'M ATTEMPTING TO FIND FISSIONABLE MATERIALS ON THE DARK WEB.

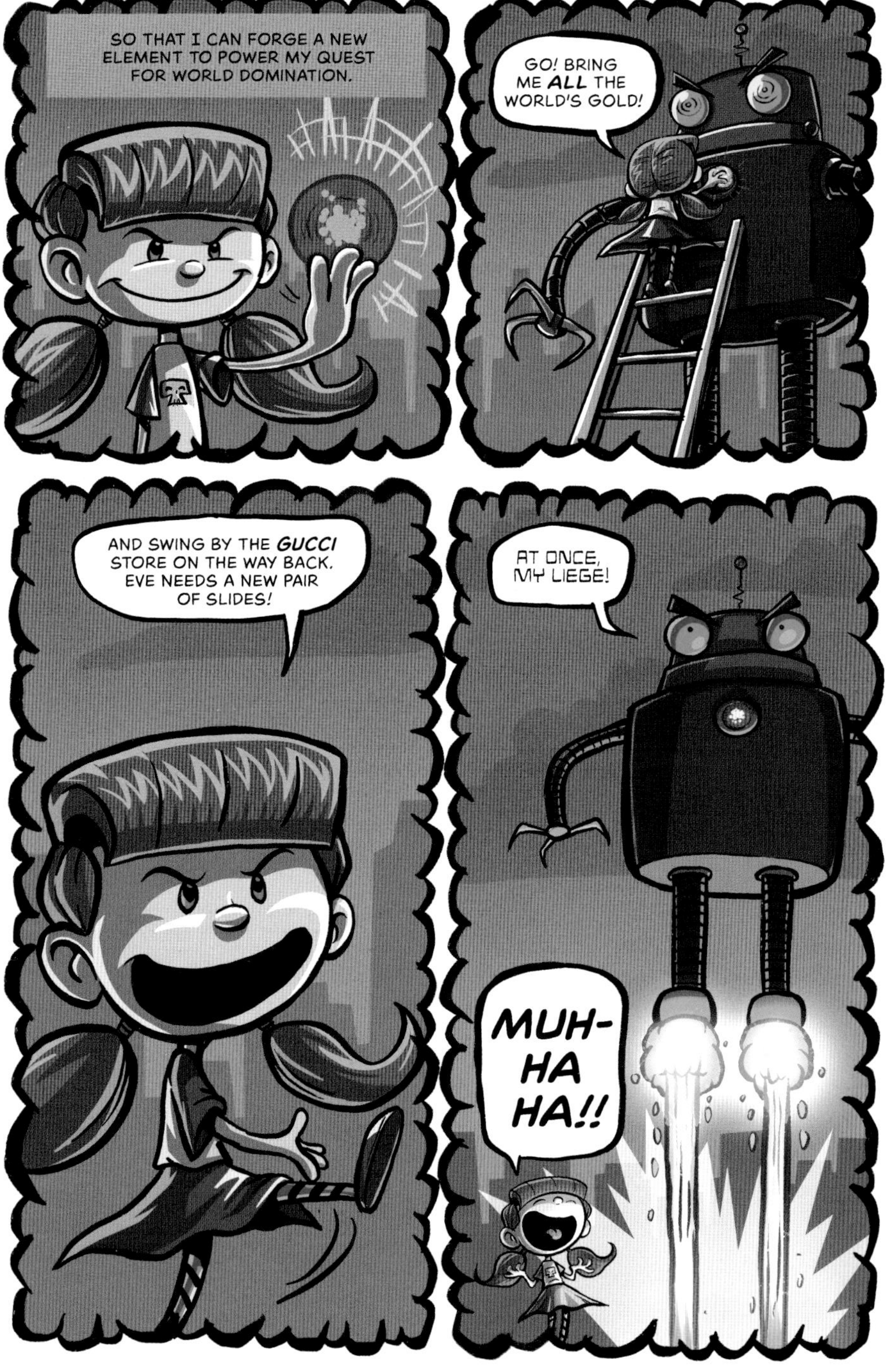
SO THAT I CAN FORGE A NEW ELEMENT TO POWER MY QUEST FOR WORLD DOMINATION.
GO! BRING ME ALL THE WORLD'S GOLD!
AND SWING BY THE GUCCI STORE ON THE WAY BACK. EVE NEEDS A NEW PAIR OF SLIDES!
AT ONCE, MY LIEGE!
MUH-HA HA!!

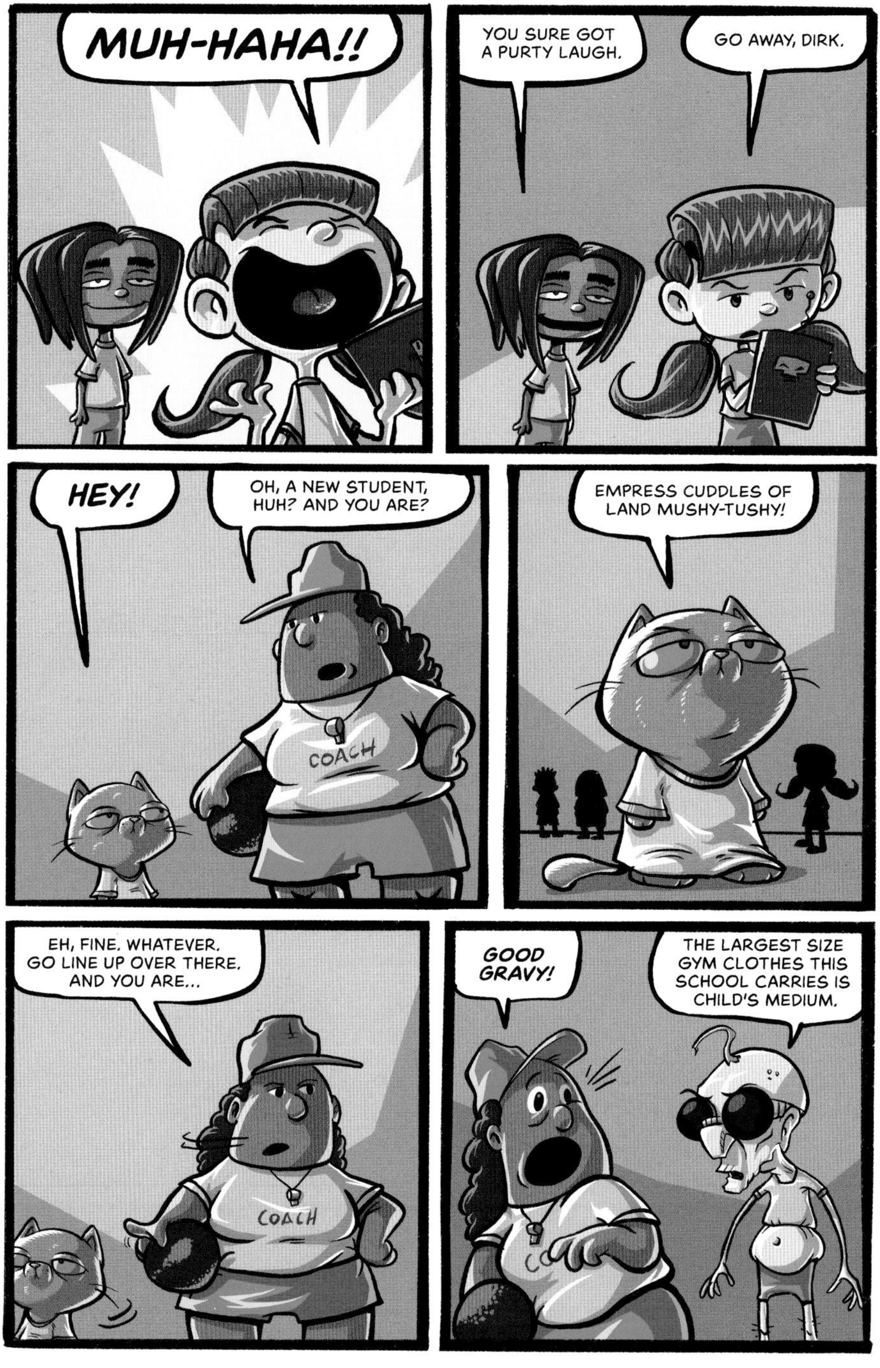
MUH-HAHA!!
YOU SURE GOT A PURTY LAUGH.
GO AWAY, DIRK.
HEY!
OH, A NEW STUDENT, HUH? AND YOU ARE?
COACH
EMPRESS CUDDLES OF LAND MUSHY-TUSHY!
EH, FINE. WHATEVER. GO LINE UP OVER THERE. AND YOU ARE...
COACH
GOOD GRAVY!
THE LARGEST SIZE GYM CLOTHES THIS SCHOOL CARRIES IS CHILD'S MEDIUM.

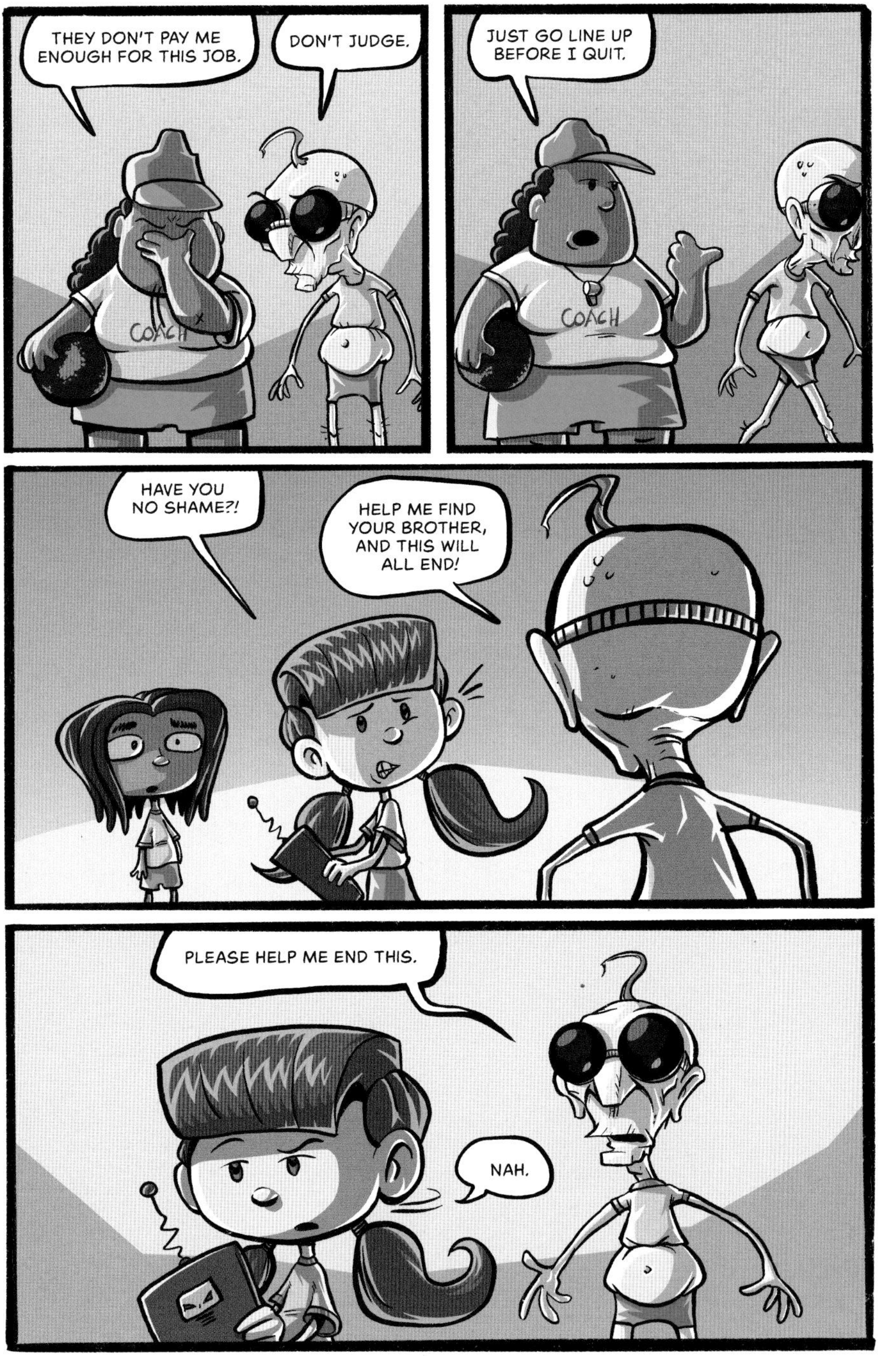
THEY DON'T PAY ME ENOUGH FOR THIS JOB.
DON'T JUDGE.
JUST GO LINE UP BEFORE I QUIT.
COACH
COACH
HAVE YOU NO SHAME?!
HELP ME FIND YOUR BROTHER, AND THIS WILL ALL END!
PLEASE HELP ME END THIS.
NAH.

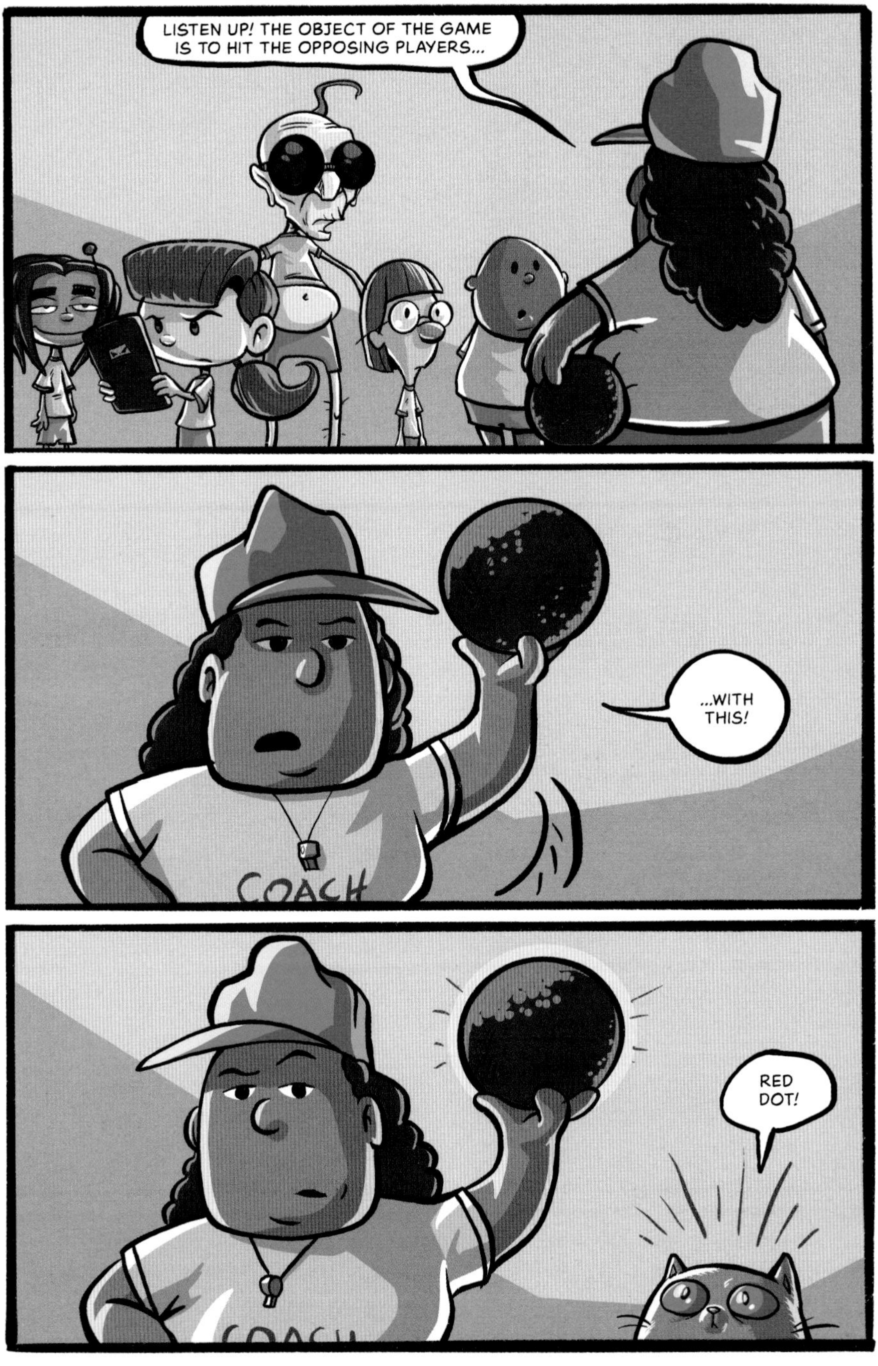
LISTEN UP! THE OBJECT OF THE GAME IS TO HIT THE OPPOSING PLAYERS...
...WITH THIS!
COACH
RED DOT!
COACH

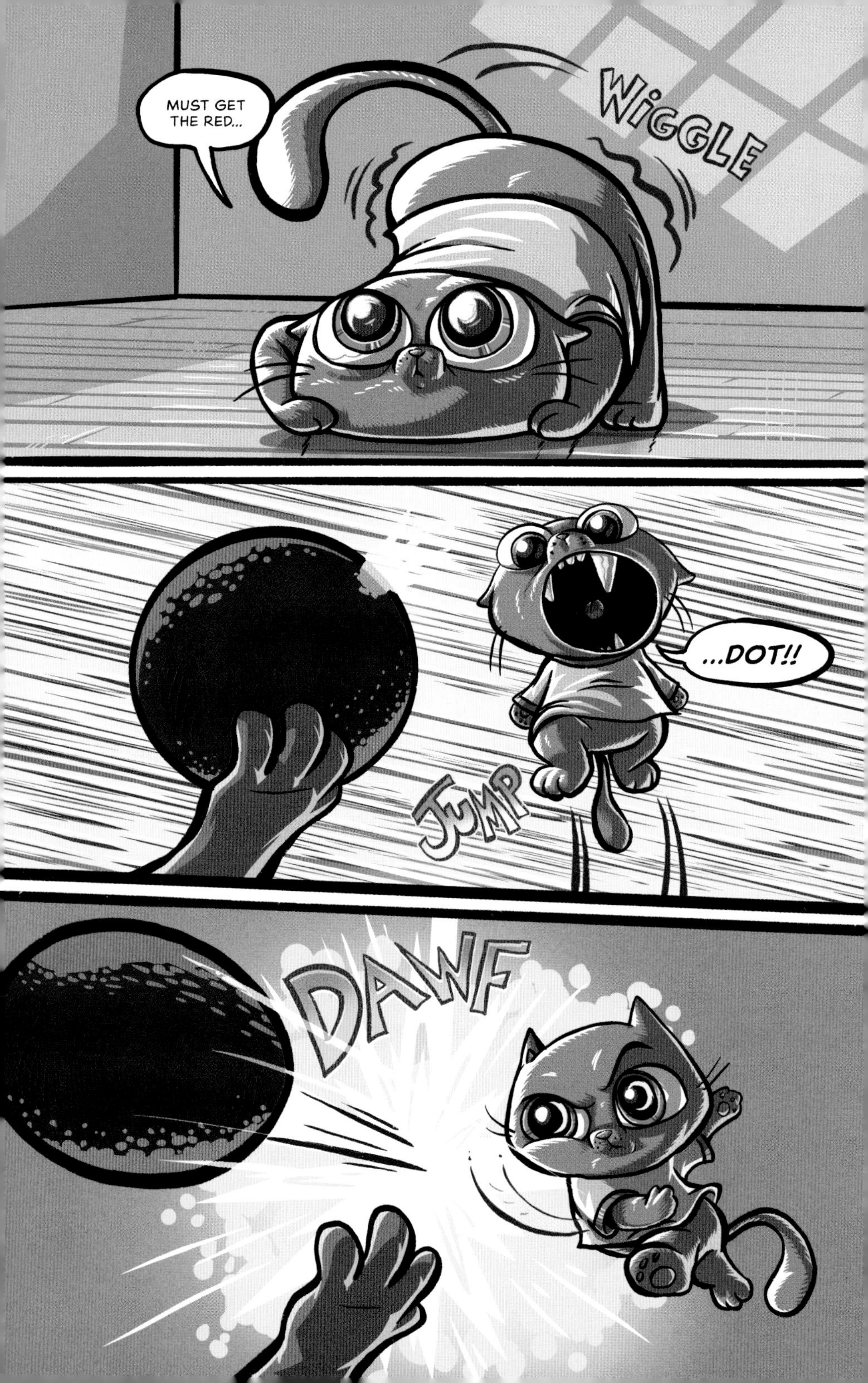
MUST GET THE RED...
WIGGLE
...DOT!!
JUMP
DAWF

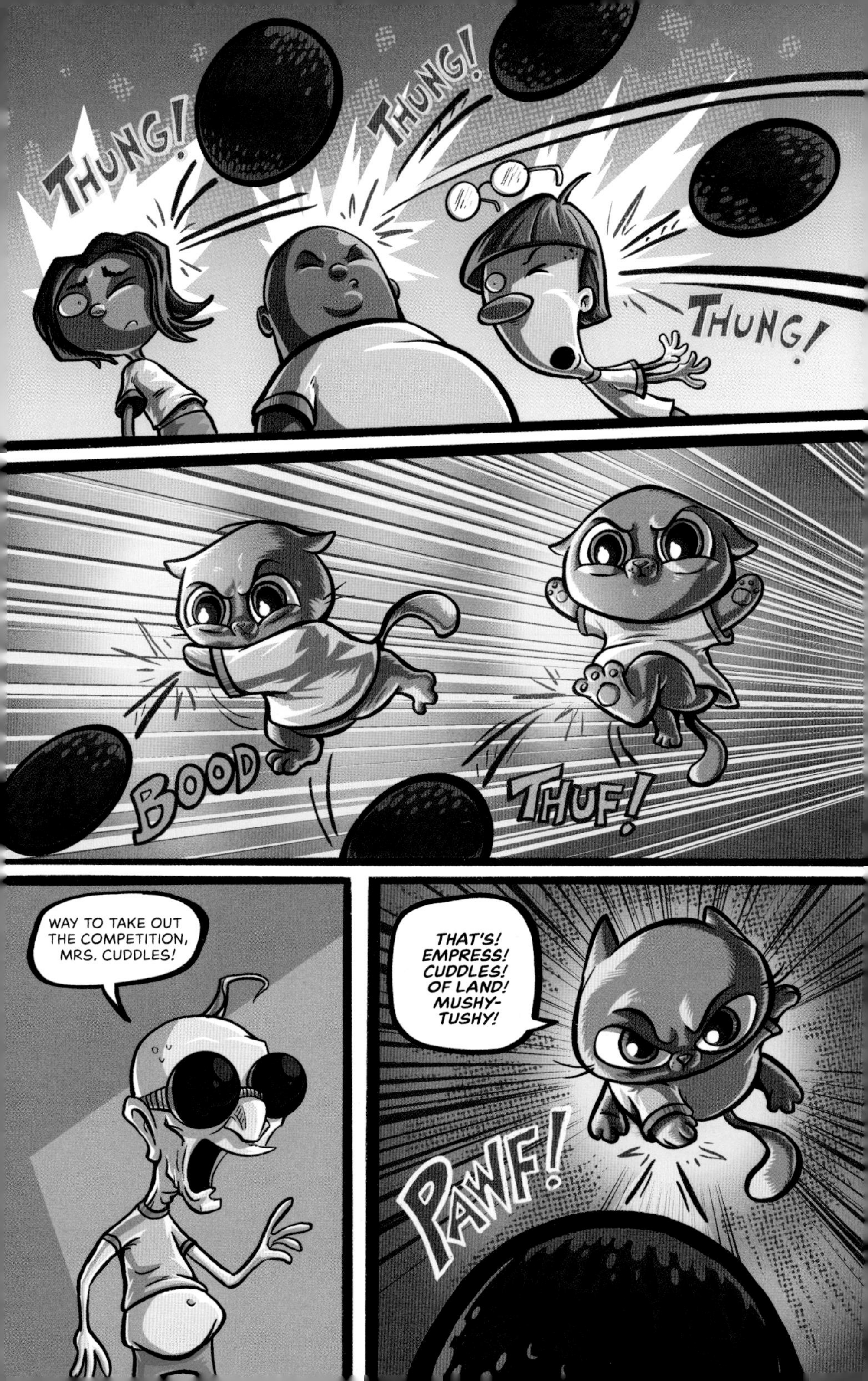
THUNG!
THUNG!
THUNG!
BOOD
THUF!
WAY TO TAKE OUT THE COMPETITION, MRS. CUDDLES!
THAT'S! EMPRESS! CUDDLES! OF LAND! MUSHY-TUSHY!
PAWF!

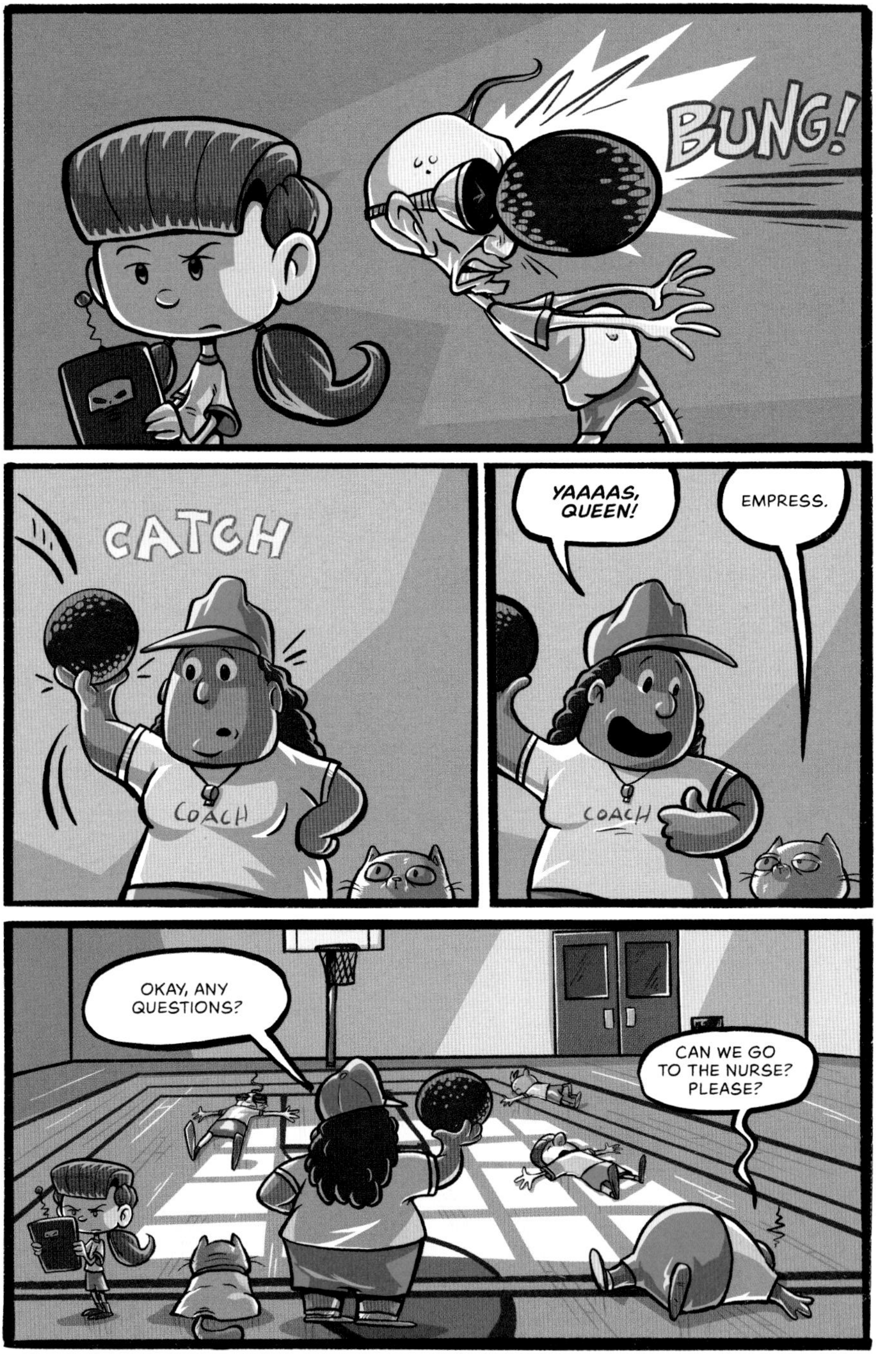
BUNG!
CATCH
YAAAAS, QUEEN!
EMPRESS.
COACH
COACH
OKAY, ANY QUESTIONS?
CAN WE GO TO THE NURSE? PLEASE?

CHAPTER 6

Let's Make a Deal

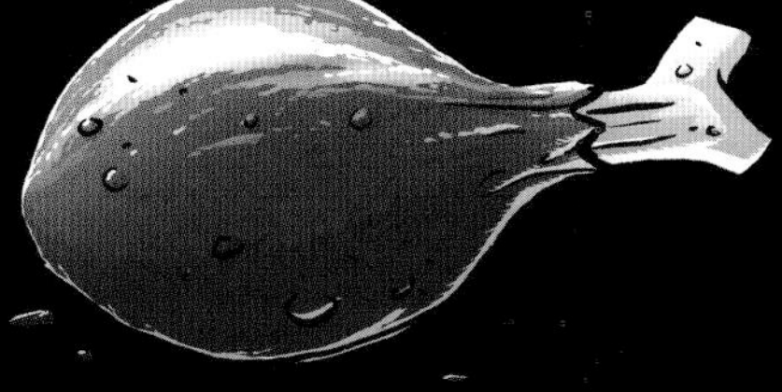

ATER, IN THE CAFETERIA...

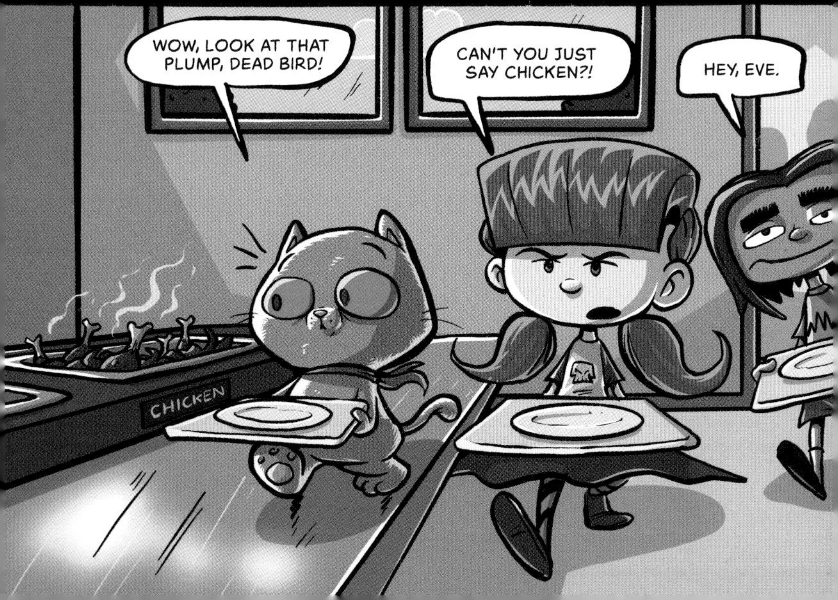
WOW, LOOK AT THAT PLUMP, DEAD BIRD!
CAN'T YOU JUST SAY CHICKEN?!
HEY, EVE.
CHICKEN

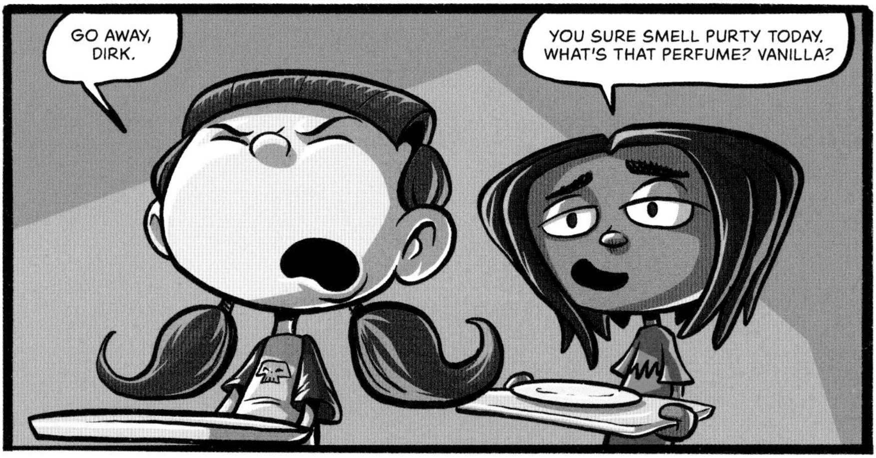
GO AWAY, DIRK.
YOU SURE SMELL PURTY TODAY. WHAT'S THAT PERFUME? VANILLA?

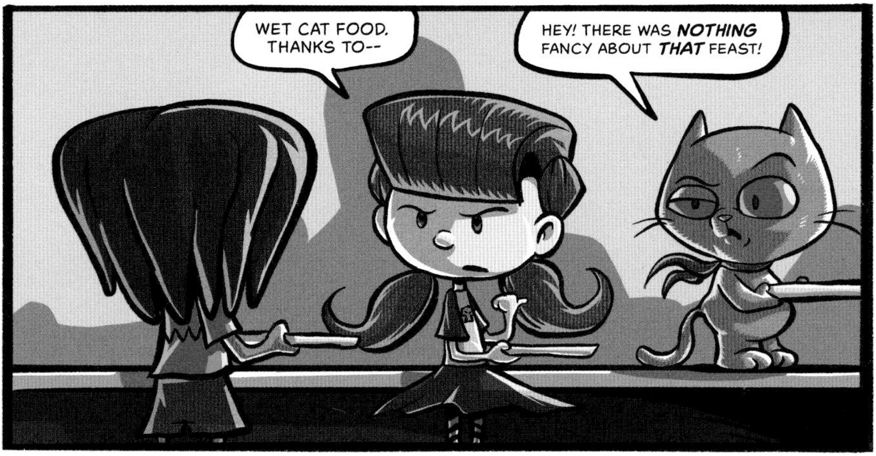
WET CAT FOOD. THANKS TO--
HEY! THERE WAS **NOTHING** FANCY ABOUT **THAT** FEAST!

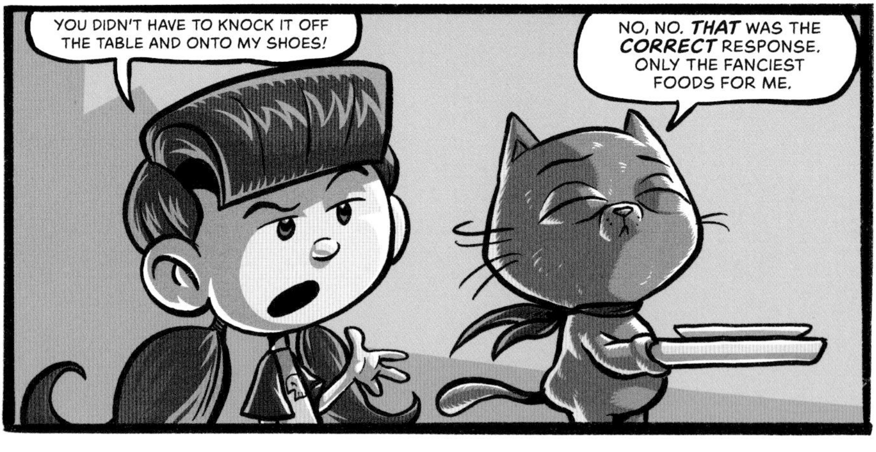
YOU DIDN'T HAVE TO KNOCK IT OFF THE TABLE AND ONTO MY SHOES!
NO, NO. **THAT** WAS THE **CORRECT** RESPONSE. ONLY THE FANCIEST FOODS FOR ME.

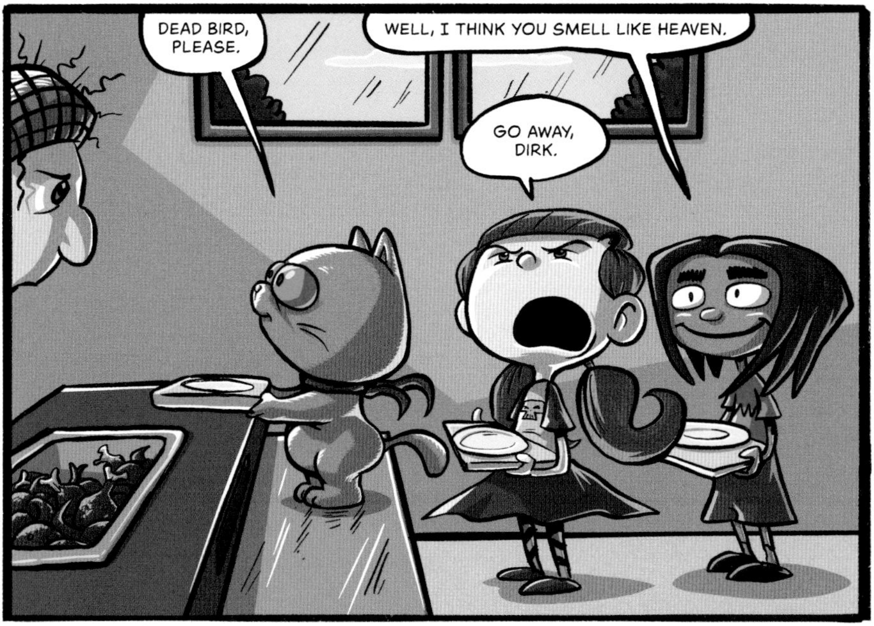
DEAD BIRD, PLEASE.
WELL, I THINK YOU SMELL LIKE HEAVEN.
GO AWAY, DIRK.

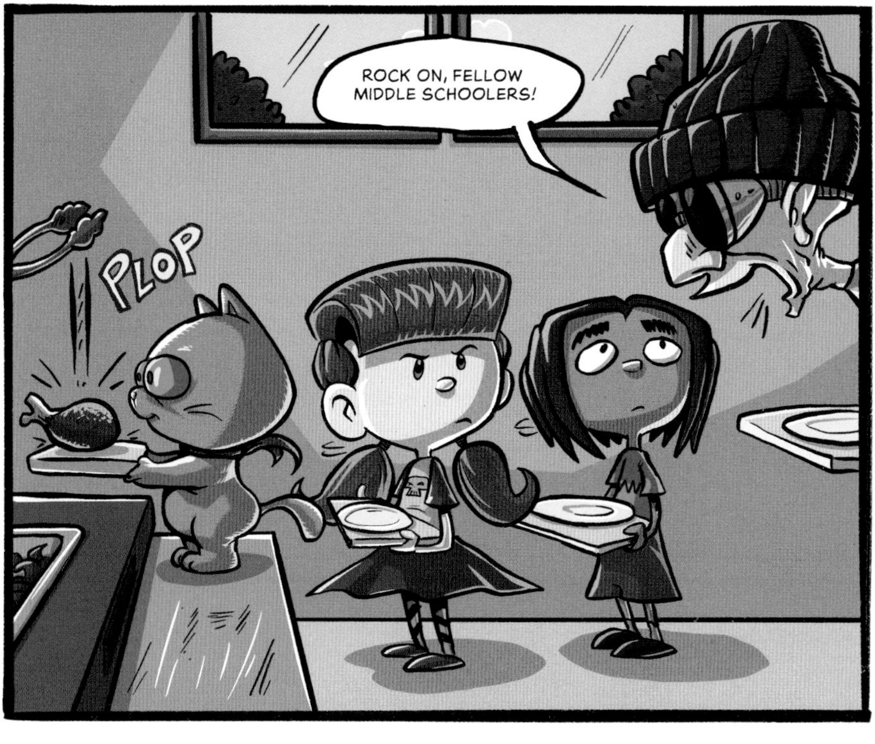
ROCK ON, FELLOW MIDDLE SCHOOLERS!
PLOP

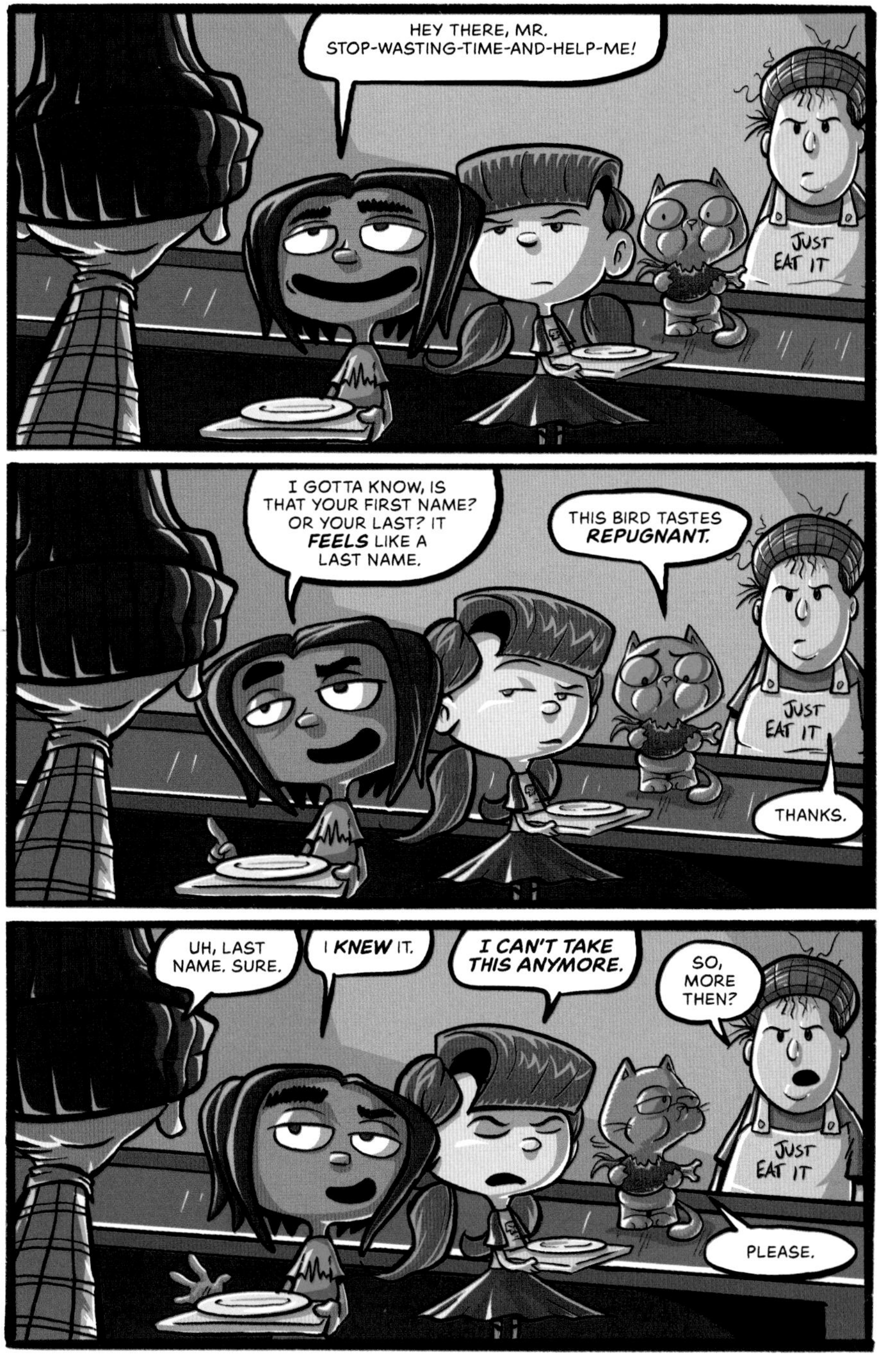
HEY THERE, MR. STOP-WASTING-TIME-AND-HELP-ME!
JUST EAT IT
I GOTTA KNOW, IS THAT YOUR FIRST NAME? OR YOUR LAST? IT **FEELS** LIKE A LAST NAME.
THIS BIRD TASTES **REPUGNANT.**
JUST EAT IT
THANKS.
UH, LAST NAME. SURE.
I **KNEW** IT.
I CAN'T TAKE THIS ANYMORE.
SO, MORE THEN?
JUST EAT IT
PLEASE.

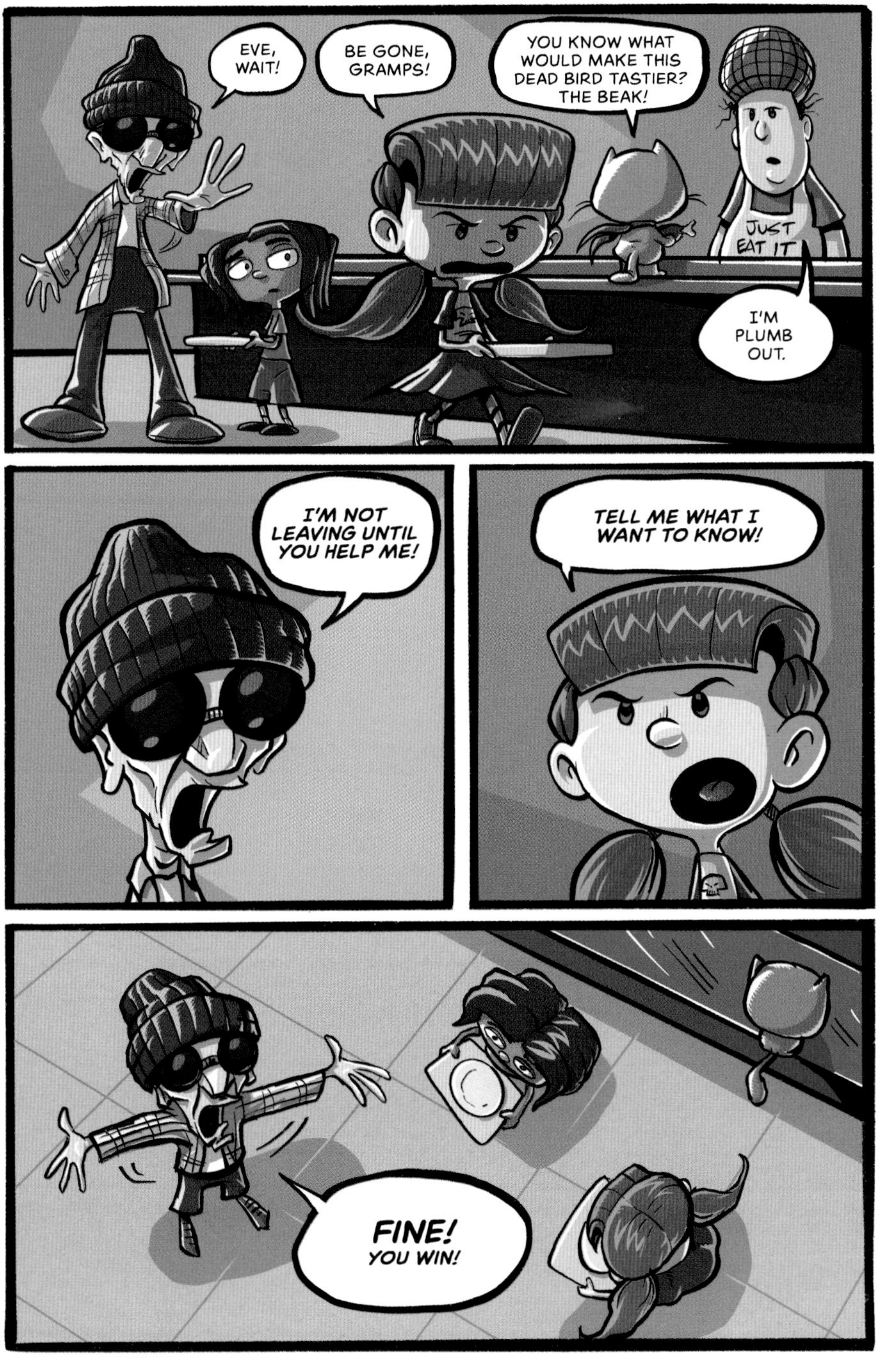
EVE, WAIT!
BE GONE, GRAMPS!
YOU KNOW WHAT WOULD MAKE THIS DEAD BIRD TASTIER? THE BEAK!
JUST EAT IT
I'M PLUMB OUT.
I'M NOT LEAVING UNTIL YOU HELP ME!
TELL ME WHAT I WANT TO KNOW!
FINE! YOU WIN!

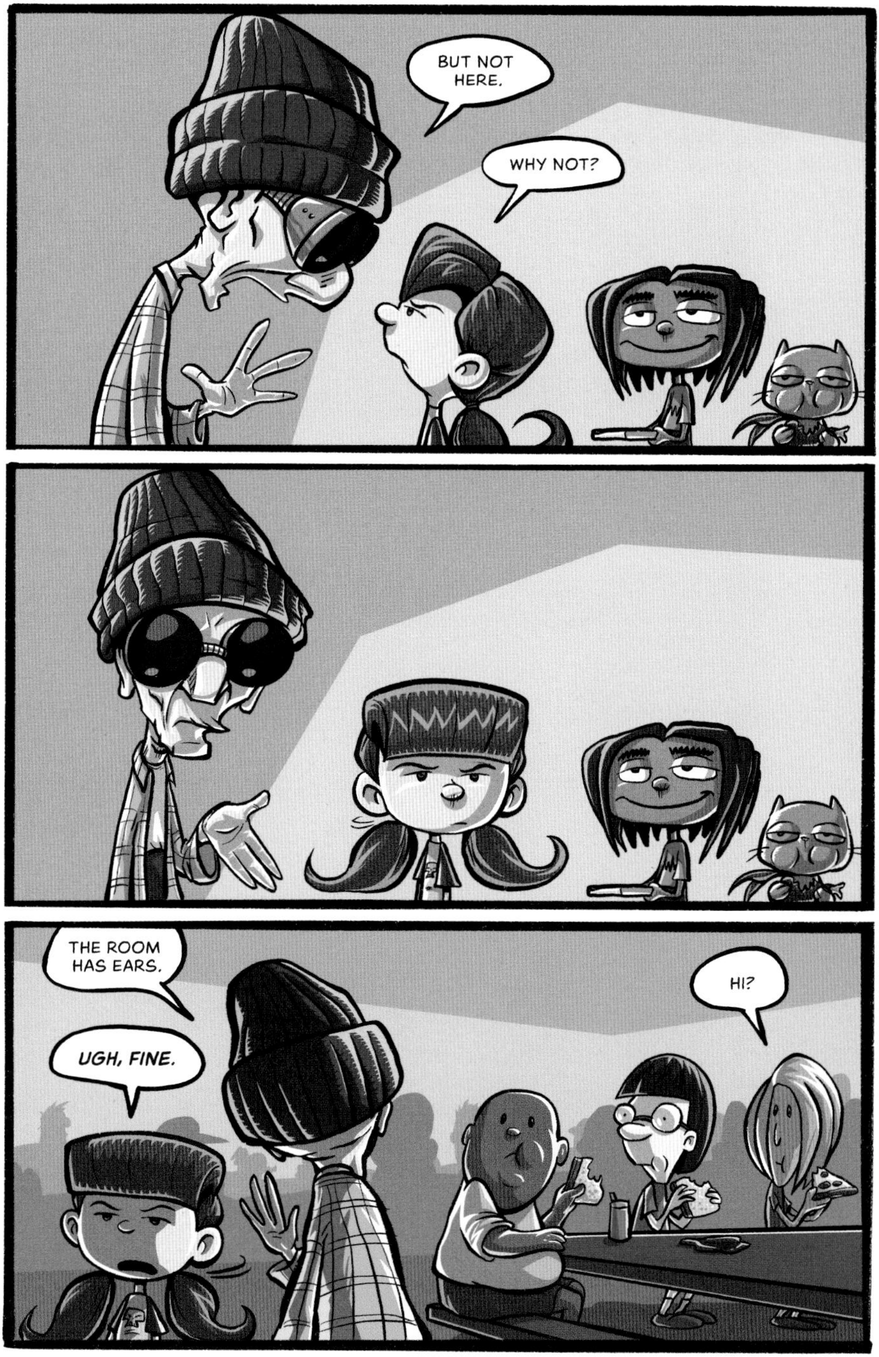
BUT NOT HERE.
WHY NOT?
THE ROOM HAS EARS.
UGH, FINE.
HI?

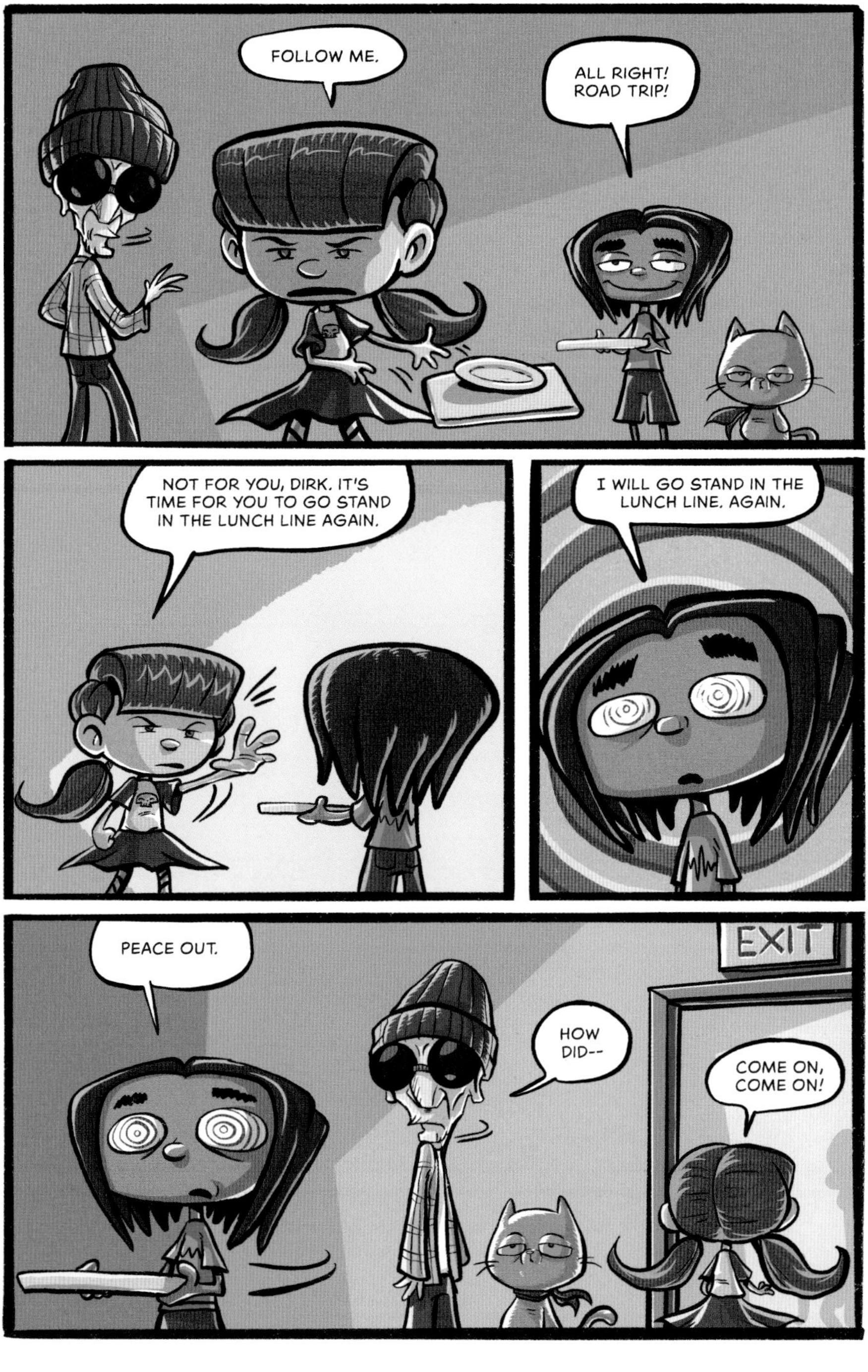
FOLLOW ME.
ALL RIGHT! ROAD TRIP!
NOT FOR YOU, DIRK. IT'S TIME FOR YOU TO GO STAND IN THE LUNCH LINE AGAIN.
I WILL GO STAND IN THE LUNCH LINE. AGAIN.
PEACE OUT.
EXIT
HOW DID--
COME ON, COME ON!

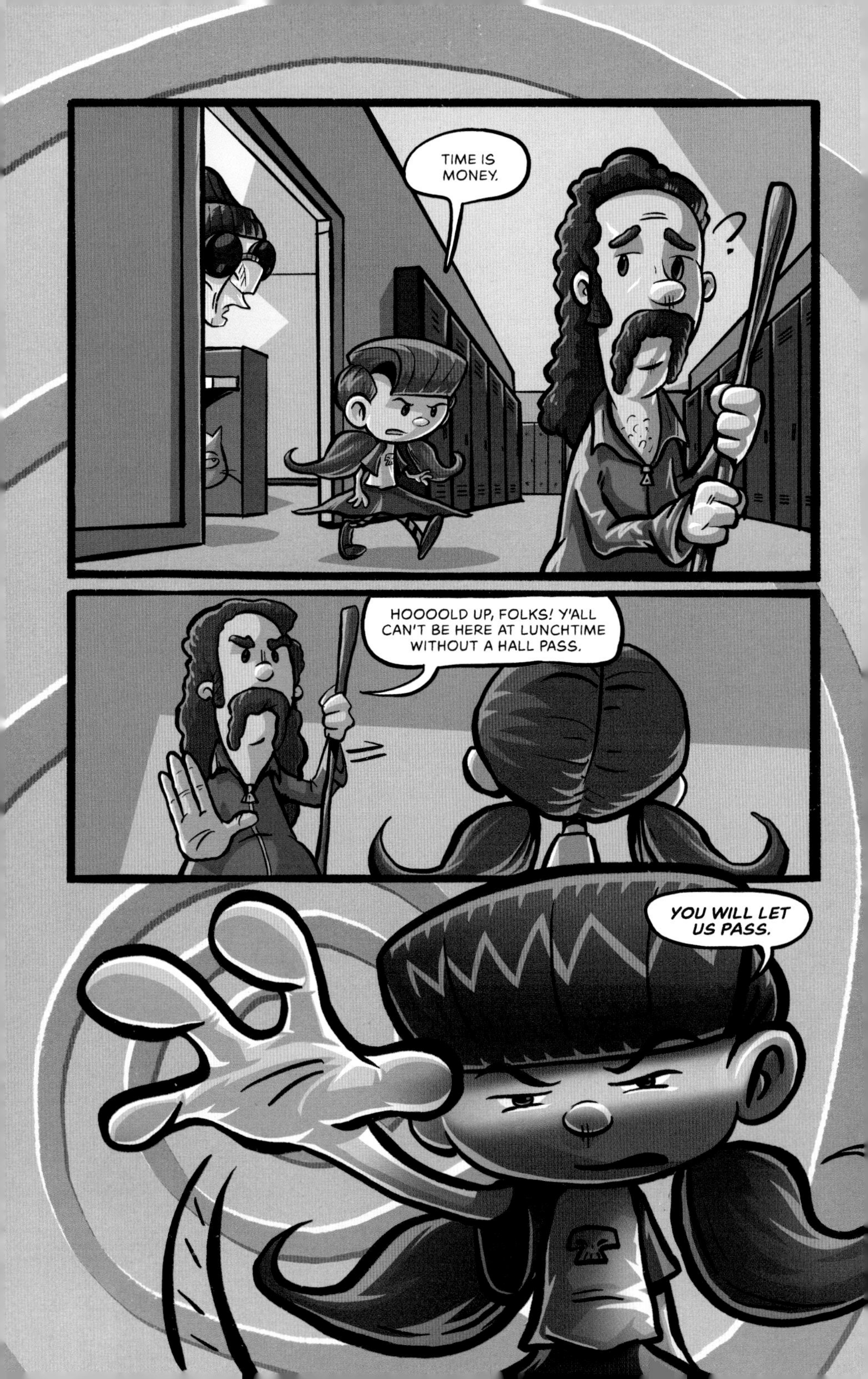
TIME IS MONEY.
HOOOOLD UP, FOLKS! Y'ALL CAN'T BE HERE AT LUNCHTIME WITHOUT A HALL PASS.
YOU WILL LET US PASS.

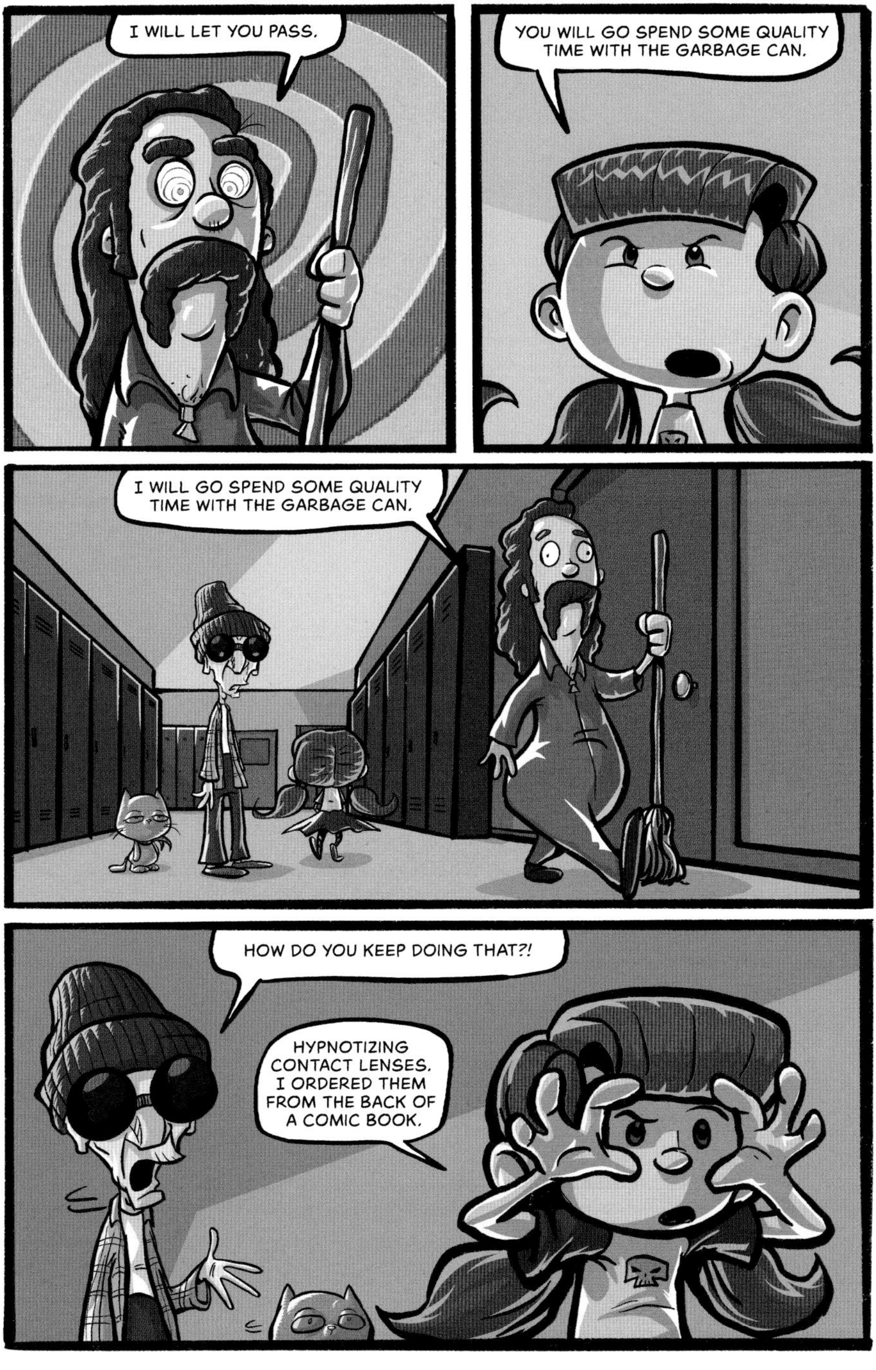
I WILL LET YOU PASS.
YOU WILL GO SPEND SOME QUALITY TIME WITH THE GARBAGE CAN.
I WILL GO SPEND SOME QUALITY TIME WITH THE GARBAGE CAN.
HOW DO YOU KEEP DOING THAT?!
HYPNOTIZING CONTACT LENSES. I ORDERED THEM FROM THE BACK OF A COMIC BOOK.

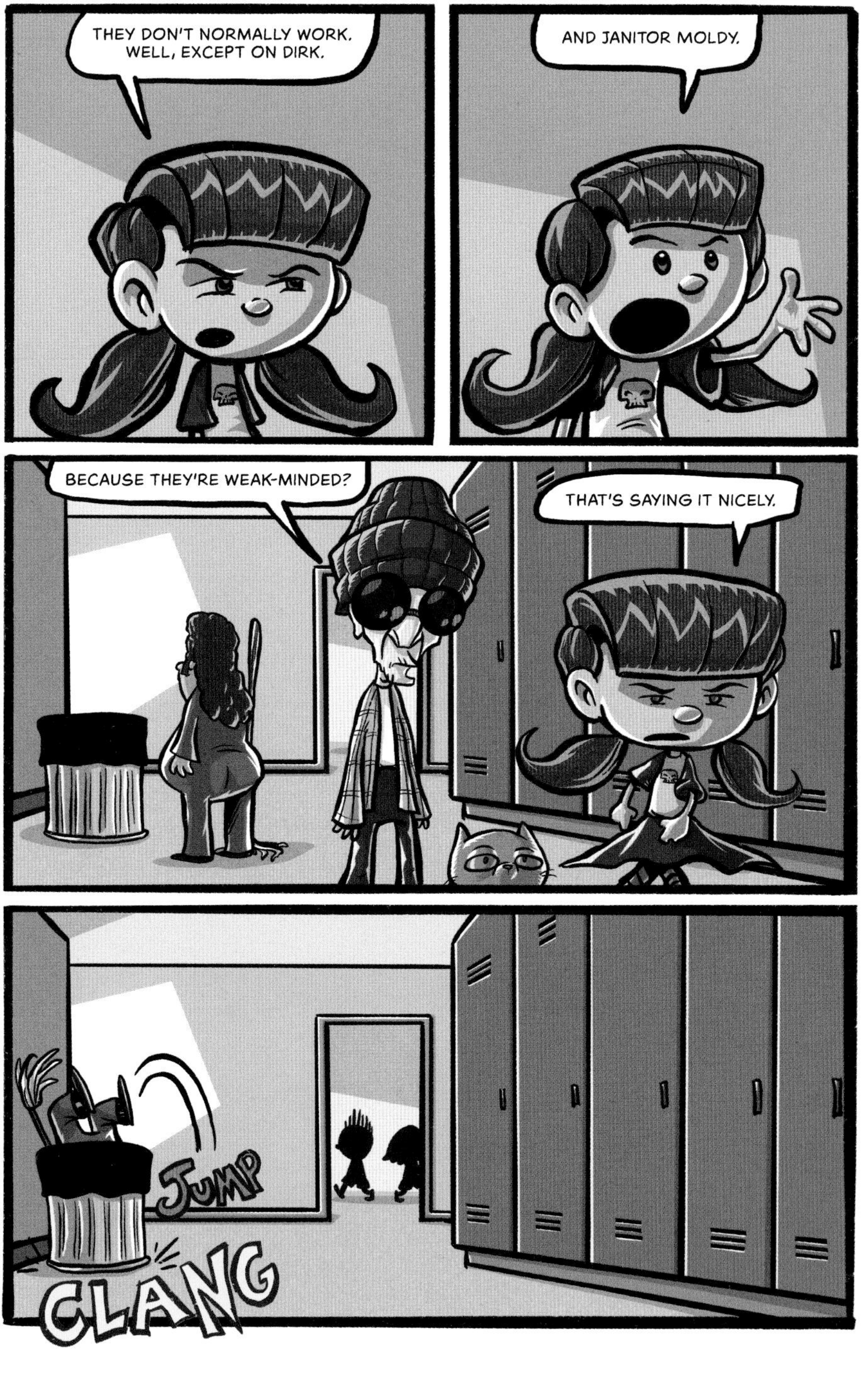
THEY DON'T NORMALLY WORK. WELL, EXCEPT ON DIRK.
AND JANITOR MOLDY.
BECAUSE THEY'RE WEAK-MINDED?
THAT'S SAYING IT NICELY.
JUMP
CLANG

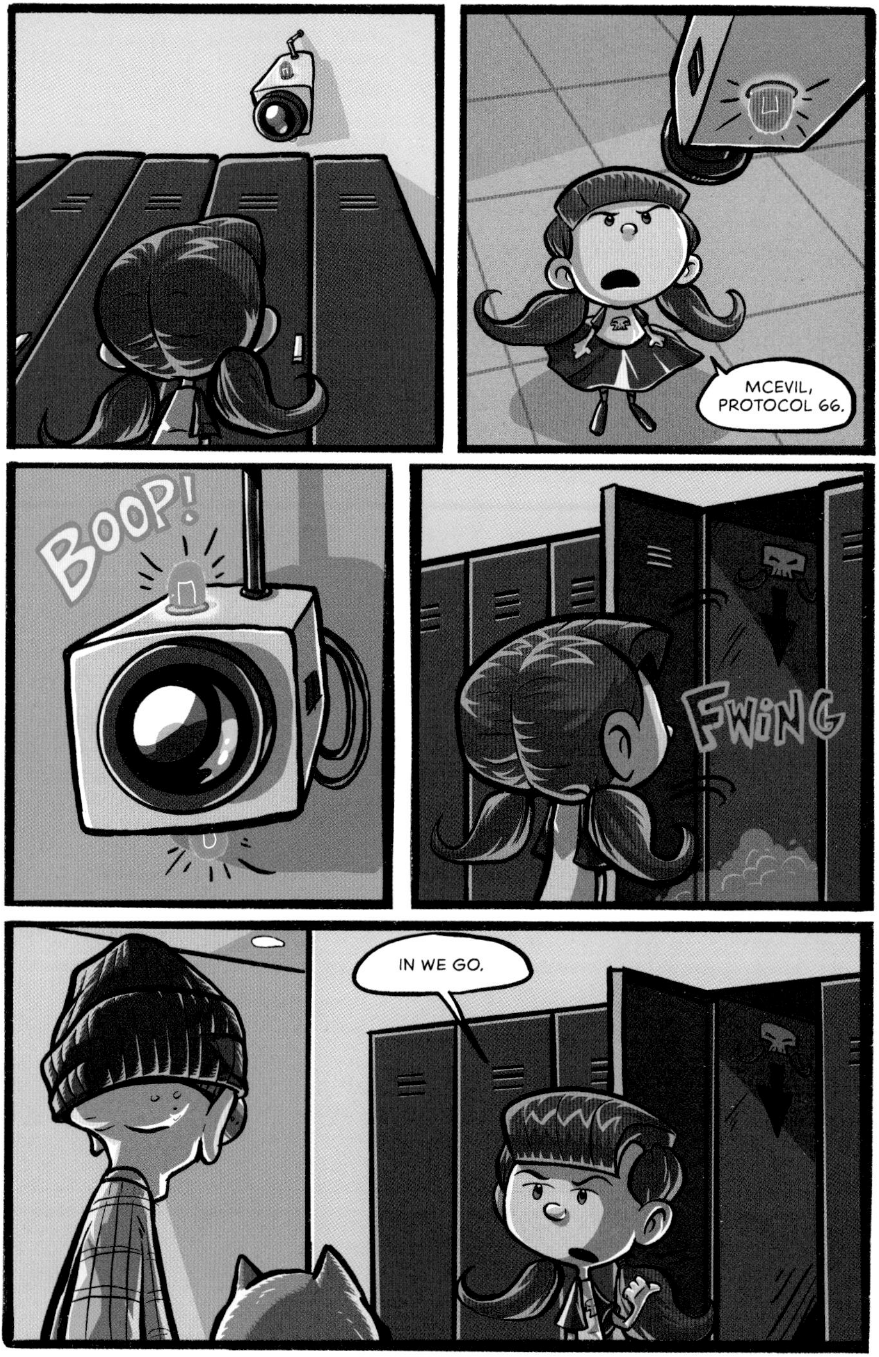
MCEVIL,
PROTOCOL 66.
BOOP!
FWING
IN WE GO.

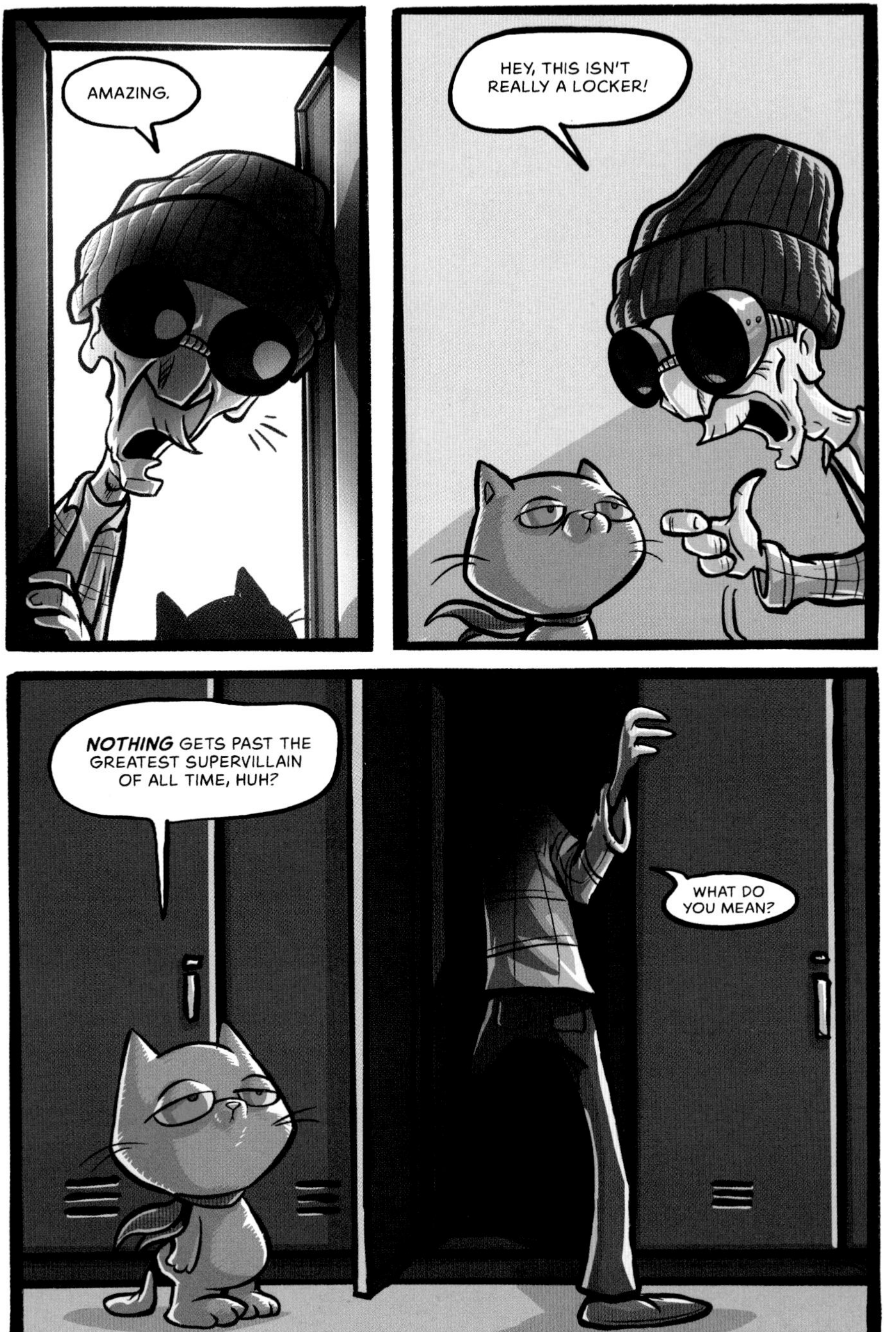
AMAZING.
HEY, THIS ISN'T REALLY A LOCKER!
NOTHING GETS PAST THE GREATEST SUPERVILLAIN OF ALL TIME, HUH?
WHAT DO YOU MEAN?

CHAPTER 7

Crystal Clear

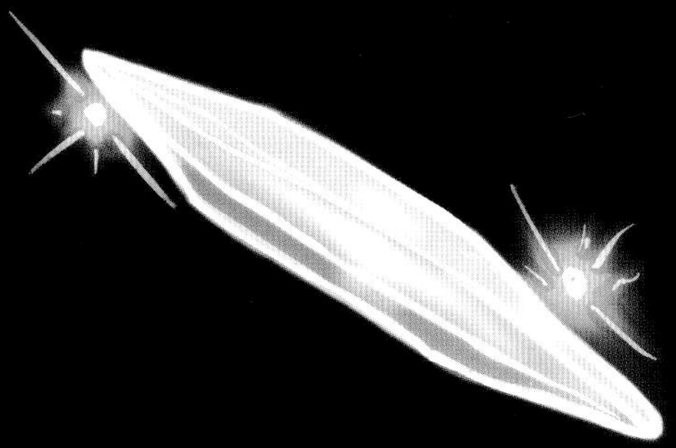

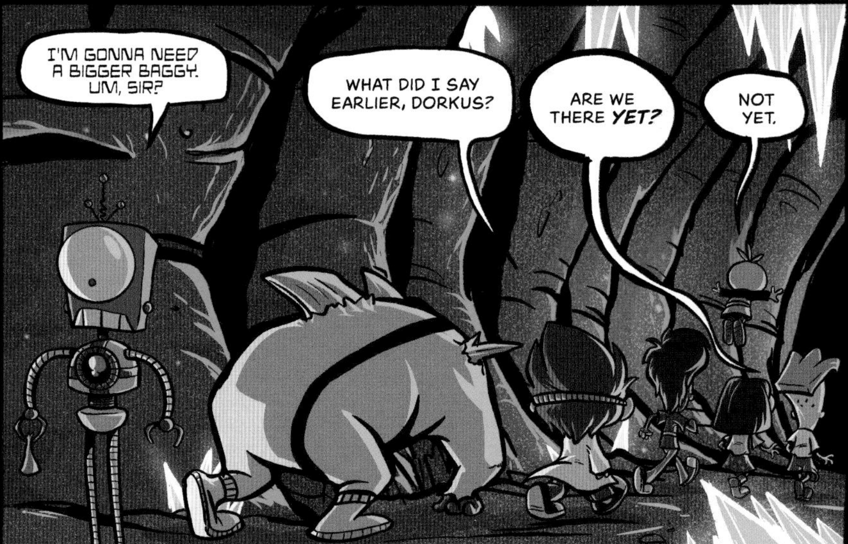
I'M GONNA NEED A BIGGER BAGGY. UM, SIR?
WHAT DID I SAY EARLIER, DORKUS?
ARE WE THERE *YET?*
NOT YET.

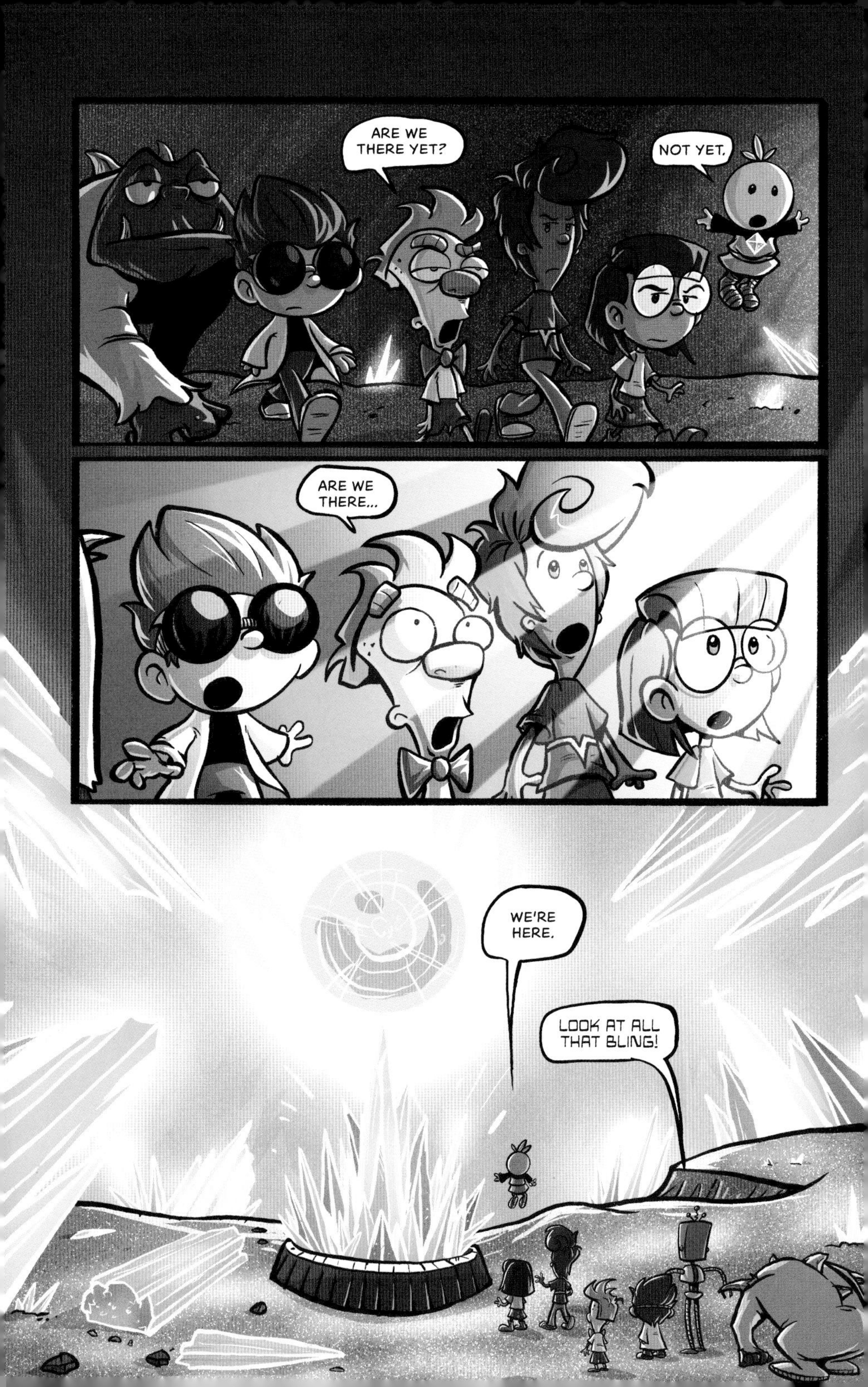
ARE WE THERE YET?
NOT YET.
ARE WE THERE...
WE'RE HERE.
LOOK AT ALL THAT BLING!

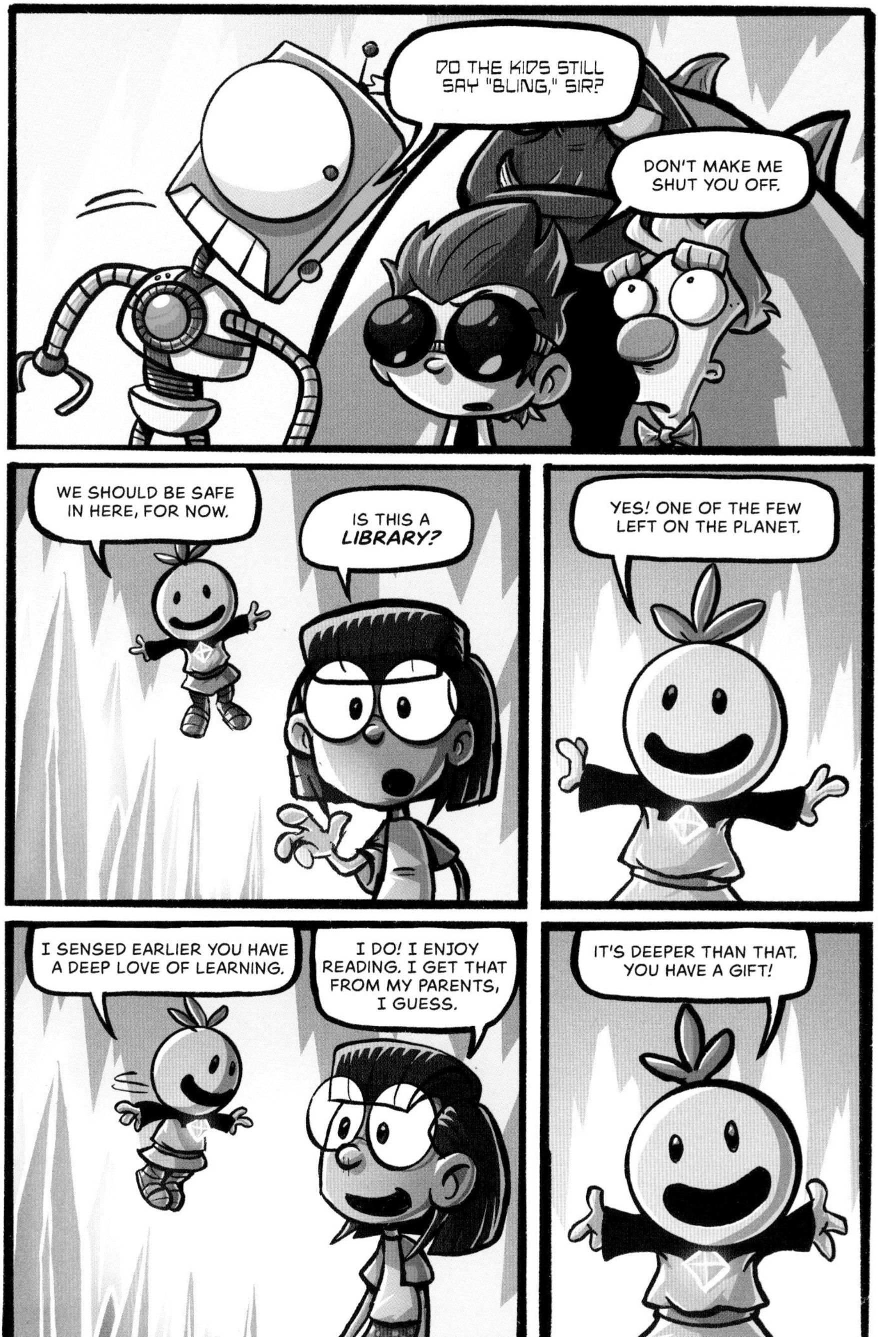
DO THE KIDS STILL SAY "BLING," SIR?
DON'T MAKE ME SHUT YOU OFF.
WE SHOULD BE SAFE IN HERE, FOR NOW.
IS THIS A *LIBRARY?*
YES! ONE OF THE FEW LEFT ON THE PLANET.
I SENSED EARLIER YOU HAVE A DEEP LOVE OF LEARNING.
I DO! I ENJOY READING. I GET THAT FROM MY PARENTS, I GUESS.
IT'S DEEPER THAN THAT. YOU HAVE A GIFT!

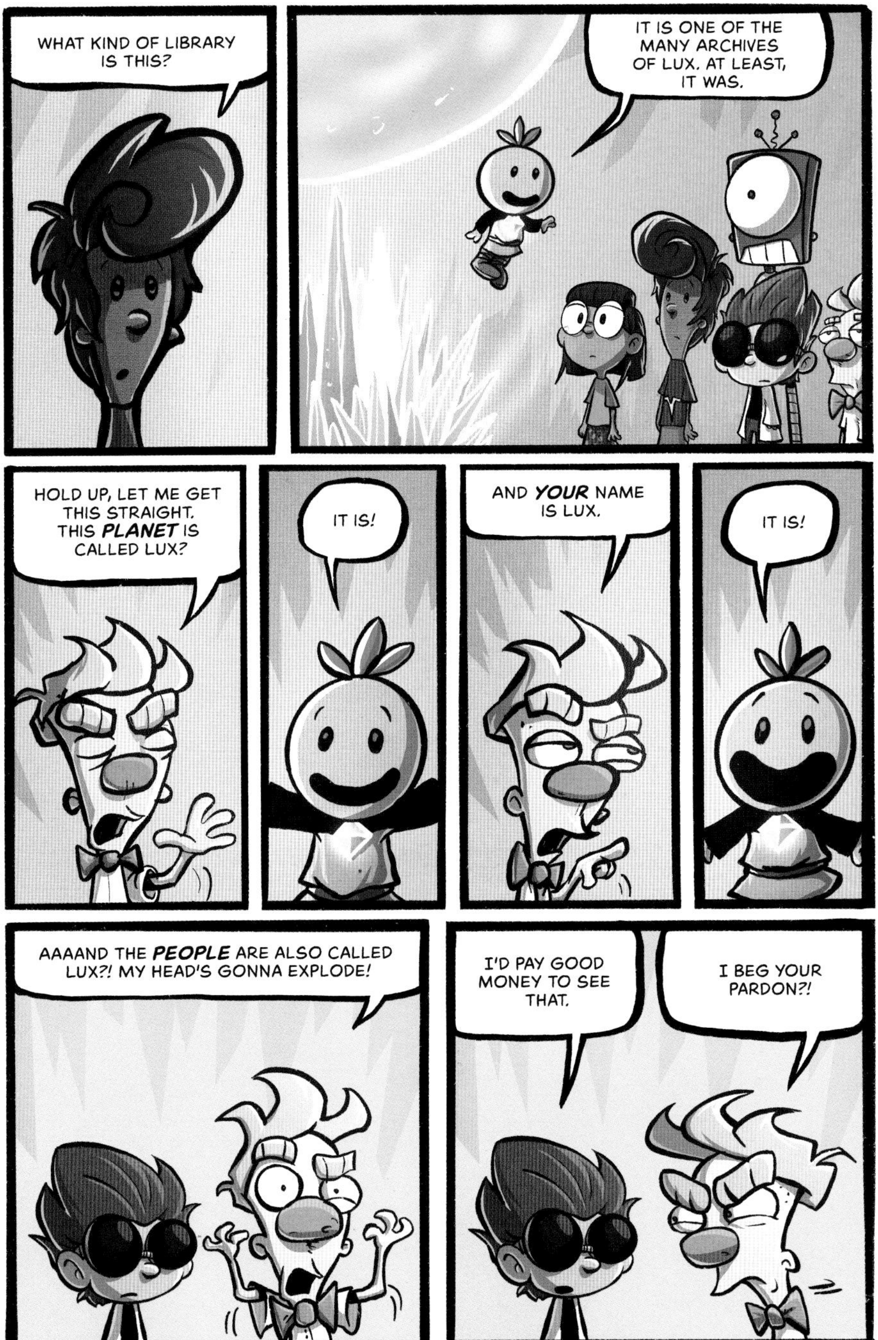
WHAT KIND OF LIBRARY IS THIS?
IT IS ONE OF THE MANY ARCHIVES OF LUX. AT LEAST, IT WAS.
HOLD UP, LET ME GET THIS STRAIGHT. THIS PLANET IS CALLED LUX?
IT IS!
AND YOUR NAME IS LUX.
IT IS!
AAAAND THE PEOPLE ARE ALSO CALLED LUX?! MY HEAD'S GONNA EXPLODE!
I'D PAY GOOD MONEY TO SEE THAT.
I BEG YOUR PARDON?!

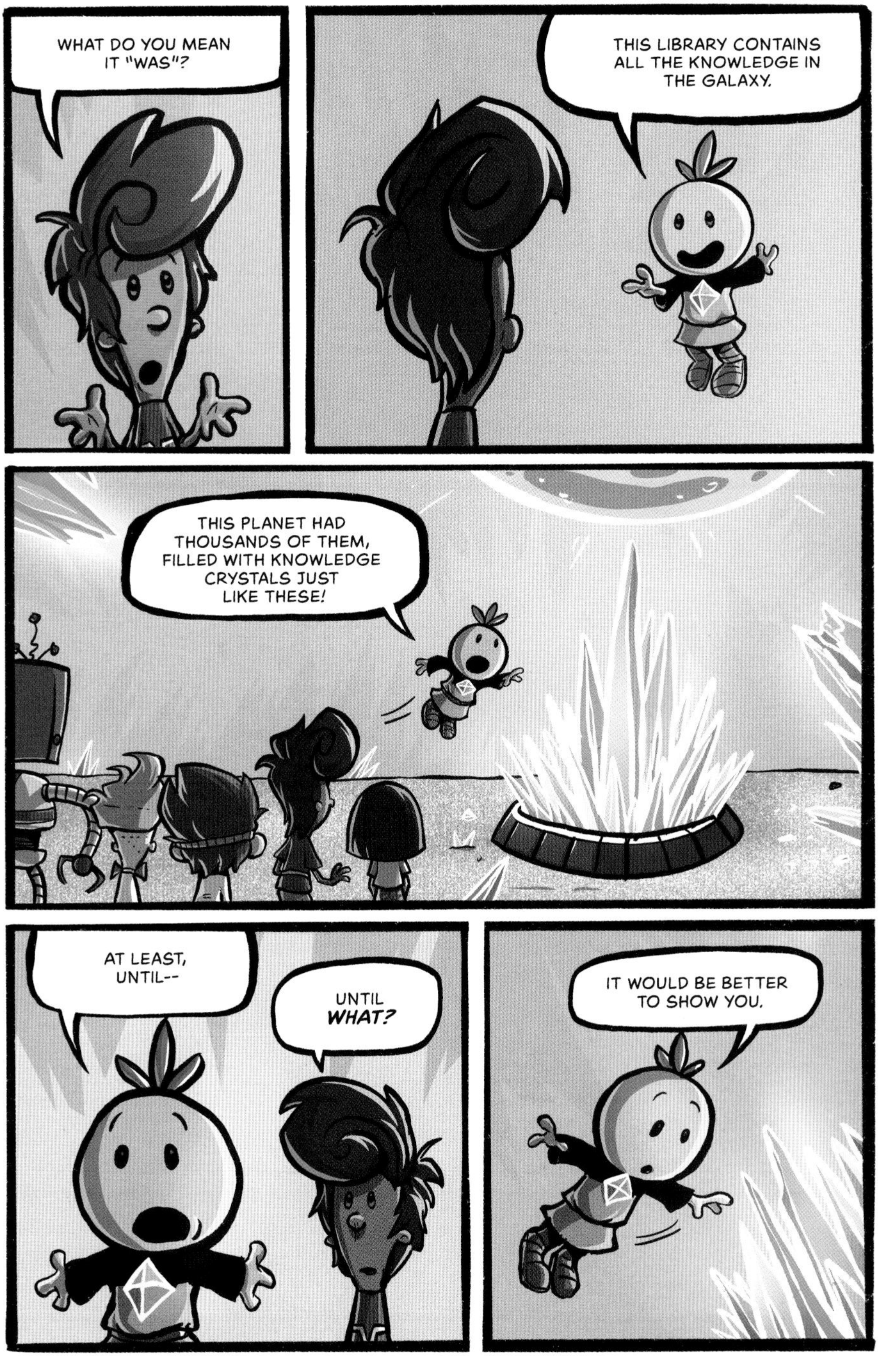
WHAT DO YOU MEAN IT "WAS"?
THIS LIBRARY CONTAINS ALL THE KNOWLEDGE IN THE GALAXY.
THIS PLANET HAD THOUSANDS OF THEM, FILLED WITH KNOWLEDGE CRYSTALS JUST LIKE THESE!
AT LEAST, UNTIL--
UNTIL *WHAT?*
IT WOULD BE BETTER TO SHOW YOU.

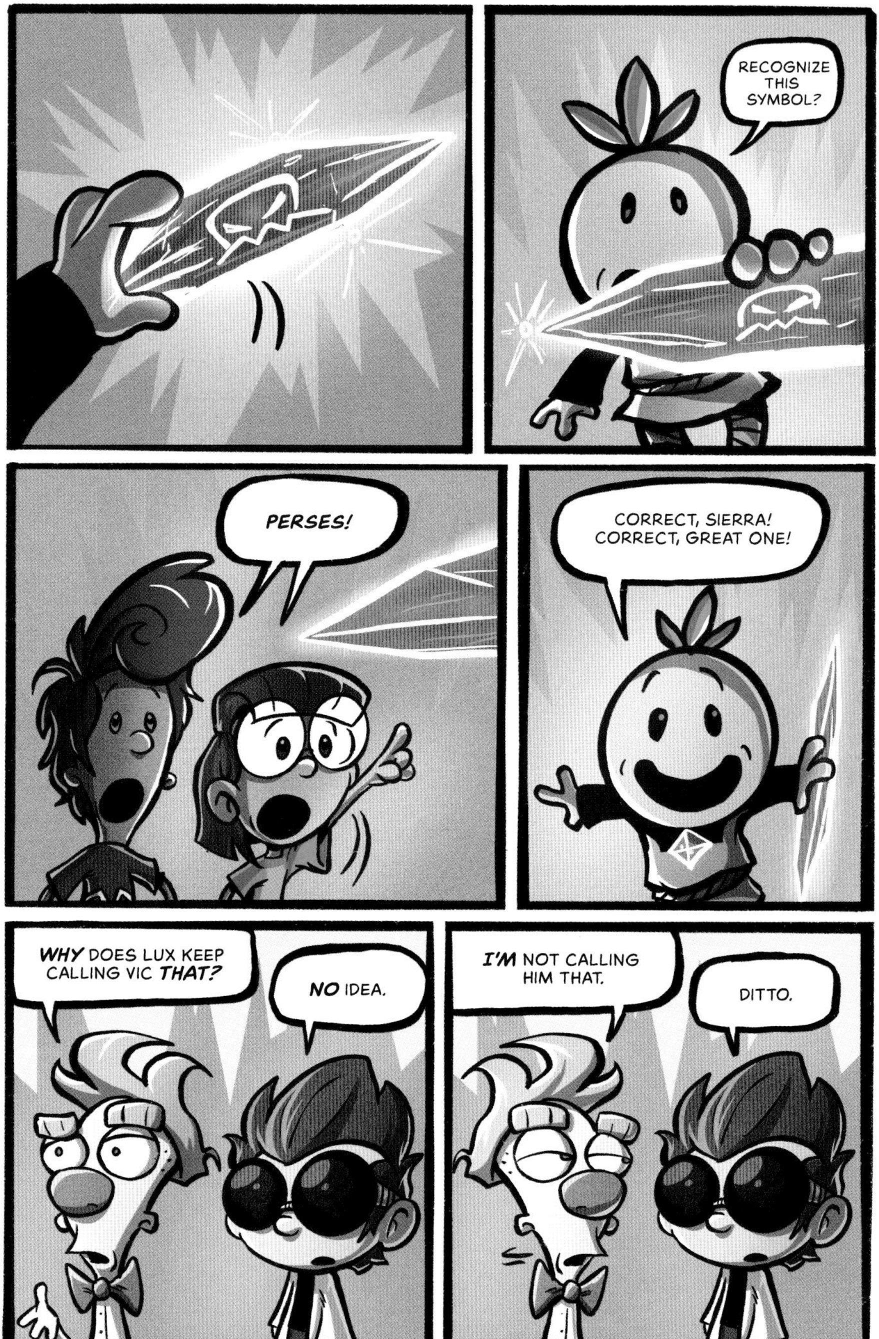
RECOGNIZE THIS SYMBOL?
PERSES!
CORRECT, SIERRA! CORRECT, GREAT ONE!
WHY DOES LUX KEEP CALLING VIC THAT?
NO IDEA.
I'M NOT CALLING HIM THAT.
DITTO.

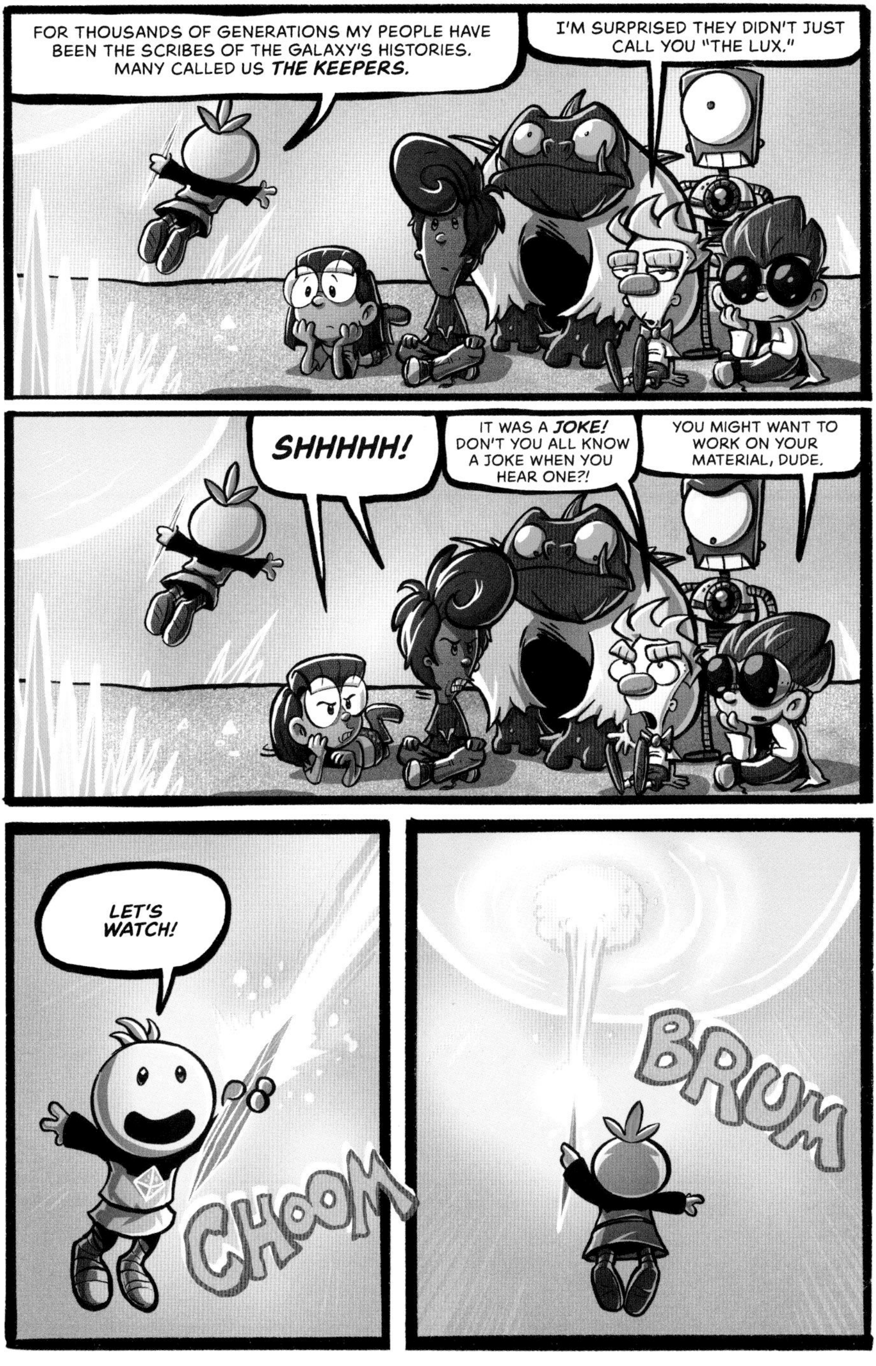

FOR THOUSANDS OF GENERATIONS MY PEOPLE HAVE BEEN THE SCRIBES OF THE GALAXY'S HISTORIES. MANY CALLED US THE KEEPERS.
I'M SURPRISED THEY DIDN'T JUST CALL YOU "THE LUX."
SHHHHH!
IT WAS A JOKE! DON'T YOU ALL KNOW A JOKE WHEN YOU HEAR ONE?!
YOU MIGHT WANT TO WORK ON YOUR MATERIAL, DUDE.
LET'S WATCH!
CHOOM
BRUM

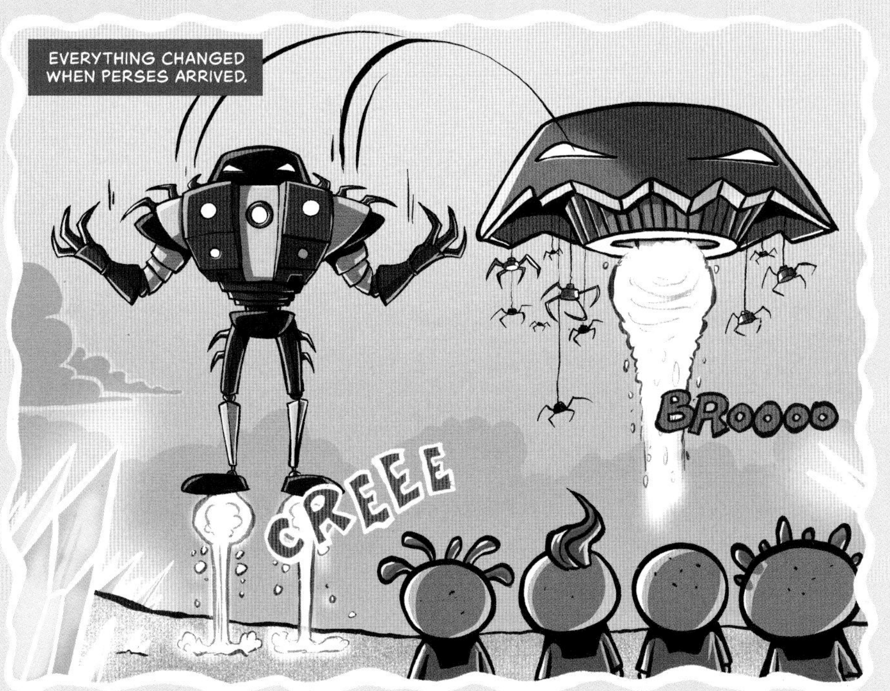
EVERYTHING CHANGED WHEN PERSES ARRIVED.
BROOOO
CREEE

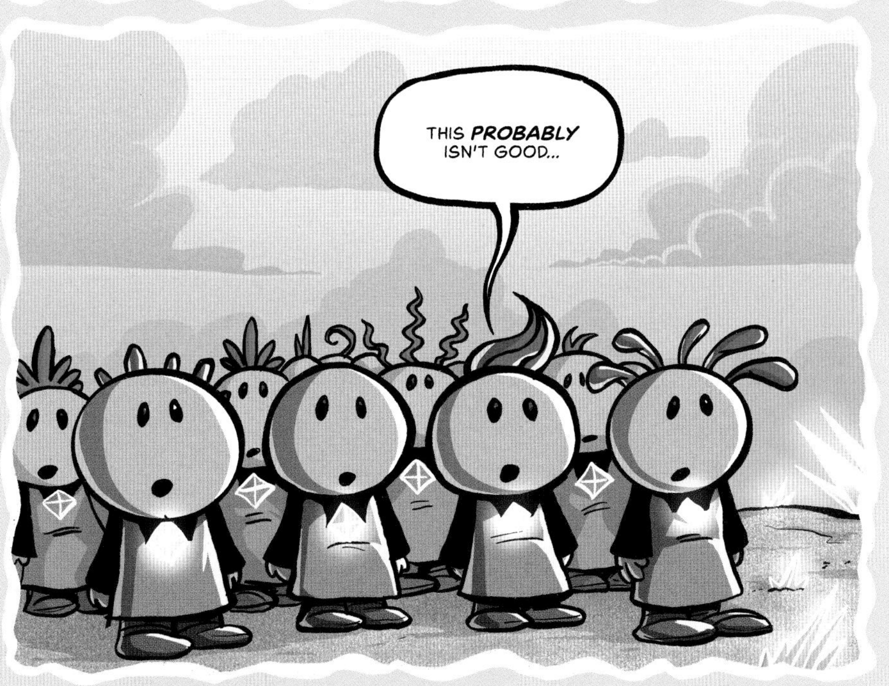
THIS *PROBABLY* ISN'T GOOD...

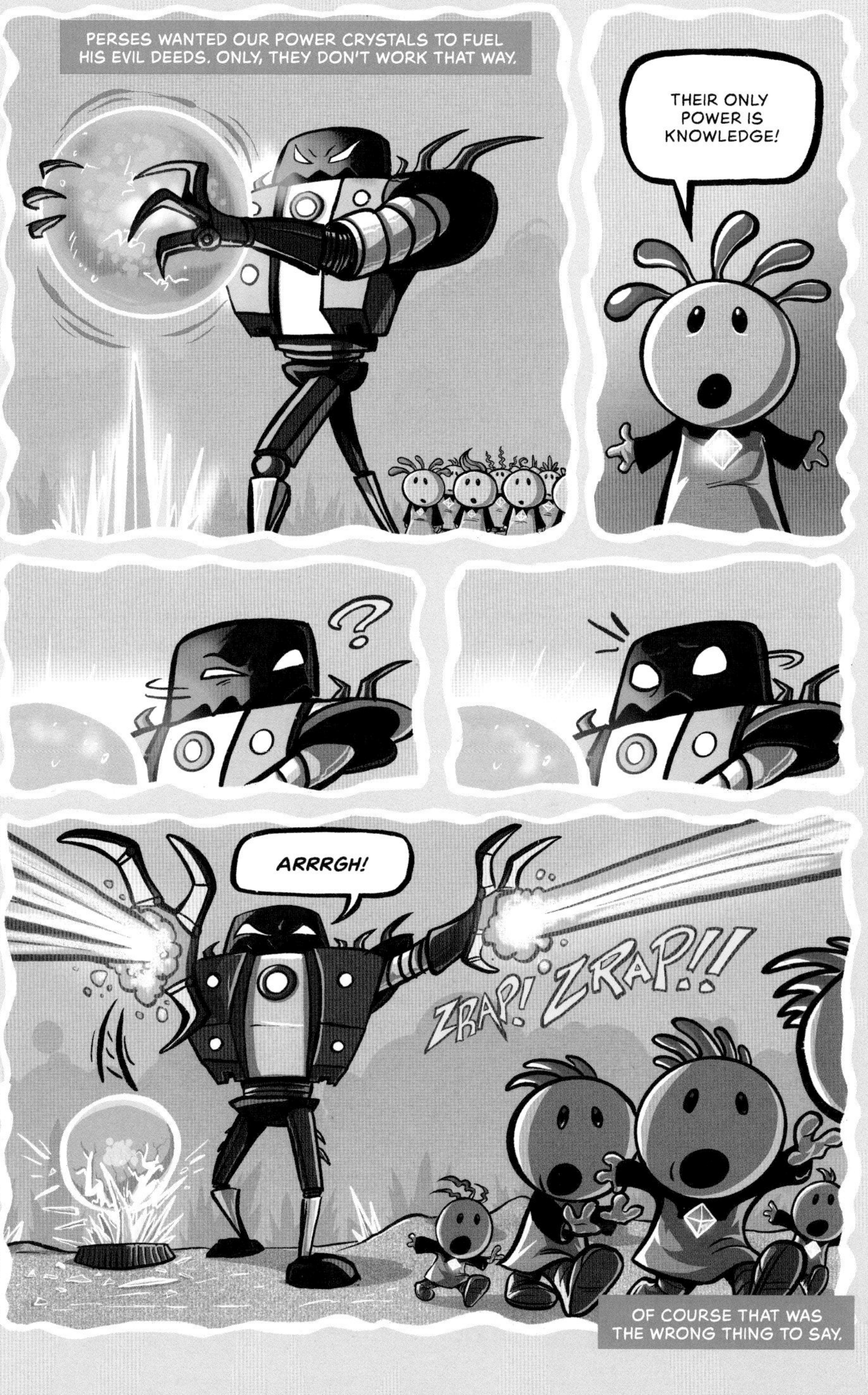
PERSES WANTED OUR POWER CRYSTALS TO FUEL HIS EVIL DEEDS. ONLY, THEY DON'T WORK THAT WAY.
THEIR ONLY POWER IS KNOWLEDGE!
?
ARRRGH!
ZRAP! ZRAP!!
OF COURSE THAT WAS THE WRONG THING TO SAY.

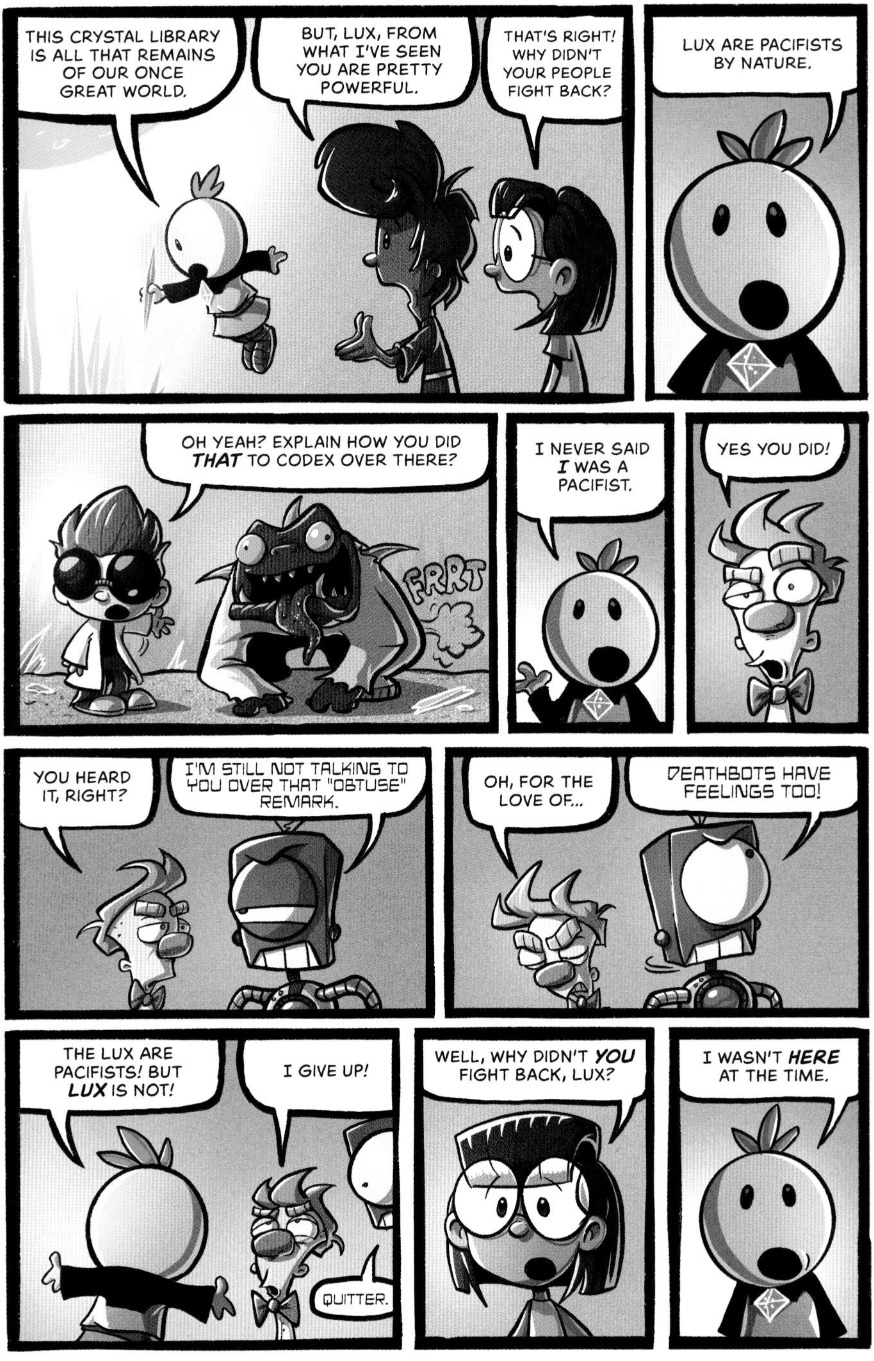
THIS CRYSTAL LIBRARY IS ALL THAT REMAINS OF OUR ONCE GREAT WORLD.
BUT, LUX, FROM WHAT I'VE SEEN YOU ARE PRETTY POWERFUL.
THAT'S RIGHT! WHY DIDN'T YOUR PEOPLE FIGHT BACK?
LUX ARE PACIFISTS BY NATURE.
OH YEAH? EXPLAIN HOW YOU DID THAT TO CODEX OVER THERE?
FRRT
I NEVER SAID I WAS A PACIFIST.
YES YOU DID!
YOU HEARD IT, RIGHT?
I'M STILL NOT TALKING TO YOU OVER THAT "OBTUSE" REMARK.
OH, FOR THE LOVE OF...
DEATHBOTS HAVE FEELINGS TOO!
THE LUX ARE PACIFISTS! BUT LUX IS NOT!
I GIVE UP!
QUITTER.
WELL, WHY DIDN'T YOU FIGHT BACK, LUX?
I WASN'T HERE AT THE TIME.

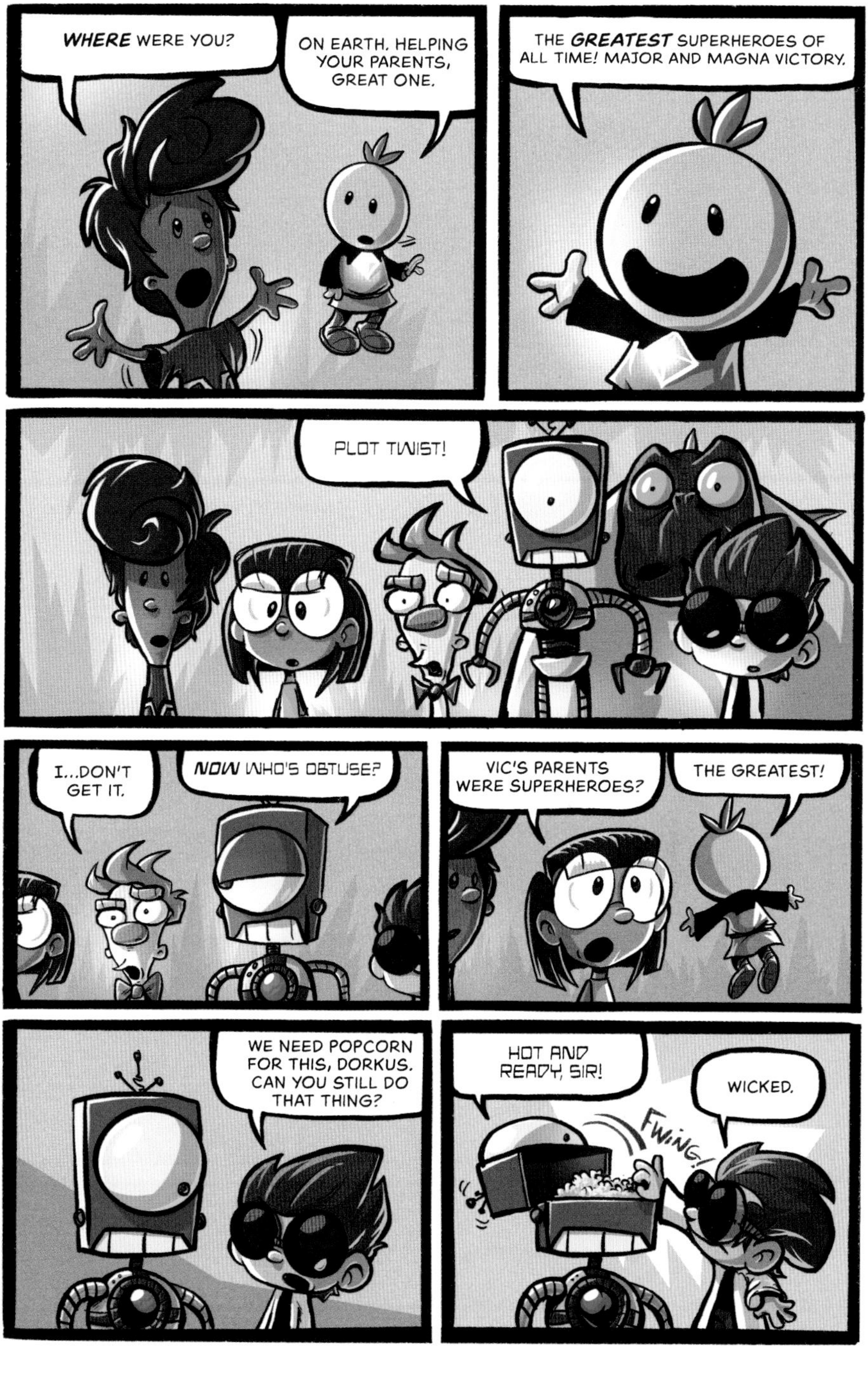
WHERE WERE YOU?
ON EARTH, HELPING YOUR PARENTS, GREAT ONE.
THE GREATEST SUPERHEROES OF ALL TIME! MAJOR AND MAGNA VICTORY.
PLOT TWIST!
I...DON'T GET IT.
NOW WHO'S OBTUSE?
VIC'S PARENTS WERE SUPERHEROES?
THE GREATEST!
WE NEED POPCORN FOR THIS, DORKUS. CAN YOU STILL DO THAT THING?
HOT AND READY, SIR!
FWING!
WICKED.

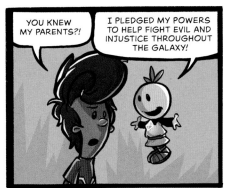

YOU KNEW MY PARENTS?!

I PLEDGED MY POWERS TO HELP FIGHT EVIL AND INJUSTICE THROUGHOUT THE GALAXY!

WHAT HAPPENED?

LIKE I SAID, THEY WERE SUMMONED TO EARTH FOR A CRISIS.

SUMMONED? WEREN'T THEY ALREADY ON EARTH?

NO, GREAT ONE.

LUX WAS ALSO THEIR HOME. *YOUR* HOME.

ARE YOU SAYING VIC'S AN...

...ALIEN?!

Riiiii...

...iip!

I KNEW IT!

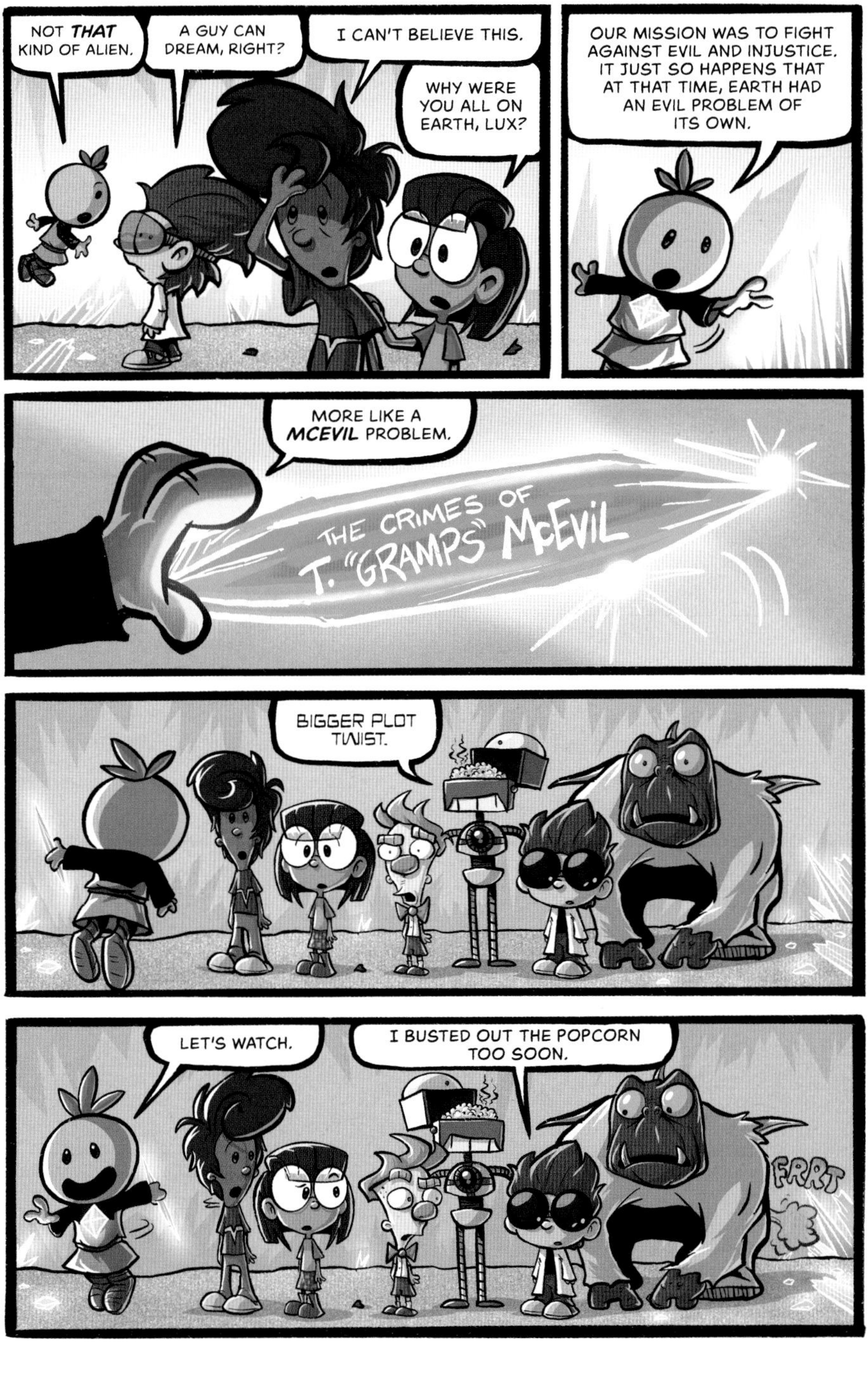
NOT *THAT* KIND OF ALIEN.
A GUY CAN DREAM, RIGHT?
I CAN'T BELIEVE THIS.
WHY WERE YOU ALL ON EARTH, LUX?
OUR MISSION WAS TO FIGHT AGAINST EVIL AND INJUSTICE. IT JUST SO HAPPENS THAT AT THAT TIME, EARTH HAD AN EVIL PROBLEM OF ITS OWN.
MORE LIKE A *MCEVIL* PROBLEM.
THE CRIMES OF T. "GRAMPS" McEVIL
BIGGER PLOT TWIST.
LET'S WATCH.
I BUSTED OUT THE POPCORN TOO SOON.
FRRT

CHAPTER 8

A Certain Point of View

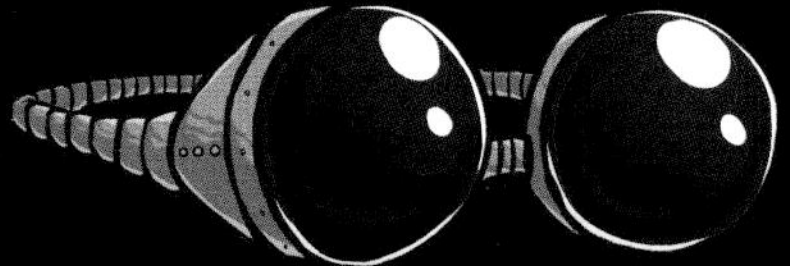

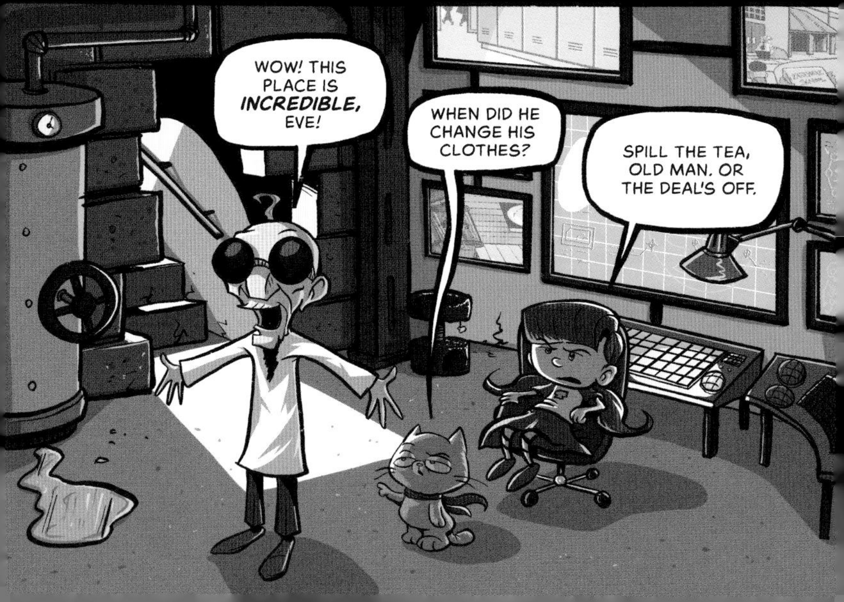
WOW! THIS PLACE IS *INCREDIBLE,* EVE!
WHEN DID HE CHANGE HIS CLOTHES?
SPILL THE TEA, OLD MAN, OR THE DEAL'S OFF.

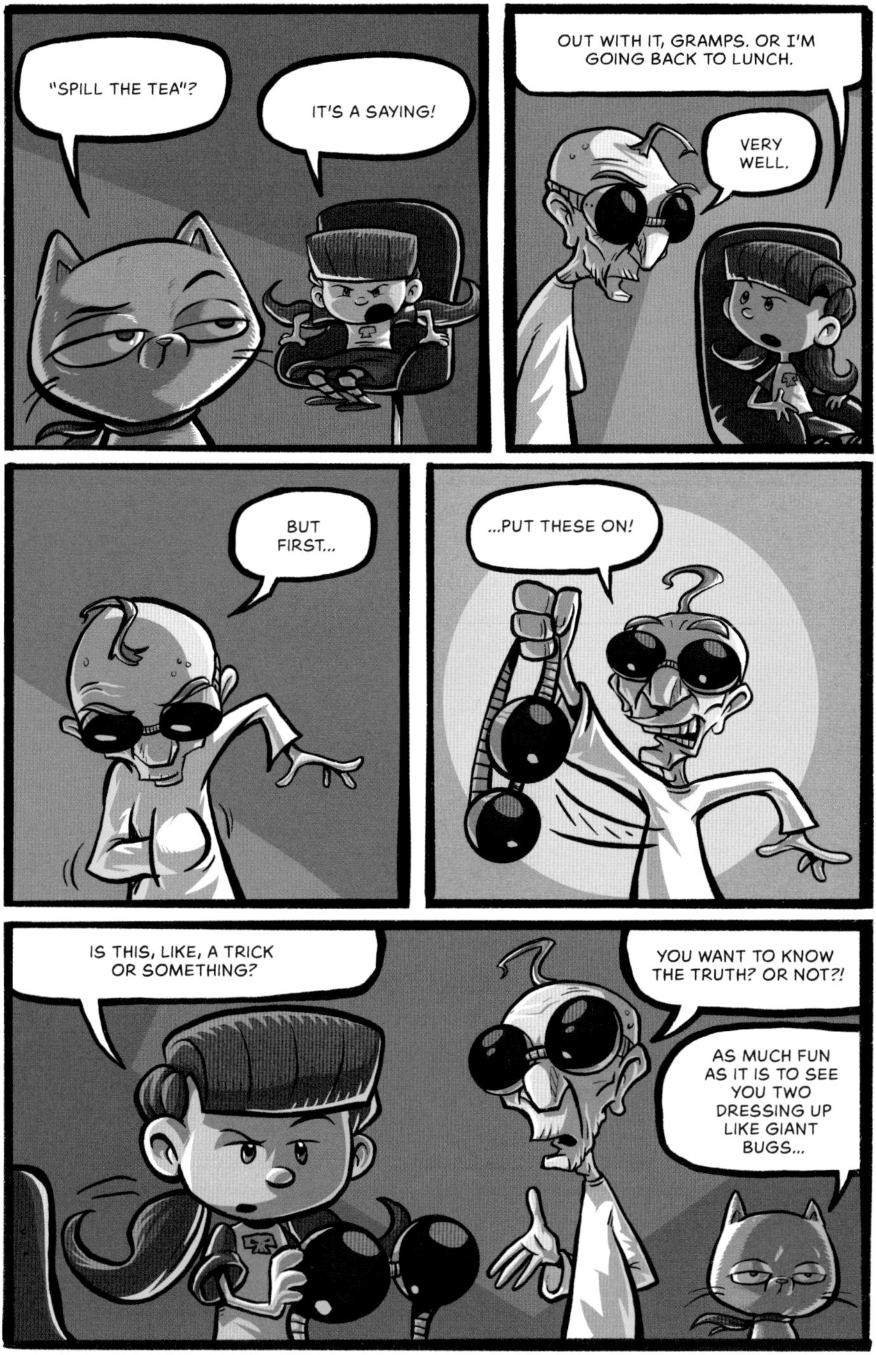
"SPILL THE TEA"?
IT'S A SAYING!
OUT WITH IT, GRAMPS. OR I'M GOING BACK TO LUNCH.
VERY WELL.
BUT FIRST...
...PUT THESE ON!
IS THIS, LIKE, A TRICK OR SOMETHING?
YOU WANT TO KNOW THE TRUTH? OR NOT?!
AS MUCH FUN AS IT IS TO SEE YOU TWO DRESSING UP LIKE GIANT BUGS...

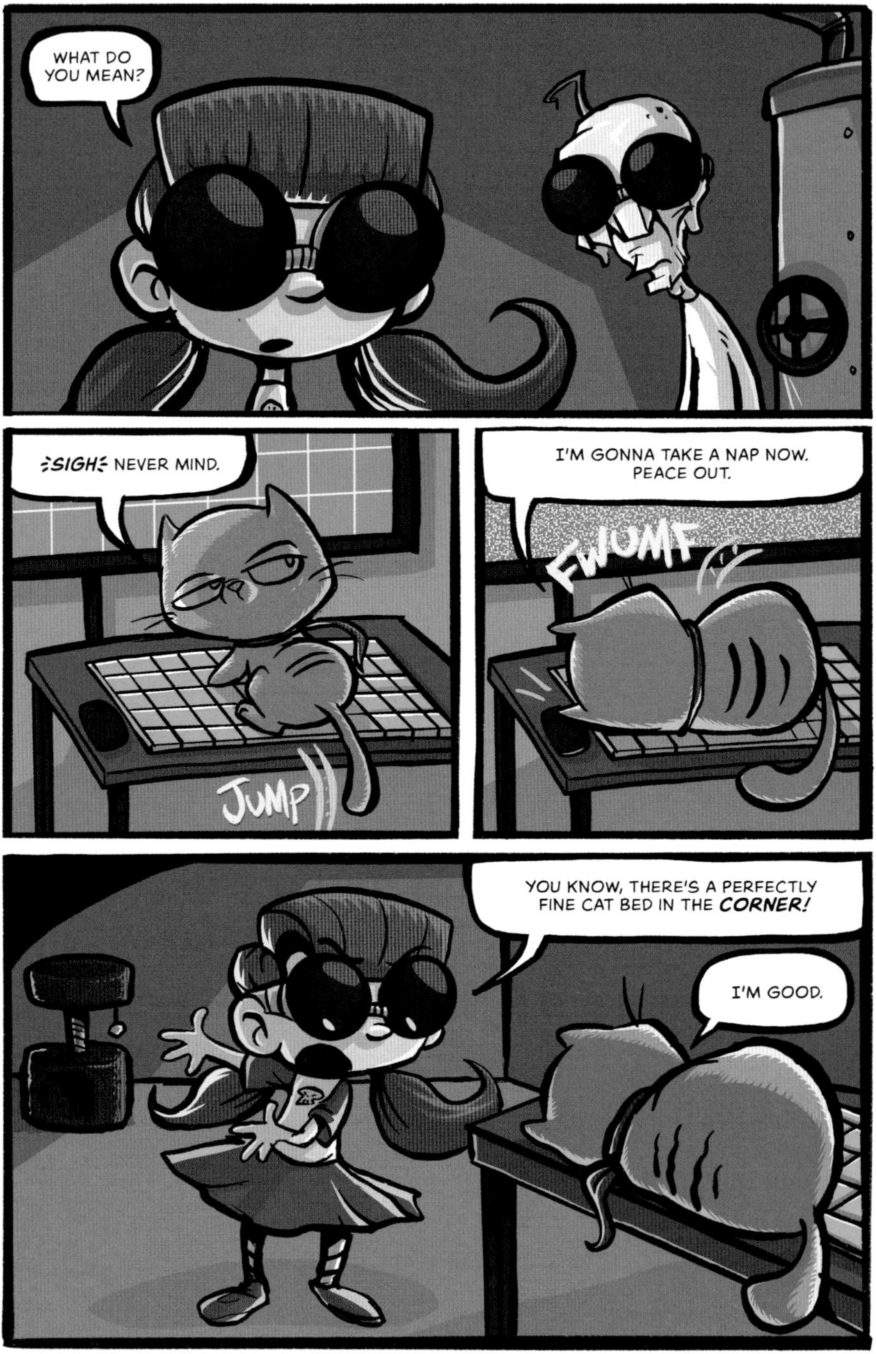
WHAT DO YOU MEAN?
SIGH NEVER MIND.
JUMP
I'M GONNA TAKE A NAP NOW. PEACE OUT.
FWUMF
YOU KNOW, THERE'S A PERFECTLY FINE CAT BED IN THE **CORNER!**
I'M GOOD.

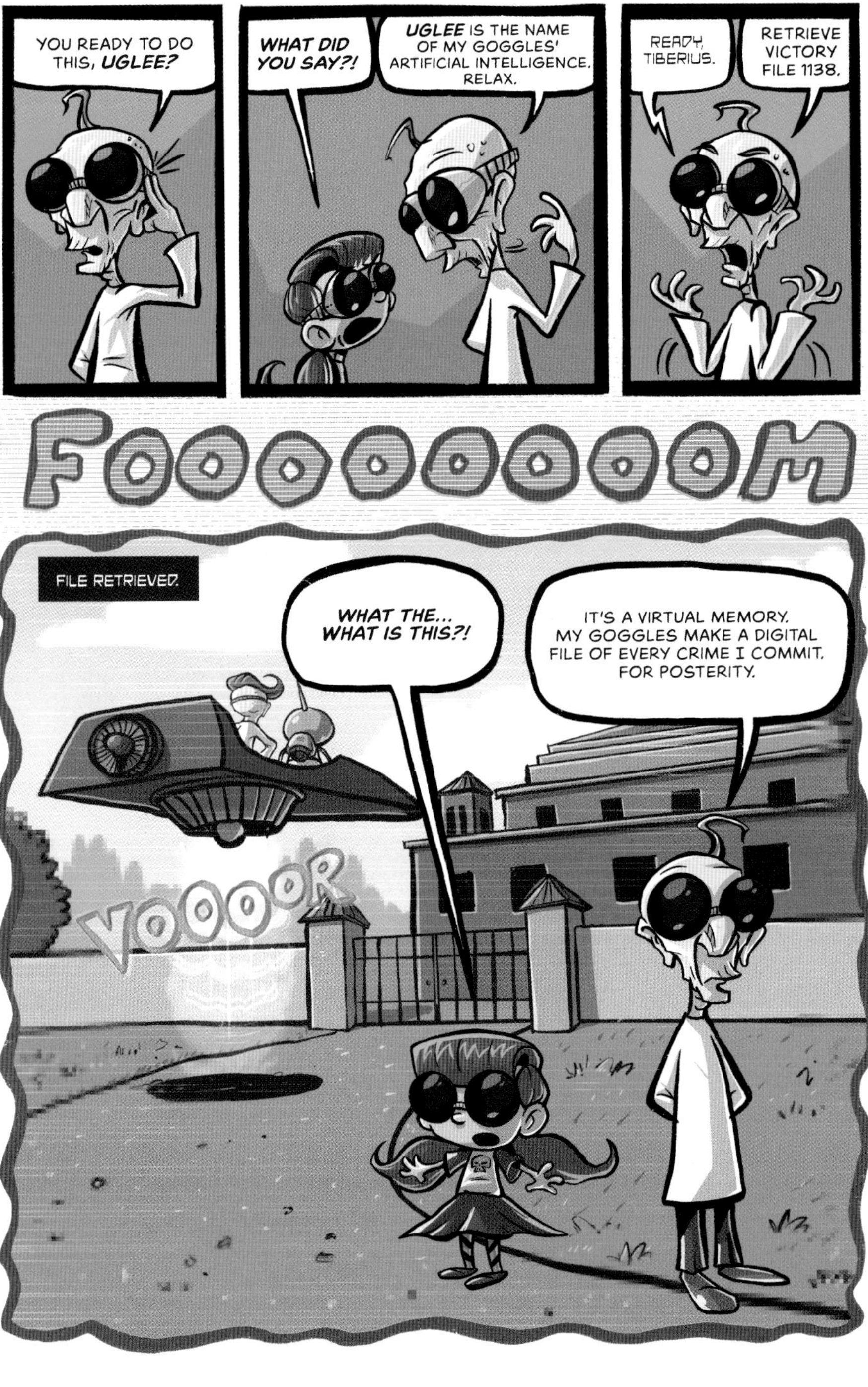
YOU READY TO DO THIS, UGLEE?
WHAT DID YOU SAY?!
UGLEE IS THE NAME OF MY GOGGLES' ARTIFICIAL INTELLIGENCE. RELAX.
READY, TIBERIUS.
RETRIEVE VICTORY FILE 1138.
FOOOOOOOOM
FILE RETRIEVED.
WHAT THE... WHAT IS THIS?!
IT'S A VIRTUAL MEMORY. MY GOGGLES MAKE A DIGITAL FILE OF EVERY CRIME I COMMIT. FOR POSTERITY.
VOOOOR

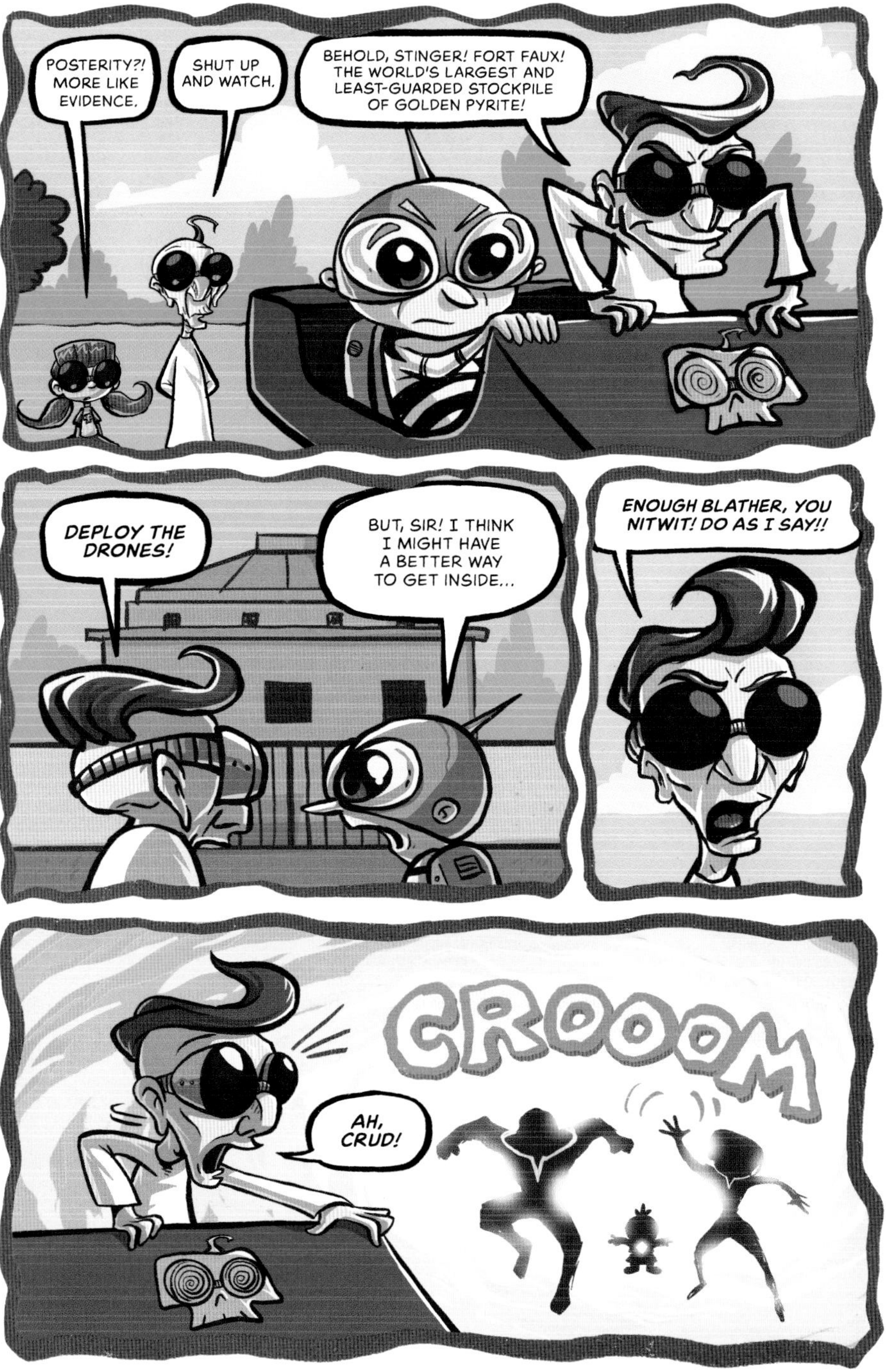
POSTERITY?! MORE LIKE EVIDENCE.
SHUT UP AND WATCH.
BEHOLD, STINGER! FORT FAUX! THE WORLD'S LARGEST AND LEAST-GUARDED STOCKPILE OF GOLDEN PYRITE!
DEPLOY THE DRONES!
BUT, SIR! I THINK I MIGHT HAVE A BETTER WAY TO GET INSIDE...
ENOUGH BLATHER, YOU NITWIT! DO AS I SAY!!
CROOOM
AH, CRUD!

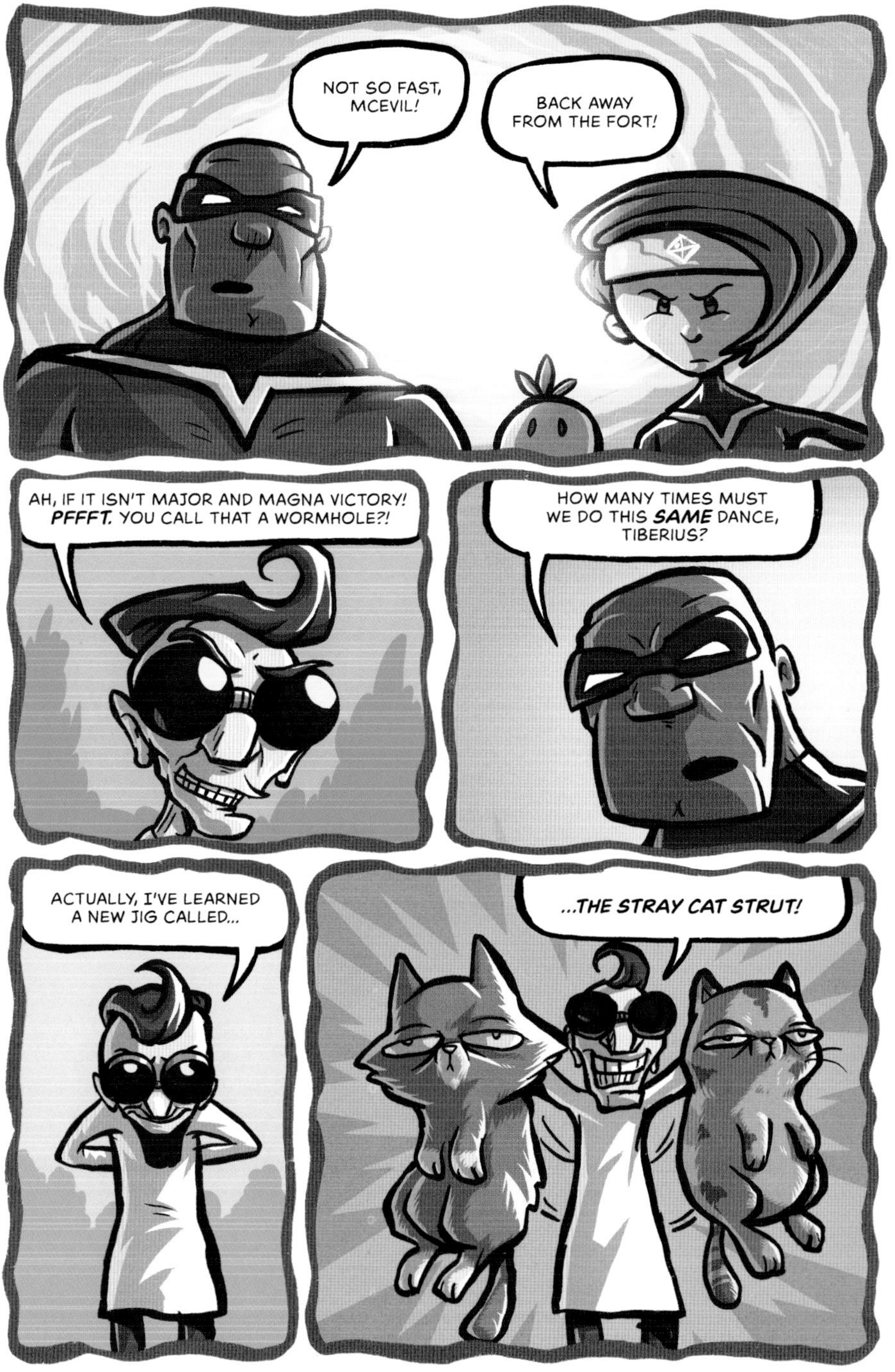
NOT SO FAST, MCEVIL!
BACK AWAY FROM THE FORT!
AH, IF IT ISN'T MAJOR AND MAGNA VICTORY! **PFFFT.** YOU CALL THAT A WORMHOLE?!
HOW MANY TIMES MUST WE DO THIS ***SAME*** DANCE, TIBERIUS?
ACTUALLY, I'VE LEARNED A NEW JIG CALLED...
...THE STRAY CAT STRUT!

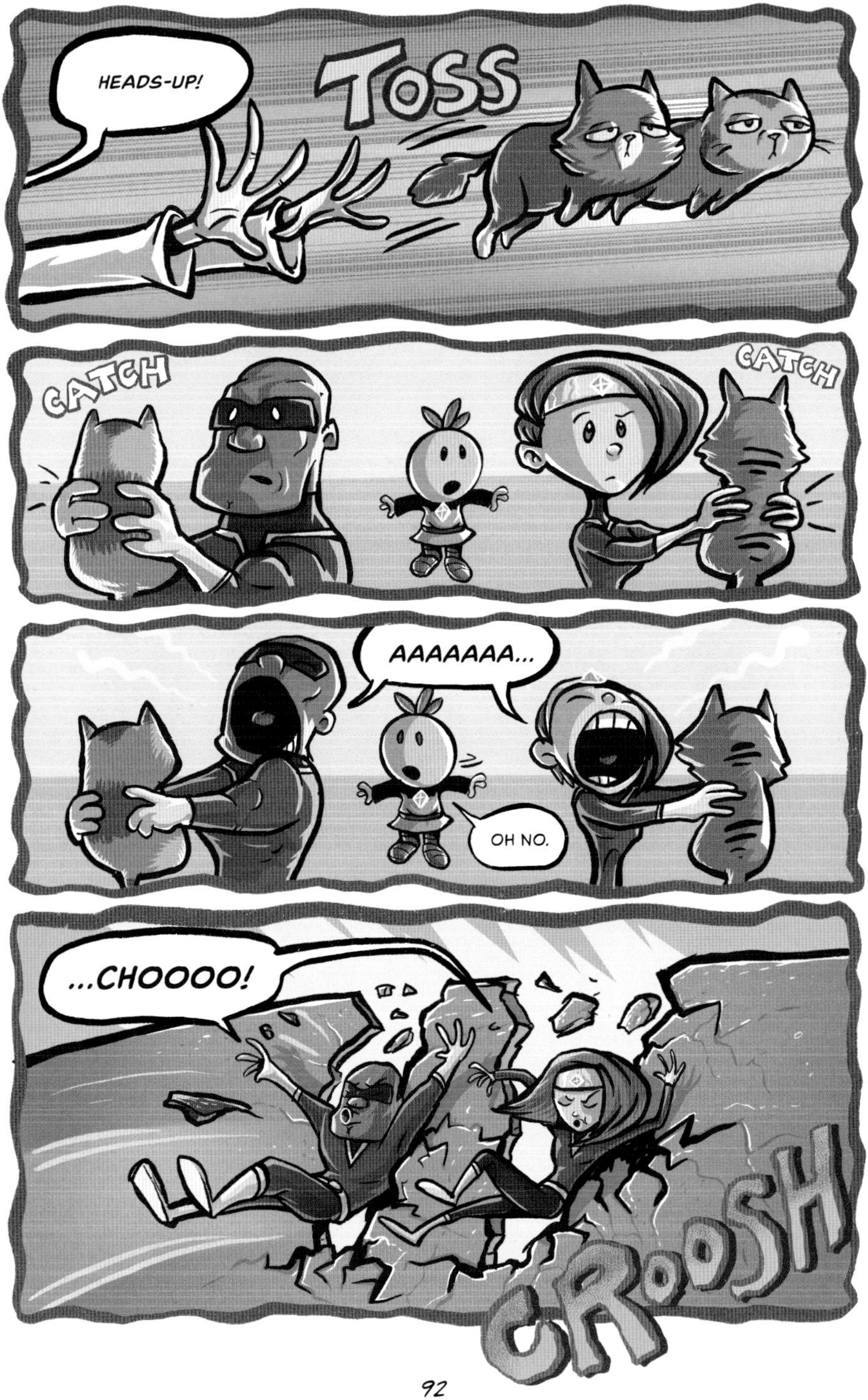
HEADS-UP!
TOSS
CATCH
CATCH
AAAAAAA...
OH NO.
...CHOOOO!
CROOSH

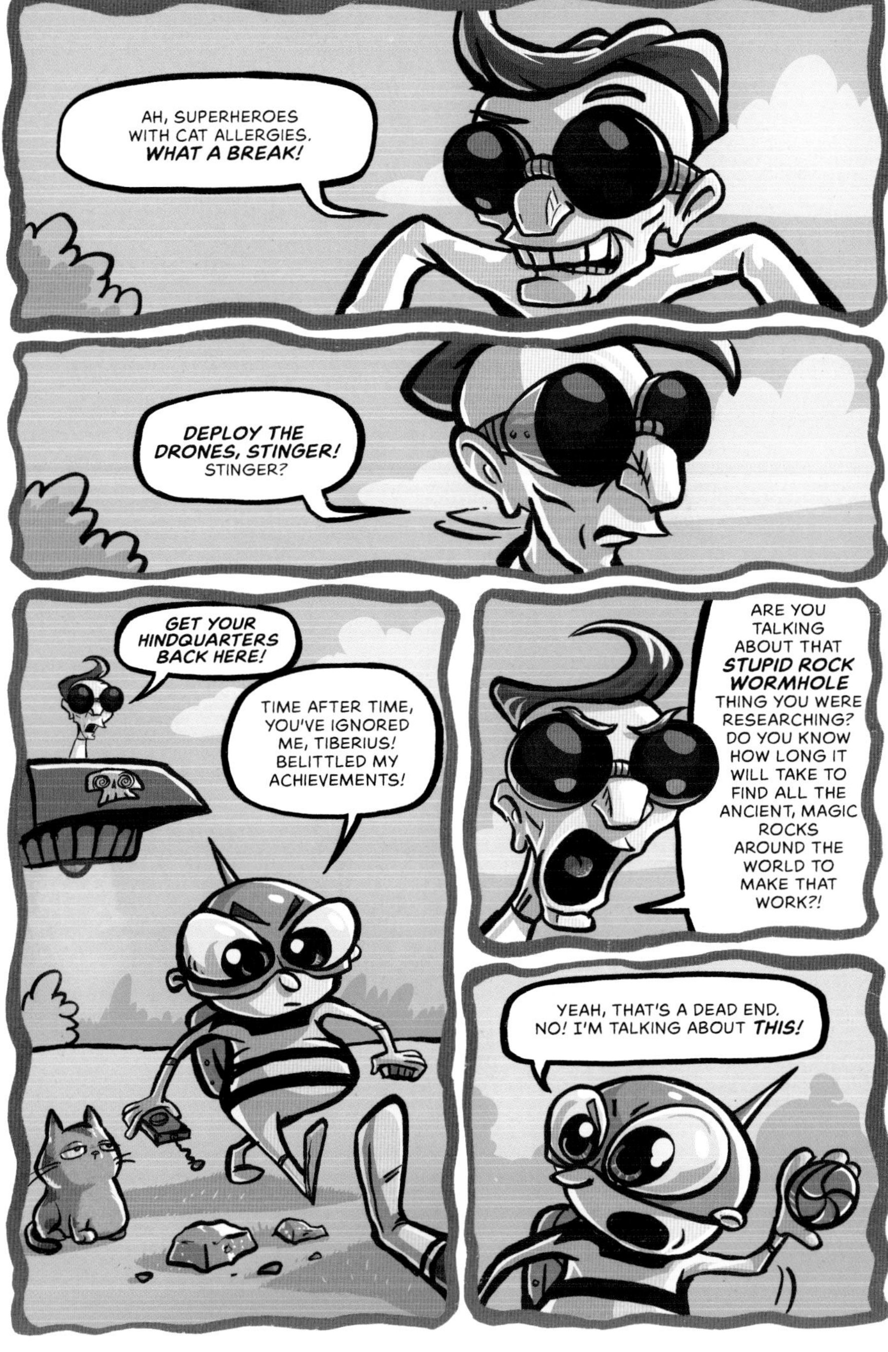
AH, SUPERHEROES WITH CAT ALLERGIES. **WHAT A BREAK!**
DEPLOY THE DRONES, STINGER! STINGER?
GET YOUR HINDQUARTERS BACK HERE!
TIME AFTER TIME, YOU'VE IGNORED ME, TIBERIUS! BELITTLED MY ACHIEVEMENTS!
ARE YOU TALKING ABOUT THAT **STUPID ROCK WORMHOLE** THING YOU WERE RESEARCHING? DO YOU KNOW HOW LONG IT WILL TAKE TO FIND ALL THE ANCIENT, MAGIC ROCKS AROUND THE WORLD TO MAKE THAT WORK?!
YEAH, THAT'S A DEAD END. NO! I'M TALKING ABOUT **THIS!**

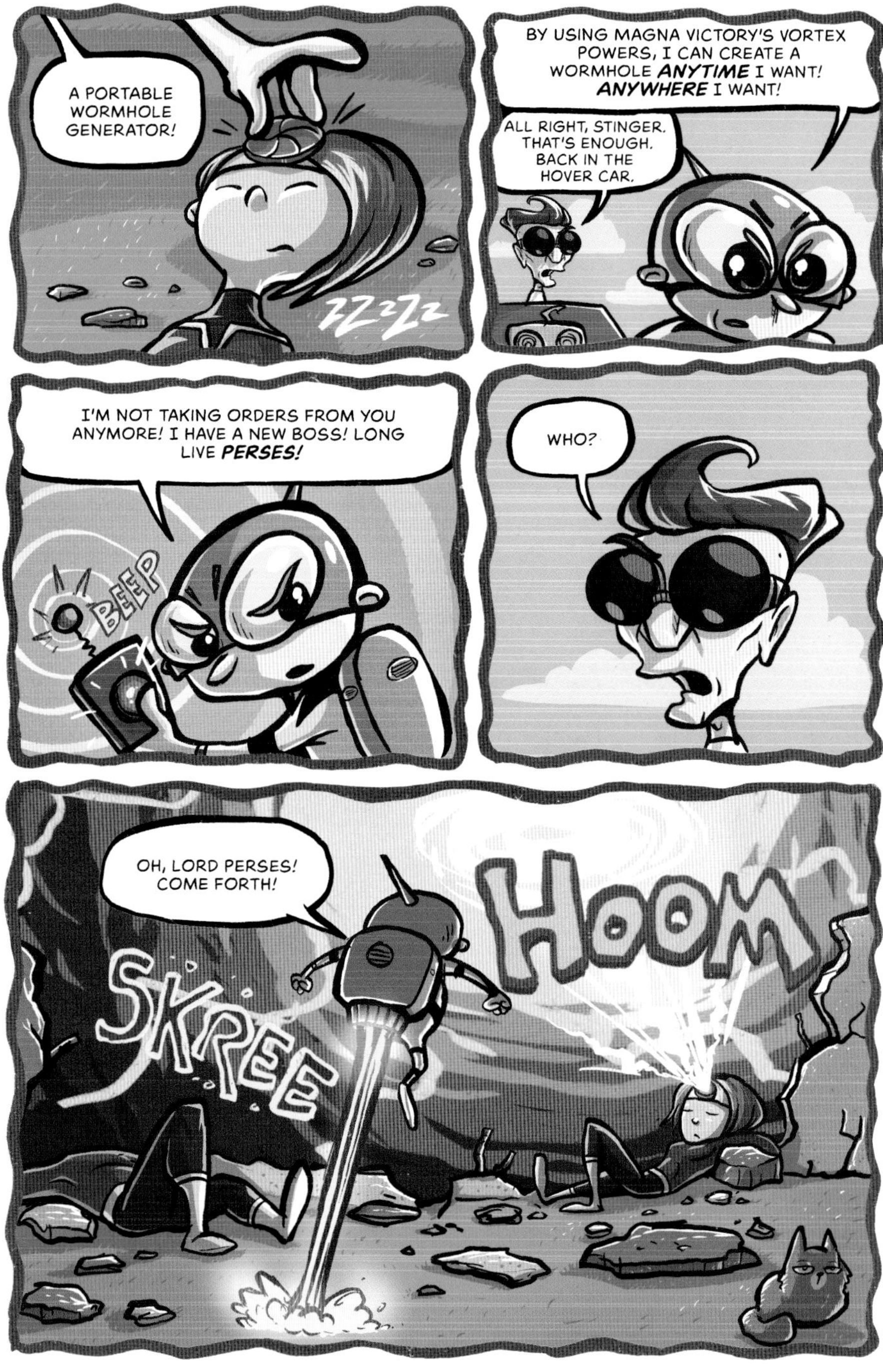
A PORTABLE WORMHOLE GENERATOR!
ZZZZZ
BY USING MAGNA VICTORY'S VORTEX POWERS, I CAN CREATE A WORMHOLE **ANYTIME** I WANT! **ANYWHERE** I WANT!
ALL RIGHT, STINGER. THAT'S ENOUGH. BACK IN THE HOVER CAR.
I'M NOT TAKING ORDERS FROM YOU ANYMORE! I HAVE A NEW BOSS! LONG LIVE **PERSES!**
BEEP
WHO?
OH, LORD PERSES! COME FORTH!
HOOM
SKREE

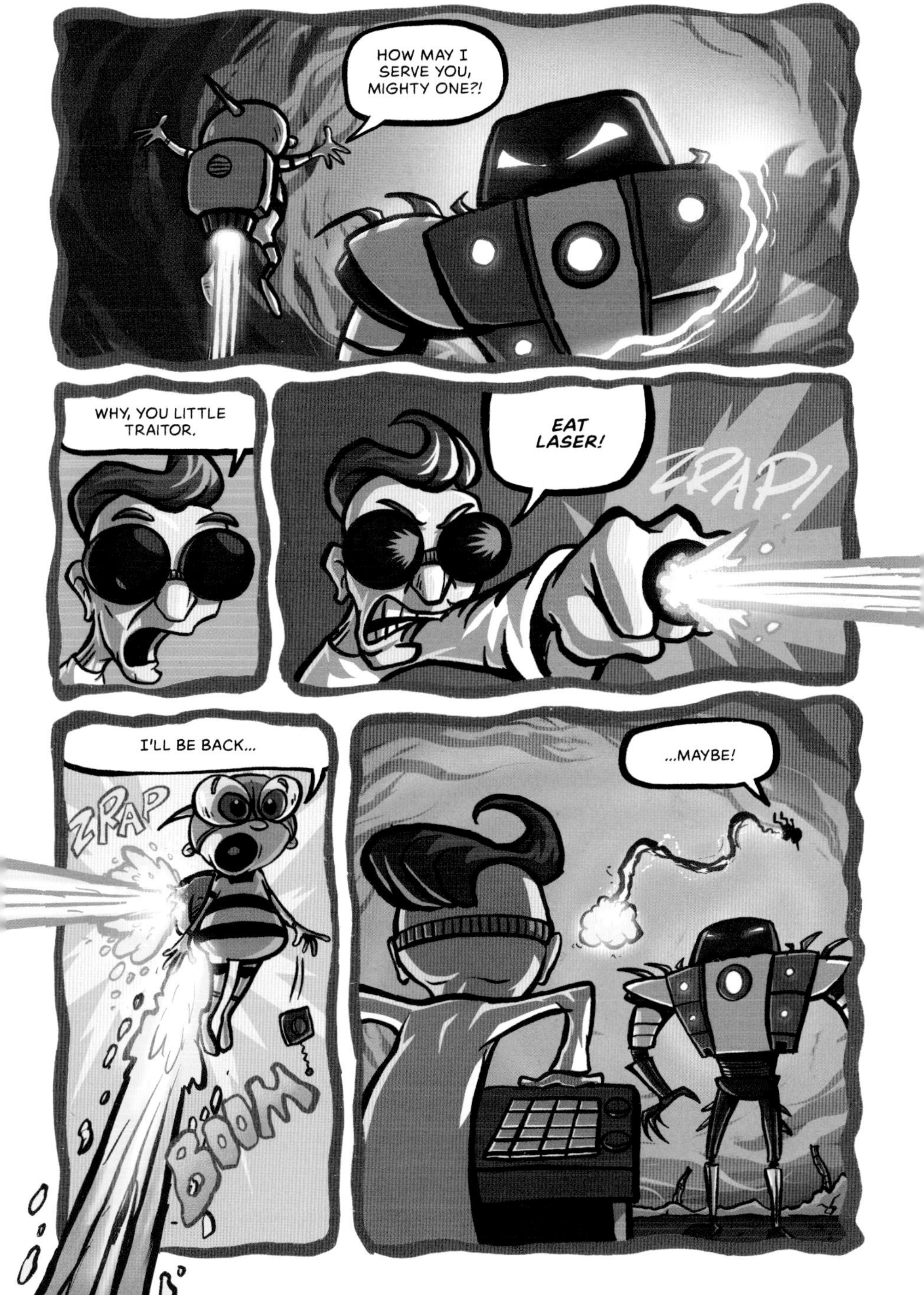
HOW MAY I SERVE YOU, MIGHTY ONE?!
WHY, YOU LITTLE TRAITOR.
EAT LASER!
ZRAP!
I'LL BE BACK...
ZRAP
BOOM
...MAYBE!

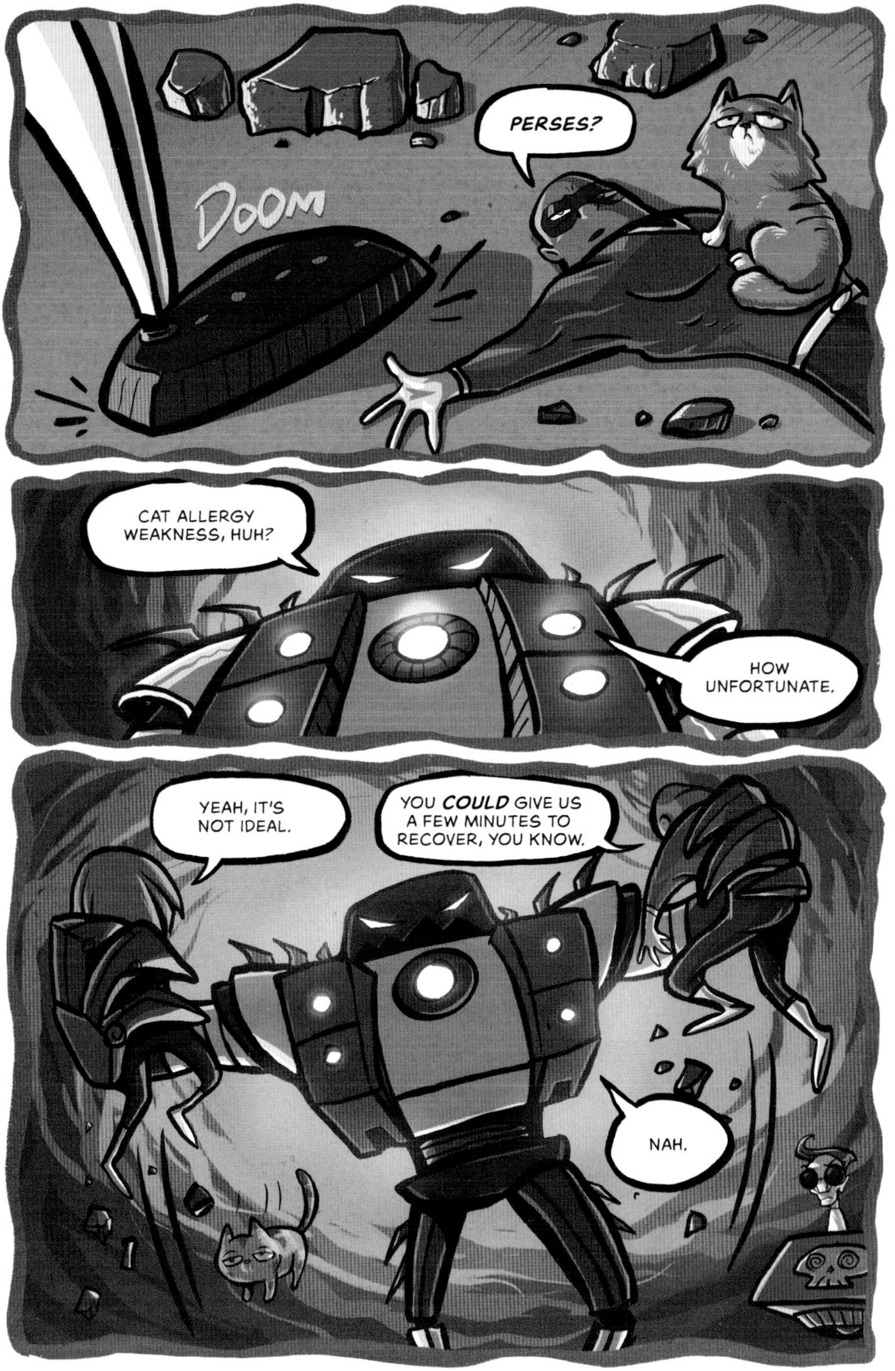
DOOM
PERSES?
CAT ALLERGY WEAKNESS, HUH?
HOW UNFORTUNATE.
YEAH, IT'S NOT IDEAL.
YOU **COULD** GIVE US A FEW MINUTES TO RECOVER, YOU KNOW.
NAH.

CHAPTER 9

Mistakes Were Made

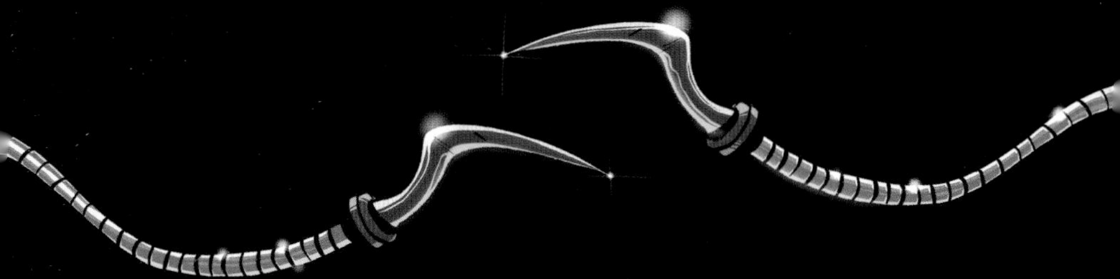

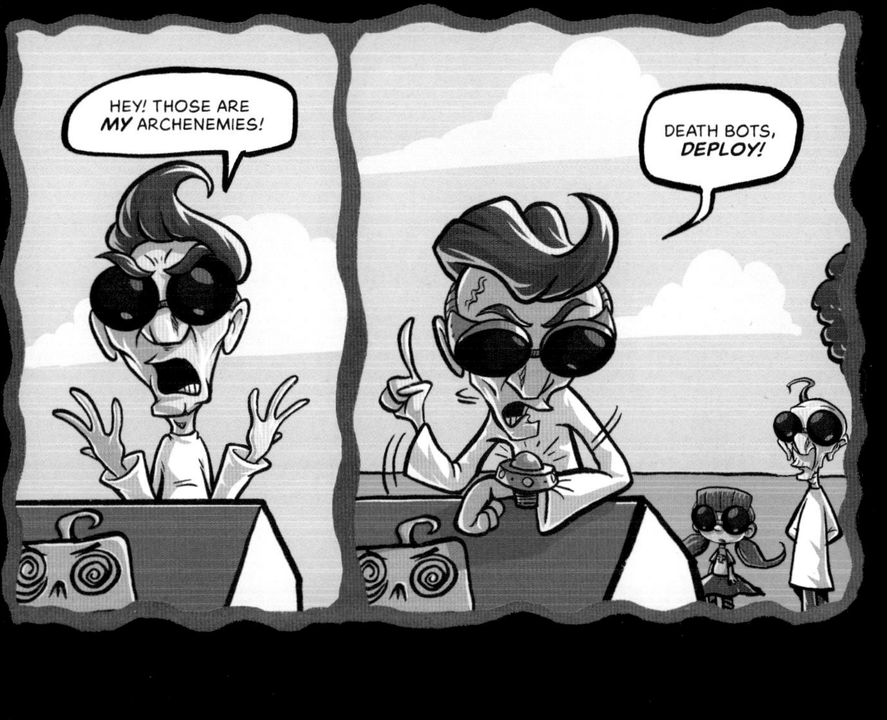
HEY! THOSE ARE *MY* ARCHENEMIES!
DEATH BOTS, *DEPLOY!*

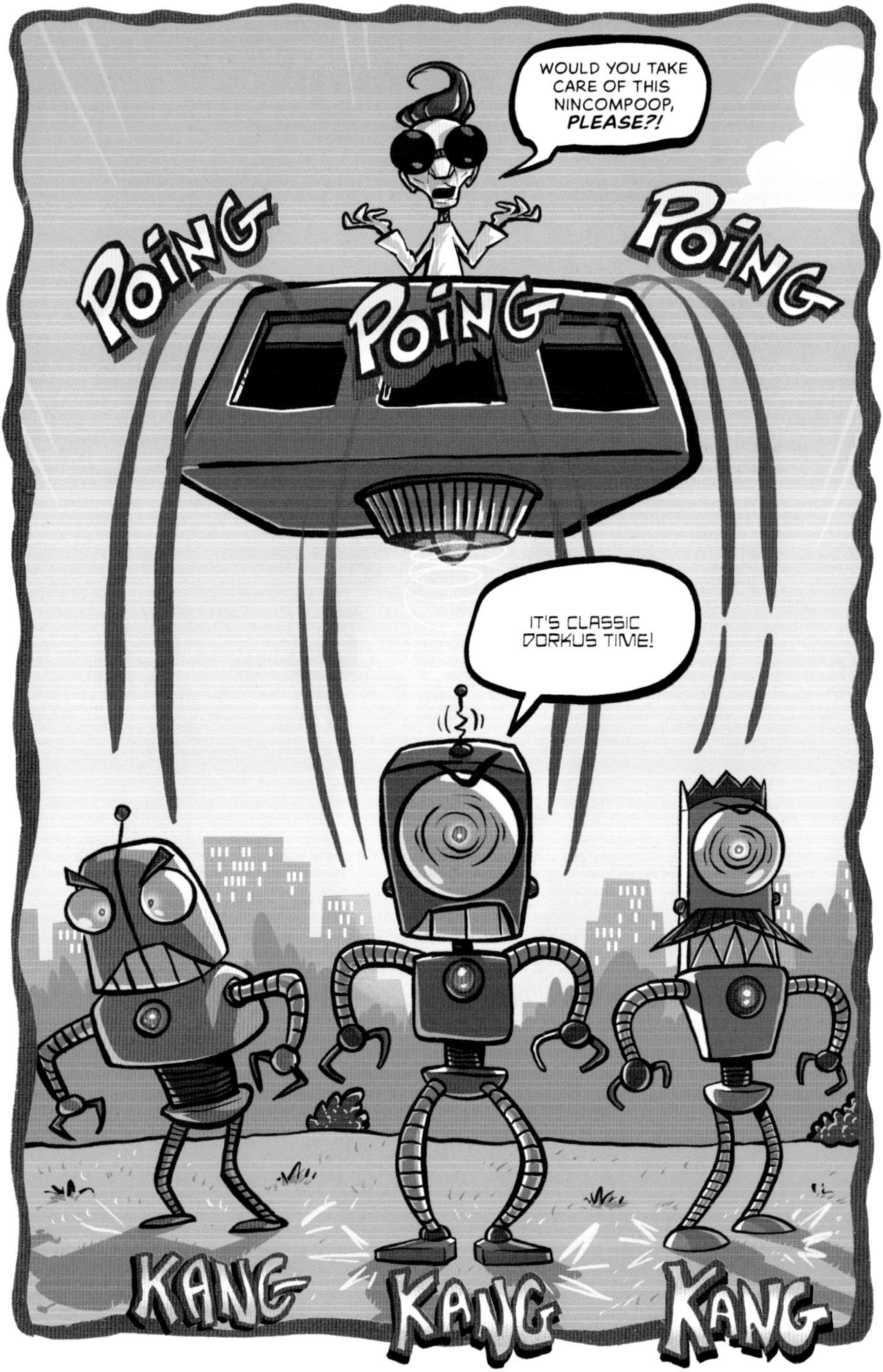
WOULD YOU TAKE CARE OF THIS NINCOMPOOP, PLEASE?!
POING
POING
POING
IT'S CLASSIC DORKUS TIME!
KANG
KANG
KANG

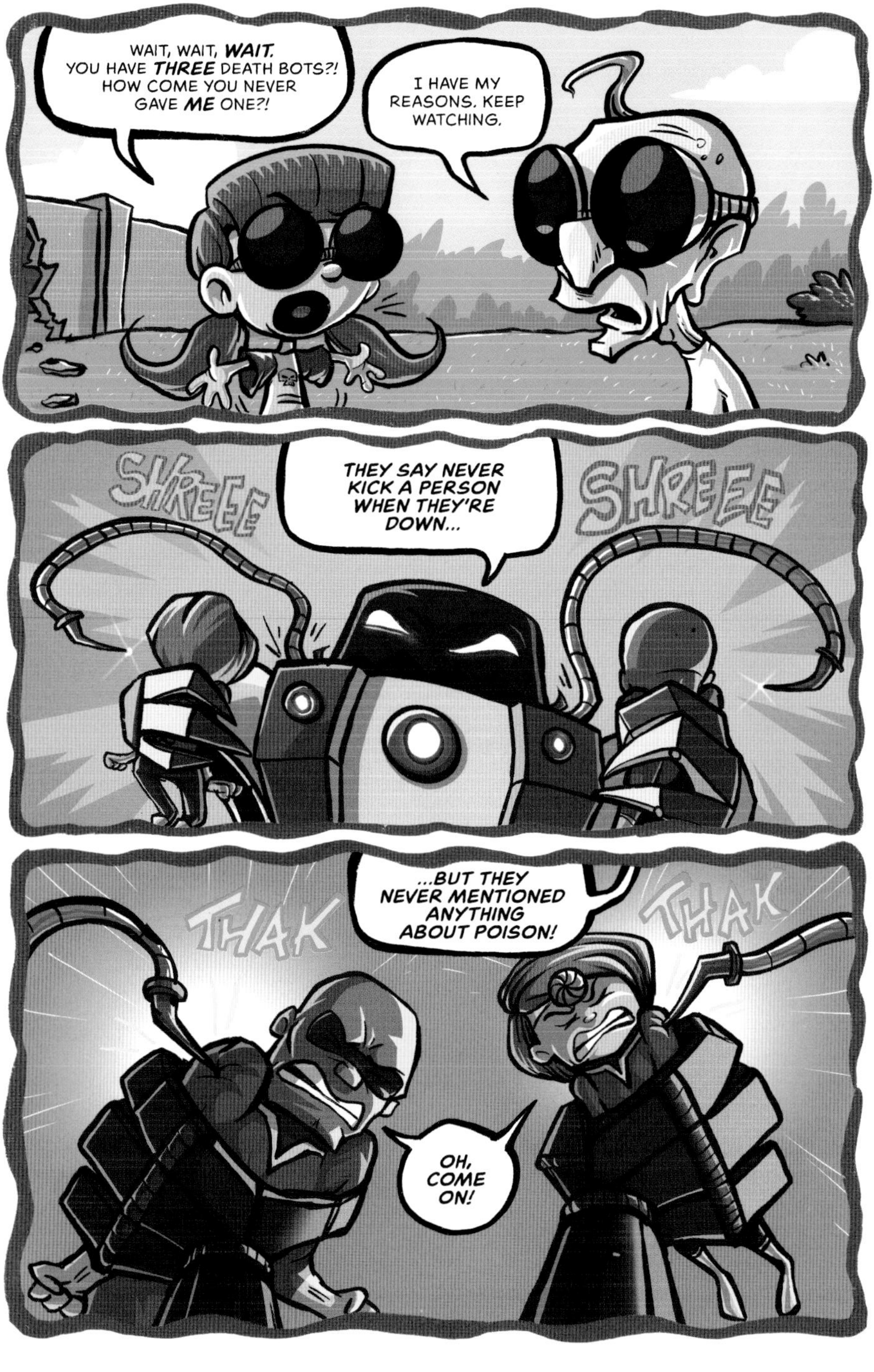
WAIT, WAIT, WAIT. YOU HAVE THREE DEATH BOTS?! HOW COME YOU NEVER GAVE ME ONE?!
I HAVE MY REASONS. KEEP WATCHING.
SHREEE
THEY SAY NEVER KICK A PERSON WHEN THEY'RE DOWN...
SHREEE
THAK
...BUT THEY NEVER MENTIONED ANYTHING ABOUT POISON!
THAK
OH, COME ON!

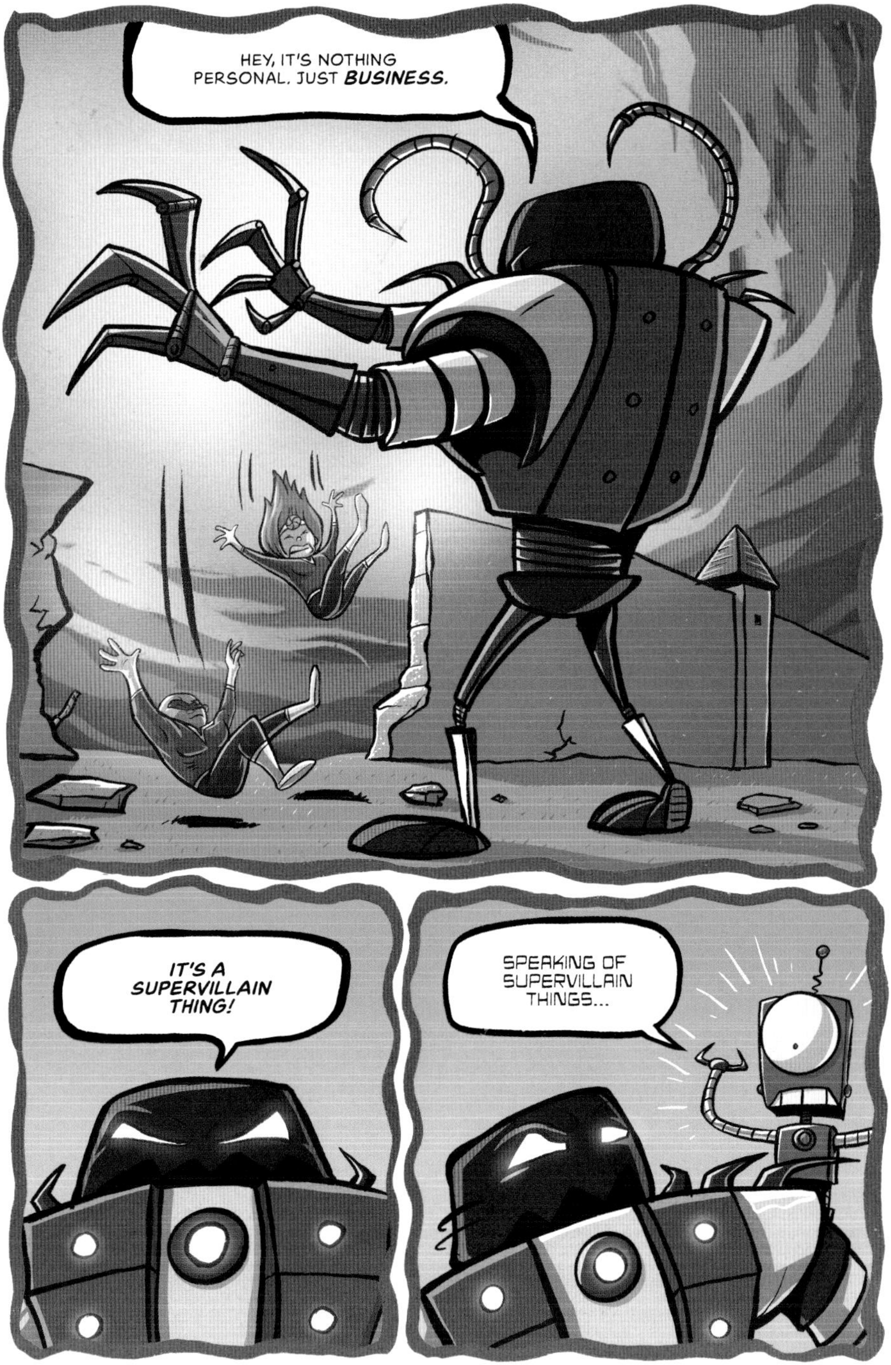
HEY, IT'S NOTHING PERSONAL. JUST **BUSINESS.**
IT'S A SUPERVILLAIN THING!
SPEAKING OF SUPERVILLAIN THINGS...

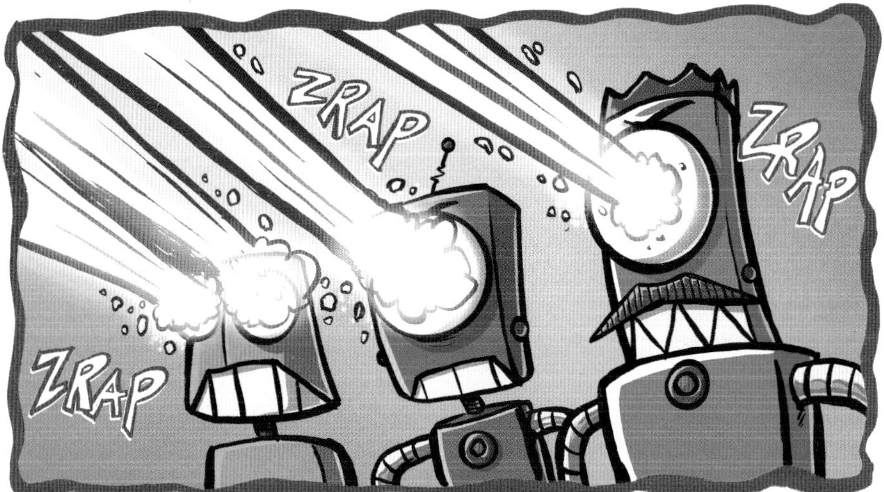
ZRAP
ZRAP
ZRAP

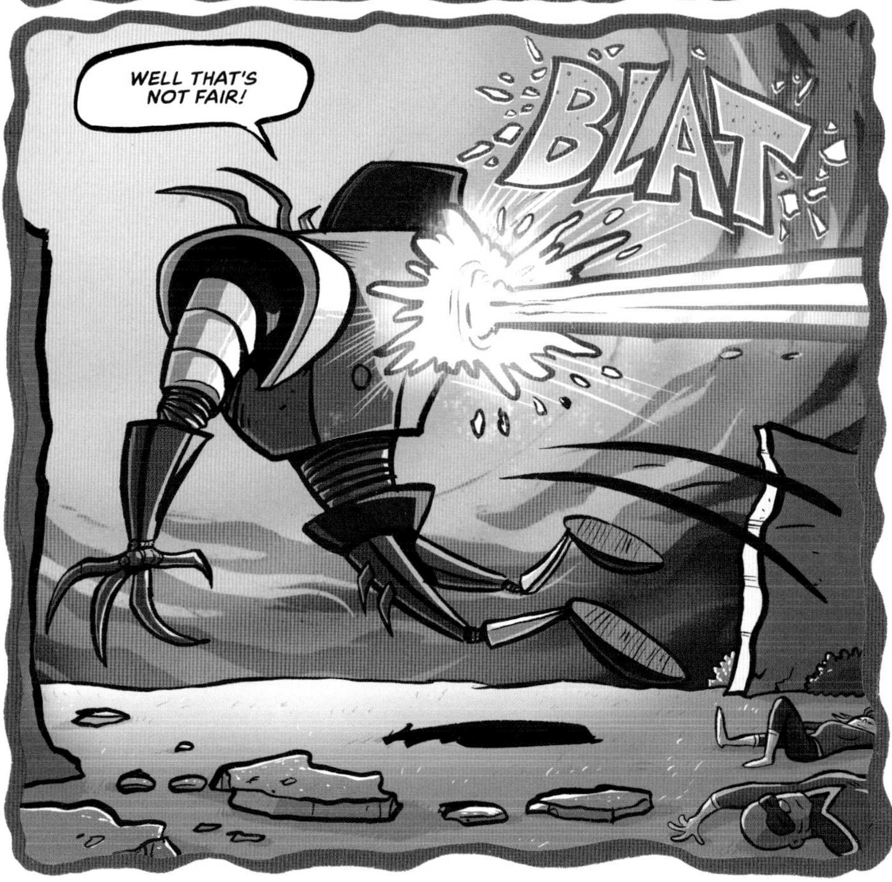
WELL THAT'S NOT FAIR!
BLAT

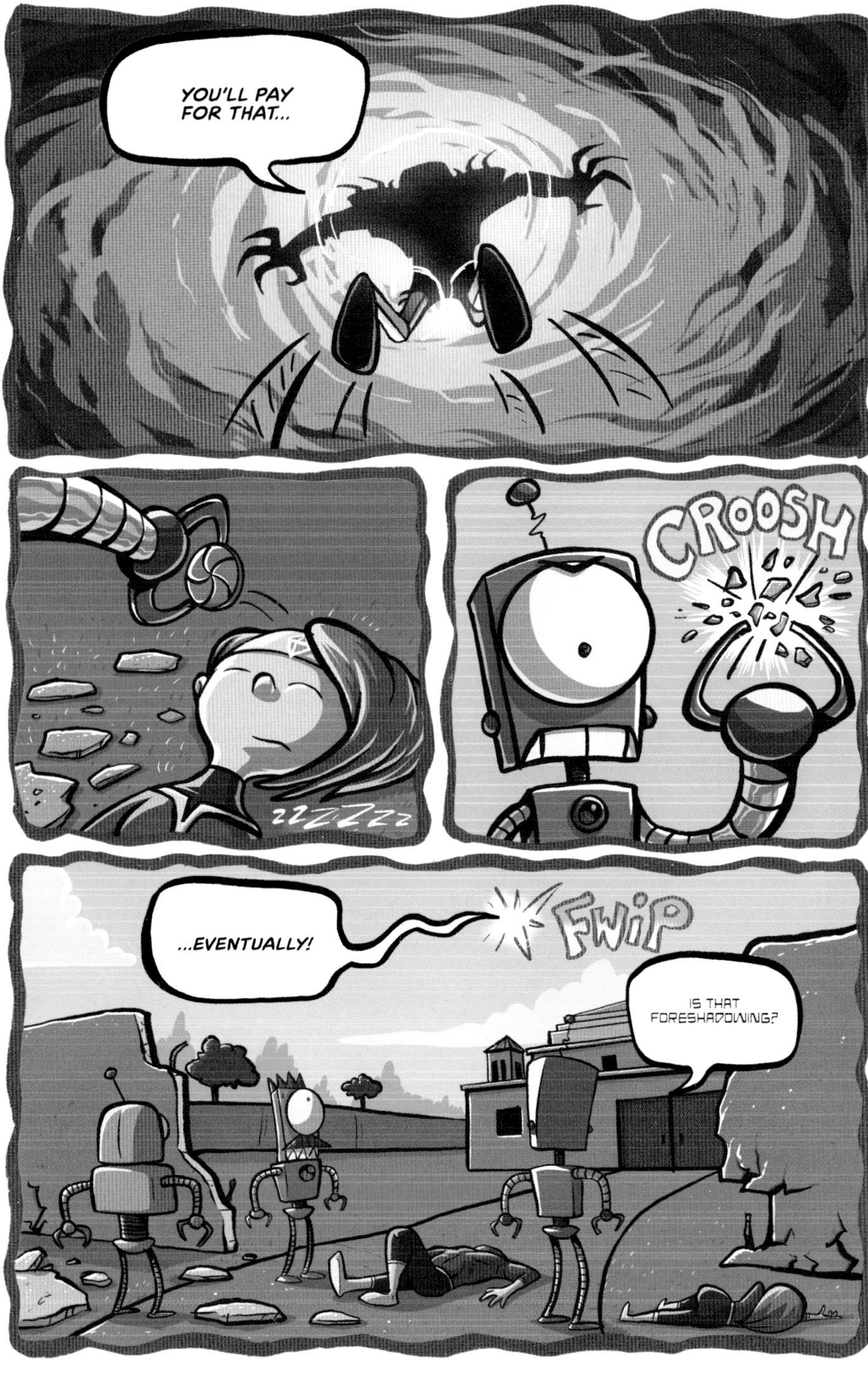
YOU'LL PAY FOR THAT...
ZZZZZZ
CROOSH
...EVENTUALLY!
FWIP
IS THAT FORESHADOWING?

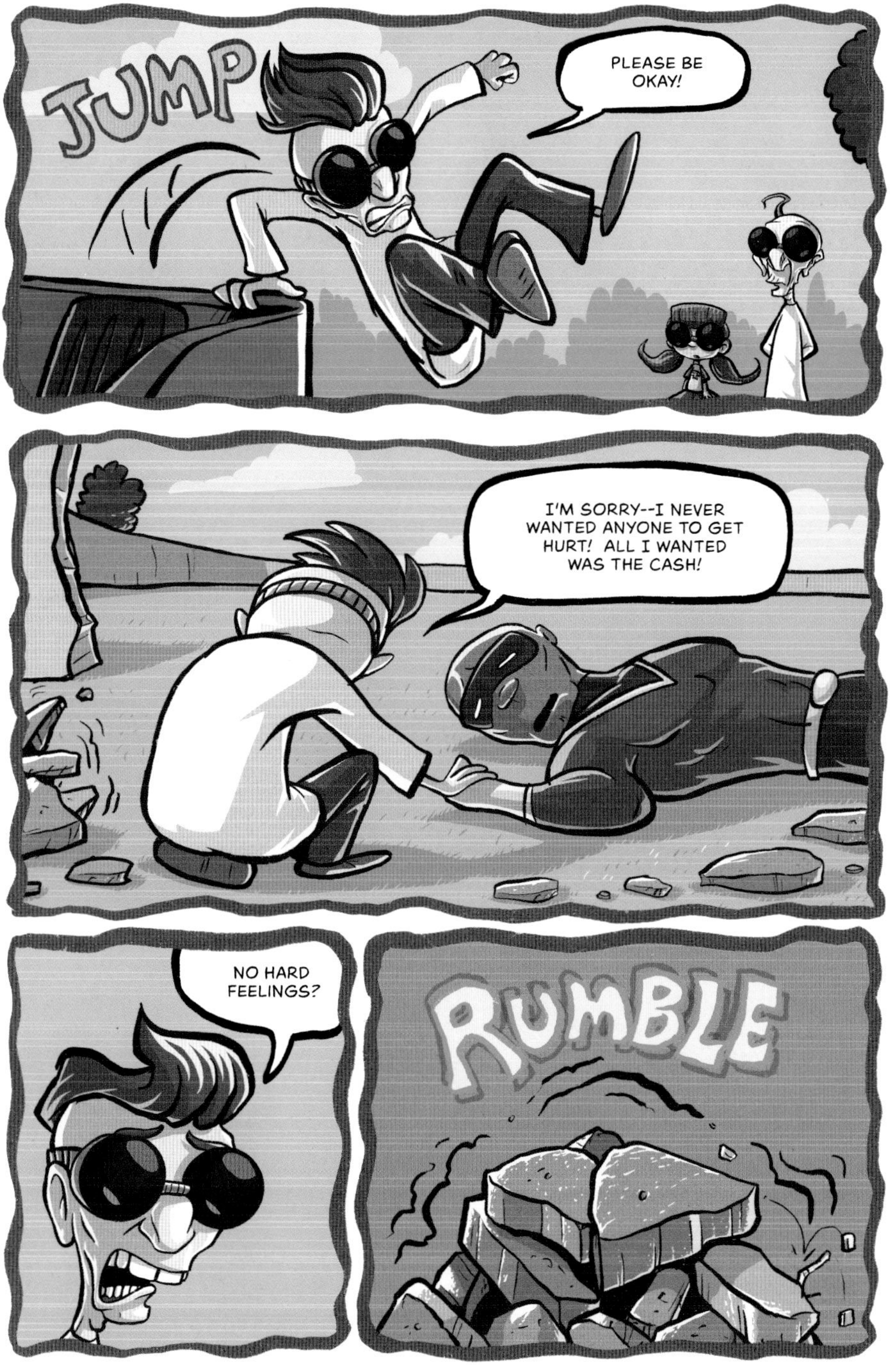
JUMP
PLEASE BE OKAY!
I'M SORRY--I NEVER WANTED ANYONE TO GET HURT! ALL I WANTED WAS THE CASH!
NO HARD FEELINGS?
RUMBLE

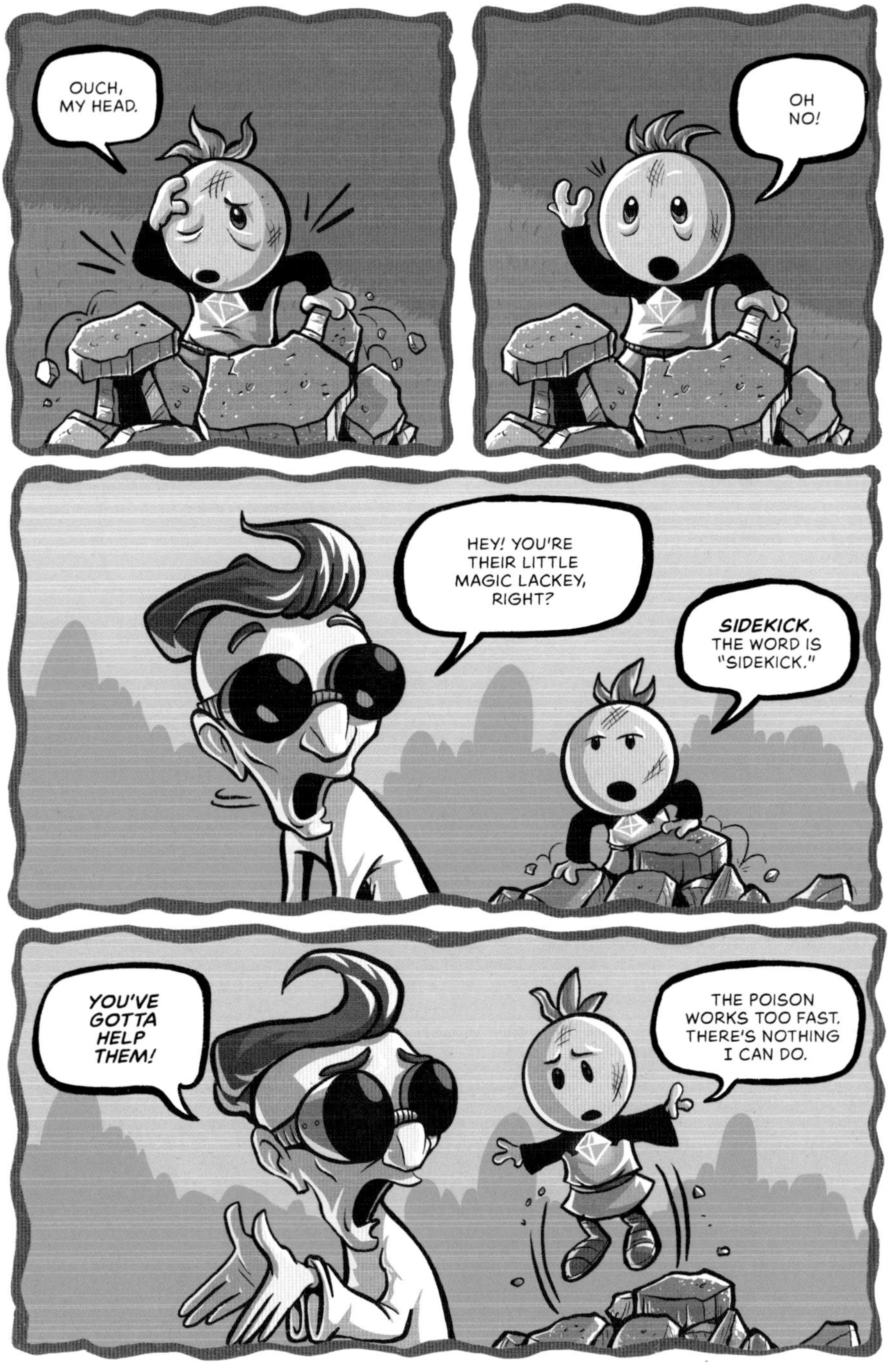
OUCH, MY HEAD.
OH NO!
HEY! YOU'RE THEIR LITTLE MAGIC LACKEY, RIGHT?
SIDEKICK. THE WORD IS "SIDEKICK."
YOU'VE GOTTA HELP THEM!
THE POISON WORKS TOO FAST. THERE'S NOTHING I CAN DO.

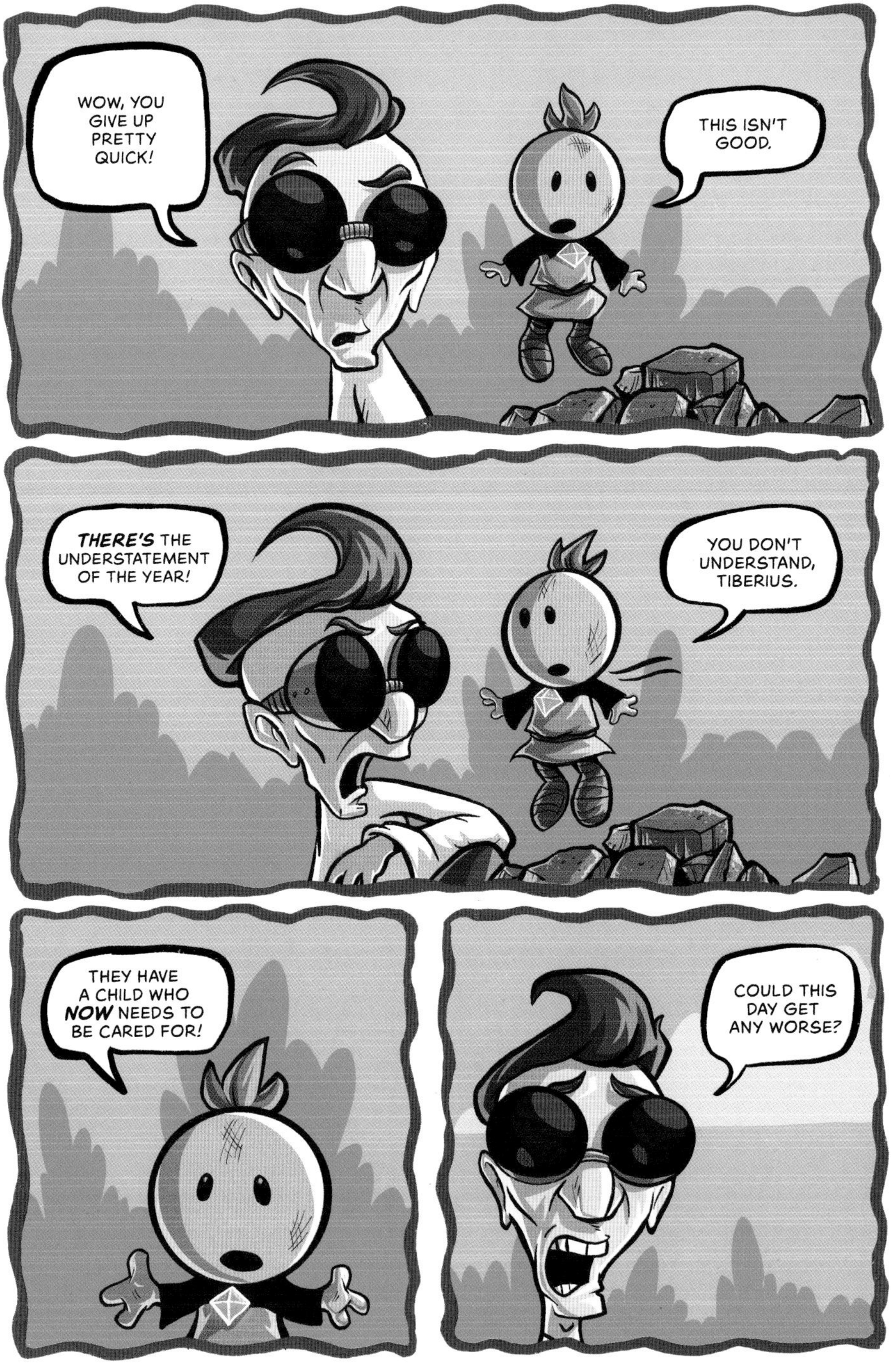
WOW, YOU GIVE UP PRETTY QUICK!
THIS ISN'T GOOD.
THERE'S THE UNDERSTATEMENT OF THE YEAR!
YOU DON'T UNDERSTAND, TIBERIUS.
THEY HAVE A CHILD WHO *NOW* NEEDS TO BE CARED FOR!
COULD THIS DAY GET ANY WORSE?

T-TIBERIUS...
I WILL MAKE THIS RIGHT.
I PROMISE.
ORDERS, SIR?
I KNOW WHAT I HAVE TO DO.

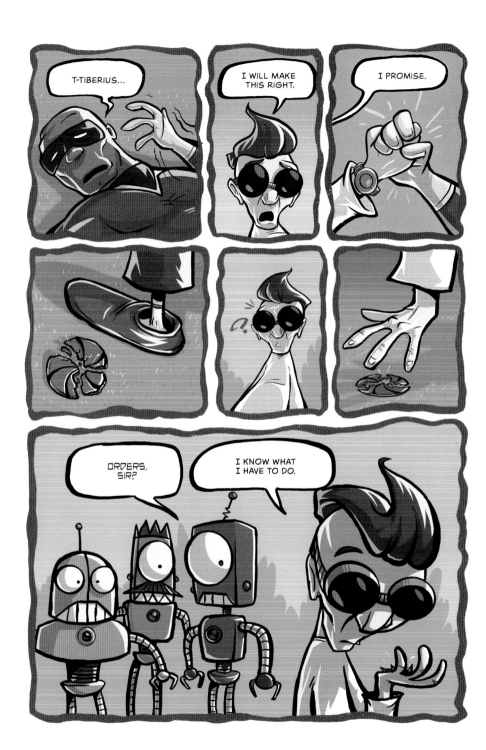

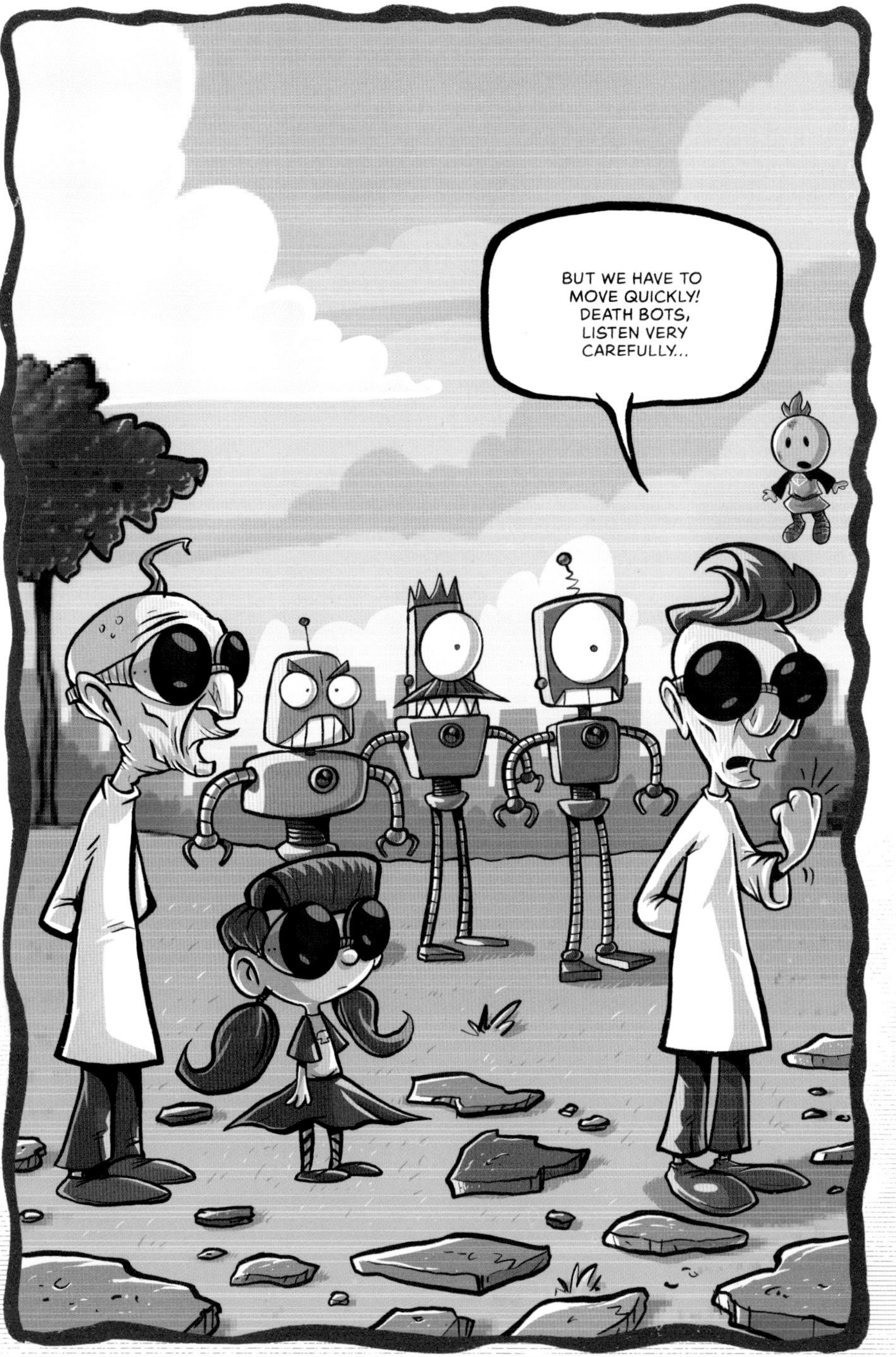
BUT WE HAVE TO MOVE QUICKLY! DEATH BOTS, LISTEN VERY CAREFULLY...

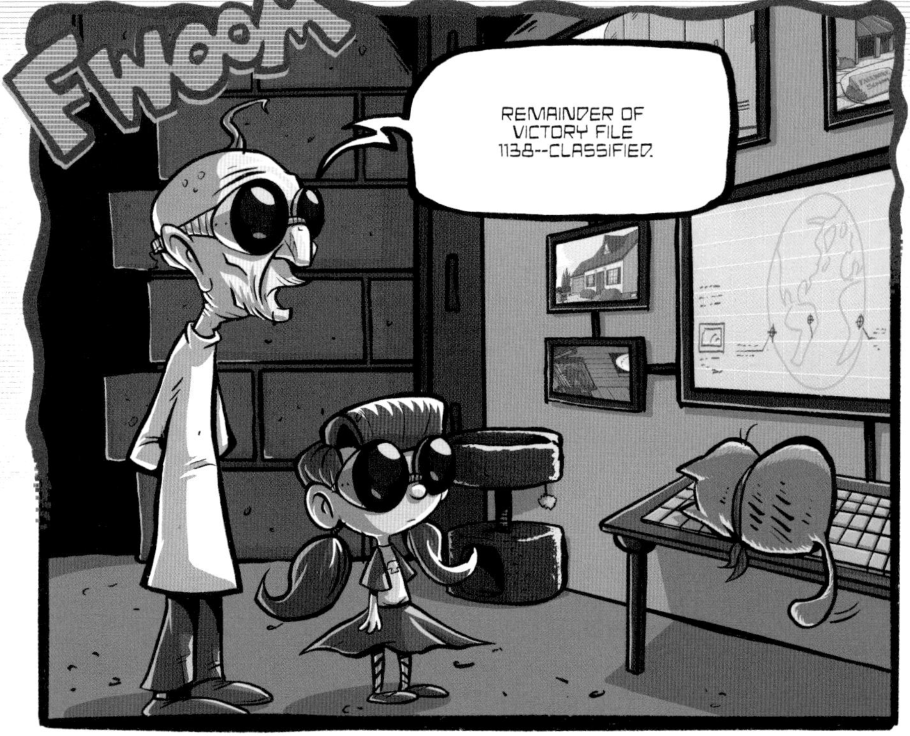
FWOOM
REMAINDER OF VICTORY FILE 1138--CLASSIFIED.

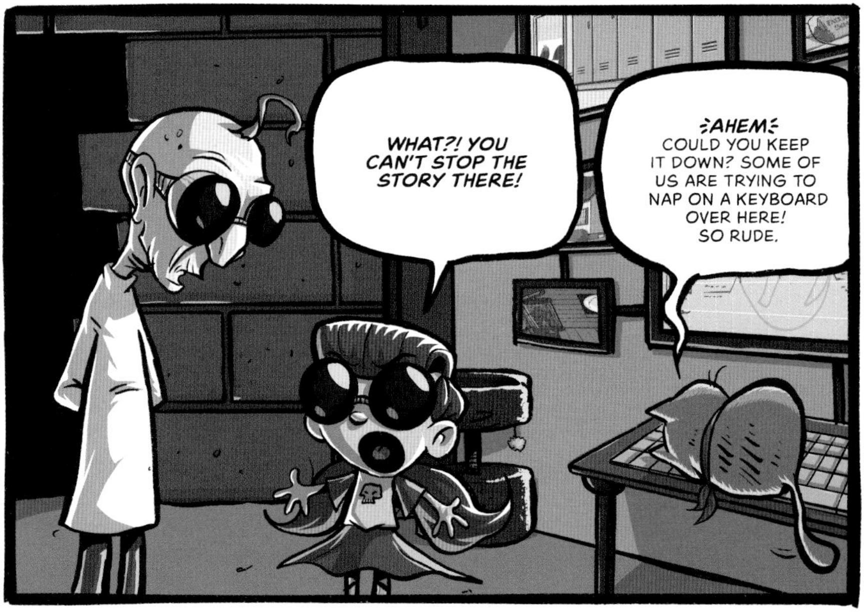
WHAT?! YOU CAN'T STOP THE STORY THERE!
AHEM
COULD YOU KEEP IT DOWN? SOME OF US ARE TRYING TO NAP ON A KEYBOARD OVER HERE! SO RUDE.

CHAPTER 10

The Long Way Home

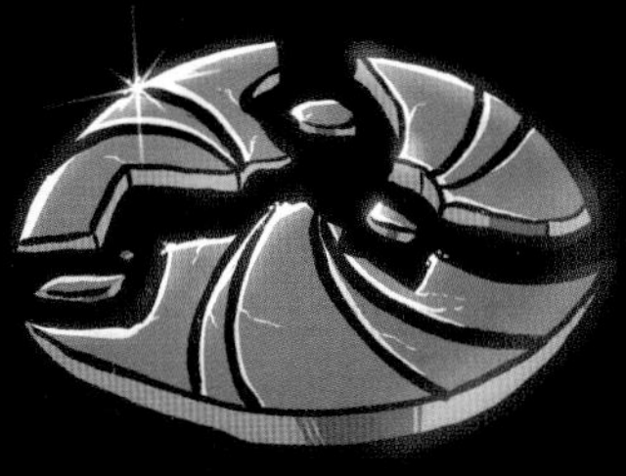

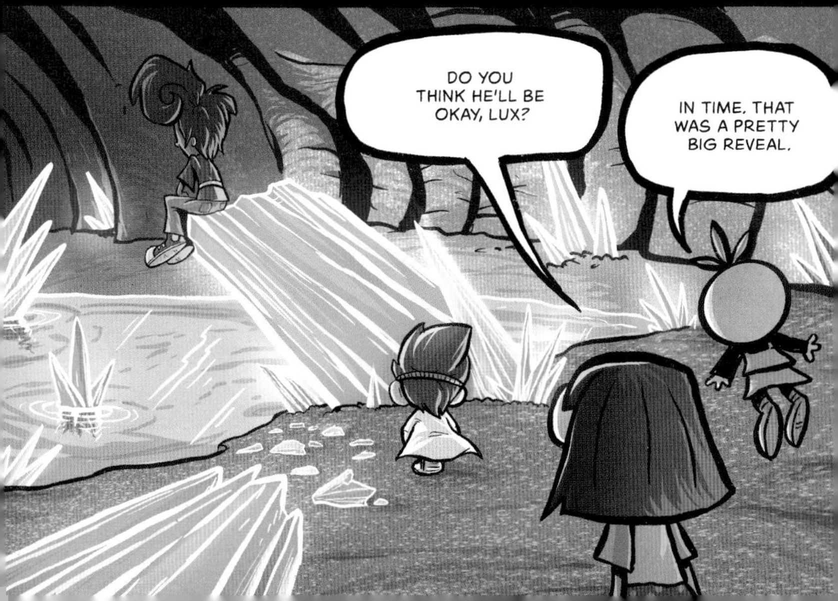
DO YOU THINK HE'LL BE OKAY, LUX?
IN TIME. THAT WAS A PRETTY BIG REVEAL.

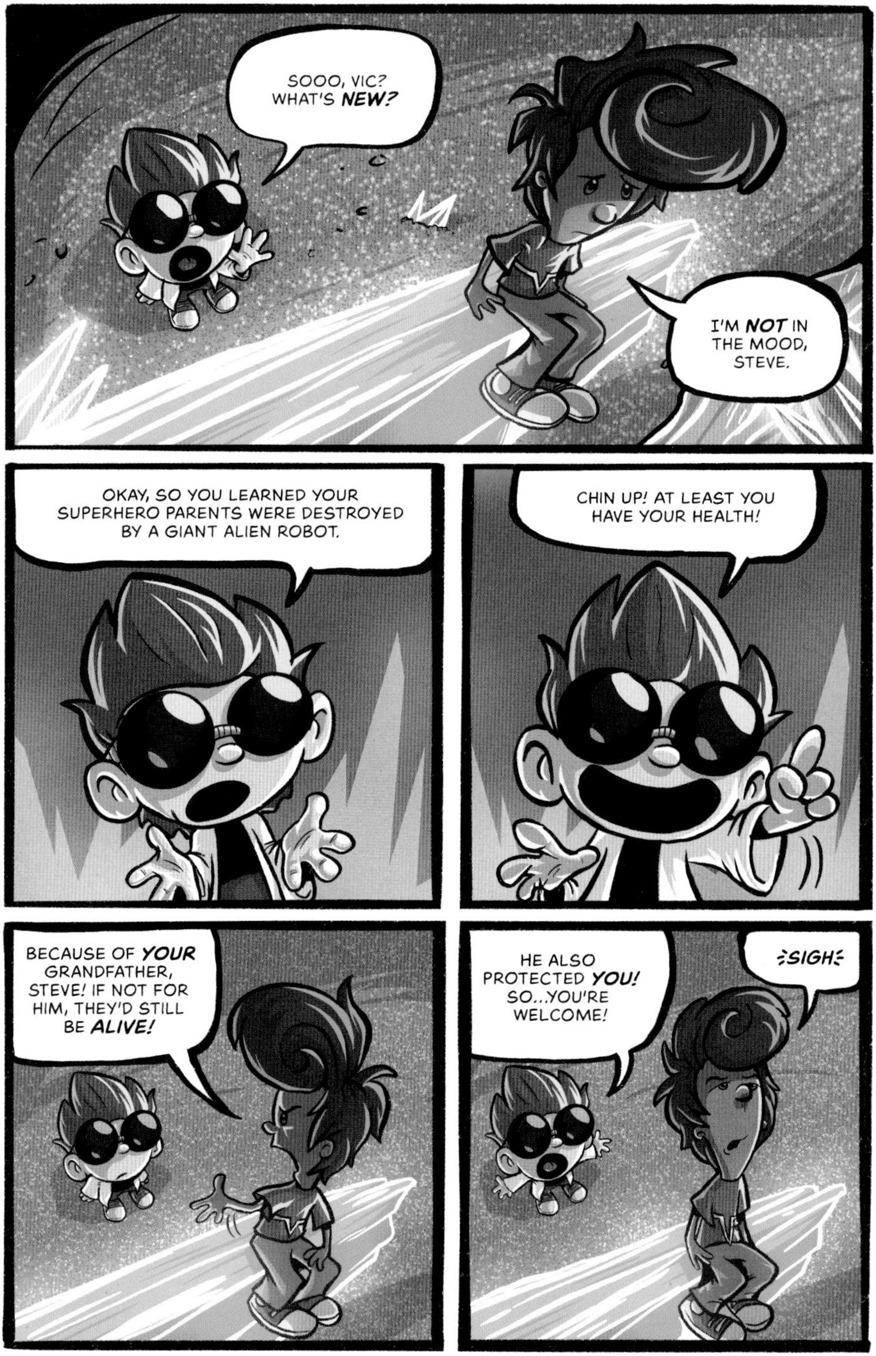
SOOO, VIC? WHAT'S NEW?
I'M NOT IN THE MOOD, STEVE.
OKAY, SO YOU LEARNED YOUR SUPERHERO PARENTS WERE DESTROYED BY A GIANT ALIEN ROBOT.
CHIN UP! AT LEAST YOU HAVE YOUR HEALTH!
BECAUSE OF YOUR GRANDFATHER, STEVE! IF NOT FOR HIM, THEY'D STILL BE ALIVE!
HE ALSO PROTECTED YOU! SO...YOU'RE WELCOME!
SIGH

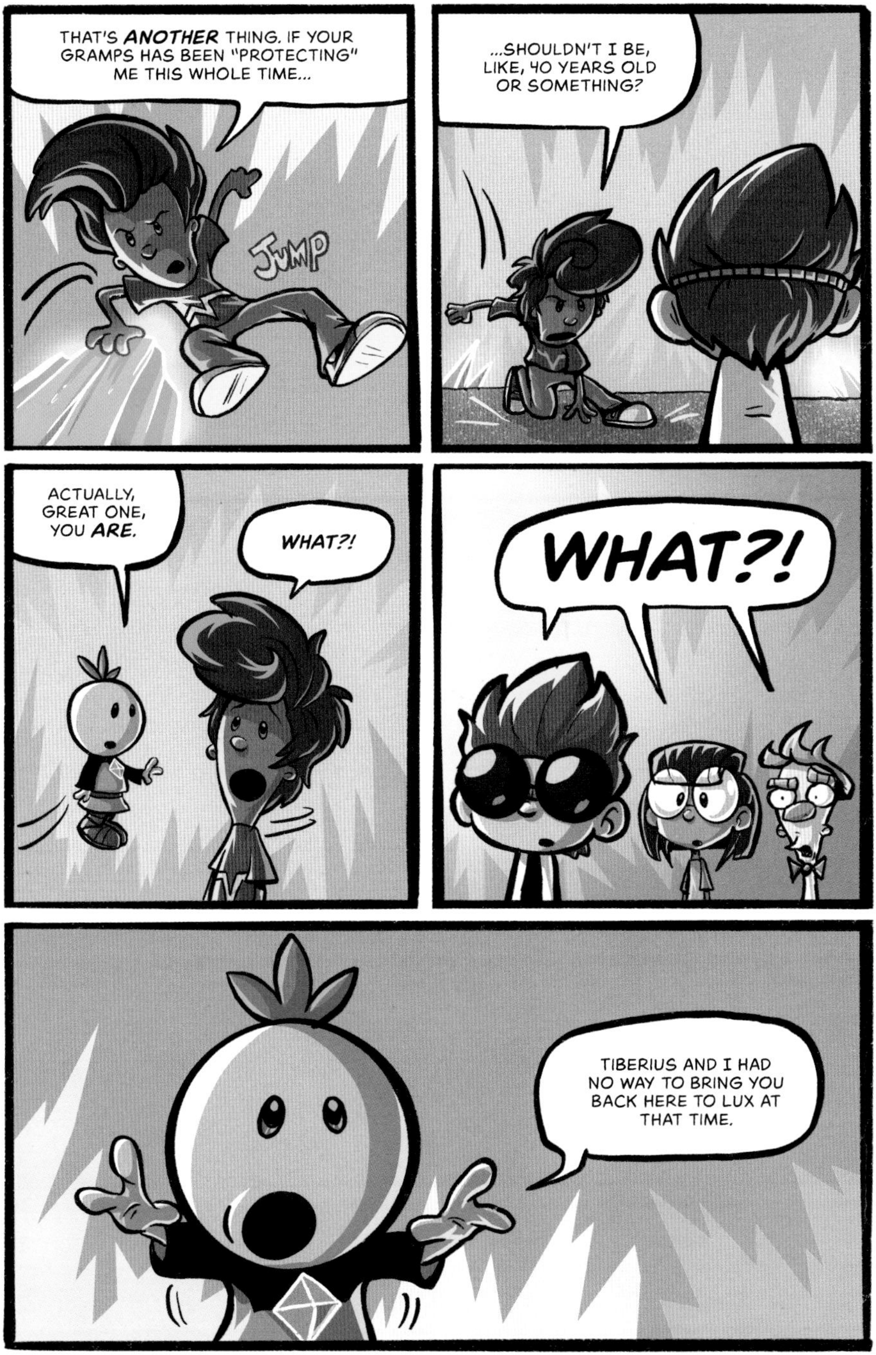
THAT'S **ANOTHER** THING. IF YOUR GRAMPS HAS BEEN "PROTECTING" ME THIS WHOLE TIME...
JUMP
...SHOULDN'T I BE, LIKE, 40 YEARS OLD OR SOMETHING?
ACTUALLY, GREAT ONE, YOU **ARE**.
WHAT?!
WHAT?!
TIBERIUS AND I HAD NO WAY TO BRING YOU BACK HERE TO LUX AT THAT TIME.

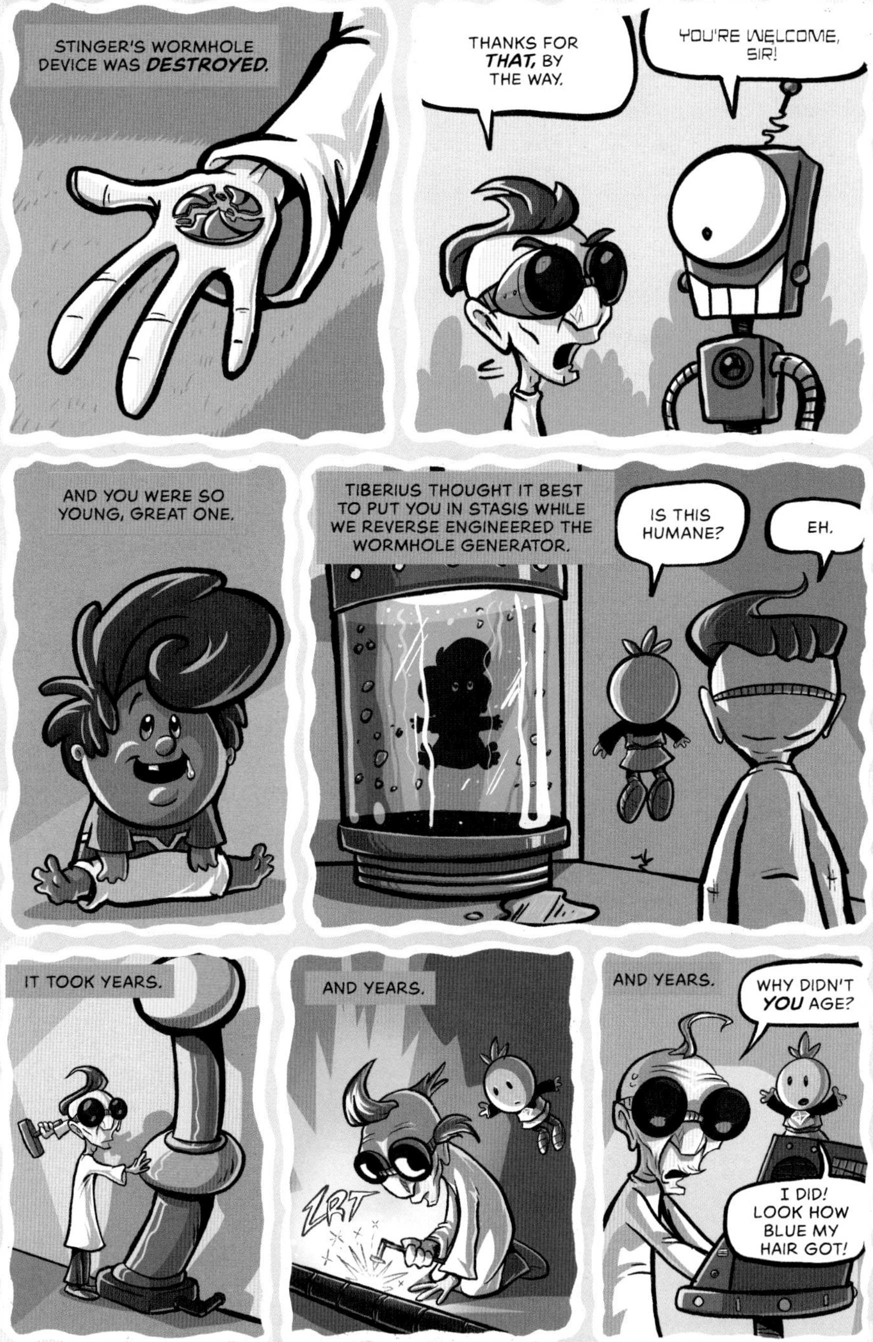
STINGER'S WORMHOLE DEVICE WAS ***DESTROYED.***
THANKS FOR ***THAT,*** BY THE WAY.
YOU'RE WELCOME, SIR!
AND YOU WERE SO YOUNG, GREAT ONE.
TIBERIUS THOUGHT IT BEST TO PUT YOU IN STASIS WHILE WE REVERSE ENGINEERED THE WORMHOLE GENERATOR.
IS THIS HUMANE?
EH.
IT TOOK YEARS.
AND YEARS.
ZRT
AND YEARS.
WHY DIDN'T ***YOU*** AGE?
I DID! LOOK HOW BLUE MY HAIR GOT!

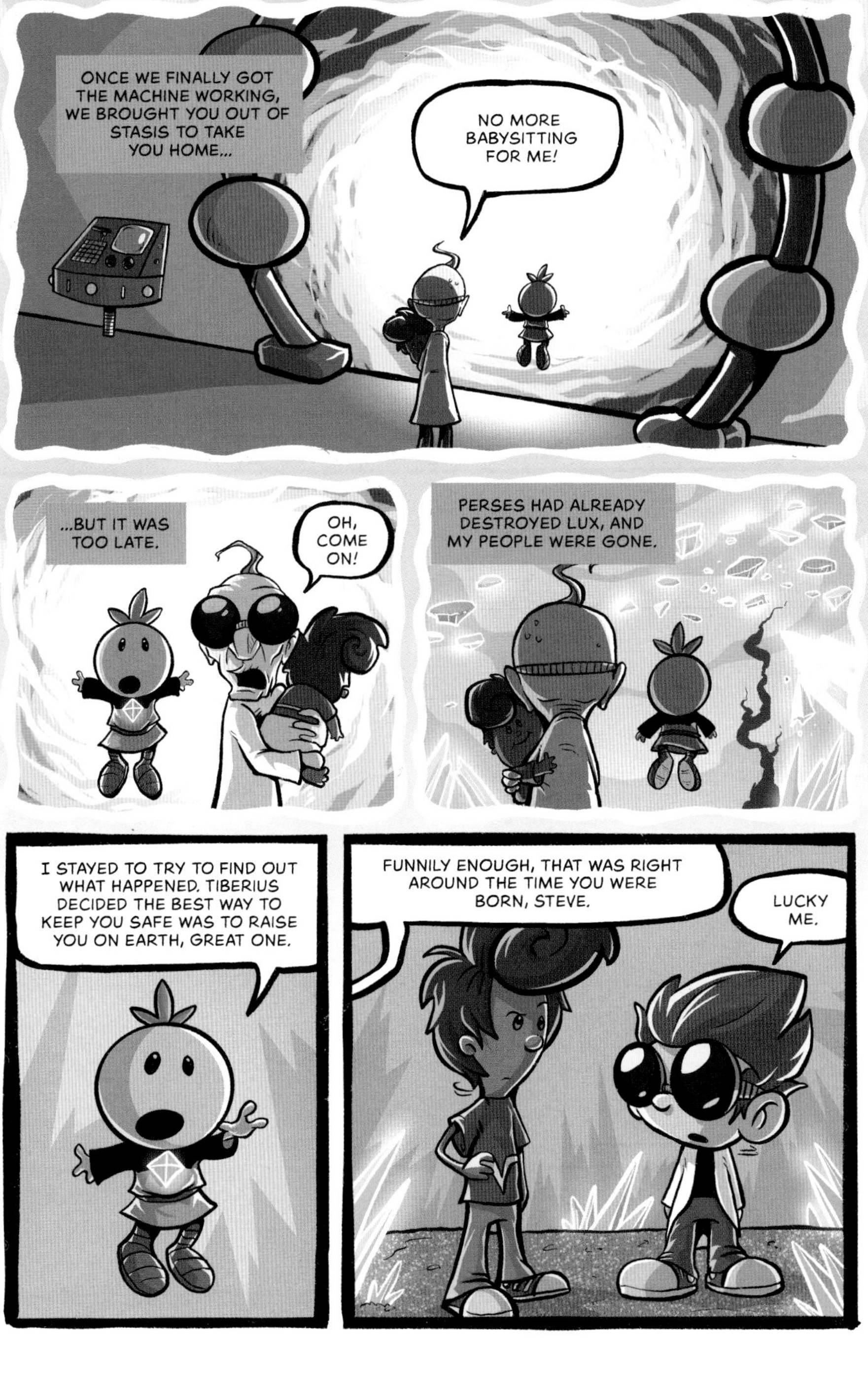
ONCE WE FINALLY GOT THE MACHINE WORKING, WE BROUGHT YOU OUT OF STASIS TO TAKE YOU HOME...
NO MORE BABYSITTING FOR ME!
...BUT IT WAS TOO LATE.
OH, COME ON!
PERSES HAD ALREADY DESTROYED LUX, AND MY PEOPLE WERE GONE.
I STAYED TO TRY TO FIND OUT WHAT HAPPENED. TIBERIUS DECIDED THE BEST WAY TO KEEP YOU SAFE WAS TO RAISE YOU ON EARTH, GREAT ONE.
FUNNILY ENOUGH, THAT WAS RIGHT AROUND THE TIME YOU WERE BORN, STEVE.
LUCKY ME.

WE ALL MAKE CHOICES IN LIFE. SOME GOOD, SOME BAD.

WHATEVER YOU MAY THINK OF TIBERIUS MCEVIL, KNOW THAT HE *DID* ABANDON VILLAINY.

AND HE'S BEEN PRETENDING TO BE BAD FOR A VERY LONG TIME SO AS NOT TO RAISE SUSPICION ABOUT WHAT HE WAS REALLY DOING: TAKING CARE OF YOU TWO.

NEVER JUDGE A PERSON BY THE MISTAKES OF YESTERDAY. IT'S WHAT WE DO TODAY THAT MATTERS.

RIGHT, STEVE?

HEY, AFTER ALL THAT'S HAPPENED, I *TOTALLY* LEARNED MY LESSON. I AM *DONE* WITH VILLAINY.

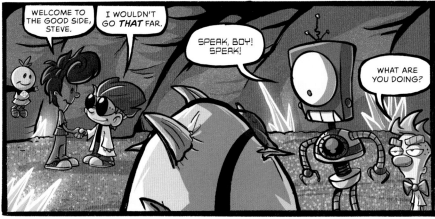

WELCOME TO THE GOOD SIDE, STEVE.

I WOULDN'T GO *THAT* FAR.

SPEAK, BOY! SPEAK!

WHAT ARE YOU DOING?

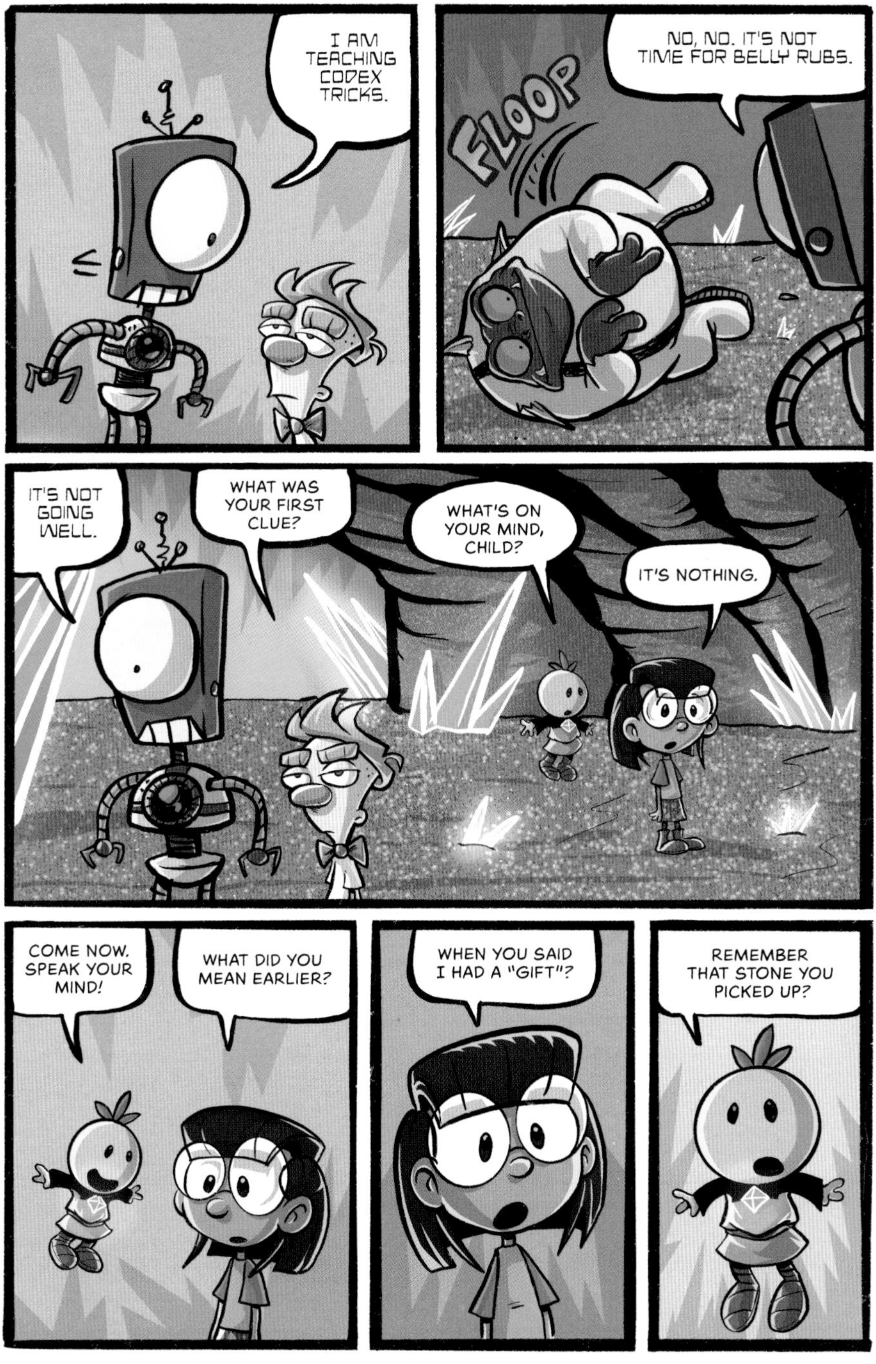

I AM TEACHING CODEX TRICKS.
FLOOP
NO, NO. IT'S NOT TIME FOR BELLY RUBS.
IT'S NOT GOING WELL.
WHAT WAS YOUR FIRST CLUE?
WHAT'S ON YOUR MIND, CHILD?
IT'S NOTHING.
COME NOW. SPEAK YOUR MIND!
WHAT DID YOU MEAN EARLIER?
WHEN YOU SAID I HAD A "GIFT"?
REMEMBER THAT STONE YOU PICKED UP?

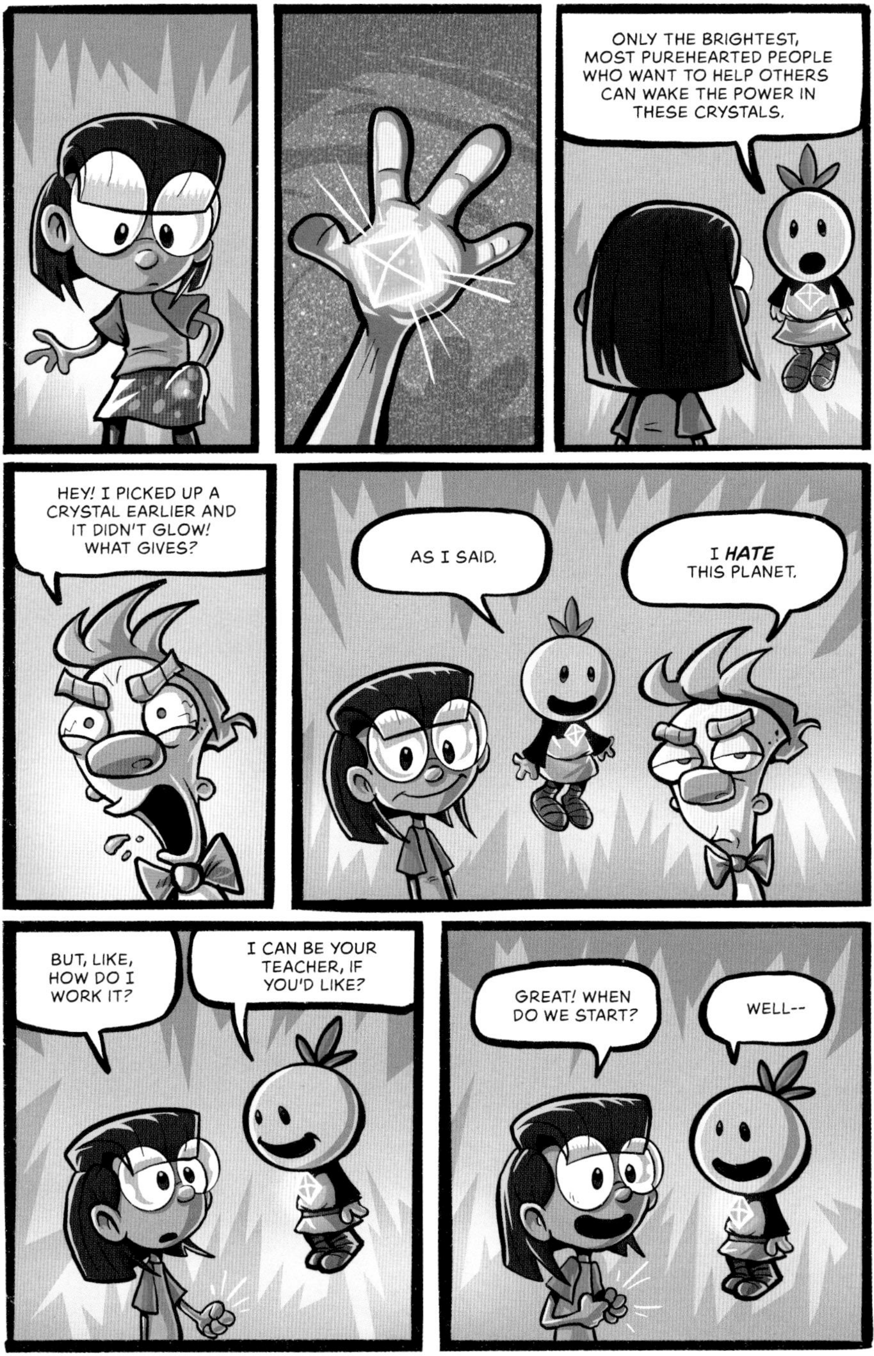
ONLY THE BRIGHTEST, MOST PUREHEARTED PEOPLE WHO WANT TO HELP OTHERS CAN WAKE THE POWER IN THESE CRYSTALS.
HEY! I PICKED UP A CRYSTAL EARLIER AND IT DIDN'T GLOW! WHAT GIVES?
AS I SAID.
I **HATE** THIS PLANET.
BUT, LIKE, HOW DO I WORK IT?
I CAN BE YOUR TEACHER, IF YOU'D LIKE?
GREAT! WHEN DO WE START?
WELL--

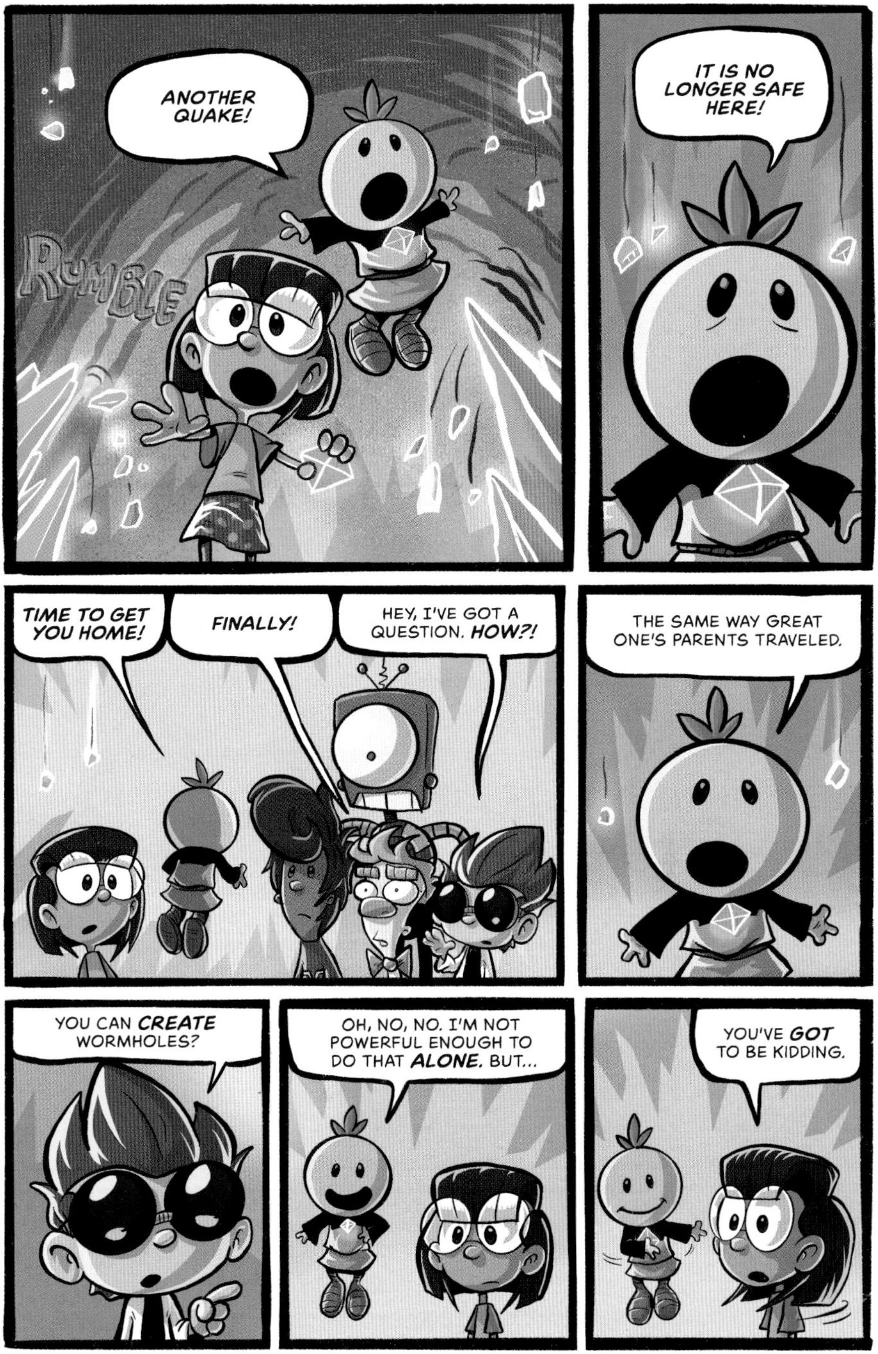
ANOTHER QUAKE!
RUMBLE
IT IS NO LONGER SAFE HERE!
TIME TO GET YOU HOME!
FINALLY!
HEY, I'VE GOT A QUESTION. HOW?!
THE SAME WAY GREAT ONE'S PARENTS TRAVELED.
YOU CAN CREATE WORMHOLES?
OH, NO, NO. I'M NOT POWERFUL ENOUGH TO DO THAT ALONE. BUT...
YOU'VE GOT TO BE KIDDING.

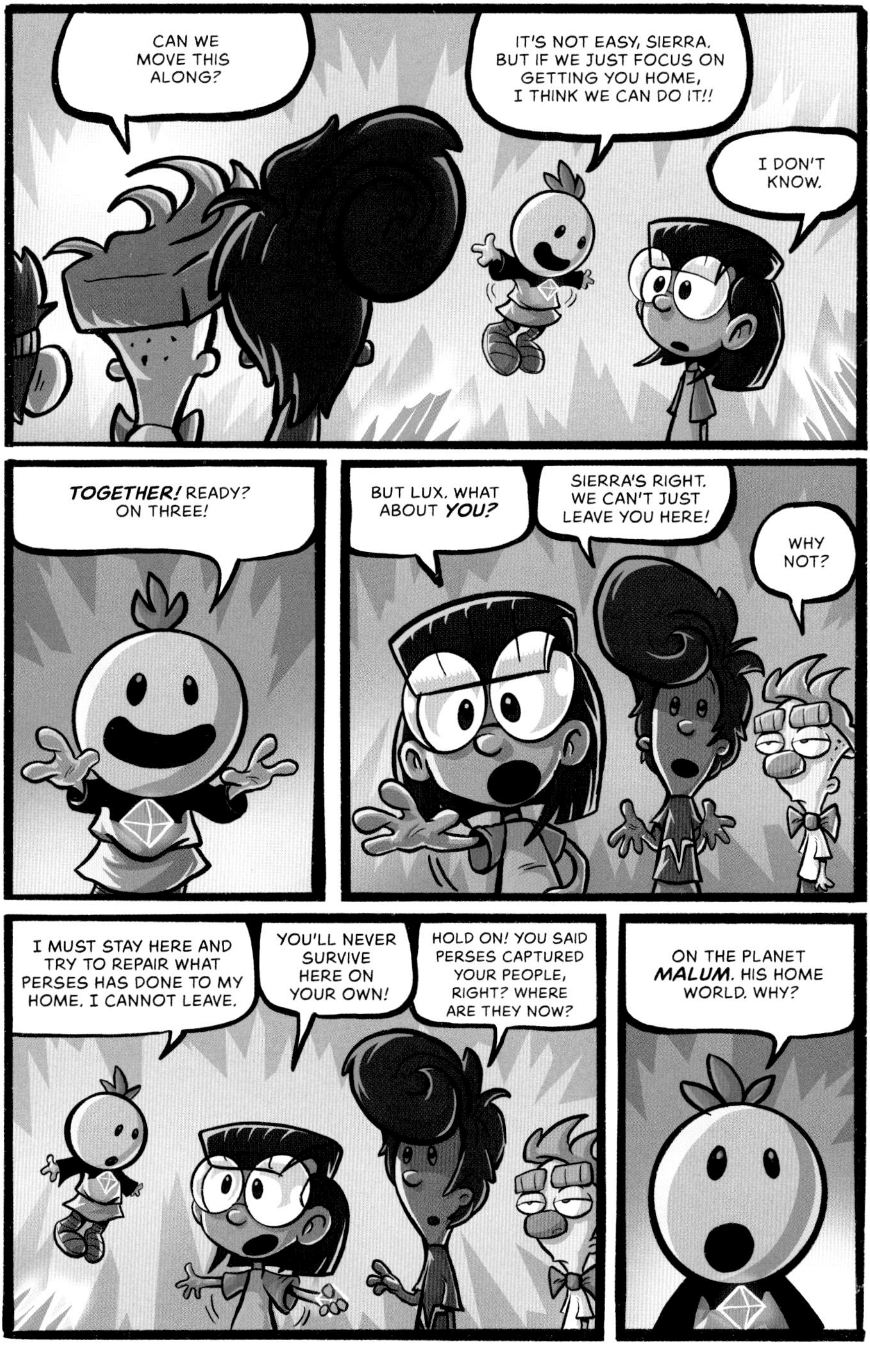

CAN WE MOVE THIS ALONG?
IT'S NOT EASY, SIERRA. BUT IF WE JUST FOCUS ON GETTING YOU HOME, I THINK WE CAN DO IT!!
I DON'T KNOW.
TOGETHER! READY? ON THREE!
BUT LUX, WHAT ABOUT YOU?
SIERRA'S RIGHT. WE CAN'T JUST LEAVE YOU HERE!
WHY NOT?
I MUST STAY HERE AND TRY TO REPAIR WHAT PERSES HAS DONE TO MY HOME. I CANNOT LEAVE.
YOU'LL NEVER SURVIVE HERE ON YOUR OWN!
HOLD ON! YOU SAID PERSES CAPTURED YOUR PEOPLE, RIGHT? WHERE ARE THEY NOW?
ON THE PLANET MALUM. HIS HOME WORLD. WHY?

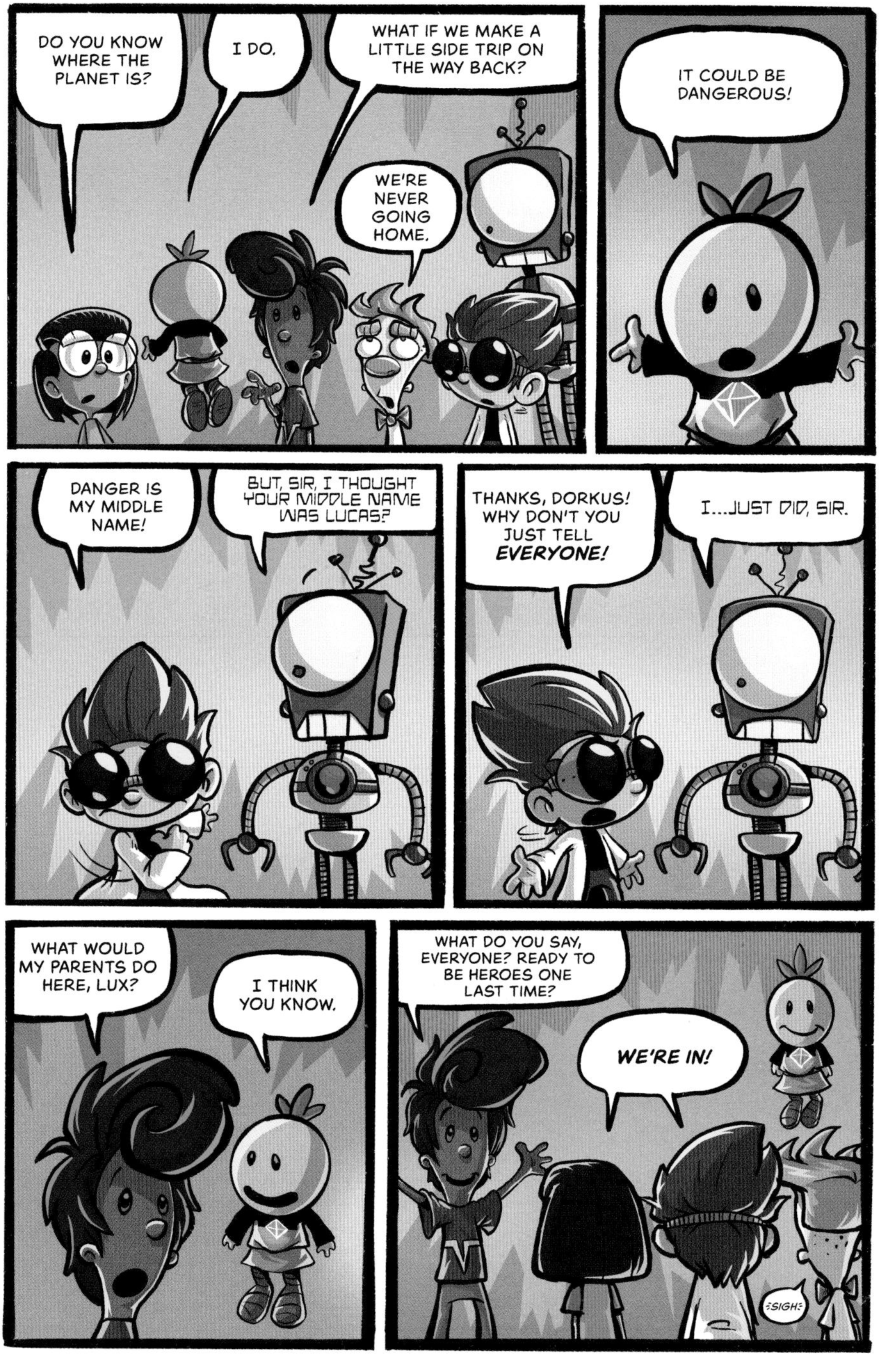
DO YOU KNOW WHERE THE PLANET IS?
I DO.
WHAT IF WE MAKE A LITTLE SIDE TRIP ON THE WAY BACK?
WE'RE NEVER GOING HOME.
IT COULD BE DANGEROUS!
DANGER IS MY MIDDLE NAME!
BUT, SIR, I THOUGHT YOUR MIDDLE NAME WAS LUCAS?
THANKS, DORKUS! WHY DON'T YOU JUST TELL EVERYONE!
I...JUST DID, SIR.
WHAT WOULD MY PARENTS DO HERE, LUX?
I THINK YOU KNOW.
WHAT DO YOU SAY, EVERYONE? READY TO BE HEROES ONE LAST TIME?
WE'RE IN!
SIGH

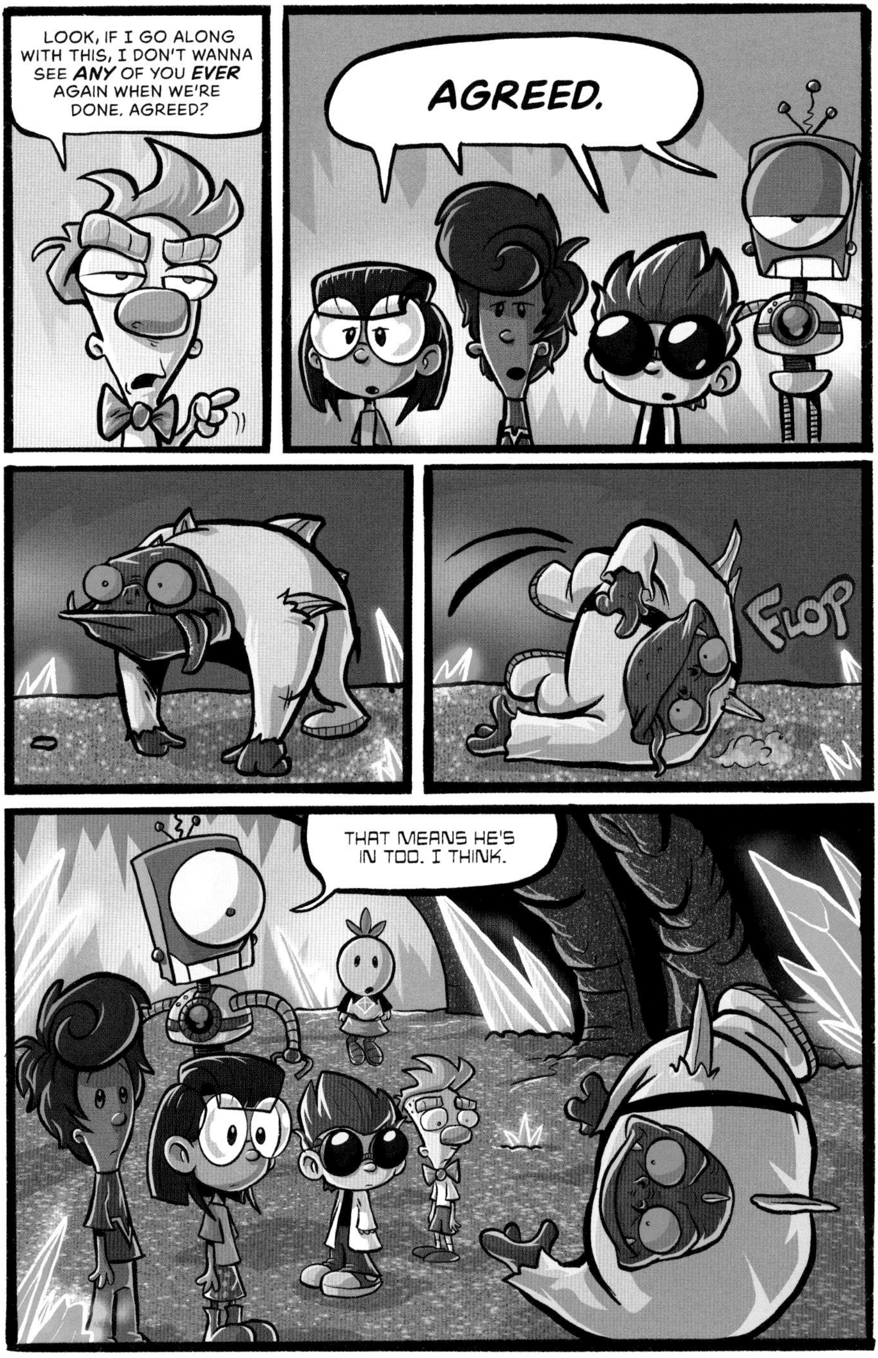
LOOK, IF I GO ALONG WITH THIS, I DON'T WANNA SEE ANY OF YOU EVER AGAIN WHEN WE'RE DONE. AGREED?
AGREED.
FLOP
THAT MEANS HE'S IN TOO. I THINK.

CHAPTER 11

In the Dumps

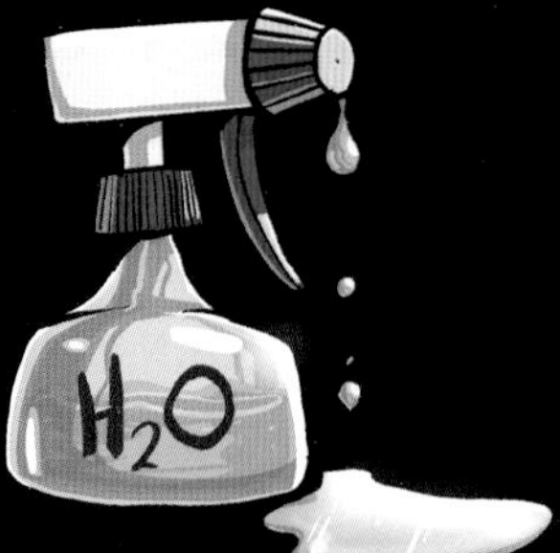
H_2O

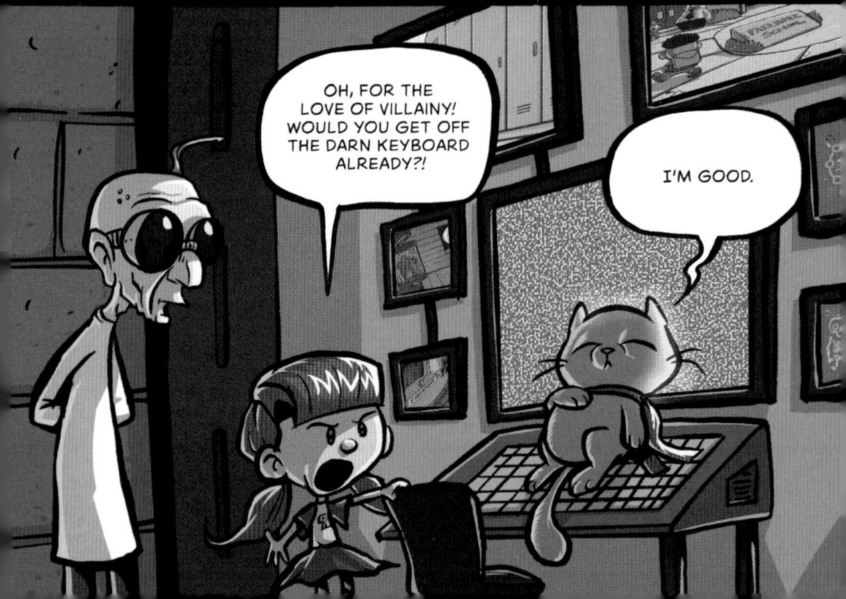
OH, FOR THE LOVE OF VILLAINY! WOULD YOU GET OFF THE DARN KEYBOARD ALREADY?!
I'M GOOD.

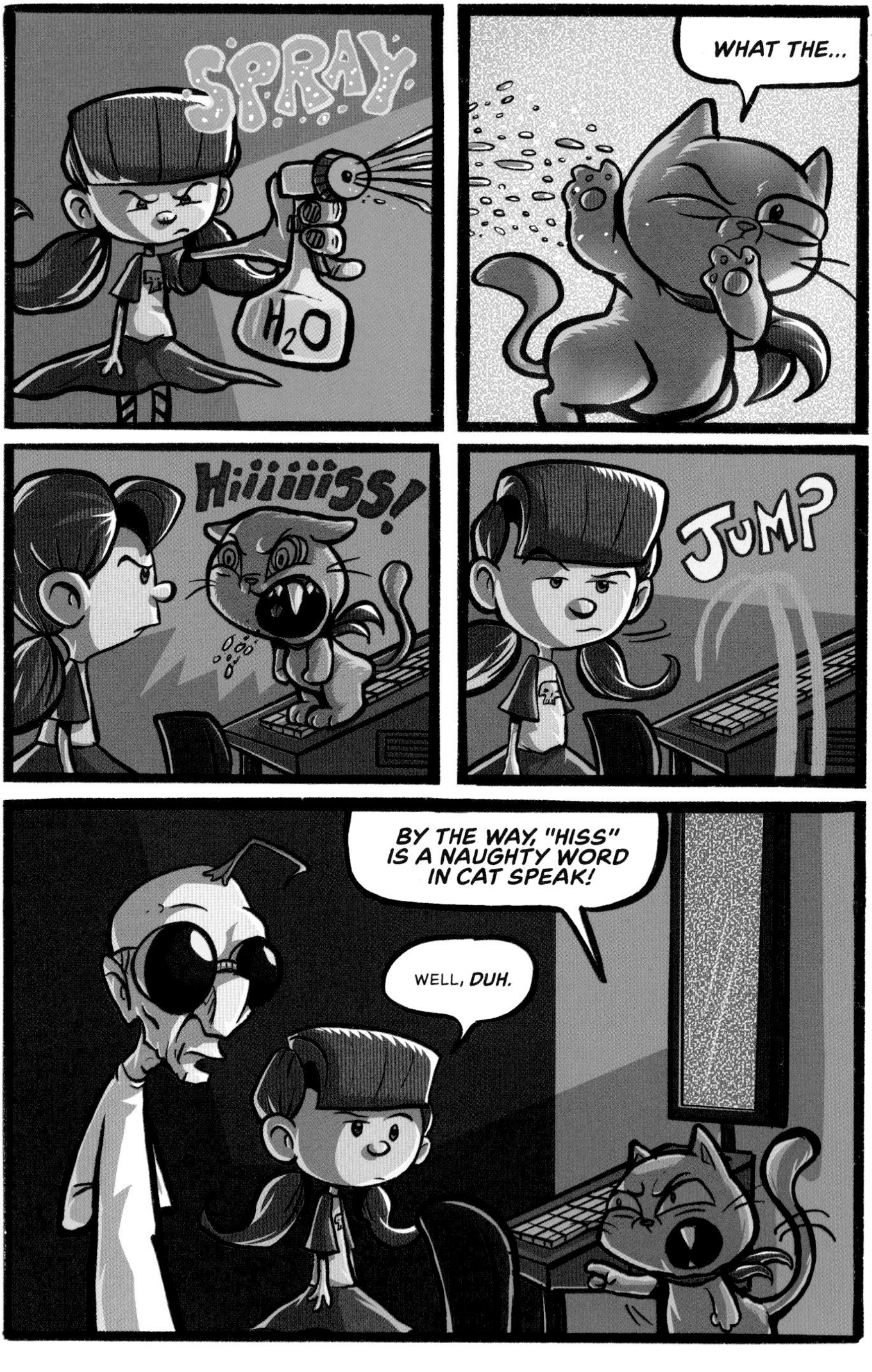
SPRAY
H2O
WHAT THE...
HIIIIIISS!
JUMP
BY THE WAY, "HISS" IS A NAUGHTY WORD IN CAT SPEAK!
WELL, DUH.

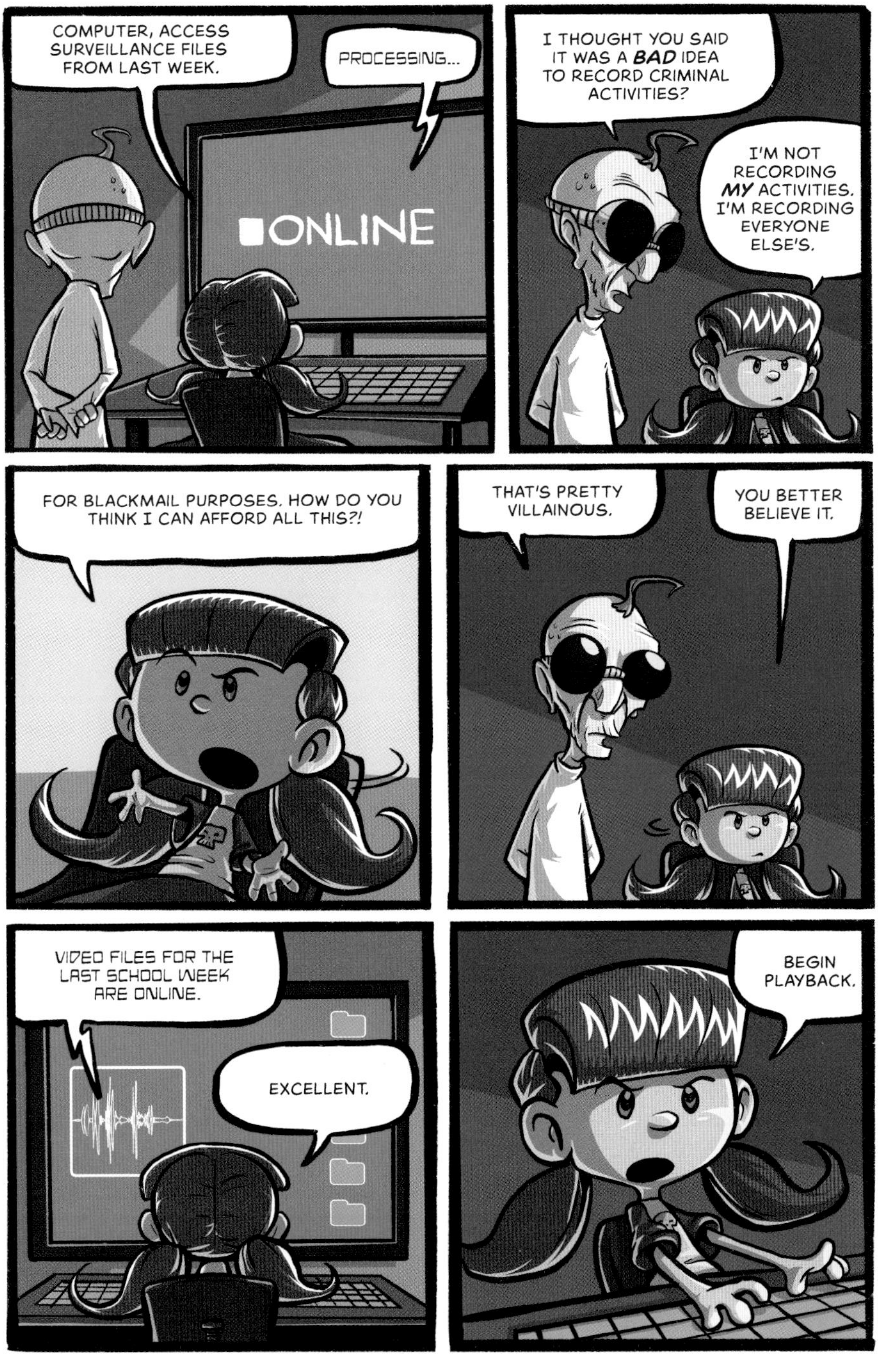
COMPUTER, ACCESS SURVEILLANCE FILES FROM LAST WEEK.
PROCESSING...
ONLINE
I THOUGHT YOU SAID IT WAS A **BAD** IDEA TO RECORD CRIMINAL ACTIVITIES?
I'M NOT RECORDING **MY** ACTIVITIES. I'M RECORDING EVERYONE ELSE'S.
FOR BLACKMAIL PURPOSES. HOW DO YOU THINK I CAN AFFORD ALL THIS?!
THAT'S PRETTY VILLAINOUS.
YOU BETTER BELIEVE IT.
VIDEO FILES FOR THE LAST SCHOOL WEEK ARE ONLINE.
EXCELLENT.
BEGIN PLAYBACK.

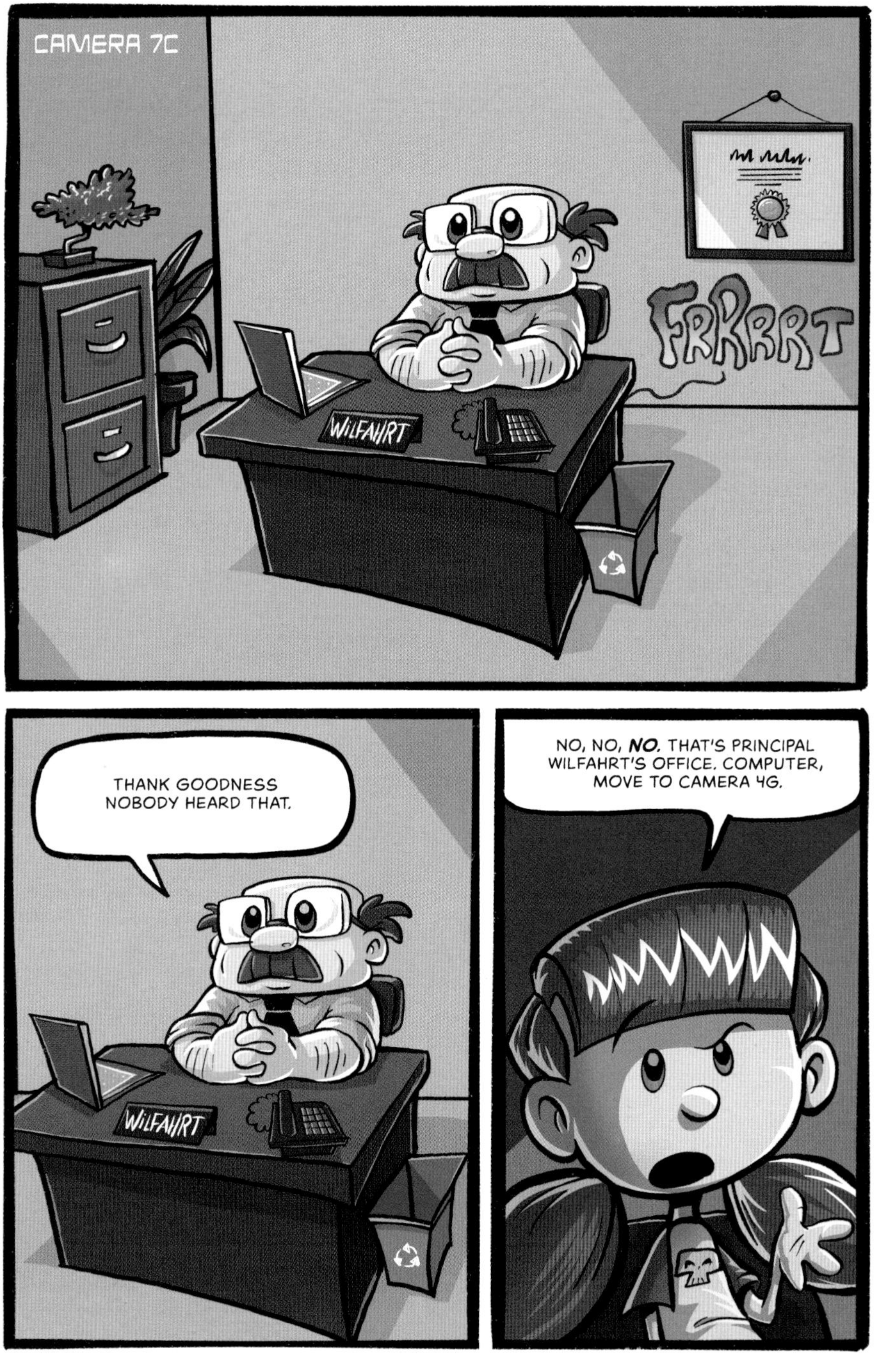
CAMERA 7C
WILFAHRT
FRRRRT
THANK GOODNESS NOBODY HEARD THAT.
WILFAHRT
NO, NO, ***NO.*** THAT'S PRINCIPAL WILFAHRT'S OFFICE. COMPUTER, MOVE TO CAMERA 4G.

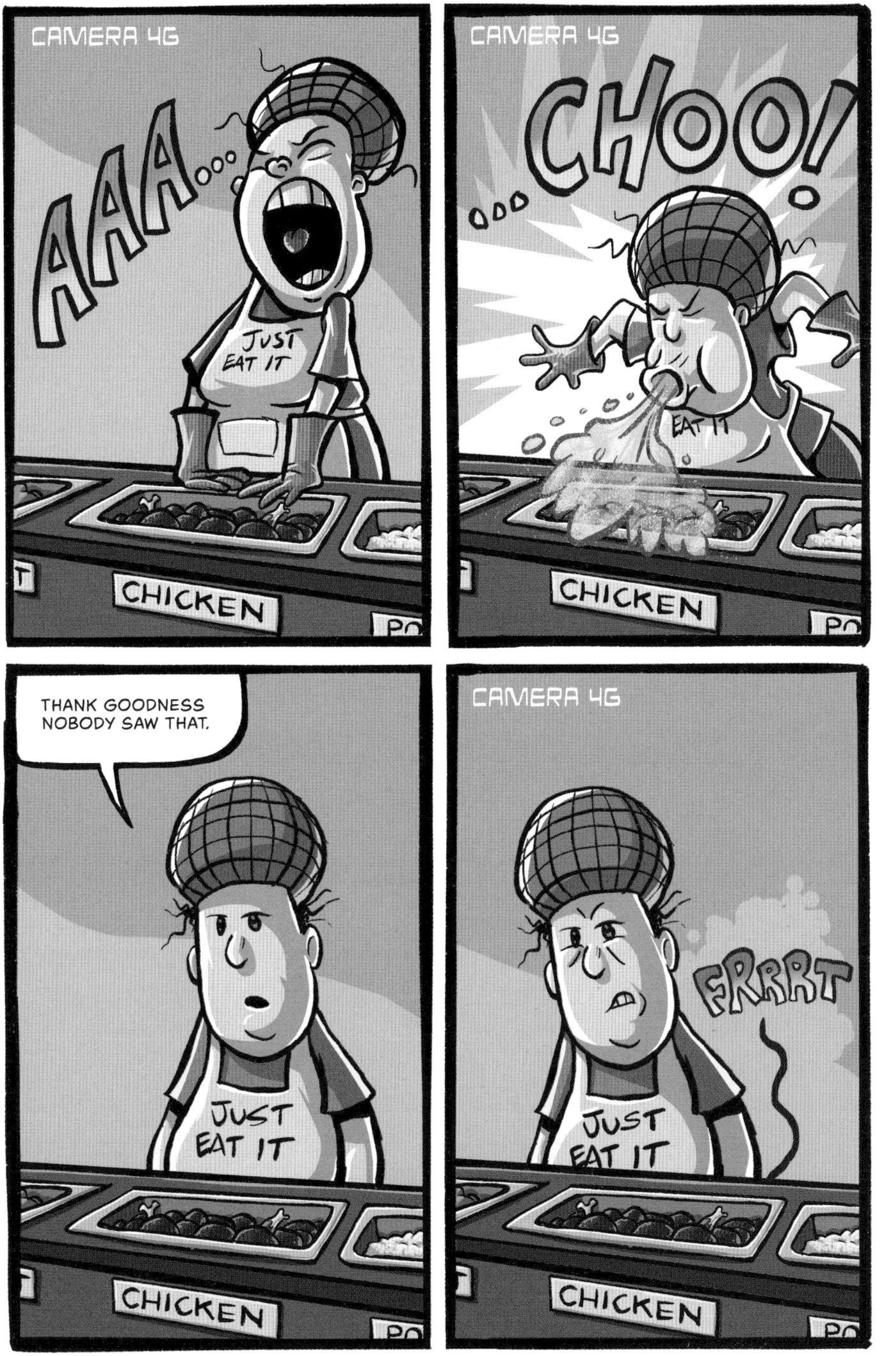
CAMERA 4G
AAA...
JUST EAT IT
CHICKEN
CAMERA 4G
...CHOO!
EAT IT
CHICKEN
THANK GOODNESS NOBODY SAW THAT.
JUST EAT IT
CHICKEN
CAMERA 4G
FRRRT
JUST EAT IT
CHICKEN

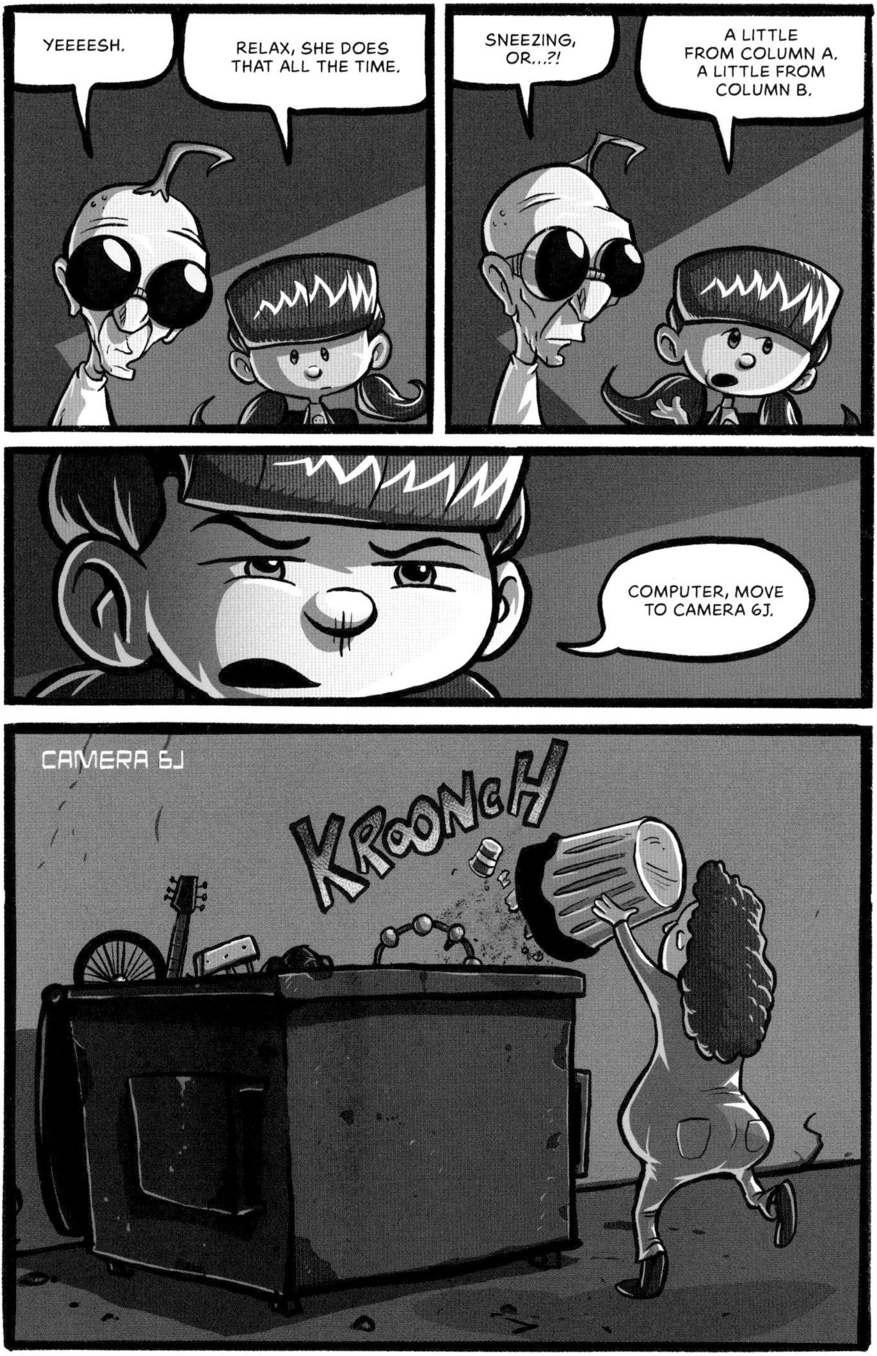
YEEEESH.
RELAX, SHE DOES THAT ALL THE TIME.
SNEEZING, OR...?!
A LITTLE FROM COLUMN A. A LITTLE FROM COLUMN B.
COMPUTER, MOVE TO CAMERA 6J.
CAMERA 6J
KROONCH

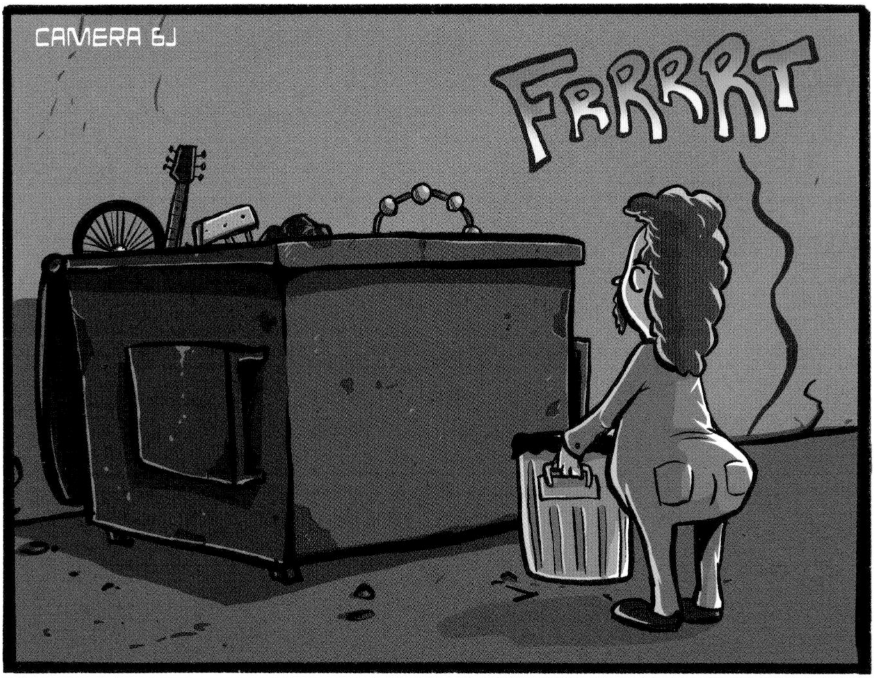
CAMERA 6J
FRRRRT

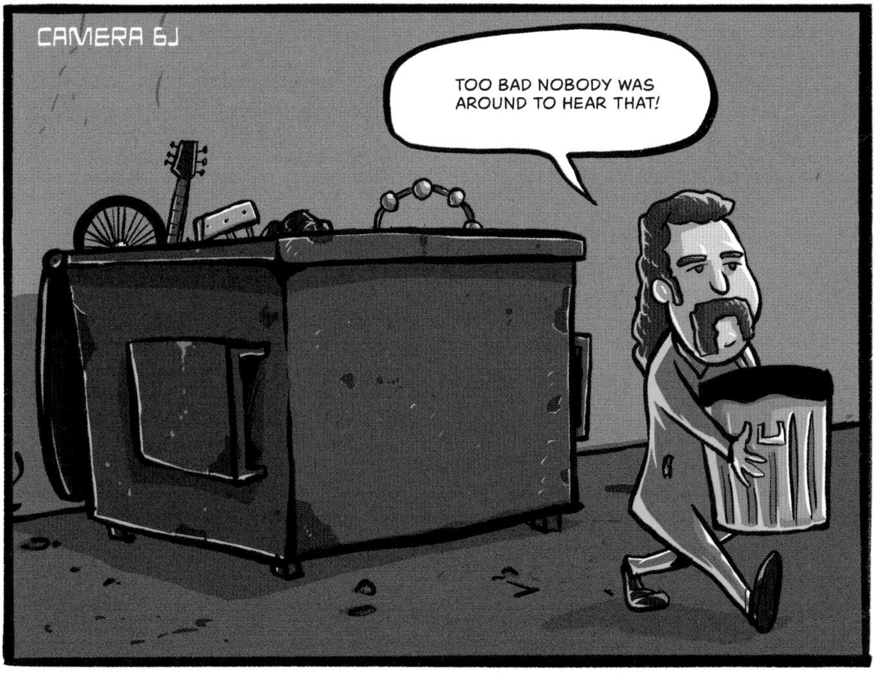
CAMERA 6J
TOO BAD NOBODY WAS AROUND TO HEAR THAT!

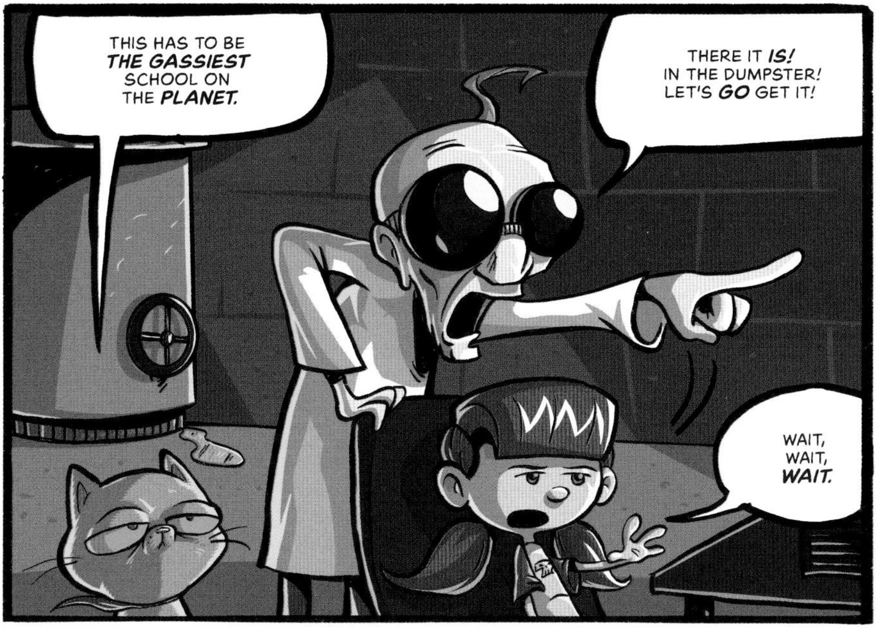
THIS HAS TO BE THE GASSIEST SCHOOL ON THE PLANET.
THERE IT IS! IN THE DUMPSTER! LET'S GO GET IT!
WAIT, WAIT, WAIT.

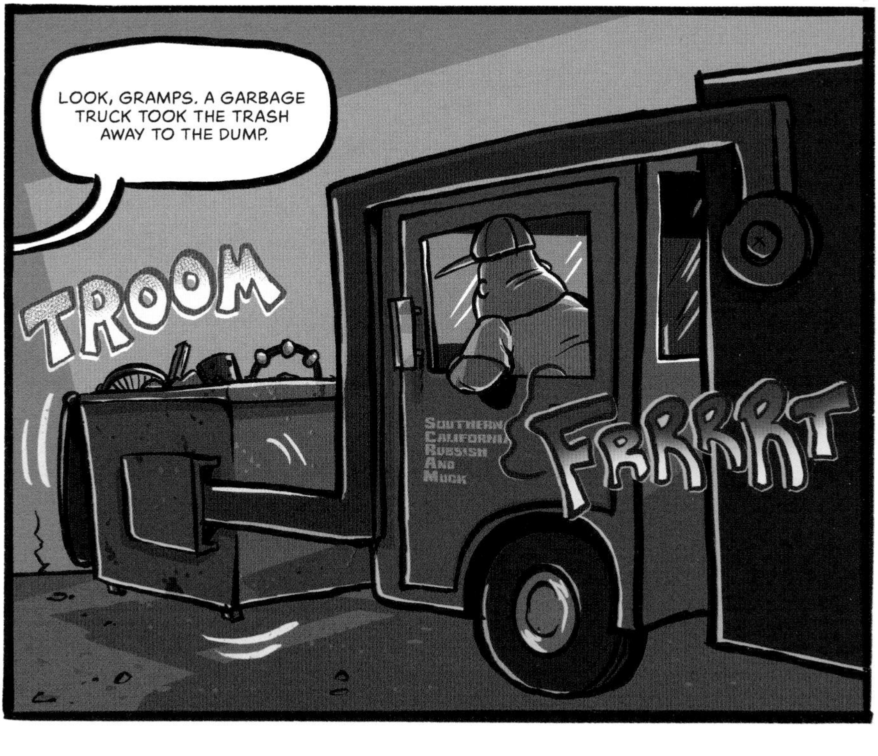
LOOK, GRAMPS. A GARBAGE TRUCK TOOK THE TRASH AWAY TO THE DUMP.
TROOM
SOUTHERN CALIFORNIA RUBBISH AND MUCK
FRRRRT

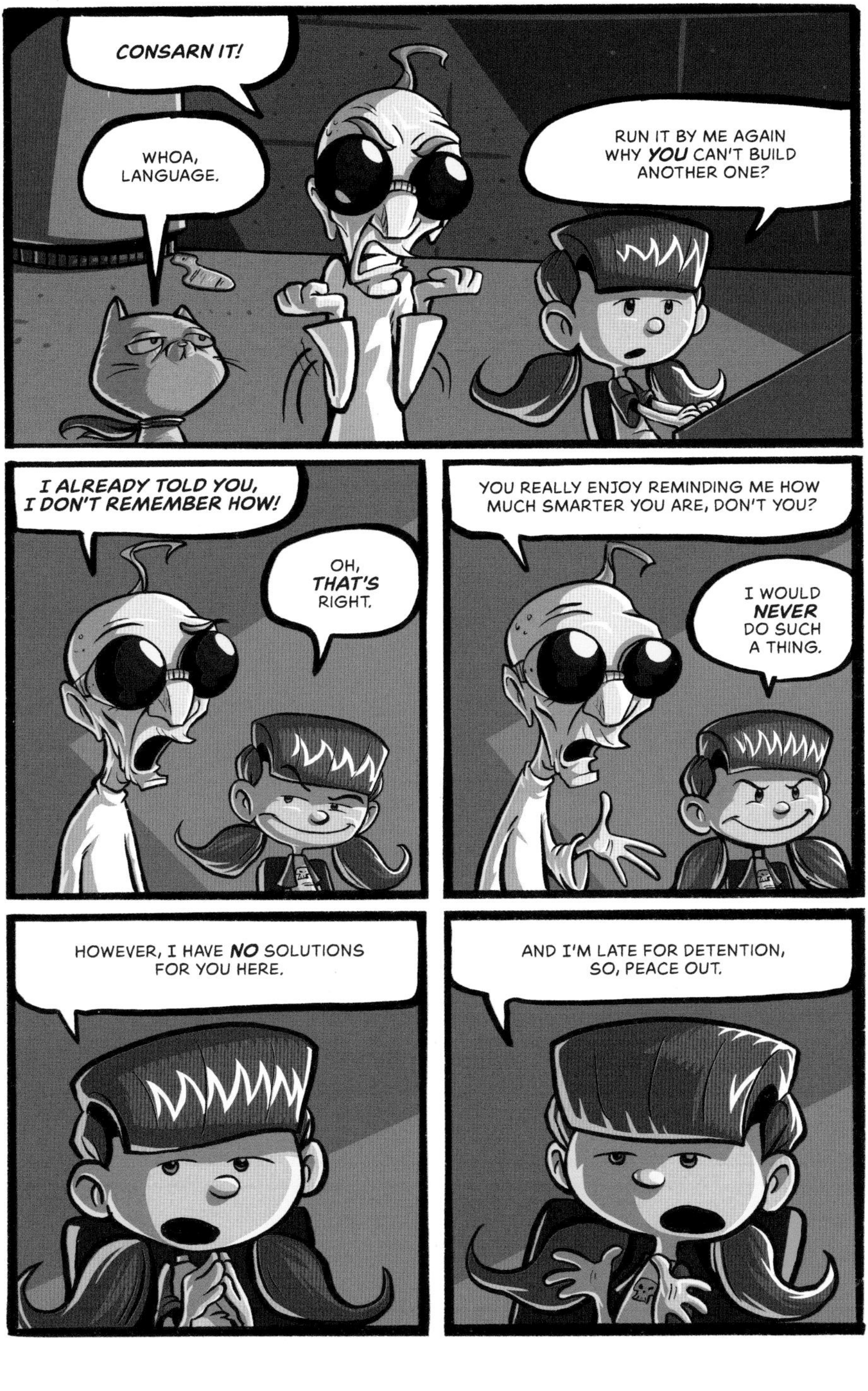
CONSARN IT!
WHOA, LANGUAGE.
RUN IT BY ME AGAIN WHY YOU CAN'T BUILD ANOTHER ONE?
I ALREADY TOLD YOU, I DON'T REMEMBER HOW!
OH, THAT'S RIGHT.
YOU REALLY ENJOY REMINDING ME HOW MUCH SMARTER YOU ARE, DON'T YOU?
I WOULD NEVER DO SUCH A THING.
HOWEVER, I HAVE NO SOLUTIONS FOR YOU HERE.
AND I'M LATE FOR DETENTION, SO, PEACE OUT.

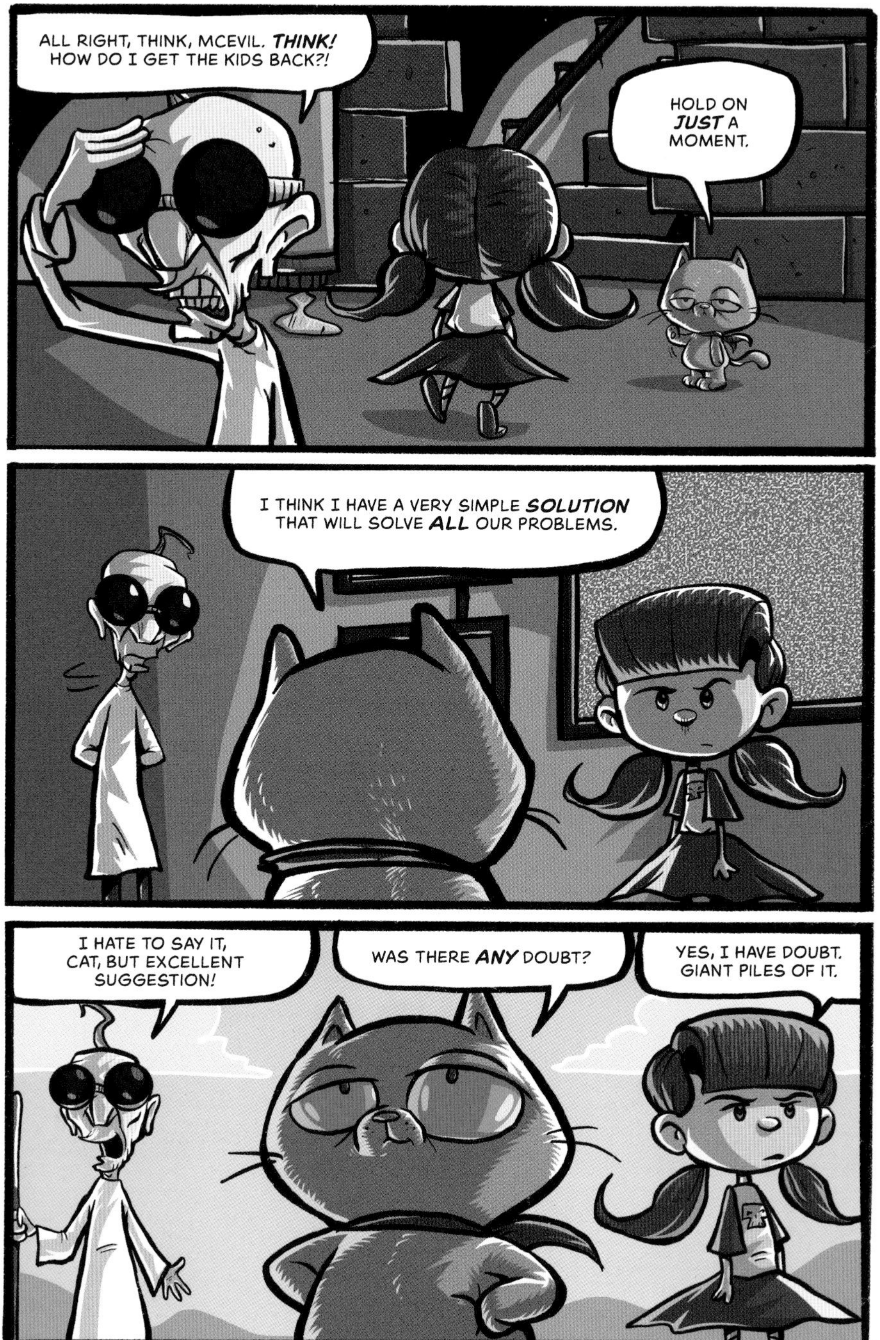
ALL RIGHT, THINK, MCEVIL. THINK! HOW DO I GET THE KIDS BACK?!
HOLD ON JUST A MOMENT.
I THINK I HAVE A VERY SIMPLE SOLUTION THAT WILL SOLVE ALL OUR PROBLEMS.
I HATE TO SAY IT, CAT, BUT EXCELLENT SUGGESTION!
WAS THERE ANY DOUBT?
YES, I HAVE DOUBT. GIANT PILES OF IT.

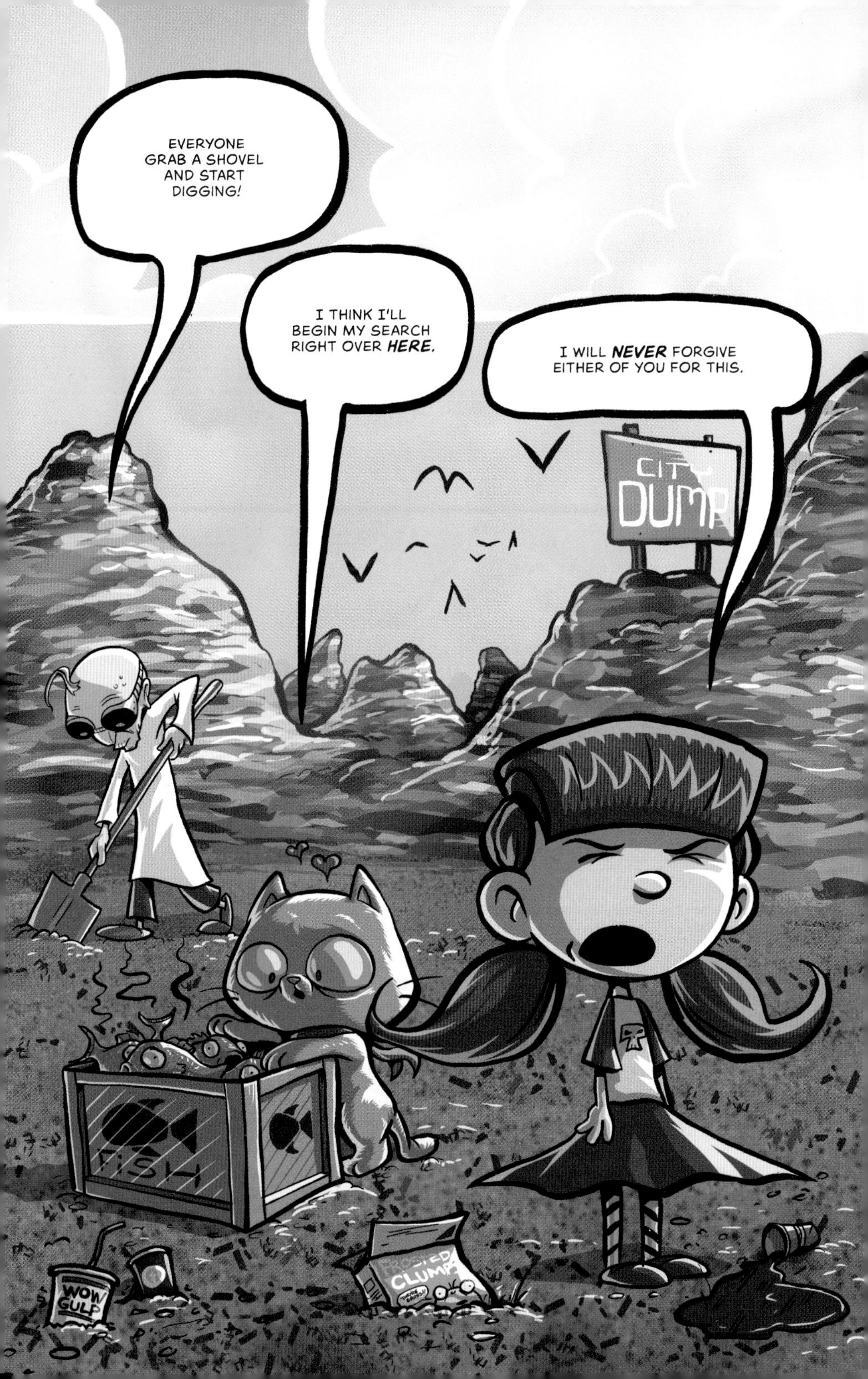
EVERYONE GRAB A SHOVEL AND START DIGGING!
I THINK I'LL BEGIN MY SEARCH RIGHT OVER HERE.
I WILL NEVER FORGIVE EITHER OF YOU FOR THIS.
CITY DUMP
FISH
WOW GULP
FROSTED CLUMPS

CHAPTER 12
Side Trip

PLANET MALUM

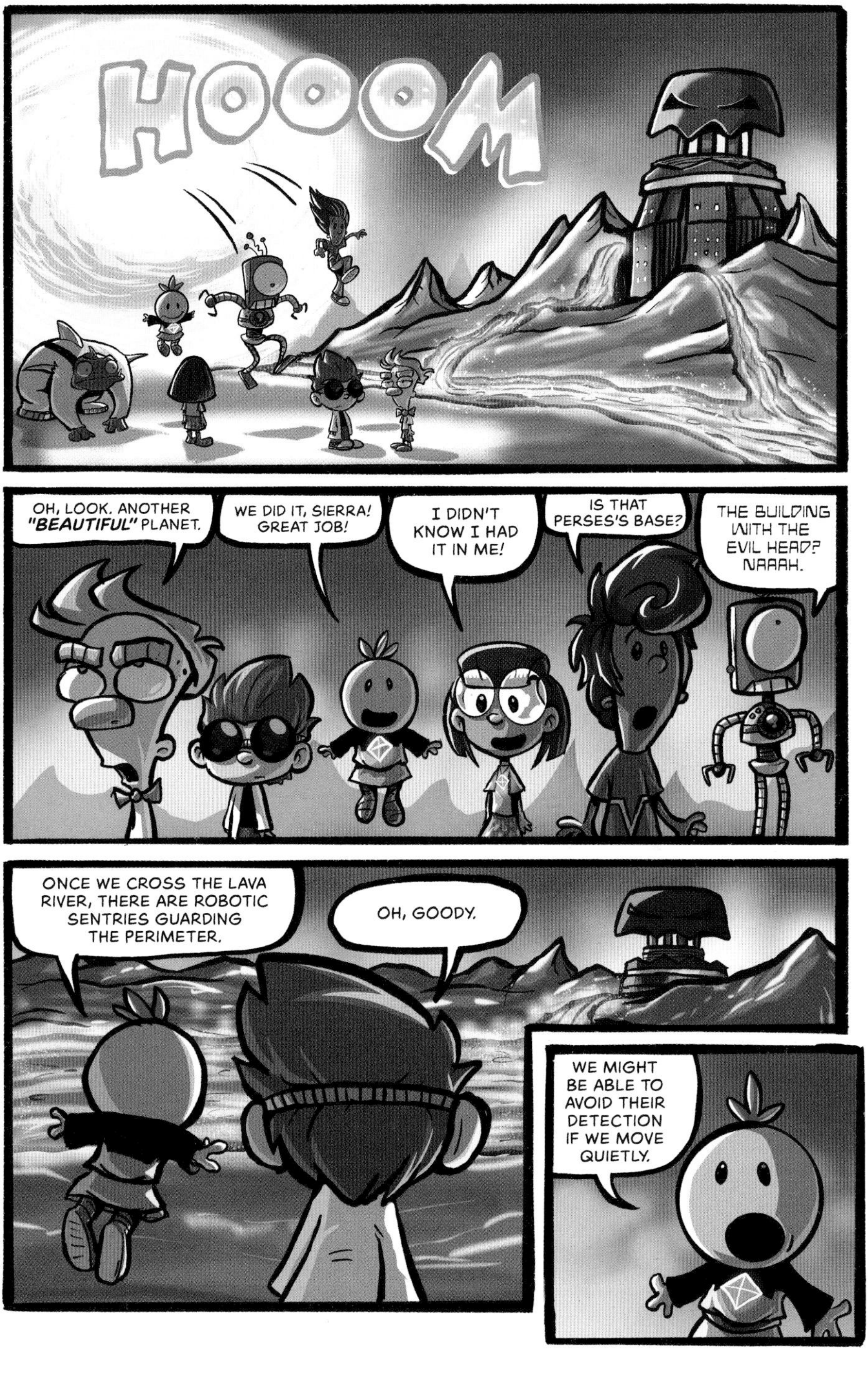
HOOOM
OH, LOOK. ANOTHER "BEAUTIFUL" PLANET.
WE DID IT, SIERRA! GREAT JOB!
I DIDN'T KNOW I HAD IT IN ME!
IS THAT PERSES'S BASE?
THE BUILDING WITH THE EVIL HEAD? NAAAH.
ONCE WE CROSS THE LAVA RIVER, THERE ARE ROBOTIC SENTRIES GUARDING THE PERIMETER.
OH, GOODY.
WE MIGHT BE ABLE TO AVOID THEIR DETECTION IF WE MOVE QUIETLY.

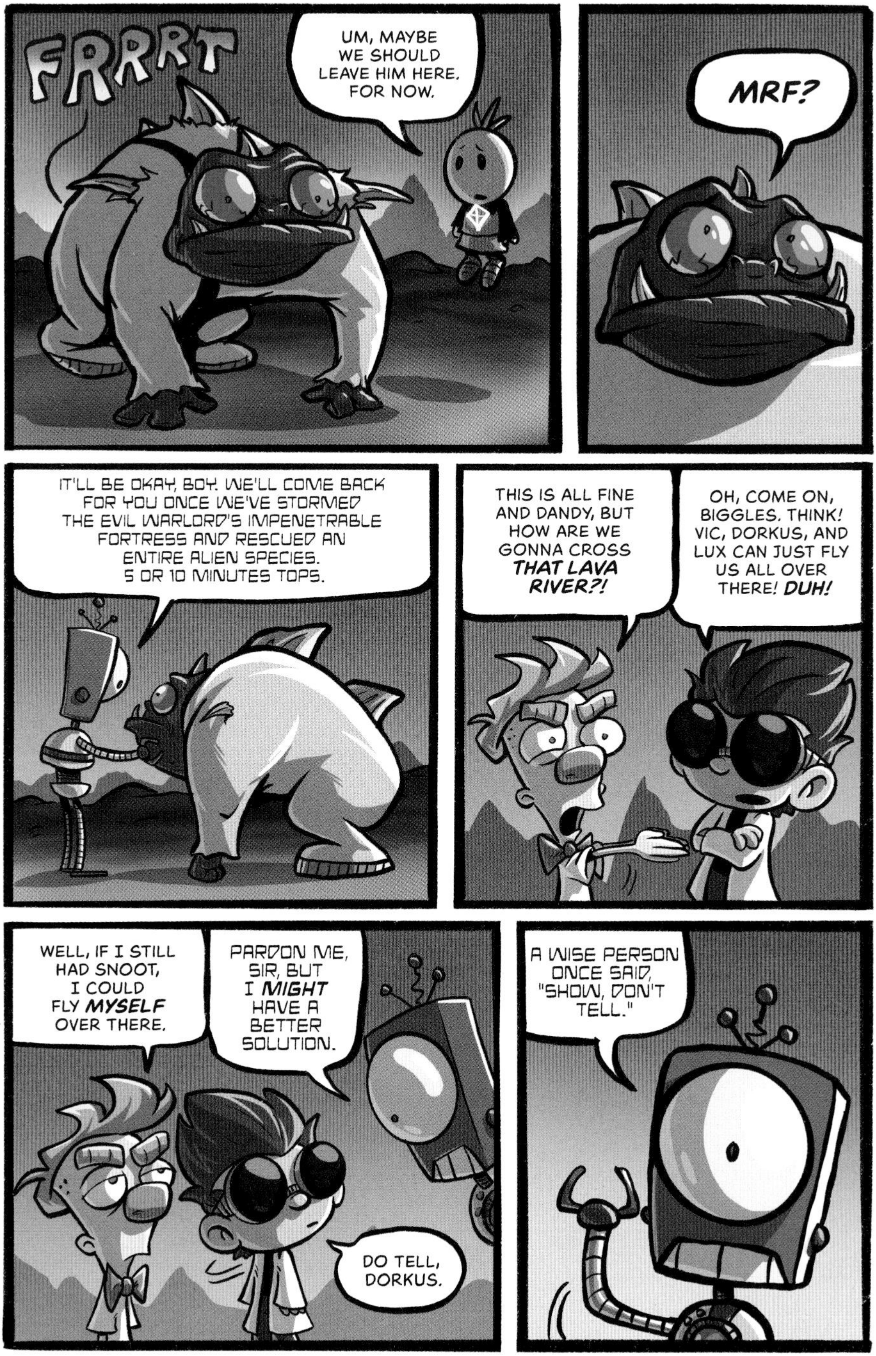
FRRRT
UM, MAYBE WE SHOULD LEAVE HIM HERE. FOR NOW.
MRF?
IT'LL BE OKAY, BOY. WE'LL COME BACK FOR YOU ONCE WE'VE STORMED THE EVIL WARLORD'S IMPENETRABLE FORTRESS AND RESCUED AN ENTIRE ALIEN SPECIES. 5 OR 10 MINUTES TOPS.
THIS IS ALL FINE AND DANDY, BUT HOW ARE WE GONNA CROSS *THAT LAVA RIVER?!*
OH, COME ON, BIGGLES. THINK! VIC, DORKUS, AND LUX CAN JUST FLY US ALL OVER THERE! *DUH!*
WELL, IF I STILL HAD SNOOT, I COULD FLY *MYSELF* OVER THERE.
PARDON ME, SIR, BUT I *MIGHT* HAVE A BETTER SOLUTION.
DO TELL, DORKUS.
A WISE PERSON ONCE SAID, "SHOW, DON'T TELL."

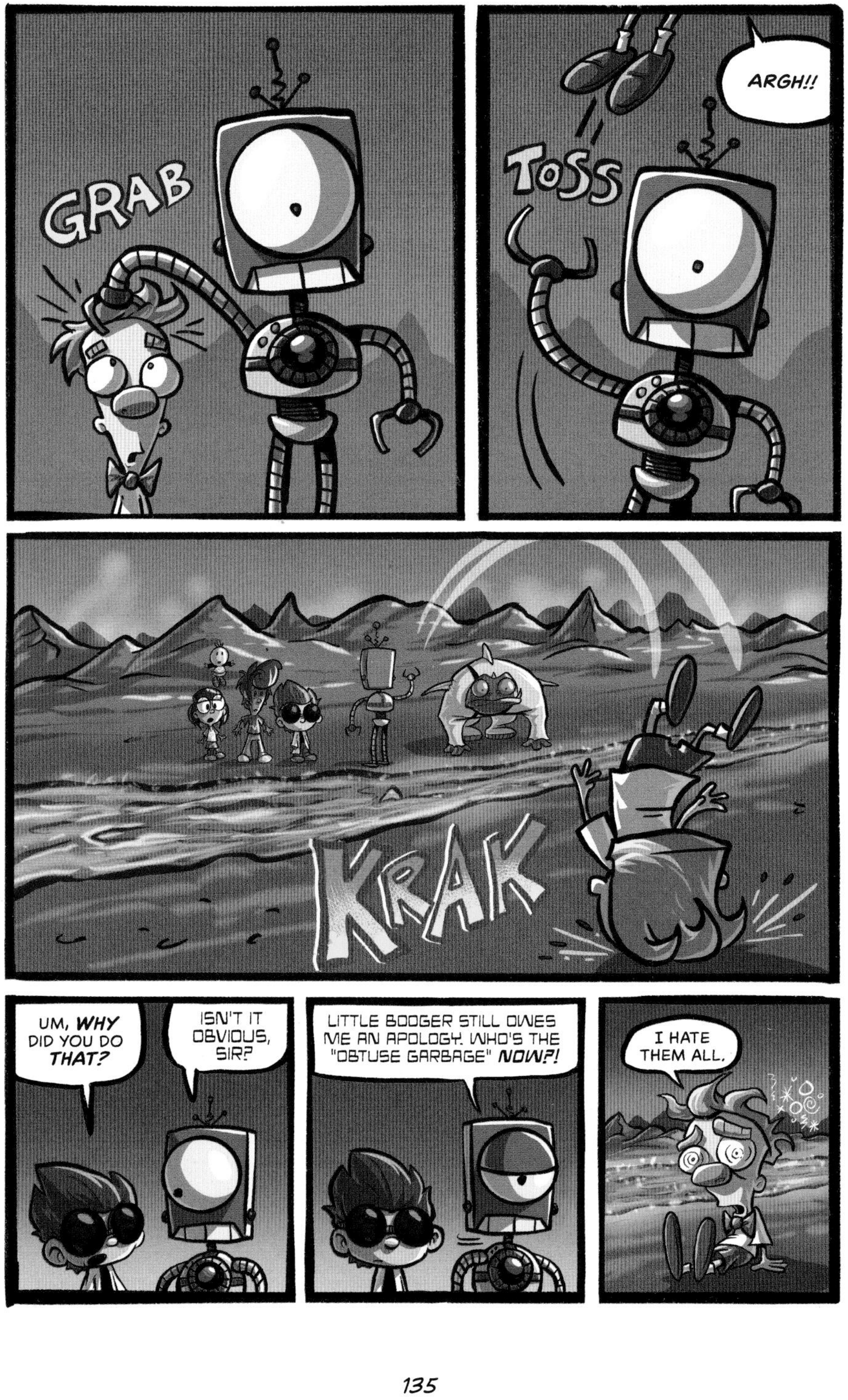
GRAB
TOSS
ARGH!!
KRAK
UM, WHY DID YOU DO THAT?
ISN'T IT OBVIOUS, SIR?
LITTLE BOOGER STILL OWES ME AN APOLOGY. WHO'S THE "OBTUSE GARBAGE" NOW?!
I HATE THEM ALL.

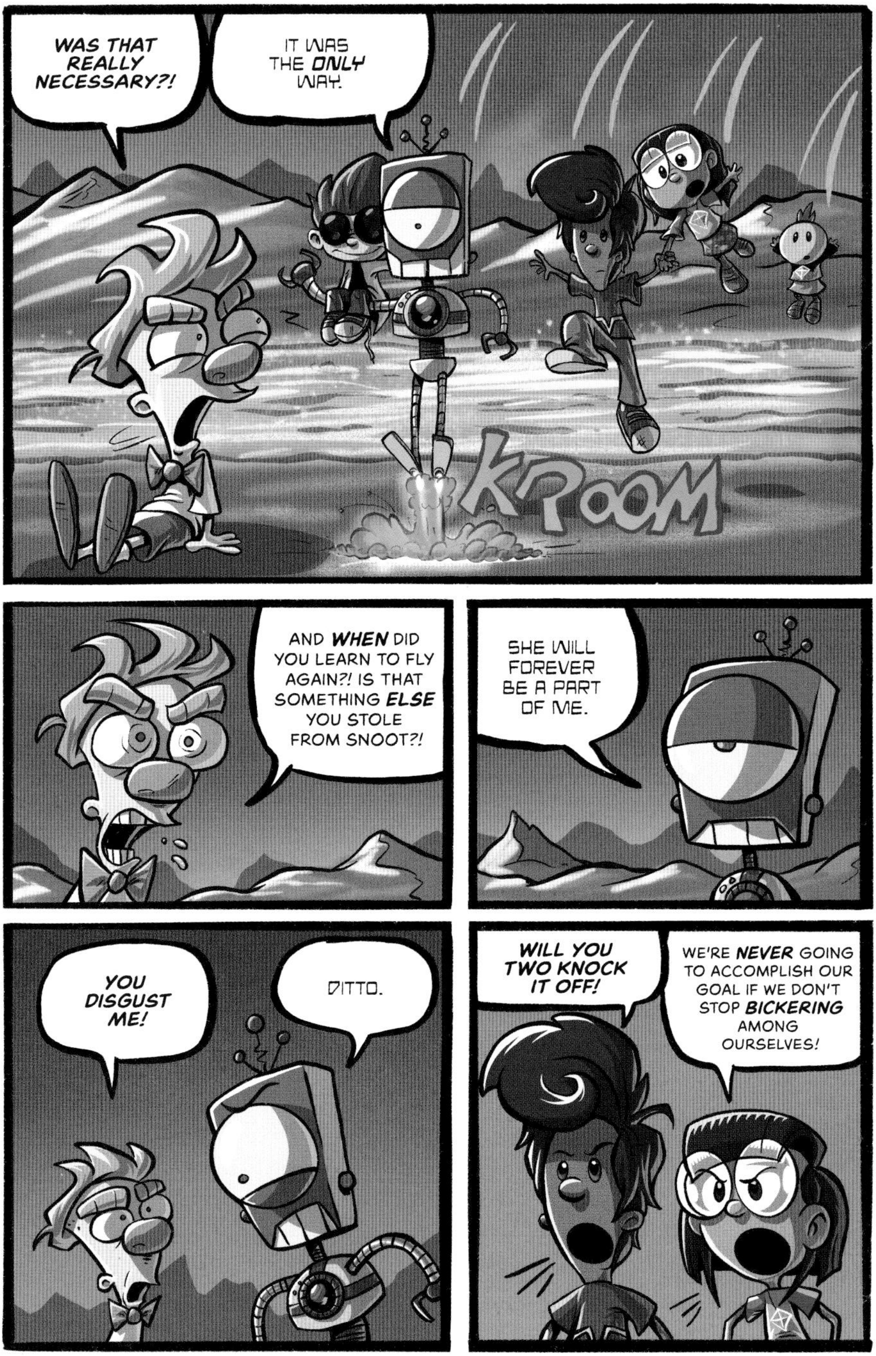
WAS THAT REALLY NECESSARY?!
IT WAS THE ONLY WAY.
KROOM
AND WHEN DID YOU LEARN TO FLY AGAIN?! IS THAT SOMETHING ELSE YOU STOLE FROM SNOOT?!
SHE WILL FOREVER BE A PART OF ME.
YOU DISGUST ME!
DITTO.
WILL YOU TWO KNOCK IT OFF!
WE'RE NEVER GOING TO ACCOMPLISH OUR GOAL IF WE DON'T STOP BICKERING AMONG OURSELVES!

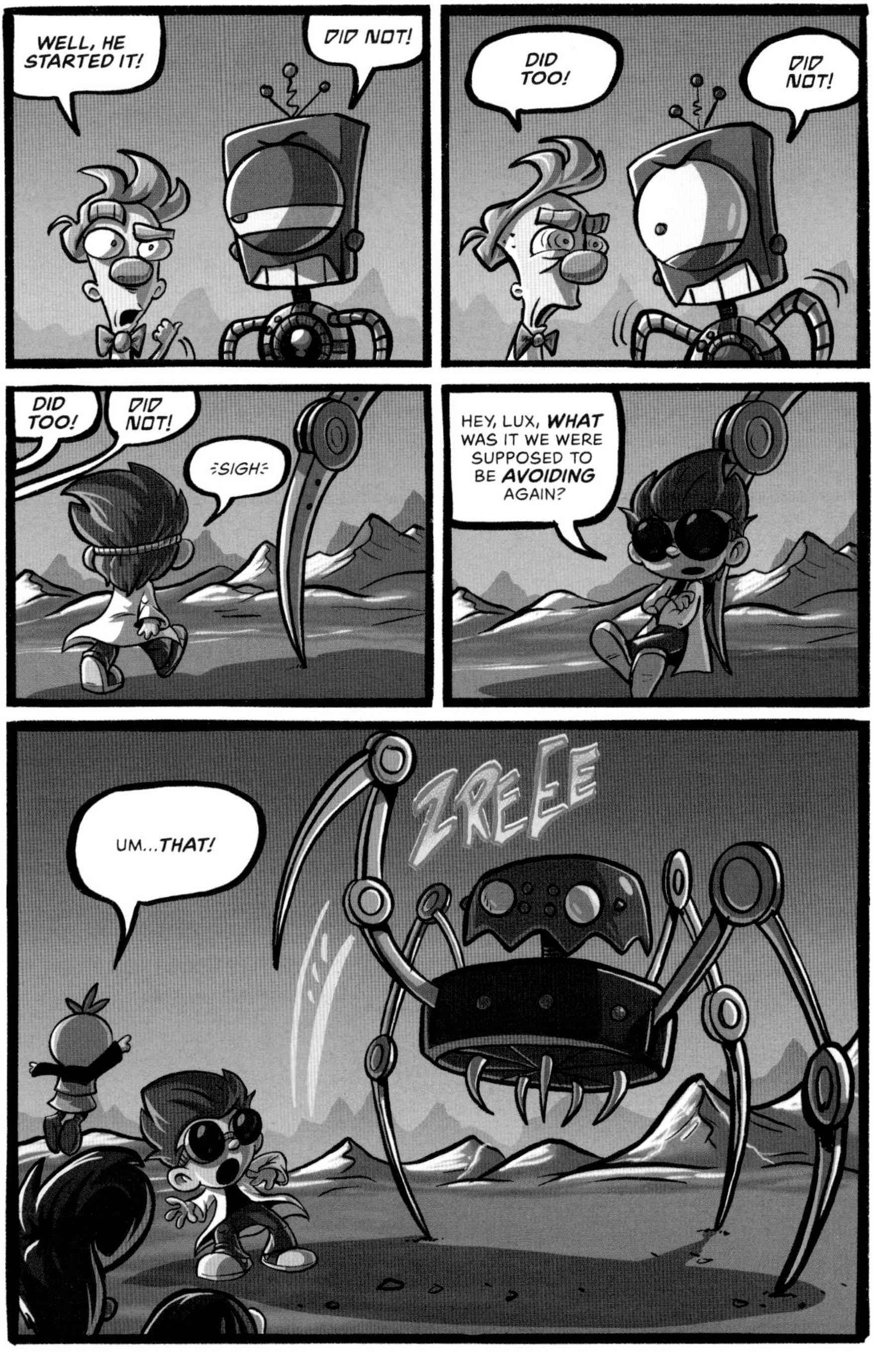
WELL, HE STARTED IT!
DID NOT!
DID TOO!
DID NOT!
DID TOO!
DID NOT!
SIGH
HEY, LUX, WHAT WAS IT WE WERE SUPPOSED TO BE AVOIDING AGAIN?
UM...THAT!
ZREEE

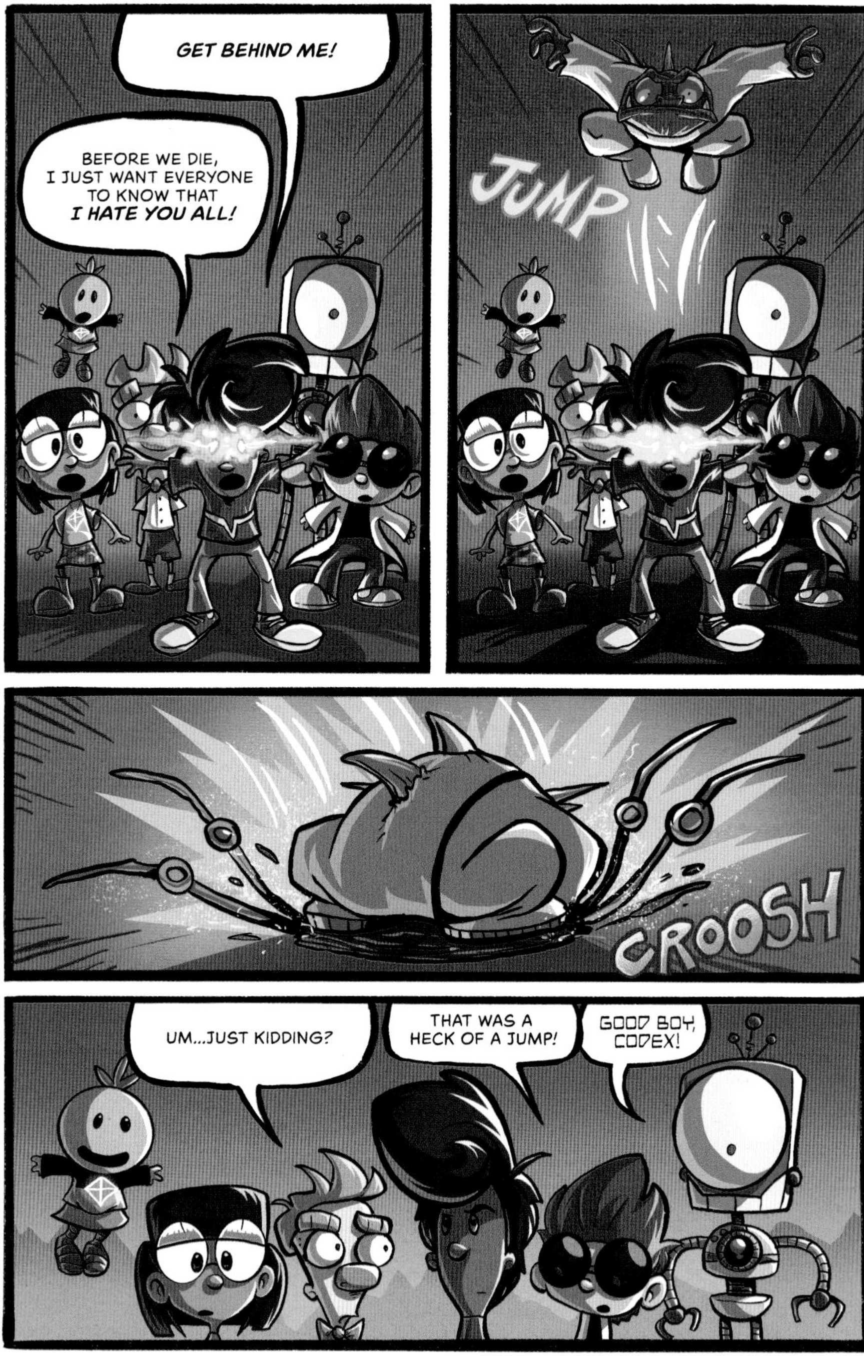
GET BEHIND ME!
BEFORE WE DIE, I JUST WANT EVERYONE TO KNOW THAT *I HATE YOU ALL!*
JUMP
CROOSH
UM...JUST KIDDING?
THAT WAS A HECK OF A JUMP!
GOOD BOY, CODEX!

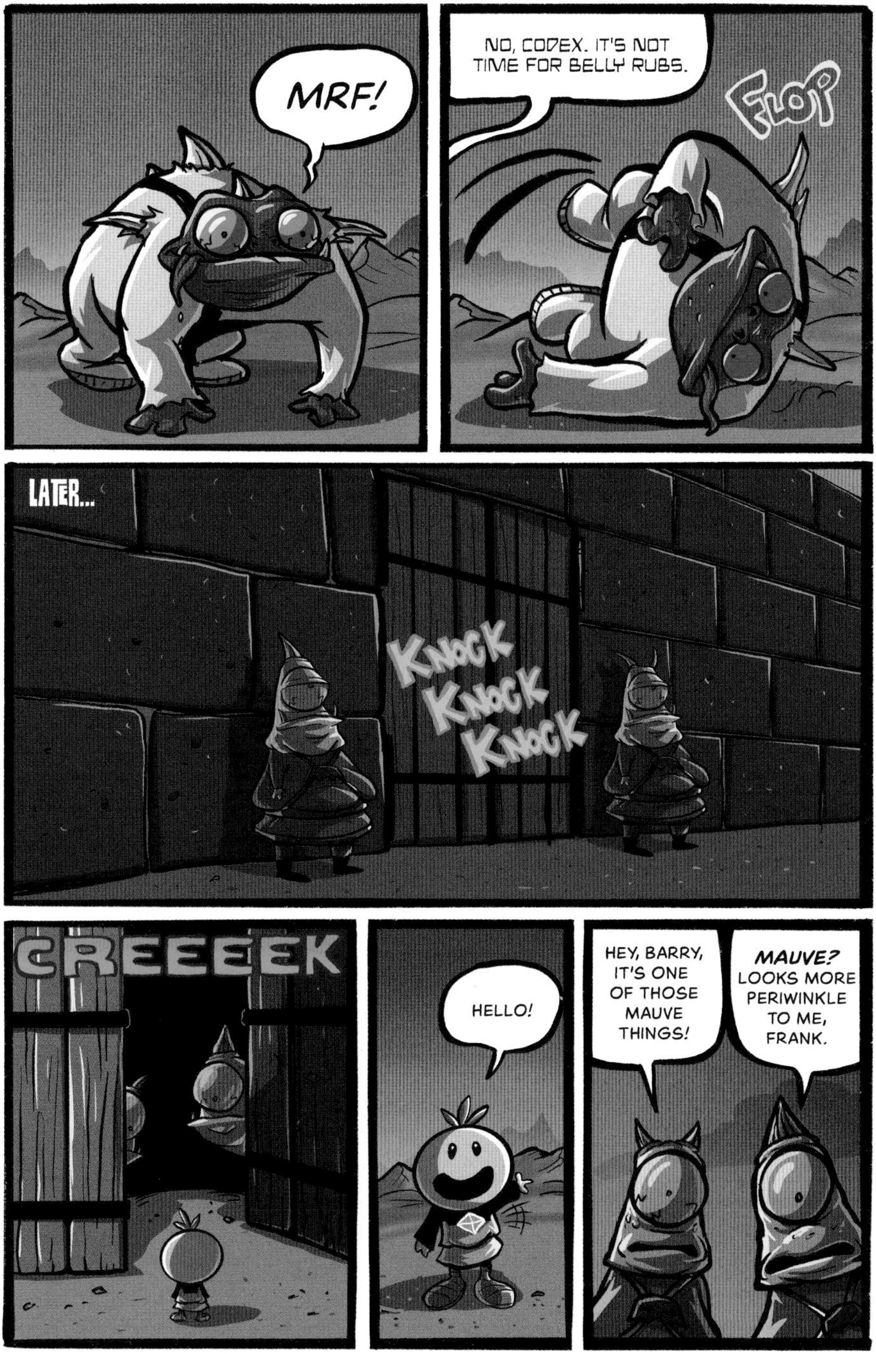
MRF!
NO, CODEX. IT'S NOT TIME FOR BELLY RUBS.
FLOP
LATER...
KNOCK KNOCK KNOCK
CREEEEK
HELLO!
HEY, BARRY, IT'S ONE OF THOSE MAUVE THINGS!
MAUVE? LOOKS MORE PERIWINKLE TO ME, FRANK.

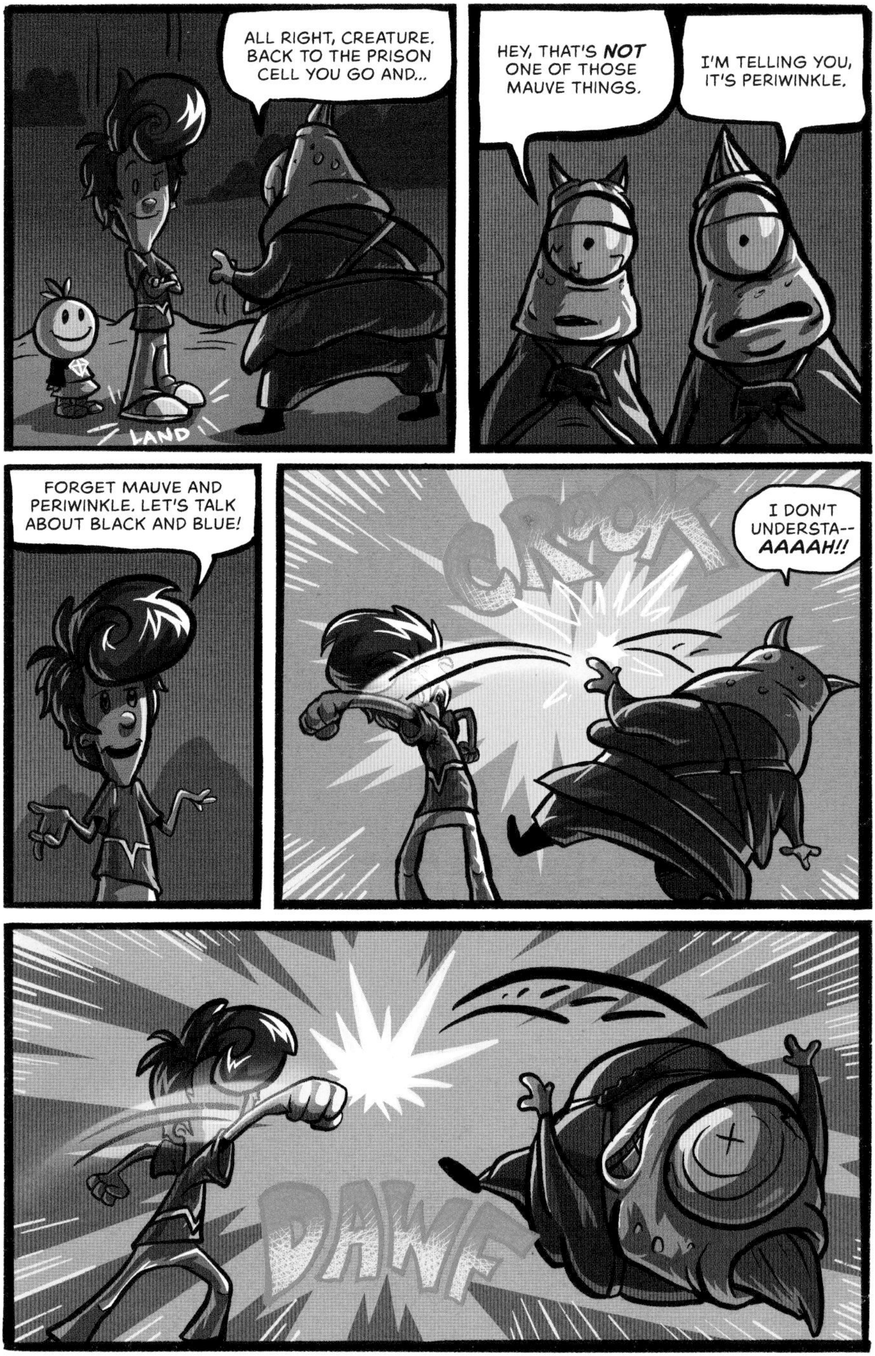
ALL RIGHT, CREATURE. BACK TO THE PRISON CELL YOU GO AND...
LAND
HEY, THAT'S **NOT** ONE OF THOSE MAUVE THINGS.
I'M TELLING YOU, IT'S PERIWINKLE.
FORGET MAUVE AND PERIWINKLE. LET'S TALK ABOUT BLACK AND BLUE!
CROOK
I DON'T UNDERSTA-- ***AAAAH!!***
DAWF

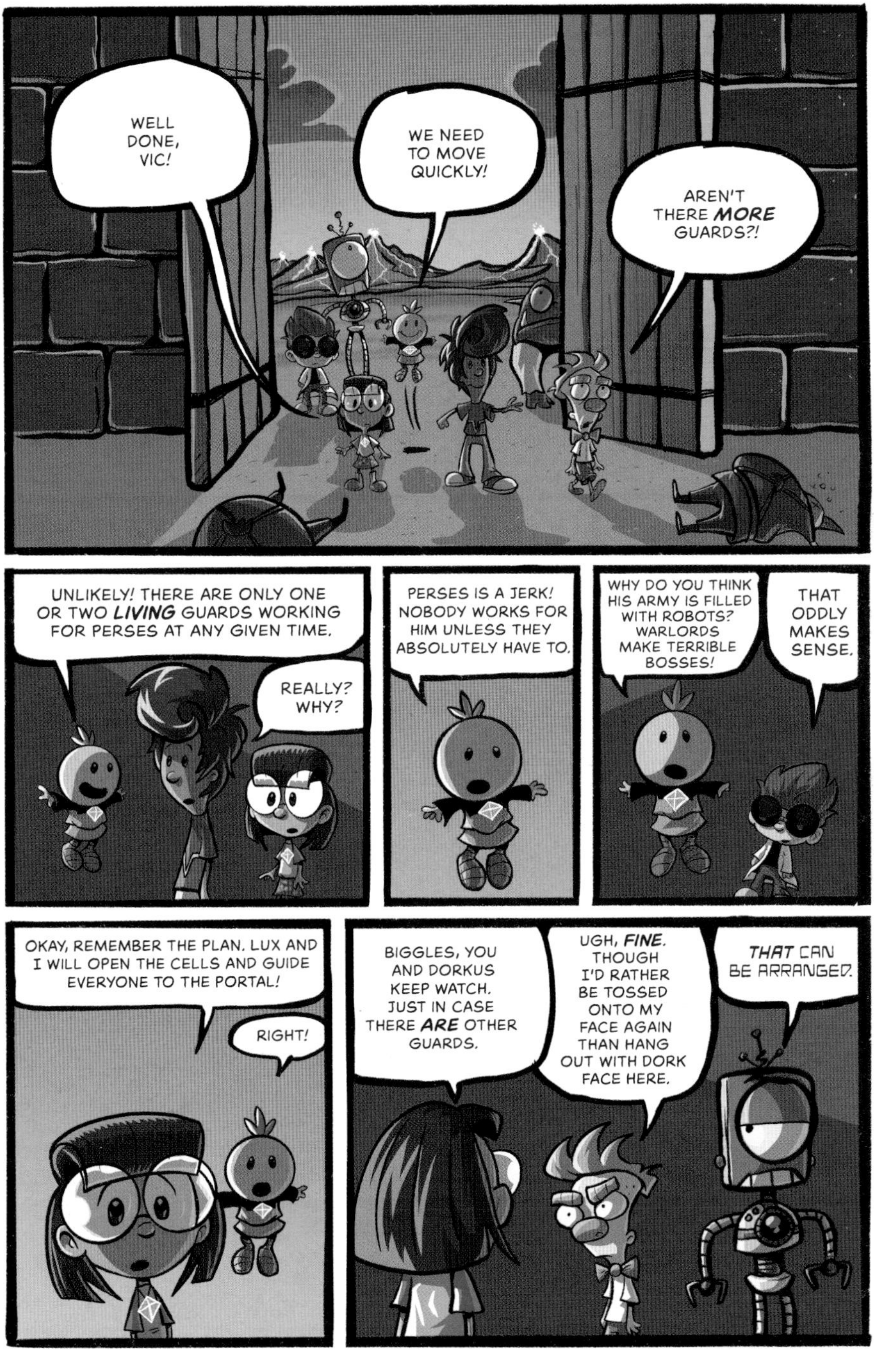
WELL DONE, VIC!
WE NEED TO MOVE QUICKLY!
AREN'T THERE MORE GUARDS?!
UNLIKELY! THERE ARE ONLY ONE OR TWO LIVING GUARDS WORKING FOR PERSES AT ANY GIVEN TIME.
REALLY? WHY?
PERSES IS A JERK! NOBODY WORKS FOR HIM UNLESS THEY ABSOLUTELY HAVE TO.
WHY DO YOU THINK HIS ARMY IS FILLED WITH ROBOTS? WARLORDS MAKE TERRIBLE BOSSES!
THAT ODDLY MAKES SENSE.
OKAY, REMEMBER THE PLAN. LUX AND I WILL OPEN THE CELLS AND GUIDE EVERYONE TO THE PORTAL!
RIGHT!
BIGGLES, YOU AND DORKUS KEEP WATCH. JUST IN CASE THERE ARE OTHER GUARDS.
UGH, FINE. THOUGH I'D RATHER BE TOSSED ONTO MY FACE AGAIN THAN HANG OUT WITH DORK FACE HERE.
THAT CAN BE ARRANGED.

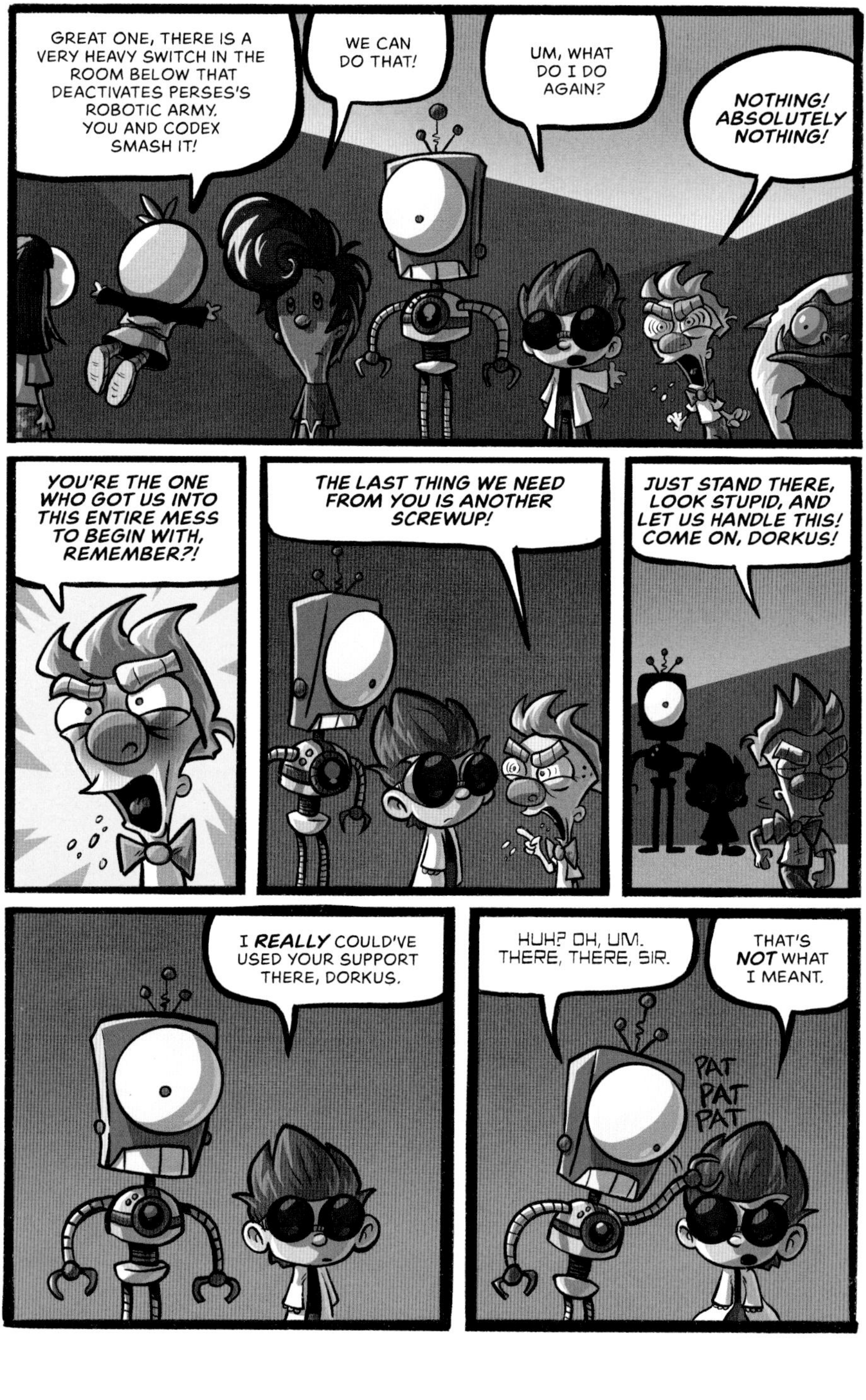
GREAT ONE, THERE IS A VERY HEAVY SWITCH IN THE ROOM BELOW THAT DEACTIVATES PERSES'S ROBOTIC ARMY. YOU AND CODEX SMASH IT!
WE CAN DO THAT!
UM, WHAT DO I DO AGAIN?
NOTHING! ABSOLUTELY NOTHING!
YOU'RE THE ONE WHO GOT US INTO THIS ENTIRE MESS TO BEGIN WITH, REMEMBER?!
THE LAST THING WE NEED FROM YOU IS ANOTHER SCREWUP!
JUST STAND THERE, LOOK STUPID, AND LET US HANDLE THIS! COME ON, DORKUS!
I REALLY COULD'VE USED YOUR SUPPORT THERE, DORKUS.
HUH? OH, UM. THERE, THERE, SIR.
PAT PAT PAT
THAT'S NOT WHAT I MEANT.

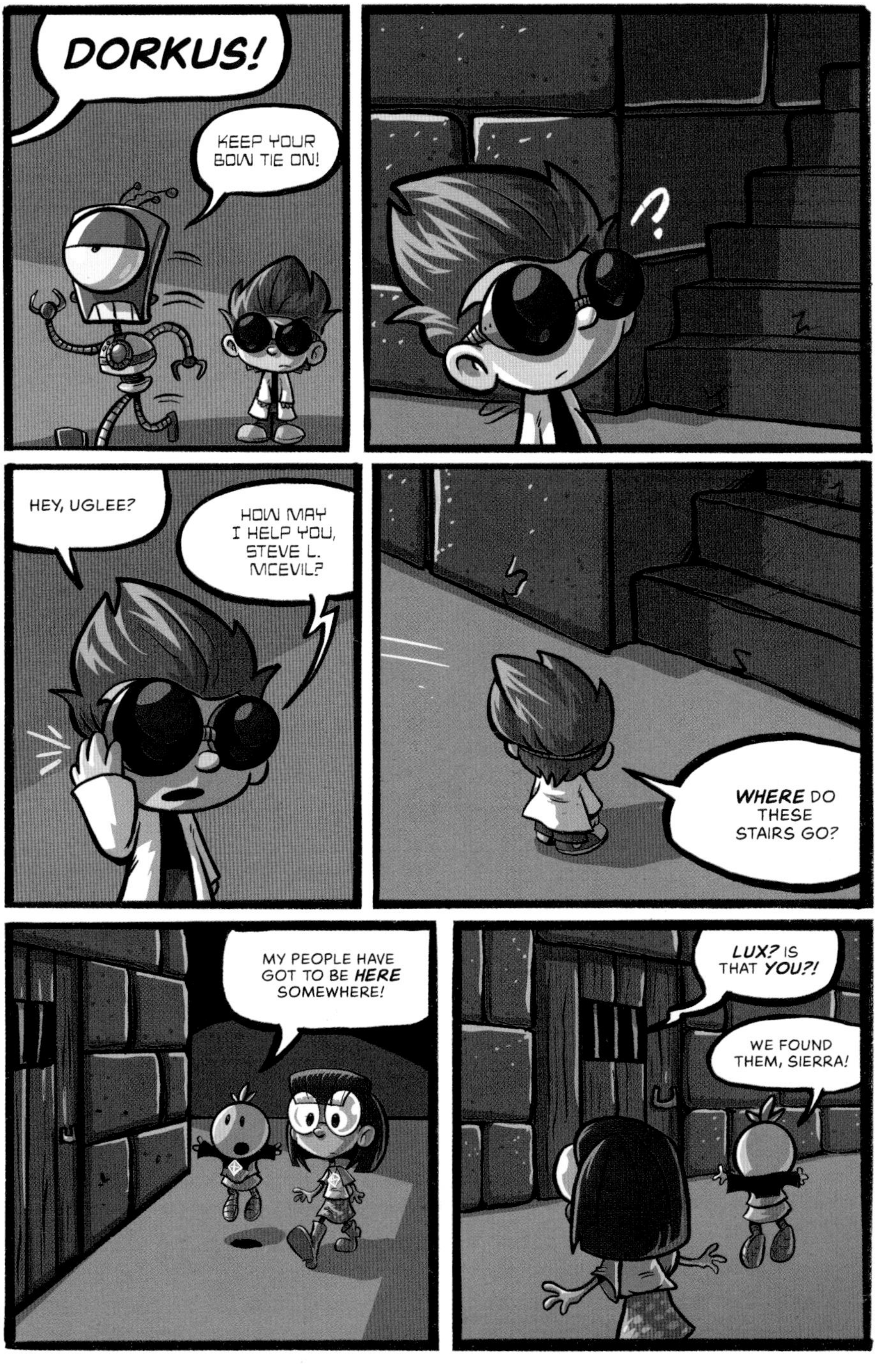
DORKUS!
KEEP YOUR BOW TIE ON!
?
HEY, UGLEE?
HOW MAY I HELP YOU, STEVE L. MCEVIL?
WHERE DO THESE STAIRS GO?
MY PEOPLE HAVE GOT TO BE HERE SOMEWHERE!
LUX? IS THAT YOU?!
WE FOUND THEM, SIERRA!

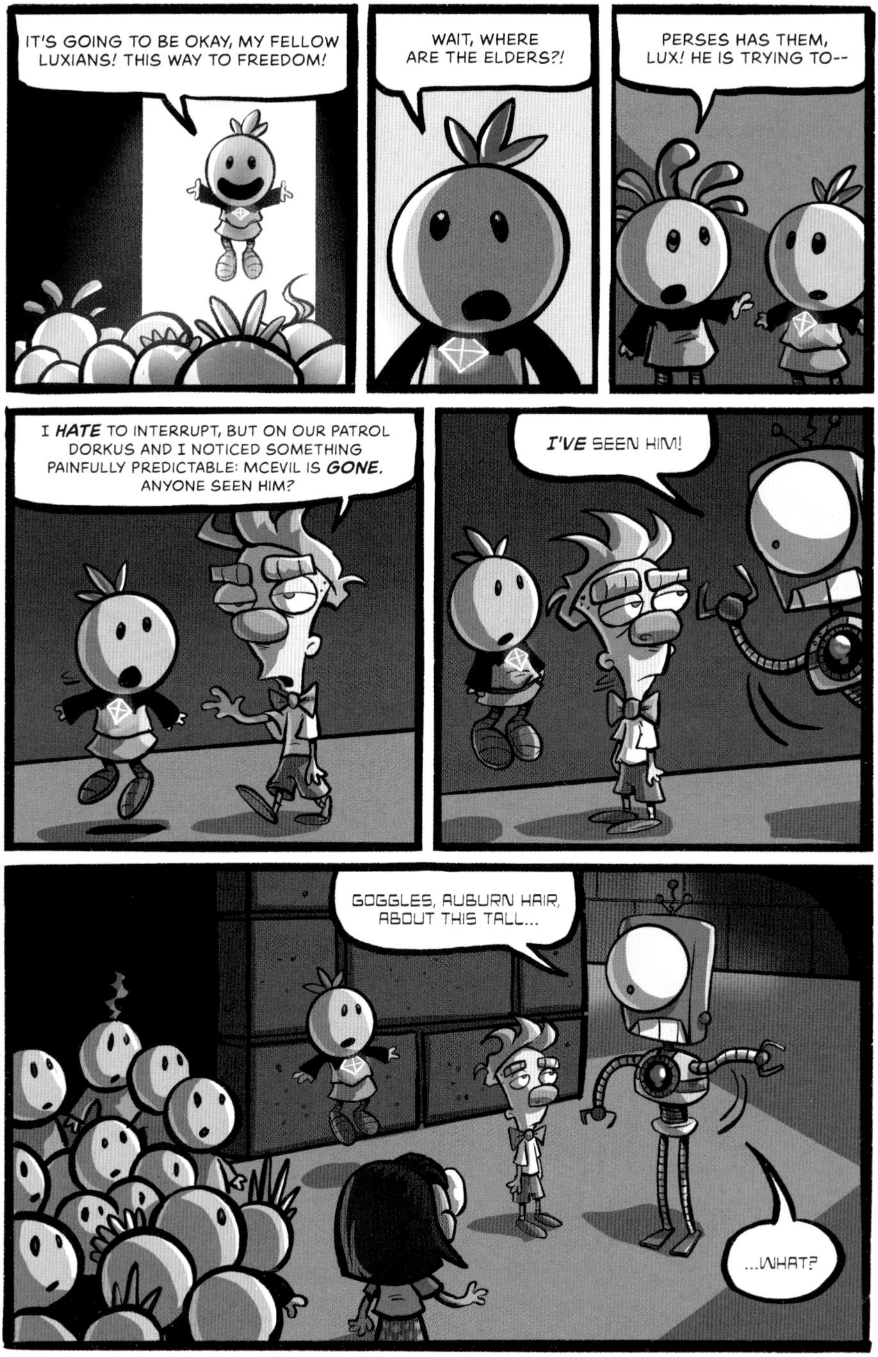
IT'S GOING TO BE OKAY, MY FELLOW LUXIANS! THIS WAY TO FREEDOM!
WAIT, WHERE ARE THE ELDERS?!
PERSES HAS THEM, LUX! HE IS TRYING TO--
I **HATE** TO INTERRUPT, BUT ON OUR PATROL DORKUS AND I NOTICED SOMETHING PAINFULLY PREDICTABLE: MCEVIL IS **GONE.** ANYONE SEEN HIM?
I'VE SEEN HIM!
GOGGLES, AUBURN HAIR, ABOUT THIS TALL...
...WHAT?

CHAPTER 13

Talkin' Trash

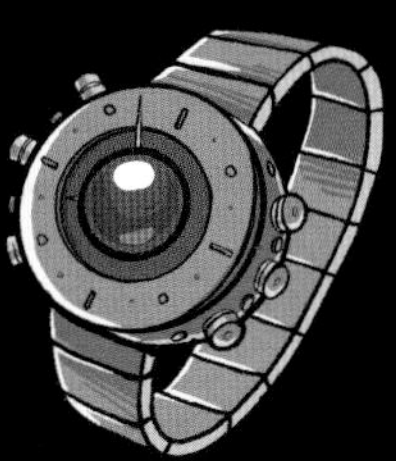

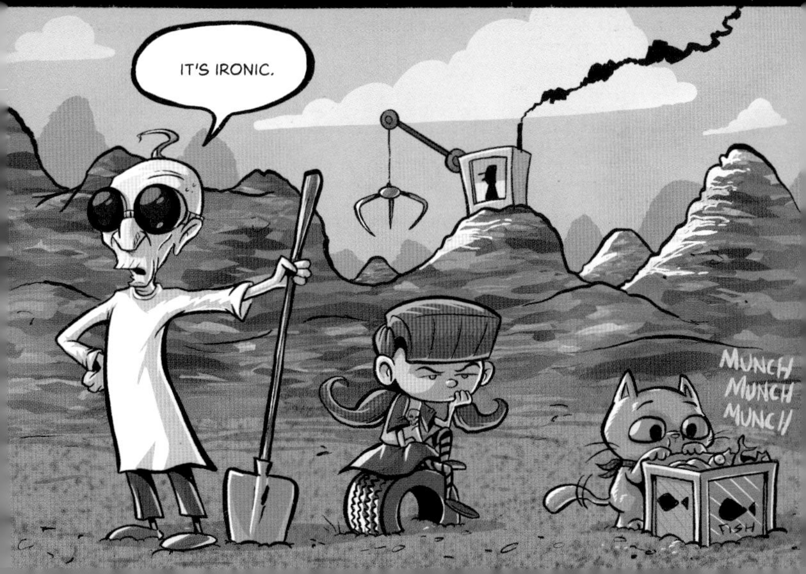
IT'S IRONIC.
MUNCH MUNCH MUNCH
FISH

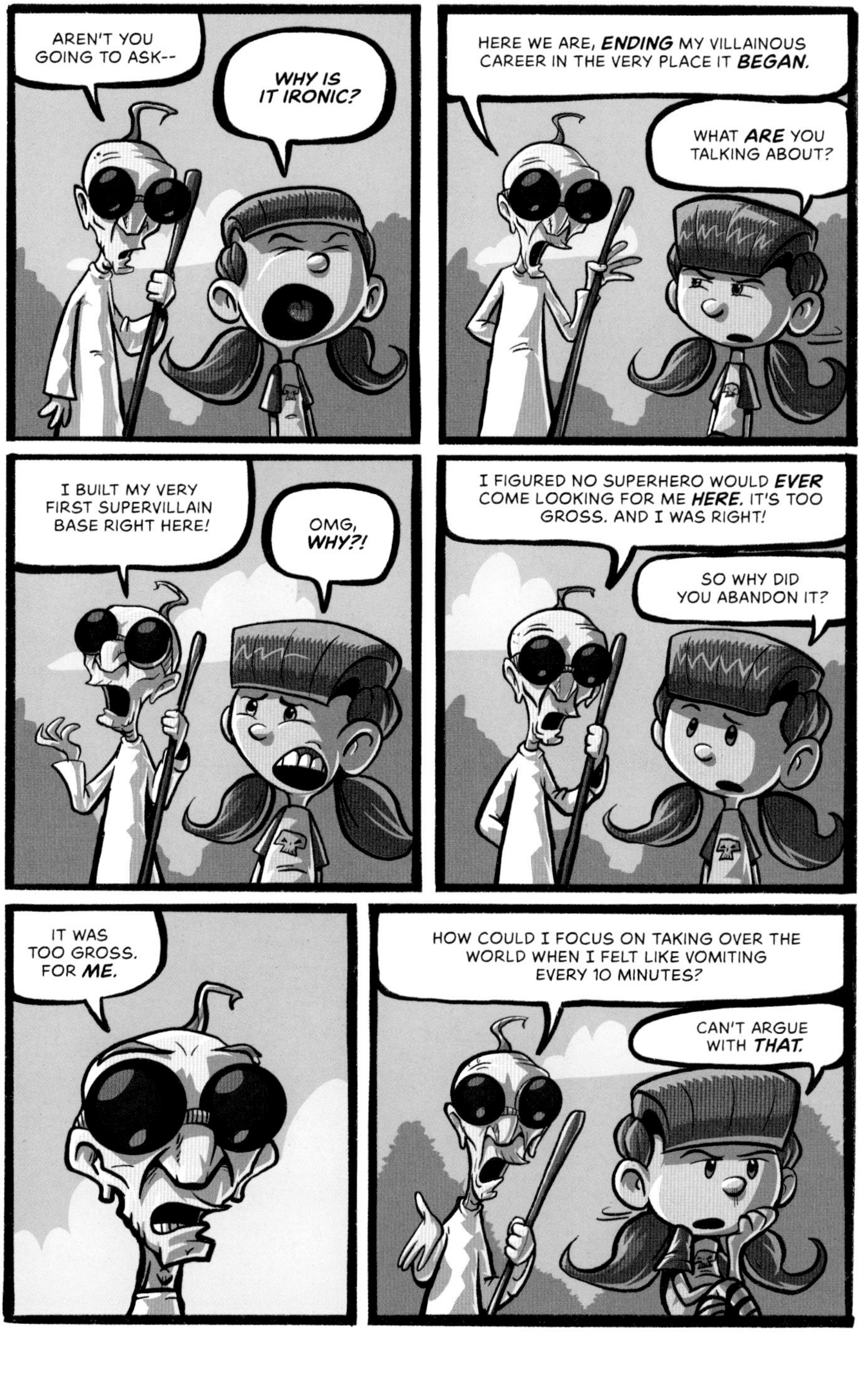
AREN'T YOU GOING TO ASK--
WHY IS IT IRONIC?
HERE WE ARE, ENDING MY VILLAINOUS CAREER IN THE VERY PLACE IT BEGAN.
WHAT ARE YOU TALKING ABOUT?
I BUILT MY VERY FIRST SUPERVILLAIN BASE RIGHT HERE!
OMG, WHY?!
I FIGURED NO SUPERHERO WOULD EVER COME LOOKING FOR ME HERE. IT'S TOO GROSS. AND I WAS RIGHT!
SO WHY DID YOU ABANDON IT?
IT WAS TOO GROSS. FOR ME.
HOW COULD I FOCUS ON TAKING OVER THE WORLD WHEN I FELT LIKE VOMITING EVERY 10 MINUTES?
CAN'T ARGUE WITH THAT.

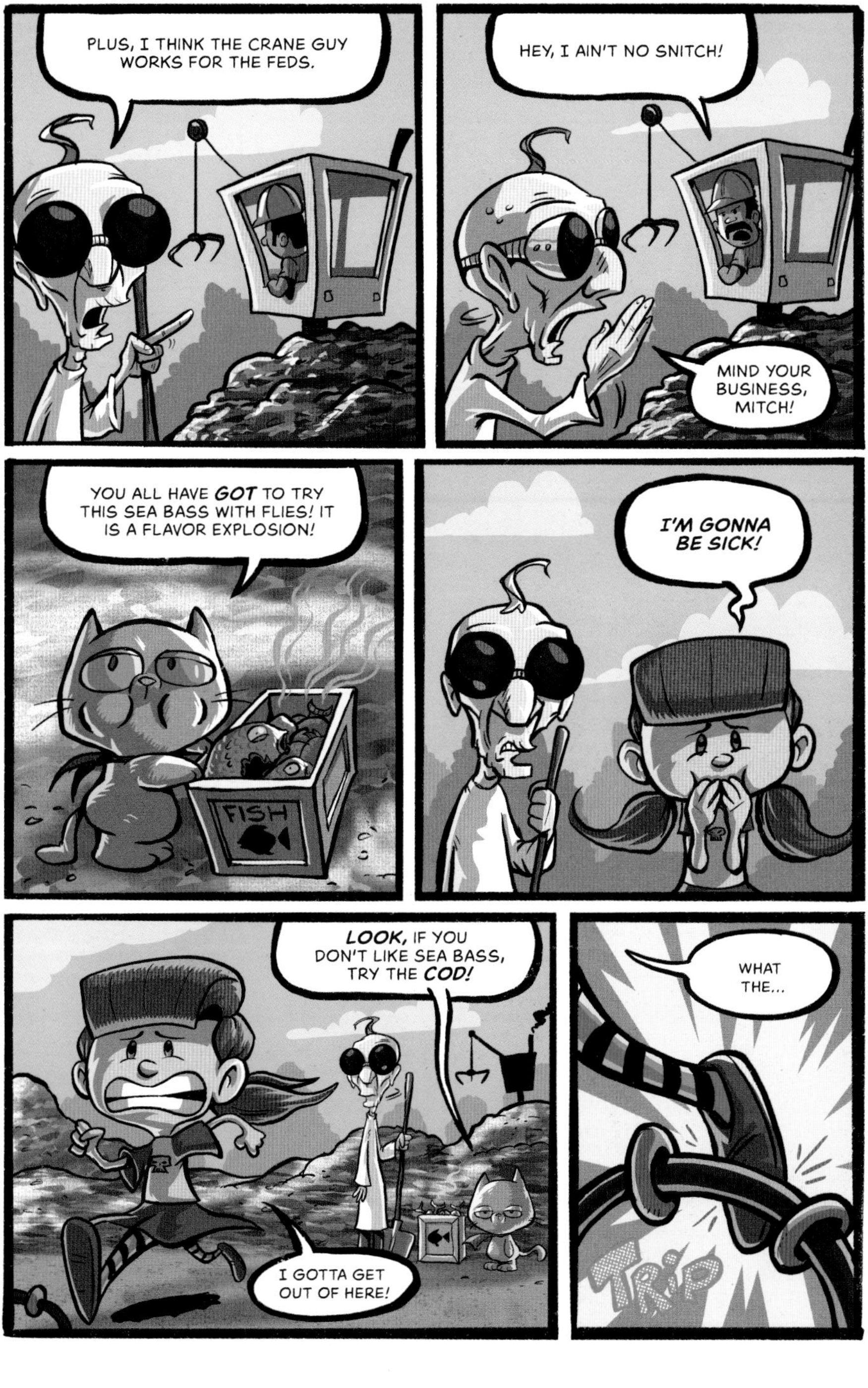
PLUS, I THINK THE CRANE GUY WORKS FOR THE FEDS.
HEY, I AIN'T NO SNITCH!
MIND YOUR BUSINESS, MITCH!
YOU ALL HAVE GOT TO TRY THIS SEA BASS WITH FLIES! IT IS A FLAVOR EXPLOSION!
FISH
I'M GONNA BE SICK!
LOOK, IF YOU DON'T LIKE SEA BASS, TRY THE COD!
I GOTTA GET OUT OF HERE!
WHAT THE...
TRIP

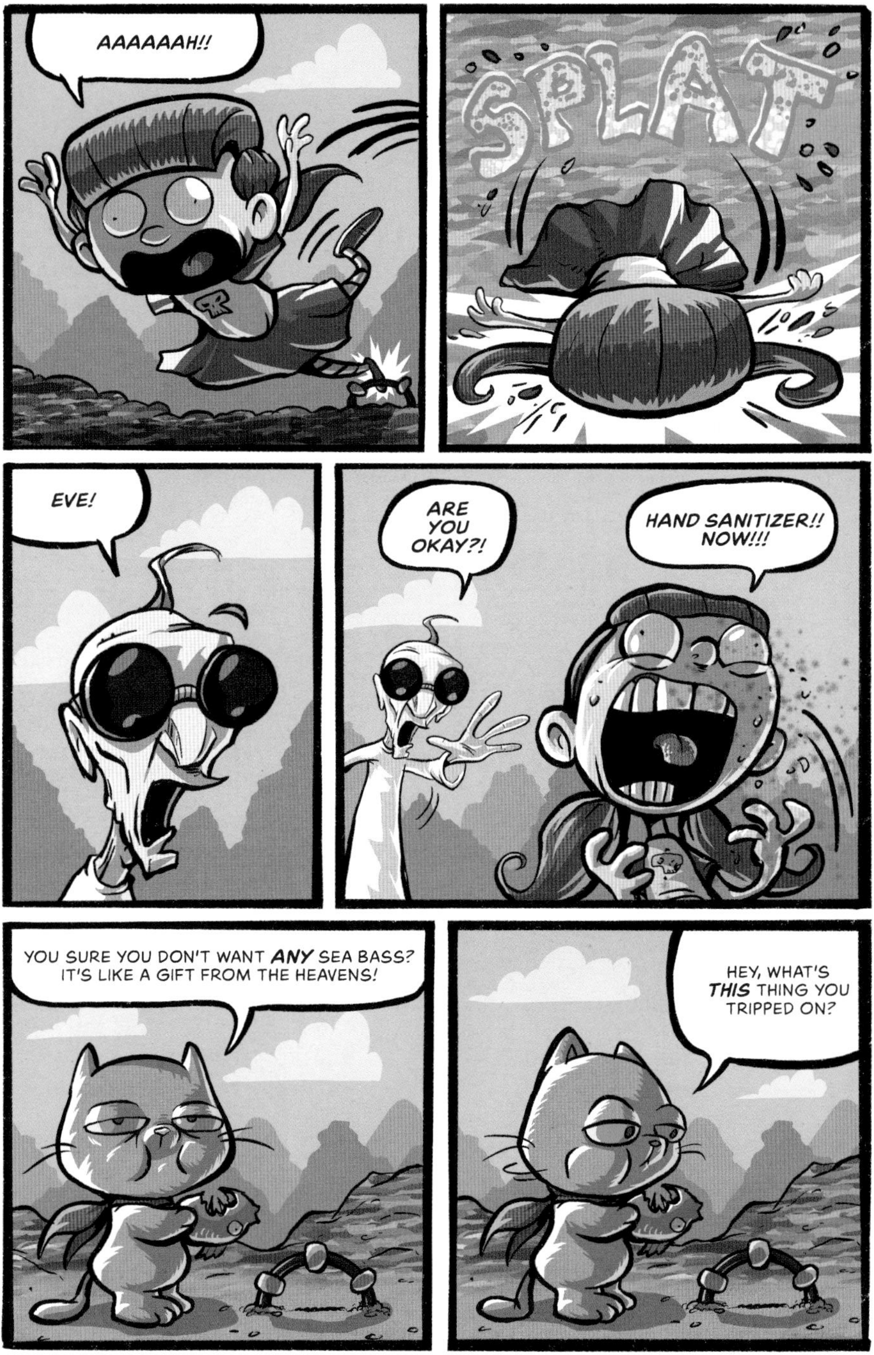
AAAAAAH!!
SPLAT
EVE!
ARE YOU OKAY?!
HAND SANITIZER!! NOW!!!
YOU SURE YOU DON'T WANT **ANY** SEA BASS? IT'S LIKE A GIFT FROM THE HEAVENS!
HEY, WHAT'S **THIS** THING YOU TRIPPED ON?

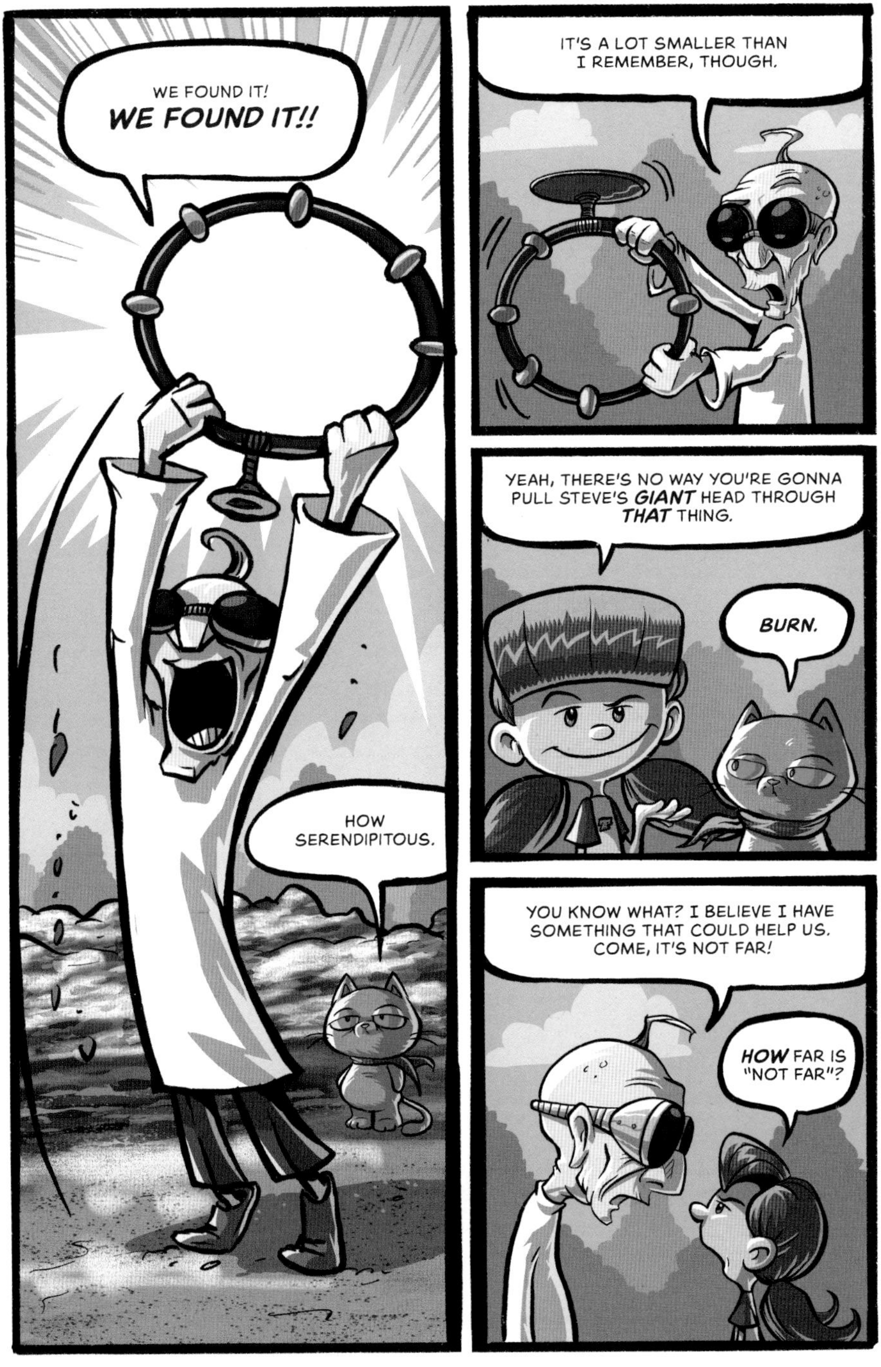
WE FOUND IT!
WE FOUND IT!!
HOW SERENDIPITOUS.
IT'S A LOT SMALLER THAN I REMEMBER, THOUGH.
YEAH, THERE'S NO WAY YOU'RE GONNA PULL STEVE'S GIANT HEAD THROUGH THAT THING.
BURN.
YOU KNOW WHAT? I BELIEVE I HAVE SOMETHING THAT COULD HELP US. COME, IT'S NOT FAR!
HOW FAR IS "NOT FAR"?

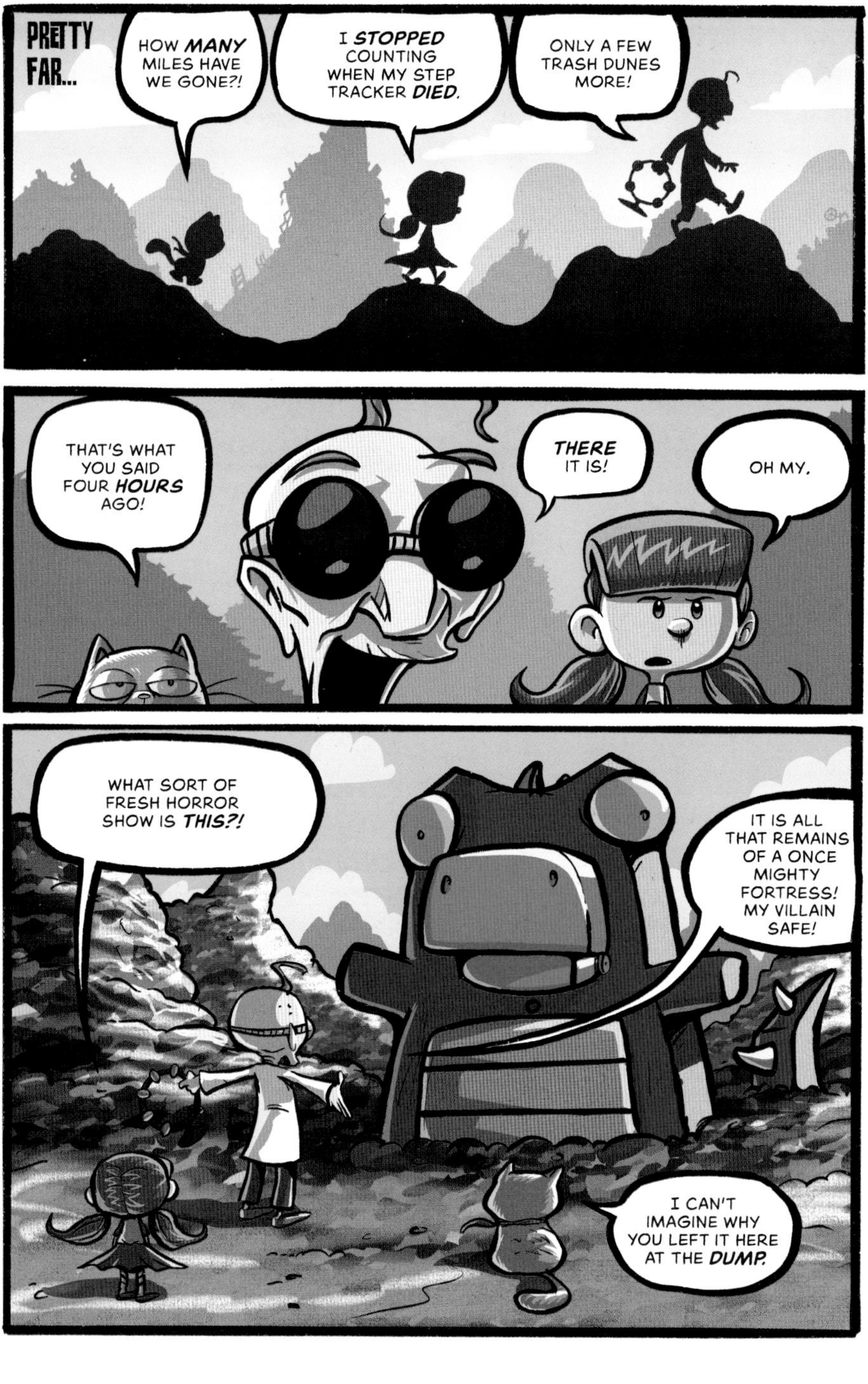
PRETTY FAR...
HOW MANY MILES HAVE WE GONE?!
I STOPPED COUNTING WHEN MY STEP TRACKER DIED.
ONLY A FEW TRASH DUNES MORE!
THAT'S WHAT YOU SAID FOUR HOURS AGO!
THERE IT IS!
OH MY.
WHAT SORT OF FRESH HORROR SHOW IS THIS?!
IT IS ALL THAT REMAINS OF A ONCE MIGHTY FORTRESS! MY VILLAIN SAFE!
I CAN'T IMAGINE WHY YOU LEFT IT HERE AT THE DUMP.

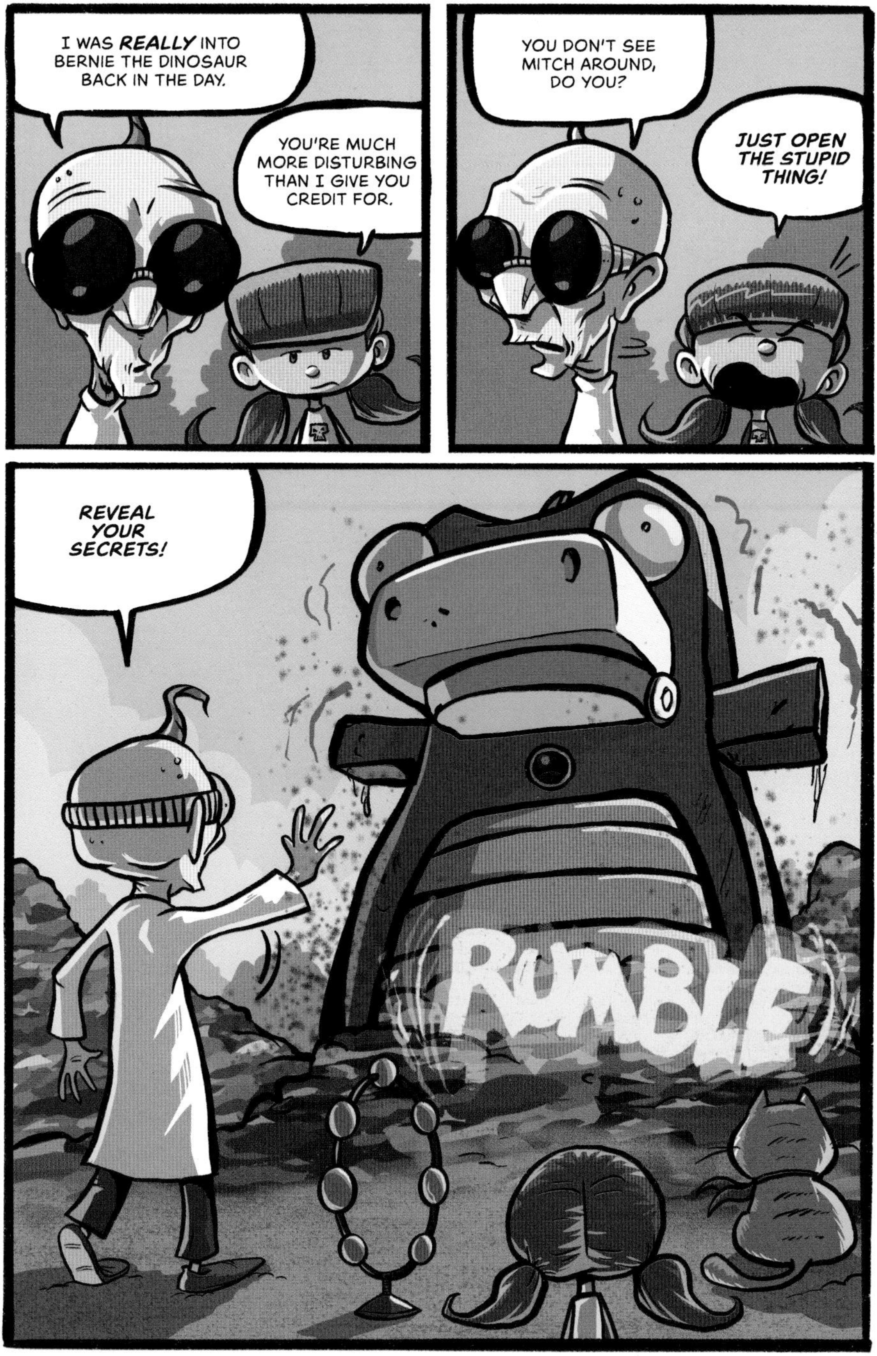
I WAS **REALLY** INTO BERNIE THE DINOSAUR BACK IN THE DAY.
YOU'RE MUCH MORE DISTURBING THAN I GIVE YOU CREDIT FOR.
YOU DON'T SEE MITCH AROUND, DO YOU?
JUST OPEN THE STUPID THING!
REVEAL YOUR SECRETS!
RUMBLE

IDENTIFY!

WELL, **THAT'S** GONNA GIVE ME NIGHTMARES FOR A MONTH.

SAME HERE.

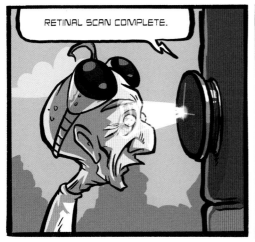

RETINAL SCAN COMPLETE.

WELCOME BACK, TIBERIUS MCEVIL.

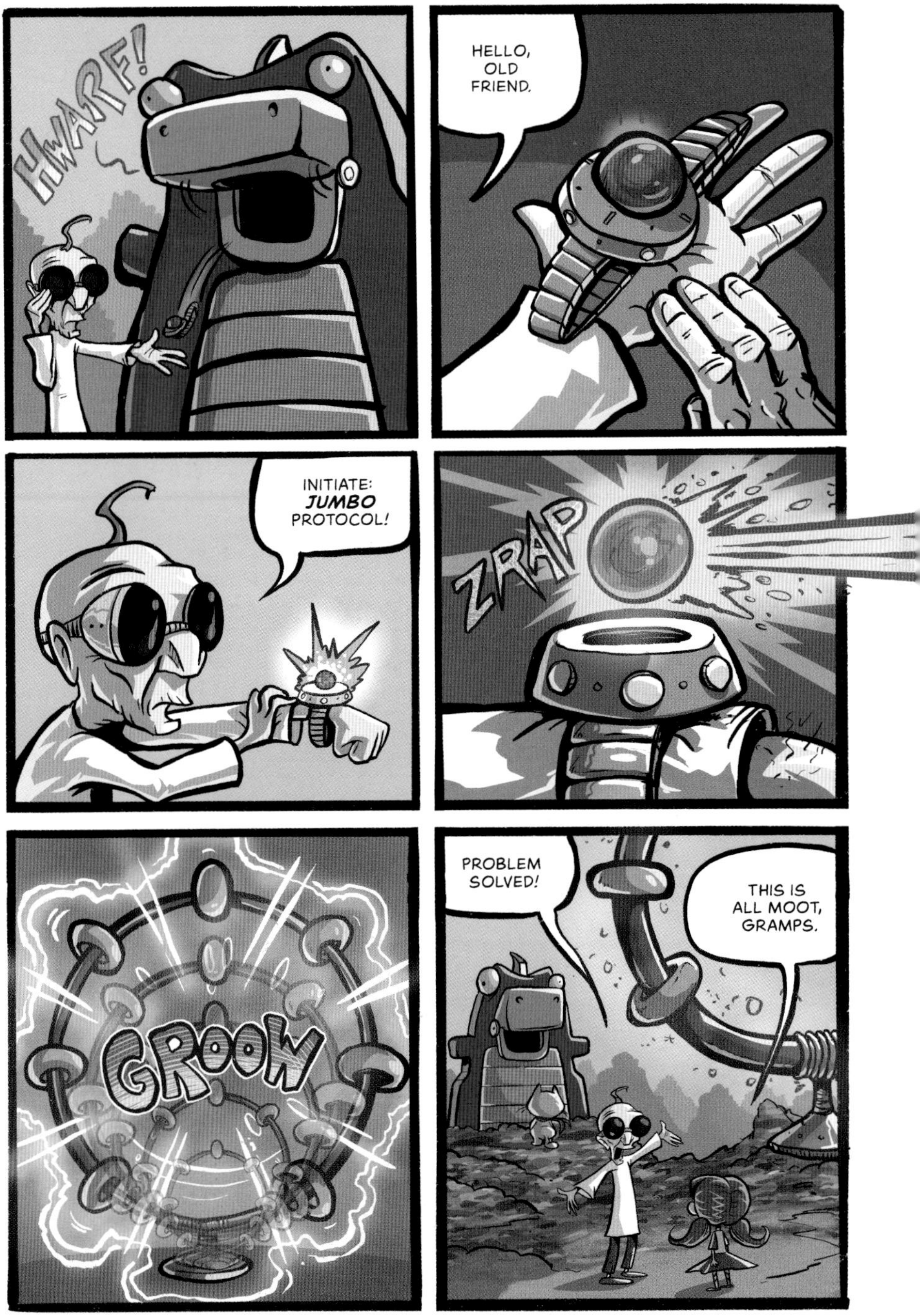
HWARF!
HELLO, OLD FRIEND.
INITIATE: ***JUMBO*** PROTOCOL!
ZRAP
GROOW
PROBLEM SOLVED!
THIS IS ALL MOOT, GRAMPS.

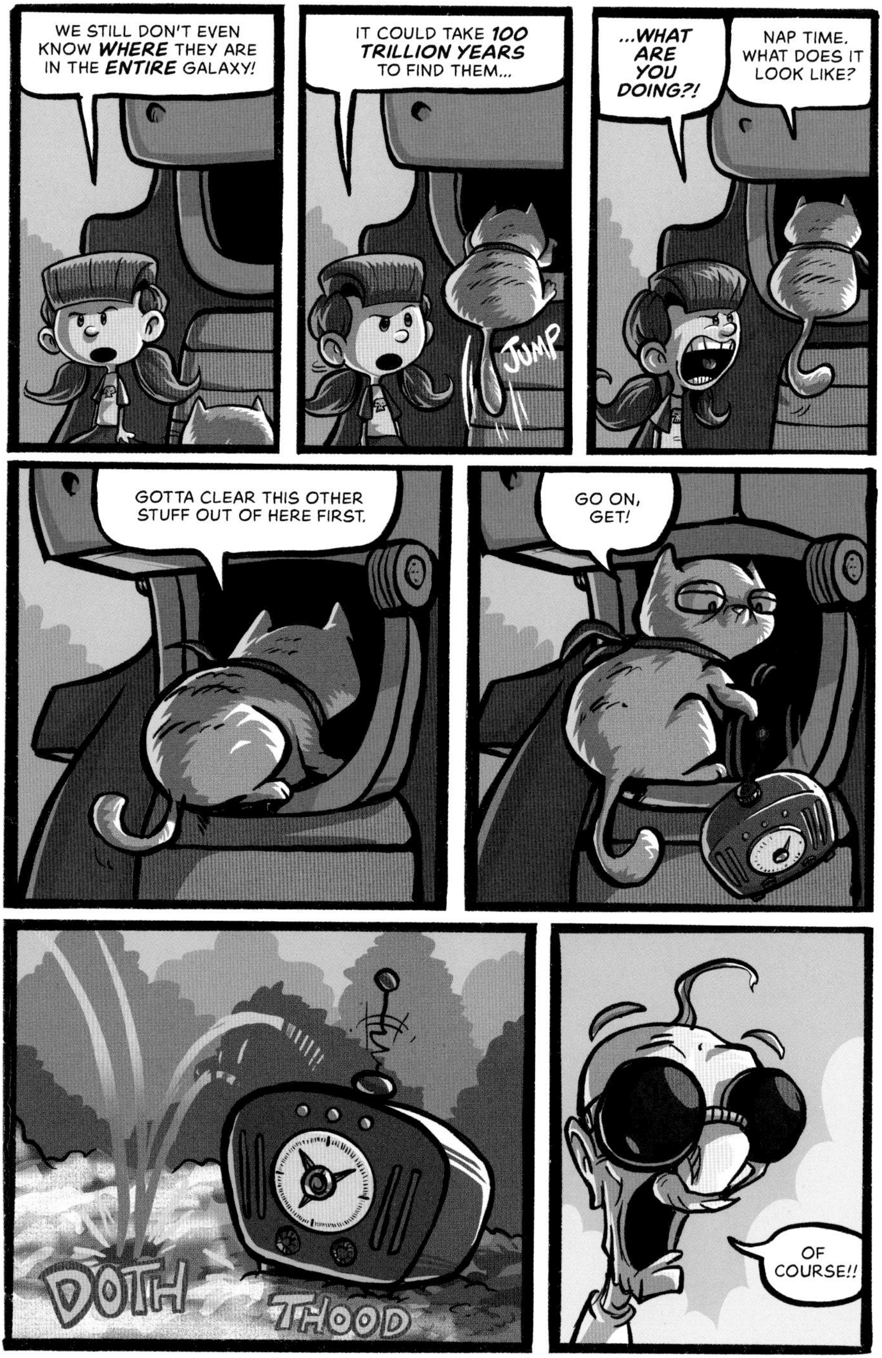
WE STILL DON'T EVEN KNOW **WHERE** THEY ARE IN THE **ENTIRE** GALAXY!
IT COULD TAKE **100 TRILLION YEARS** TO FIND THEM...
JUMP
...WHAT ARE YOU DOING?!
NAP TIME. WHAT DOES IT LOOK LIKE?
GOTTA CLEAR THIS OTHER STUFF OUT OF HERE FIRST.
GO ON, GET!
DOTH
THOOD
OF COURSE!!

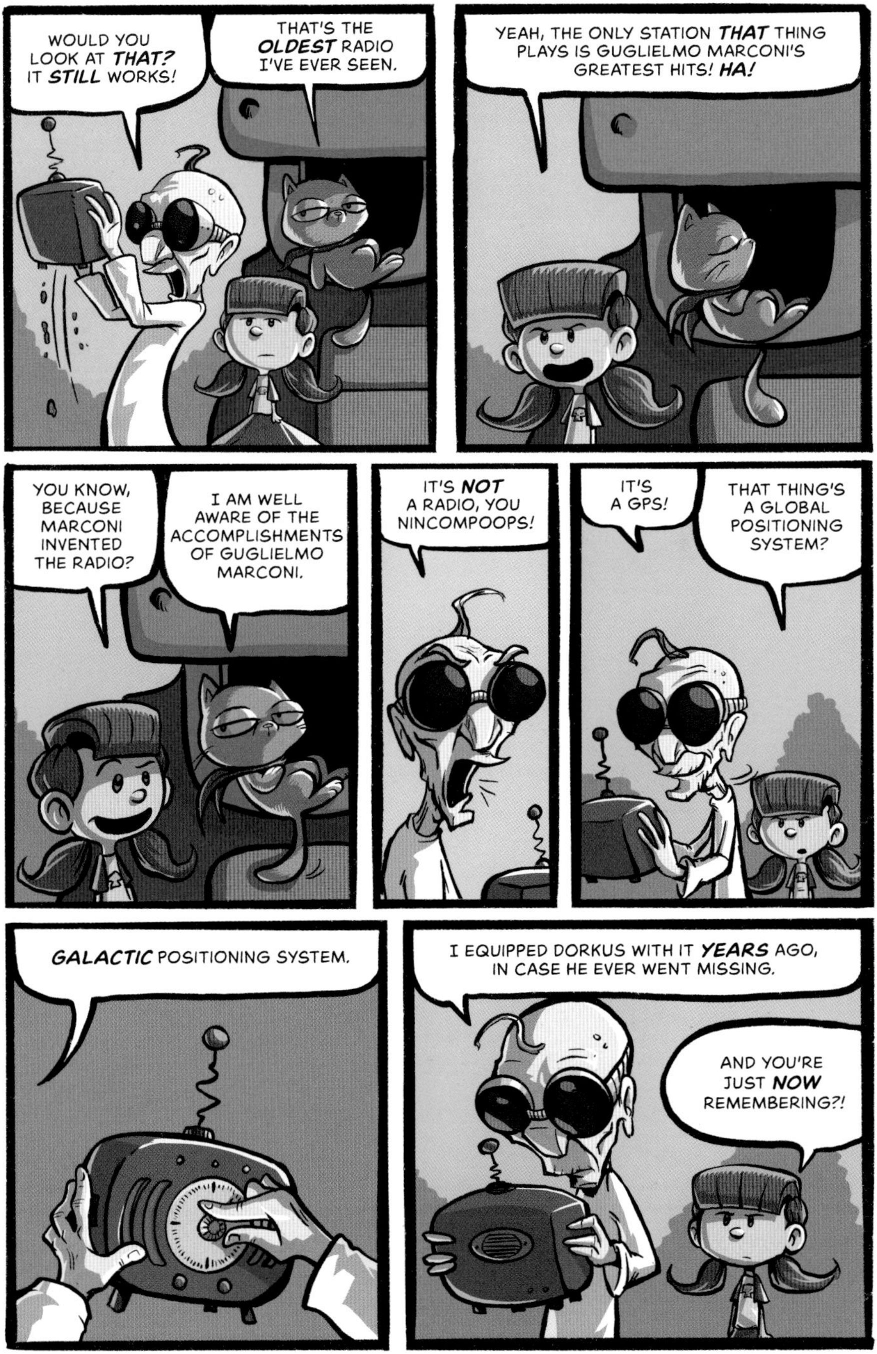
WOULD YOU LOOK AT THAT? IT STILL WORKS!
THAT'S THE OLDEST RADIO I'VE EVER SEEN.
YEAH, THE ONLY STATION THAT THING PLAYS IS GUGLIELMO MARCONI'S GREATEST HITS! HA!
YOU KNOW, BECAUSE MARCONI INVENTED THE RADIO?
I AM WELL AWARE OF THE ACCOMPLISHMENTS OF GUGLIELMO MARCONI.
IT'S NOT A RADIO, YOU NINCOMPOOPS!
IT'S A GPS!
THAT THING'S A GLOBAL POSITIONING SYSTEM?
GALACTIC POSITIONING SYSTEM.
I EQUIPPED DORKUS WITH IT YEARS AGO, IN CASE HE EVER WENT MISSING.
AND YOU'RE JUST NOW REMEMBERING?!

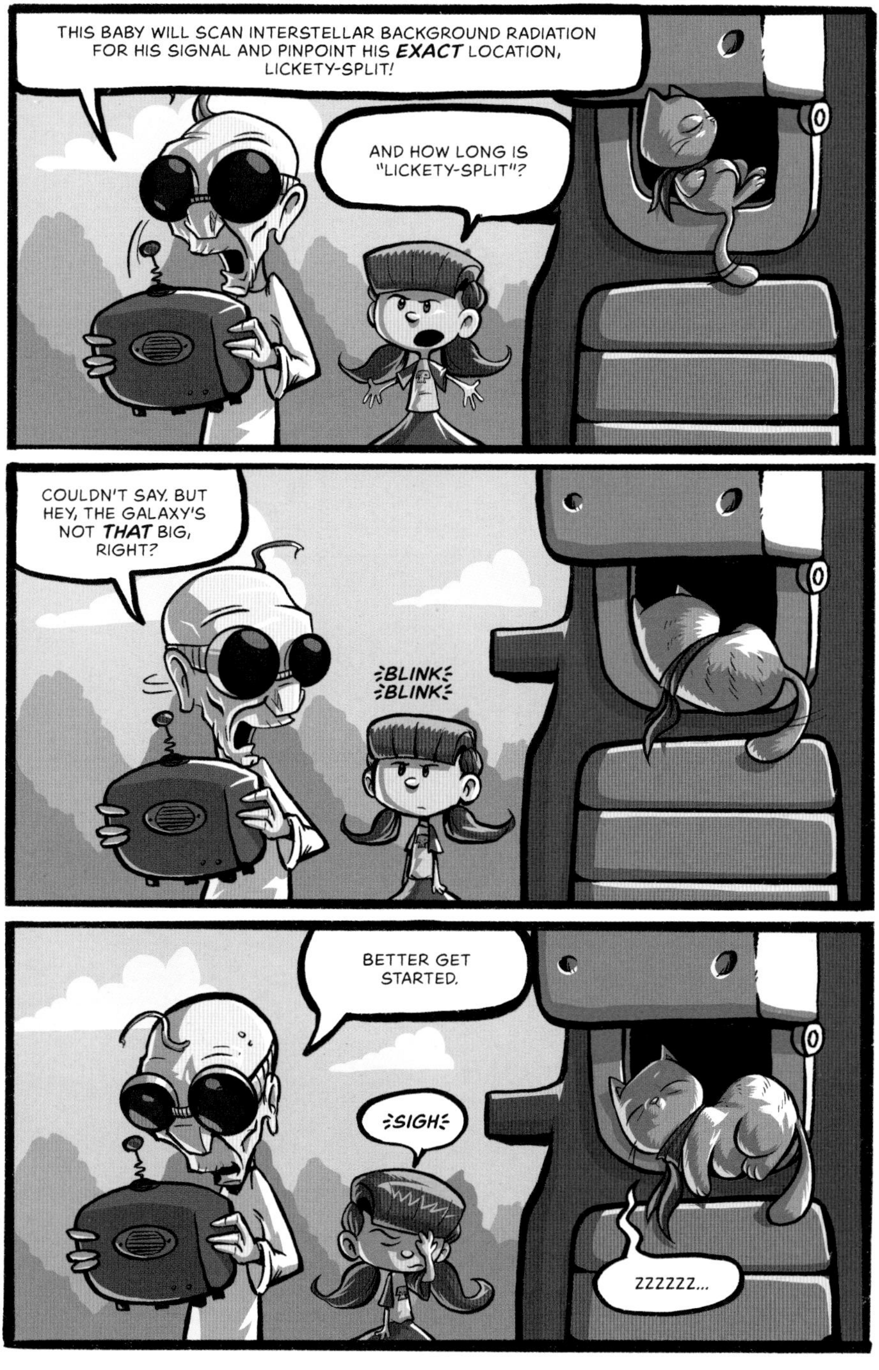
THIS BABY WILL SCAN INTERSTELLAR BACKGROUND RADIATION FOR HIS SIGNAL AND PINPOINT HIS **EXACT** LOCATION, LICKETY-SPLIT!
AND HOW LONG IS "LICKETY-SPLIT"?
COULDN'T SAY. BUT HEY, THE GALAXY'S NOT **THAT** BIG, RIGHT?
BLINK BLINK
BETTER GET STARTED.
SIGH
ZZZZZZ...

CHAPTER 14

Enter the Destroyer

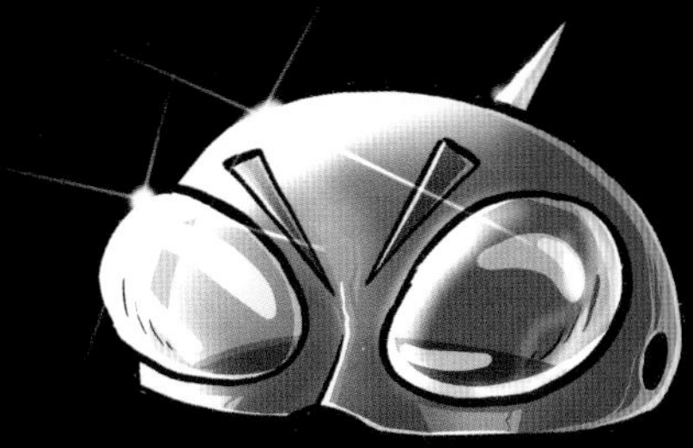

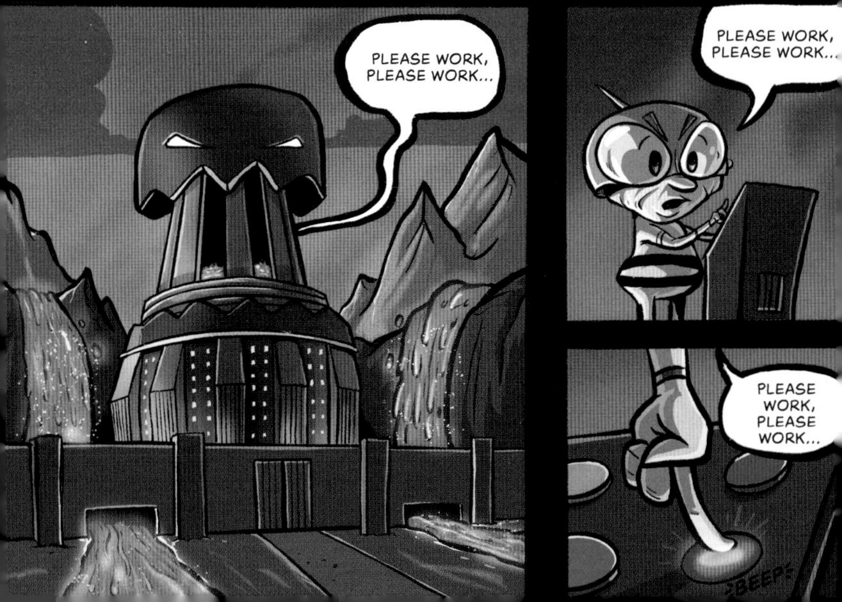
PLEASE WORK, PLEASE WORK...
PLEASE WORK, PLEASE WORK...
PLEASE WORK, PLEASE WORK...
BEEP

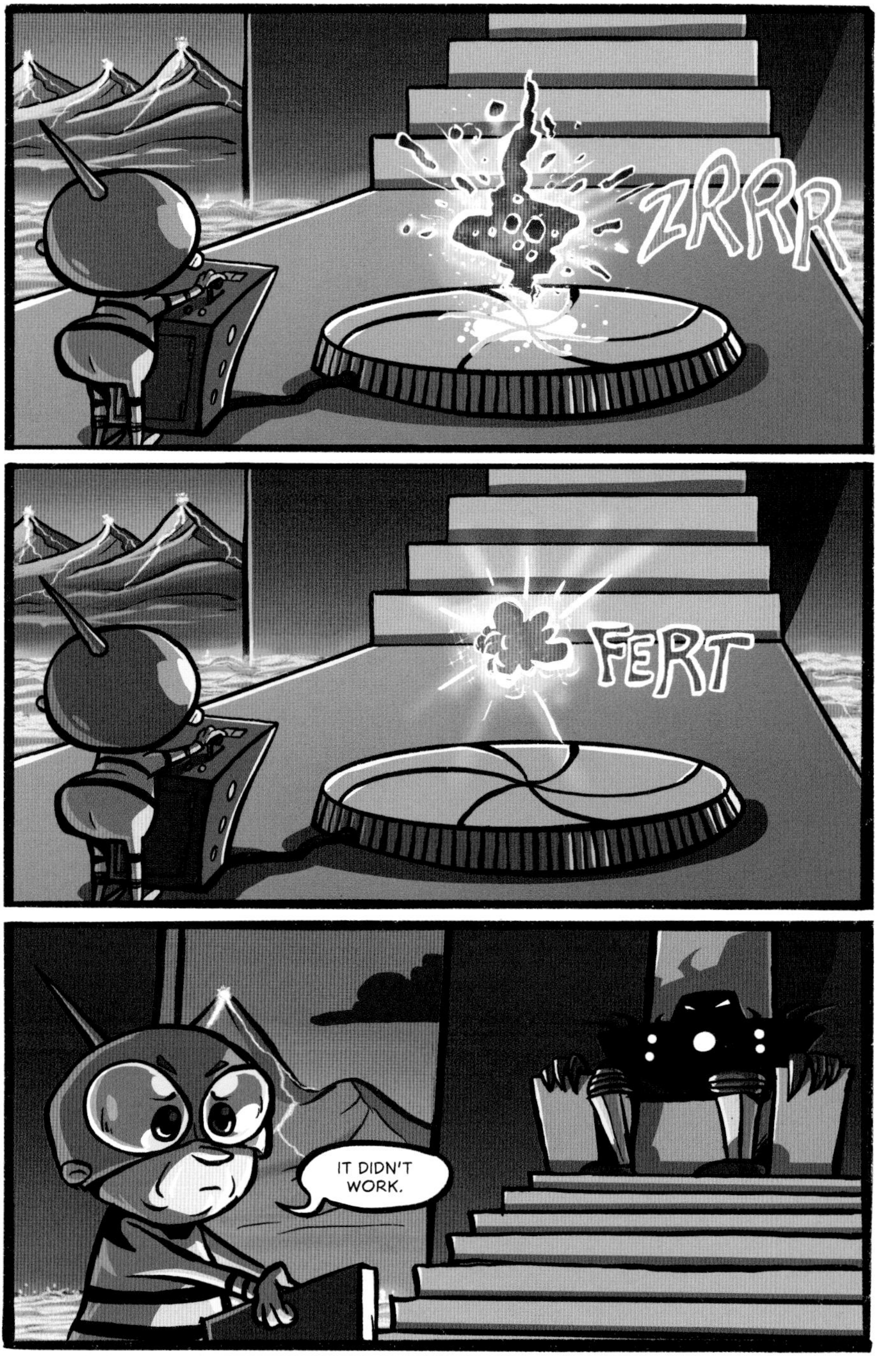
ZRRRR
FERT
IT DIDN'T WORK.

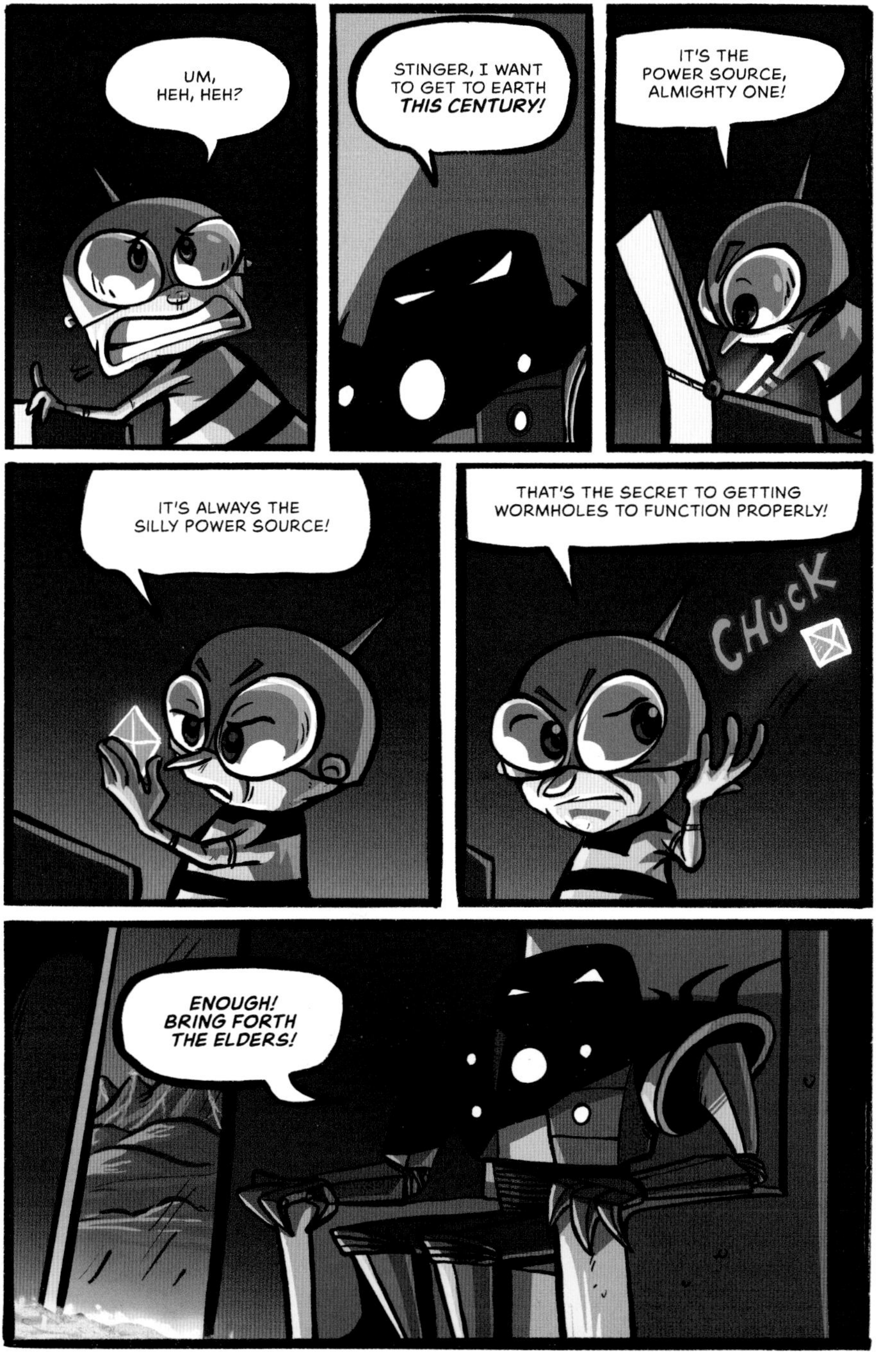

UM, HEH, HEH?
STINGER, I WANT TO GET TO EARTH *THIS CENTURY!*
IT'S THE POWER SOURCE, ALMIGHTY ONE!
IT'S ALWAYS THE SILLY POWER SOURCE!
THAT'S THE SECRET TO GETTING WORMHOLES TO FUNCTION PROPERLY!
CHUCK
ENOUGH! BRING FORTH THE ELDERS!

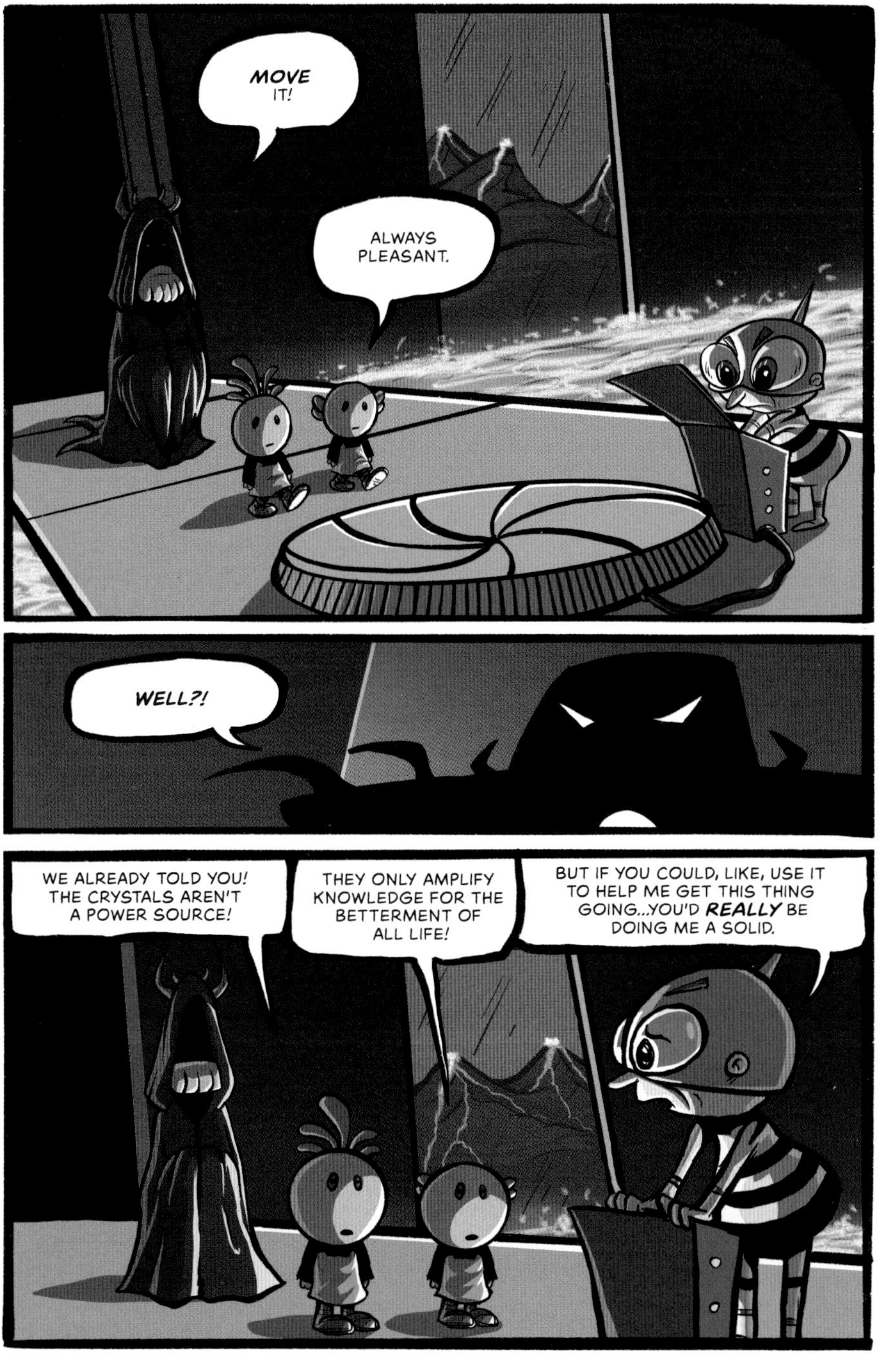
MOVE IT!
ALWAYS PLEASANT.
WELL?!
WE ALREADY TOLD YOU! THE CRYSTALS AREN'T A POWER SOURCE!
THEY ONLY AMPLIFY KNOWLEDGE FOR THE BETTERMENT OF ALL LIFE!
BUT IF YOU COULD, LIKE, USE IT TO HELP ME GET THIS THING GOING...YOU'D REALLY BE DOING ME A SOLID.

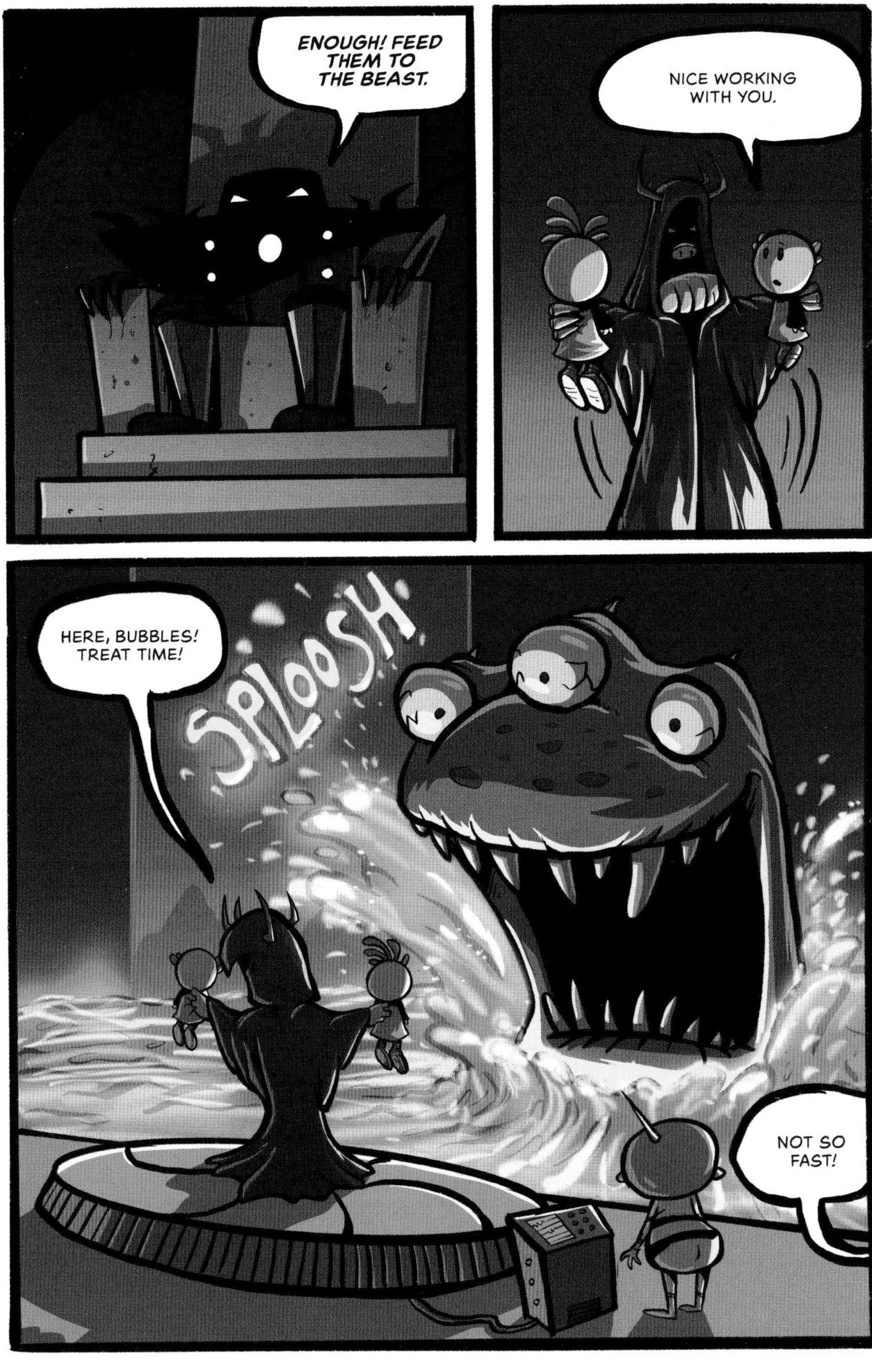
ENOUGH! FEED THEM TO THE BEAST.
NICE WORKING WITH YOU.
HERE, BUBBLES! TREAT TIME!
SPLOOSH
NOT SO FAST!

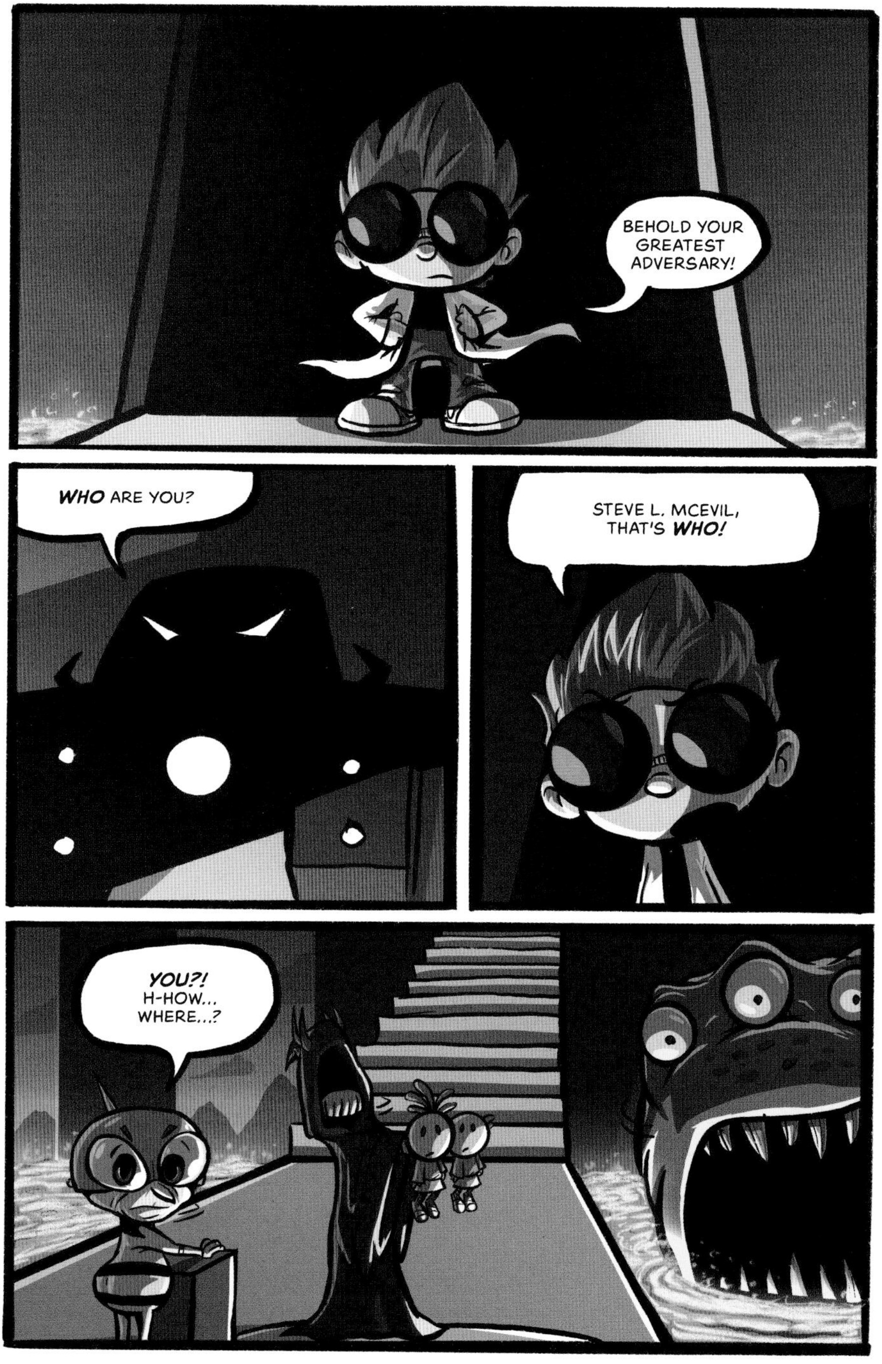
BEHOLD YOUR GREATEST ADVERSARY!
WHO ARE YOU?
STEVE L. MCEVIL, THAT'S WHO!
YOU?! H-HOW... WHERE...?

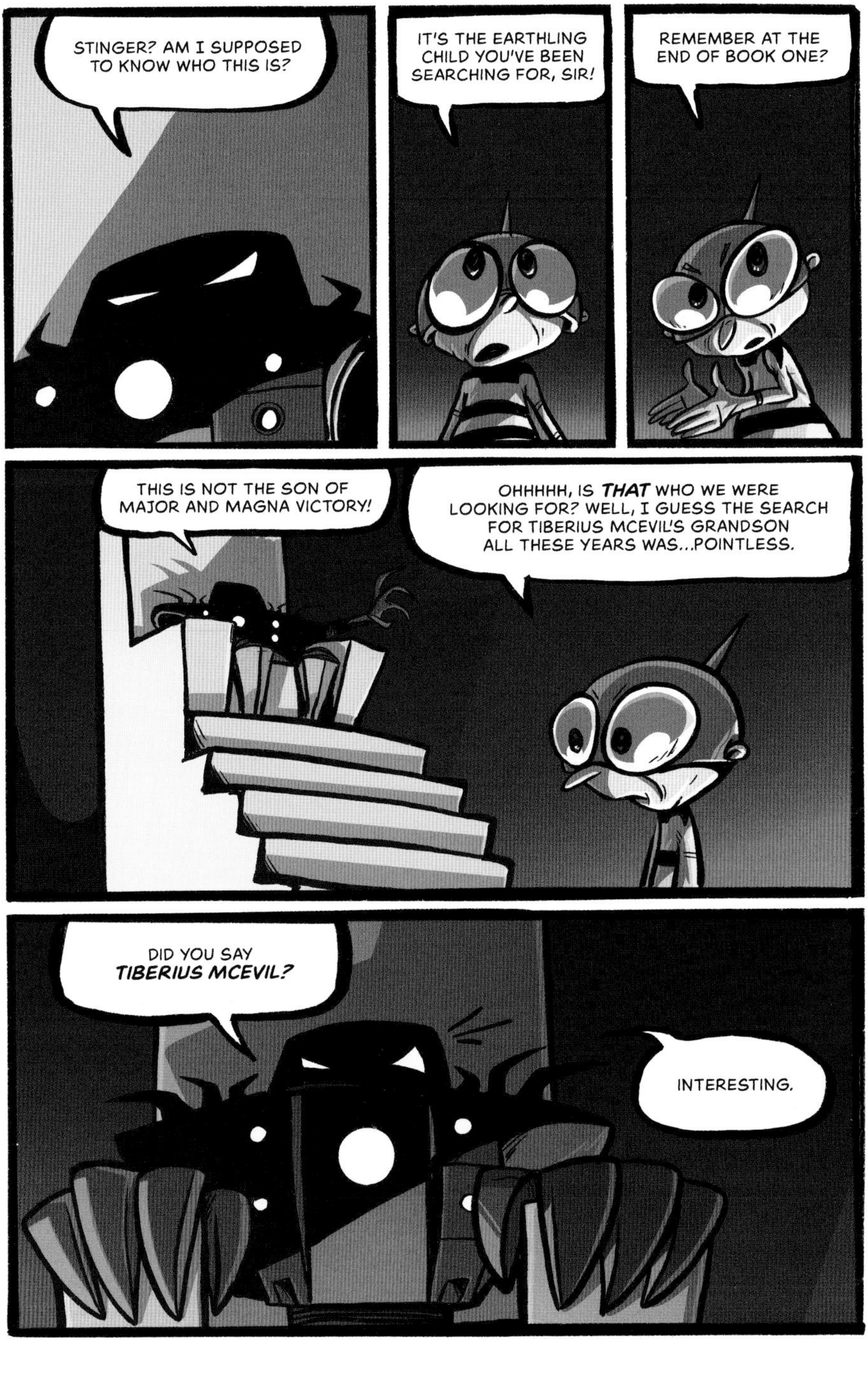
STINGER? AM I SUPPOSED TO KNOW WHO THIS IS?
IT'S THE EARTHLING CHILD YOU'VE BEEN SEARCHING FOR, SIR!
REMEMBER AT THE END OF BOOK ONE?
THIS IS NOT THE SON OF MAJOR AND MAGNA VICTORY!
OHHHHH, IS **THAT** WHO WE WERE LOOKING FOR? WELL, I GUESS THE SEARCH FOR TIBERIUS MCEVIL'S GRANDSON ALL THESE YEARS WAS...POINTLESS.
DID YOU SAY **TIBERIUS MCEVIL?**
INTERESTING.

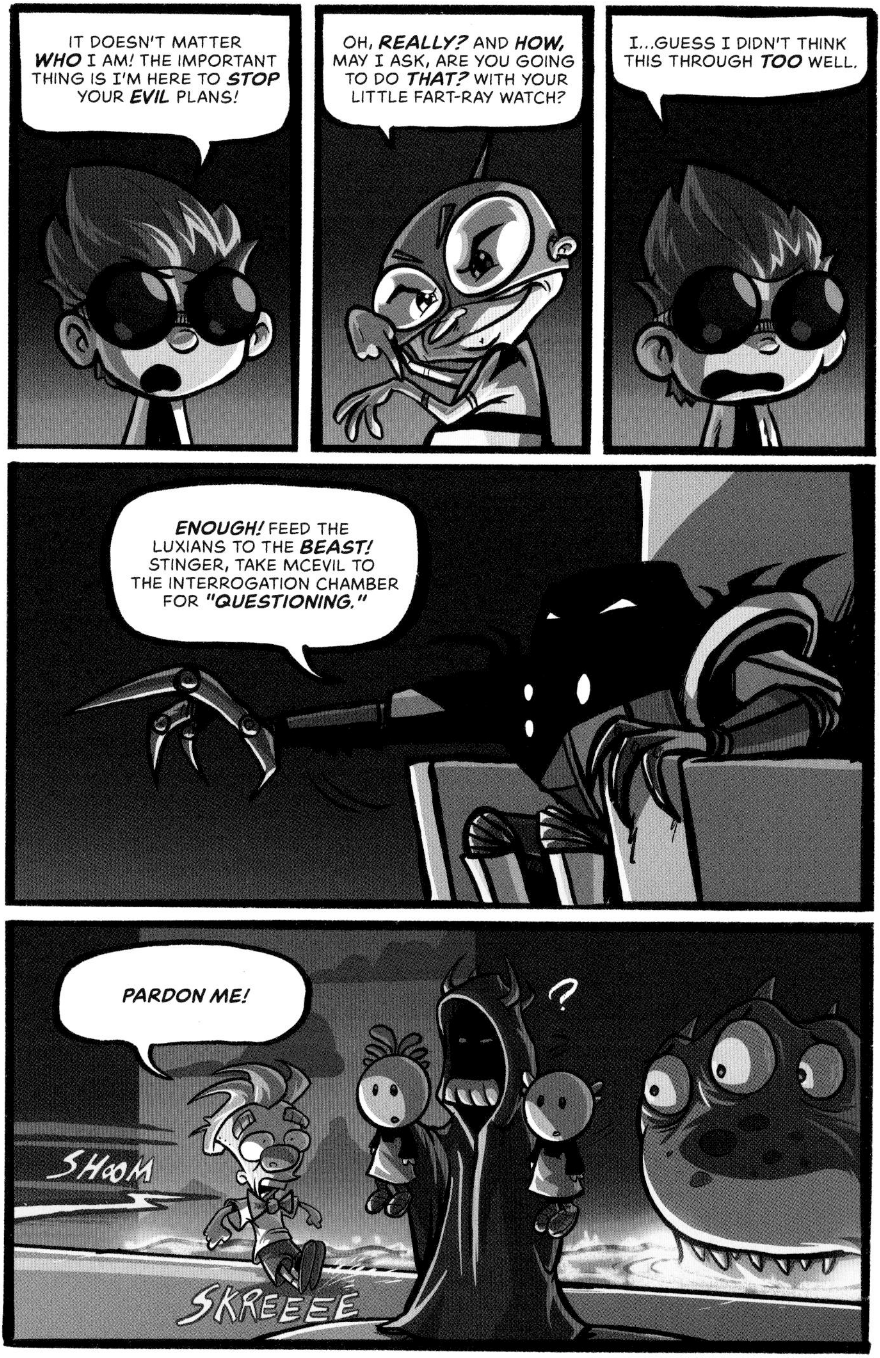
IT DOESN'T MATTER **WHO** I AM! THE IMPORTANT THING IS I'M HERE TO **STOP** YOUR **EVIL** PLANS!
OH, **REALLY?** AND **HOW,** MAY I ASK, ARE YOU GOING TO DO **THAT?** WITH YOUR LITTLE FART-RAY WATCH?
I...GUESS I DIDN'T THINK THIS THROUGH **TOO** WELL.
ENOUGH! FEED THE LUXIANS TO THE **BEAST!** STINGER, TAKE MCEVIL TO THE INTERROGATION CHAMBER FOR **"QUESTIONING."**
PARDON ME!
?
SHOOM
SKREEEEE

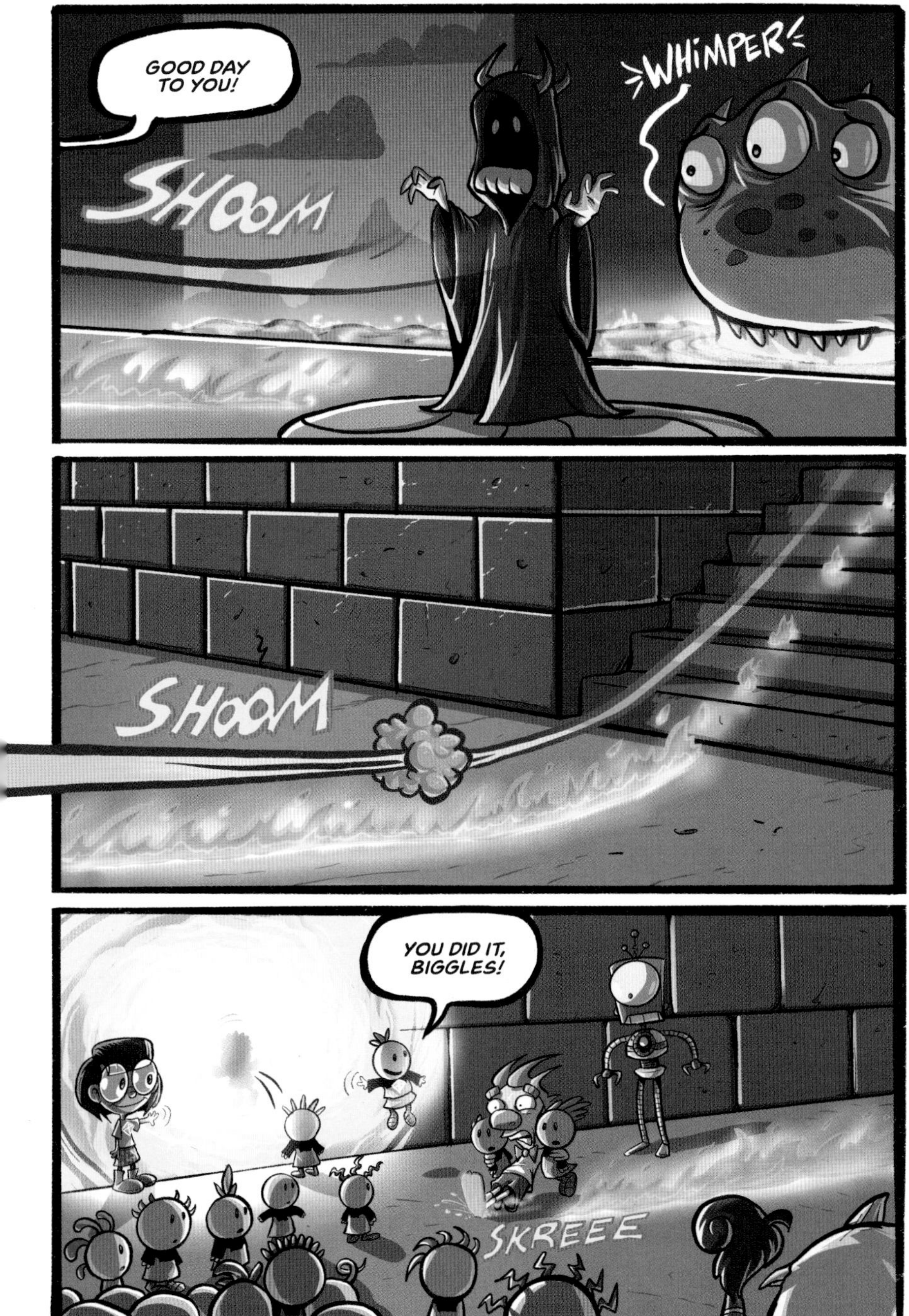
GOOD DAY TO YOU!
WHIMPER
SHOOM
SHOOM
YOU DID IT, BIGGLES!
SKREEE

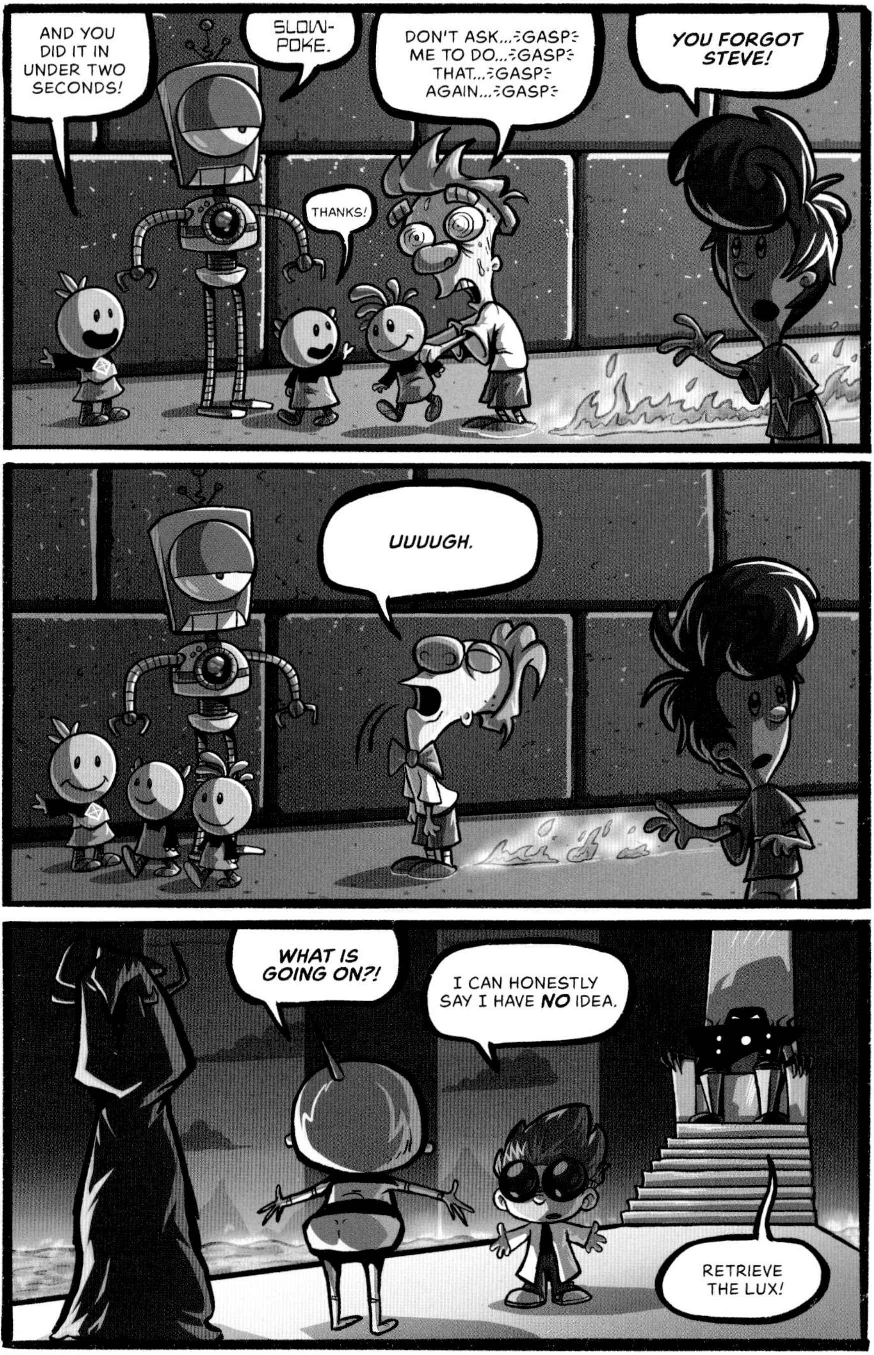
AND YOU DID IT IN UNDER TWO SECONDS!
SLOW-POKE.
THANKS!
DON'T ASK... ≈GASP≈ ME TO DO... ≈GASP≈ THAT... ≈GASP≈ AGAIN... ≈GASP≈
YOU FORGOT STEVE!
UUUUGH.
WHAT IS GOING ON?!
I CAN HONESTLY SAY I HAVE NO IDEA.
RETRIEVE THE LUX!

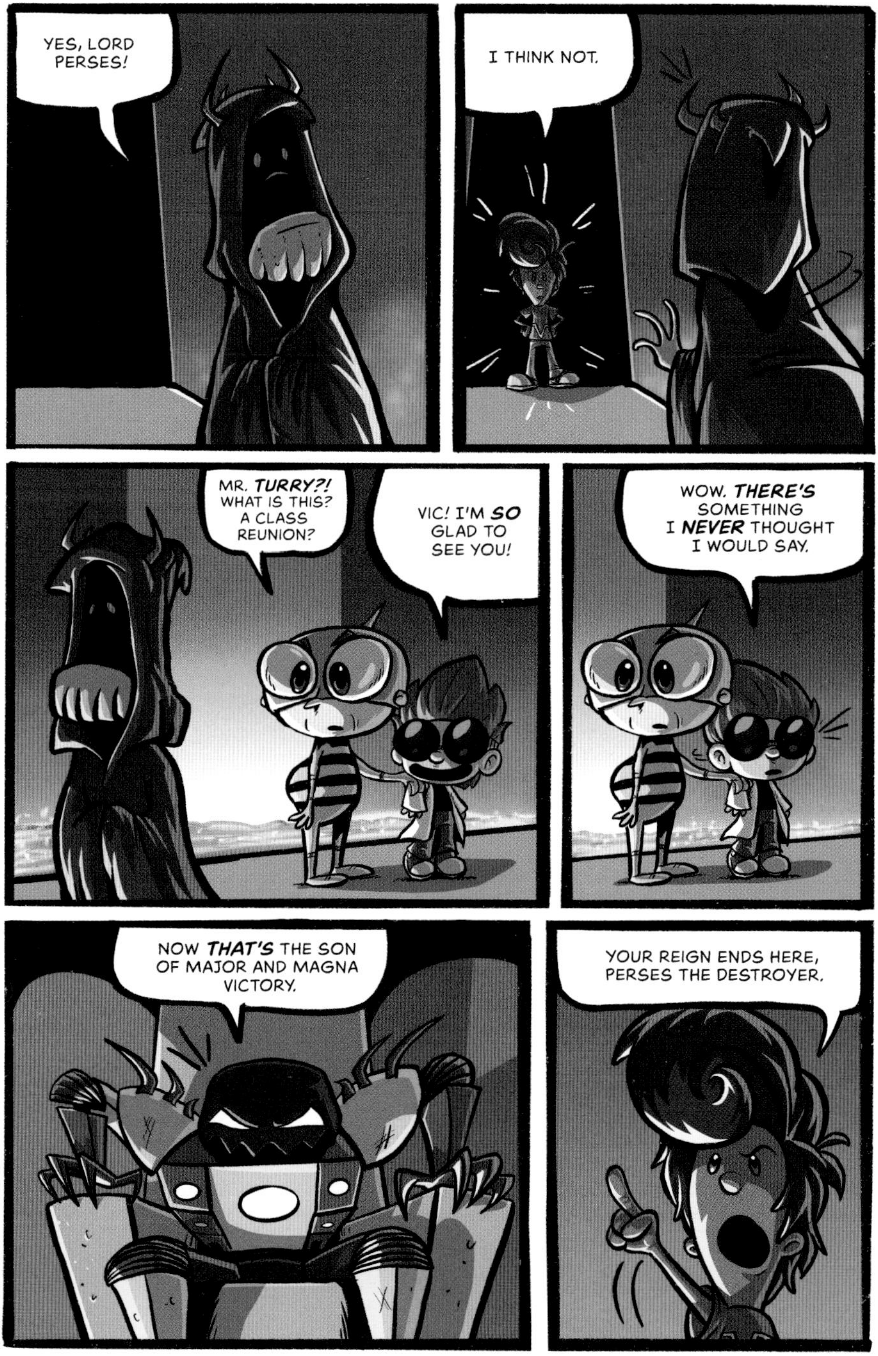

YES, LORD PERSES!
I THINK NOT.
MR. TURRY?! WHAT IS THIS? A CLASS REUNION?
VIC! I'M SO GLAD TO SEE YOU!
WOW. THERE'S SOMETHING I NEVER THOUGHT I WOULD SAY.
NOW THAT'S THE SON OF MAJOR AND MAGNA VICTORY.
YOUR REIGN ENDS HERE, PERSES THE DESTROYER.

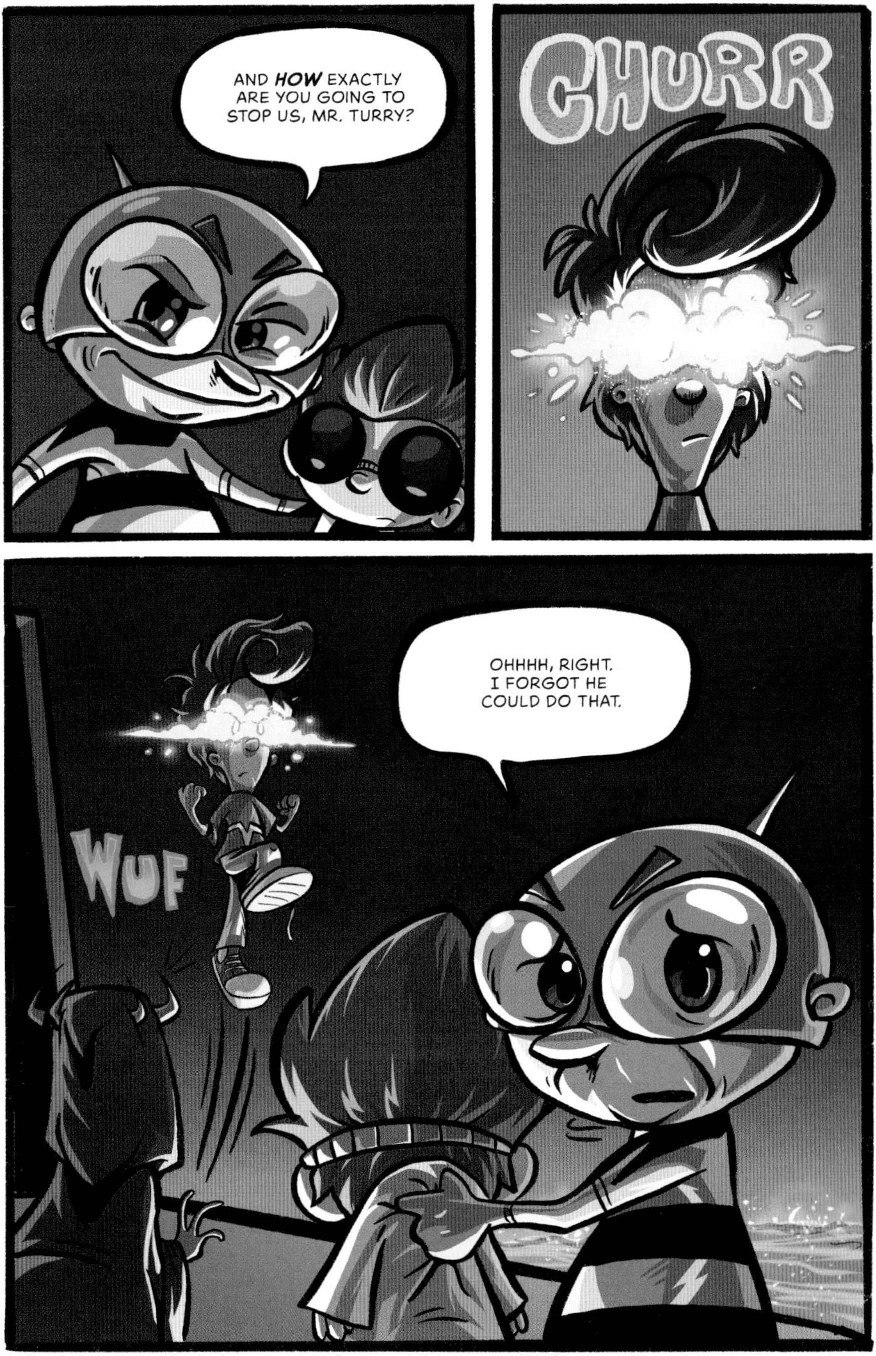
AND HOW EXACTLY ARE YOU GOING TO STOP US, MR. TURRY?
CHURR
OHHHH, RIGHT. I FORGOT HE COULD DO THAT.
WUF

CHAPTER 15
War and Pieces

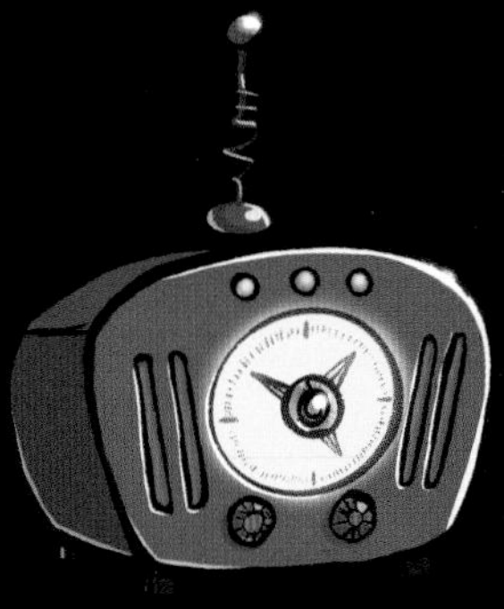

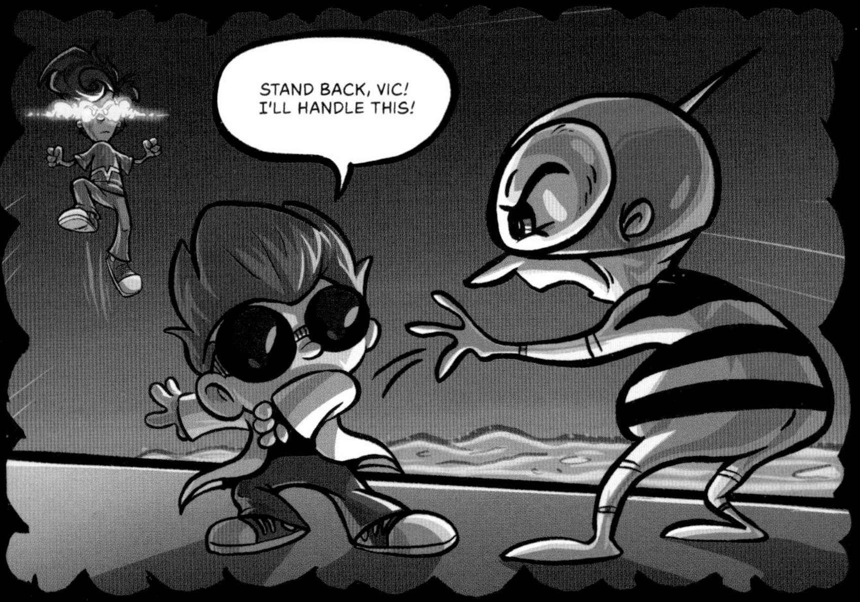
STAND BACK, VIC! I'LL HANDLE THIS!

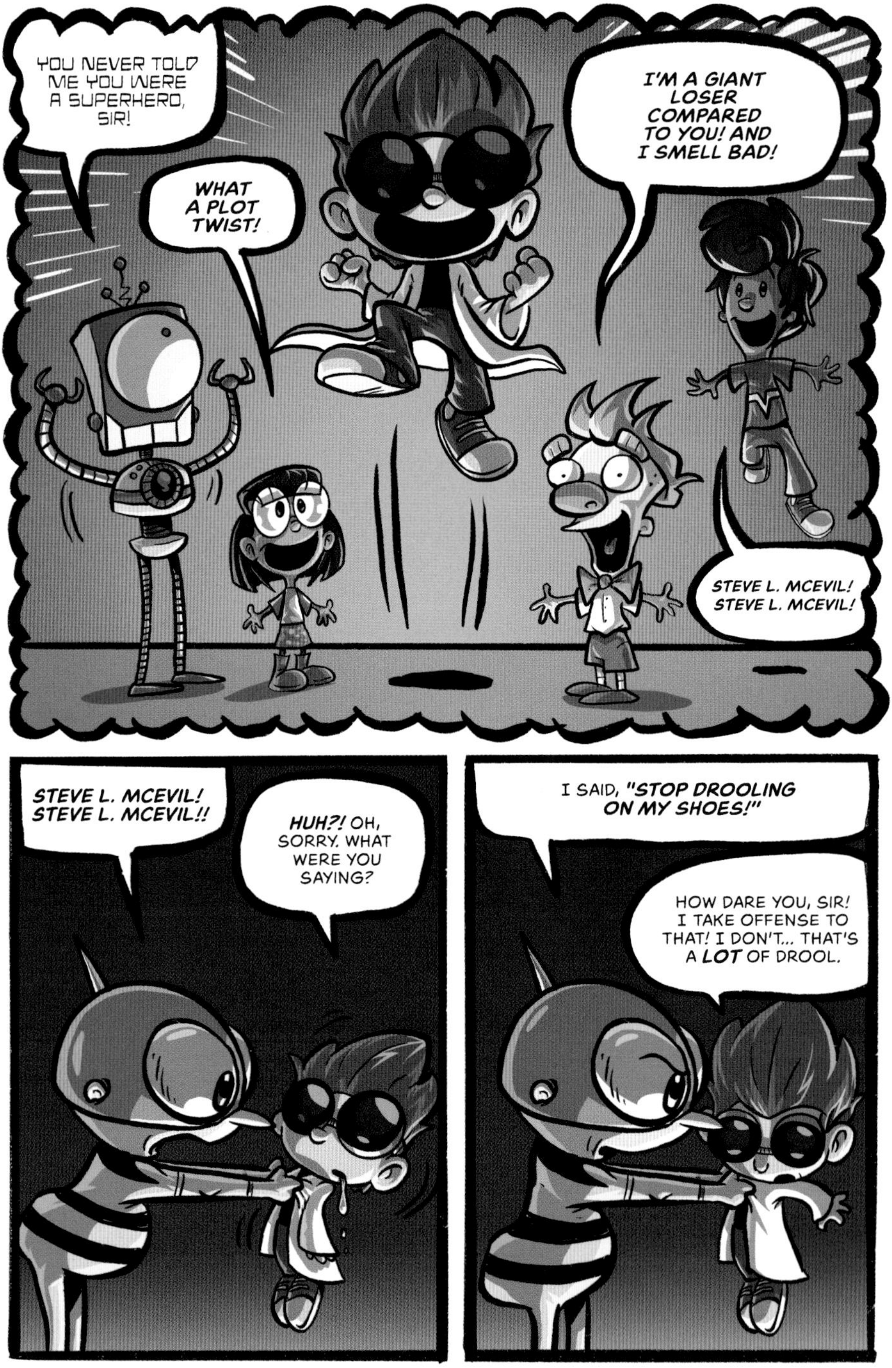
YOU NEVER TOLD ME YOU WERE A SUPERHERO, SIR!
WHAT A PLOT TWIST!
I'M A GIANT LOSER COMPARED TO YOU! AND I SMELL BAD!
STEVE L. MCEVIL! STEVE L. MCEVIL!
STEVE L. MCEVIL! STEVE L. MCEVIL!!
HUH?! OH, SORRY. WHAT WERE YOU SAYING?
I SAID, "STOP DROOLING ON MY SHOES!"
HOW DARE YOU, SIR! I TAKE OFFENSE TO THAT! I DON'T... THAT'S A LOT OF DROOL.

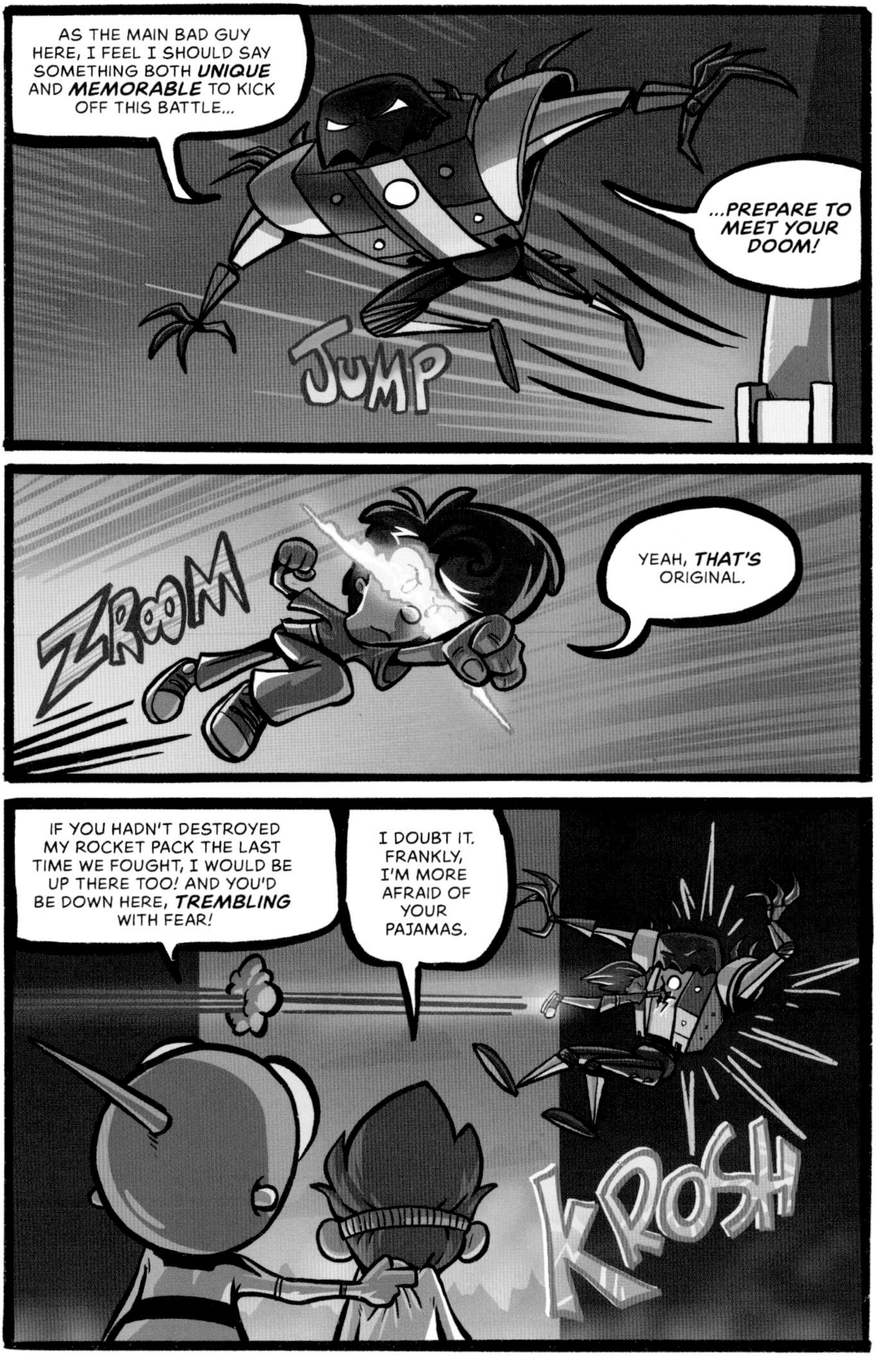
AS THE MAIN BAD GUY HERE, I FEEL I SHOULD SAY SOMETHING BOTH UNIQUE AND MEMORABLE TO KICK OFF THIS BATTLE...
...PREPARE TO MEET YOUR DOOM!
JUMP
ZROOM
YEAH, THAT'S ORIGINAL.
IF YOU HADN'T DESTROYED MY ROCKET PACK THE LAST TIME WE FOUGHT, I WOULD BE UP THERE TOO! AND YOU'D BE DOWN HERE, TREMBLING WITH FEAR!
I DOUBT IT. FRANKLY, I'M MORE AFRAID OF YOUR PAJAMAS.
KROSH

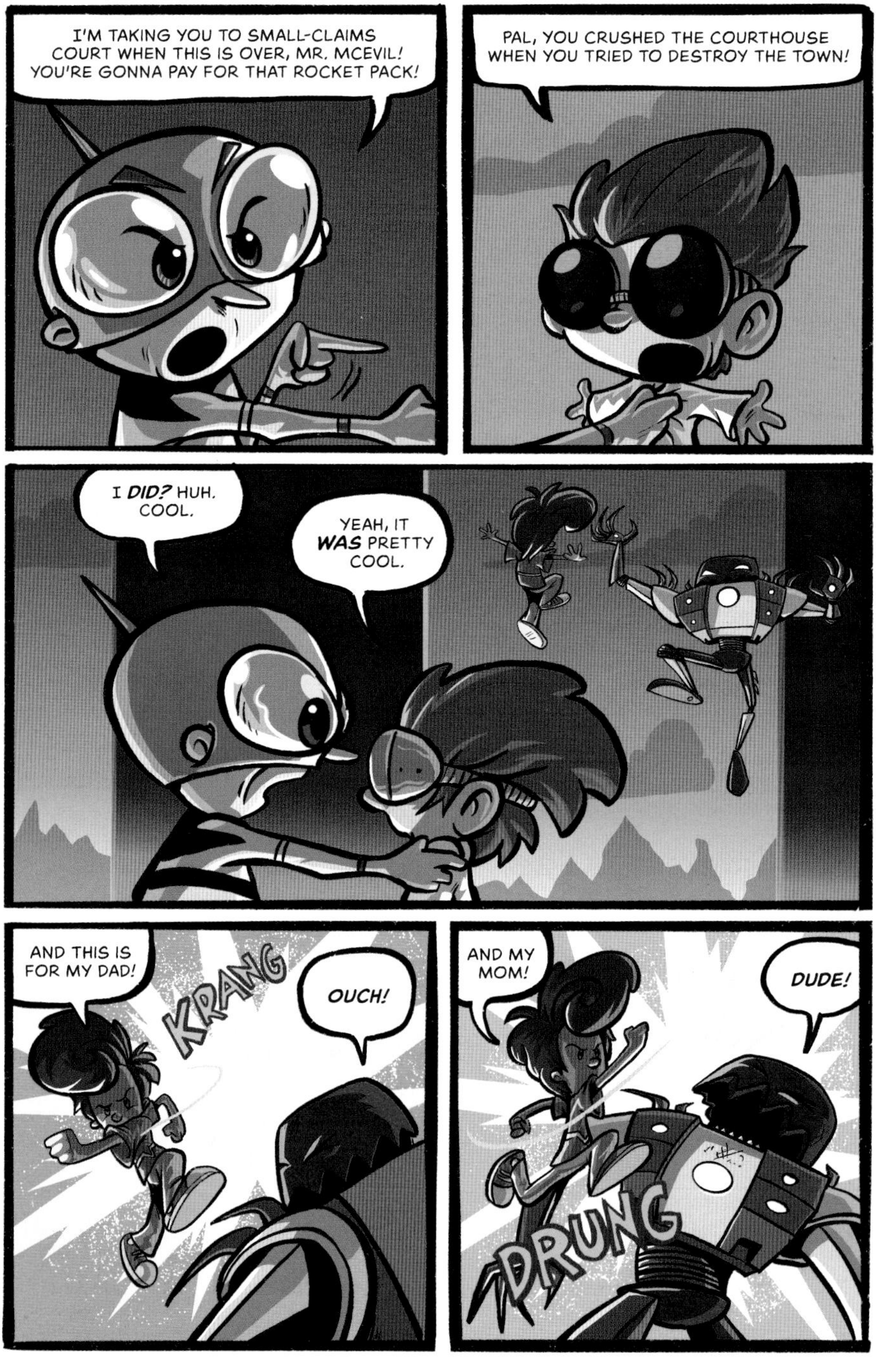
I'M TAKING YOU TO SMALL-CLAIMS COURT WHEN THIS IS OVER, MR. MCEVIL! YOU'RE GONNA PAY FOR THAT ROCKET PACK!
PAL, YOU CRUSHED THE COURTHOUSE WHEN YOU TRIED TO DESTROY THE TOWN!
I DID? HUH. COOL.
YEAH, IT WAS PRETTY COOL.
AND THIS IS FOR MY DAD!
KRANG
OUCH!
AND MY MOM!
DUDE!
DRUNG

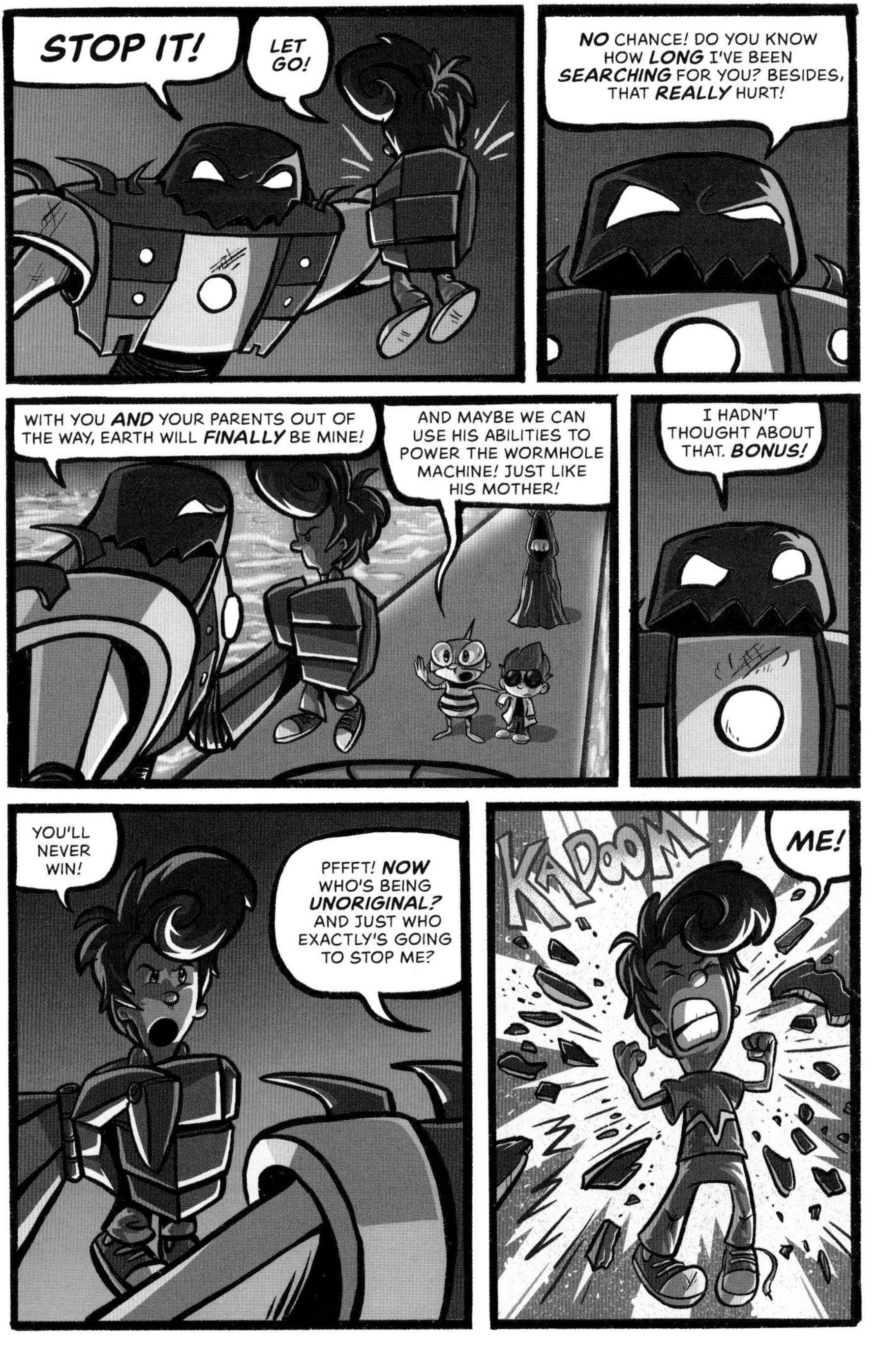
STOP IT!
LET GO!
NO CHANCE! DO YOU KNOW HOW LONG I'VE BEEN SEARCHING FOR YOU? BESIDES, THAT REALLY HURT!
WITH YOU AND YOUR PARENTS OUT OF THE WAY, EARTH WILL FINALLY BE MINE!
AND MAYBE WE CAN USE HIS ABILITIES TO POWER THE WORMHOLE MACHINE! JUST LIKE HIS MOTHER!
I HADN'T THOUGHT ABOUT THAT. BONUS!
YOU'LL NEVER WIN!
PFFFT! NOW WHO'S BEING UNORIGINAL? AND JUST WHO EXACTLY'S GOING TO STOP ME?
KADOOM
ME!

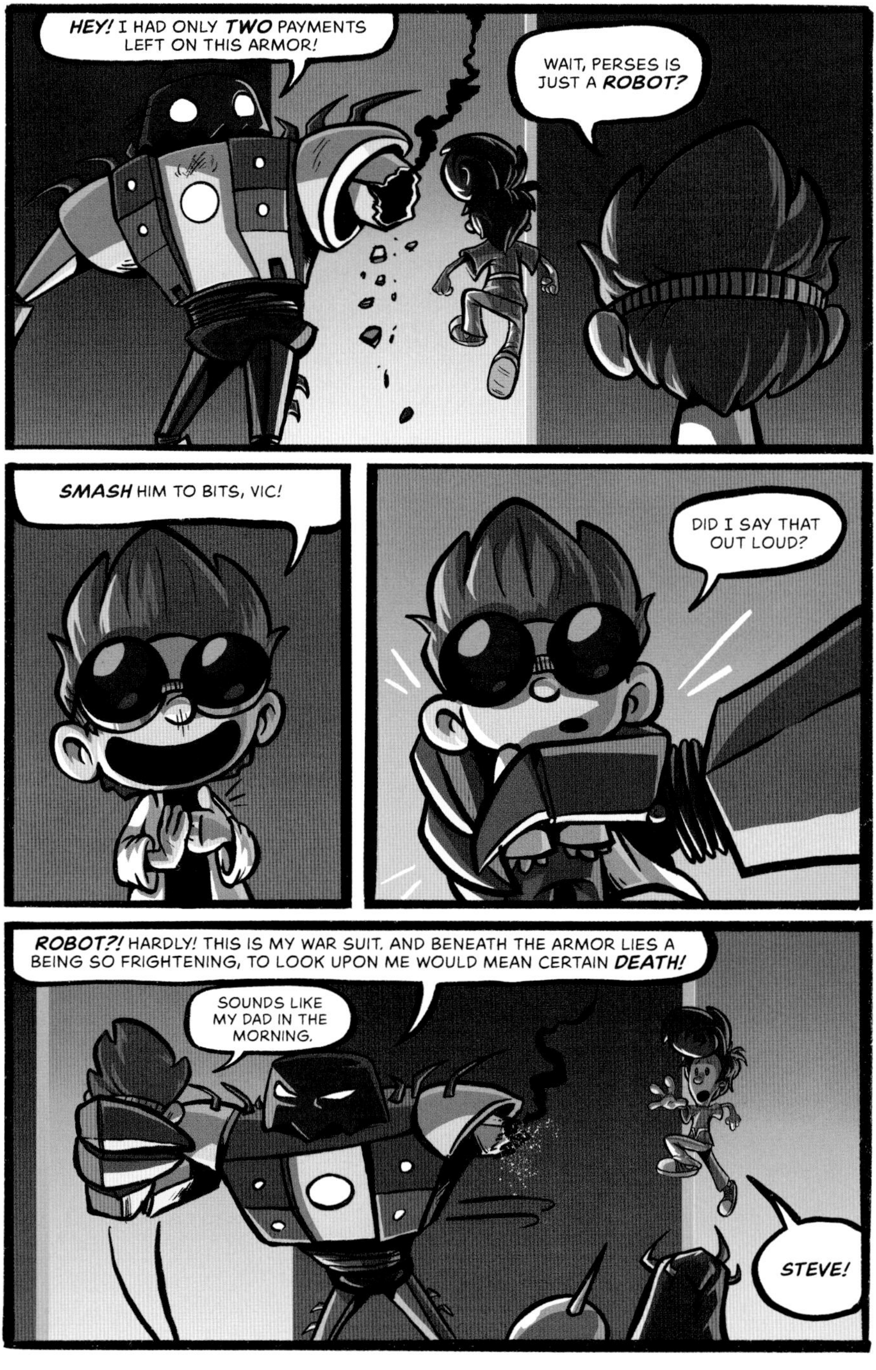
HEY! I HAD ONLY TWO PAYMENTS LEFT ON THIS ARMOR!
WAIT, PERSES IS JUST A ROBOT?
SMASH HIM TO BITS, VIC!
DID I SAY THAT OUT LOUD?
ROBOT?! HARDLY! THIS IS MY WAR SUIT. AND BENEATH THE ARMOR LIES A BEING SO FRIGHTENING, TO LOOK UPON ME WOULD MEAN CERTAIN DEATH!
SOUNDS LIKE MY DAD IN THE MORNING.
STEVE!

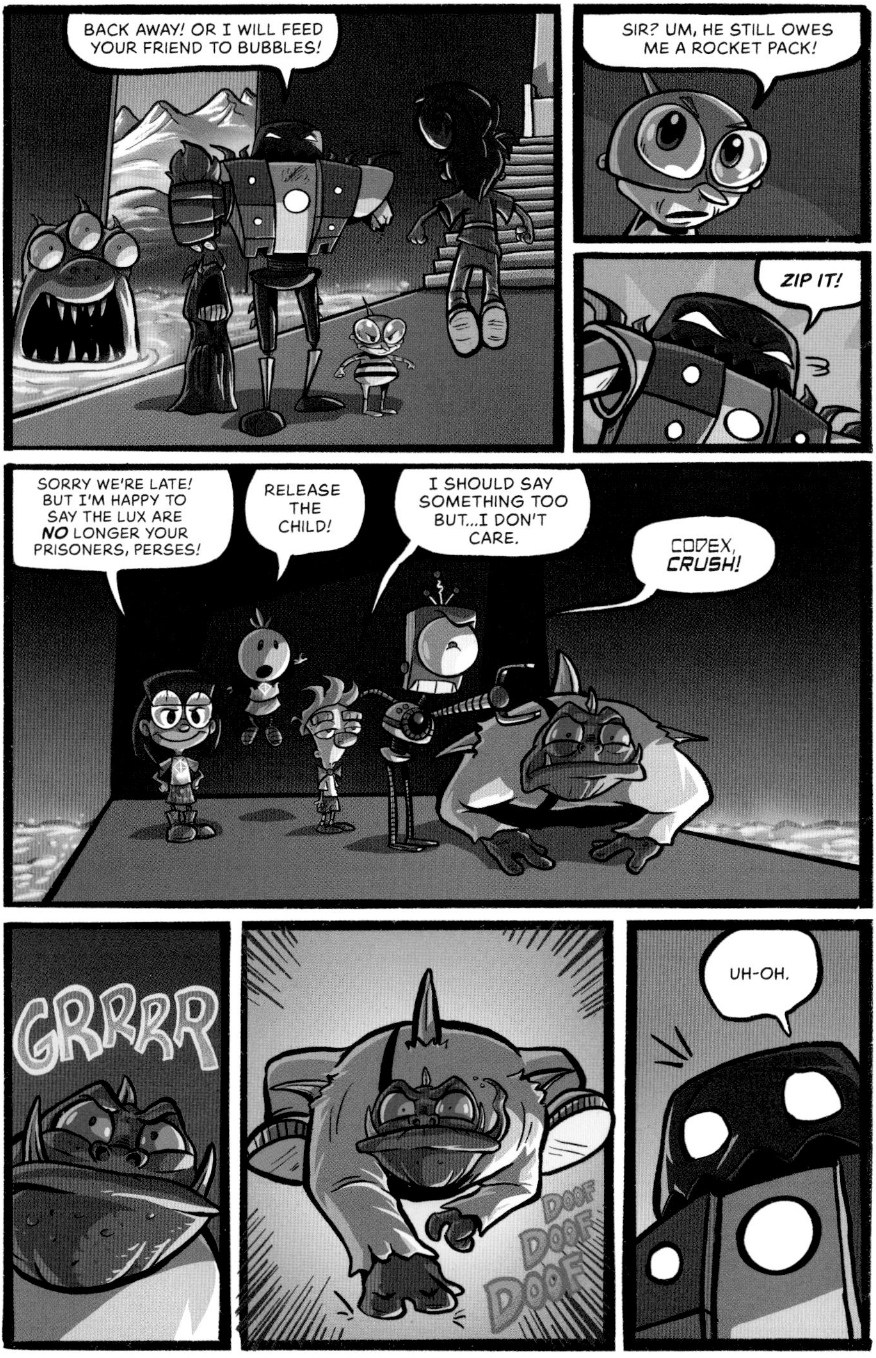
BACK AWAY! OR I WILL FEED YOUR FRIEND TO BUBBLES!
SIR? UM, HE STILL OWES ME A ROCKET PACK!
ZIP IT!
SORRY WE'RE LATE! BUT I'M HAPPY TO SAY THE LUX ARE NO LONGER YOUR PRISONERS, PERSES!
RELEASE THE CHILD!
I SHOULD SAY SOMETHING TOO BUT...I DON'T CARE.
CODEX, CRUSH!
GRRRR
DOOF DOOF DOOF
UH-OH.

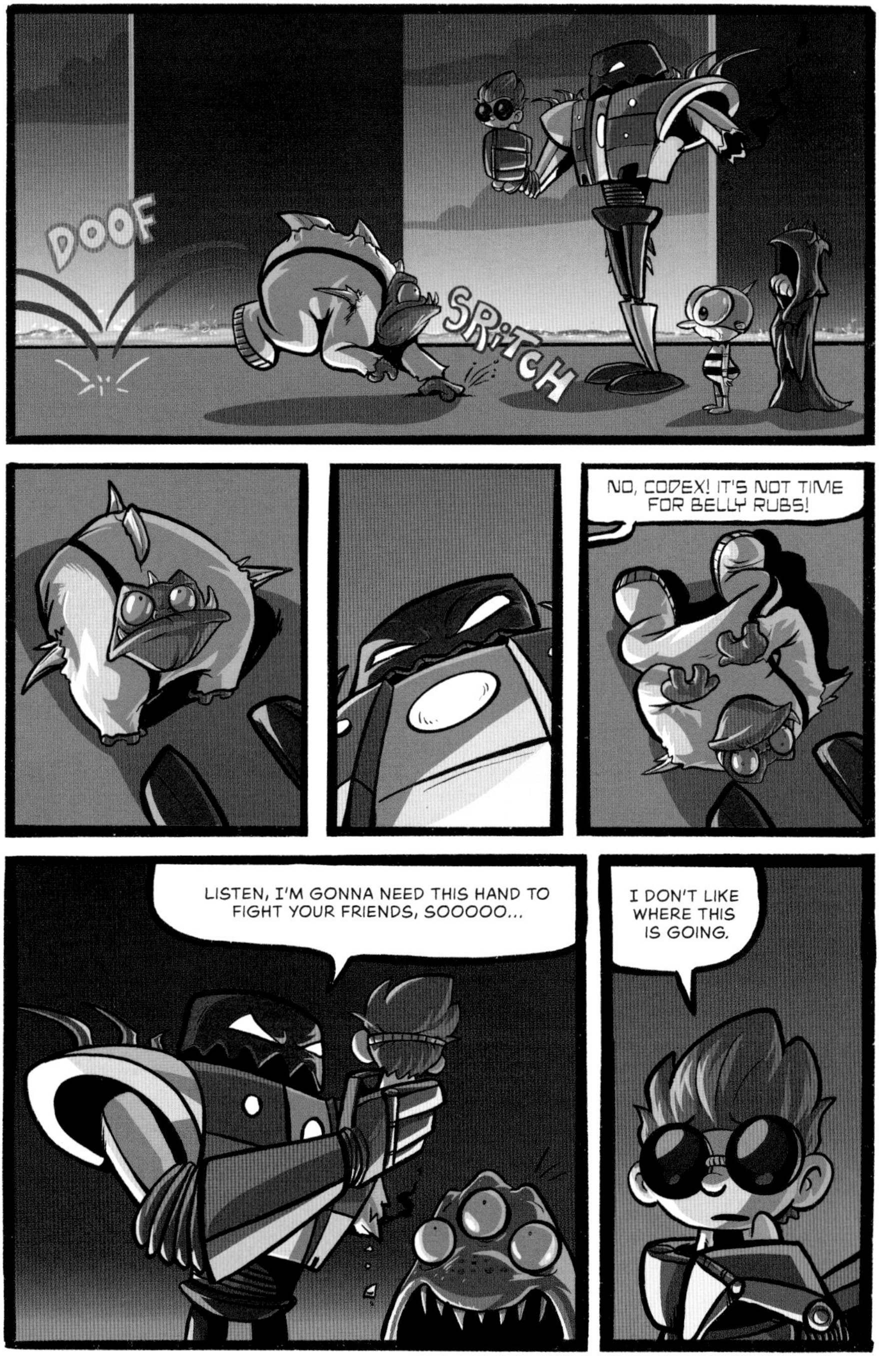
DOOF
SRITCH
NO, CODEX! IT'S NOT TIME FOR BELLY RUBS!
LISTEN, I'M GONNA NEED THIS HAND TO FIGHT YOUR FRIENDS, SOOOOO...
I DON'T LIKE WHERE THIS IS GOING.

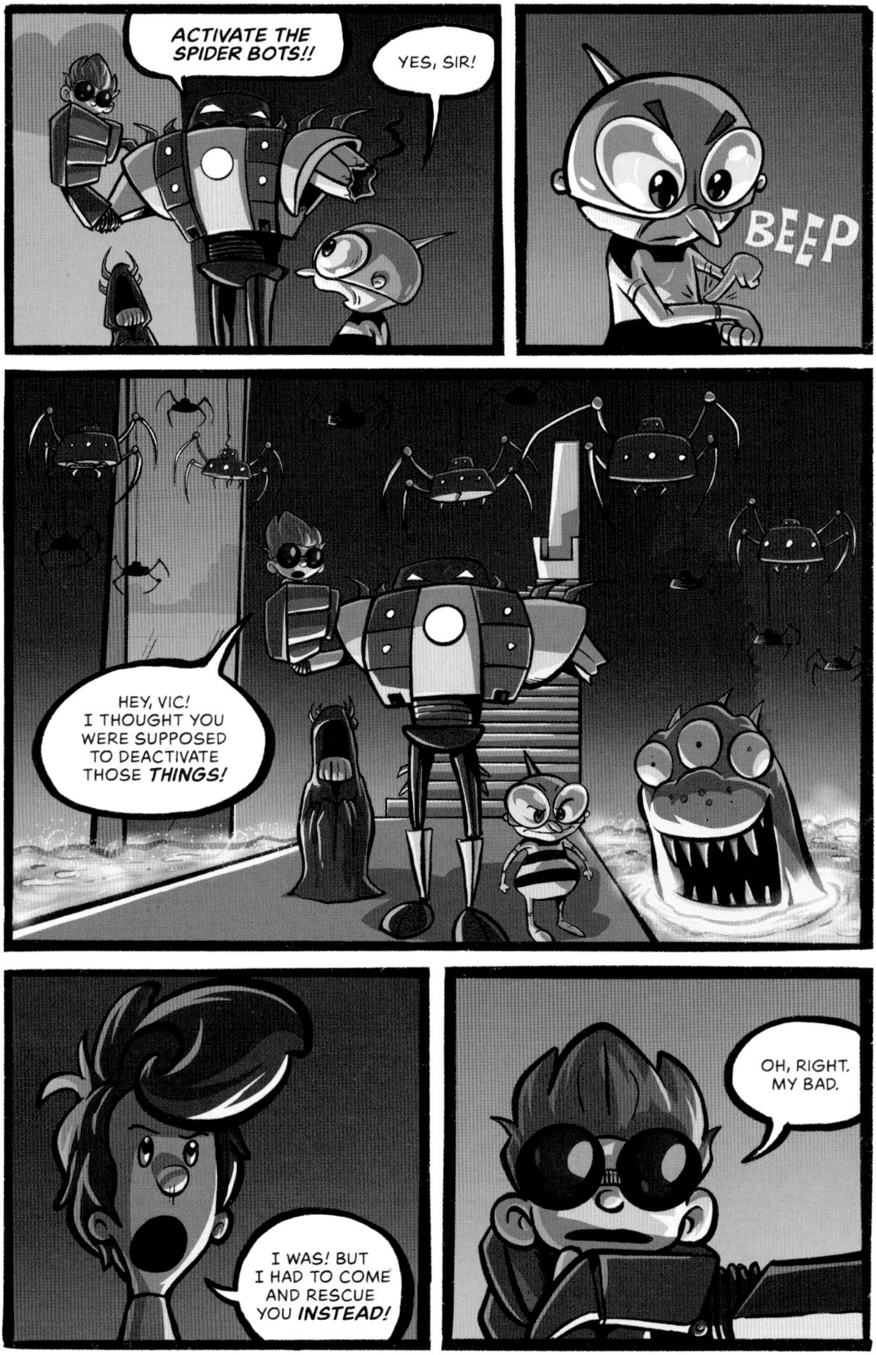
ACTIVATE THE SPIDER BOTS!!
YES, SIR!
BEEP
HEY, VIC! I THOUGHT YOU WERE SUPPOSED TO DEACTIVATE THOSE THINGS!
I WAS! BUT I HAD TO COME AND RESCUE YOU INSTEAD!
OH, RIGHT. MY BAD.

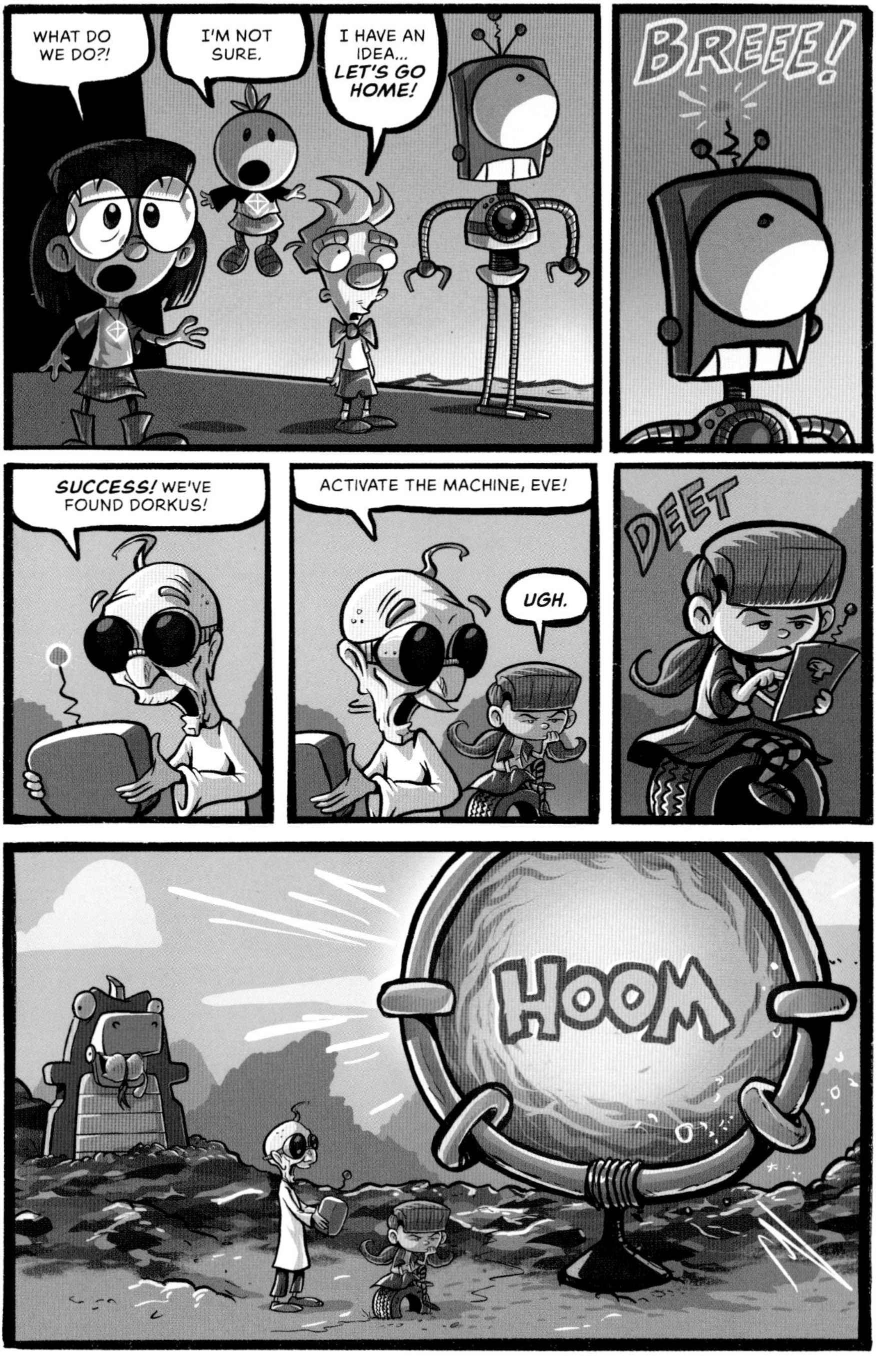
WHAT DO WE DO?!
I'M NOT SURE.
I HAVE AN IDEA... LET'S GO HOME!
BREEE!
SUCCESS! WE'VE FOUND DORKUS!
ACTIVATE THE MACHINE, EVE!
UGH.
DEET
HOOM

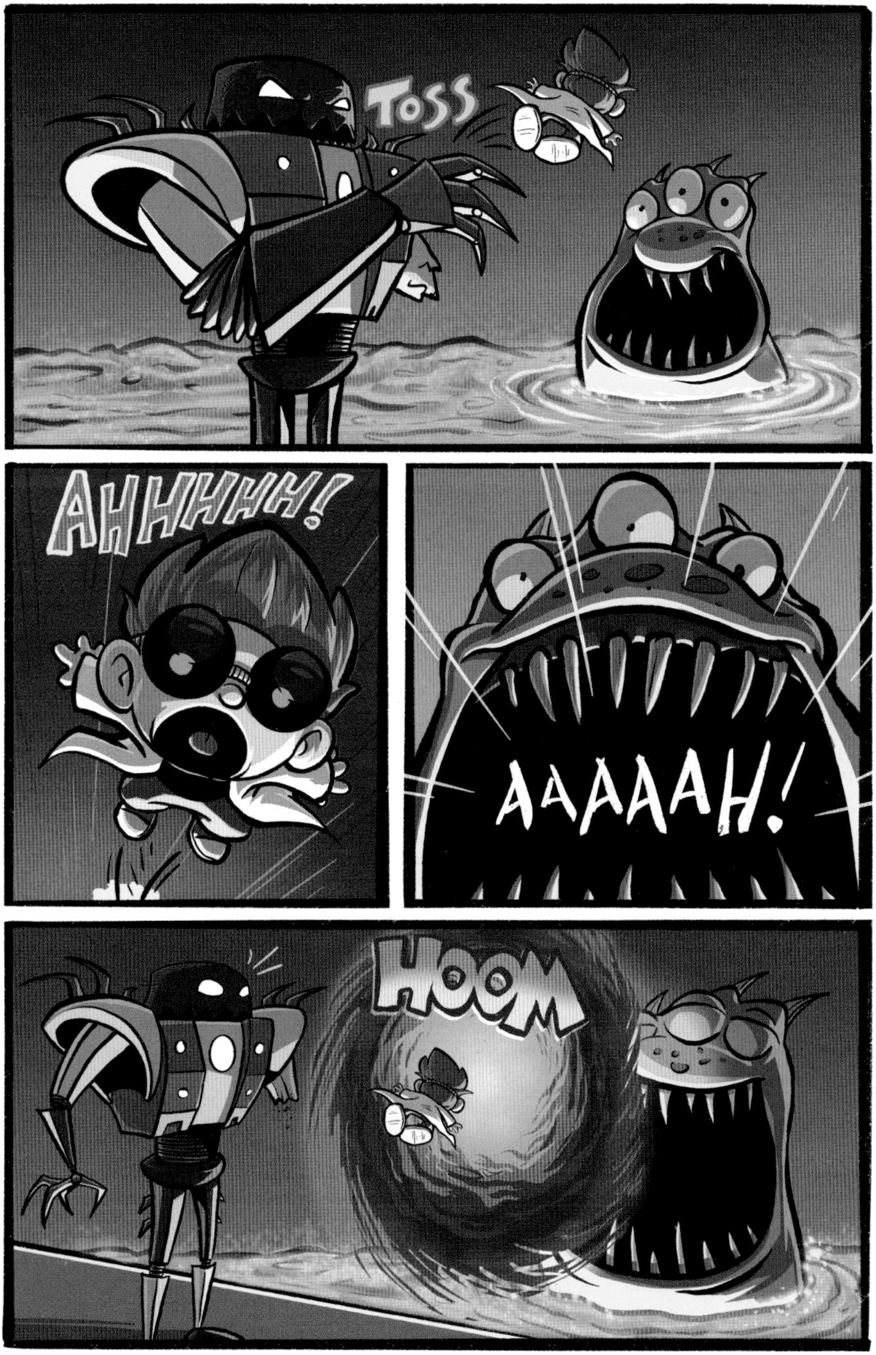
TOSS
AHHHHH!
AAAAAH!
HOOM

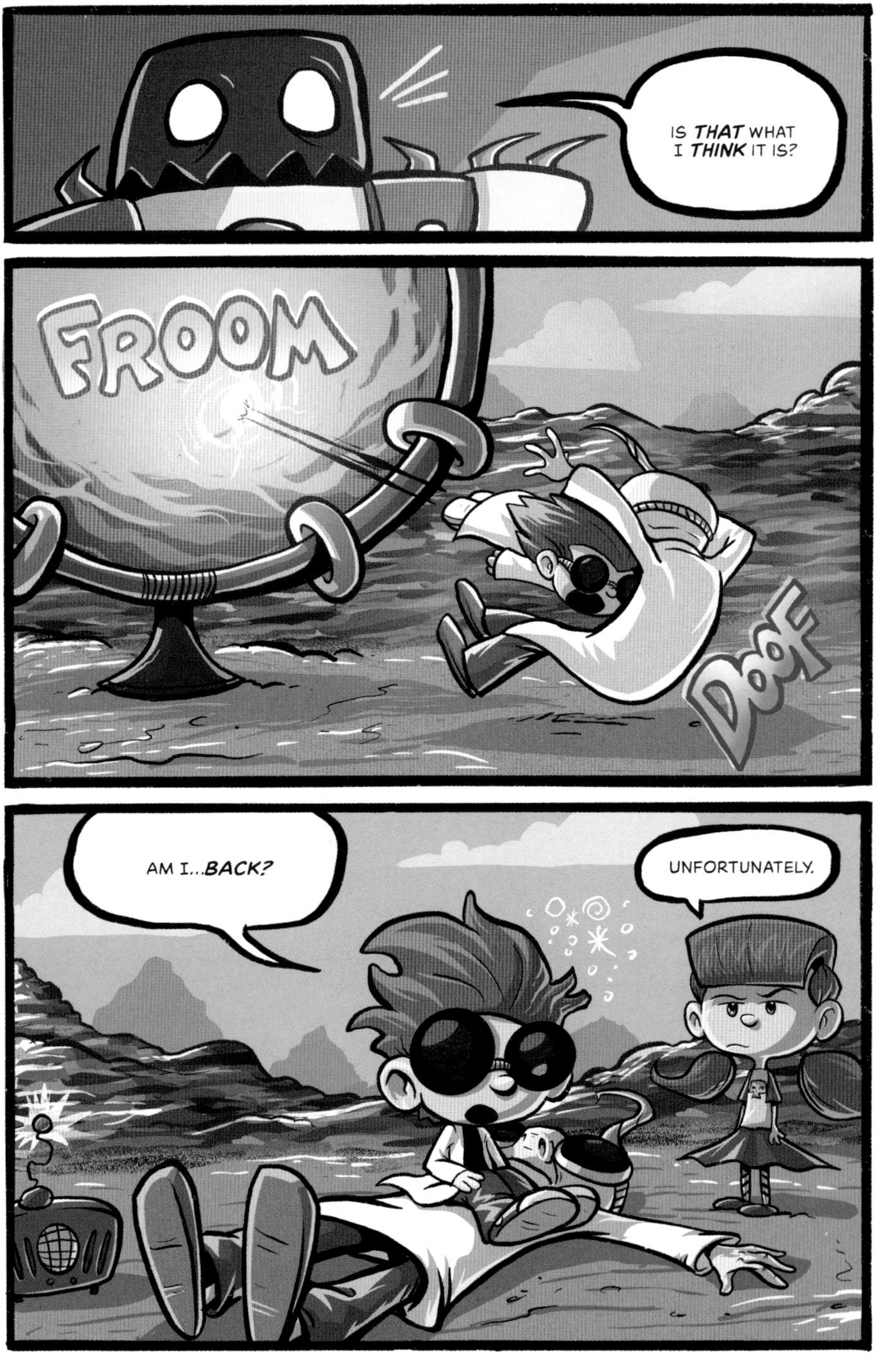
IS THAT WHAT I THINK IT IS?
FROOM
DOOF
AM I...BACK?
UNFORTUNATELY.

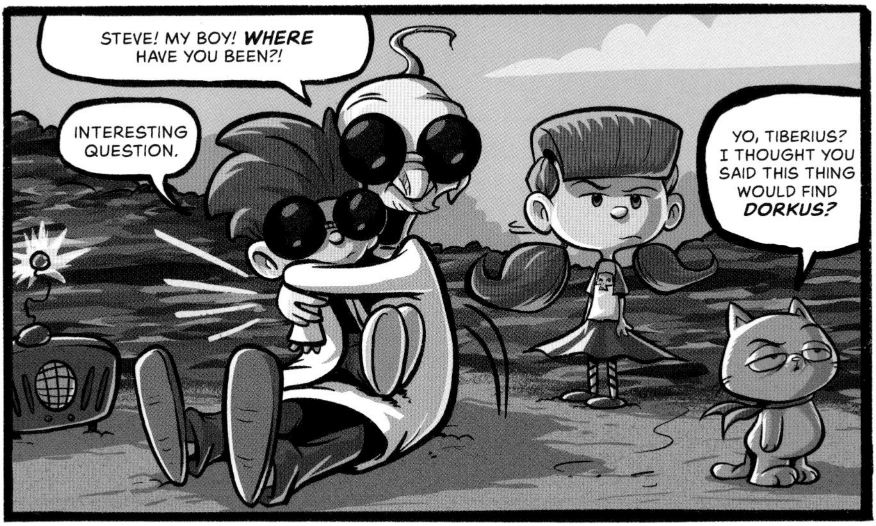
STEVE! MY BOY! **WHERE** HAVE YOU BEEN?!
INTERESTING QUESTION.
YO, TIBERIUS? I THOUGHT YOU SAID THIS THING WOULD FIND **DORKUS?**

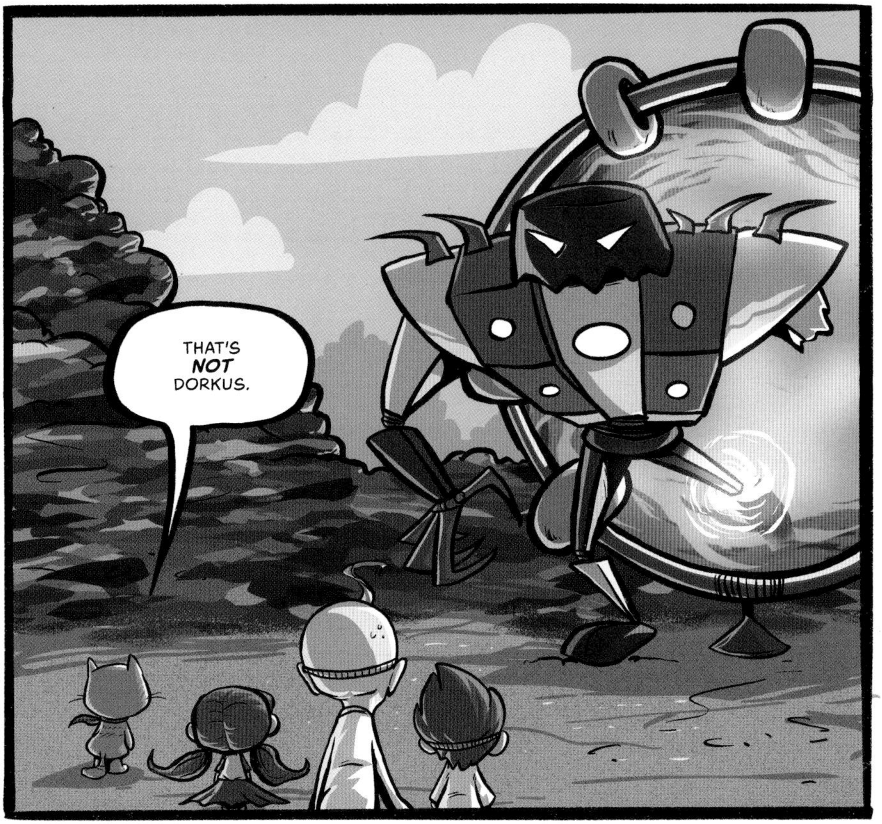
THAT'S **NOT** DORKUS.

CHAPTER 16

Home Is Where the Hurt Is

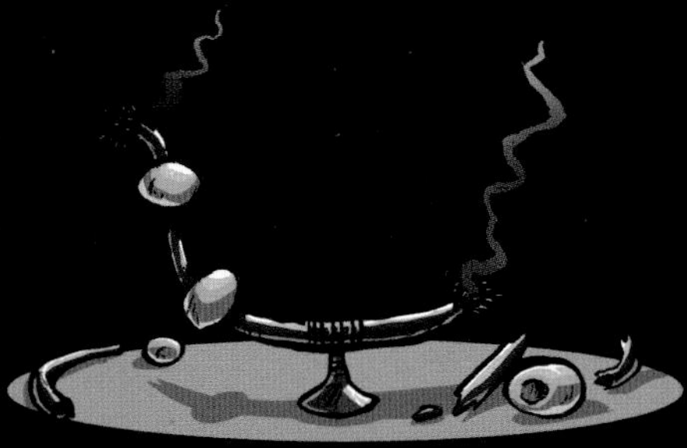

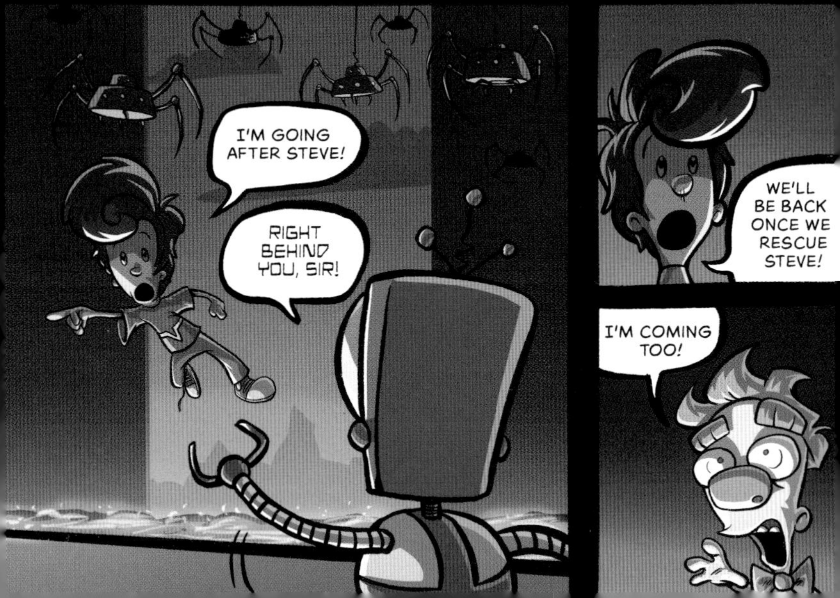
I'M GOING AFTER STEVE!
RIGHT BEHIND YOU, SIR!
WE'LL BE BACK ONCE WE RESCUE STEVE!
I'M COMING TOO!

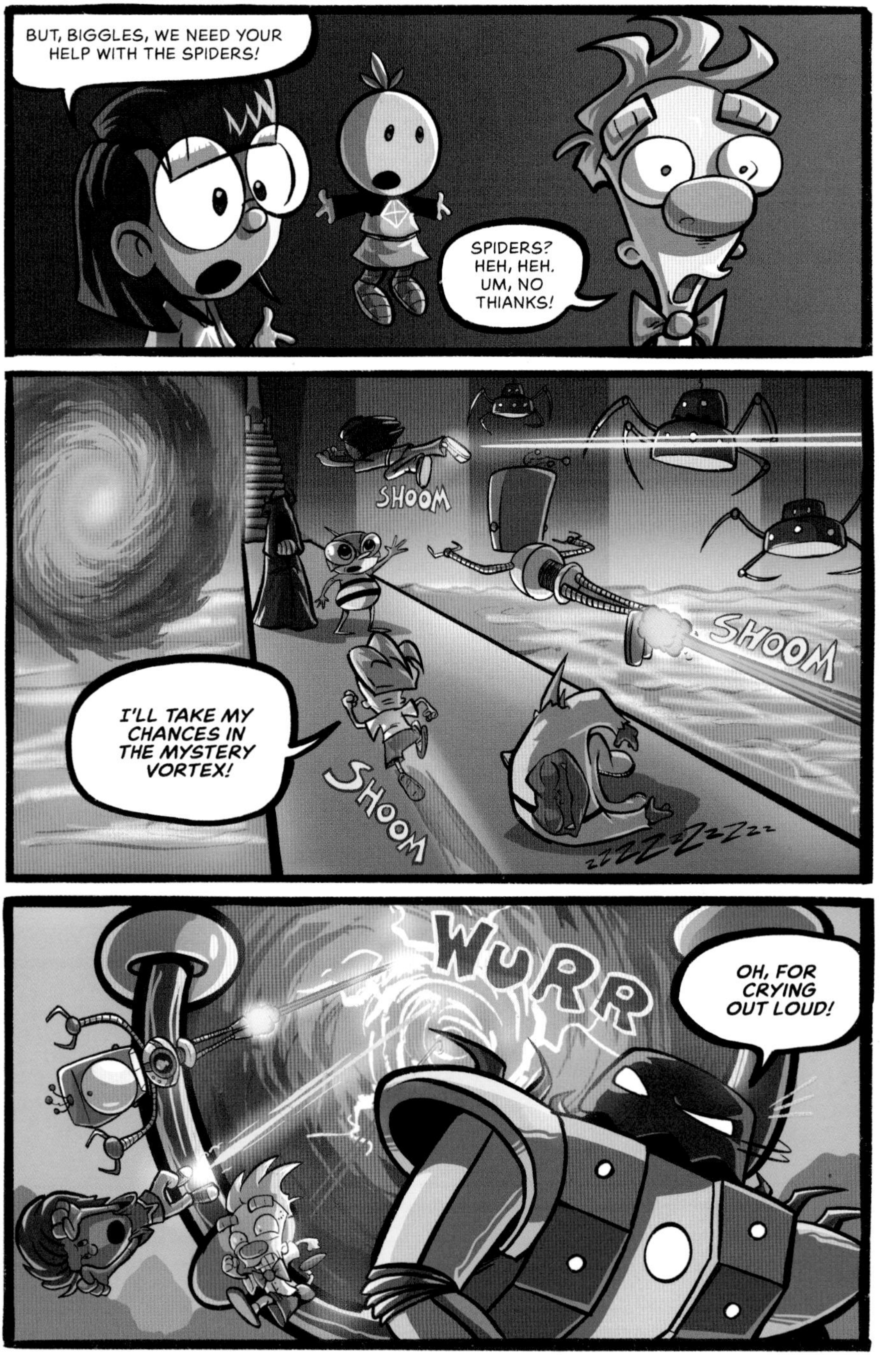
BUT, BIGGLES, WE NEED YOUR HELP WITH THE SPIDERS!
SPIDERS? HEH, HEH. UM, NO THIANKS!
SHOOM
SHOOM
I'LL TAKE MY CHANCES IN THE MYSTERY VORTEX!
SHOOM
ZZZZZZZZZ
WURR
OH, FOR CRYING OUT LOUD!

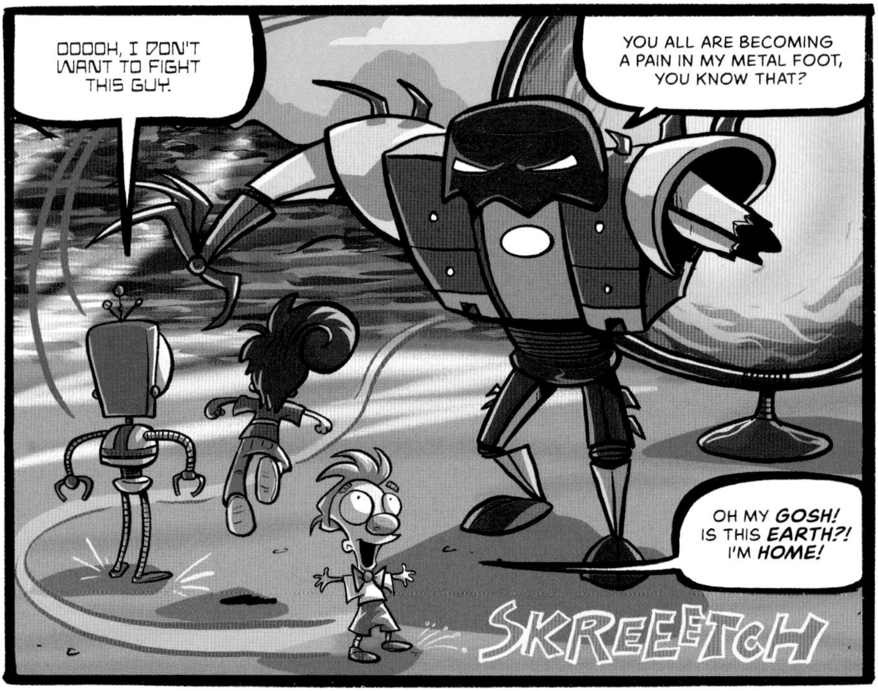
OOOOH, I DON'T WANT TO FIGHT THIS GUY.
YOU ALL ARE BECOMING A PAIN IN MY METAL FOOT, YOU KNOW THAT?
OH MY GOSH! IS THIS EARTH?! I'M HOME!
SKREEETCH

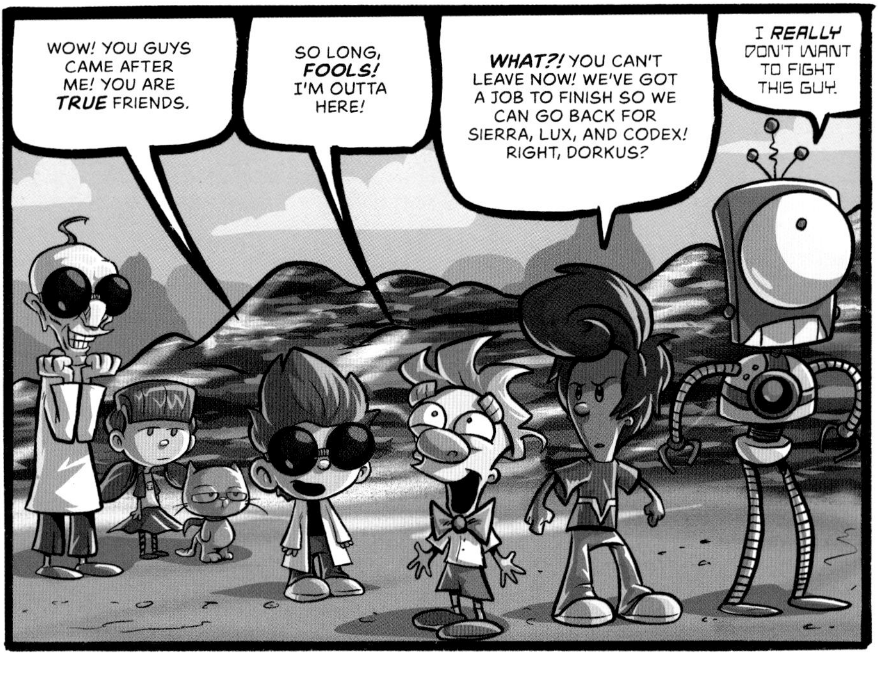
WOW! YOU GUYS CAME AFTER ME! YOU ARE TRUE FRIENDS.
SO LONG, FOOLS! I'M OUTTA HERE!
WHAT?! YOU CAN'T LEAVE NOW! WE'VE GOT A JOB TO FINISH SO WE CAN GO BACK FOR SIERRA, LUX, AND CODEX! RIGHT, DORKUS?
I REALLY DON'T WANT TO FIGHT THIS GUY.

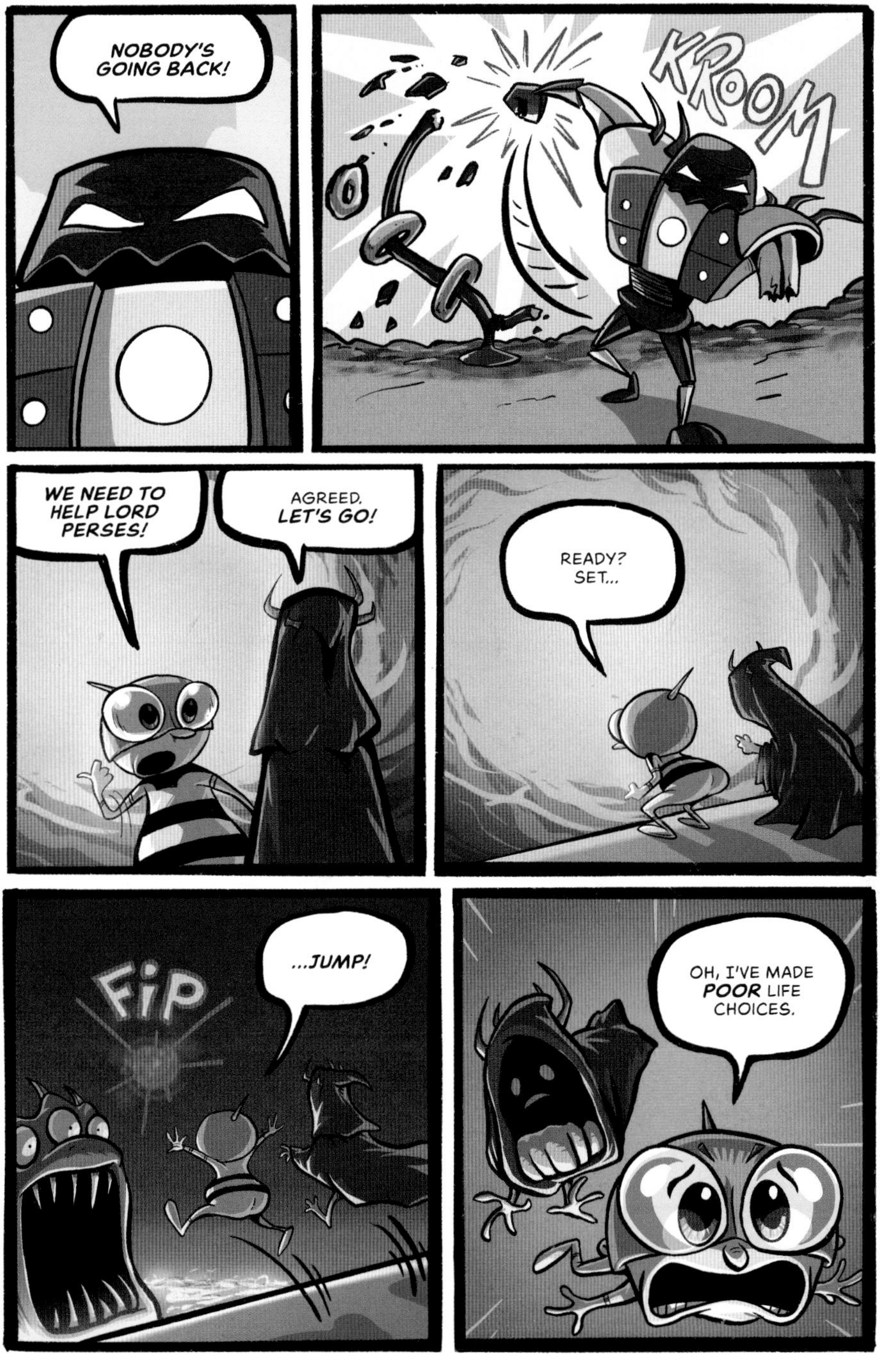
NOBODY'S GOING BACK!
KROOM
WE NEED TO HELP LORD PERSES!
AGREED. LET'S GO!
READY? SET...
FiP
...JUMP!
OH, I'VE MADE POOR LIFE CHOICES.

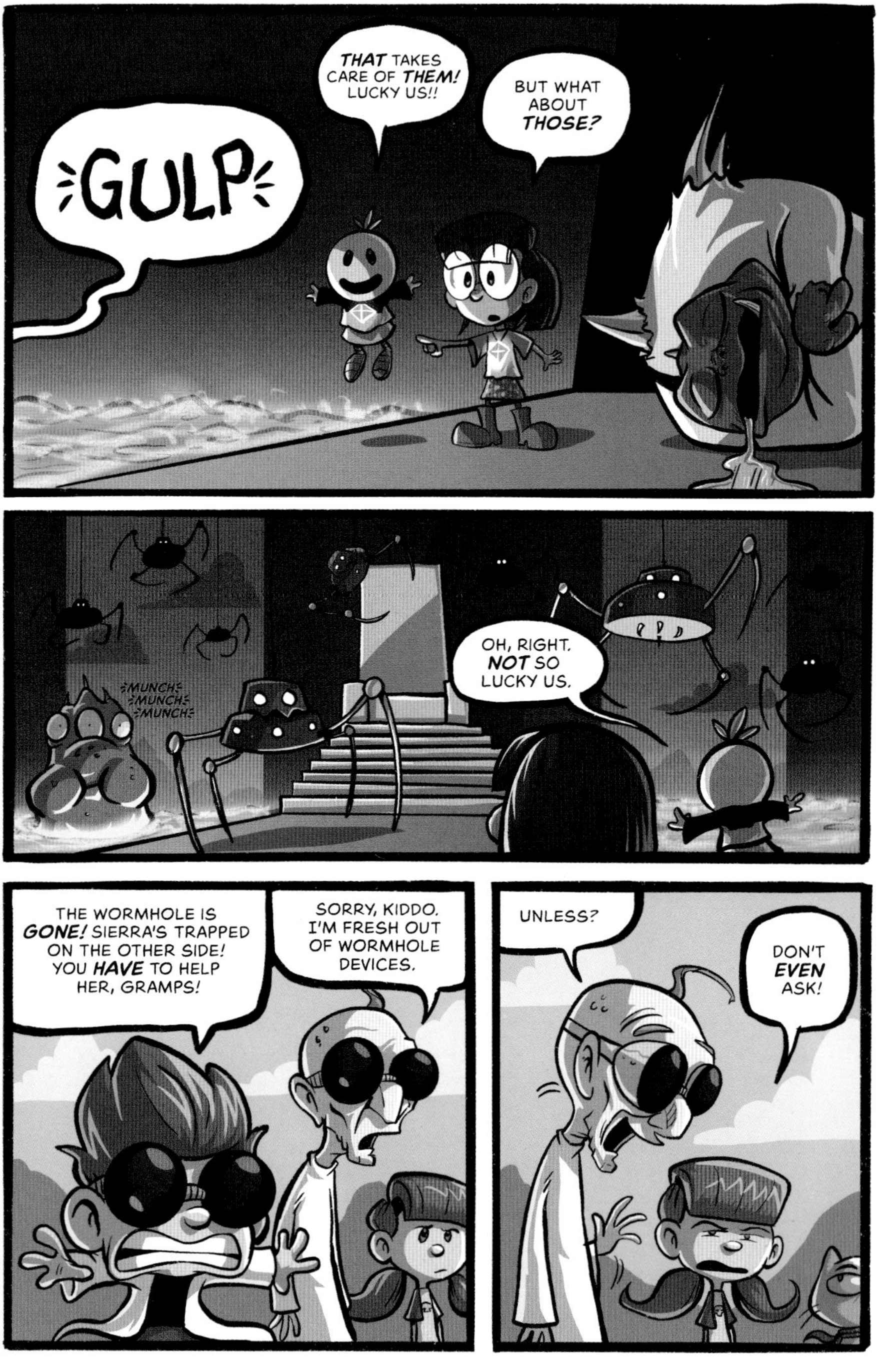
GULP
THAT TAKES CARE OF THEM! LUCKY US!!
BUT WHAT ABOUT THOSE?
MUNCH MUNCH MUNCH
OH, RIGHT. NOT SO LUCKY US.
THE WORMHOLE IS GONE! SIERRA'S TRAPPED ON THE OTHER SIDE! YOU HAVE TO HELP HER, GRAMPS!
SORRY, KIDDO. I'M FRESH OUT OF WORMHOLE DEVICES.
UNLESS?
DON'T EVEN ASK!

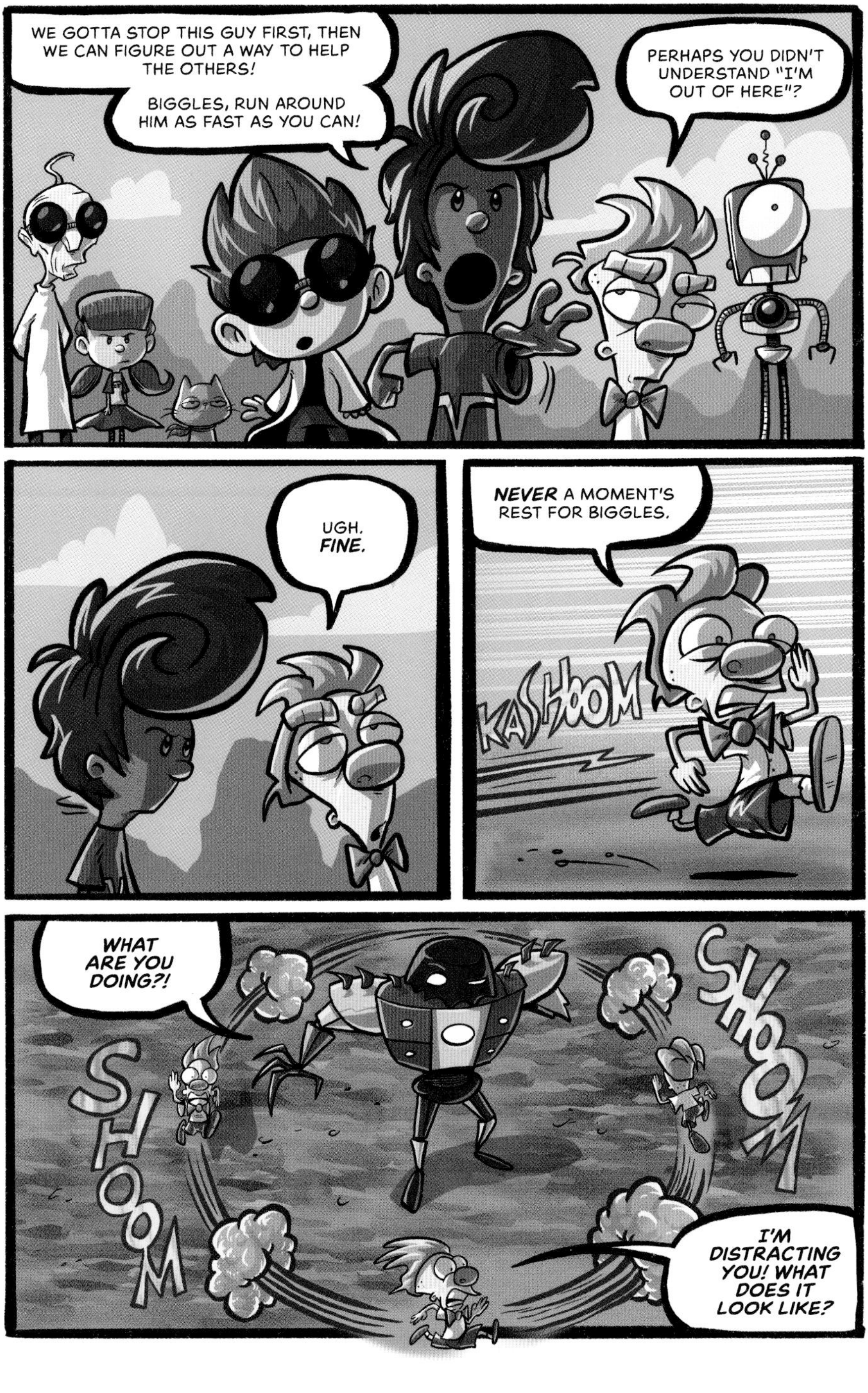

WE GOTTA STOP THIS GUY FIRST, THEN WE CAN FIGURE OUT A WAY TO HELP THE OTHERS!
BIGGLES, RUN AROUND HIM AS FAST AS YOU CAN!
PERHAPS YOU DIDN'T UNDERSTAND "I'M OUT OF HERE"?
UGH. *FINE.*
NEVER A MOMENT'S REST FOR BIGGLES.
KASHOOM
WHAT ARE YOU DOING?!
SHOOM
SHOOM
I'M DISTRACTING YOU! WHAT DOES IT LOOK LIKE?

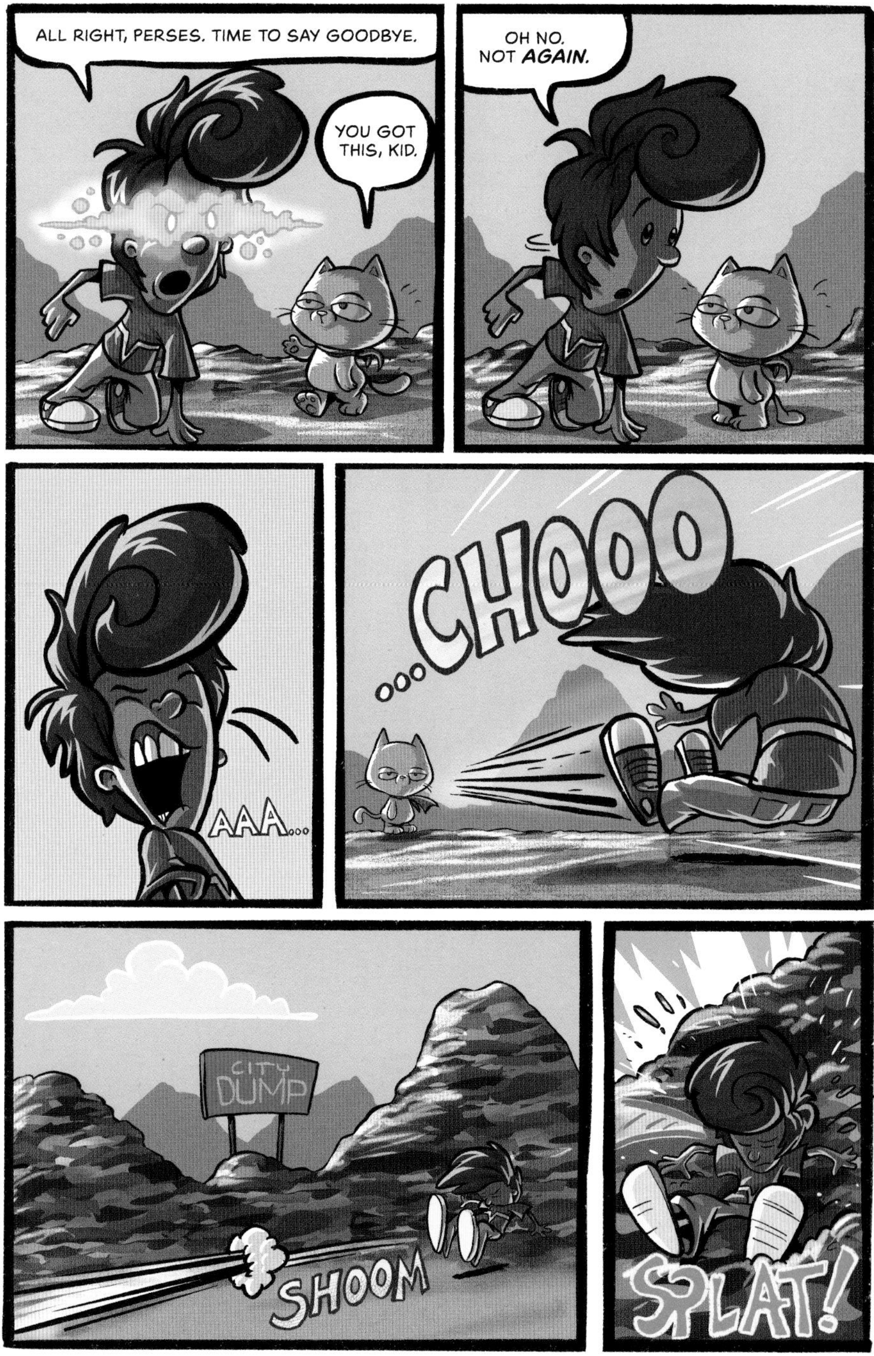
ALL RIGHT, PERSES. TIME TO SAY GOODBYE.
YOU GOT THIS, KID.
OH NO. NOT **AGAIN.**
AAA...
...CHOOO
CITY DUMP
SHOOM
SPLAT!

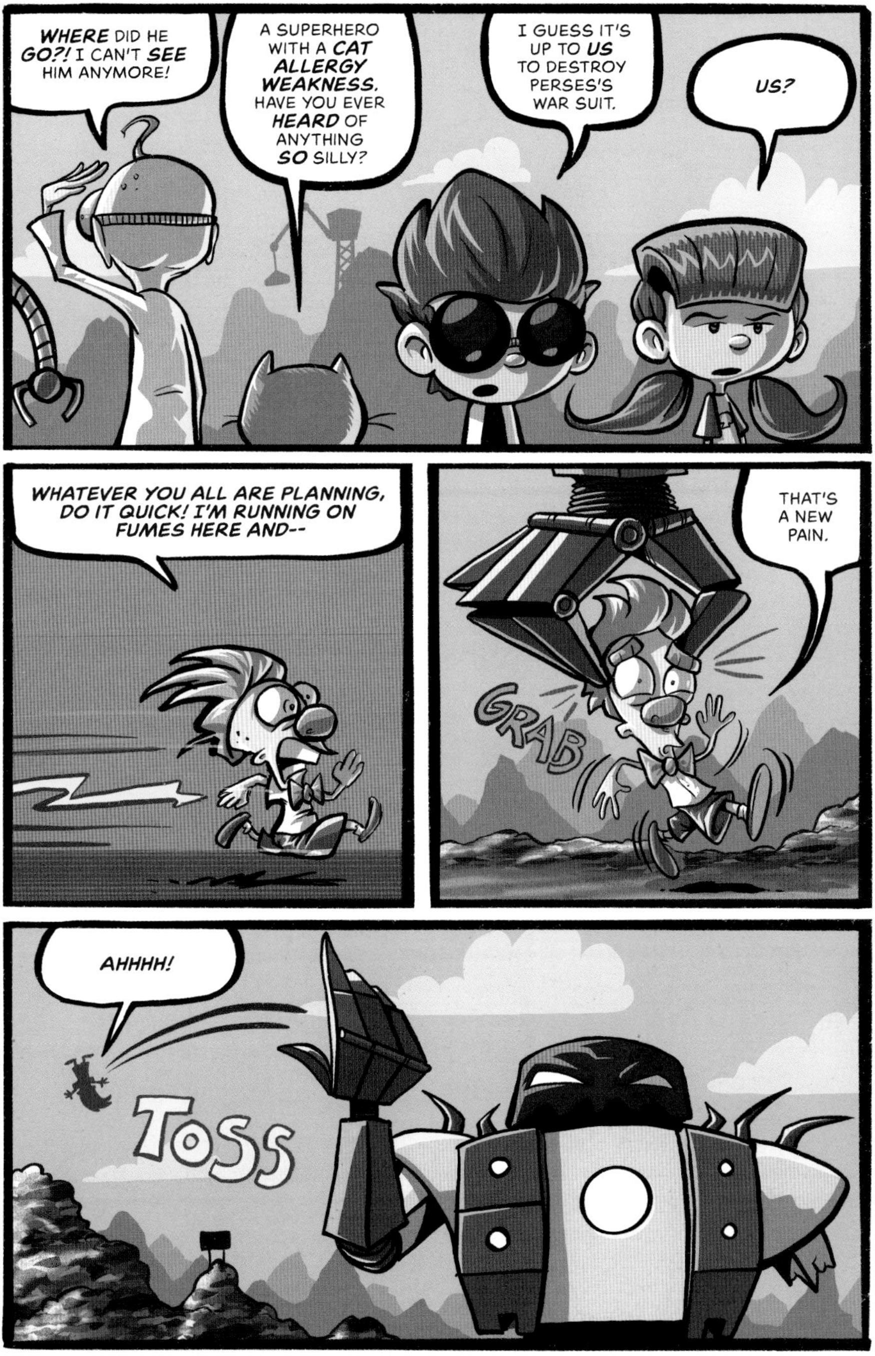
WHERE DID HE GO?! I CAN'T SEE HIM ANYMORE!
A SUPERHERO WITH A CAT ALLERGY WEAKNESS. HAVE YOU EVER HEARD OF ANYTHING SO SILLY?
I GUESS IT'S UP TO US TO DESTROY PERSES'S WAR SUIT.
US?
WHATEVER YOU ALL ARE PLANNING, DO IT QUICK! I'M RUNNING ON FUMES HERE AND--
THAT'S A NEW PAIN.
GRAB
AHHHH!
TOSS

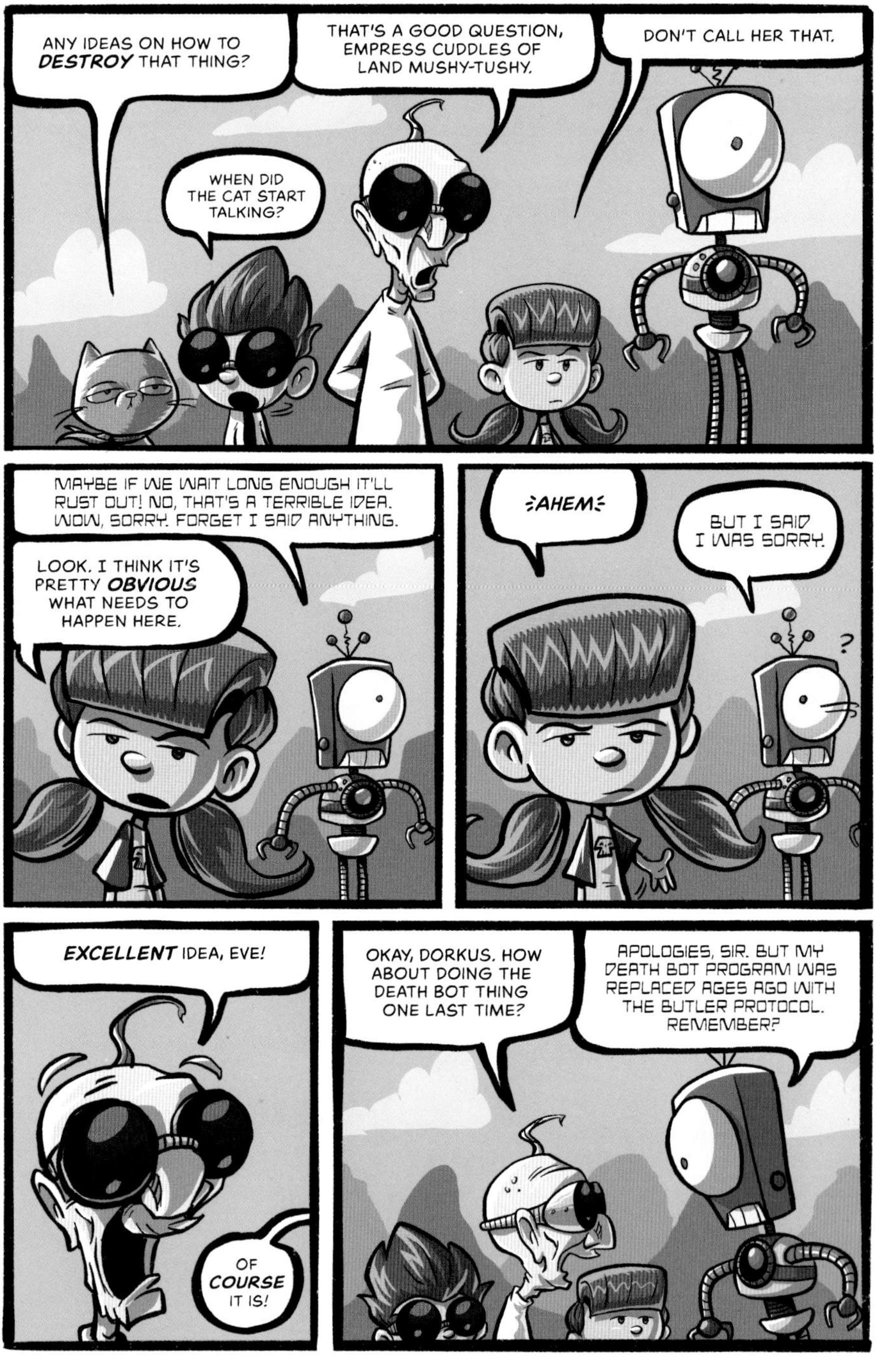
ANY IDEAS ON HOW TO DESTROY THAT THING?
WHEN DID THE CAT START TALKING?
THAT'S A GOOD QUESTION, EMPRESS CUDDLES OF LAND MUSHY-TUSHY.
DON'T CALL HER THAT.
MAYBE IF WE WAIT LONG ENOUGH IT'LL RUST OUT! NO, THAT'S A TERRIBLE IDEA. WOW, SORRY. FORGET I SAID ANYTHING.
LOOK. I THINK IT'S PRETTY OBVIOUS WHAT NEEDS TO HAPPEN HERE.
AHEM
BUT I SAID I WAS SORRY.
?
EXCELLENT IDEA, EVE!
OF COURSE IT IS!
OKAY, DORKUS. HOW ABOUT DOING THE DEATH BOT THING ONE LAST TIME?
APOLOGIES, SIR. BUT MY DEATH BOT PROGRAM WAS REPLACED AGES AGO WITH THE BUTLER PROTOCOL. REMEMBER?

SPEAKING OF WHICH, MAY I GET YOU A BEVERAGE, SIR?

TRUST ME, DORKUS! INITIATE: *JUMBO* PROTOCOL!

ZRAP

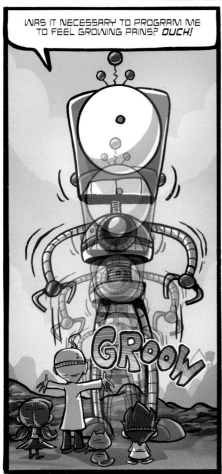

WAS IT NECESSARY TO PROGRAM ME TO FEEL GROWING PAINS? *OUCH!*

GROOW

YOU'RE GOING TO NEED A COPILOT FOR THIS, DORKUS!

COPILOT? WHO'S DUMB ENOUGH TO TAKE *THAT* JOB?

GRAB

SHOULD'VE KEPT MY MOUTH SHUT.

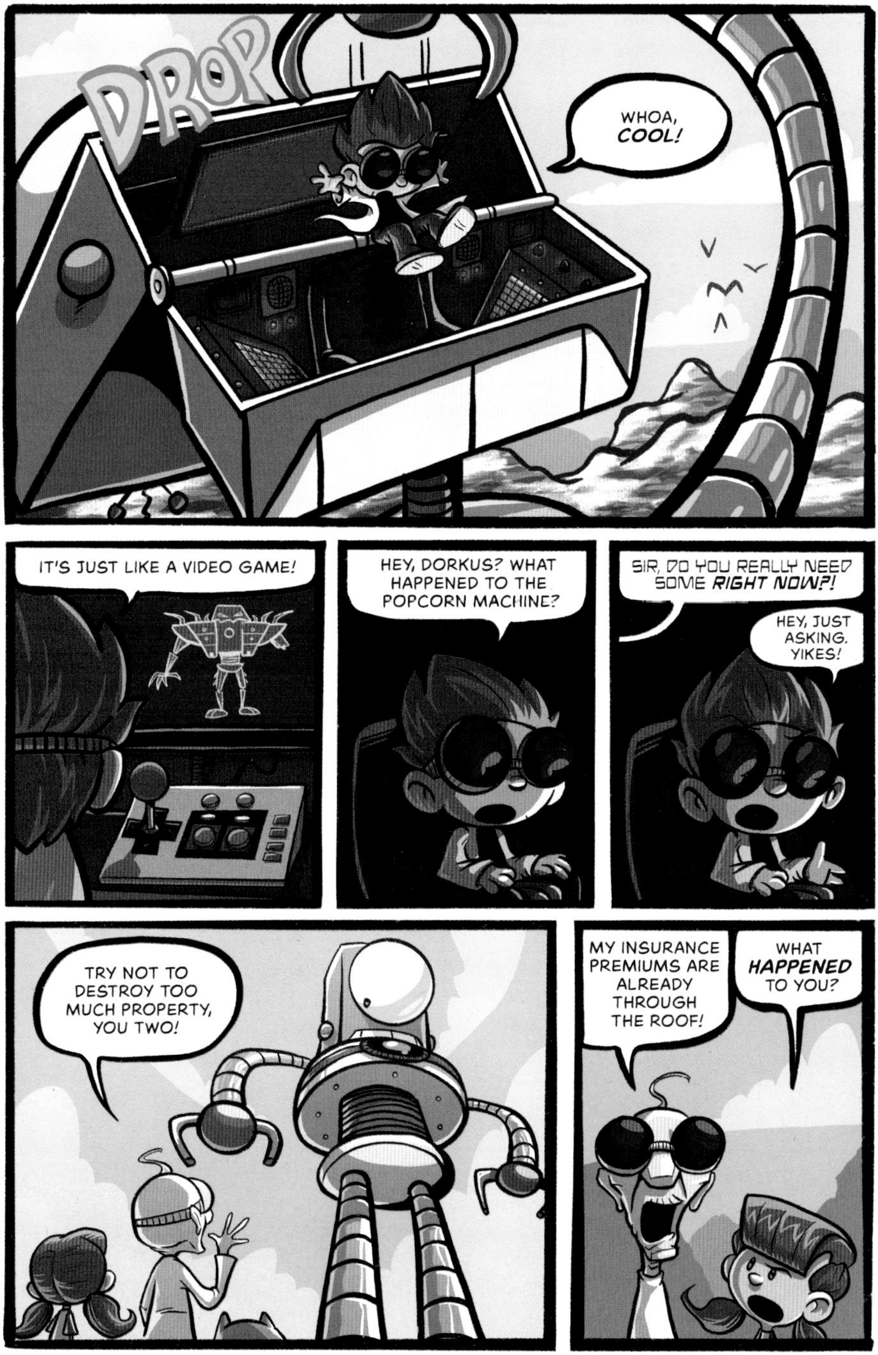
DROP
WHOA, COOL!
IT'S JUST LIKE A VIDEO GAME!
HEY, DORKUS? WHAT HAPPENED TO THE POPCORN MACHINE?
SIR, DO YOU REALLY NEED SOME RIGHT NOW?!
HEY, JUST ASKING. YIKES!
TRY NOT TO DESTROY TOO MUCH PROPERTY, YOU TWO!
MY INSURANCE PREMIUMS ARE ALREADY THROUGH THE ROOF!
WHAT HAPPENED TO YOU?

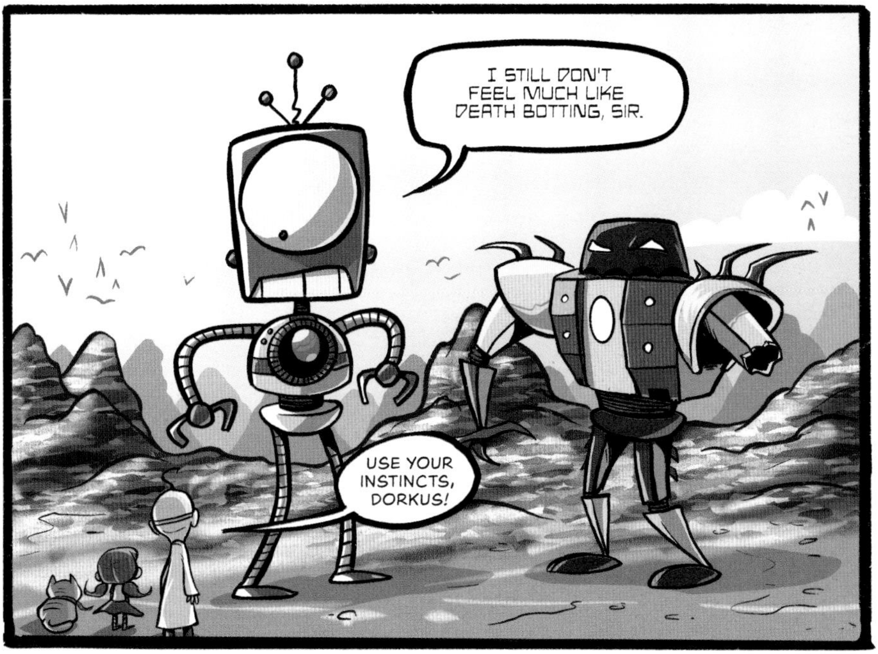
I STILL DON'T FEEL MUCH LIKE DEATH BOTTING, SIR.
USE YOUR INSTINCTS, DORKUS!

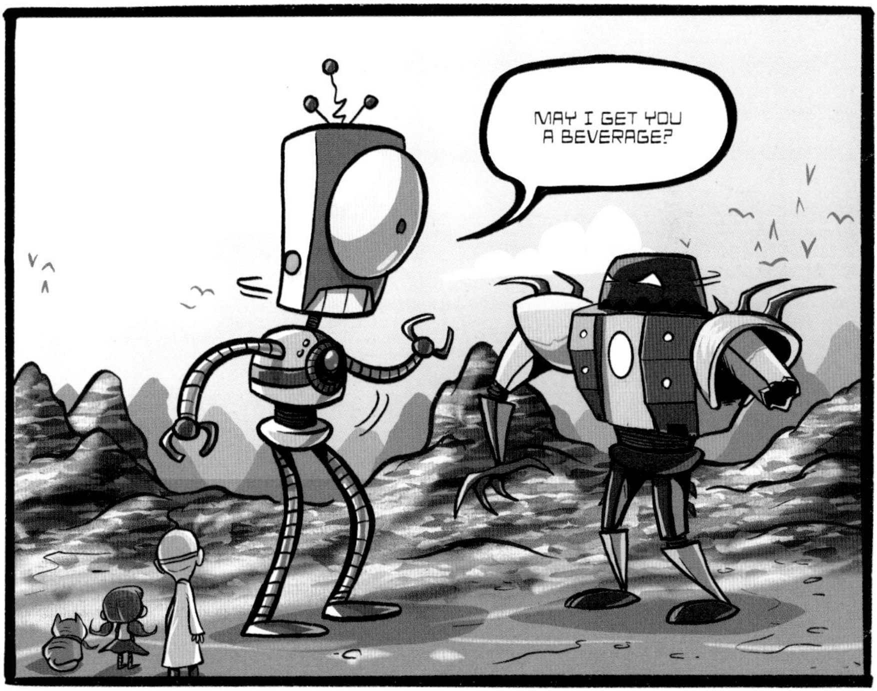
MAY I GET YOU A BEVERAGE?

CHAPTER 17

Brawl Things Considered

PREPARE YOURSELF FOR THE GREATEST BATTLE OF ALL TIME!
DOOM
DOOM
DOOM
WHAT THE...
NUDGE

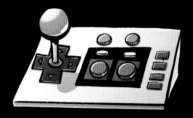

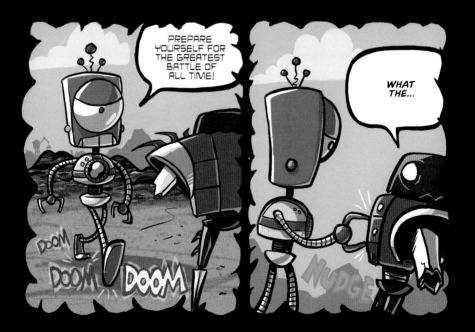

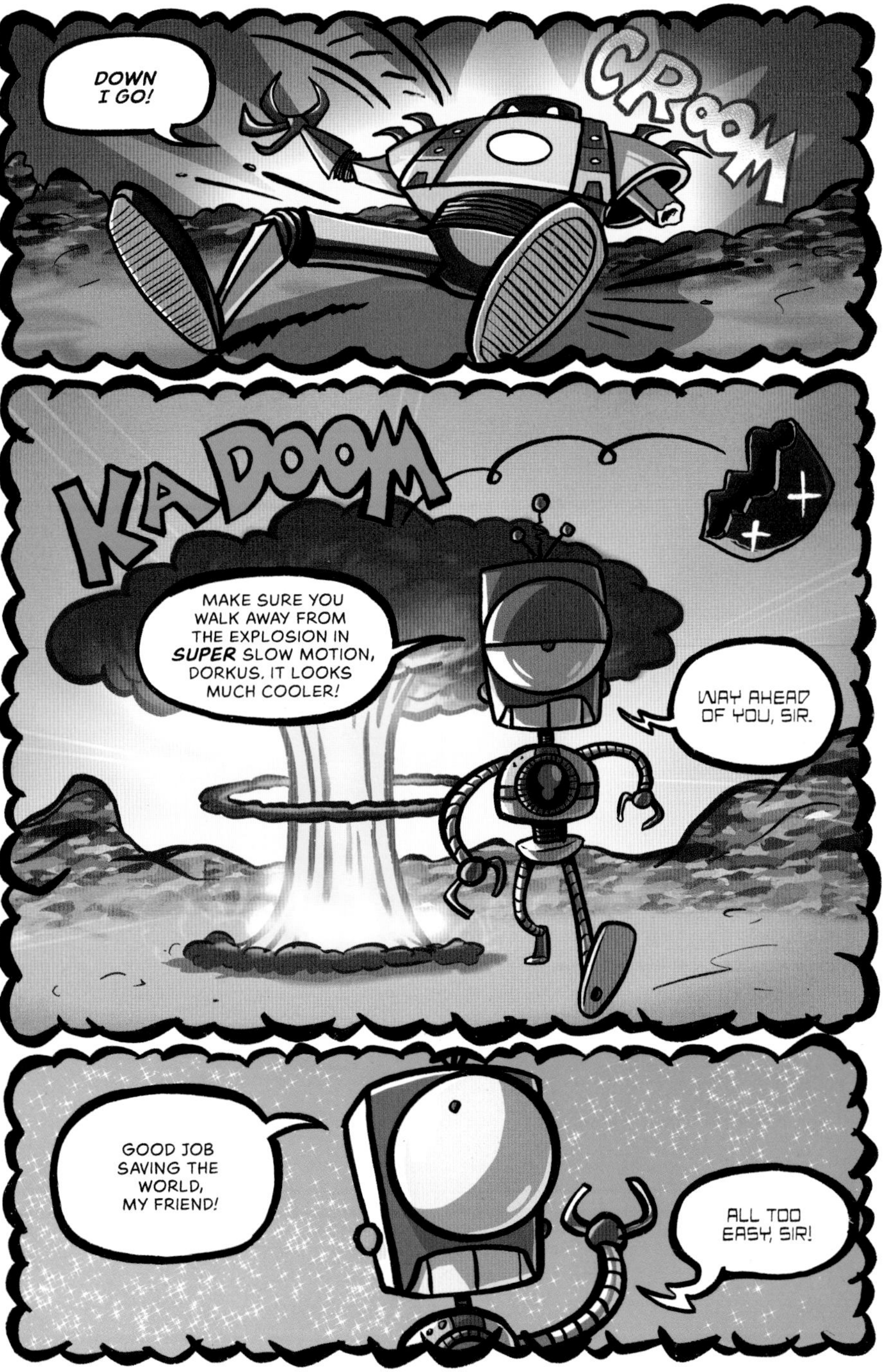
DOWN I GO!
CROOM
KADOOM
MAKE SURE YOU WALK AWAY FROM THE EXPLOSION IN SUPER SLOW MOTION, DORKUS. IT LOOKS MUCH COOLER!
WAY AHEAD OF YOU, SIR.
GOOD JOB SAVING THE WORLD, MY FRIEND!
ALL TOO EASY, SIR!

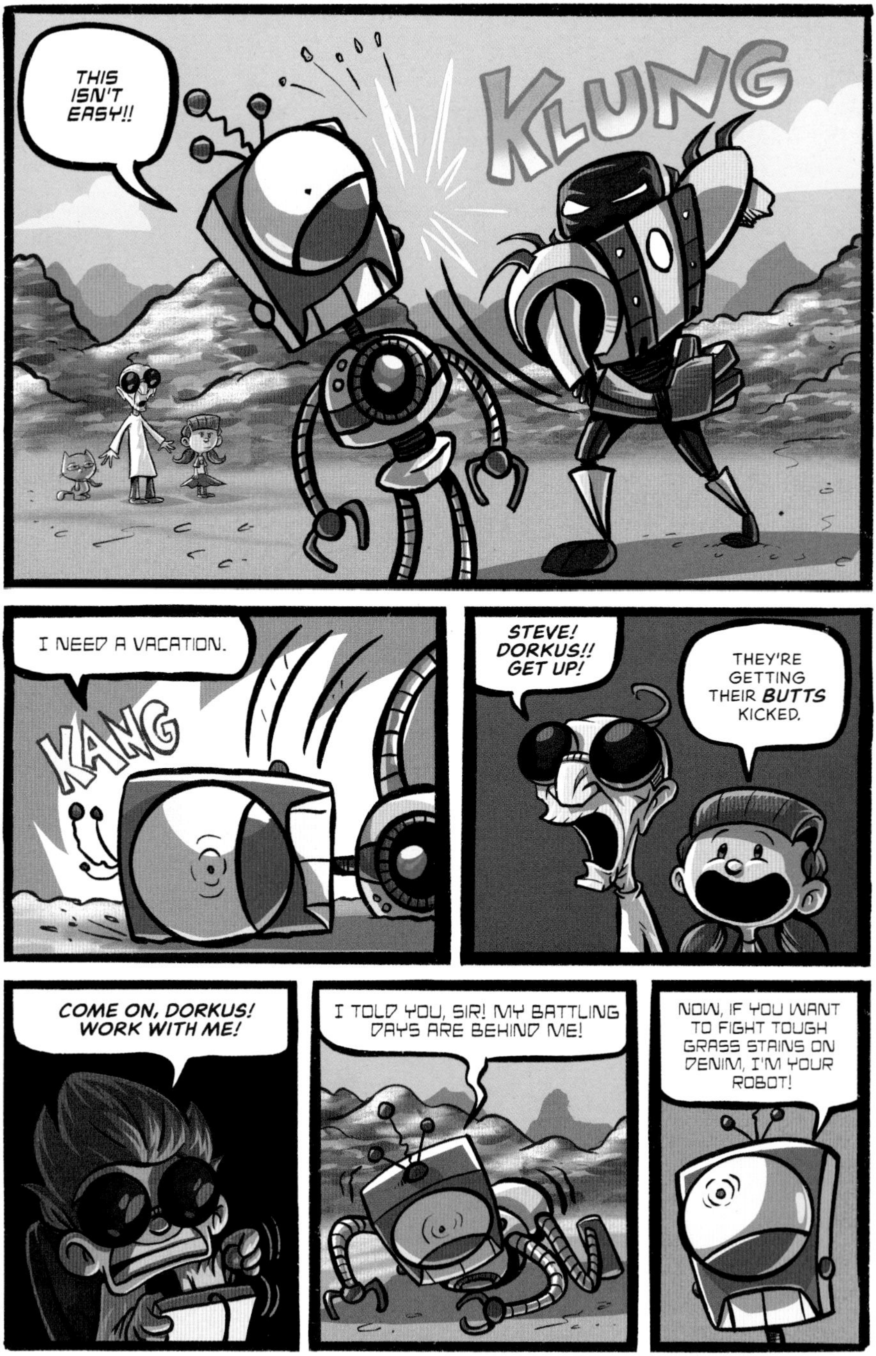
THIS ISN'T EASY!!
KLUNG
I NEED A VACATION.
KANG
STEVE! DORKUS!! GET UP!
THEY'RE GETTING THEIR **BUTTS** KICKED.
COME ON, DORKUS! WORK WITH ME!
I TOLD YOU, SIR! MY BATTLING DAYS ARE BEHIND ME!
NOW, IF YOU WANT TO FIGHT TOUGH GRASS STAINS ON DENIM, I'M YOUR ROBOT!

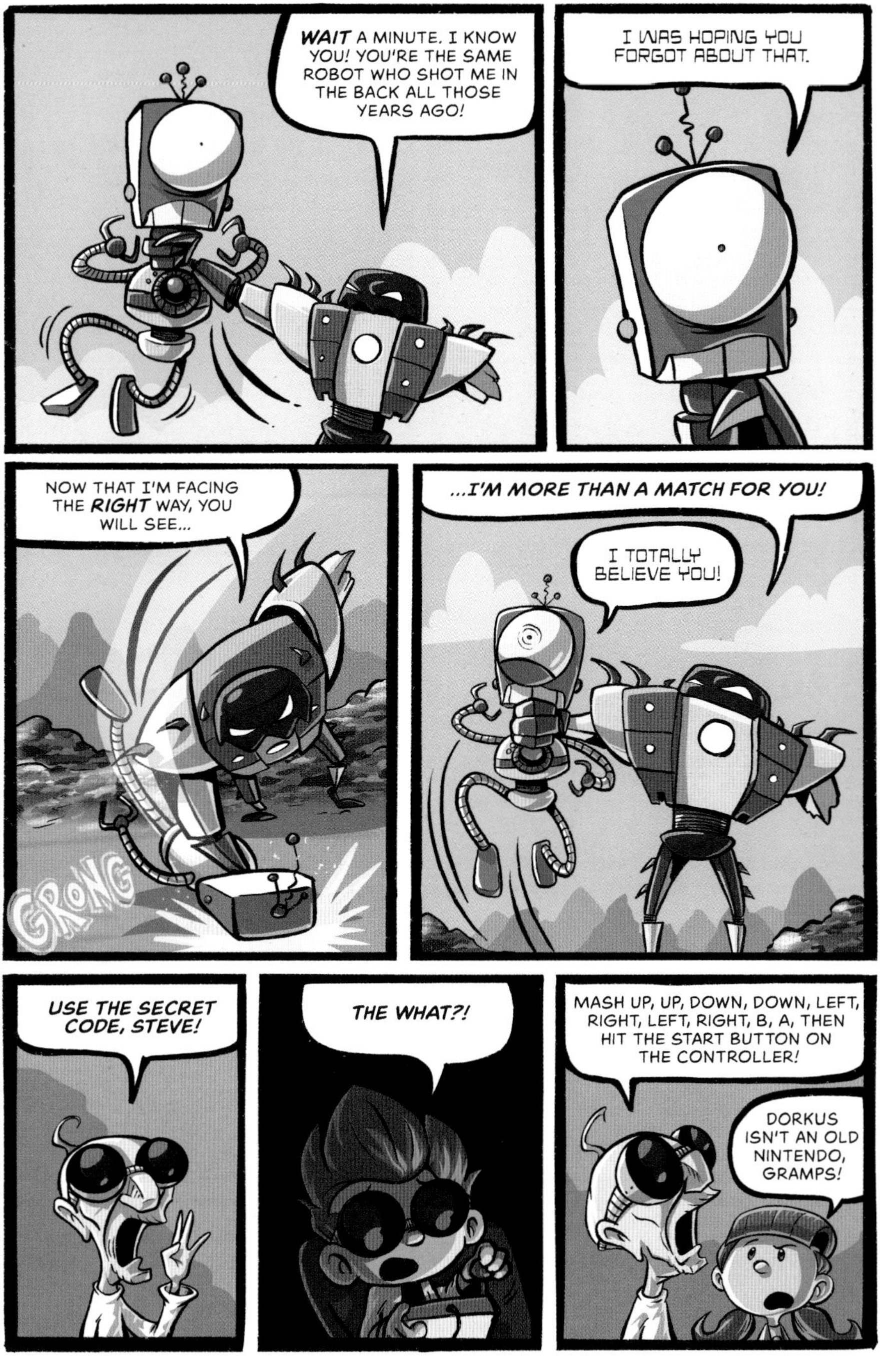
WAIT A MINUTE. I KNOW YOU! YOU'RE THE SAME ROBOT WHO SHOT ME IN THE BACK ALL THOSE YEARS AGO!
I WAS HOPING YOU FORGOT ABOUT THAT.
NOW THAT I'M FACING THE RIGHT WAY, YOU WILL SEE...
GRONG
...I'M MORE THAN A MATCH FOR YOU!
I TOTALLY BELIEVE YOU!
USE THE SECRET CODE, STEVE!
THE WHAT?!
MASH UP, UP, DOWN, DOWN, LEFT, RIGHT, LEFT, RIGHT, B, A, THEN HIT THE START BUTTON ON THE CONTROLLER!
DORKUS ISN'T AN OLD NINTENDO, GRAMPS!

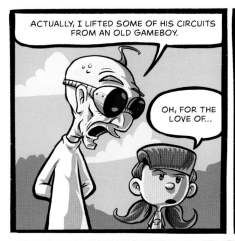

ACTUALLY, I LIFTED SOME OF HIS CIRCUITS FROM AN OLD GAMEBOY.

OH, FOR THE LOVE OF...

UP, UP, DOWN, DOWN, LEFT, LEFT...

...DOWN, NO, *WAIT!* LET ME START OVER.

OKAY, ENOUGH OF THIS SILLY *GAME.*

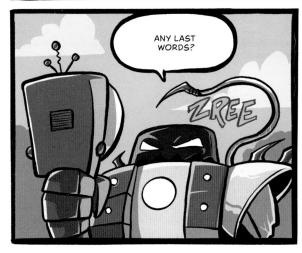

ANY LAST WORDS?

ZREE

I DON'T WANT TO PLAY ANYMORE.

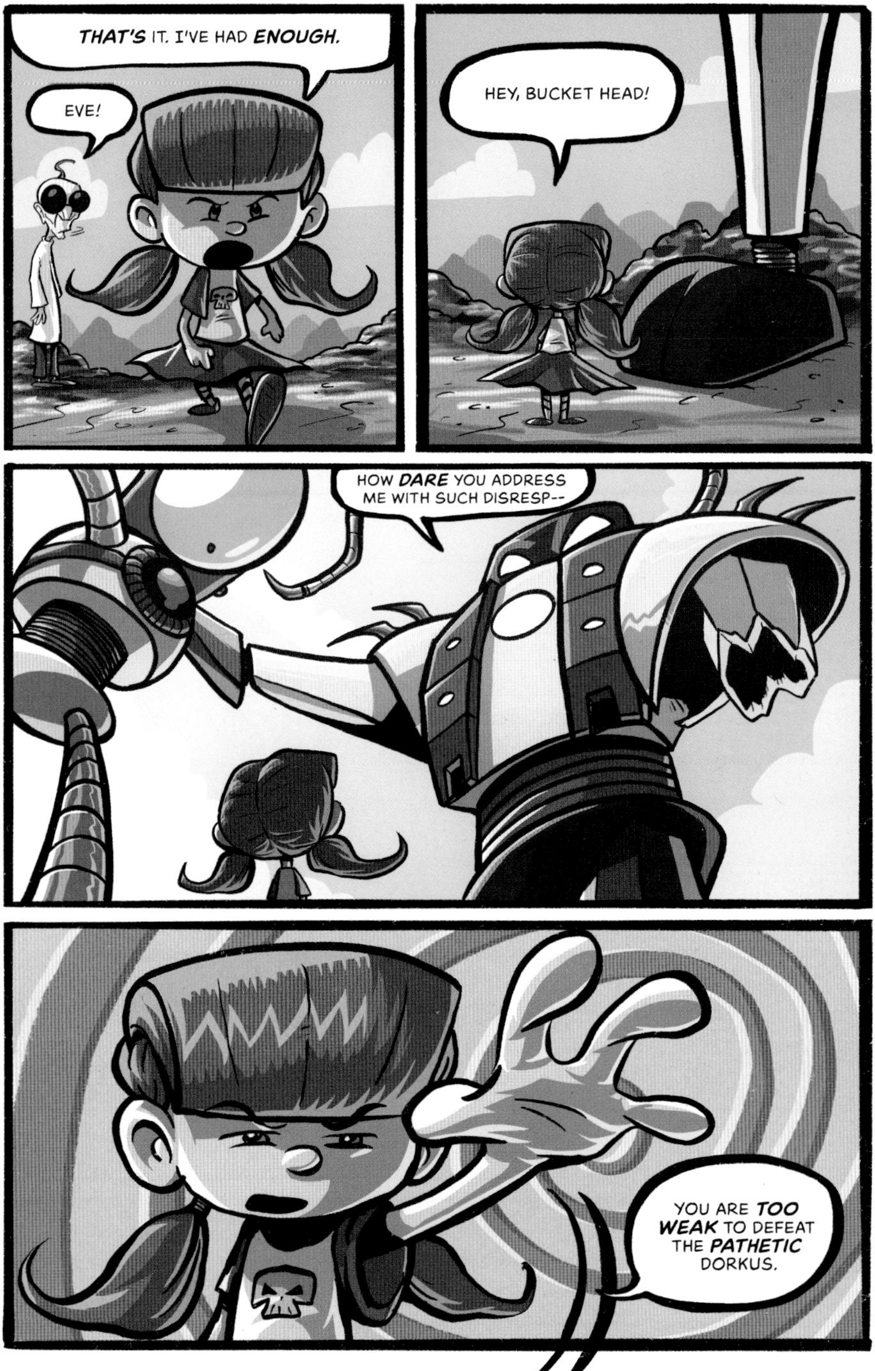
THAT'S IT. I'VE HAD ENOUGH.
EVE!
HEY, BUCKET HEAD!
HOW DARE YOU ADDRESS ME WITH SUCH DISRESP--
YOU ARE TOO WEAK TO DEFEAT THE PATHETIC DORKUS.

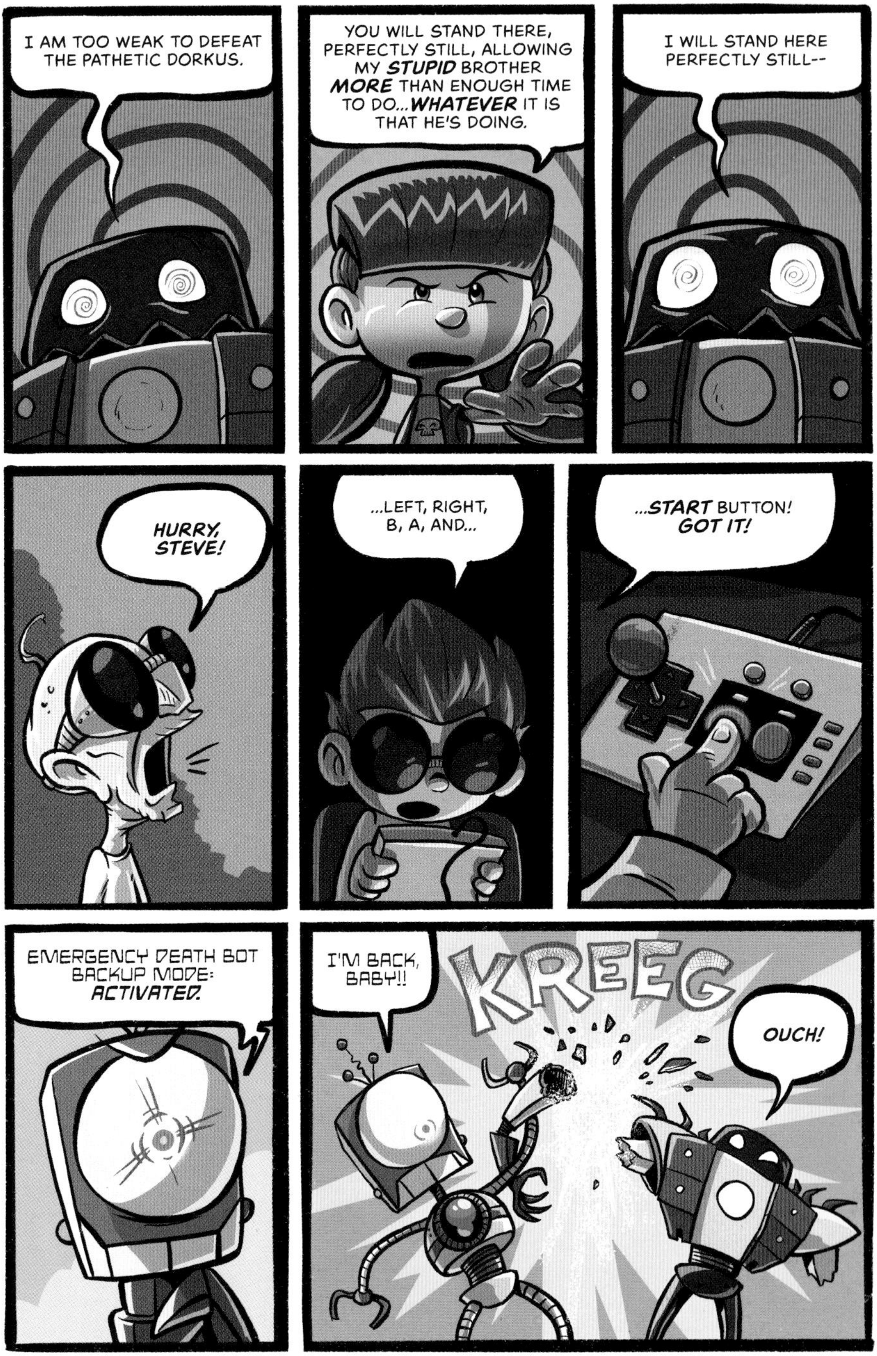
I AM TOO WEAK TO DEFEAT THE PATHETIC DORKUS.
YOU WILL STAND THERE, PERFECTLY STILL, ALLOWING MY STUPID BROTHER MORE THAN ENOUGH TIME TO DO...WHATEVER IT IS THAT HE'S DOING.
I WILL STAND HERE PERFECTLY STILL--
HURRY, STEVE!
...LEFT, RIGHT, B, A, AND...
...START BUTTON! GOT IT!
EMERGENCY DEATH BOT BACKUP MODE: ACTIVATED.
I'M BACK, BABY!!
KREEG
OUCH!

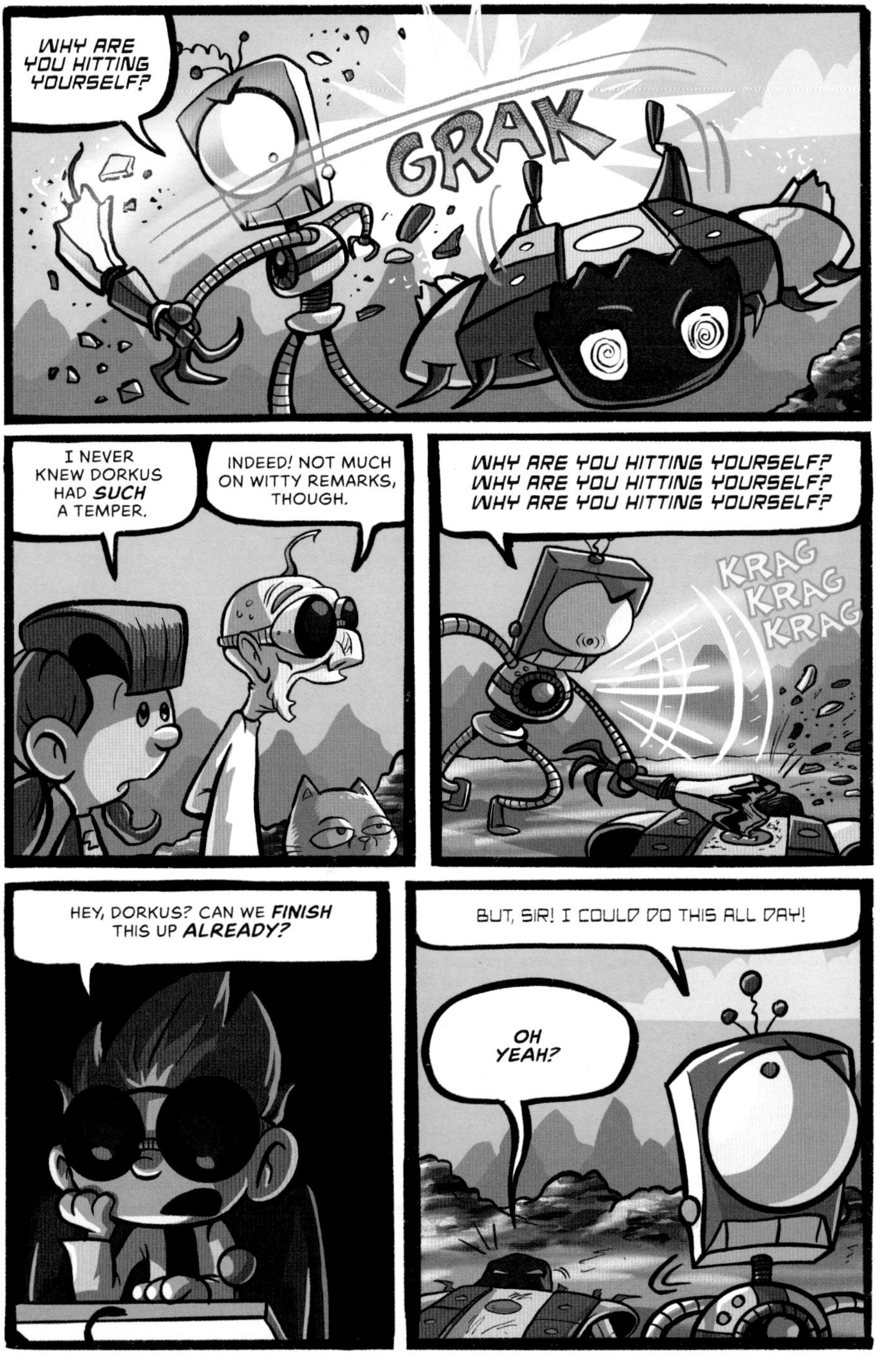
WHY ARE YOU HITTING YOURSELF?
GRAK
I NEVER KNEW DORKUS HAD SUCH A TEMPER.
INDEED! NOT MUCH ON WITTY REMARKS, THOUGH.
WHY ARE YOU HITTING YOURSELF?
WHY ARE YOU HITTING YOURSELF?
WHY ARE YOU HITTING YOURSELF?
KRAG
KRAG
KRAG
HEY, DORKUS? CAN WE FINISH THIS UP ALREADY?
BUT, SIR! I COULD DO THIS ALL DAY!
OH YEAH?

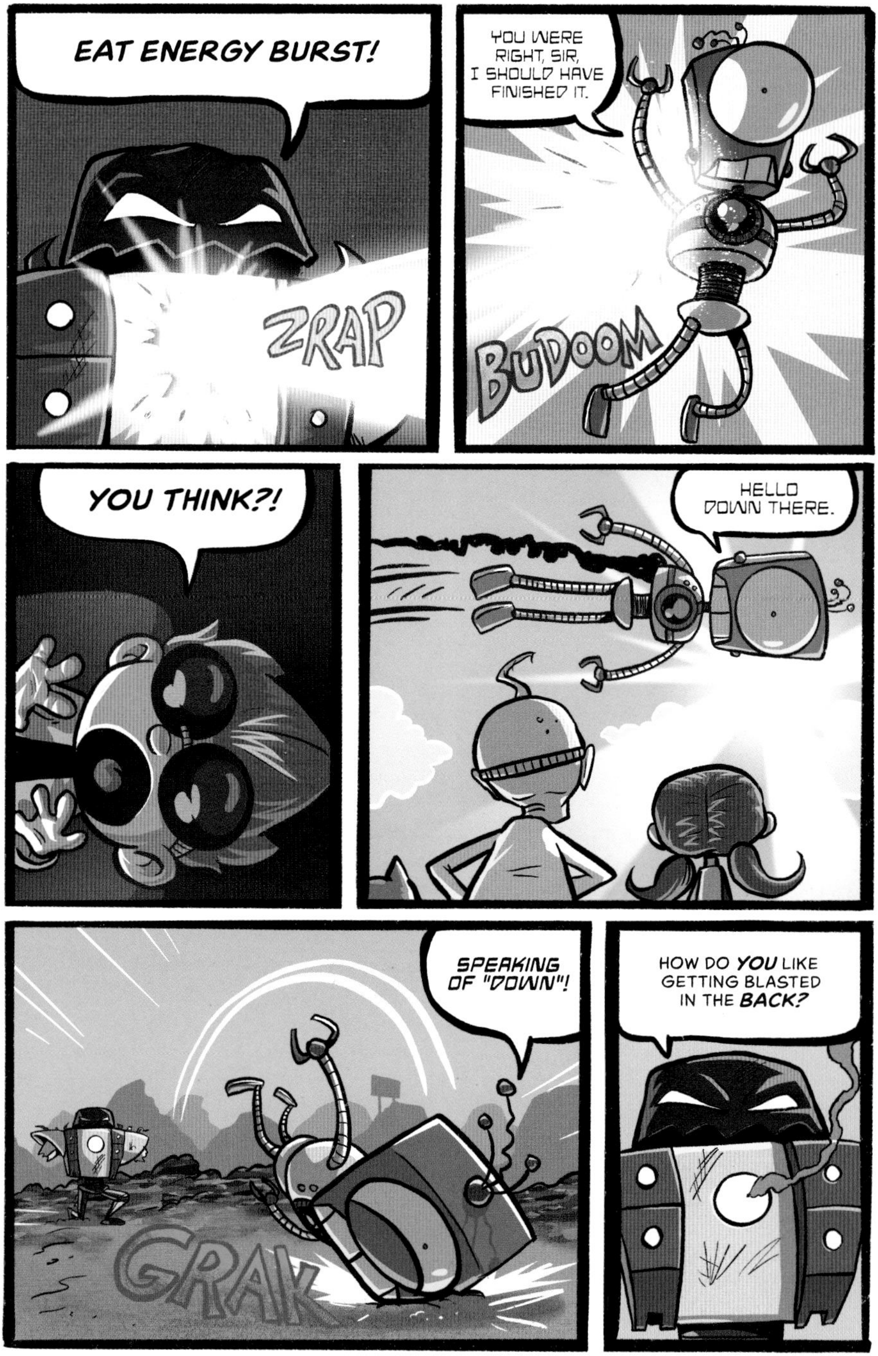
EAT ENERGY BURST!
ZRAP
YOU WERE RIGHT, SIR, I SHOULD HAVE FINISHED IT.
BUDOOM
YOU THINK?!
HELLO DOWN THERE.
SPEAKING OF "DOWN"!
GRAK
HOW DO YOU LIKE GETTING BLASTED IN THE BACK?

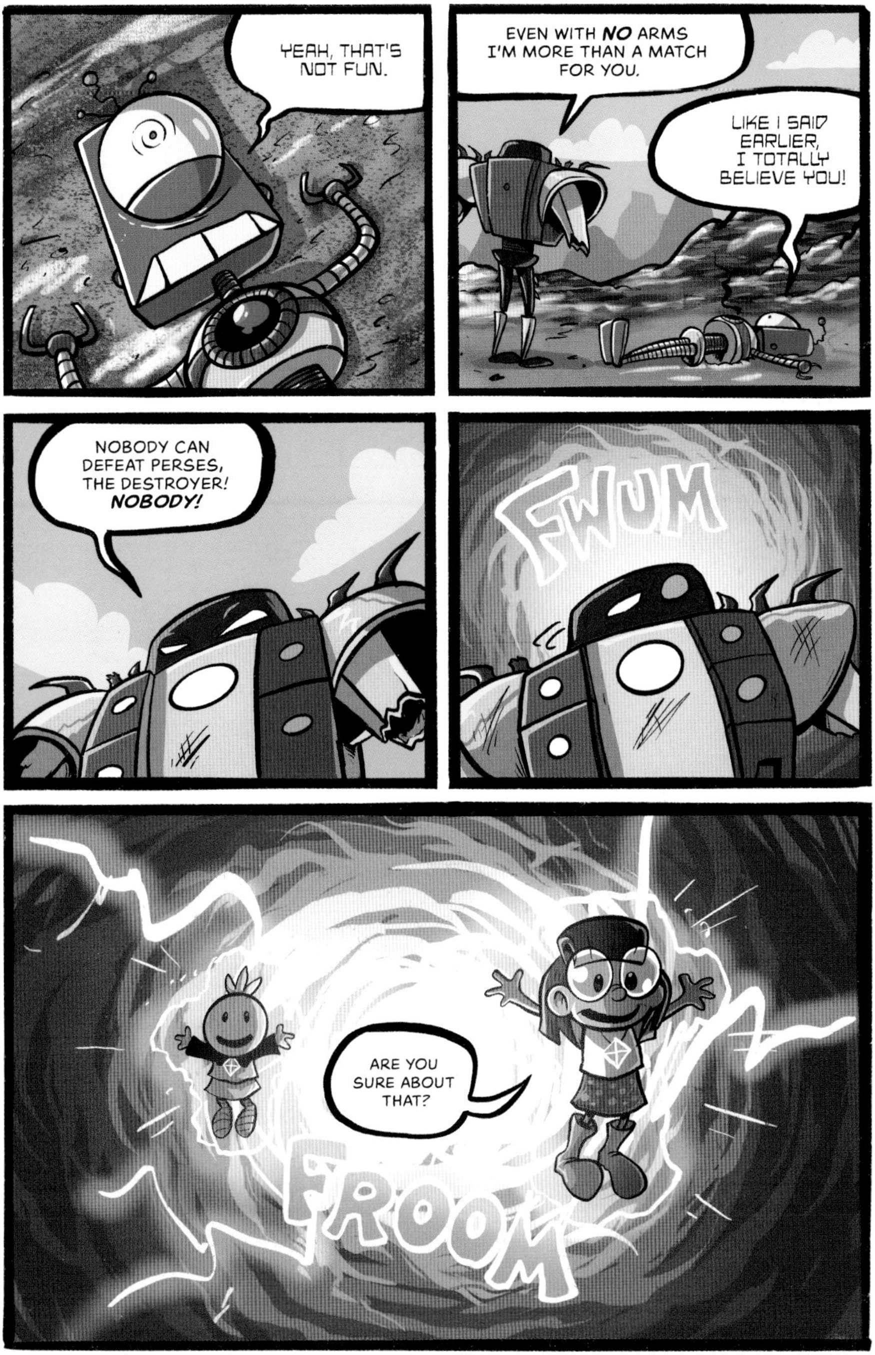
YEAH, THAT'S NOT FUN.
EVEN WITH **NO** ARMS I'M MORE THAN A MATCH FOR YOU.
LIKE I SAID EARLIER, I TOTALLY BELIEVE YOU!
NOBODY CAN DEFEAT PERSES, THE DESTROYER! ***NOBODY!***
FWUM
ARE YOU SURE ABOUT THAT?
FROOM

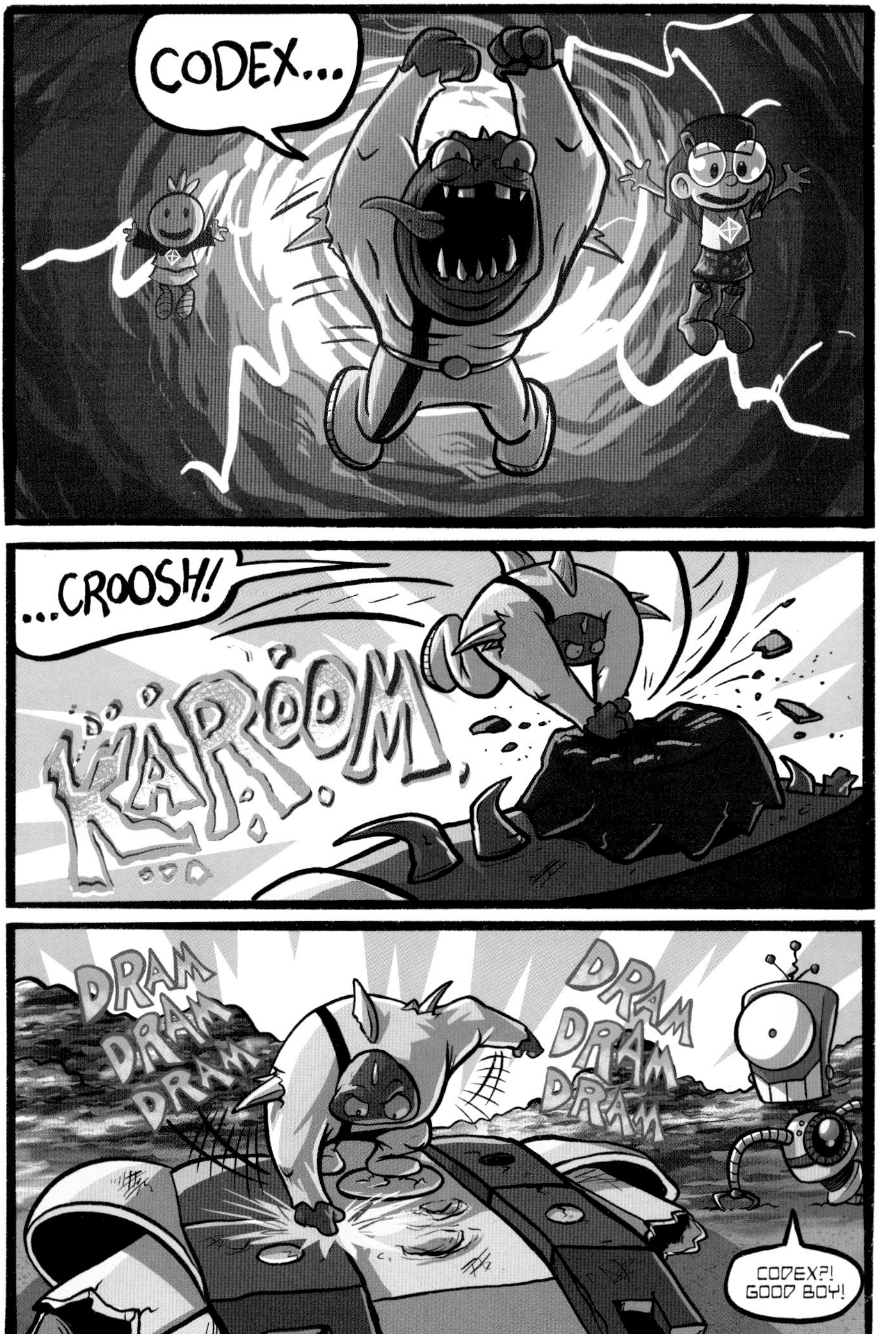
CODEX...
...CROOSH!
KAROOM
DRAM DRAM DRAM
DRAM DRAM DRAM
CODEX?! GOOD BOY!

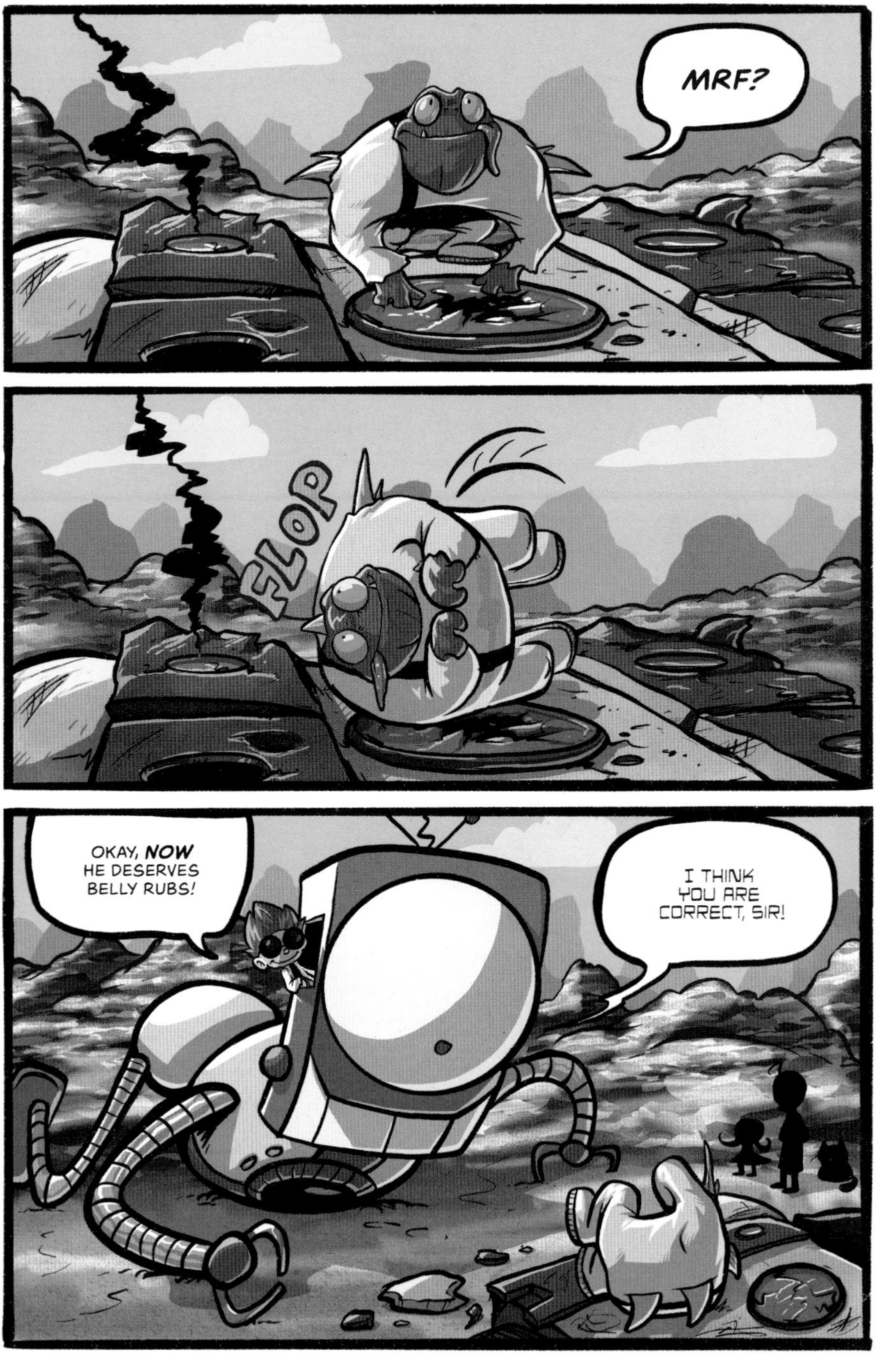
MRF?
FLOP
OKAY, **NOW** HE DESERVES BELLY RUBS!
I THINK YOU ARE CORRECT, SIR!

CHAPTER 18

Parental Guidance Suggested

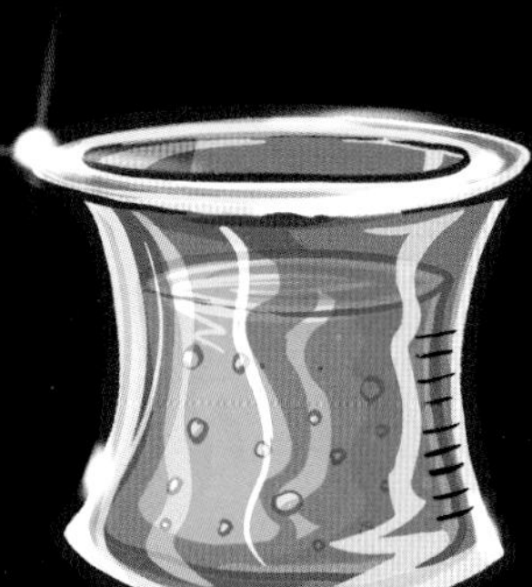

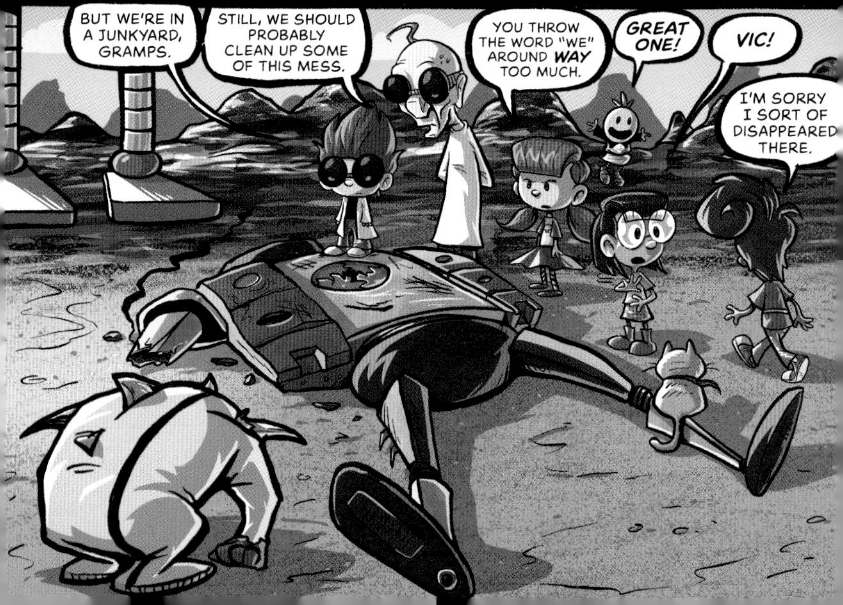
BUT WE'RE IN A JUNKYARD, GRAMPS.
STILL, WE SHOULD PROBABLY CLEAN UP SOME OF THIS MESS.
YOU THROW THE WORD "WE" AROUND **WAY** TOO MUCH.
GREAT ONE!
VIC!
I'M SORRY I SORT OF DISAPPEARED THERE.

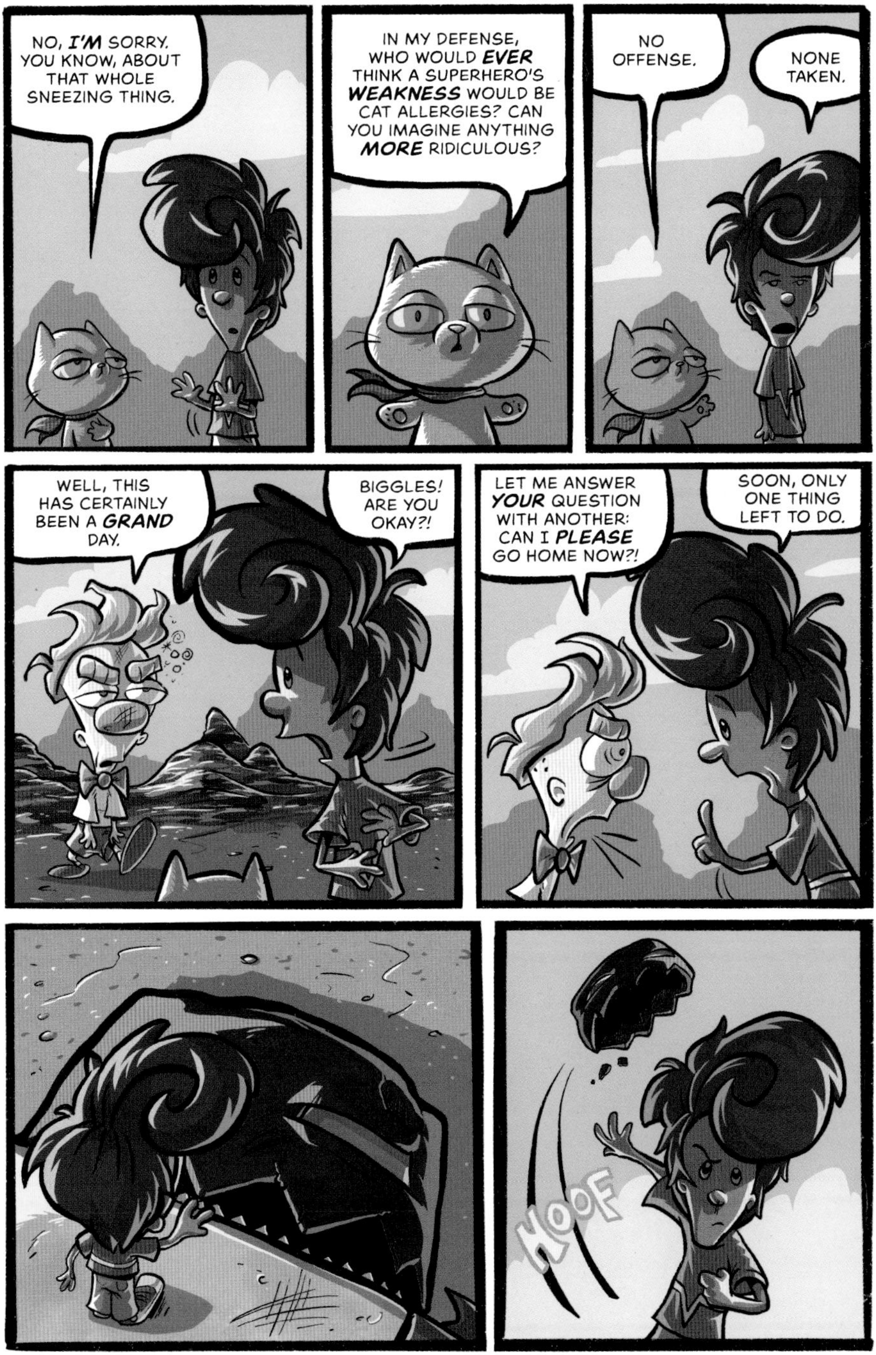
NO, ***I'M*** SORRY. YOU KNOW, ABOUT THAT WHOLE SNEEZING THING.
IN MY DEFENSE, WHO WOULD ***EVER*** THINK A SUPERHERO'S ***WEAKNESS*** WOULD BE CAT ALLERGIES? CAN YOU IMAGINE ANYTHING ***MORE*** RIDICULOUS?
NO OFFENSE.
NONE TAKEN.
WELL, THIS HAS CERTAINLY BEEN A ***GRAND*** DAY.
BIGGLES! ARE YOU OKAY?!
LET ME ANSWER ***YOUR*** QUESTION WITH ANOTHER: CAN I ***PLEASE*** GO HOME NOW?!
SOON, ONLY ONE THING LEFT TO DO.
HOOF

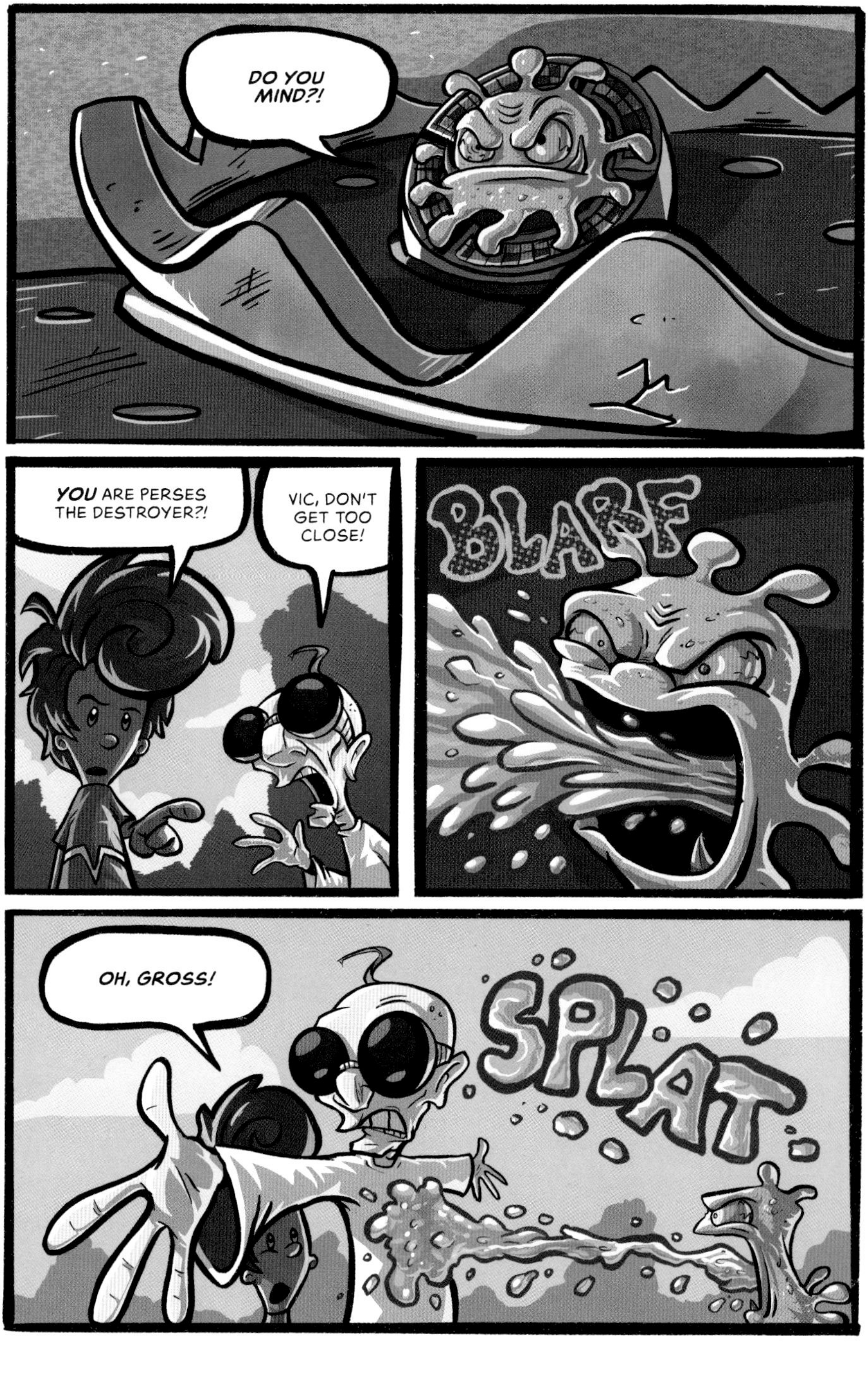
DO YOU MIND?!
YOU ARE PERSES THE DESTROYER?!
VIC, DON'T GET TOO CLOSE!
BLARF
OH, GROSS!
SPLAT

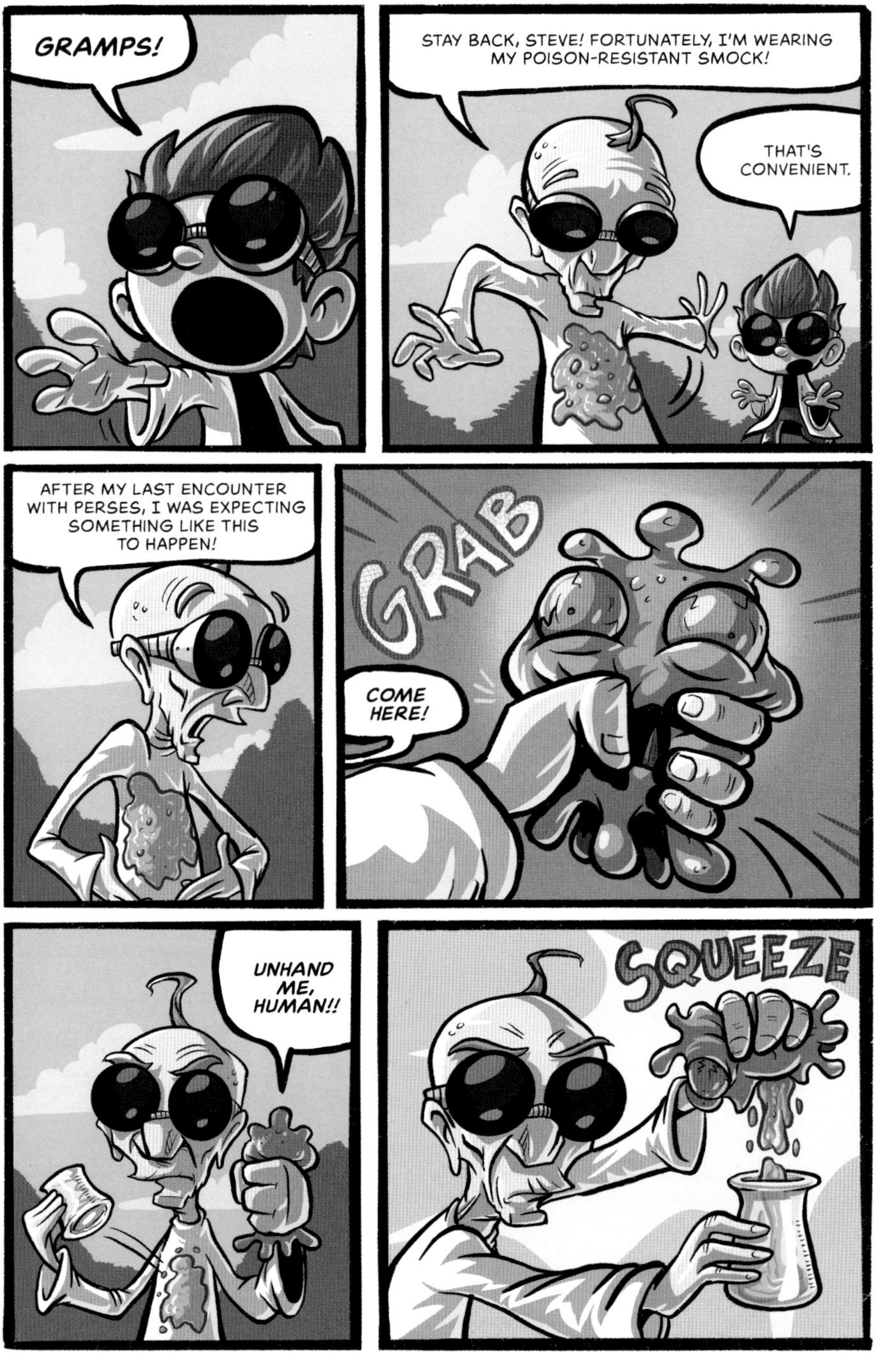
GRAMPS!
STAY BACK, STEVE! FORTUNATELY, I'M WEARING MY POISON-RESISTANT SMOCK!
THAT'S CONVENIENT.
AFTER MY LAST ENCOUNTER WITH PERSES, I WAS EXPECTING SOMETHING LIKE THIS TO HAPPEN!
GRAB
COME HERE!
UNHAND ME, HUMAN!!
SQUEEZE

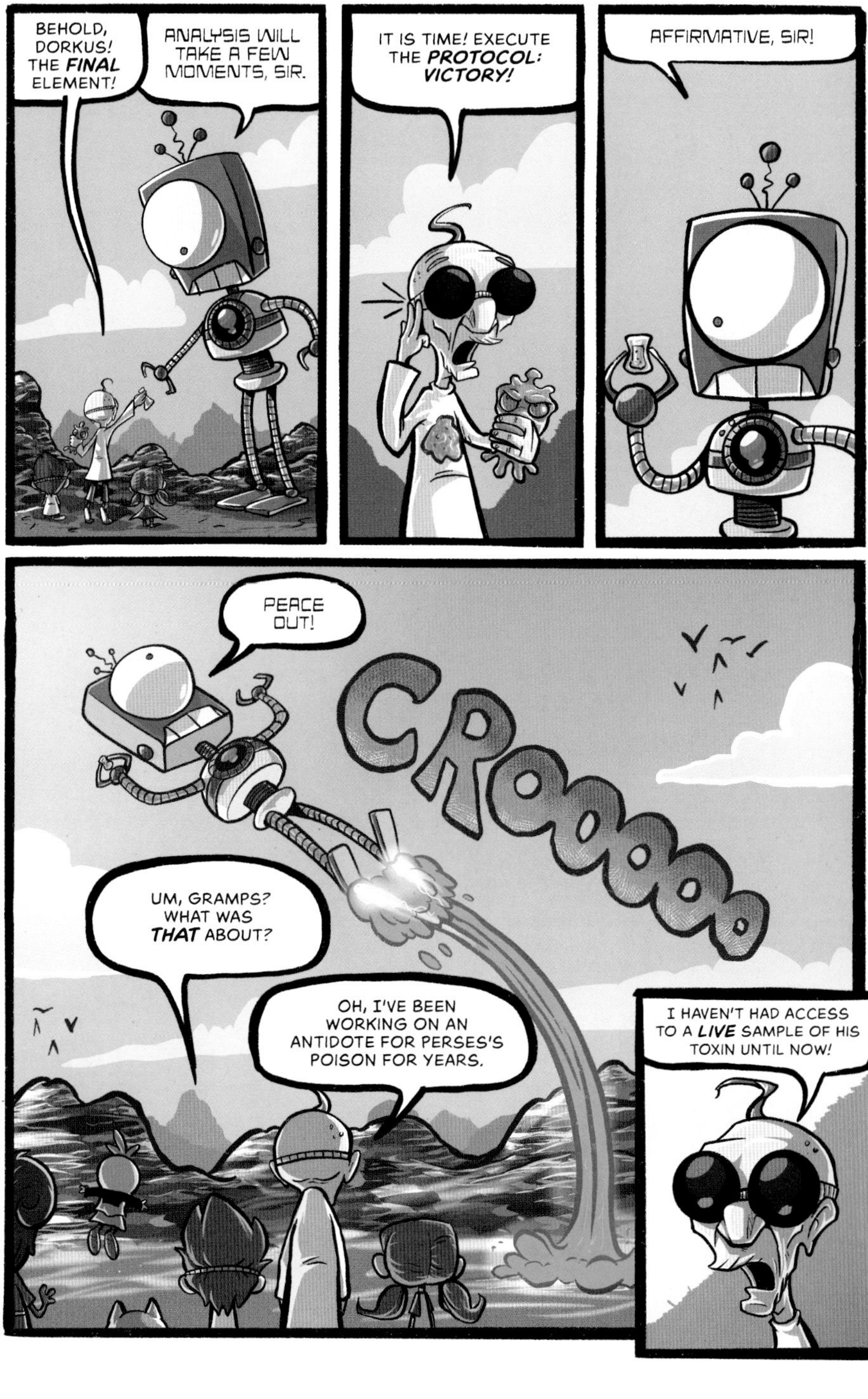
BEHOLD, DORKUS! THE *FINAL* ELEMENT!
ANALYSIS WILL TAKE A FEW MOMENTS, SIR.
IT IS TIME! EXECUTE THE *PROTOCOL: VICTORY!*
AFFIRMATIVE, SIR!
PEACE OUT!
CROOOOOO
UM, GRAMPS? WHAT WAS *THAT* ABOUT?
OH, I'VE BEEN WORKING ON AN ANTIDOTE FOR PERSES'S POISON FOR YEARS.
I HAVEN'T HAD ACCESS TO A *LIVE* SAMPLE OF HIS TOXIN UNTIL NOW!

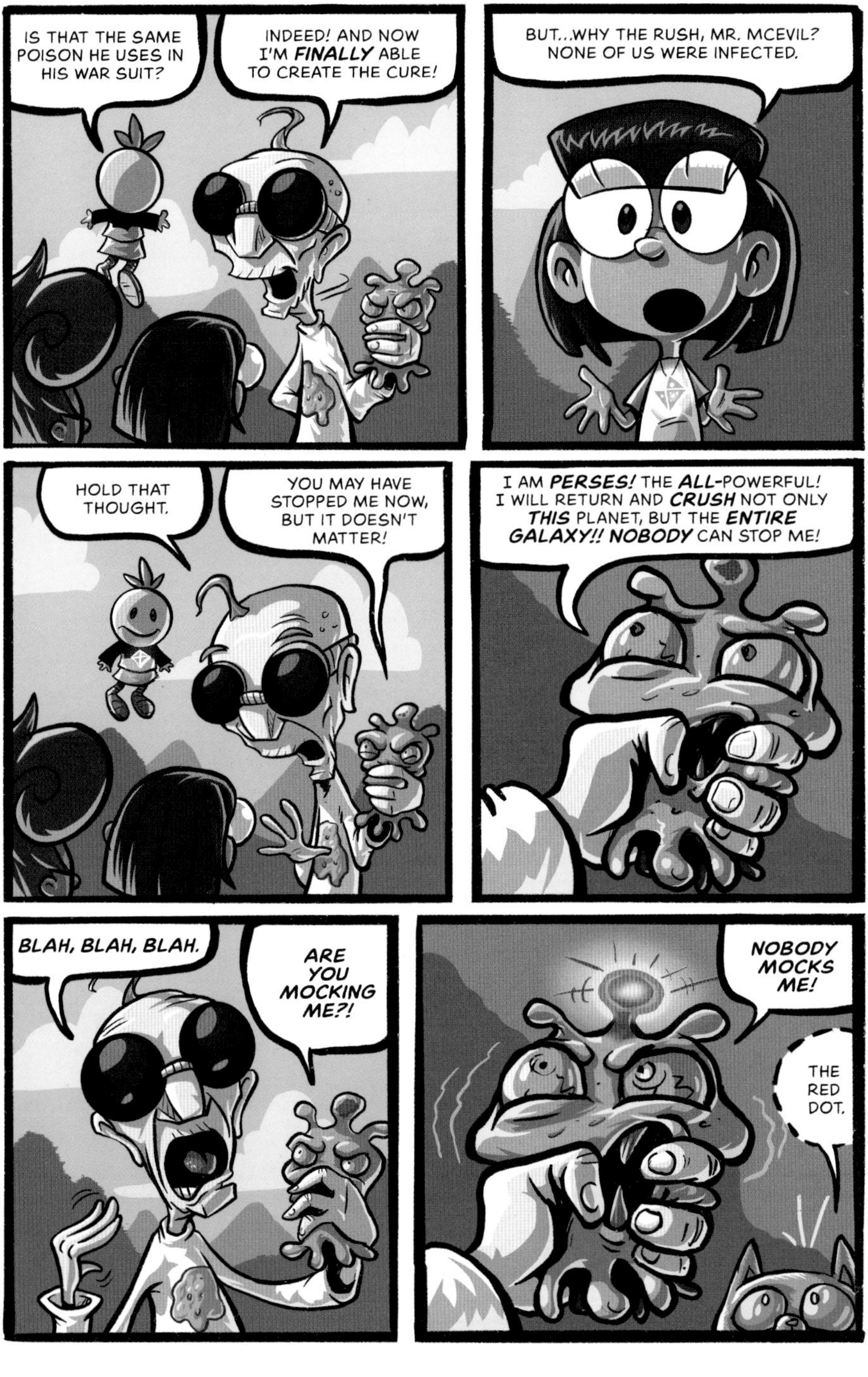
IS THAT THE SAME POISON HE USES IN HIS WAR SUIT?
INDEED! AND NOW I'M FINALLY ABLE TO CREATE THE CURE!
BUT...WHY THE RUSH, MR. MCEVIL? NONE OF US WERE INFECTED.
HOLD THAT THOUGHT.
YOU MAY HAVE STOPPED ME NOW, BUT IT DOESN'T MATTER!
I AM PERSES! THE ALL-POWERFUL! I WILL RETURN AND CRUSH NOT ONLY THIS PLANET, BUT THE ENTIRE GALAXY!! NOBODY CAN STOP ME!
BLAH, BLAH, BLAH.
ARE YOU MOCKING ME?!
NOBODY MOCKS ME!
THE RED DOT.

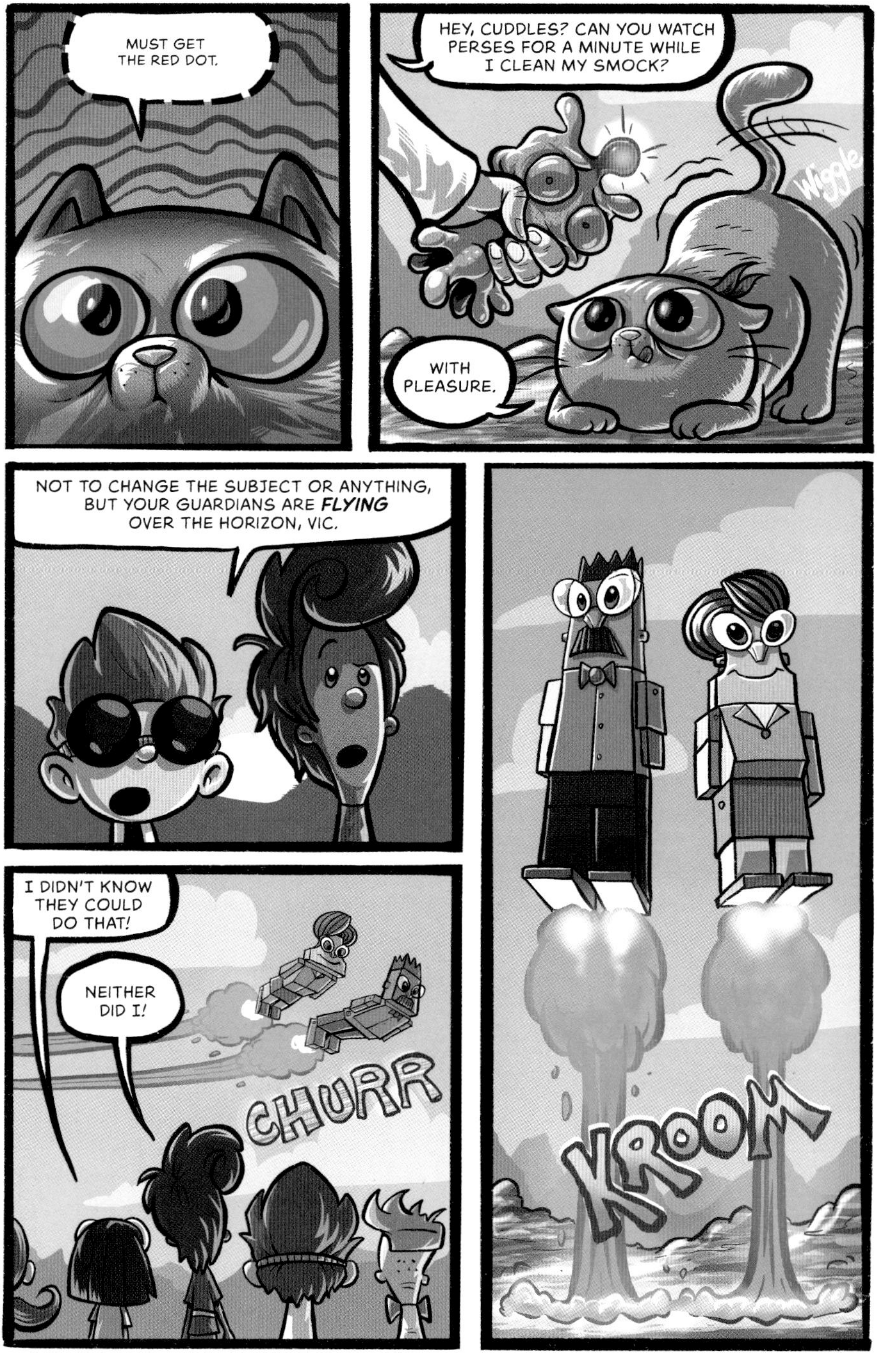
MUST GET THE RED DOT.
HEY, CUDDLES? CAN YOU WATCH PERSES FOR A MINUTE WHILE I CLEAN MY SMOCK?
Wiggle
WITH PLEASURE.
NOT TO CHANGE THE SUBJECT OR ANYTHING, BUT YOUR GUARDIANS ARE FLYING OVER THE HORIZON, VIC.
I DIDN'T KNOW THEY COULD DO THAT!
NEITHER DID I!
CHURR
KROOM

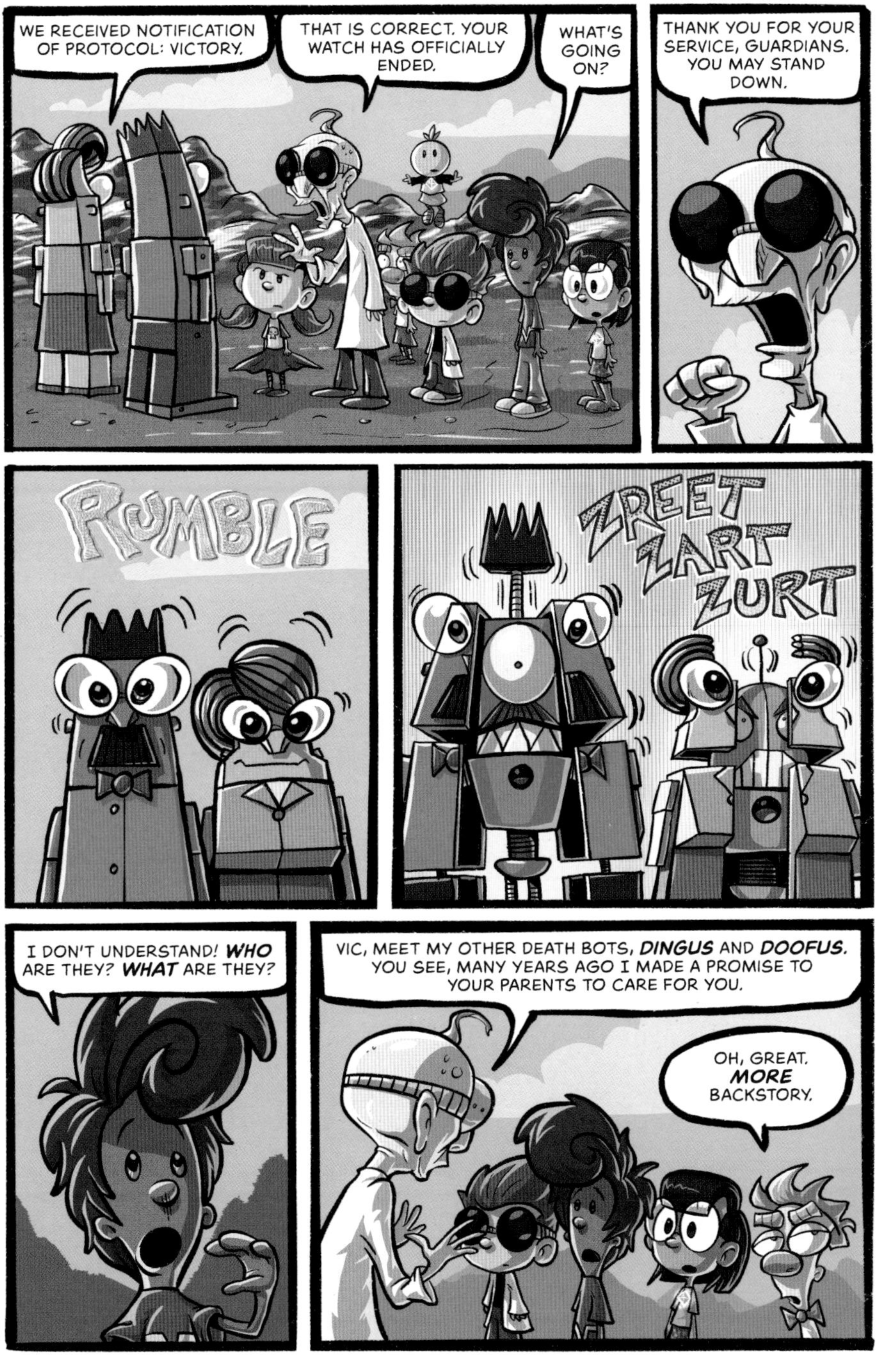
WE RECEIVED NOTIFICATION OF PROTOCOL: VICTORY.
THAT IS CORRECT. YOUR WATCH HAS OFFICIALLY ENDED.
WHAT'S GOING ON?
THANK YOU FOR YOUR SERVICE, GUARDIANS. YOU MAY STAND DOWN.
RUMBLE
ZREET ZART ZURT
I DON'T UNDERSTAND! ***WHO*** ARE THEY? ***WHAT*** ARE THEY?
VIC, MEET MY OTHER DEATH BOTS, ***DINGUS*** AND ***DOOFUS.*** YOU SEE, MANY YEARS AGO I MADE A PROMISE TO YOUR PARENTS TO CARE FOR YOU.
OH, GREAT. ***MORE*** BACKSTORY.

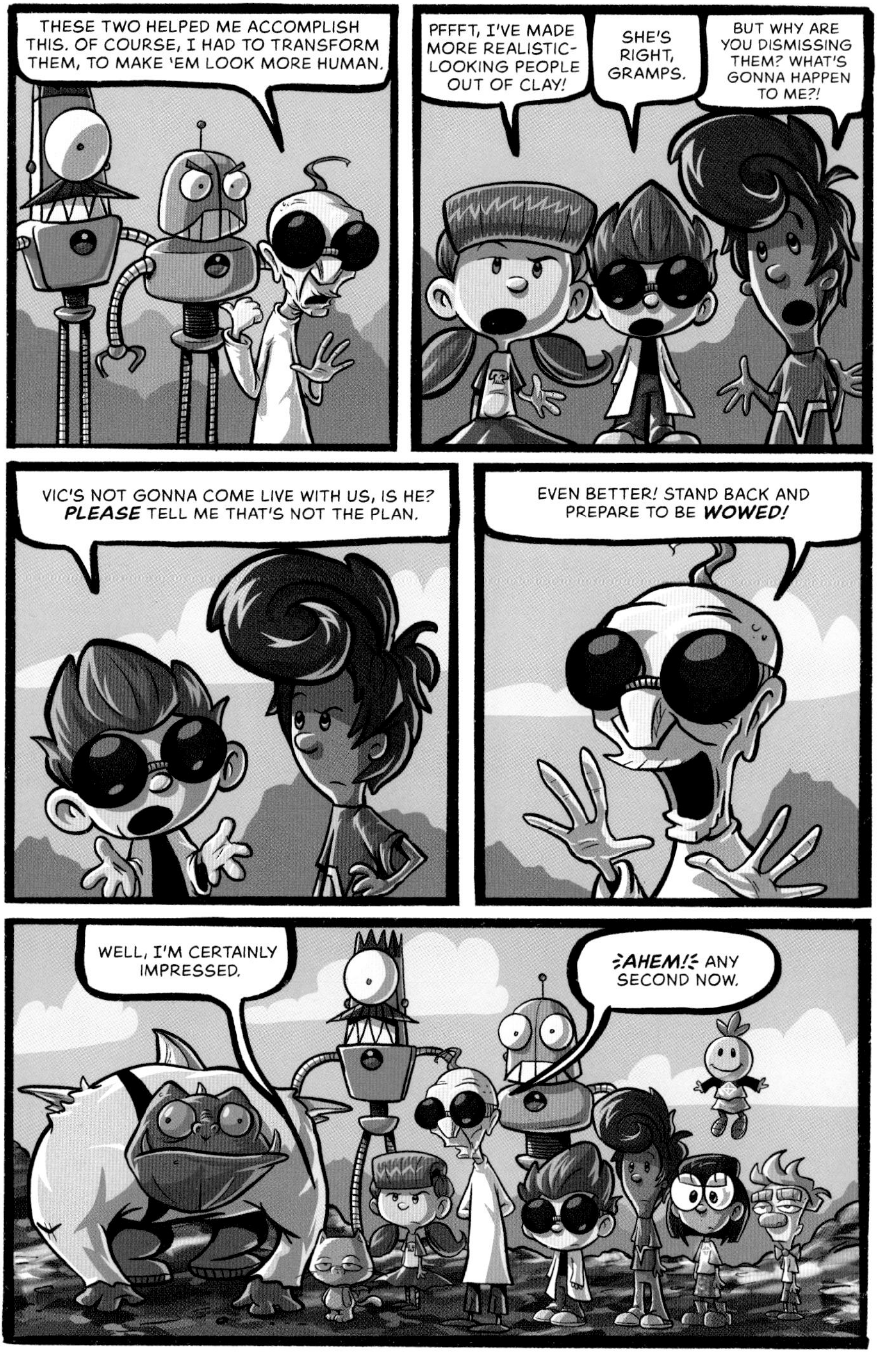
THESE TWO HELPED ME ACCOMPLISH THIS. OF COURSE, I HAD TO TRANSFORM THEM, TO MAKE 'EM LOOK MORE HUMAN.
PFFFT, I'VE MADE MORE REALISTIC-LOOKING PEOPLE OUT OF CLAY!
SHE'S RIGHT, GRAMPS.
BUT WHY ARE YOU DISMISSING THEM? WHAT'S GONNA HAPPEN TO ME?!
VIC'S NOT GONNA COME LIVE WITH US, IS HE? ***PLEASE*** TELL ME THAT'S NOT THE PLAN.
EVEN BETTER! STAND BACK AND PREPARE TO BE ***WOWED!***
WELL, I'M CERTAINLY IMPRESSED.
AHEM! ANY SECOND NOW.

MANY SECONDS LATER...

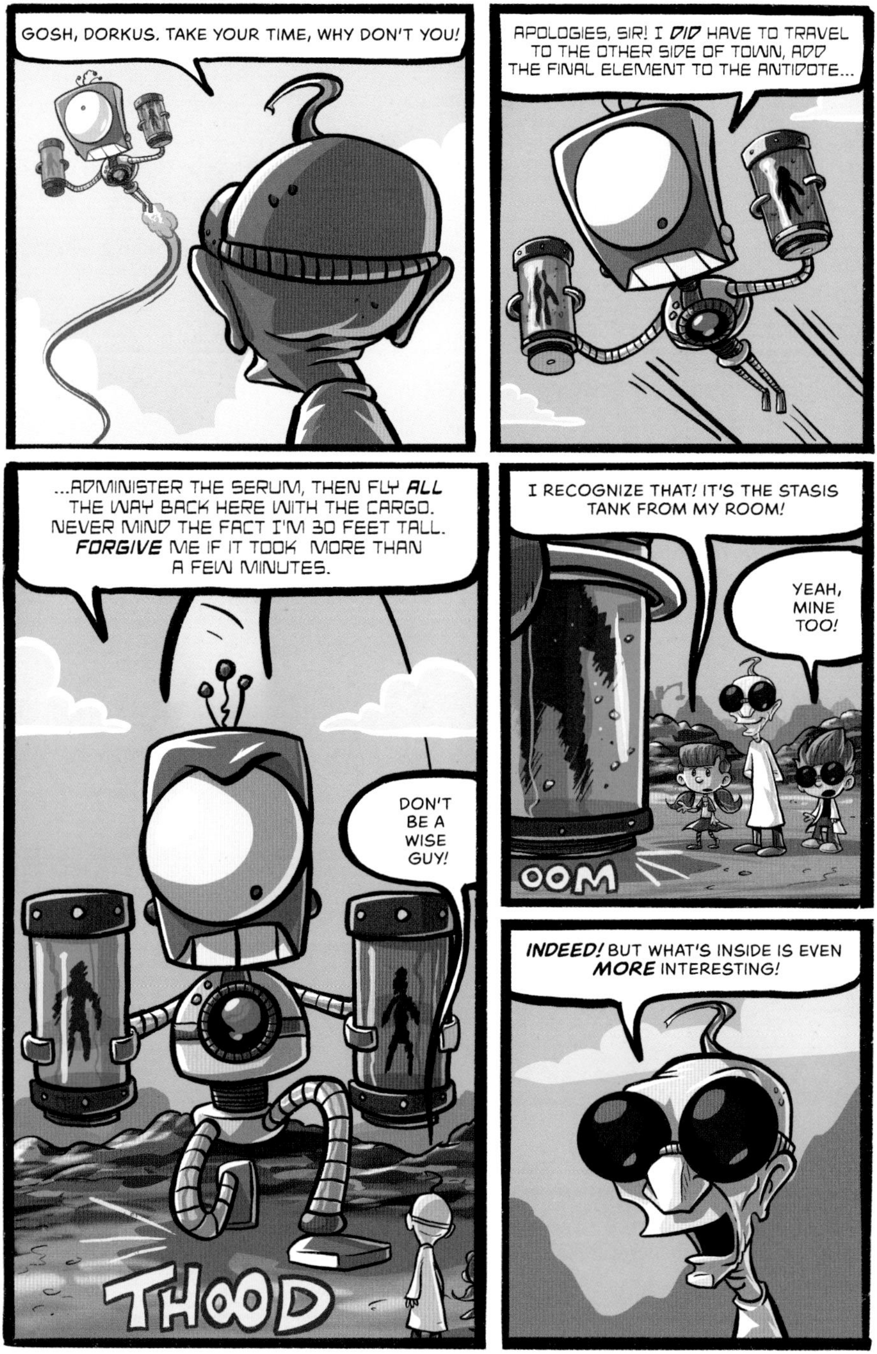

GOSH, DORKUS. TAKE YOUR TIME, WHY DON'T YOU!
APOLOGIES, SIR! I *DID* HAVE TO TRAVEL TO THE OTHER SIDE OF TOWN, ADD THE FINAL ELEMENT TO THE ANTIDOTE...
...ADMINISTER THE SERUM, THEN FLY *ALL* THE WAY BACK HERE WITH THE CARGO. NEVER MIND THE FACT I'M 30 FEET TALL. *FORGIVE* ME IF IT TOOK MORE THAN A FEW MINUTES.
DON'T BE A WISE GUY!
THOOD
I RECOGNIZE THAT! IT'S THE STASIS TANK FROM MY ROOM!
YEAH, MINE TOO!
OOM
INDEED! BUT WHAT'S INSIDE IS EVEN *MORE* INTERESTING!

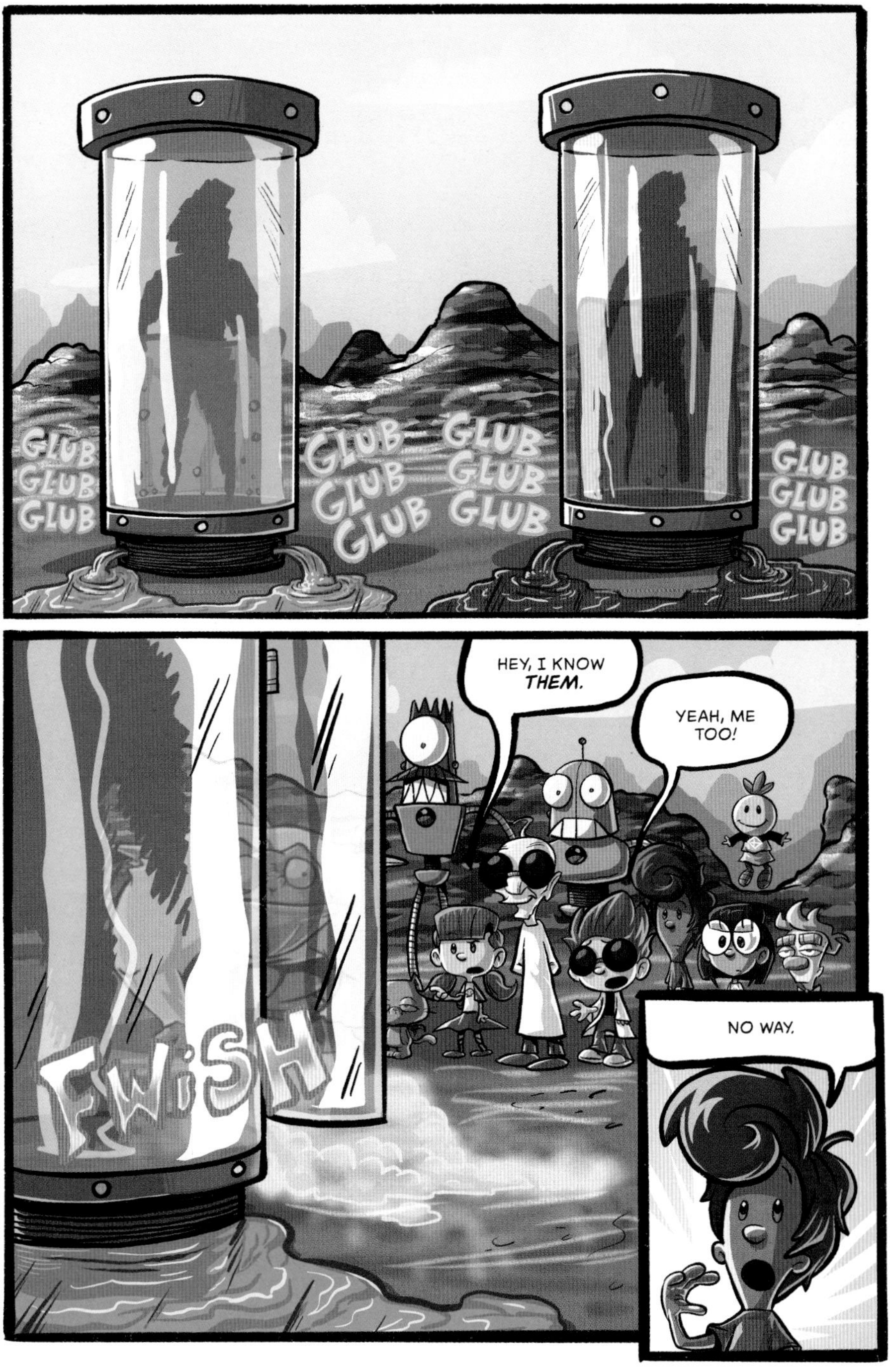
GLUB GLUB GLUB
GLUB GLUB GLUB
GLUB GLUB GLUB
GLUB GLUB GLUB
FWISH
HEY, I KNOW *THEM.*
YEAH, ME TOO!
NO WAY.

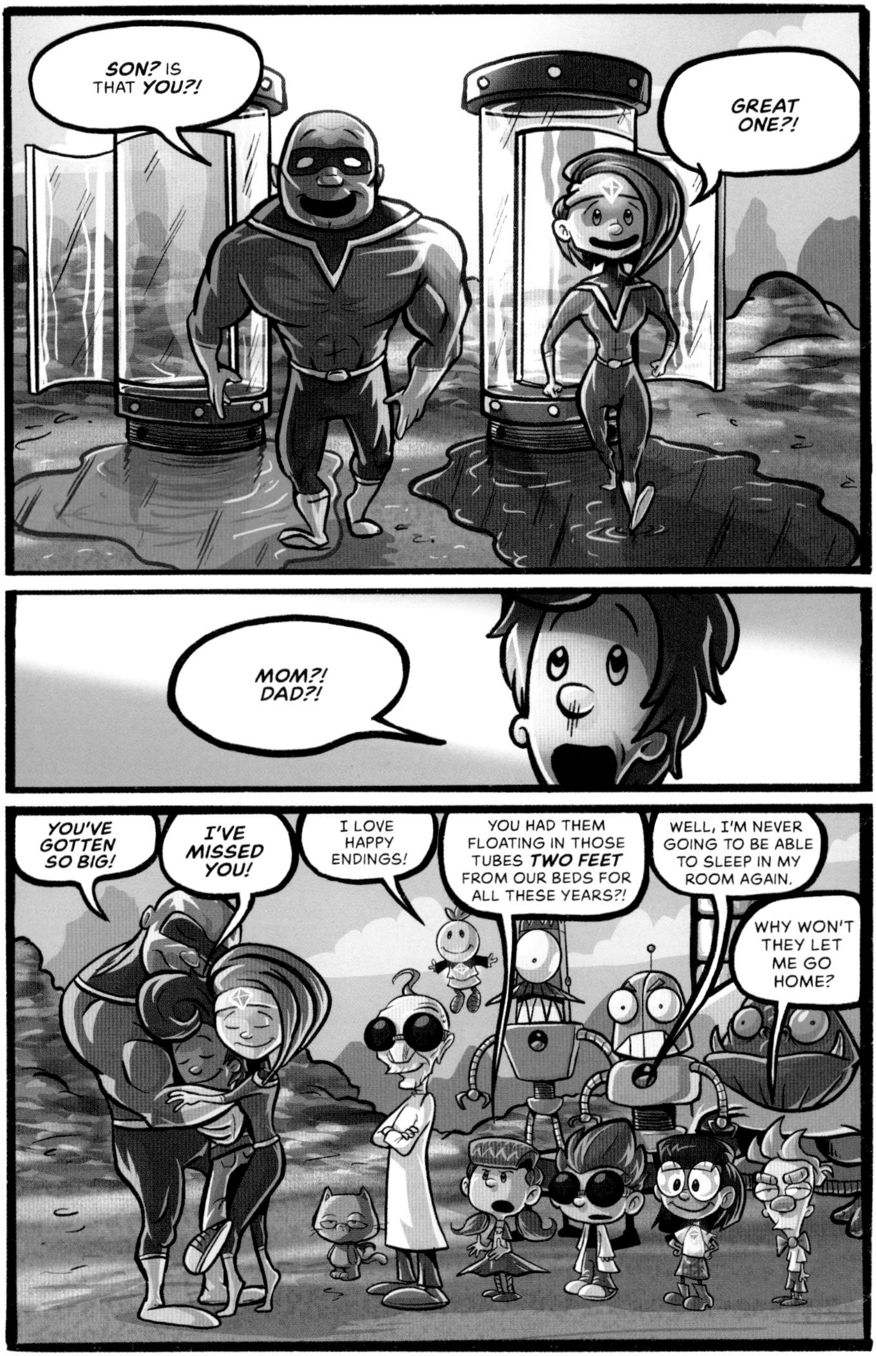
SON? IS THAT YOU?!
GREAT ONE?!
MOM?! DAD?!
YOU'VE GOTTEN SO BIG!
I'VE MISSED YOU!
I LOVE HAPPY ENDINGS!
YOU HAD THEM FLOATING IN THOSE TUBES TWO FEET FROM OUR BEDS FOR ALL THESE YEARS?!
WELL, I'M NEVER GOING TO BE ABLE TO SLEEP IN MY ROOM AGAIN.
WHY WON'T THEY LET ME GO HOME?

CHAPTER 19
All Good Things

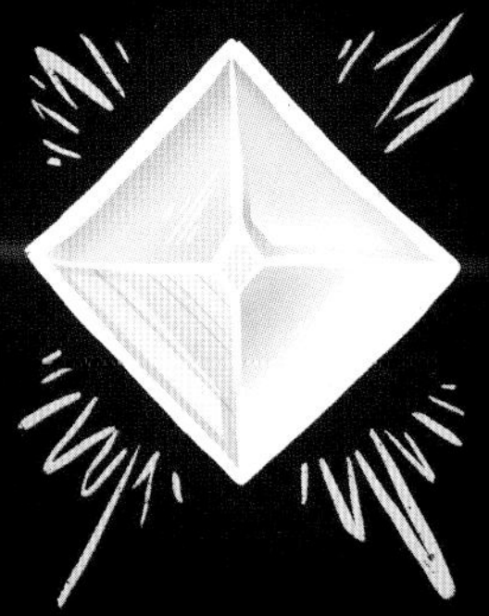

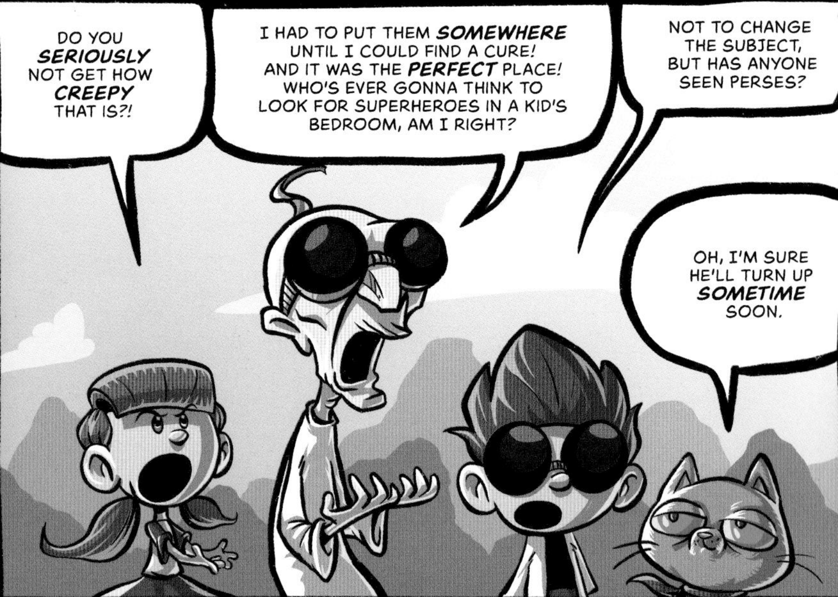
DO YOU *SERIOUSLY* NOT GET HOW *CREEPY* THAT IS?!
I HAD TO PUT THEM *SOMEWHERE* UNTIL I COULD FIND A CURE! AND IT WAS THE *PERFECT* PLACE! WHO'S EVER GONNA THINK TO LOOK FOR SUPERHEROES IN A KID'S BEDROOM, AM I RIGHT?
NOT TO CHANGE THE SUBJECT, BUT HAS ANYONE SEEN PERSES?
OH, I'M SURE HE'LL TURN UP *SOMETIME* SOON.

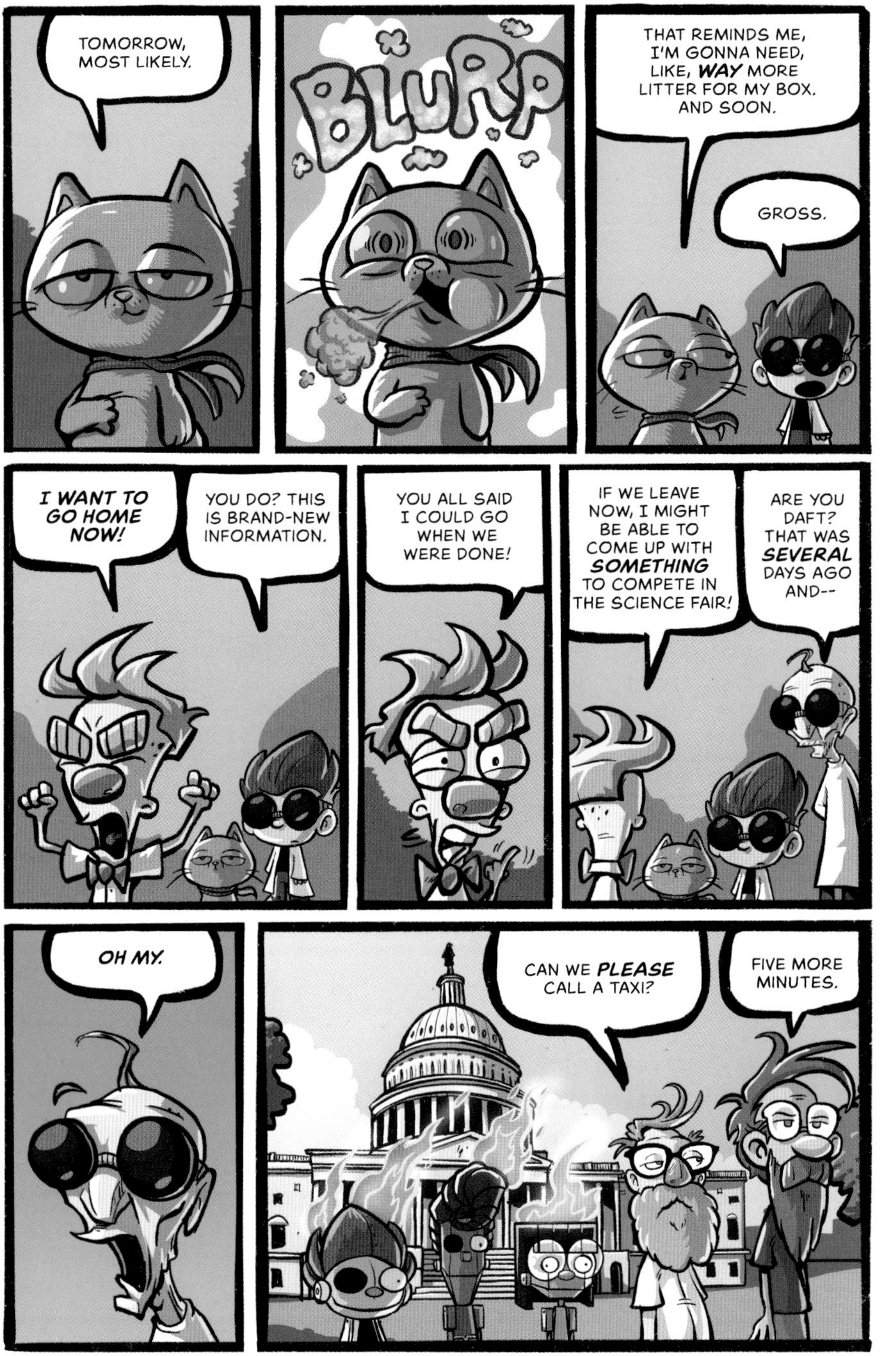
TOMORROW, MOST LIKELY.
BLURP
THAT REMINDS ME, I'M GONNA NEED, LIKE, WAY MORE LITTER FOR MY BOX. AND SOON.
GROSS.
I WANT TO GO HOME NOW!
YOU DO? THIS IS BRAND-NEW INFORMATION.
YOU ALL SAID I COULD GO WHEN WE WERE DONE!
IF WE LEAVE NOW, I MIGHT BE ABLE TO COME UP WITH SOMETHING TO COMPETE IN THE SCIENCE FAIR!
ARE YOU DAFT? THAT WAS SEVERAL DAYS AGO AND--
OH MY.
CAN WE PLEASE CALL A TAXI?
FIVE MORE MINUTES.

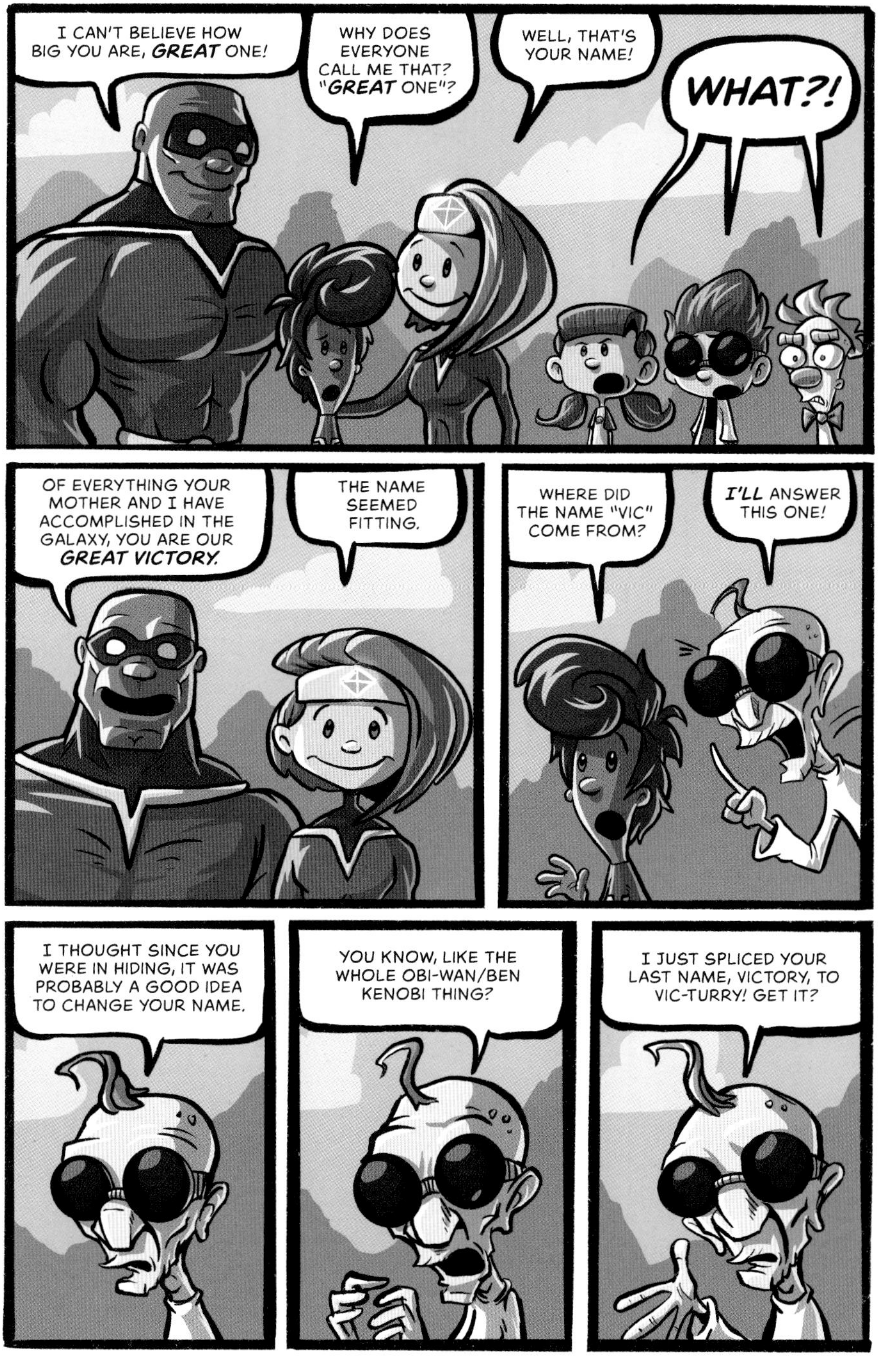
I CAN'T BELIEVE HOW BIG YOU ARE, GREAT ONE!
WHY DOES EVERYONE CALL ME THAT? "GREAT ONE"?
WELL, THAT'S YOUR NAME!
WHAT?!
OF EVERYTHING YOUR MOTHER AND I HAVE ACCOMPLISHED IN THE GALAXY, YOU ARE OUR GREAT VICTORY.
THE NAME SEEMED FITTING.
WHERE DID THE NAME "VIC" COME FROM?
I'LL ANSWER THIS ONE!
I THOUGHT SINCE YOU WERE IN HIDING, IT WAS PROBABLY A GOOD IDEA TO CHANGE YOUR NAME.
YOU KNOW, LIKE THE WHOLE OBI-WAN/BEN KENOBI THING?
I JUST SPLICED YOUR LAST NAME, VICTORY, TO VIC-TURRY! GET IT?

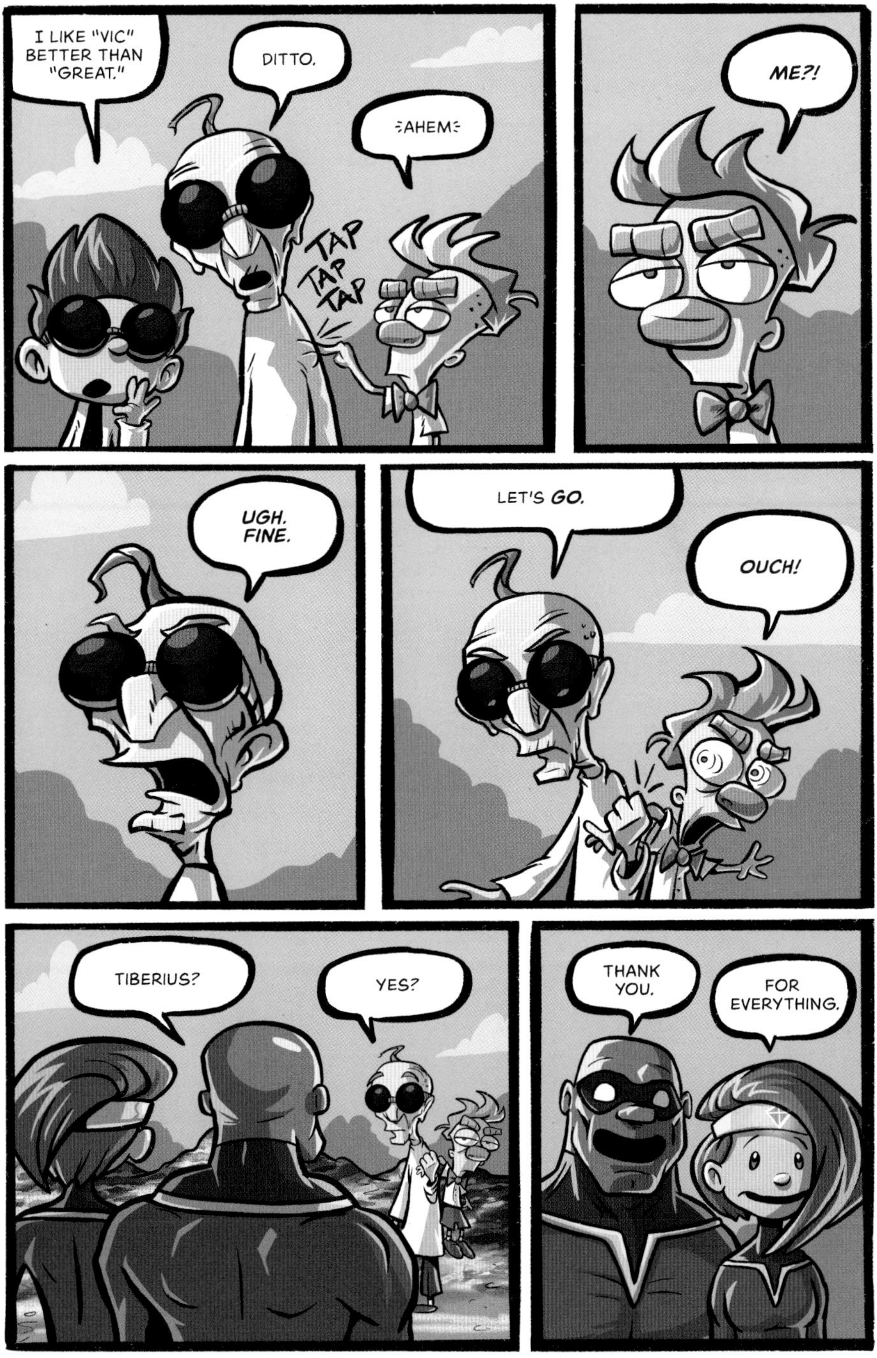
I LIKE "VIC" BETTER THAN "GREAT."
DITTO.
AHEM
TAP TAP TAP
ME?!
UGH. FINE.
LET'S GO.
OUCH!
TIBERIUS?
YES?
THANK YOU.
FOR EVERYTHING.

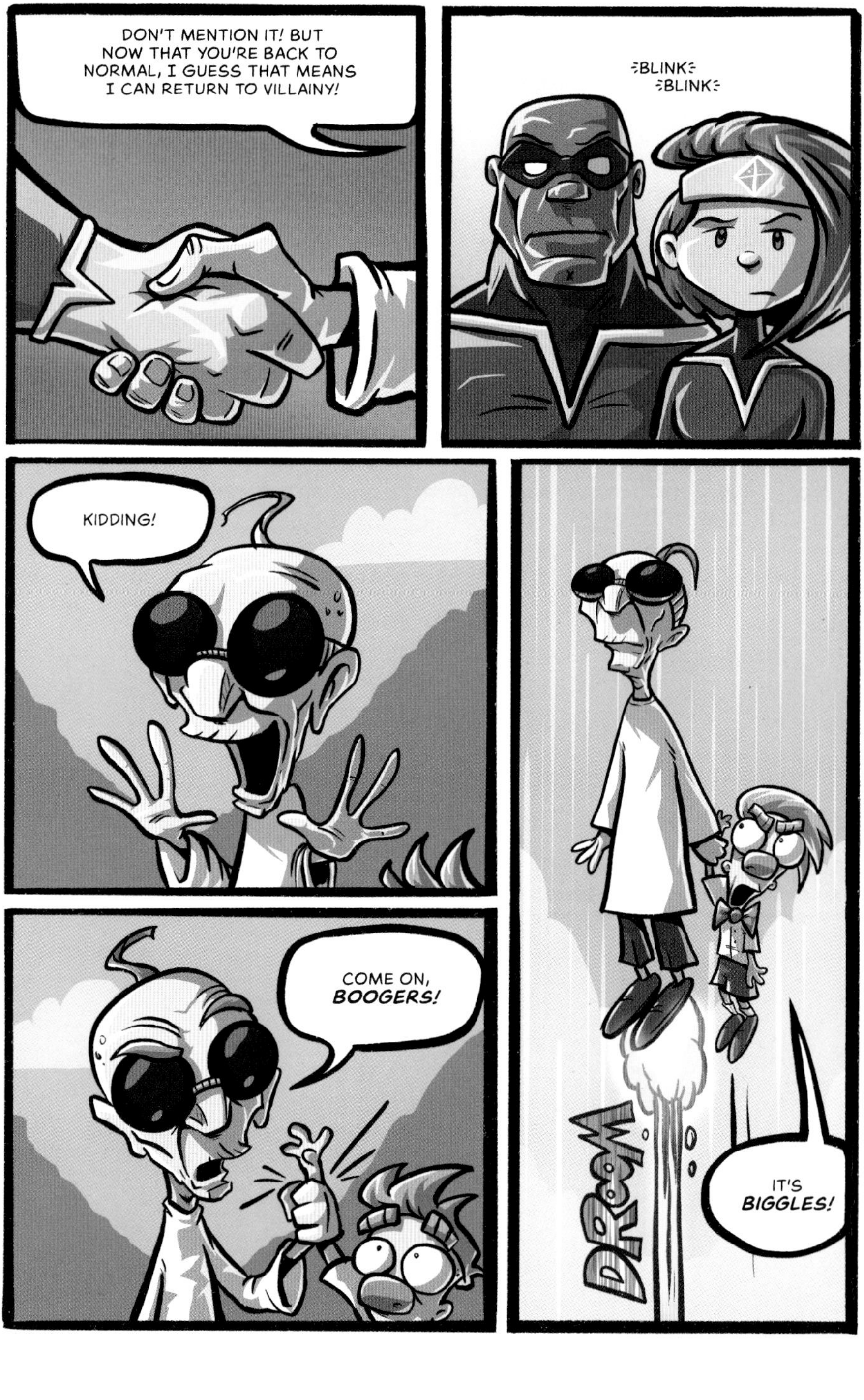
DON'T MENTION IT! BUT NOW THAT YOU'RE BACK TO NORMAL, I GUESS THAT MEANS I CAN RETURN TO VILLAINY!
BLINK BLINK
KIDDING!
COME ON, BOOGERS!
DROOM
IT'S BIGGLES!

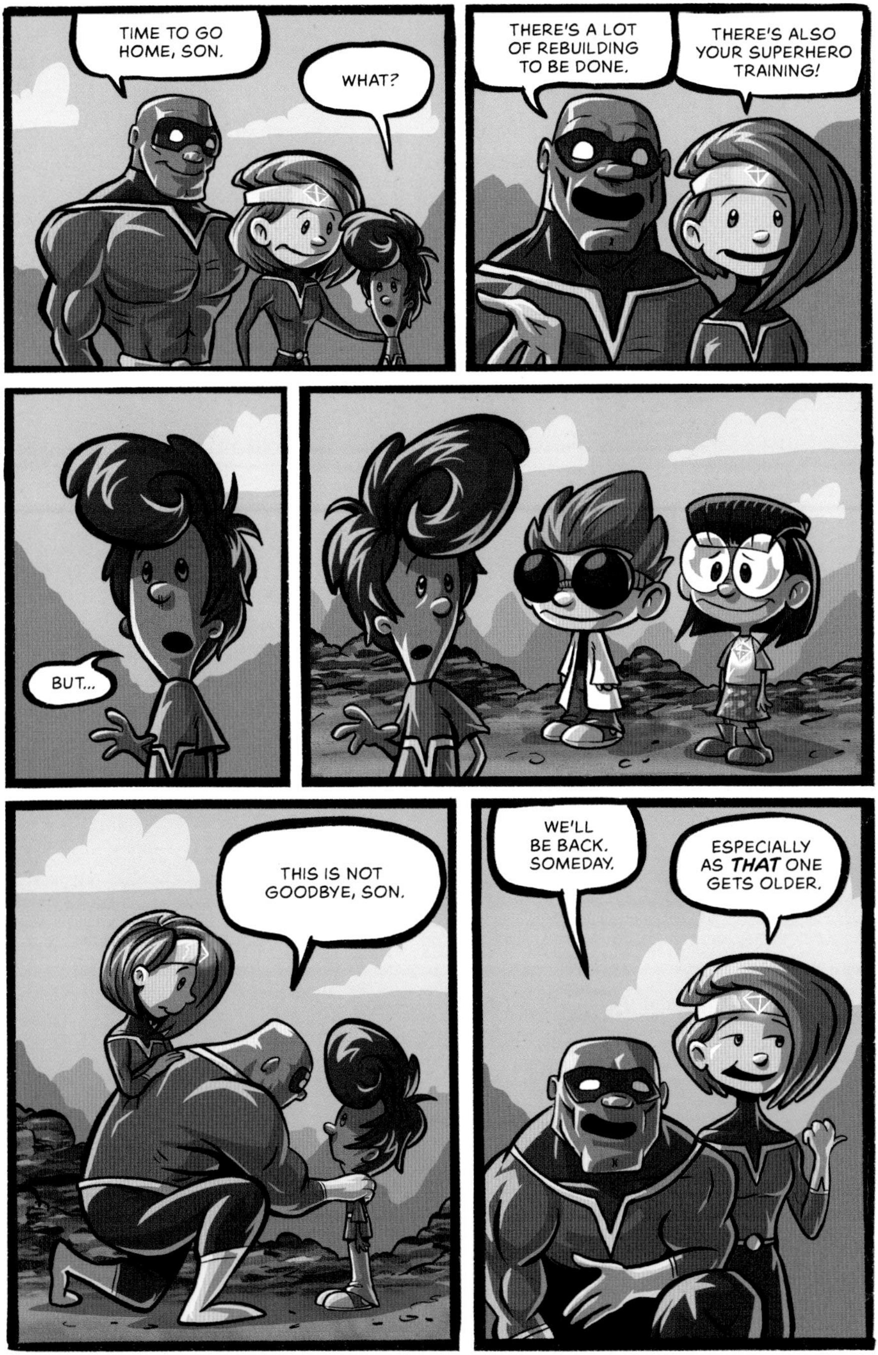
TIME TO GO HOME, SON.
WHAT?
THERE'S A LOT OF REBUILDING TO BE DONE.
THERE'S ALSO YOUR SUPERHERO TRAINING!
BUT...
THIS IS NOT GOODBYE, SON.
WE'LL BE BACK. SOMEDAY.
ESPECIALLY AS **THAT** ONE GETS OLDER.

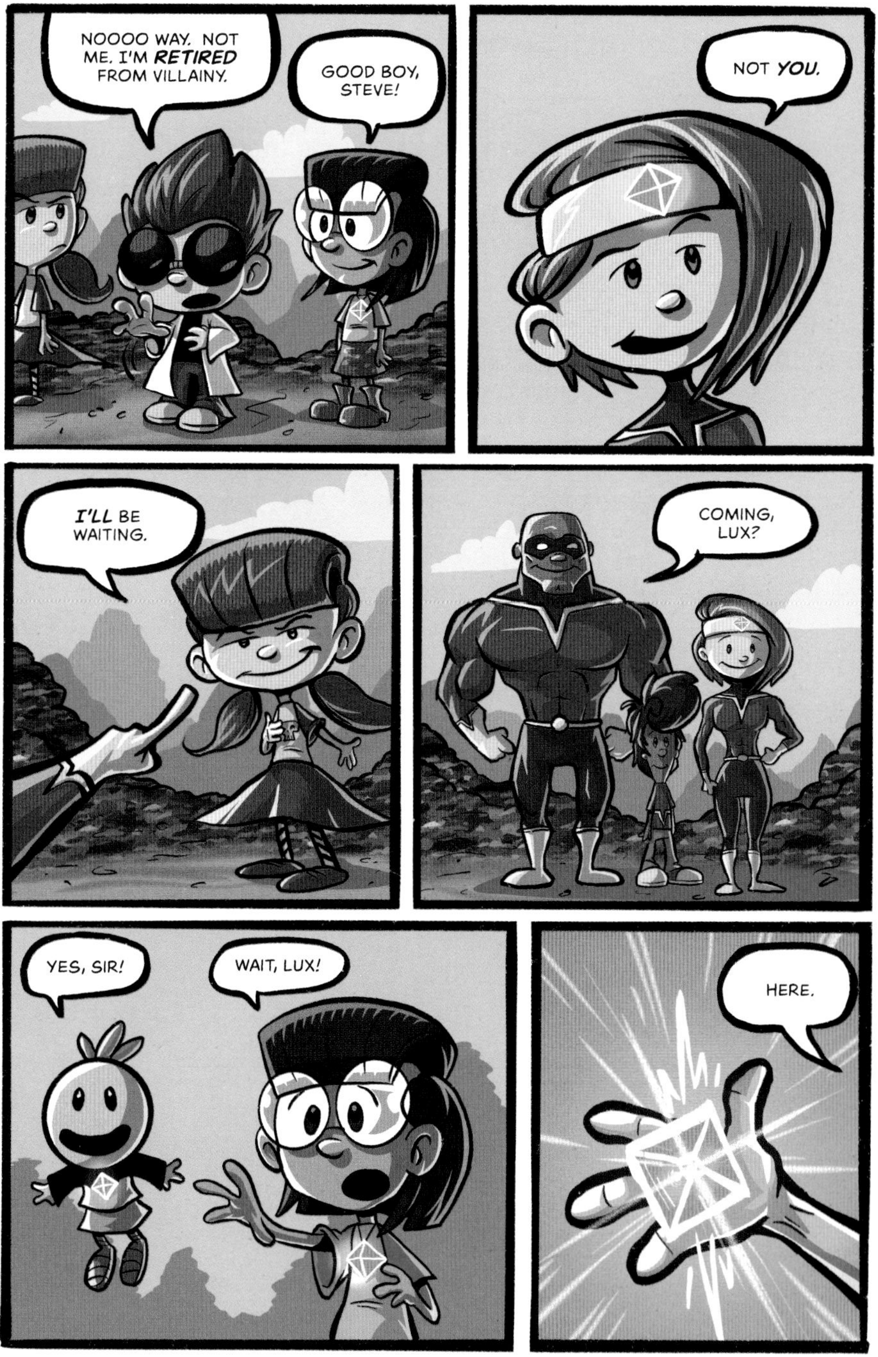
NOOOO WAY. NOT ME. I'M **RETIRED** FROM VILLAINY.
GOOD BOY, STEVE!
NOT **YOU.**
I'LL BE WAITING.
COMING, LUX?
YES, SIR!
WAIT, LUX!
HERE.

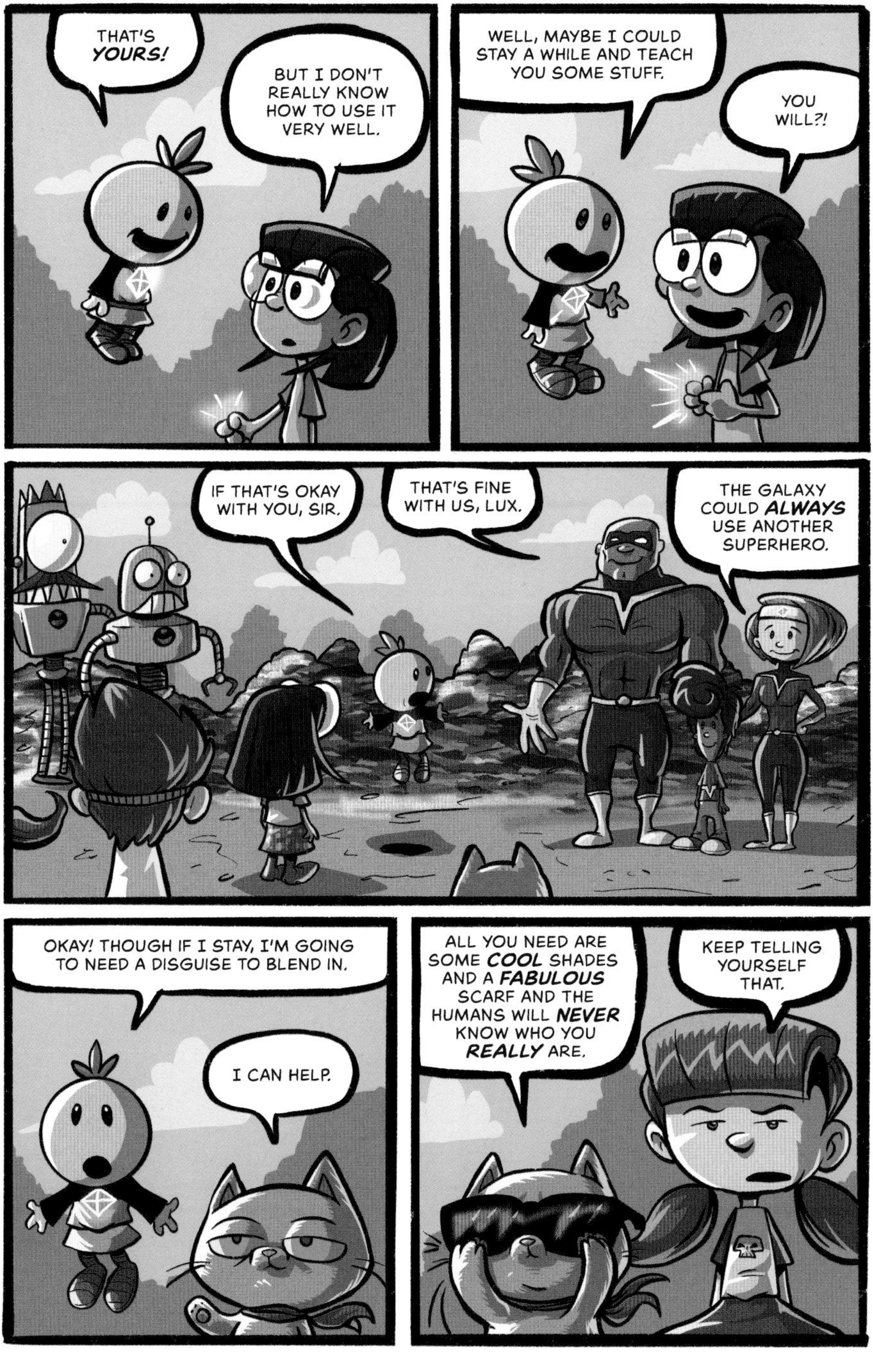
THAT'S YOURS!
BUT I DON'T REALLY KNOW HOW TO USE IT VERY WELL.
WELL, MAYBE I COULD STAY A WHILE AND TEACH YOU SOME STUFF.
YOU WILL?!
IF THAT'S OKAY WITH YOU, SIR.
THAT'S FINE WITH US, LUX.
THE GALAXY COULD ALWAYS USE ANOTHER SUPERHERO.
OKAY! THOUGH IF I STAY, I'M GOING TO NEED A DISGUISE TO BLEND IN.
I CAN HELP.
ALL YOU NEED ARE SOME COOL SHADES AND A FABULOUS SCARF AND THE HUMANS WILL NEVER KNOW WHO YOU REALLY ARE.
KEEP TELLING YOURSELF THAT.

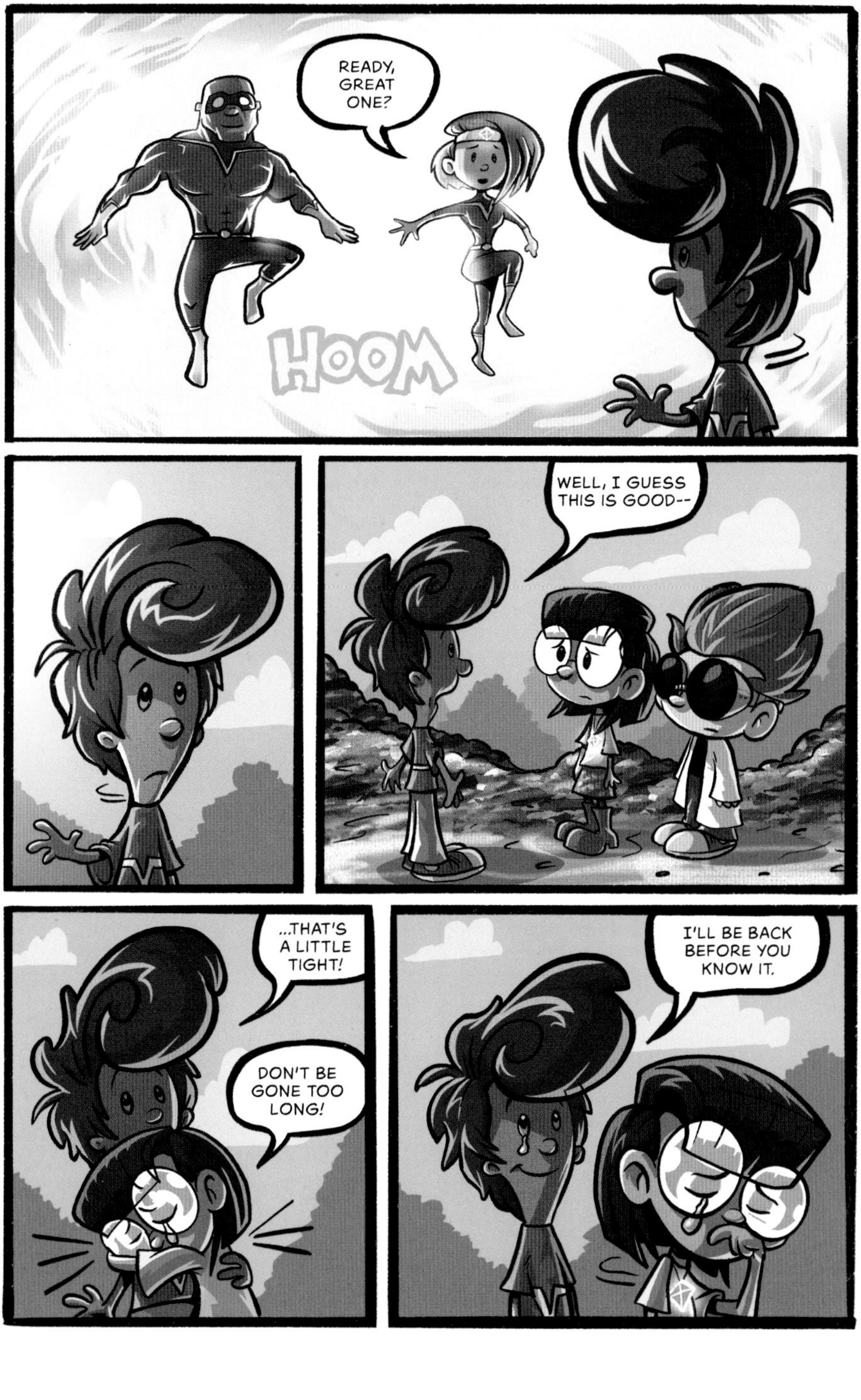
READY, GREAT ONE?
HOOM
WELL, I GUESS THIS IS GOOD--
...THAT'S A LITTLE TIGHT!
DON'T BE GONE TOO LONG!
I'LL BE BACK BEFORE YOU KNOW IT.

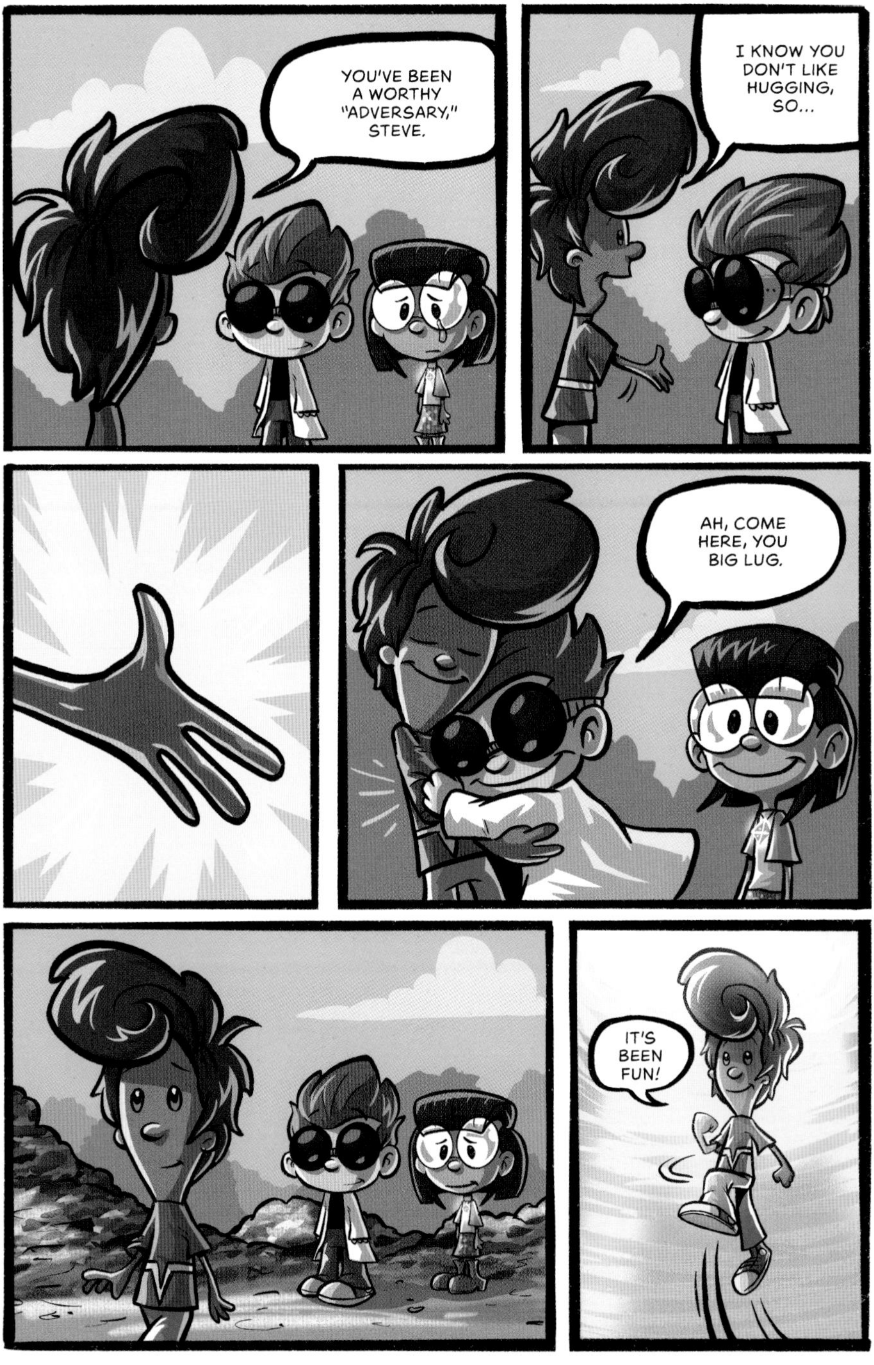
YOU'VE BEEN A WORTHY "ADVERSARY," STEVE.
I KNOW YOU DON'T LIKE HUGGING, SO...
AH, COME HERE, YOU BIG LUG.
IT'S BEEN FUN!

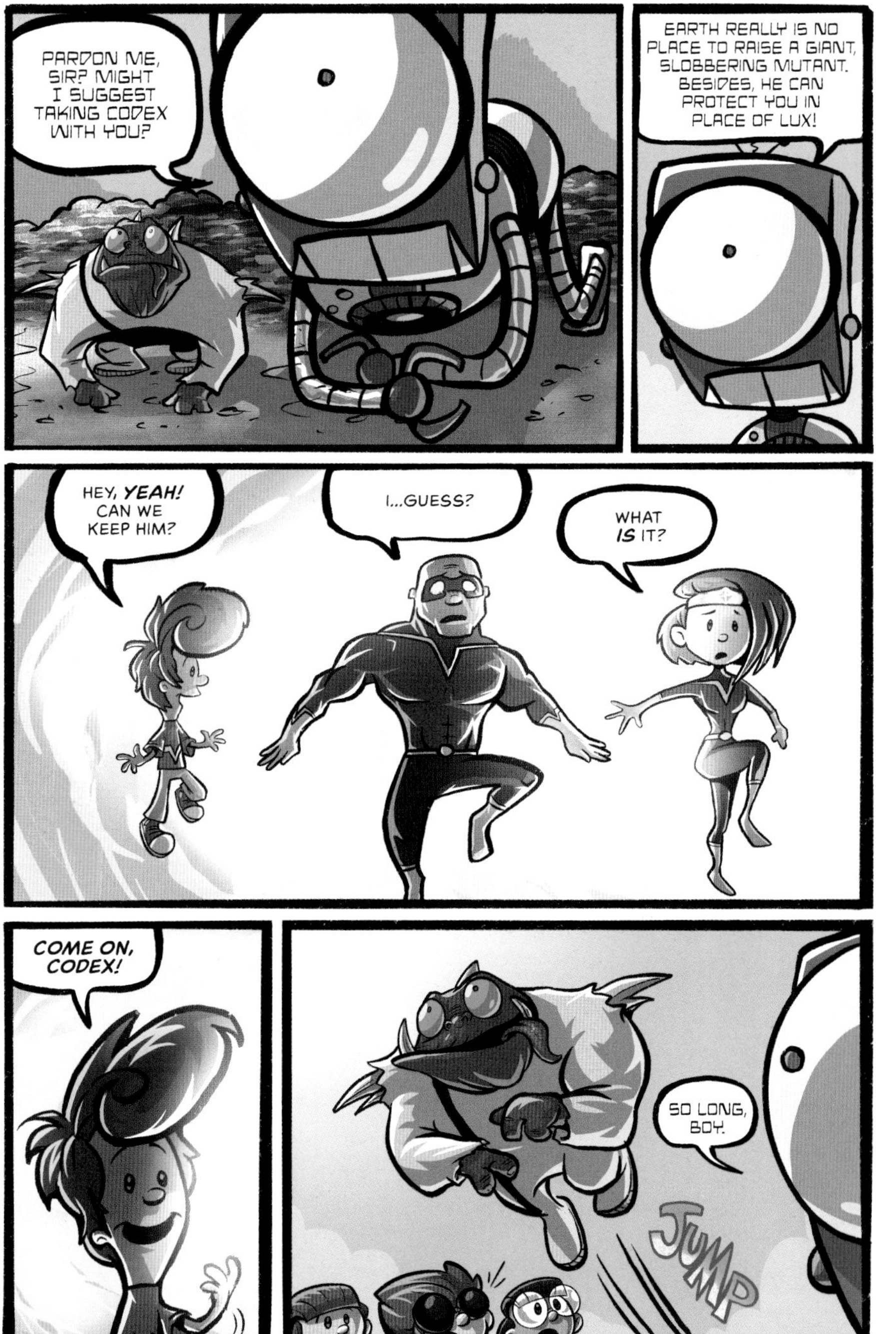
PARDON ME, SIR? MIGHT I SUGGEST TAKING CODEX WITH YOU?
EARTH REALLY IS NO PLACE TO RAISE A GIANT, SLOBBERING MUTANT. BESIDES, HE CAN PROTECT YOU IN PLACE OF LUX!
HEY, YEAH! CAN WE KEEP HIM?
I...GUESS?
WHAT IS IT?
COME ON, CODEX!
SO LONG, BOY.
JUMP

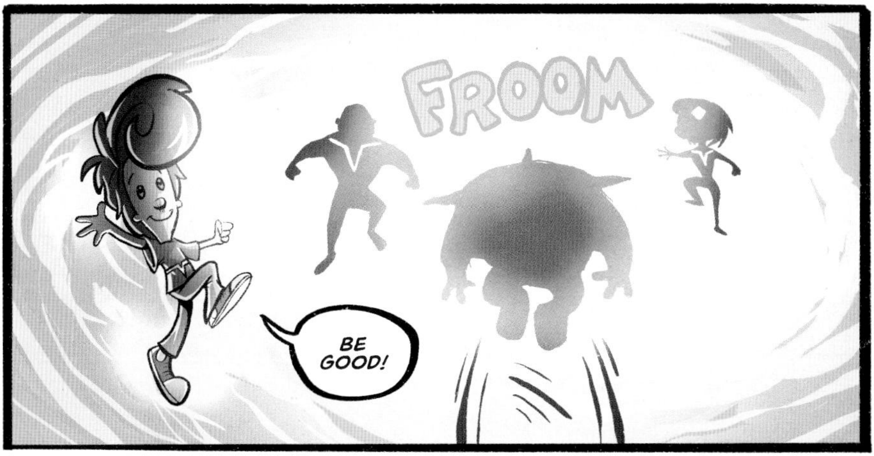
FROOM
BE GOOD!
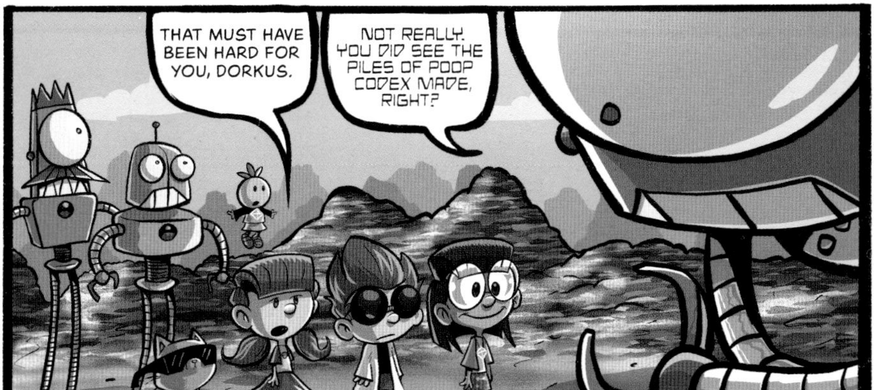
THAT MUST HAVE BEEN HARD FOR YOU, DORKUS.
NOT REALLY. YOU DID SEE THE PILES OF POOP CODEX MADE, RIGHT?
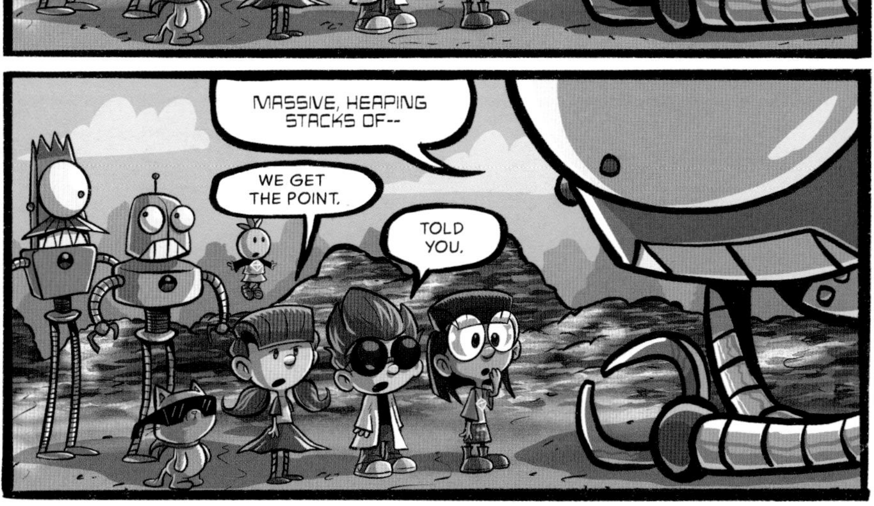
MASSIVE, HEAPING STACKS OF--
WE GET THE POINT.
TOLD YOU.

CHAPTER 20
The Next Generation

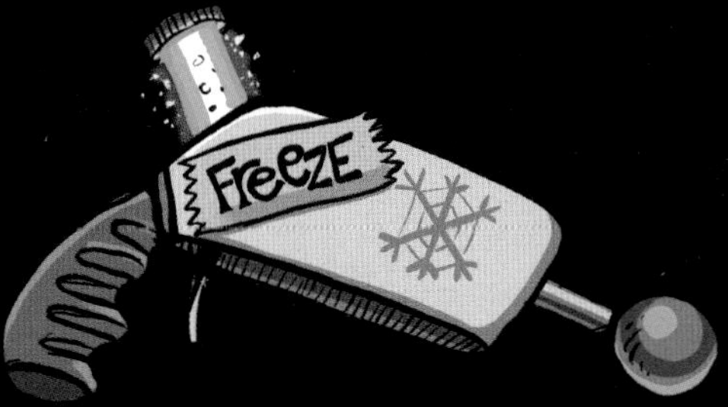
FREEZE

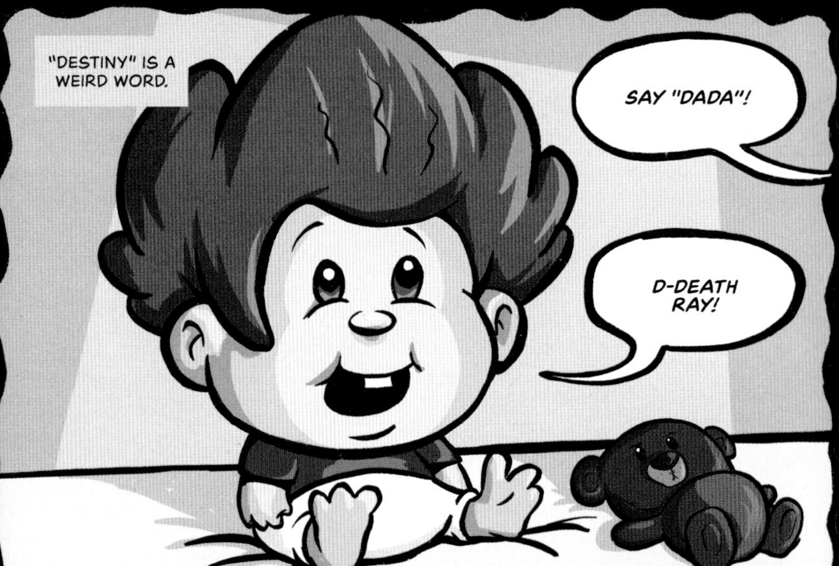
"DESTINY" IS A WEIRD WORD.
SAY "DADA"!
D-DEATH RAY!

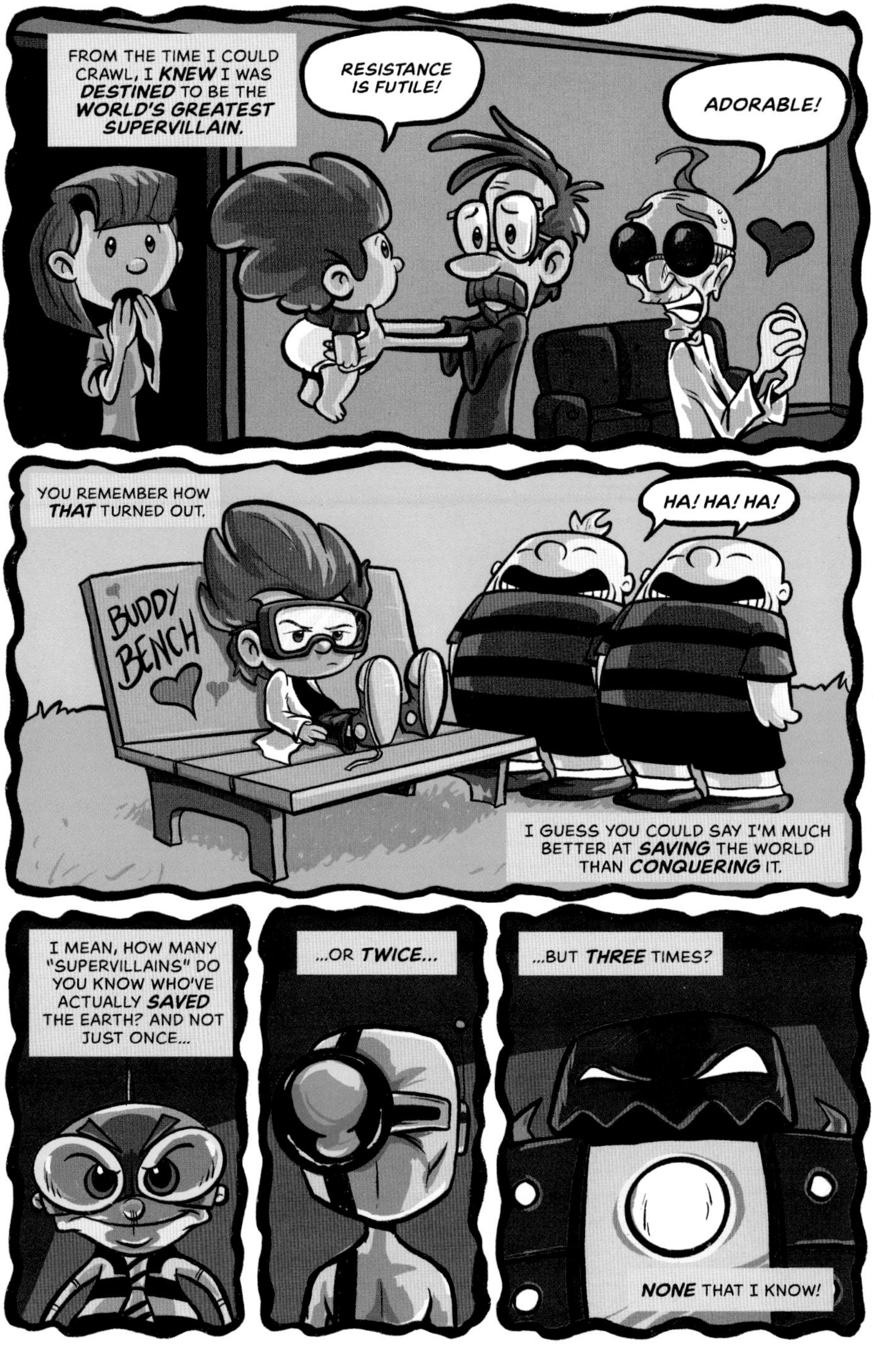
FROM THE TIME I COULD CRAWL, I **KNEW** I WAS **DESTINED** TO BE THE **WORLD'S GREATEST SUPERVILLAIN.**
RESISTANCE IS FUTILE!
ADORABLE!
YOU REMEMBER HOW **THAT** TURNED OUT.
HA! HA! HA!
BUDDY BENCH
I GUESS YOU COULD SAY I'M MUCH BETTER AT **SAVING** THE WORLD THAN **CONQUERING** IT.
I MEAN, HOW MANY "SUPERVILLAINS" DO YOU KNOW WHO'VE ACTUALLY **SAVED** THE EARTH? AND NOT JUST ONCE...
...OR **TWICE**...
...BUT **THREE** TIMES?
NONE THAT I KNOW!

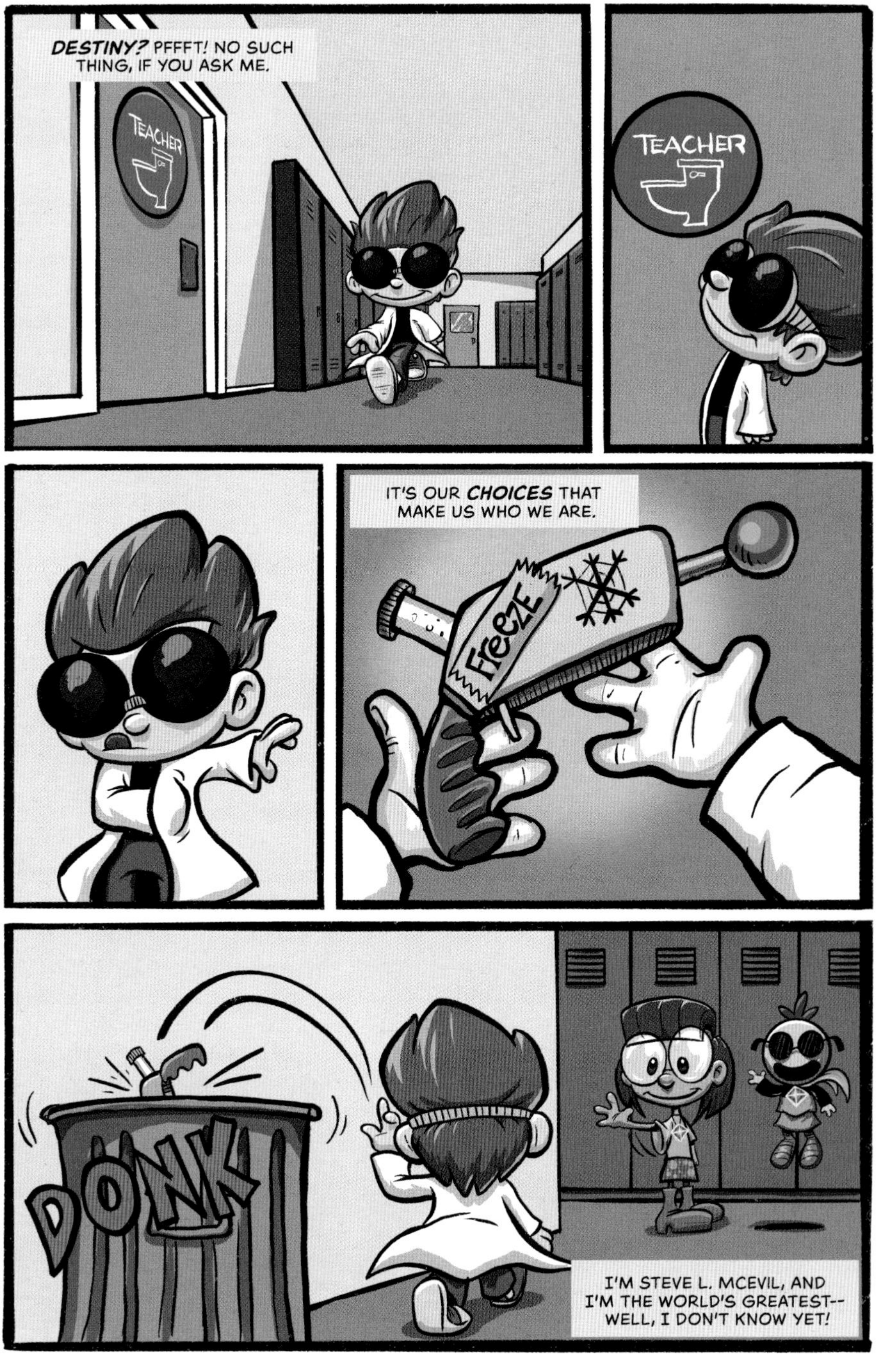

DESTINY? PFFFT! NO SUCH THING, IF YOU ASK ME.
TEACHER
TEACHER
IT'S OUR CHOICES THAT MAKE US WHO WE ARE.
FREEZE
DONK
I'M STEVE L. MCEVIL, AND I'M THE WORLD'S GREATEST-- WELL, I DON'T KNOW YET!

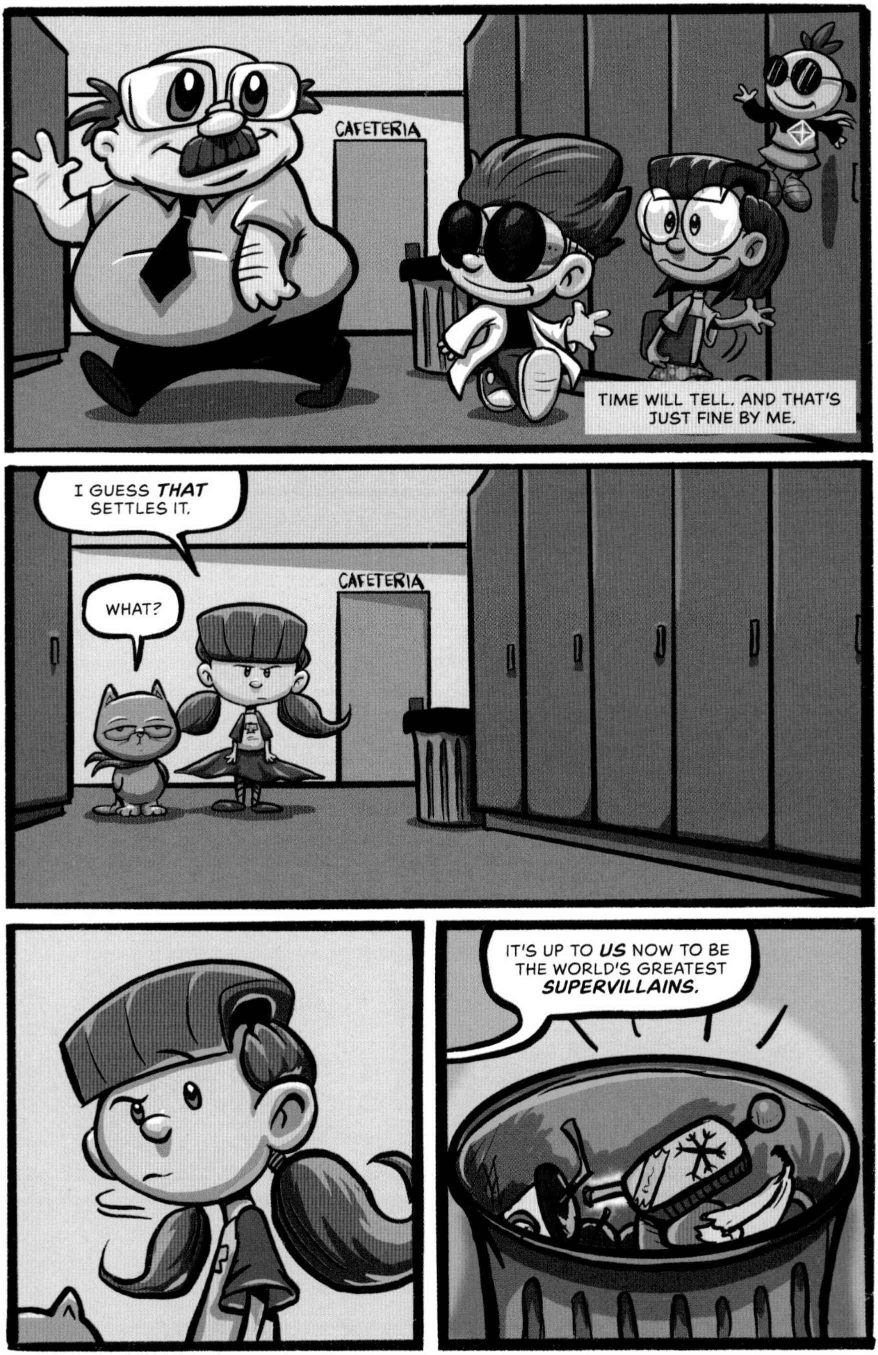
CAFETERIA
TIME WILL TELL. AND THAT'S JUST FINE BY ME.
I GUESS *THAT* SETTLES IT.
CAFETERIA
WHAT?
IT'S UP TO *US* NOW TO BE THE WORLD'S GREATEST *SUPERVILLAINS.*

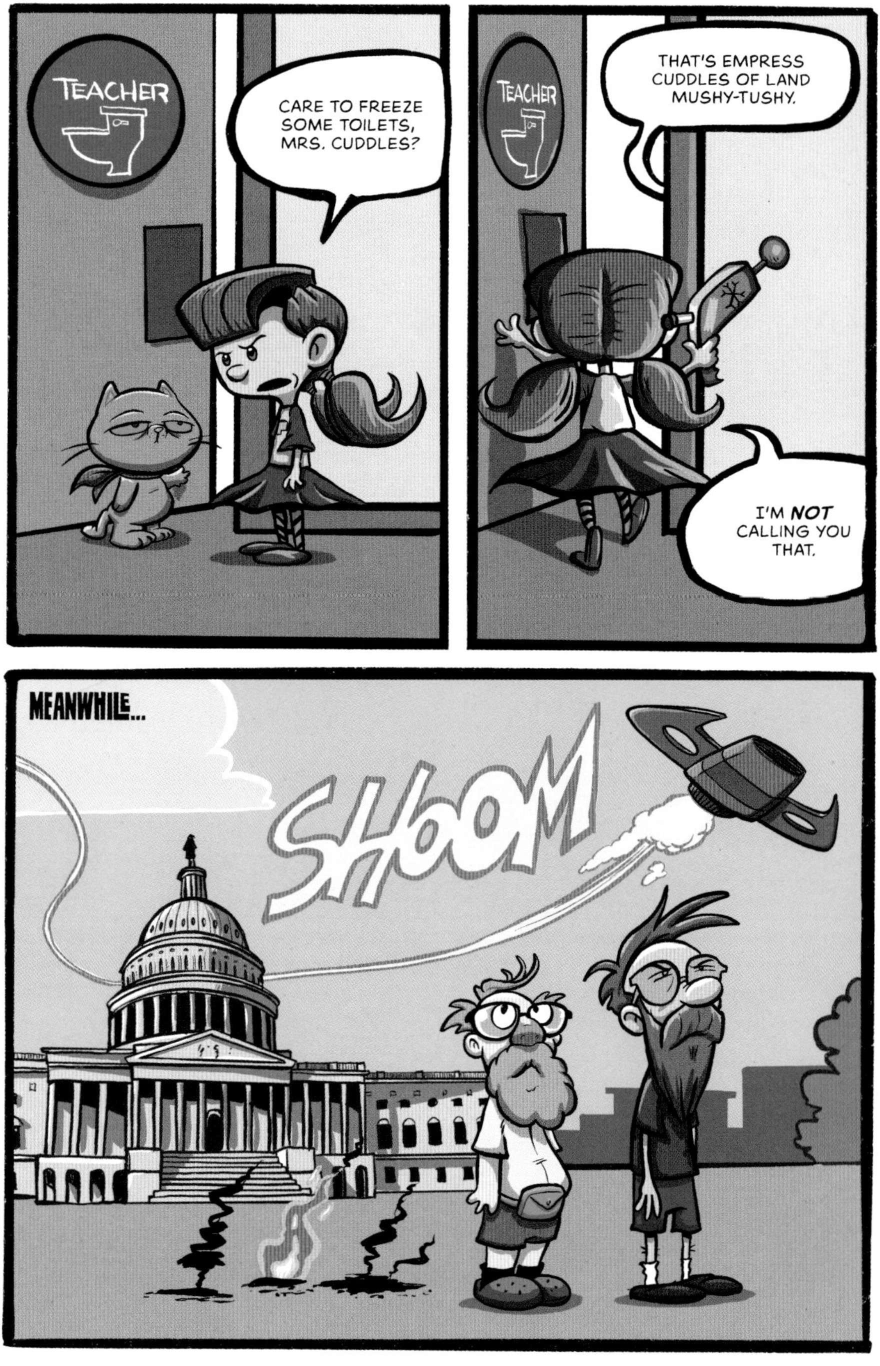
TEACHER
CARE TO FREEZE SOME TOILETS, MRS. CUDDLES?
TEACHER
THAT'S EMPRESS CUDDLES OF LAND MUSHY-TUSHY.
I'M **NOT** CALLING YOU THAT.
MEANWHILE...
SHOOM

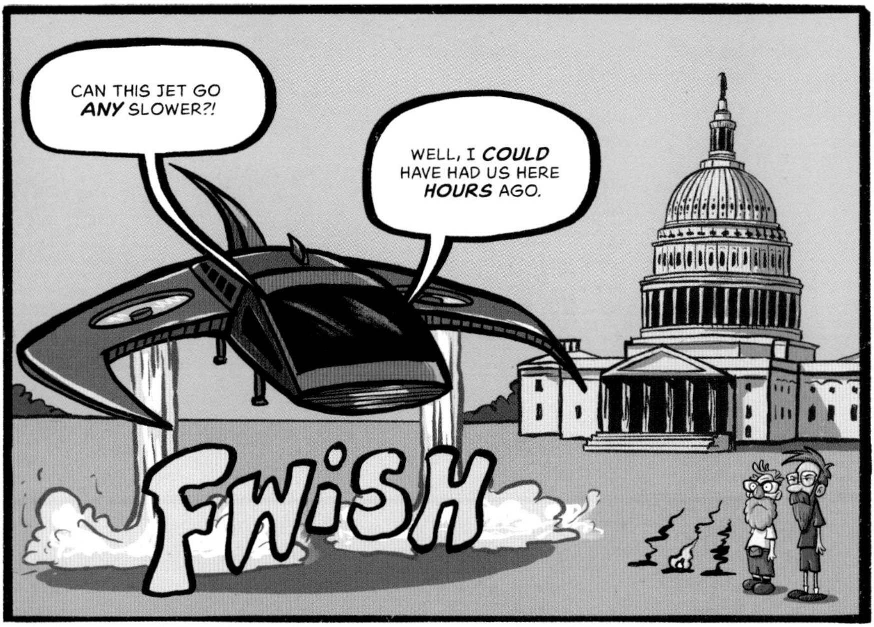
CAN THIS JET GO **ANY** SLOWER?!
WELL, I **COULD** HAVE HAD US HERE **HOURS** AGO.
FWISH

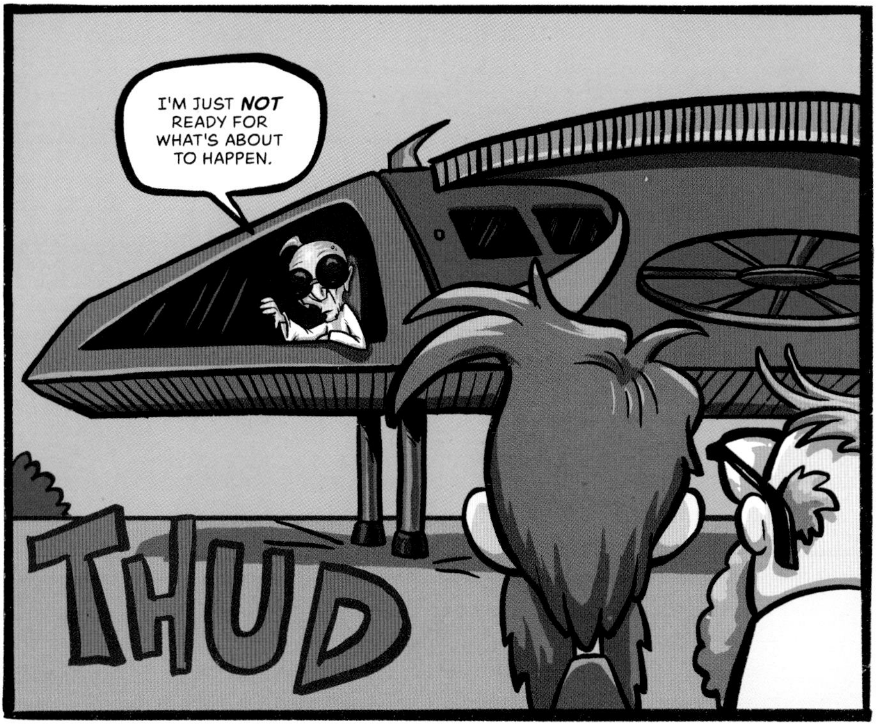
I'M JUST **NOT** READY FOR WHAT'S ABOUT TO HAPPEN.
THUD

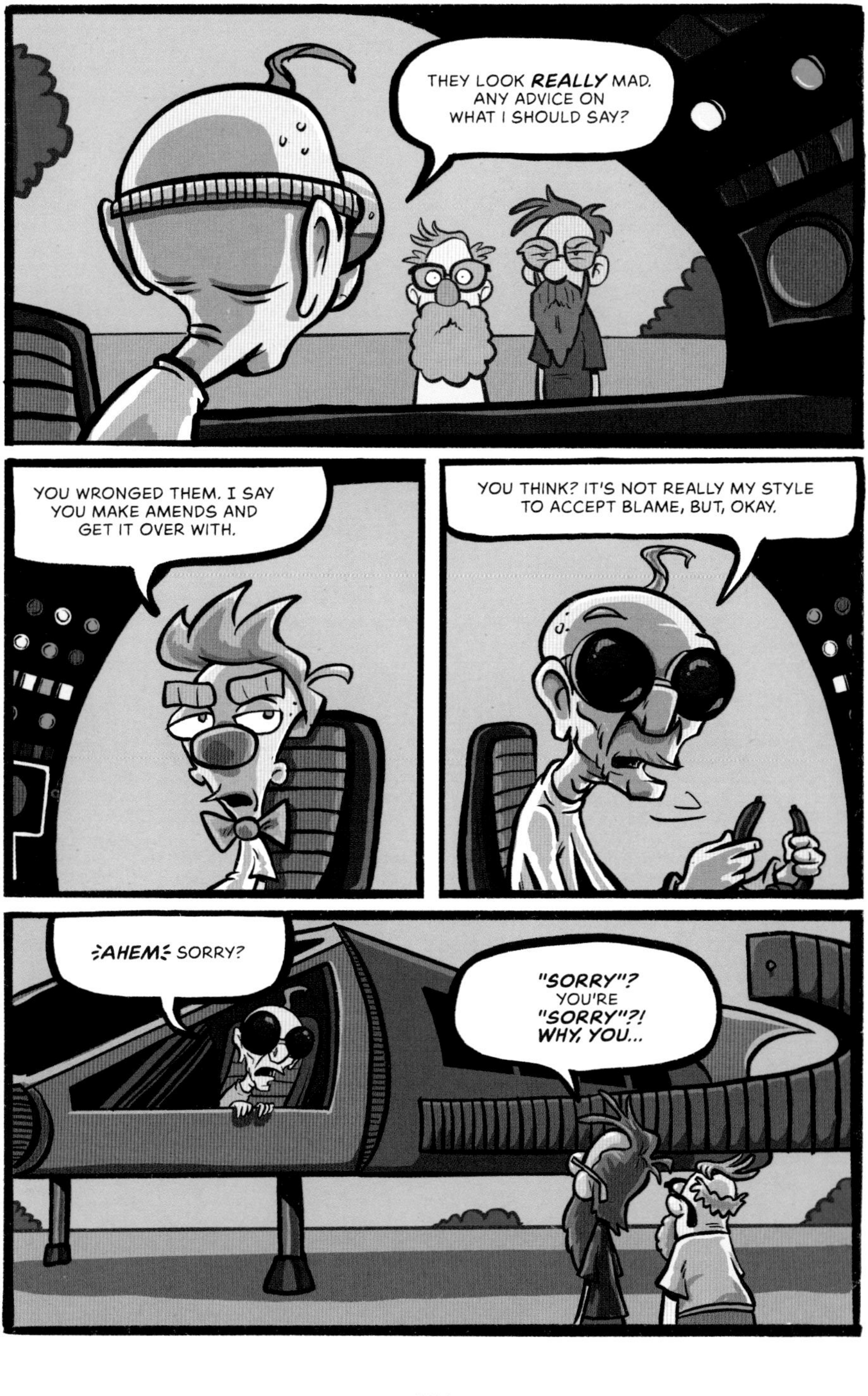
THEY LOOK **REALLY** MAD. ANY ADVICE ON WHAT I SHOULD SAY?
YOU WRONGED THEM. I SAY YOU MAKE AMENDS AND GET IT OVER WITH.
YOU THINK? IT'S NOT REALLY MY STYLE TO ACCEPT BLAME, BUT, OKAY.
AHEM SORRY?
"SORRY"? YOU'RE **"SORRY"?! WHY, YOU...**

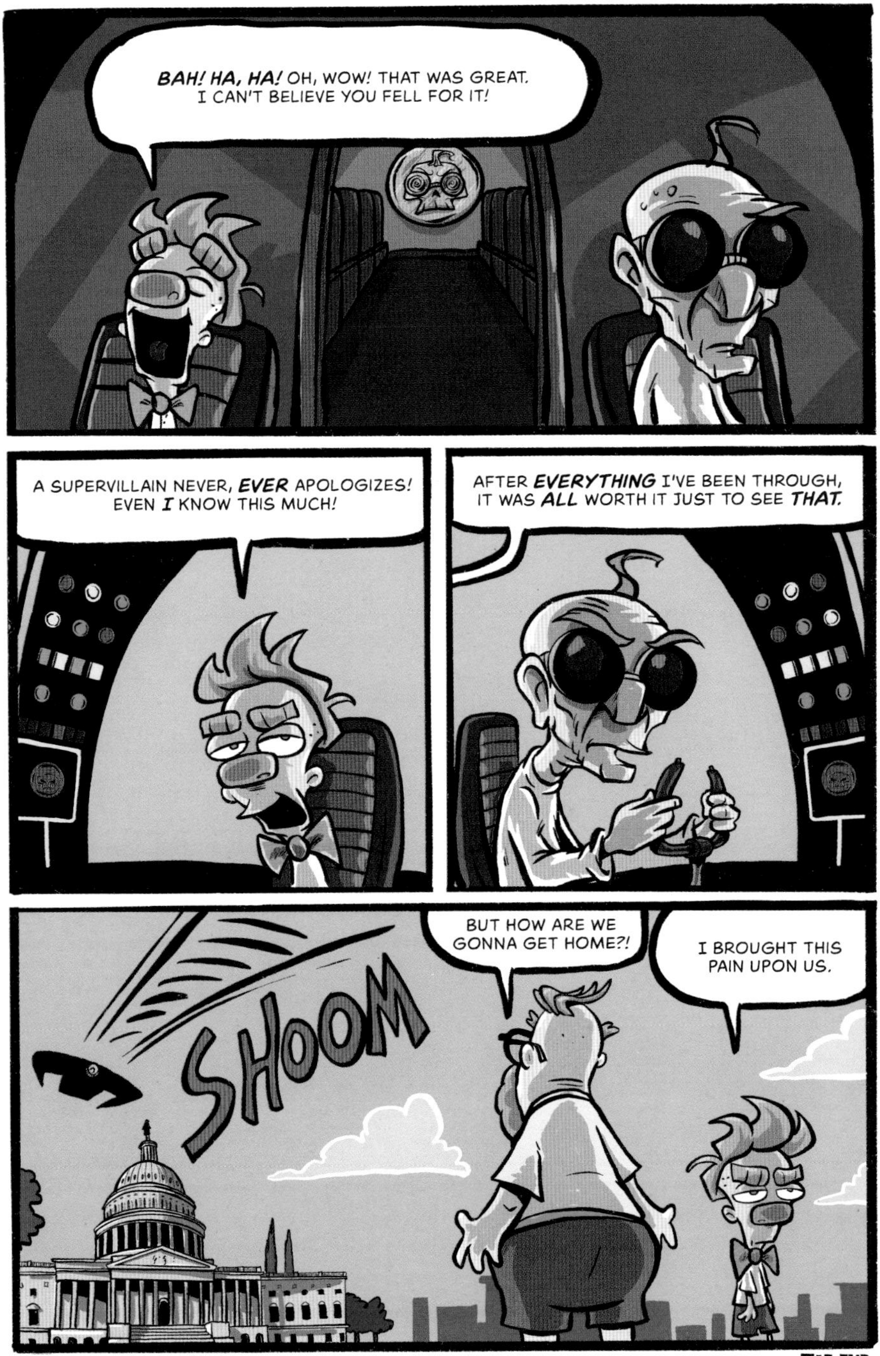
BAH! HA, HA! OH, WOW! THAT WAS GREAT. I CAN'T BELIEVE YOU FELL FOR IT!
A SUPERVILLAIN NEVER, EVER APOLOGIZES! EVEN I KNOW THIS MUCH!
AFTER EVERYTHING I'VE BEEN THROUGH, IT WAS ALL WORTH IT JUST TO SEE THAT.
SHOOM
BUT HOW ARE WE GONNA GET HOME?!
I BROUGHT THIS PAIN UPON US.

THE END

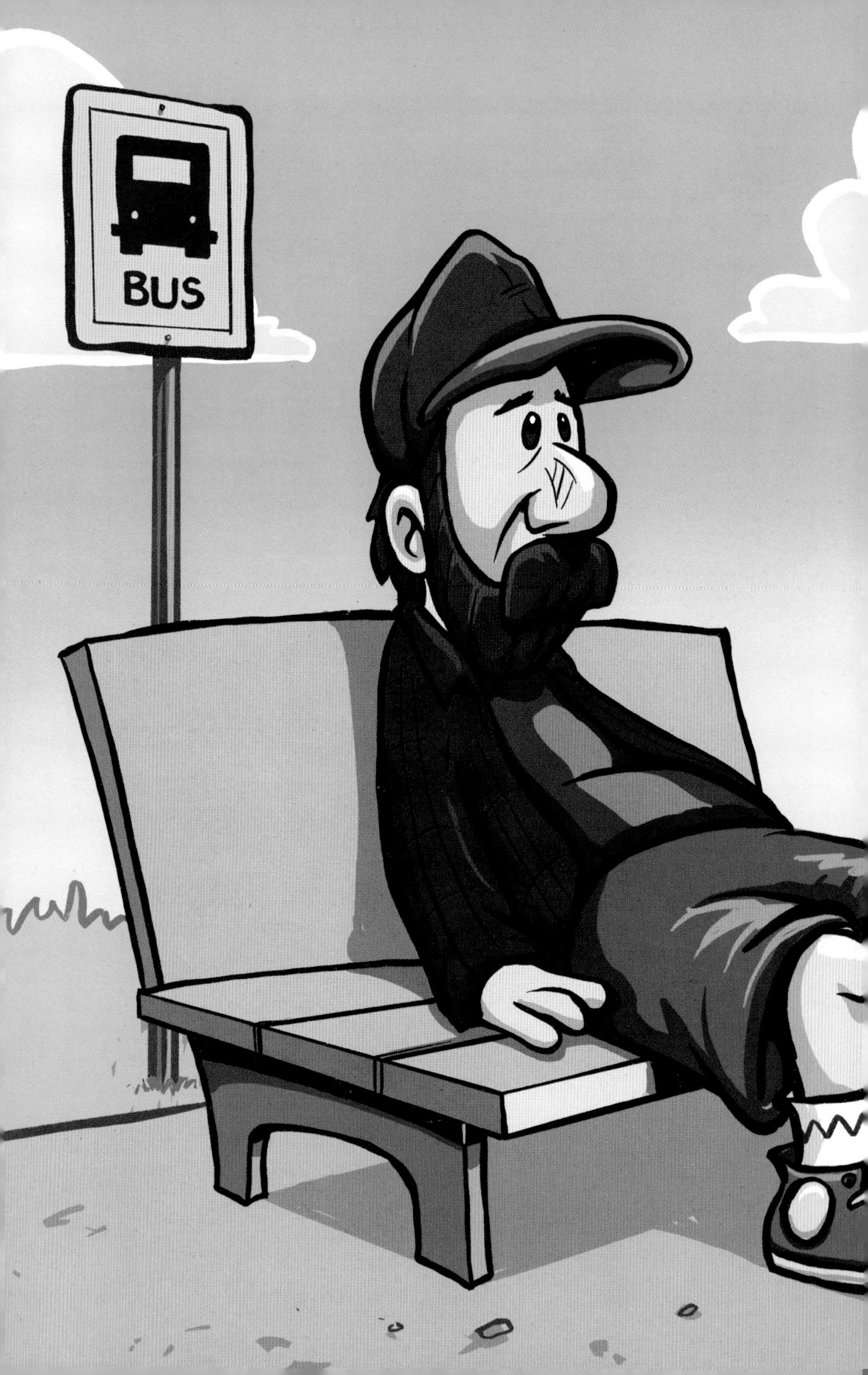
BUS

Lucas Turnbloom grew up on the shores of Hawaii during the magical era known as the 1980s. There, he spent his days watching stuff like *Star Wars, ThunderCats, Transformers,* and *Teenage Mutant Ninja Turtles,* while also reading comics like *Peanuts, Garfield, The Far Side,* and *Calvin and Hobbes.* It was during these formative years Lucas realized he wanted to be a professional cartoonist.

Lucas resides in San Diego with his wife, two sons, and one temperamental cat. When Lucas isn't cartooning, he plays loud guitar, collects embarrassing amounts of action figures, or seeks crucial naps.

Follow Lucas's comic adventures on X,
Instagram, Facebook, Threads, or Bluesky:
@LucasTurnbloom

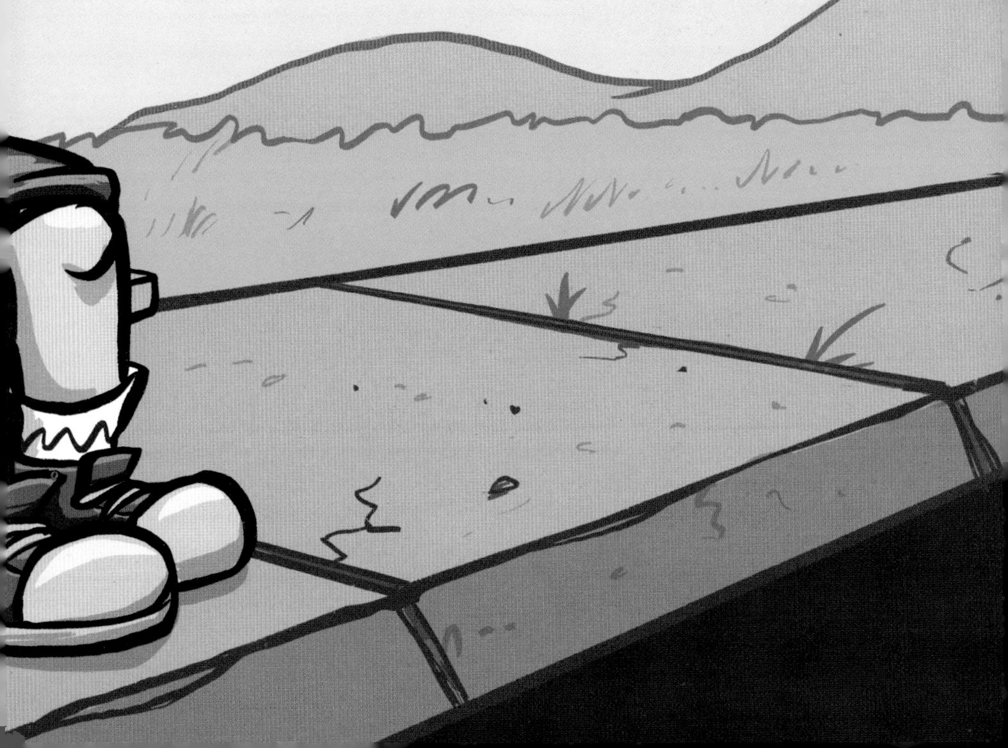

HOW TO DRAW EVE L. McEVIL!

Grab your PENCIL and let's draw!

TIPS: A) Follow the steps in order; B) Don't press your pencil down on the paper too hard; C) Make lots of little lines to complete your shapes; D) Have fun!

1. LIGHTLY sketch one oval for her head and two others for her ears.

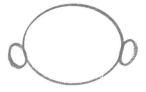

2. Add a marshmallow rectangle for her bangs and two ovals for the sides of her hair.

3. Make two ovals for her pigtails, with two triangles at the tips.

4. Add a square for her neck, a trapezoid for her upper body, and two triangles for sleeves.

5. Draw two thin rectangles for arms. Add three small ovals on the ends of each for her fingers.

6. Add one giant trapezoid for her dress.

7. Draw two small rectangles for legs and two ovals for feet.

8. Draw a line for her mouth and an oval for her nose. Include two half circles for her eyes with lines for eyelids.
(Don't forget the eyebrows, the skull on her shirt, and the lines on her pants.)

9. Grab a PEN and trace over ONLY the pencil lines you wish to KEEP.
(Make sure the bottom of her dress is a wavy line!)

10. Erase the pencil lines and BAM! That's how we draw Eve L. McEvil! Remember, the more attitude the better!

GET CAUGHT UP WITH THE McEVILS!

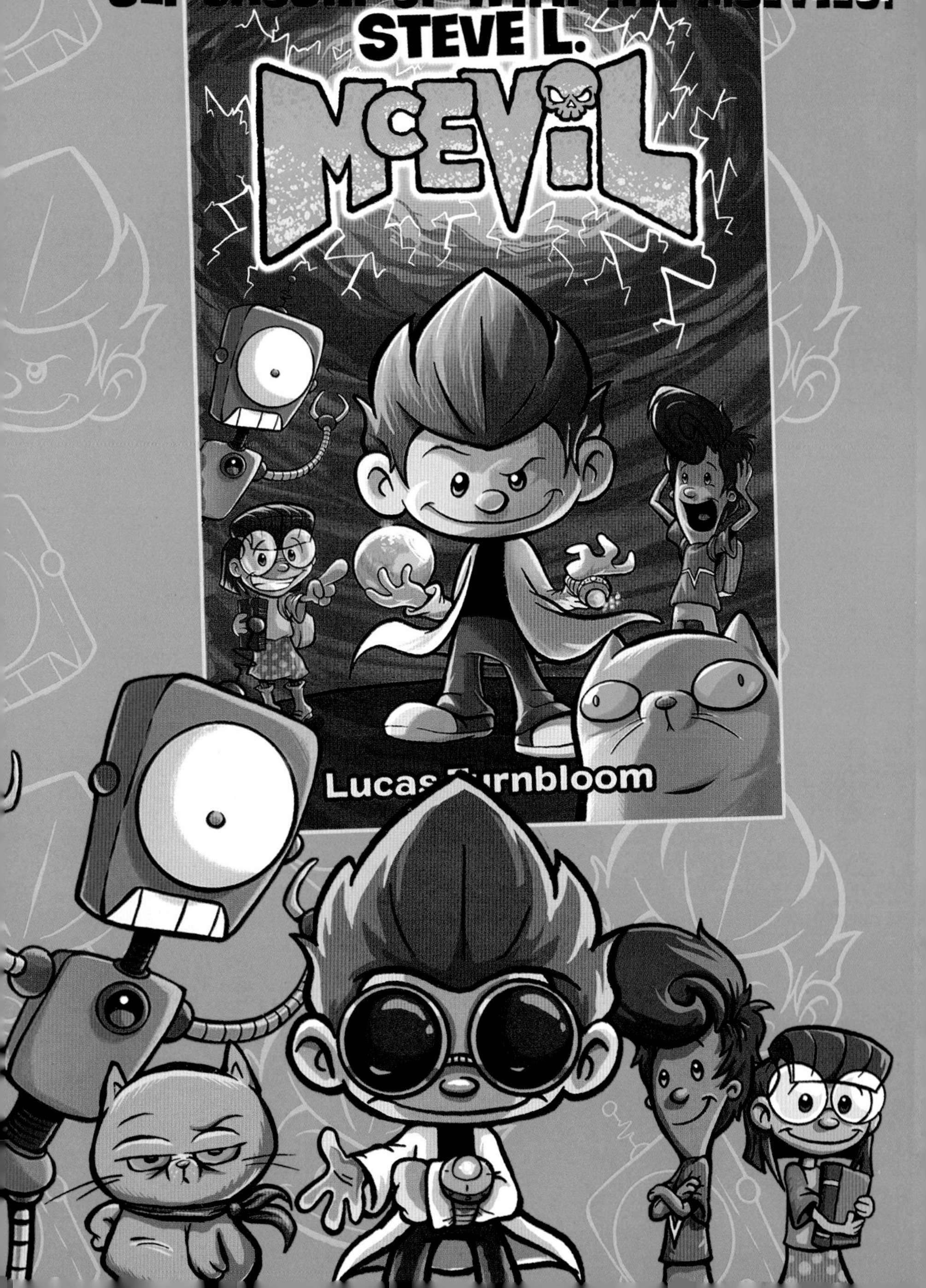
STEVE L.
McEVIL
STEVE L.
Lucas Turnbloom

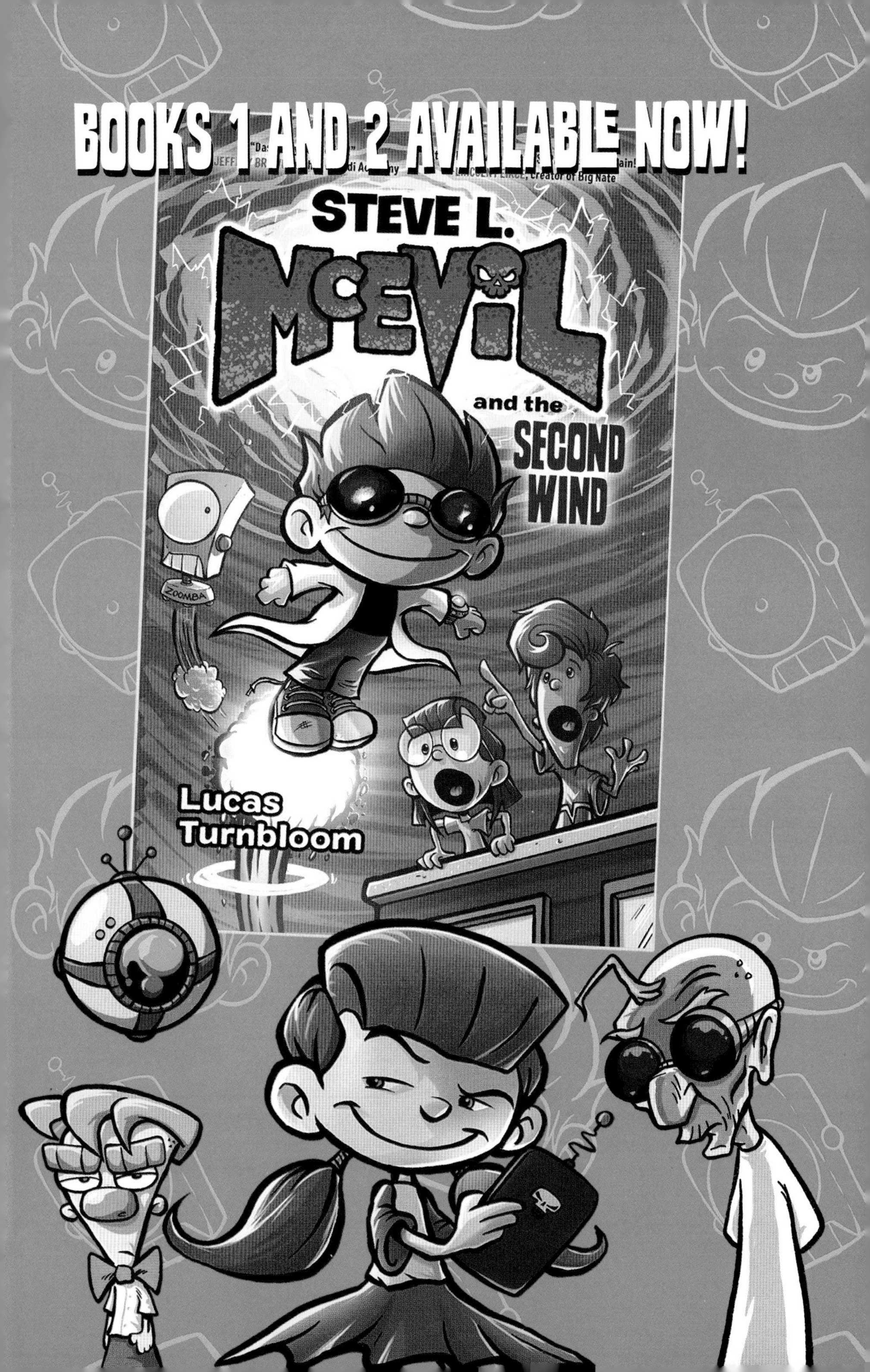
BOOKS 1 AND 2 AVAILABLE NOW!
STEVE L. McEVIL
and the SECOND WIND
ZOOMBA
Lucas Turnbloom

"BEDTIME"

MY NAME IS *STEVE L. McEVIL*, AND I AM THE *WORLD'S GREATEST SUPERVILLAIN*.

I MEAN, I *WILL* BE. SOMEDAY.

@LUCASTURNBLOOM

LIGHTS OUT!

CLICK

TIK
TIK
TAK

IT'S HARD TO TAKE OVER THE WORLD WHEN YOU *STILL* HAVE A BEDTIME.

STEVELMCEVIL.COM

Follow STEVE L. McEVIL's WEBCOMIC adventures at www.SteveLMcEvil.com

SPECIAL THANKS

ZOE LAPIERRE FOR HER COLOR ASSISTANCE.
ALEX TURNBLOOM AND *AIDEN TURNBLOOM* FOR THEIR INKING SKILLS.

ACKNOWLEDGMENTS

MAKING A GRAPHIC NOVEL IS NO EASY TASK. CREATING *STEVE L. MCEVIL AND THE TWISTED SISTER* WOULD NOT HAVE BEEN POSSIBLE WITHOUT THESE VERY IMPORTANT PEOPLE.

MY COLORIST, *MARC LAPIERRE*, WITHOUT HIS AMAZING COLORING SKILLS, THIS BOOK WOULDN'T LOOK HALF AS GOOD AS IT DOES. HE'S INCREDIBLE. FOLLOW HIM ON INSTAGRAM AT @MARCTOONS

ART TEAM *BOB BIANCHINI* AND *JULES BUCKLEY* AND EDITORIAL TEAM *DANIELA CORTES* AND *LINDSAY WAGNER* FOR THEIR TIRELESS WORK ON THE MCEVIL SERIES. THEY HAVE MADE THESE BOOKS MORE BEAUTIFUL THAN I COULD'VE HOPED. FOR THAT I'M GRATEFUL!

MY EDITOR, *PHOEBE YEH*, THIS BOOK SERIES WOULD NOT BE WHAT IT IS WITHOUT YOU. THANK YOU FOR PUSHING ME WHEN I NEEDED IT, FOR BEING THERE WHEN I NEEDED YOU, AND FOR YOUR PATIENCE. YOU GUIDED ME THROUGH MY OMNIPRESENT IMPOSTOR SYNDROME, AND I COULDN'T HAVE ASKED FOR A BETTER EDITOR.

MY AGENT, *JUDY HANSEN*, WHO HAS BEEN MUCH MORE THAN AN AGENT. THANK YOU FOR BELIEVING IN ME WHEN I STOPPED BELIEVING IN MYSELF. FOR BEING MY GUIDE AND SOMETIMES THERAPIST! I WOULDN'T BE DOING THIS WITHOUT YOU. FROM THE BOTTOM OF MY HEART, THANK YOU.

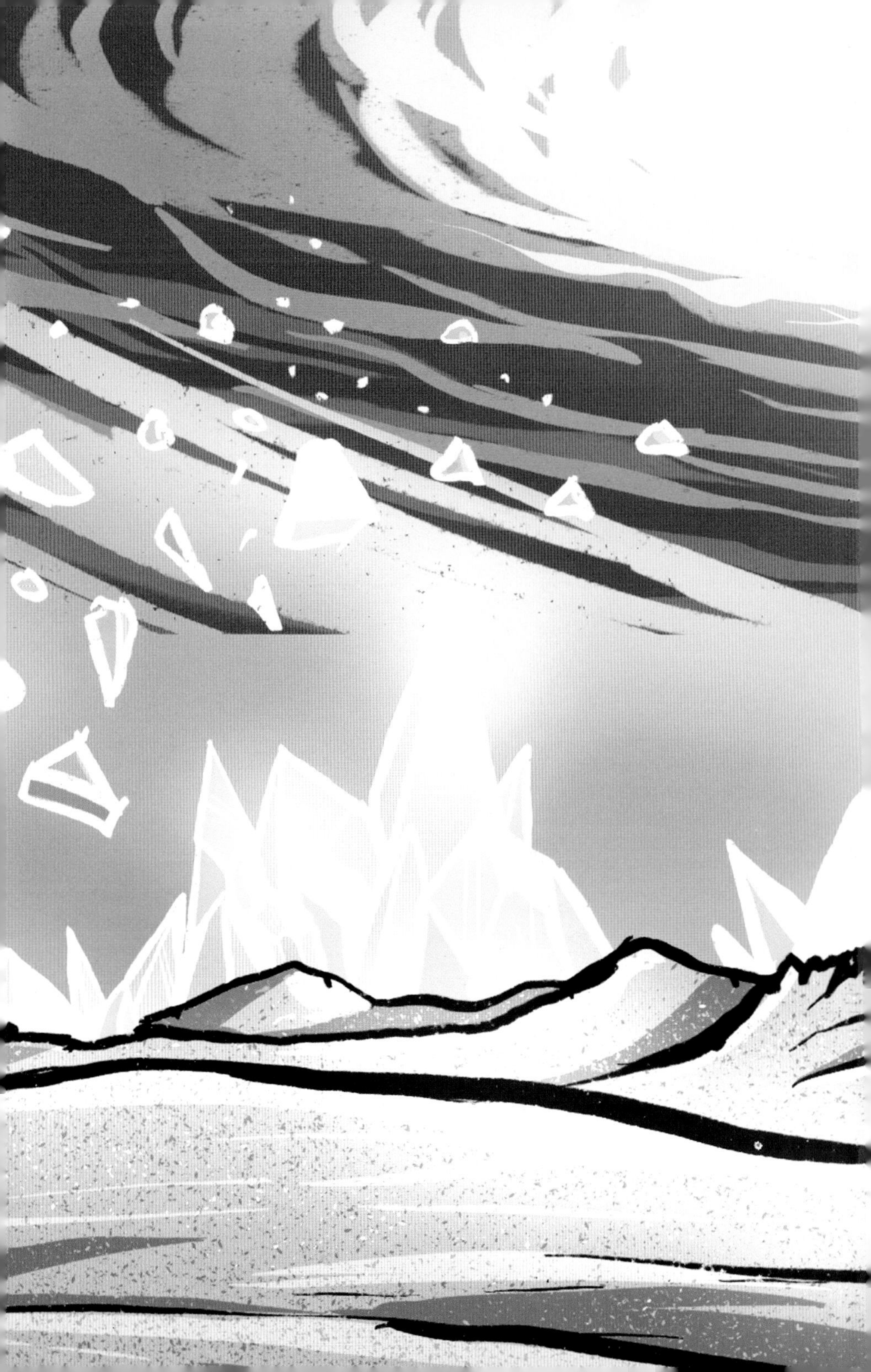